Pike's Peak

OTHER BOOKS BY FRANK WATERS

Midas of the Rockies (1937)
People of the Valley (1941)
The Man Who Killed the Deer (1942)
The Colorado (1946)
The Yogi of Cockroach Court (1947)
Masked Gods: Navaho and Pueblo Ceremonialism (1950)
The Earp Brothers of Tombstone (1960)
Book of the Hopi (1963)
Leon Gaspard (1964)
The Woman at Otowi Crossing (1966)
Pumpkin Seed Point (1969)

PIKE'S PEAK:

a family saga

Frank Waters

SAGE BOOKS

THE SWALLOW PRESS INC.

CHICAGO

Printed in the United States of America

First Edition
Second Printing 1971

This book is printed on 100% recycled paper.

Sage Books are published by
The Swallow Press Incorporated
1139 South Wabash Avenue
Chicago, Illinois 60605

ISBN 0-8040-0503-6
LIBRARY OF CONGRESS CATALOG CARD NUMBER 77-150753

CONTENTS

BOOK ONE

The Wild Earth's Nobility

PART I

SILVER

1

In the dusk it loomed before him now as it had the first time he had glimpsed it from the broad and muddy Arkansas far out on the buffalo plains below: like something risen from the depths of dreamless sleep to the horizon of wakeful consciousness, without clear outline yet embodying the substance of a hope and meaning that seemed strangely familiar as it was vague. Even its discoverer, Zebulon Pike, had first mistaken it for a cloud floating rootless above the upturned blue horizon — a great snowy peak too high for any man to climb. Yet many after him had tried to measure its fatal fascination. Rogier himself had vaguely intended to continue with the caravan on that wide-beaten trail, already called old, down toward Santa Fe. But like thousands of fools from the little towns along the Missouri a decade before, their wagon sheets emblazoned with the ridiculous slogan "Pike's Peak or Bust," he had been drawn toward it like a helpless moth to a flame. Not by the illusion of gold, that perpetual Pike's Peak Bust of greedy mankind, but by a single snowy peak. No more than that.

So he had turned north with a few other wagons to crawl up the Fontaine-qui-Bouille to the new little settlement at its foot. The barren stretch of plains kept breaking in tawny waves against the blue mountain wall as ineffectually as time. Still the peak loomed higher every day, its snowcap flushing pink at dawn, its majestic slopes shining like polished silver in the moonlight, its seamy crags baring teeth to every storm. If it had a single shape or meaning he had not yet found it. At once mystifying and alluring, beautiful and terrifying, it still held him here like a mammoth lodestone whose secret and ineffable power he had no will to resist.

"HEE-YAH!"

The sharp gutteral cry roused Rogier from his reverie in the shadow of the porch where his heavy square-built body lounged motionless in a chair, his gaze enmeshed in the vast web of twilight translucent between the row of cottonwoods and the enigmatic face of the peak before him. The cry flashed like lightning across his somber mood, illuminating a crawl of figures along the creek. With it sounded the slip of hoofs upon the stones. Sharply outlined, a horse reared on its haunches, one forefoot knocking at the sky. He could see the slim body of its rider, the single lash of a brutal arm. Then making the leap, Indian and horse cleared the slippery bank to the right of a group of laboring squaws and disappeared beyond the trees as if the night had opened to their call.

Joseph Rogier tipped his chair down to all four legs and leaned forward. A band of Blue Cloud Arapahoes was crawling past to its encampment down the creek. It was not yet too dark to make out the heavily laden squaws and the ponies drawing still more dunnage lashed to spruce tepee poles dragging on the ground. The confused murmur of their voices washed up to him on the breeze with occasionally the neigh of a horse and the cry of a child. The papooses never made a sound. Bound on cradleboards strapped to their mothers' backs, they might have been little mummies embalmed in their casts.

For days such bands had been passing by. Arapahoes and Cheyennes from out on the Great Plains, making for the mouth of the canyon at the foot of the high peak where every fall they gathered to drop offerings in the sacred springs, and to trade with the mountain Utes. There was seldom trouble except when too much whiskey got around, recalling to young bucks the difference between their tribes. Then the school and court house bells began to ring.

People farther out than Rogier could hear them in the thin, rarefied air, gentle mellow notes breaking against the somber mountain wall; and hearing, men and women and children went to stay in the courthouse until the Indians had passed by.

Rogier knew everyone enjoyed the occasion; it made them feel they were pioneers in a Wild West that was no more. Women gossiping over their sewing and basket lunches. Children playing "Cowboy and Indian" on the grass and stealing to ambush behind the lilacs. Young men forever cleaning rifles and hanging openmouthed upon the words of old men (past thirty) come from the Civil War. Their interminable talk of the Union Saved and the Great American Empire so accentuated Rogier's deep sense of exile that he never went in, himself. A Southerner of French Huguenot descent, born an aristocrat and an individualist, he abhorred their crude provincialism and at the same time suffered his lack of their proclaimed nationalism.

His father had borne all the graces and vices that a South Carolina gentleman was expected to bear during the decades preceding the Civil War. Daniel Lee Rogier owned a large rice plantation upriver from Charleston, maintained a gentlemanly acquaintance with his wife and three sons that was naturally and charmingly noncommittal, and lavished his caresses and outspoken admiration upon his horses and hunting dogs. With the death of his wife he left his youngest son Joseph, a child of eight, to be reared in the Negro quarters and dedicated himself wholly to his career of rum and debt.

His success as a drunkard and an ineffectual planter was soon complete. It was aided by his best friend and closest neighbor, Dr. Lascelles, to whom he pledged the extent of his plantation as security for his conniving oldest son's alleged gambling debts. With the changing wisdom of successive generations men live by the single code necessary for their type of existence; and their catchwords are State, Church, Fame, Courage, or Six Per Cent. Daniel Lee Rogier with others of his time subscribed his life to Honor as the light illuminating his every deed. It was the first thing in his mind that morning when a house servant opened his study doors to a group of lawyers and creditors and went to fetch the rum. Rogier took one glance at the face of Dr. Lascelles and knew that they had come to escort him down the road to ruin. Rising from his desk, he turned to look out the open window upon his spacious rice paddies extending beyond the outhouses and slave quarters to the river.

"A divine mornin', gentlemen," he observed quietly.

The preliminaries were delicately brief. One of the men took a sip of excellent Southern rum and looked up from the sheaf of papers. "Dr. Lascelles advises us of the considerable extent to which you have pledged security for equally large obligations, Mr. Rogier"

"He has my word, suh."

"You wish to contest the regrettable action necessary?"

"You have my word, suh!"

A short silence filled the room. Dr. Lascelles drew an easy breath. Rogier remained standing.

"Then you will be prepared to conclude arrangements, Mr. Rogier?"

He bowed. It was as if all his weaknesses, his life of charming uselessness fell from him with that needless, foolish gesture. As though a man lived a long life of emptiness, like a lonely monk walking his cloisters, awaiting the one moment of fulfillment and knowing the sound of his call.

The vultures moved in quickly. The boy Joseph was ten years old when the Rogier plantation on its estuary, with all the black children of its soil, the white-porticoed house, kitchen, slave quarters, carriage house, stables, and blacksmith shop, passed out of his father's hands at a word and a gesture that had taken generations to make casual. At his father's death soon afterward, he was bound out by his oldest brother to learn the carpenter trade in Roanoke, Virginia, and went there in a tow shirt. He always remembered that tow shirt and others like it. Not for seven years did he have a coat of his own to cover them. It was homespun for him by a widow with a lame daughter his own age. The girl with a club foot taught him to read and write, then kissed him and sent him to Maryland for his first job.

In Baltimore he worked fourteen hours a day in a carpenter shop, and during his two years there squeezed in three months' schooling. With an aptitude for arithmetic, he evolved a method of his own for making computations on a steel square. When Civil War broke out, Rogier ran away to avoid conscription by either side.

It was perhaps then it suddenly struck him – a strange conviction of his solitary exile upon an insubstantial world fraught with fleshly folly and the fraility of human knowledge. If for the first time in his life he felt both the elation and the disturbing falsity of his complete individual freedom, he also found himself with nothing to love nor strive for, no allegiance to any creed or land, no star to guide him across the empty earth.

At St. Joseph, Missouri he got off the train. It was night and he was ill. His hands, his knees trembled. Every few moments as he walked along the drab, dark streets beside the river he stopped and sat down upon his carpet bag to wipe the sweat from his face. Three squares farther on he came to a boarding house with a lamp burning in the window. He knocked and a woman let him in. Next morning he could not get up. That afternoon the woman told him he had the fever and dragged him up into the attic. For days he lay on a pallet of quilts and blankets spread on the floor. At intervals the woman handed water and food up through the trap door. Only in mid-afternoon when all the boarders were gone and the children were playing outside did she crawl up the ladder to his room.

"Well, young fella, still takin' youah naps reg'lar-like?" she would inquire; and then with a chuckle, "Thank Gawd, suh, youah quiet enough, and not a sign of anything ketchin' on the place! Now s'posin' you turn over for a wash. Ovah you do, suh!"

There was something about Rogier's sickness infinitely repugnant to him. It was as if a stealthy fate had struck him down as he had emerged into the brilliance of his freedom; a shameful affliction that condemned him to lonely darkness. And the woman, Mrs. White, was its accomplice. Yet he listened for her footsteps like a lover awaiting his mistress, and received her with the same bright eyes and silent tongue. Only when it was over between them, the doctoring, washing, and cleaning, and she settled back in her blue gingham that had regained its faded color wherever water had splashed, did he feel at ease.

Mrs. White was a slight, little-boned woman from Louisville, Kentucky whose father, Captain De Vinney, had been one of the oldest steamboat captains on the Mississippi. Her first husband had been a wealthy furniture dealer who outfitted boats plying on the river. A short time after he had died from drinking too much sour wine at a boat christening, his warehouse burned. Mrs. White gave the insurance money to her son Ansil to take to her brother-in-law in New Orleans to invest for her. The lad got off the boat there too late at night to catch the ferry to his uncle's home in Algiers, and went to a hotel. Put into a room out of which had just been carried a sick man, he caught yellow fever and died before his uncle learned of his whereabouts. "Leastways, that's what my brother-in-law says. The money was never found," she explained in her casual matter-of-fact voice that betrayed a profound and unmoved knowledge of mankind. With her two remaining children, both girls, she had moved to St. Jo and married Mr. White; and when he had run off to the war, she had opened her boarding house.

"He never said what State he was goin' to fight for, and I ain't heard from him yet. What side do you belong on, North or South, suh?"

Rogier was propped up against the wall in a posture of indefinable aloofness that involuntarily had brought the "suh" to her lips despite his threadbare clothes and coarse hands. "I reckon I just don't rightly belong anywhere, Mrs. White," he said quietly.

He seldom broke his noncommittal silence. Only once he asked briefly, "I wonder why you've been doing so much for me?"

A woman so inured to the vicissitudes of a troublesome existence that human tragedies took on the aspect of mere daily faults, so naturally responsive with a sympathy which was wordless because it was involuntary, Mrs. White seemed surprised at his allegation of kindness. She turned on her knees before the trap-door opening to face him. "I reckon it's because it ain't in you to ask no he'p or expect any, suh."

Upon his recovery Rogier obtained work with a construction firm. A few months later Mr. Powell, the architect and builder, had come to the house to see him. It was evening and Rogier, the last boarder to come in, was eating alone at the table. Mrs. White, quick to meet the astounding occasion of employer coming to employee, hurried into the parlor to light the twisted glass chimney lamps. But Mr. Powell walked directly into the dining room. Rogier rose and shook hands. Then he sat down and continued eating. Mr. Powell sat down beside him and began to talk. The building was not progressing. There were delays and more delays. Something had got into the men. He had to have somebody who could take over the whole thing and keep it going. A firm hand and a head for construction. He had thought of Rogier—he had a way with the men. Finishing supper, Rogier crossed his fork and knife on the plate. "Beginning tomorrow morning I'll see that things get along, Mr. Powell," he said.

A couple of years later Mrs. White's husband showed up. At the close of the war he had wandered down into Mexico where he had been imprisoned for a year. Returning home, he suffered so badly with his maggot-infested feet he could hardly walk. For hours he sat with his feet under the pump to ease the pain. Eventually a friend, a wagonmaker by trade, offered him work in the next county. All the family, Mr. and Mrs. White and her two daughters, Molly and Martha, with Rogier and the other boarders, gathered in the parlor to discuss the impending change.

"I don't know about the girls," began Mrs. White. "As fuh as Molly goes, she's way past schoolin' anyhow. But take Martha now—" Rogier interrupted. "Don't worry about her," he said in his quiet persuasive voice. "You're going to leave Martha here with me. I know a house that'll suit us first rate."

A month later when the Whites left, Rogier married Mrs. White's youngest daughter, Martha. She was a small wiry girl, sixteen years old, and deaf in one ear from an early attack of brain fever. Her habit of listening with her head turned, and the omnipresent string of black beads around her throat – a reminder of the rosaries worn by the Sisters of the Sacred Heart Convent where she had gone to school – accentuated her pose of early maturity. What drew Rogier to her was a mystery neither of them knew. But what held him, even after the birth of two daughters, was the nervous force that surcharged her small body and her great capacity for simply living, both of which she devoted to him.

Old for his age, Rogier accepted his family with equanimity and responsibility, and only to himself admitted the rank heresy of the continuing conviction of his secret exile on a still strange and lonely earth. It was this that had led him across the plains to the high snowy beacon that had suddenly loomed up before him like an etiolated projection of his own hidden longing.

Darkness now had obscured both the Peak and the last straggle of Indians. Rogier got up from his chair on the porch and went inside. In the big square kitchen he lit a lamp, and stirred up a supper of cold porridge with fresh wild raspberries and cream. Then, as he had done every night for two weeks, he settled down to read Martha's last letter. The news had thoroughly penetrated every fiber of his thoughts. She and their two girls, Ona and Sally Lee, were on their way to join him. With them was coming Martha's older sister, Molly, and her two boys, Bob and Hiney, to rejoin her husband, Tom Hines. They were all coming on the new railroad and they hoped everything would be ready for them. Martha as usual had addressed her scrawled note to him with "B. N."—"Big Nigger." The nickname made him smile. He took it as a compliment, remembering the only friends he had known as a child, those great black men who were children yet, maintaining their childlike dignity and divine human sympathy.

As he sat there, waiting with patient anticipation for the morrow when their train was due, he heard hoofbeats outside. The rider jumped off, threw back the door, and stalked inside. It was Tom Hines, young, lean, excited, carrying a rifle in the crook of his left arm.

"Hi, Joe! Haven't forgot what tomorrow is, have you?"

"No, Tom. The house is all ready for them."

"So's mine! Hope they're on the train all right." He was one of those men who never quite succeed in growing up and who appear at their best when affecting boyish enthusiasm — a role that was always changing with new ventures. "I'll bet Molly and the kids will be glad to see me!" His eyes were bright, his face flushed, as he still stood there with his rifle.

"What's the gun for, Tom?" asked Rogier quietly. "Been out hunting?"

With the question Tom changed into another role. "Indians! Never saw so many as this time. There's goin' to be trouble sure and I aim to protect my family. I've never got me a Redskin yet, but this time I'm goin' to!"

"They're peaceful people when they're let alone. Won't you sit awhile?"

"No Joe. I'll meet you at the depot tomorrow, eh? I just rode by now to see if I could get a five from you. Somethin' to celebrate our first night on. Sure, I've got flour and salt and lard, all that, but you know—"

Rogier got up and from a cookie jar took out a five-dollar bill. Tom almost grabbed it from his hand in his eagerness to get away. Rogier from the door watched him swing on his broomtail mare and gallop away. Then again he sat down on his chair on the porch.

Down the creek at the crossing of the Big Ditch a faint glowing pink marked the Indian encampment. In nights past Rogier had walked down there to watch the stomp dancing. Flamelight and pulsing drum; they created a world into which leaped strong lean figures naked to the waist and with that in their faces he never saw elsewhere. A simple and peaceful people, contrary to hotbloods like Tom and his kind; strange only to intruding whites like himself because of all America's many breeds and races they alone were an inalienable part of this vast and naked rock-ribbed earth.

What its rhythm was, the meaning of its hidden spirit, they alone somehow mirrored it as had that rider making the leap an hour before. The black silhouette of horse and rider, the eerie cry, remained burnt into his mind. Rogier did not know why. No more than why the earliest recollection of a child is not the great event but only the queer turning of a single phrase, like the odd disquieting remembrance of the gesture of a loved woman's hand long after she has faded from his mind. He only knew that he could never erase that instant's picture from his memory. The wild rearing horse and its slim rider, arm upraised, exultant in the night. The upright feather stuck into his hair—a single feathered plume descended to him who wore it, not defiantly as men flaunt the faded cockades of their decadent heritage, but proudly, like the everlasting insignia of the wild earth's nobility.

The disturbing sense of beauty in the night was echoed by the throb of the far-off drums. In the luminous purity of the moonlight he could make out again the pale, silvery sheen of the great peak. It too seemed to throb in unison with the pulse beat of the drums, with the living land itself.

2

Near eight o'clock next morning on the depot platform in Denver City, two Englishmen stood discussing the toy train drawn up at the siding before them. It was the Denver and Rio Grande narrow-gauge, projected to run between Denver and Mexico City. The diminutive locomotive was appropriately named *Montezuma* and the two passenger coaches *Denver* and *El Paso*. The undertone of pride in the two men's voices had some justification. Most of the capital required for construction of the initial seventy-six miles of line to Colorado Springs had been raised in London and the rails had been bought in England. Still they argued over a curve of two chains radius, a gradient of one in ninety-two, and whether the train would run or not. The toot of a whistle and the ting-a-ling of a bell that reminded them of "Muffins all hot!" in London, stopped their conjectures. They knocked out their pipes and sauntered toward the "baby railroad."

Down the platform behind them hurried two women weighed down with carpet bags, bundles and lunch baskets, and four children. "Go on! Can't you hurry none?" the smaller woman cried to her two young girls. Her short straight mouth bit off the words in exasperation as though they were another bit of black ribbon dangling from her rusty black bonnet.

"Yeah; go on, boys. Quit bothering your cousins," the older woman called easily to the two boys loafing along beside the two girls. It was a drawl that belonged to her large body, wide-featured face, and air of genial, tolerant strength.

Arriving at the coach, Mrs. Rogier inquired breathlessly, "Is this our train?" The conductor took a chew of tobacco with deliberate concern. "Well, Ma'am, it belongs to the D & RG."

Mrs.Rogier dropped her carpetbag. "Why, of all the –"

"Get on, Martha," Sister Molly's deep voice interrupted, as she hoisted the bags up the steps. Then turning with a grin to the conductor, "Tell us when we get to Colorado Springs, won't you, Mister?"

"Sure," he called back. "We don't go no farther."

The coach was an odd little car with a seat on one side to accommodate one person and one on the other side large enough for two, the seats alternating so that the car could keep its balance. The two girls, Ona and Sally Lee, each took a single seat. Molly Hines' two boys, quarreling over who should sit next to the window, crawled into the double seat across from Sally Lee.

"You just settle yourselves down quick!" Sister Molly flung at them. "Bob, you quit figitin' around. And Hiney, you quit ticklin' Sally Lee with your toes before I step on 'em!"

The two women sat across the aisle from Ona with all the luggage. At the first jerk of the train as it pulled out of the depot, Mrs. Rogier began rearranging and restacking the carpetbags, bundles, and baskets. Imperious and inflexible as one enlightened by the sense of command, she assumed toward her sister an unconscious attitude of unwarranted superiority. Sister Molly, carelessly unconcerned, watched her with tolerant humor, wondering why a man like Joseph Rogier had ever married such a fussy woman. Still it was quite evident that Mrs. Rogier often wondered why Sister Molly had married a man like Tom Hines.

Her few years in southern Missouri, terrible with human mockery, had made Molly a woman. The Whites were neighbors to a bunch of Union soldier outlaws headed by Jessie James and Cole Younger. One day they brought in an old man to shoot at sunrise.

Molly played cards with a Union officer to save his life while the old man sat praying on a cracker box. Molly won, she was sure, because the next day was her birthday. All the outlaws got up early next morning, laughing and talking as they led the old man over the hill. Happy and excited, Molly cooked a gingerbread birthday cake for them. A few hours later the men returned with the old man's body and ordered White to make a coffin.

A short time later Molly married a man named Henry who took her to Kansas City on a wedding trip. After dinner a few evenings later he went out of the hotel to buy a cigar. He never came back.

Soon afterward she married Tom Hines. He was a handsome man who staggered through life blind and smiling; weak without seeming ineffective, likeable because of his faults, and always busy at cross-purposes. With their marriage Sister Molly's life opened into full flower. It was as if all her life she had walked at the edge of a vast chasm of frustration and silent despair. And then, with one divining look of love, she saw in Tom Hines the miasmic nobility, the divine promise of all human life, and dedicated her own to its preservation.

"God, I do love him," she murmured as though he were already close enough to whisper.

"I suppose you do," Mrs. Rogier answered. "I only hope he's got the house finished for you. It's been long enough."

She folded her small hands together in a complacent gesture that showed she had no doubt about her own home. Nor did Sister Molly. Rogier would have his house done, his business started. And then, in a sudden hot rush, came the feeling she didn't care about anything if Tom were there waiting.

"Tom ought to get along better out here," observed Mrs. Rogier.

Sister Molly knew what she meant and was truly grateful. "And don't think Tom ain't either. He thinks everything of Joe, the way he brought him out and helpin' him get started. And Tom's goin' to get along. I just know it, Martha!" Her large coarse face assumed a mask of faith and courage to cover the secret contradiction that had instantly replaced her words.

"I hope so. We all got to start a new life. We got to be somebody!"

The indomitable ambition of the little woman seemed so futilely set against the wall of mountains rising into view that Sister Molly turned her face away.

It had been a long and tiresome trip on the Kansas Pacific to Denver where they had changed trains. Herds of thousands of buffalo, stray remnants of the tens, the hundreds of thousands being killed off. Bunches of graceful, leaping antelope. Prairie-dog towns counted off on the children's fingers. But always the same flat and endless plain. Sister Molly could see no beauty in its empty, arid waste; in the tumbleweeds rolling across the land as if of their own momentum; in the steadily receding horizon. The crude towns where they stopped to eat seemed brutal and unreal. Men, men everywhere. And always eating. Buffalo tongue, buffalo hump, antelope steak, beefsteak. Always men and meat. "We're in Colorado now," a man told her, sniffing out the open window. "It don't look no different, but it's got the feel. Kinda cold. And the wind." Then one sunrise she awakened to see the far, faint rise of mountains. Forbiddingly unreal, they kept rising to block their path at Denver.

Now on the little narrow-gauge they were crawling south along the eastern side of that great blue wall; creeping across grassy slopes between huge cliffs, past castellated rocks of red sandstone, white limestone, and blue shale half-hidden by groves of pine like the ruins of ancient castles in another world called old because it was so much newer. Colorado, the land of colored rock. And then at last Pike's Peak, white and shining, rising more than 14,000 feet above tidewater. The coach was silent as if a blast of wind from its summit had frozen every voice.

A sudden childish shout aroused the coach. "Indians! Hiney, here they are!" He and the two girls rushed across the aisle to stare out the window with Bob. A few men on the coach turned their heads briefly, then sank back to their pipes. Outside, the long line of Indians straggled on. At the end of the column struggled small ponies dragging dunnage lashed to tepee poles, accompanied by squaws carrying their papooses on their backs. Ahead of them were the older men, beclouded in dust, beset with dogs and flies, and enveloped in a dreary aura of weariness. Only at the front of the column a few young bucks yelled and lashed their ponies into a short run beside the coach as the train rolled past.

"Reckon we'll be gettin' in soon. Are your things ready?" asked Mrs. Rogier with her unavoidable assurance.

A queer feeling swept down upon Sister Molly. She could not tear her gaze from the massive peak. Its lower slopes smokily clothed in pine, it reached out like a shadow falling on the plain. "Oh, my God! I hope he's here!" she whispered in a hoarse voice.

He was there on the platform to sweep her into his arms for a hearty hug the instant they got off the train. Beside him stood Rogier to greet his own family with equal affection but less demonstrativeness. At last the hugs and kisses, the excited shouts, were over. Rogier led them to a carriage he had hired for the occasion.

"How can we afford it? Sure it didn't cost too much?" asked Mrs. Rogier sharply.

"Get in. Get in!" He settled in the front seat, taking the reins and lighting a cigar while Tom stowed in the luggage. Then Tom got in beside him, holding his rifle between his knees.

"We're goin' to show you the town first!" announced Tom proudly as they drove off.

The new town had an incomparably beautiful setting. It was located on the flat plain only six miles east of the foot of Pike's Peak. Here at the mouths of its yawning canyons and Ute Pass leading through the mountains bubbled the many iron and soda springs to which the Indians, since time immemorial, had made pilgrimage. Already a small resort was growing up there, named Manitou after the Indians' Great Spirit.

"We won't go over there now. The Indians are gatherin' and they might be trouble," explained Tom, patting his rifle. "Unless of course we do somethin' about it!" Taking it up from between his knees, he sighted along the barrel to a spot about halfway between Manitou and town. That's where Colorado City is—the first capital of Colorado before Denver. Oh, you got lots to see, all right, just as soon as I get me a team and buggy."

Rogier drove slowly up the low hill behind the railroad depot and past a hotel of two stories, covered by a mansard roof with five dormer windows, and with a spacious veranda in front. "That's General Palmer's Colorado Springs Hotel," continued Tom. "He's the one that started Colorado Springs here and built the Denver and

Rio Grande. Rich as all get out, him and all his English cronies. Look there!" He pointed to the ladies sitting on the veranda and then to an English nursemaid strolling behind an English dogcart out in front. "Blasted Britishers all of them! That's why us folks call the town Little London."

"I don't see why," muttered Mrs. Rogier.

"It takes a lot of money to build a town and railroad, and most all of it was raised in England," said Rogier quietly. "So naturally there's quite an English colony here. I don't know but what they're doin' a good job. They're quite likely to make the town into a real spa, the Saratoga of the West. It's a new country. There's plenty of room for all of us."

"But I want to see Indians!" yelled Bob.

There were many to see now, as Rogier drove slowly down spaciously wide Pike's Peak Avenue fronting the hotel and the great peak rising behind it. The dusty street was lined with small stores, leather, harness, and butcher shops, riding horses and teams snubbed to hitching racks. Big Indian bucks idled from door to door. Blanketed squaws sat on every corner with their buffalo robes spread out for sale. Little London! What an anomaly it was, this tidy English colony set in the midst of the crude American West!

"It's growin' fast. We'll get along here first rate," said Rogier quietly, whipping up his team to turn northward towards the outskirts of town.

The sun was sinking behind the mountains when he drew up at the Hines' place. It reminded the girl Ona of an old tramp man she once had seen sitting and smiling beside the dusty road. Small and ungainly, its clapboards stuck out every which-a-way. Weeds and sunflowers grew high everywhere around it. Even the flat roof of the kitchen was covered with earth and sprouted a wild growth of oats.

"Wait'll I light the lamp so's you can see it better!" Tom jumped out, ran inside, and came back to help Sister Molly out of the carriage. All the others trooped in behind them. The light of the lamp in the kitchen revealed a stack of unwashed dishes on the iron cookstove, and the unmade beds in the room beyond. Catching Mrs. Rogier's quick look, Tom laughed. "Why, I was so excited about seein' Molly and the boys this mornin' I never bothered about them dishes and covers!" He wrapped his arms about Molly

"It ain't nothin' but a pioneer's home, but you can bet your bottom dollar we're going to have us a house as big and fancy as them Englishmen!"

"I don't care, Tom! This one's fine. Jes' so's we can all be together!"

"That we are, right now, and we're going to celebrate!"

On the kitchen table sat a bottle of Three Star Hennessy surrounded by three small boxes of candy. The candy he hurriedly gave to Molly and the two boys, then opened the bottle of whiskey.

"We're not goin' to stay," Mrs. Rogier said resolutely. "Molly's got the dishes and beds to do, supper to cook, and things to settle. So've I when I get home."

"Oh stay, Martha. We're all here together for the first time to start a new life. I'll rustle up somethin'."

"I want to go home. I'm hungry," wailed little Sally Lee in a petulant voice.

"I'll have a drink with Tom before we go," said Rogier. "How about it, Molly?"

Pleased and excited, she set out three glasses. "Open your candy now, boys, and pass it around."

Tom took his drink down neat and quick, and poured himself another. "Here's to my wife and kids, and you all too! It's goin' to be a great life. Here's to it!"

Rogier smiled gently and set down his empty glass. Then catching Mrs. Rogier's sharp glance, he rose to his feet. "Well, I've got three more of the family to settle in a new house, too. We'll see you in the mornin'."

Tom and Molly, arms around each other, watched the carriage drive away.

3

Ona always remembered their first house. It sat alone in the prairie north of the end of Tejon Street. Built like a Maltese cross, as her mother always said, it had a long narrow room sticking out on each side of the big square kitchen, a porch to the south, and a storeroom with a big cellar underneath, to the north. Seen from the creek where she played among the cottonwoods, the house seemed bigger than it was. Especially at dusk when the sun, dropping behind the mountains, brought on a swift pale night without twilight. Then the house seemed even bigger, the sharp edges of its ramshackle outline, its sloping roof, blurred like fresh inked lines into the dark. On summer nights the yellow radiance of the lamp trickled out of the open doorway and lay liquiscent in queerly shaped puddles on the porch. On cold winter nights the lamp sat in the window, small and white, like a silver stud on a bridle strap. It was only when seen from the other side, a tiny speck against the great purple mountains, that the house appeared for what it really was.

Every day Ona and her mother walked to town, stopping by the Hines' place to pick up Sister Molly. It was only a couple of miles or so and on the way they passed the College Reservation, a big piece of land bought by government scrip and set aside for a college.

"Joe's biddin' on the first building, Cutler Academy," Mrs. Rogier said proudly. "My! A college already!"

"He's gettin' a good start, contractin' so soon," Sister Molly agreed.

Mrs. Rogier nodded her black bonnet curtly. "Since Joe's so busy he can't use our six acres and has offered them to Tom to work with his; I don't see why Tom don't."

"Oh, Tom's pretty busy too, he's gone all day long. Besides, he ain't cut out for farmin'; he likes to be around people. Next spring he says he's goin' out on a huntin' trip. He was talkin' to two men who have been out on the plains since last December and have just come in. They brought in more than 600 buffalo, wolf, and antelope hides; and they got $2 apiece for them."

"Well, he'll get more lonesome than he would farmin'," observed Mrs. Rogier drily.

In town Ona lagged behind. There was so much to see, all of it different. The hotel, its cool veranda crowded with Easterners and Britishers wearing such nice clean clothes and giving off an air of opulence and comfort. And across from it, Sample's Boarding House. The long narrow building with its rooms each opening upon the long wooden porch was the rendezvous of all the teamsters, miners, traders, and riff-raff of the town. Teams and wagons of all descriptions, from a buckboard to an old covered wagon, stood out in front. As Ona passed by she could see the porch floor strewn with whips, spurs, saddles, and other gear.

Of all the stores she liked the butcher shops best. In front of every one hung marbled carcasses of deer, antelope, bear, and buffalo. These markets were the favorite lounging places of the Indians. Early in the morning the squaws would arrive and unstrap their papooses from their backs, leaning the cradle boards with their little living mummies against the wall. There were old men wrapped in blankets and a queer dignity; young bucks strutting back and forth. Despite Tom's constant preaching against them, they didn't look very mean or dangerous to Ona; just kind of dirty and lazy.

Wherever she went she was aware of the mountains. They seemed so close you could walk to them to play. From Cheyenne

Mountain and the Devil's Horn to the south, they extended to Cameron's Cone and Pike's Peak with the Bottomless Pit between, and then northward in an unbroken wall as far as she could see. Pike's Peak was the highest. You could tell that by a line drawn across it. Below the line the peak was dark with pine and spruce and cedar; above it, the peak rose bare and white. Timberline. That's what it was called.

But Ona liked the prairies and plains too. Early one morning soon after their arrival she took all the children out for a picnic: little Sally Lee, Bob and Hiney, and the Siegerfries girl Marion. The Siegerfries family lived on two of Tom's mortgaged six acres. Marion brought along their old blind mule. It was good she did, for if Sally Lee or Hiney became tired they could ride on her; besides she could carry their lunch of bread and butter with jam, apples, pickles, and pie.

They walked down the creek to the long irrigation ditch called the Big Ditch, where the Indians always camped on their way to the mountains. Then they straggled eastward toward a low range of wooded bluffs out on the prairie. Austin Bluffs was split by a gunsight notch called Templeton's Gap. It was a great lightning and storm center, Marion said. Last year there had been a cloudburst over it. The water came down with such great force that it gouged a great hole in the earth, causing the mud to roll out in balls ranging in size from that of a walnut to a squash, all hard as if they had been baked in an oven.

"That's where we'll go! To get us some of them mud balls!" everybody decided.

So now they all walked faster, laughing and throwing stones, beside the plodding blind mule. The bundle of lunch tied to a rope looped around the mule was continually sliding down and hanging under her belly.

"Let her hang," said Bob practically. "It can't balance on her backbone nohow." He and Marion walked together now, leading the mule. They were great friends although with her starched sunbonnet she topped him several inches. Hiney and Sally Lee kept close together too, leaving Ona alone. She always felt alone, no matter how many people were around. It was an awful feeling sometimes, when just for an instant you imagined you were dead and invisible, walking with them like a ghost, or spying on them through the keyhole of a dark closed-up room. She would be glad to grow up and not feel that way then.

Still it was good to be out on the prairies, watching the buffalo or gramma grass waving in the wind, and seeing bright clumps of purple lupines and bluebells, crimson Indian paintbrush, wild yucca, onions, and locoweed. Prairie dogs barked from their mounds. Plump meadow larks sang deliriously, ignoring a hawk that hung as if suspended from the cloudless sky. A rabbit ran out from a bush. Innumerable horny toads crawled through the warm sand, some with yellow bellies which caused warts.

"Hurry up! Come on!" shouted Marion. "We've found a red-ant hill!"

When Ona reached them, Bob was on his knees frantically digging into a large pebbly mound. Ona knew what he was after – garnets. She liked to think of the big red ants bringing the flinty blood-red stones up from way down in the ground to build into their hills, and the Indians coming along later to dig them out and sell them in town. Her mother had bought her a little jar of them. To carry all they were going to find here, the children ate up the pickles in their big jar. But digging was hard without a shovel, and the big red ants swarmed bitingly over their legs. So they gave it up, and tied bunches of wildflowers into the rope around the old mule, making a garland of red, white, and blue.

Farther on they ate their lunch although it was hardly mid-morning. Then Bob, who had wandered off, started to yell and wave his arms. They all jumped up and ran to him.

"I've cornered a rattler!" he yelled. "Hiney, you turn over that big stone with Ona. And when he comes out, Marion, you keep pushing his head down with a stick while I grab him by the tail! Don't hurt him none!"

The snake was really big and beautiful with six or seven rattles. Bob carried him by the tail while Marion kept pushing down his head with a stick. Ona led the blind, garlanded mule with Sally Lee and Hiney mounted on her back.

It was then they heard the indistinct sound of hoofbeats. "Do like the Indians do!" commanded Bob authoritatively. "Lay down and put your ear to the ground!"

Obediently Ona sprawled down, ear to the ground. Then looking up from this ludicrous posture of strained attention, she saw two mounted horsemen galloping toward them over a far rise. The men were upon them in a jiffy, flinging off their panting horses, grabbing Hiney and Sally Lee off the old mule to put on their own mounts.

"Leggo that snake, you kids! Now come on, all of you! There's no time to be lost!"

An overwhelming presentiment of evil, like a black choking pall from the cloudless sky, caught up Ona. In it they hurried home. One horseman carrying Sally Lee and leading the old mule. The other horseman carrying Hiney and lashing the mule with a whip. Ona, Marion, and Bob took turns riding her double while the other trotted behind. Ona was sorry for her. "She's old and blind, and can't see where she's goin'. Quit beatin' her so hard!"

"None of your back talk now!" the man said, lashing the old mule again. "You oughta be glad we're savin' you from bein' scalped! Come on, I say!"

Even before they reached home, Ona could hear the courthouse bells ringing in town. Tom and Sister Molly were waiting for them with Mrs. Rogier in front of the house. Tom rushed forward, gun in hand, to take the two smaller children out of the saddles.

"You got the news?" asked one of the horsemen. "It was Charlie, the herd boy. Scalped on Mount Washington."

"I'm takin' 'em all in to town right now!" answered Tom, patting his rifle. "Don't you worry no more about us!"

Charlie was one of the town herd boys, twelve or fourteen years old maybe, about Ona's own age. Every morning he would collect a number of families' cows to drive out to pasture, bringing them back each night. It seemed impossible that the lazy Indians she'd seen loafing in town had scalped him on Mount Washington, a low hill on the prairie just southeast of town. Tom wasted no words on an explanation of how it may have happened. He was in a raging hurry to escort them all to safety in the courthouse.

"Git your stuff together and let's get goin'! We'll go by the Siegerfries place, and then right to town. There's no tellin' when the whole band of murderin' Redskins will sweep by!"

Despite the black cloud of evil still surrounding her, Ona could detect the pleasurable air of excitement he exuded. She was surprised that her mother seemed immune to it. "You all go ahead," she told Tom stubbornly. "Me and the two girls are goin' to wait here for Joe."

"He's in town waitin' to protect all the gatherin' citizens! Listen to them bells!"

"Protectin' all them Eastern and English ladies drinkin' tea in the hotel? No! If there's any protectin' to do, Joe had better come home and do it!"

"Martha's right," said Sister Molly. "Maybe it's a false alarm anyway."

"You come on! When we see Joe we'll send him back."

Ona watched them go, the four Hines and Marion, with a feeling of abandon tinctured with a curious admiration for her mother's stubborn independence.

Whatever Mrs. Rogier thought, she kept it to herself. She fixed lunch and after it was eaten put the two girls to work on household chores. While they were still busy with these in mid-afternoon, a shrill eerie cry was heard. Both Mrs. Rogier and Ona knew instantly what it was. The Indians were less than a mile away; there was no time nor way to flee to town. Quickly Mrs. Rogier closed the windows, barred the doors, and hurried the two girls with bread and candles down into the cellar.

Looking out the window over which Mrs. Rogier was hanging a blanket, they both could see the band of Indians crossing the creek at the cottonwoods and riding toward the house. The older men jogged along leisurely, sleepy in the warm sunshine. Behind them followed the long ungainly file of laden ponies and overloaded squaws splashing at the creek. Then a dozen young braves on barebacked ponies swept up to gallop around the house, yelling with arms upraised and then crouching low or hanging to the sides of their mounts. It was a brave show though none of the squaws nor their sleepy elders appeared to notice them. They only succeeded in raising the dogs in cry. Down in the dark cellar the noise was ominously fearful, the high pitched yells broken into a staccato by palms clapped to mouths, the thunder of hoofs and the dust sifting through the window, the barking of dogs. Ona raised up the corner of the blanket to look out.

"Ona!" Mrs. Rogier called out low and sharp, and when the girl did not answer slapped her on the cheek. As she flinched, Ona clumsily yanked down the blanket from the window. Instantly Mrs. Rogier pulled her down to lie on the floor. She did not even scold, they were so still. But the hoofbeats stopped, and suddenly as out of a dream, a red-brown face grinned in the window. There sounded blows upon the door and the east window tinkled into pieces. Mrs. Rogier closed her straight short mouth and covered up Sally Lee with a blanket. "Stop that whimperin' and go to sleep!" Then she marched upstairs with Ona cringing at her heels.

The house was filling with Indians. Even the old men were dismounting to crowd into the big kitchen behind the young ones, leaving the squaws massed outside the door. To Ona they looked like the ones she had seen so often in town, old dark wrinkled faces impassively staring out from the striped blankets, sharp young faces grimacing with devilish delight as they threw out shiny new kettles and fresh scrubbed pots to the waiting squaws. Mrs. Rogier stood straight and still with indignation, her head cocked to one side, apprehensively listening for Sally Lee.

The young bucks now discovered the feather bed in the next room. Whooping in positive enjoyment, they wrestled on it, stripped it of blankets, slit it with their knives, and threw handfuls of feathers swirling through the house. Through all this their wrinkled elders stood in a corner, weary, sleepy, and disinterested, as if they had seen it an incalculable number of times. Two of them kept munching apples.

The young braves had opened the flour bin. They demanded pancakes. For an hour Mrs. Rogier stood over the red-hot stove, growing whiter with anger every minute as she ladled up cakes to the savage horde. They knew what hotcakes were, all right, thought Ona. Drowned in syrup, covered with handsful of sugar! When her food was all gone, and with it most of her pots and pans, Mrs. Rogier could stand no more. Little and thin, she flailed at the savages with thin arms. The Indians laughed and hollered, thrusting her down upon a chair. Whenever she tried to stand up, they thrust her down again. Then imagining she heard a whimper from Sally Lee downstairs, her imagination gave way. She sat weeping stonily, wiping the tears from her red-lidded eyes. Ona, holding her hand, remained standing beside her as if petrified, a small stone image in calico set up stiffly among the warm-colored bodies guttering among themselves like splendid beasts at play. Something about her indomitable silence and stony face impressed the council of old men in the corner. They silently held the gaze of their sharp black eyes upon her.

It was then that Ona noticed him for the first time, as he moved toward her. He was a young man, tall and straight as an arrow but powerfully built. He was naked to the waist and she could see the sharp outline of his muscular breasts. His face, with its Roman nose and high cheekbones, glowed rose-red. His hair was straight and coarse and black, like the mane of a horse, and his eyes were piercing black. Stooping slightly, he caught her up like a feather and swung her sideways so that another young brave could catch her by the arms. He then grasped her by the ankles and the two of them began swinging her toward the hot stove. Closer. Closer. Suddenly, with one hand, he pulled up her calico dress and on the next slow swing pressed her naked bottom against the hot iron of the stove. It all happened instantly and at once. She could feel the sharp pain of the burn on her right buttock, the faint odor of singeing white flesh; and at the same time the steady fixed stare of his black eyes into her own, a stare that seemed to penetrate so deep into her that for instant they became one.

Then they set her on her feet, the shorter young Indian still holding her by the wrists. Ona didn't notice her mother writhing on her chair in the grip of other Indians. Nor did she pay any attention to the steady stare of the old men in the corner, muttering appreciatively because she hadn't cried out. She stood looking vaguely at the young brave who had burned her, aware only of the sharp pain of her burned behind creeping down like a slow glow to her crotch, and feeling a warm trickle down the inner side of one leg.

The short Indian holding her wrists gave a sudden jerk and grunted, "Hagh!" He wanted to swing her against the stove again till she hollered. But the tall one, still looking at her, pushed him back till he released her arms. She went back to stand beside her mother and to stare back at him. That sharp, rose-brown face with its slightly flaring nostrils and piercing black eyes had something about it she would never understand nor ever forget; a look at once more repellently wild and curiously intimate than anything she had ever known. The warm trickle down her leg scared her. She didn't know what it meant either.

4

Rogier, sitting in the little board shanty he used for an office downtown, had heard the report of the herd boy's scalping that morning. It was a tragic occurrence of course, but also an unfortunate incident to which he did not attribute the pealing importance of the courthouse bells. The time had passed when they might have signalled a disastrous Indian uprising.

Some twenty years earlier the great peace treaty of 1851 drawn at Fort Laramie had apportioned the mountains and plains among the different tribes for as long as the grass should grow. All the buffalo plains west from Kansas and Nebraska to the Rocky Mountains, and south from the Platte to the Arkansas, had been granted to the Cheyennes and Arapahoes. To the Sioux went the land north of the Platte, and to the Kiowas and Comanches the sere plains south of the Arkansas. The high front range of the Rockies and the mountains west remained to the Utes. The Pike's Peak Rush of 1858, with thousands of white gold-seekers pouring in to found Denver, had proved the treaty false. The finishing touch had come in the election year of 1864 when a rabid ex-elder of the Methodist Episcopal Church running for election as a delegate to Congress,

John M. Chivington, had attacked a peaceful village of Cheyennes and Arapahoes at Sand Creek, not far east, with four mounted companies of Colorado Volunteers. Most of the some five hundred people in the village were women and children. Chivington's massacre of them was almost complete. He returned jubilantly to Denver, parading his troops down the street with their bloody scalps and exhibiting captive children in a carnival. Indicted by a Congressional committee but not punished for the crime, Chivington nevertheless had broken the power of the Plains tribes.

The mountain Utes, Rogier knew, were faring little better. In 1868 the federal government had reserved for them a great section of some 15,000,000 acres in southwestern Colorado, but with the rumors of gold in the region was already taking steps to recover it. Immemorial custom was still strong. Bands of Utes kept coming down the mountains every year to pitch their smoke-gray lodges near the new little resort of Manitou growing up around their tribal medicinal springs; and to join them for trade straggled in stray bands of Cheyennes and Arapahoes. They were quiet and abject enough, these broken remnants of once great tribes, unless disreputable saloon keepers in Colorado City sneaked them a few bottles of whiskey. The commotion they caused was disagreeable enough, but far exceeded by the importance given it.

This was what had happened that morning. For days the encampment had been breaking up; and one small band, urged on by firewater, had run off a few head of stock on its way out of town and then had cruelly and tragically scalped the herder Charlie. Looking out the window, Rogier could see the street emptying of people, the Indians vanishing like wraiths to escape retribution and the white residents fleeing to the courthouse when the bells began to peal their warning. It was quite noticeable that the Colorado Springs Hotel was not evacuated nor barricaded against assault; the ladies on the veranda simply removed inside to continue their games of whist and bézique. So Rogiér, discounting the alarm, had remained in his office. He had work to do.

Early that afternoon, more annoyed than alarmed by the emptiness of the street, he walked down to the courthouse. A crowd of people had assembled on the lawn, all pervaded with a growing air of excitement. Several outlying ranchers had come in with reports that the fleeing bands of Indians had committed depredations of all sorts, running off stock, breaking up wagons, and shooting through the windows. There was no telling when more people, like the herd boy, would be killed.

In the crowd Rogier saw Tom hurrying from group to group with his rifle. In a moment he came up to Rogier. A flush of excitement illumined his clear tanned face. His blue eyes glowed. The men were dividing into two parties, he announced; one to pursue the Indians and the other to stay here at home to protect the women and children. "Come on. Where's your gun? You're goin', aint you, Joe?" he demanded, looming up straight and tall.

Before Rogier could answer, Molly and her two boys came up. "Where's Martha and the girls? You brought 'em down here, didn't you Joe?"

"Why no, Molly. I haven't been home. I had to finish some figurin' on that south wall."

"My God, man!" exclaimed Tom. "They're home waitin' for you to come and protect them after we saved the girls from bein' scalped by that bunch that killed Charlie!"

A worried frown flitted over Rogier's face as he listened to Sister Molly. "I'll go right on up." Then noticing her face bent to her husband's worn-out boots, he added, "First, though, let's see about some new boots, Tom. You can't ride off this way."

"Naw!" laughed Tom self-consciously. He had been talking for several weeks about a new pair of boots "the minute I draw five aces."

"Tom! Don't be stubborn. You can pay Joe back in no time. And please be careful. Don't forget me and the boys, Tom."

Rogier turned away from the look in Sister Molly's eyes with the forlorn hope that someday Tom might see how priceless was his possession. Tom followed him across the street for a new pair of boots. And then, because he was Tom, they bought a bottle of Hennessy in case of a rattlesnake bite or something. Now a bugle was blowing for the men to form. Mounting every available horse and bearing every conceivable kind of weapon, the avengers of small Charlie wheeled into line. At its head Lieutenant Crestmore, an ex-officer in the British Navy, waved aloft a bright saber, his most cherished possession. Behind him rode five members of the English colony in the red-coated attire in which they rode to hounds after coyotes on the plains – Tanzt breeches, Busvine habits, and tailored English riding boots. Tom, brown-faced and smiling, waved back from his borrowed piebald, the finest and bravest gentleman of them all.

Rogier clumped home as quickly as possible on a left-over, swaybacked livery nag. The crowd of Indians massed around the house revealed, to his shame, his neglect of his family. He swung off his nag with a tense square-cut face, pushed through the crowd of squaws, and stalked into the kitchen.

"Joe!" Mrs. Rogier, with red-rimmed eyes, was squirming on a chair beside the hot stove. Ona was standing beside her, holding her hand and facing the two young bucks who had just seared her bottom. Against the wall stood a group of old men.

"You're all right, Martha," Rogier answered almost curtly, walking up to her and giving her a pat on the shoulder. Then he moved close to the stove and its convenient poker. Unbuttoning his coat and leaning an arm on the mantel, he faced the old men with a steady stare.

The afternoon was warm and all the Indians were full of food; they looked torpid and bored. The short young buck, however, wanted a little more fun. He advanced a step, took Ona by the wrists, and waited for the slim one to grab her legs. The latter did not move; he was still caught in Ona's mesmerized stare. Rogier slowly took down his arm from the mantelpiece, then suddenly reached out and caught the short buck by the wrist. As the Indian released Ona and straightened, Rogier stooped and twisted, lifting the Indian off his feet. Then with a half-turn of his wide workman's shoulders he flung the Indian out the door. It was a neat display of strength, but Mrs. Rogier heard and saw the rip of his coat under the armpits. A murmurous chorus of grunts from the old men filled the room. Rogier stood still, his right hand dangling against his leg inches from the iron poker.

The young Indian hit the ground outside in a sprawl and rebounded to his feet instantly. As he approached the doorway the old men broke out into noisy talk, pointing to the lacerated flesh where his arm had been torn by a nail. There was an instant of ominous stillness, like a deep pool nurturing a geyser of trouble. It was abruptly broken by the tall young buck still curiously held immobile by the rapt stare of the young girl in front of him. He pivoted about on mocassined feet, gave a high pitched yell, and strode out the door, giving the other Indian a derisive push on the chest. The old men turned and walked out behind him, followed by other young bucks tumbling everything on the floor that remained erect. The squaws outside scattered in all directions, and in a few minutes the whole band was straggling off.

Mrs. Rogier shut up her sniffle as quickly as if she had been on a stage and the curtain had rung down, and gave Rogier a sharply accusing look before running down to the cellar after Sally Lee. "Well! It's about time you were gettin' home! You might have known something like this was goin' to happen with all them Indians passin' by!"

When she came back up the stairs Rogier gave her a consoling hug. "I'm sorry, Martha, but no harm's been done."

"No harm!" She pointed tragically at the tumbled down furniture bestrewn with flour and salt and feathers. "All my new pots and pans gone. The feather bed ruined. Flour bin emptied. Not a speck of food left in the house. And Ona! They burned her against the stove. Right on her bare behind. Look here!"

Scooping up a handful of lard from a tumbled can she hastened over to Ona and lifted her calico dress. The girl stood helplessly still, looking down with a shamefaced and uncomprehending stare at the sparse trickle of blood down her leg. Mrs. Rogier, upon seeing it, let out a scream of pity and rage. Flinging down the girl's upraised skirt, and grabbing her in a tight motherly embrace, she gave vent at last to all her fright and indignation. "Her first blood-lettin'! Those red devils scared her into it! Because you wouldn't come home to protect your family like Tom!"

Rogier listened quietly to her impassioned tirade; and when she finally released Ona, he put his hand gently on her head. "Every girl has to learn about this thing, Ona. You're not hurt. I'm only sorry you were scared."

"I wasn't real scared when they burned me. I knew I wasn't goin' to be scalped. It was just –" Her voice dwindled off into silence. She could not explain to anyone the strange fusion of feelings in that mysterious moment: the searing pain on the right side of her bottom, the warm glow in her crotch, the knifing stare of those wild but intimate eyes – the wildness and the fear, the sweetness and sudden familiarity, all of it mixed together all at once.

That evening Sigerfries brought over Sister Molly and her two boys in his wagon. The scare was over now that the fighting party was pursuing the Indians, and most of the townspeople had gone home from the courthouse, leaving only the outlying ranchers to stay all night. "I just had to come. I worried all day about you," said Sister Molly surveying the torn-up house. "It's a good thing I did. There's plenty of work for all of us."

"There's no bed to sleep on, nothin' to cook, and nothin' to cook it in. Oh, I'm glad you came!" Mrs. Rogier began to sniffle, recounting all their misfortunes.

"My dad's goin' to shoot himself an Indian! That's where he went!" proclaimed Bob.

"I hope not," Rogier said quietly. "One killing's enough."

"You get to work now sweepin' this floor!" ordered Sister Molly. "Come on. Let's all pitch in."

Worn out at last, they had a few scraps for supper and all went to bed on the floor. Sister Molly lay sleepless in the darkness. "I reckon I'm worryin' about Tom," she said as if to herself. "Oh, I hope nothin' happens to him!"

"Nothing's goin' to happen to anybody," came Rogier's quiet voice. "It's all over. Isn't it, Ona?"

Ona, her burned bottom rubbed with lard, was asleep and dreaming a dream that had no meaning at all.

Late the next day Tom returned home with the avenging party. His breath smelled of whiskey, he was tired and in a bad mood. Leaning his gun in the corner, he went to bed supperless without saying a word about the expedition. Rogier learned from others what had happened. The party had ridden out on the plains, following the retreating band of Indians. There was no one qualified to track them, and going had been slow with all the livery stable nags. Nevertheless about dusk the party had come upon a band of Indians making camp. Some of the men wanted to attack at once. The others held back. They were tired and hungry after their long day's ride, and night was coming on. Besides, they argued, how did they know this was the band which had murdered the herd boy?

Lieutenant Crestmore ended the argument by riding with a few men to the encampment for a parley. The Indians disclaimed any knowledge of the scalping. "They're lying. Indians always lie," he was advised by one of his staff. "Tell 'em we're goin' to punish them anyway!"

The lieutenant delivered his ultimatum. The Indians must give up the man who had killed the boy by daybreak or they would be attacked. He then rode back and ordered camp pitched for the night. The men gathered grass and chips for fires and cooked supper. Afterwards they sat cleaning their rifles and revolvers, and talking over the cavalry tactics they would use. "But it looks like they're goin' to turn over our man," said one. "You don't see any war dance goin' on around their fires or hear any war-whoops, do you?"

"That's all right too!" said another. "We'll march him back to the courthouse and have a public hangin' on the lawn!"

The night dragged by, the men watching the steadily burning Indian fires with mounting excitement. Promptly at the first light of day the bugle sounded. The men saddled and mounted, and under Lieutenant Crestmore the column split into two detachments to surround the Indian camp. The column gradually closed in, then waited for the lieutenant and his aides in their red coats to receive the decision of the Indians to fight or to deliver their prisoner. Crestmore rode back with discomfiting news. There wasn't an Indian in the camp. During the night one Indian had remained to keep the fires burning, and the rest had fled. Grumbling, out of sorts, and without provisions for a long chase, the column had turned back home.

5

Late next spring came the opportunity Rogier had been waiting for. It opened the door of his shanty in the person of a slimly built young man of twenty-five with mild blue eyes and a diffident manner. "Doin' all right, Joe?" he asked, squatting on a chair in front of Rogier's drawing table.

Rogier grinned. "I'm biddin' on the Academy. Suppose you are too, Stratton. Somebody's got to get it if it isn't you." Older, stockily built and more mature, he did not look like a man facing his ex-employer.

Young Winfield Scott Stratton had come out West from Jeffersonville, Indiana shortly before Rogier and set up shop as a carpenter, contractor, and builder. A jim-dandy carpenter, he had no trouble landing jobs in the booming new settlement. He put in the woodwork on the new stone Episcopal church and built several first-class houses including one bought by W.S. Jackson for his bride, Helen Hunt. Rogier, arriving in town stone broke, had worked for him as a journeyman carpenter. The two men got along as well as could be expected from their difference in temperaments. Stratton was moody, unpredictable, and hot tempered. In an instant his mild blue eyes would flame blue fire, and his diffident manner would erupt into a volcano of thrashing fists. He had quarreled and broken off with two previous partners and Rogier was glad to set up in business for himself as soon as he got on his feet. Stratton, owing him a hundred dollars in back wages, remained friendly and often dropped by for a talk.

This morning he came to the point immediately. "No, I'm not biddin' on the Academy. No more building for me. I'm off to Baker's Park."

The look on Rogier's face betrayed his shocked amazement. Ten or twelve years before, a man named John Baker had heard from Navajos that there was gold in the San Juan mountains of southwestern Colorado, one of the wildest regions in America. Gathering a group of men, Baker worked northward from New Mexico into a tiny valley walled by lofty peaks and watered by the Animas River. Although almost all the men perished, it was reliably reported they had picked rubies and garnets off the ground; and D.C. Collier of Central City staked his reputation as a noted geologist that the region would prove to be the most extensive diamond field in the world.

Such wild tales had not been forgotten. The government had abrogated its treaty with Ouray, the Ute chief, throwing the region wide open. More and more prospectors kept climbing over Stony Pass and down through Cunningham Gulch. With the discovery of the Little Giant silver lode in Arrestra Gulch the rush began. Towns were building up – Silverton, Howardsville, Eureka – and the country was now swarming with men. One of them had just come to Colorado Springs to offer the opportunity of a lifetime – a wonderful claim just filed and ready to be worked, the Yretaba Silver Lode in Cunningham Gulch. Within a few days several prominent men in town began to form a company to work the Yretaba. This was the venture on which Stratton was itching to embark.

"You'd sell out your contracting business, an enterprisin' and successful young fellow like you, to run off on a wild goose chase like this?" asked Rogier.

"It's not a wild goose chase, Joe. When I was a kid in Indiana I heard of gold on Pike's Peak. Right then I could see it plain as day, like a dream in broad daylight. A big snowy peak and on it gold nuggets big as walnuts waitin' to be picked up! That's why I came here, Joe. Something tells me I'm going to hit it. Big!"

That great and lofty peak, the beacon for a generation of men with all their foolhardy hopes. "The Pike's Peak Bust! It should have warned you, Stratton."

"I've sold my two lots and I'm still short of the $3,000 for my share. What do you say, Joe? You can take over my office, the whole business. $1,500."

"Well, building is my line, and I'm not interested in gold, silver, mining, nothin' like that." He opened his strong box and taking out a packet of bank notes laid them on the table in front of Stratton. "This is all the cash I've got. $500. I could give you a note for $1,000."

"Good enough, Joe. I can raise the rest of the cash on your note. Now, do you want papers, option and so on?"

Rogier grinned. "I reckon our word's as good as paper."

A few days later Stratton left for the San Juans to make his fortune. Rogier moved into his vacated office on Pike's Peak Avenue. It was an excellent location: a big room with an open skylight on the top floor of one of the few two-story buildings in town. On the glass pane of the door was now painted:

JOSEPH ROGIER
Contractor and Builder

It had taken him some time to decide upon the lettering. The simplicity of the sparse wording, the solid forcefulness of the black Roman letters, pleased him; they gave the feeling he wanted them to express.

Now on his first morning in the office, he ambled around like a bear in a new den accustoming himself for a long winter. On the shelf along the wall he had placed the few books he had collected: arithmetics, engineering handbooks on structural design and stresses and strains, a number of geologies, and with these several books on various religions which Mrs. Rogier had been glad to see removed from the house. On the opposite wall was thumb-tacked a plat of the Colorado Springs Settlement. The names of the cross streets south of Pike's Peak Avenue bore Spanish names from the earliest influence south of the settlement: Huerfano, Cucharas, Vermejo, Moreno. Those to the north had been taken from the

French trapper element: Bijou, St. Vrain, Cache la Poudre. The principal north and south avenues – Wahsatch, Nevada, Cascade – were named for mountain ranges. Rogier regarded with ironic amusement the effort to perpetuate the memory of those *coureurs des bois* and *conquistadores* who had entered these fabled Shining Mountains to rape their treasures of beaver and gold. The day of the Spanish and the French had forever passed. Now the English and Americans had come, so cocksure of their permanence they had made haste to name some streets after mountains before the ranges were trampled under foot and forgotten. As if that high peak out the window would not outlive their own dust and memory, a mute witness of their own greedy and inauspicious lives. Yes, dom it! It was a great land, long as time and wide as the imagination, with the rhythm of its own being. Always conscious of a sense of uplift, Rogier looked down as if from great height upon the slow evolution of his kind from their cenozoic ooze. He could see them crawling upon the slimy land, slinking into the steamy jungle as he had seen men vanishing into the half-light of the Carolina swamps, then emerging slowly out upon the wide grassy lowlands of the Mississippi basin. Always westward and upward until they stood at last upon this great arid plateau fronted by lofty mountains raised like a pulpit before which they could shout their everlasting queries at the empty sky above. This was the end of their hegira. Not a land new and raw to be molded at their will, but one so old it had outlived the forests imbedded in the limestone cliffs just west of town. A land to be lived with, not conquered.

Rogier was brought up short at his drafting board. Spread out on it was a blueprint of the first school building proposed for the College Reservation. Cutler Academy. English Gothic, of course, and to be constructed of gray stone. And imposingly big and durable building, and for a college too. The foresight of its planners humbled him, he was so conscious of his own lack of education. Straddling the high stool before the drafting board, he slid his coarse, calloused thumb up and down a T-square of hand-polished bird's eye maple he had brought from Maryland. He held one end of it down on the board, lifted the other to test its supple strength, and then released it to whack resoundingly on the dusty yellow paper. Dom it! Whatever was to go inside the Academy or to come out, he was the man to build its walls.

An hour or more later he was interrupted by a woman's step sounding outside the door and the rap of her knuckles against the door. Martha! It was so unlike her to come to town to see him that Rogier smiled with pleasure as he opened the door.

"Why, mornin' Molly!" he said in surprise upon seeing it was she.

"Mornin' Joe," she answered dully, standing big, gaunt, and hollow-eyed before him with a bunch of bluebells dangling in her hand.

"Come in, Molly," he said kindly. "It's nice of you to come down to see the place. I thought it might be Martha."

Listlessly she scuffed into the room, laying the flowers upon his desk. "I fetched 'em for your new office." Rogier, aware that she knew his dislike of picked flowers yet appreciating her gesture, acknowledged the gift with his silence. It was obvious she was in trouble. The wrinkles in her faded gingham dress showed it had been slept in. Her black hair, caught at the back, was uncombed and strands of it kept falling over her face. Pushing them back from her dull eyes, she slumped down on a chair.

"What's the trouble, Molly? Bob?"

Her oldest boy Bob was like Tom, always running away from home and playing with firearms. That winter he had shot himself twice with Tom's rifle, once through the hand and the last time in the head while looking down the barrel. The doctor's probing had extracted the ball, and the accident had ended the prized ownership of Tom's rifle. He was his mother's obvious favorite, but Sister Molly said nothing.

"Hiney – Hiney's gettin' along all right, isn't he, Molly?"

A slight, straight-haired little lad, eleven years old, he went about with a shy grin and an amazing self-assurance. With the printing of the region's first newspaper, Hiney had obtained the job of delivering copies along the route to Colorado City and Manitou by horseback. Some time ago he had been thrown and was brought home with a slight concussion. Although he had recovered, he occasionally still suffered its effects.

"No, Joe. But it's Tom." Sister Molly paused and raised her chin resolutely. "Yesterday mornin' Hiney got another one of them spells. Couldn't remember nothin' at all, even who he was. The doctor always said there was nothin' much to do when he got that way but use the medicine and to come after him. So I give Tom all the money in the house to get some more medicine and bring home the doctor. He ain't come home yet!"

"I'm sure nothing serious has happened to him."

Sister Molly's slumped body stiffened under the wrinkled gingham as if she were calling forth all her strength to staunchly uphold a new and devastating conviction. "That's the trouble, Joe. I know nothin's happened to Tom." For an instant she lowered her glance as if in acknowledgment of his shamefulness. It was but a last momentary flinching from the truth, and when she raised her eyes Rogier could feel the force of conviction. "It's been comin' a long time, like I knew it would but couldn't believe until I gave Tom that money. It was two silver dollars in a pickle jar put up on the the top shelf – bein' saved for a rainy day. Tom never knew it was there till I climbed up after it and put it in his hand and told him to hurry. And then the way he looked at me, Joe, I knew! I tell you I knew we was done!"

Her voice rang out clear and strong with all the conviction of a pent-up truth. "I kept thinkin' of it all afternoon when I sat there beside Hiney with his wet face. Tom didn't come back. Bob wasn't around either. So when the herd boy brought our cow back, I sent him after the doctor. Pretty soon the doctor left, sayin' Hiney would be all right. Then Bob came and ate some bread and ham and went to bed. That's all there was to eat. Tom never bothered whether there was much or nothin' to eat in the house. I thought of lots of other things too, after I blew out the lamp. A night's a long time, Joe, when you sit lookin' out the window at the prairies empty in the moonlight and thinkin' just one thing. And all the time things fittin' together like pieces of wood in a puzzle."

She stared past Rogier on his stool and out into the morning sunlight as if seeing painted on the cloudless sky the completed tangram of her fate. "I ain't never complained, or I ain't whinin' now," her eyes came back to him unafraid," 'cause a woman don't want much. But she's got to have a man who'll stick by her and see things through. And I never have. Never! And neither has Mom. In all our family, clear through, we been standin' all we can bear. I'm done! I love Tom, but I tell you, Joe, so help me God, I know we're done!"

Rogier unstraddled his legs and got off his high stool. "You're upset, Molly. Tuckered out and worried sick. Go home and rest. I'm goin' over to Colorado City to see a man. I'll keep a lookout for Tom. Here." He gave her a random handful of silver dollars. "On your way home buy the little tike somethin' from Martha and the girls."

"Joe!" She stood up, rattling the coins in her hand. "Be square with me. That's why I come. Not for these!"

Rogier gave her a keen gray glance that cut through her pride. "You should have been born a Rogier," he said curtly. "If I hadn't been, I'd have thanked your mother for savin' my life."

He moved toward the door. Sister Molly stood still until he looked around. "Joe, what'll I do?"

"What can you do?" he answered her bluntly and simply, with all honesty in his steady gaze and held back the open door to let her pass.

Colorado City, strung out along the creek bottoms midway between Little London and Manitou at the base of the peak, was the sort of place Tom was sure to be. A convenient stop to water horses and men, its short and crowded streets gave an illusion of bustling importance deriving from the fact that while saloons were barred in the plains town, here almost every building swung open its half-doors to any thirsty stranger's push. Tom was not in Jake Becker's saloon nor in either of the two large beer gardens. Rogier continued his search, turning down on one of the side streets leading to the creek. It was an unsavory area of wooden shanties and Rogier sauntered along the cowpaths between saloons. The hitching rack in front of Levy's was lined solid with teams so he pushed open the doors.

In the middle of the floor four teamsters were rolling dice on top of a table; one of them had his arm upraised in the hierophantic attitude of opportuning the favor of his fate. The long mahogany bar was spotted with men exchanging news and drinks. A group of women, their cheeks rosy with paint, noted Rogier's arrival and stood up at mechanical attention with set, stiff smiles. Rogier dismissed their invitations with a quick glance. He had caught sight of Tom lounging dejectedly at a corner table off to his right. Casually Rogier turned his back and strolled to the bar.

He had not finished his drink before Tom got up and ambled toward him. Rogier watched him in the mirror. For an instant Tom stood beside him, his sober red eyes carrying the look of a whipped dog. Then he laid his hand on Rogier's shoulder.

Rogier set down his glass and turned around slowly. "Oh, hello, Tom."

"What you doin' down here, Joe?'"

"Over to see a man and dropped in to hear all the news. Have a drink – my own brand?" Without waiting for an answer he called to the bartender, "A raw lemonade with a dash of sherry."

Tom shuffled his feet, his quick eyes apprehensive of derision in the faces in the mirror. Then picking up his glass, he followed Rogier to a table at the window. For a time he floundered around on his chair trying to get settled. Finally giving up the attempt, he sat up straight. "Damnit to hell! I'm all in! I wasn't home last night!"

His mere statement of one night's absence appeared to have no effect upon the man before him. It sounded so weak and foolish to his own ears that he made haste to supplement it. "No! And by God I oughta been. I was supposed to have gone right back with some medicine for Hiney yesterday afternoon. And I ain't been back since. What do you think of that?"

Rogier lit a cigar without answering him. Tom continued more slowly now. "I left word at the doctor's office and went out to get some medicine. It was our last two dollars, but hell! – a man can't go home without takin' a sick kid somethin' more than medicine. Can he? I thought I'd take him a real whip like he'd been wantin'. One that a Mexican had over at Sample's Boardin' House, braided leather with a silver handle. Well, when I got there and started playin' for it, my luck just turned cold on me. Those damn Mex playin' cards did the trick. With all them *espadas, oros* and *copas* you never know what you're doin'." He leaned forward, both hands on the table. "I didn't quit till I was cleaned cold. Every time that damn greaser slapped down a greasy card hollerin' out, '*Suerte, Senor!*' I thought of Hiney sufferin' and waitin' for his dad to bring him somethin'. So I slapped down mine too, every time. The damn luck! You can't beat it. I was so ashamed I couldn't go home. So I sat here all night. And I owe four dollars for drinks."

Outside, two curs tangled in the street, their yaps and snarls sounding clamorous applause through the open windows. There was a sudden sound of whips and curses, and all was still again.

"Hiney got over his spell. I saw Molly this mornin'," Rogier said quietly.

Tom contracted suddenly, like a turtle drawing within his shell. "Did she say anything about me?"

"She seemed worried, wonderin' what had happened to you."

Tom struggled with his remorse and heroically overcame it. "I reckon. She's always worryin' about me." He grinned, feeling better. "And I'll bet she is mad as a wet hen!"

"She wasn't, but if I were you I'd be gettin' back." Rogier stood up. "Want a ride?"

Tom settled back as though a spasmodic pain had ripped him up the belly. "Sit down a minute before we go. Maybe you can kind of straighten out things in my mind."

Rogier sat down again, steeling himself against Tom's words.

"What the hells' wrong with me, Joe? That makes me stay out like last night when I was worryin' about bein' home, and everything else? I'm just as good as anybody else. I can throw any man my size as many times as he can throw me. I ain't nasty nice like Perkins in the bank, and I ain't overly mean either. Everybody likes me and I don't hold a grudge long myself. But I don't seem to get along. What's the matter with me, Joe?"

Rogier sat still, his face giving an air of flinty indifference as it did whenever he was deeply affected.

"Even Molly is beginnin' to look at me funny, Joe. Like I was no good. Christ! I try hard enough. Why, they ain't a thing in town I ain't tried, but nothin' appeals to me overly much. That's what's worryin' me. Unless –

"Yes?"

"Luck!" Tom's voice rang out suddenly clear and sharp, as though the secret of men's souls, the hidden key to their success or failure, had been revealed to him in an instant flash. "Luck's been savin' me from bein' a carpenter, a blacksmith, a trapper and Indian trader, a banker, a business man, all those dull jobs. This whole damn world is bein' spun around by God like a roulette wheel. He don't have anything to do with which slot the ball falls into. It's luck that picks the slot. And it's been savin' me one!"

"And which one is that, Tom?"

Tom leaned forward. "You remember hearin' some float was picked up by a fellow herding cattle in Wet Mountain Valley flankin' the east wall of the Sangre de Cristos not more'n a hundred miles south of here? Nobody did anything about it till a prospector finally sunk his pick into the hill it come from. Chloride of silver, rich enough to eat! The Humbolt and Pocahontas were opened on the spot, and in the last six months three hundred thousand dollars have been pulled out. Rosita, their camp, already is a town of 2,000 people, with two hotels, a brewery, and a cheese factory. A fellow just told me so. These mountains are full of silver, Joe. That's what luck's savin' for me. To hit a bonanza. And I'm going to name her the 'Molly Hines'!"

How quickly his mood changed. He was like quicksilver himself. "Well, let's be takin' home," said Rogier wearily, rising to go.

Sister Molly was waiting in front of the door when they approached. After a few hours' sleep and in a fresh gingham dress, she seemed like herself again.

"I'm just stoppin to ask about Hiney," said Rogier.

"Sleepin' like a little log."

A tacit agreement of understanding was signed in their glance. Each of them knew the other would never refer to their morning's talk. Tom stood grinning with embarrassment, ready to fling his arms around Molly with a laugh or to snap back surlily, at either provocation.

"So long, Tom."

Rogier went home for supper. Afterwards the girls played quietly while Mrs. Rogier, pregnant again, read from her Big Book. Rogier could not get settled. All the talk, talk, talk of the day had driven him to the deep need of solitude. To let the disconcerting news and conjectures evaporate and leave their residual truth for him to weigh with clearer thought. "I've got to go down town for a while." he said kindly. "I won't be gone too late."

In his office he did not light the lamp but sat at the open window, staring out into the moonlight. How diaphanous, how phosphorescent it was, with the strange alchemy of turning green, blue, or lilac all it touched. Not of the light of living day nor of the darkness of night, but containing something of them both. More penetrating and more inescapable than light itself because it had no direct source, but emanated from everywhere. The high peak looming up at the end of the street shone with a silvery incandescence like the moon itself, mysteriously silver, casting over all the shadowed town, over himself, the same moon-madness. That's what it was, this lure of silver in the Uncompahgres, the Sangre de Cristos, the San Juans, in all the ranges of these high Rockies, a queer moon-madness. Rogier could not blame Stratton, Tom nor all the thousands of men for succumbing to its strange malady. Even he, alone and troubled, could recognize with some misgivings the uncontrollable quickening of his blood at the rumors of the new strikes.

6

Early in July the men who had gone down to the San Juan region returned with the report that the Yretaba Silver Lode foisted upon them was a worthless claim. Yet so entrancing were the deep gulches dotted with camps and claims they were raising money to buy into other claims. the Ouray, Rocky Mountain Chief, and Silver Wing.

Two weeks later Stratton pushed open the door of Rogier's office. He had lost his hat and his long hair was uncombed. His wornout boots were tied with string. His torn shirt and overalls were damp. "I just got in, but I was so dirty I stopped to wash my clothes in the creek," he explained diffidently. "We busted, you know."

"So I heard. Well, maybe it's just as well you got it out of your system, Stratton. Now how about some new clothes and a good hot meal? Then we'll talk about your gettin' back into business."

"I told you I was done when I left here, Joe! The Yretaba was no good, but you should see the silver showin's down there. My God, man! The King Solomon Mountain is so seamed with mineral veins they can be seen two miles away. Everybody calls Begole's discovery the Mineral Farm, and what a farm it is! Rich veins spread out over forty acres! There's a hill black with oxide of manganese they call the Nigger Baby. Full of lead carbonates rich in silver. And in the Uncompahgre range more towns are springing up. Ouray, Telluride, Ophir, Rico. Silver, Joe! That's for me. No more buildin'!"

"Think it over on a night's sleep," cautioned Rogier, giving him some money. "We'll talk about it tomorrow."

The next day Stratton returned still insistent. He soon raised a new grubstake and took off with an old freighter over Ute Pass and up Chalk Creek toward the head of the Arkansas. Here below Granite, fronting the Sawatch Range, another new strike had been reported and Stratton intended to be in on the ground floor.

Rogier ignored the growing excitement; he was too busy. A recognized builder now in a fast growing town, he was finishing the School for the Deaf and Blind, laying foundations for the Academy, and preparing estimates for a new two-story Courthouse on the corner of Nevada and Kiowa.

That fall Mrs. Rogier gave birth to their third daughter, Mary Ann, and settled down to a hard winter. Smothering the earth with a fresh and flocculent whiteness the instant a roof edge or tree tip emerged to view, clinging with tenacious and icy fingers upon its helpless prey, the winter could not be shaken off. Each morning the sun rose scowling, but like the scowl of a man without the inward fire of righteous anger it became placid, without the warmth of conviction, and retreated redly between the great snowy peaks. The mountains reared silver above the prairies like a wall of ice shutting off a white and frozen sea. Herds of antelope gathered from the plains outside the town. Deer came down from the mountains and were to be found in anybody's back yard. Seven grizzly bears were killed above Manitou.

Even Tom tired of the easy slaughter long before his shed was filled with frozen meat. All morning he loafed in the saloons at Colorado City or stood watching the gambling in Sample's Boarding House. At home he sat glowering at Sister Molly, shrewder-tongued than himself, and thus quick to turn his plaints at everything against himself. Bitter and vindictive, they worried at each other's minds and spirits like wolves tearing at a carcass. Tom was loud and swore profusely, beating at her with the crude clubs of many thwarted ambitions. She, with a fine-spun web of pride torn at every sally, hid her hurts and punctured his noisy arguments with the swift sting of a harsh truth.

Their only relief was their evening visit with the Rogiers. Usually they brought along Siegerfries with his wife and daughter, Marion. Ona was glad of the latter's company. Fulfilling the curse laid upon the eldest daughters of large families, she was kept busy all day doing housework, taking care of Sally Lee, and helping to tend Mary Ann.

Siegerfries was a small man with thin reddish brown hair that was never combed. Nevertheless he gave the impression of a man of good family who had known better days at home in New York. He was educated and his speech was precise. Mrs. Siegerfries and her daughter Marion were regarded by Mrs. Rogier as "common." They both always wore sunbonnets, evidently Mrs. Siegerfries' only conception of women's head-gear. Even now in winter they came in with calico sunbonnets wrapped to their heads with long wool scarfs.

The three men usually grouped together on one side of the stove. Siegerfries, a geologist, talked about the silver strikes calmly enough but with quick puffs at his pipe.

"The Saguache, the Uncompahgre, the San Juans, the Sangre de Cristos! Almost every range following down the course of the Continental Divide. I've never heard of anything like it! The whole mountain chain seems to be full of silver."

"Have you heard of the new booms in Wet Mountain Valley?" asked Tom. "A fellow named Ed Bassick wandered north of Rosita a little ways and sat down to take some sand out of his shoe. It happened to be an ant hill he was sittin' on. So, when the ants stung him in the pants he jumped up and lit into the hill with his pick, strikin' silver ore runnin' 150 ounces to the ton. That was the beginnin' of the new town, Querida. But that ain't half of it!" He hitched his chair closer. "Another Rosita fellow called Edwards hiked west a bit to a high cliff, knocked off a chunk, and had it assayed. It was full of silver and the ground around it was covered with pure horn silver. That's the Silver Cliff you're hearin' about now. It's got nearly 10,000 people, ten miles of streets, two banks, seven hotels – the third largest city in Colorado already!"

"And what about Rosita you were so excited about?" asked Rogier.

"Oh, everybody moved to Silver Cliff where the showin' was better."

Rogier chuckled. "Here today, gone tomorrow."

"I don't care!" exclaimed Tom. "I'd like to go down there and pick me out a claim while the pickin's good!"

Siegerfries turned toward him an amused stare. "Humm. All you have to do is put down your discovery shaft ten feet and do a hundred dollars worth of work every year. Five hundred dollars' worth of work will get you a patent. Maybe it'll be a mine worth developing and maybe it won't. Humph!" He spit at the woodpile.

"Too many Yretabas?" asked Rogiér quietly.

"That's the point," agreed Siegerfries. "Too many men staking out too many claims with no knowledge, no money behind them. The mountains are full of silver. No question about that. But when you find it, what then? It takes money to get it out of the ground, more money to get the ore to a smelter or to a railroad. No. These first surface showings are only an indication of what's to come. Wait'll a big district is opened up and the money gets in there for development. Then's when the real fortunes will be made."

"Hell!" said Tom. "If I knew as much about it as you, I wouldn't be grubbin' vegetables out of a couple of acres with a blind mule. I'd go and find me a silver lode!"

"The time'll come, but I'm not going to be stampeded yet. Like your friend Stratton." He turned toward Rogier. "Did I tell you he's back in town from Granite already?"

Rogier nodded. "He's working for me as a carpenter. Just long enough to save up a grubstake so he can return to the San Juan region."

Mrs. Rogier on the other side of the stove pricked up her ears at mention of his name. "That disreputable gadfly! Runnin' around with that seventeen-year-old Stewart girl, Zeurah. The whole town's buzzin' about it."

"I hope you don't add to it," said Rogier shortly. "He's a friend of mine and a good carpenter."

"You run your business the way you want to, but don't expect me to associate with people like that." She flounced out of her chair.

"Ona, let's get them sandwiches and cookies out now."

Early in March Rogier hitched up his mares and drove Mrs. Rogier and Ona down to see the site he had picked for the new house they needed. It was a flat expanse of prairie just east of town along Shook's Run. The little creek, with its bed gouged deep by the cloudburst at Templeton's Gap and deeper by the spring freshets, boasted a new plank bridge. The view of town westward was shut off by Bijou Hill. The only building visible was a wooden shack near the stream, in front of which two old men in blood-stained, tattered clothes were unpacking from two decrepit covered wagons carcasses of deer and antelope and strings of duck and geese.

"Stop the buggy this minute!" demanded Mrs. Rogier. "I can't stand the smell!"

Ona too sat holding her nose; forty years later she could still recall the stench of those bloody wagons and old men. The patriarchal Kadles, father and son, were well-known in town. They made their living hunting out on the plains, driving in periodically with filled wagons to peddle their meat from door to door.

While Rogier went to say hello to them, Mrs. Rogier sat in the buggy, her small pointed chin holding the blanket-wrap down to her breast against the wind. She was scandalized, utterly dismayed that Rogier actually intended to build their house on the exact spot where stood the Kadles' shack. Shooks Run! Living along the creek like all the common people farther down, like gypsies!

In a few minutes Rogier came back and they drove off. Evidently he had been thinking about the house a great deal. It would have to be big; they needed lots of room inside and out. The land was large as a city block, providing good pasturage for a horse or two.

"But I don't like it!" Mrs. Rogier interrupted. "I don't like the idea of people sayin' we come from the South End or are livin' along the creek. When people hear either of those two places they don't stop to think what your house looks like or what you do. They know what you are already. Living on the Kadles' campground! We'll be carrying the Kadles' name with us to the grave. Why, the ghosts of those two old men with their bloody clothes and tobacco juice runnin' down their white beards will be stompin' through the house in their smelly boots as long as it stands!"

Rogier snapped out the loose reins at the mares, and in a splatter of mud they flew along the road. He knew she was right. The best families, the old English stock which made up the best portion, were collecting to the north of town. Despite his own inborn aloofness which he recognized as a fault, he recognized the infallibility of his wife's intuition.

"I tell you, Joe," she went on, "we can't take chances in gettin' a right start. Rogier was a good name in South Carolina. Everybody that went up and down the Mississippi knew the De Vinneys. It didn't make any difference whether he drank himself to death. He had a name. Out here it's all new. Nobody knows what kind of families we're from. Especially the English folks. Maybe it's worse because we're from the South. We got to show 'em, Joe."

"Show 'em what?" He drew up the mares at a ditch, and once over, spoke again. "Well, I'll leave it to you. We can't build in the North End till we have more money. The College Reservation is going to encroach on our land and boost taxes. But by trading it now, we can build in Shook's Run." Rogier patted her arm and let the team out again. "I'll promise you this – Ona, you remember too – the minute I make enough money I'll build you the big house up in the North End you want. Meanwhile this one's to be put in your name – it's all yours."

Mrs. Rogier leaned back, folding her gloved hands. "I'll remember that."

"Well, Ona," Rogier asked. "Is it going to do or not?"

"I guess there's not much difference in looks anywhere, right now. But there ought to be some trees and lilac bushes."

Rogier nodded. He was a man difficult to cross, for he never argued; his silence seemed to smother noisy disagreement with its taciturn force. Bound to her father with the common ties of their inherent aloofness, she understood him better than did her mother. Ona was surprised at her mother's opposition. It always seemed strange that there should be so much strength of denial in the frail body sitting beside her. A bundle of nerves, really, elusive as a reed in the wind.

Nevertheless she gained a new respect for her mother through the incident. Mrs. Rogier never said another dissenting thing about the new house. When they got home they found Tom and Sister

Molly waiting, and Mrs. Rogier told them about the decision cheerfully as though she had helped to make the choice.

Tom and Sister Molly, for all their whole-hearted pleasure at the news, seemed somewhat ill at ease. Tom shuffled about awkwardly, even after Rogier asked him to boss the construction. He tried to motion Rogier to the back room. Failing this, he put his arm around Mrs. Rogier and led her off to the kitchen to hear a secret, laughing loudly. Alone with her, his face straightened instantly. He wanted to borrow five dollars.

"I got to have it, Martha," he said, pinching her chin. He sat on the kitchen table swinging his long legs while she went to the cupboard and came back. "You're a peach. Now remember, it's a secret. I wouldn't have Molly know for anything."

He kissed her on the cheek and with his arm around her, they went back into the room. Sister Molly and Rogier had moved away from the children, and stood by the window talking in low voices. Sister Molly stopped talking instantly on seeing them, stepping away from him and concealing her hand in her dress.

Mrs. Rogier wanted them to stay for supper, but Sister Molly, murmuring vaguely about getting home to the boys before dark, threw her shawl over her shoulders and stepped out the door. Tom shuffled after her. The snow was melting and the ragged smears of water splashed from the wheeltracks lay copper-red, the *colorado* of the earth itself, stained richer by the setting sun. The long roadway seemed to run with its bleeding life. Sister Molly walked in front, hurrying as if from the scene of a monstrous crime.

"What the hell's the rush?" grumbled Tom. "From what you said comin' over I didn't think you'd be rushin' back to your happy peaceful home."

"Well, you're always in a hurry to leave. Why shouldn't I be the one to hurry home?"

"You should. You appreciate what a beautiful big place it is."

"It's the best home my husband can provide for me. If he doesn't care enough to stop a leak in the roof after being asked for a month, should I blame it on the house?"

"Christ! You make me tired!" said Tom. "I just been waitin' to see how long it would take you to sing that song again. I've only heard it forty times."

Sister Molly increased her pace. Tom kept at her heels, growling. "Oh, I'll fix the damn roof before it falls in, all right. And before Martha gets her new house, too. Or else you'll be shoutin' to all the town about your own leaky roof."

Sister Molly looked around and smiled. "Jealous, Tom?"

He leapt apace with her in one stride and caught her by the arm. "Goddamn, don't you ever say I'm jealous of Joe, or I'll knock your words down your throat, wife or no wife. He's the best friend I ever had and he deserves all he'll ever get and more too."

Sister Molly stopped in the snow and took his hand off her arm. "That'll do, Tom. We think the same about Joe." Then suddenly she grabbed his arm and ran it under hers. They started walking. "Don't let's quarrel any more today, Tom. I'm almost sick from thinkin' what we've said to each other all day. And, oh Tom," she pleaded, "please let's be sensible. Forget about Joe and Martha's new house. Think of us. What are we comin' to? What are we goin' to do now?"

"You're just worryin' yourself sick over nothin'," Tom reassured her. "The kids are growin' up and we're all healthy. I ain't made a killin' and struck it rich, but I been workin' enough to make a livin', ain't I?"

"No. You haven't," answered Sister Molly, "Can't you realize that? Don't you know what we've been eating all this time?"

"Hell, yes!" laughed Tom. "I'm so sick of raspberry jam and frozen venison I could holler!"

Sister Molly's face set. "I'll tell you what we've been eating. We been eating up those six acres Joe got for you. First the mortgage on two acres to Siegerfries, then two more, and now the loan on the last piece our own house is settin' on. What'll we do when it's gone? That's all I ask. Just stop long enough to realize you're a grown man who hasn't supported a wife and two children." Her voice lowered. "I love you, Tom. I don't want much. But you must give us some kind of a living the same as any other man. I'm sick of borrowing money. And I had to borrow some from Joe to buy our supper tonight. There wasn't even any pancake flour left."

Tom turned to her with surprise. A grin spread over his face. "Well, I'll be damned! How much did you get?"

"Five dollars."

"Just what I got from Martha," muttered Tom, holding out a

gold piece on his palm.

Sister Molly stopped and stared at the coin. A dark rush of blood swept to her cheeks, and then receding, left her face pale grey in the flush of evening. Her eyes narrowing, she struck his hand with a quick blow that jumped the coin away into the snow.

Tom stood immovable, his hand still outstretched as if in a magnificent gesture of pardon or mutely imploring forgiveness. His jaw dropped as he stood listening to Sister Molly. She kept on talking; and her voice, low and even, cut at him like a whip wielded not in the frenzy of sudden anger, but with the precision of a cruel judgment coolly meted out. His arm dropped to his side. He stood there, big and clumsy, mouth open, like a man crumbling inside.

She suddenly stopped; a low sob broke from her. She dropped to her knees, hands outflung in the snow searching for the gold-piece, sobbing bitterly. "Never. Never. I'll never forgive you as long as I live!"

Tom bent slowly, as if fearful of tumbling in an empty heap, and dropped to his knees beside her. He lit matches; and their thin bright glow lit up the dusky snow patch, revealed to him the pallid grayness of her wet cheeks, her tight tense mouth. Then, burning his fingers, they each went out, and he lit another without taking his eyes from Sister Molly.

She finally found the coin. Without a word she rose and walked home in silence. Tom slushed in the mud beside her. At the door, turning to face him, she placed the gold-piece in his hand.

"Here's your money, Tom," she said quietly. "I'll not depend on you to bring home anything to eat. Go on over to Colorado City and get drunk, and bring back your excuses tomorrow."

Without a word Tom walked away. Sister Molly turned her back; she did not watch him go.

7

At last it was spring. As if with a cataclysmic shake the great peaks threw off the winter snow and reared heads and shoulders high, free and rock-naked, like immense beasts awakened with new life. The shake started one of the region's worst landslides. A quarter-mile wide, it swept down the Cone gathering trees and rocks. Suddenly the cliffs gave way. With a belching roar the turbulent stream leapt out into the clear sunshine and fell upon the pine and spruce slopes below. An angry brown torrent, it cut through the blue-clad forest like a flow of molasses and spilled into the canyon, damming up the stream with a mountain of timber and rock. Men could hear it miles away; they could see the gash from out on the plains. And as though heralded by the slide, as if born of the catastrophe with the land writhing in mighty travail, the news broke forth from the mountains.

Silver had been discovered in Leadville.

It was not the first discovery in that high region 125 miles west. Some years before, Abe Lee, one of the discouraged Forty-Niners on his way back from California, had christened the area lying at the headwaters of the Arkansas with the name of California Gulch.

Finding gold in his pan, he had jumped to his feet shouting, "I found it! I got it – the hull state of Californy in this goddam pan!"

The yield of three million dollars from the first placer mines, however, had dwindled to paltry thousands and men began to regard the gulch as an area of worthless lead. A black heavy sand cluttered up their sluices till it was almost impossible to separate gold from the gravel, and this trouble was further enhanced by the difficulty of moving out of the way heavy worthless boulders.

It was then a man named W.H. Stevens discovered a supposed lead deposit on the south side of the Gulch, naming it the Iron Mine. Samples from it assayed twenty to forty ounces of silver to the ton, revealing that the heavy sand and huge boulders were composed of a carbonate of lead forming a silver base. Thus spread the reports as more men rushed to the hills and gulches, and brought back more specimens to test. The oxide of iron imparted to one group of ores a red color; chromate of iron a yellow hue; the predominance of silica and lead in others a gray color. But chloride of silver permeated all ores.

The rush got under way. Long mule trains struggled over Ute Pass, breaking the silence with the shouts of the skinners and the pistol cracks of their long rawhide whips. The trail led on through a great mountain valley, once the hunting ground of the Utes and now known as South Park. Here the men could see the high snowy peaks of the Saguache Range, almost three miles high. Twelve glistening silver peaks, like twelve apostles robed in white. And now, gritting their teeth, the men began the steep ascent up Mosquito Pass, that "Highway of Frozen Death," to Leadville, the "Silver City in a Sea of Silver."

Within six months a dense spruce forest was hacked down to make space for the town that looked, as someone described it, like "a Monaco gambling room emptied into a Colorado spruce clearing." The hacked stumps still stuck up in the streets which ran through a clutter of log cabins, board shacks, shanties, and saloons. The first ore had been carted out by ox-teams for shipment to St. Louis. Now a sampling works and blast furnace were established, and more smelters were being built. Money was pouring in – and more was being taken out. The Iron Mine had been sold for $200,000, one share of it being bought by Levi Leiter, partner of

Marshall Field, who was beginning to make millions from it. A storekeeper and the first mayor of the new town, Horace A.W. Tabor, grubstaked two seedy German prospectors with $64.75 worth of groceries. On Fryer Hill the two prospectors, August Rische and Theodore Hook, dug a thirty-foot shaft and struck silver ore which assayed 225 ounces per ton. Naming the mine the Little Pittsburgh, Hook sold his share for $153,000 and Rische sold his for a wad of 262 $1,000 bills. Within a year the mine was capitalized at $20,000,000. Tabor, on his one-third share, began his meteoric flight to wealth and fame, becoming Lieutenant Governor of Colorado that same year and United States Senator within five years. And they were not the only ones. Day after day news of still more strikes, the Chrysolite, Robert E. Lee, Little Johnny, and the Matchless, swept through Colorado to give all men similar dreams, grand, improbable, but by the grace of God not impossible – yet niggardly in comparison to the reality that would shame their wildest imaginings.

The main inlet to that great camp, the narrow wagon road up through Ute Pass was crowded each mile and hour. More than twelve thousand mules and horses crept up, and back the grade. Their eastern terminus and principal supply depot was the settlement on the plains at the foot of Pike's Peak.

Manitou swarmed with crawling wagons like an ant hill alive with a horde of ants. Colorado City blazed with a light that stayed red, and in its flicker mule-skinners, miners, teamsters, prostitutes, and men crossbred to every purpose drank the clock around. Colorado Springs went wild – able to catch breath enough to shout. Day and night the noise kept up, of wagons pulling out for Ute Pass, of men getting ready for the trek. The D & RG couldn't haul goods in fast enough for the stores to empty across their counters. Prices jumped sky high.

Tom went almost crazy with excitement. For days on end he hung around Colorado City, listening to the talk in Jake Becker's place or in Levy's saloon; or else, in Manitou, wandering from wagon to wagon, rejecting the repeated tales of hardship, embroidering the rumors of new discoveries. And then coming home after a three-day absence, unshaven, dirty, and worn-out, he flung himself upon the bed to curse his fate, his own impotence, or the family that tied him to his home.

Siegerfries, although he did not show it, was as excited as Tom. Night after night he sat up studying reports, assays, every topographical map he could get of the Leadville district. From these he meticulously sketched the location of every strike and mine, working out the position of the major lodes and veins.

"Blanket veins," he told Rogier in his office one night when they were alone. "Look here." He spread out his sketches. "They appear in horizontal veins, varying in thickness from a few inches to great chambers forty feet in height, with iron above the ore, capped with trachyte, and covered to a hundred feet with drift."

"You're saying the ore is rich and extensive but expensive to mine?" asked Rogier thoughtfully.

"Exactly. The strikes have been made at surface outcrops. More, much more lies beneath. That's why Eastern money is pouring in to buy up all surface showings and sink to depth. You know what I'm driving at, don't you Joe?"

Rogier nodded.

"It's a boomer, Joe! The big one I've been waiting for. Throw in with me. I've sold out the land I bought from Tom, written home for all the money I can borrow. Be my partner, Joe!"

Long after he had left, Rogier sat in his office fighting for his head. A strange dormant excitement, a desire for something he could not put into words, crept into his veins, pulsed at his temples. Unable to shake it off, he paced the floor and intermittently stared out the window at the inscrutable peak which at once gave shape to his thoughts and masked their meanings. If Siegerfries were touched with the moon-madness that now completely possessed Stratton, Tom, and thousands of other helpless men, he denied the assumption. Siegerfries, cold, analytical, and immune to the possibility of glamor in his trade, was going too. Why not he? For the moment his building contracts, with the first payments for running expenses, the plans for his own new house on Shook's Run, his large family, and the growing dependence on him of Sister Molly and her two boys, all dwindled to insignificance under the appalling proximity of the great boom at Leadville. And yet something held him back. Worn out, he slept on a couch in his office.

Next morning on his way home he stopped off at Siegerfries'

house. It was still early. Marion in her omnipresent sunbonnet was out gathering wood; Mrs. Siegerfries was cooking breakfast; and Siegerfries, when Rogier entered the house, was busy packing his clothes.

"I've made up my mind. I'm not going," he said brusquely.

Siegerfries stood up and brushed back his thin, tousled hair. "I'm sorry, Joe. Keep an eye on my family while I'm gone, will you?"

"I'll do that. Good luck!"

They shook hands and Rogier walked slowly home, feeling the great weight of a repressed desire slowly dissipating within him.

The departure of Siegerfries raised Tom to a pitch of almost uncontrollable frenzy. He refused Rogier's offer to work as construction boss on the new house. Nor could he find time to fix his own roof. He was always over at Colorado City talking to mule-skinners, prospectors, and hopefuls bound for Leadville. When he did come home he would stand at the window pointing at the fold in the mountains through which wound Ute Pass, as if expecting Pikes Peak itself to burst into eruption and roll a flood of molten silver to his feet. Recounting the latest news, his voice grew husky, tremulous, and inarticulate with the vision burning in his mind. "Siegerfries went, didn't he," he would shout again and again. "He ain't crazy, is he? Wait'll he comes back!" These declamations oppressed Sister Molly even worse than his most violent quarrels. But Tom kept waiting for Siegerfries like a disciple awaiting the miraculous return of his chosen prophet. There would be no holding him back then.

Meanwhile, under the clear blue summer skies, rose the ungainly big frame house along Shook's Run. Its original plans Rogier stored away pending a proper site in the North End. For them he substituted hasty sketches as the work went on. His painstaking care and fine craftsmanship were bestowed upon the academy building on the College Reservation. The greater the stones from the quarries, the more carefully they were cut and placed, the more his mind seemed eased, as if they weighed him deep and fast, beyond all possible escape from his chosen work. Only at twilight, when the day's work was done, did he carry in his buggy a box of groceries each for Sister Molly and Mrs. Siegerfries on his way home. The house was finished by winter and the Rogiers moved in. It was an immense house, ungainly as it was, and Mrs. Rogier asked Sister Molly to move in with them. Bob and Hiney clamored to, and Tom assented, but Sister Molly was curt in her refusals. She was getting awfully touchy.

The year went by and another had begun its flight when Siegerfries came back. His wife and daughter were sitting on the broken down front steps with Sister Molly; they were dressed in patched gingham dresses, their shoes tied with twine, and looking mournfully out upon the world under the cowls of their everlasting calico sunbonnets. Sieferfries himself looked worse than a tramp and many years older. After kissing them and telling Sister Molly to bring back all her folks that evening, he laid down on the bed, duffle bag under his head.

That evening they all learned that Siegerfries had struck it rich. He talked little like a man who had plucked the apple of heart's desire, and yet he was going to take his wife and daughter back to his family in New York and build a house up along the Hudson River. He damned the Leadville region like a man who had seen the shooting of men on claims, the hardships, greed, and poverty too well to pay the price again.

"The hell with all that!" shouted Tom. "You hit it, didn't you? Just like I knew you would! Pure silver! What did it look like when you saw it? How much did you get?"

Siegerfries shrugged, then turned to Rogier. After looking over the ground carefully for months, he had staked out a claim in a remote gulch, a mere blind stab at forture. Sinking a discovery shaft through the snow, he had found a showing of silver ore. That spring he had sold it to some speculators for $30,000 without waiting to see if it would turn out good or bad. He had then put all the money into a new mine he had been hired to survey and that was being financed for development. When in one week it produced more than $100,000 in silver, with the prospect of becoming one of the best mines in Leadville, Siegerfries sold out at the first substantial offer for a price that would make him independent the rest of his life. He was never going back. It was a prosy dry tale worthy of the man, and Rogier nodded his approval.

Mrs. Siegerfries and Marion expressed little joy; they lacked the imagination to encompass their good fortune. Siegerfries had met his wife in Kansas on his way West. She was an honest, industrious woman, but uneducated and almost illiterate. Marion, gawky, freckled, and born to poverty, and with barely enough schooling to scrawl an awkward hand, was little better. Now Siegerfries had instilled a new destiny in their minds, "a home on the Hudson," wherever that was.

Mrs. Rogier, Sister Molly, and Ona helped them get ready to leave. On the day before they took the narrow-gauge, Mrs. Siegerfries brought home some new cloth and a roll of lace to make sunbonnets for herself and Marion to wear to New York. Mrs. Rogier was slightly envious and a little puzzled because it had been God's will to bestow this world's wealth not upon members of the blooded aristocracy who might have shown it with more grace, but upon people who after all were common, having no conception of headgear beyond sunbonnets trimmed for the first time with a scrap of lace.

It was left to Sister Molly to bear the brunt of their success. Tom was past all argument and appeal now. It made no difference that he watched men dribbling back down Ute Pass gaunt with hunger and hollow-eyed, broken by the immutable law that levels men to their average that fickle chance might raise one to play a horde of others false. Stone broke as he was, he was determined to go to the promised land.

The break came with an unexpected letter from Mrs. White. Mrs. Rogier was sitting with it in her lap when Rogier came home from work. "It's a letter from Mother. Read it."

Rogier looked at her sharply, noticing the slight flush in her cheeks. "Never mind. What does she say?"

"She's on her way out here."

Rogier nodded complacently. "I'll be glad to see her."

Mrs. Rogier's small foot tapped the floor nervously. "She's coming out here to live with us, and she's bringing brother's little boy Boné with her." She hesitated, never quite sure how he was going to take things. "I guess I didn't tell you I wrote her we'd be glad to take Boné. One more won't make much difference with the three children we got."

"Of course not! I owe your mother much and I was homeless as the little fellow myself."

"Well, I just thought you might be thinkin' it was comin' at a bad time now, but of course it's not as it she were comin' here to live without a cent. She says in her letter – " her fingers began picking at the pages.

"Never mind. What does she say?"

"You remember when my father died Mother gave all the insurance money to Ansil to take downriver to New Orleans, and he died of yellow fever in a hotel there, and the money was never found. Nobody knew whether it was stolen in the hotel or whether his uncle really did get it without saying so. The De Vinneys ended up pretty poor. Even the section of land in Louisville father owned was grabbed and sold for a park."

"I remember!" Rogier said impatiently. "What about your mother?"

"Well anyway some of the stolen money finally turned up. Mother got $500 apiece for me and Sister Molly, and $1,000 apiece for Ansil's and Boné's shares. She's comin' out right away: Sister Molly and I were talkin' about it just before you came."

"Where is she?"

"She left. Said she wished Mother was comin' out here without a dollar. She was terribly upset hearing about her $500. I'd think she'd welcome it like a blessing. You don't suppose Tom – " her voice dribbled away before Rogier's frown.

He sat staring past her with troubled, anxious eyes. Then he rose slowly. "Listen Martha. What Tom and Molly decide to do with their money is no concern of ours. Don't interfere."

Two weeks later the Rogiers and Hines drove down to the depot to meet the two arrivals. Mrs. White got off the train, small, indomitable, and easy-voiced as ever. With her was Boné, a small lad with black hair and blacker eyes. He looked frail and fine-strung as a corded whip and said nothing during the ride home.

Tom and Sister Molly stayed for supper. Bob and Hiney, at the Rogier house since early morning, insisted on spending the night with the girls. So Ona took the children upstairs to bed, leaving Mrs. White with her two daughters and sons-in-law sitting grouped about the lamp on the dining room table. Mrs. White talked at length of her husband who had finally, mercifully died; of the death of Boné's father; and of his mother who had run away. And then, as out of a clouded sky, she turned to her daughters a kind smile that reflected a long life that had held pain, much sorrow, and very little joy, but never the gaunt emptiness that stared back at her through Sister Molly's eyes.

"Shuh now," she drawled easily. "I'm pleased to find y'all doin' fine. Joe heah is gettin' along right smart, and Tom you look healthy as a lean hound. Molly, how you figurin' on spending youah five hundred dollahs?"

Tom started erect on his chair as if someone had jerked up his head by the hair. He flashed a quick look at Sister Molly who sat looking straight before her without blinking an eye. It was evident to all that he had not heard of the money before.

Sister Molly broke the silence with a clear calm voice. "Spendin' that $500 is goin' to be easy, Mother. But it's taken me a long time to decide on just what to buy."

"Well anyway, heah it is." Mrs. White gave a packet of banknotes to Mrs. Rogier who handed it over to Rogier to keep for her; another packet, containing Ansil and Boné's share, to Rogier; and the third packet to Sister Molly who slipped it down the bosom of her dress. Then Molly rose and put her arms around her mother. "You don't know what you've done, but you've done it for the best, Mother."

Tom stood up and pushed back his chair against the wall with a bang. "I can't stay gossipin' here all night! There's a man waitin' to see me downtown!" He strode out the door without another word.

Late next morning Sister Molly walked the two boys home. She sat down on the porch steps, chin on hand, without moving, staring at the wall of mountains. That afternoon Tom's figure appeared far down the road. She called the boys and sent them back to Rogier's on an idle errand, then got up and went inside the house. Drawing back the curtains she watched Tom slouching rapidly toward her, swinging his long arms. "Oh God," she breathed piteously, face upturned to the ceiling, "don't let him be too drunk to know what I'm goin' to say." At the first angry scratch of his steps on the gravel, she sat down stiffly at the kitchen table.

It was thus Tom found her when he flung back the door. She was confronting him with a face as colorless and immobile as if set in clay. The angry stare in his eyes was extinguished as suddenly as if she had whipped out the blaze with one glance from her own eyes. "Come here, Tom," she said quietly.

He slammed the door behind him as if to break the tension and muttered something about washing up.

"Come here!" she said again, without raising her voice.

He slouched to the table and flopped down in a chair opposite her. Sister Molly drew out from her breast the brown-paper packet and tossed it on the table between them. "Five hundred dollars in bank notes. My share from Mother. There won't be any more."

Tom did not speak nor stir a finger.

"Go ahead and shout," she continued in a level tone. "The boys won't be back for two hours and there's nobody within a mile to hear. You've been thinkin' about it all night, and in Levy's all mornin'."

"I ain't been drinking," he denied surlily.

Sister Molly let it pass. "We got something more important to talk about. Tom, we're going to settle everything right now. Understand? I can't go on like this any more."

Tom settled back, taking off his old felt hat and dropping it on the floor.

"That five hundred is yours, Tom. I ain't keepin' a cent for me and the boys. It's your last chance. You're goin' to take it and make good, or you're never comin' home to us again. She took a deep breath. "You're goin' to Leadville, Tom."

A foolish look of pain crept into Tom's face. It was suddenly replaced by a wide grin. "Molly!" He leapt up to kiss her, to throw his arms around her stiff tense body. She sat quietly without turning her face, as if unaware of his kisses.

"Aw, Molly," he muttered, sitting down again. "I'll make you proud of me. I'll come back from Leadville with ten times that much, easy. I know I'll make a strike – the Molly Hines!"

"You didn't understand," she said coldly. "If you don't make good we're through with you – me and the boys. And because we still love you, and always will, I can't take no chances with you, Tom. You're goin' like I say, or not at all. We'll finish now."

"What's up your sleeve?" he demanded.

Sister Molly raised her voice. "You're more ignorant of mining than I am. You'd rush up there and dig a hole any place the digging was easy or the view was good. You wouldn't know a rock was full of silver if you had the finest specimen in your hand. You been ravin' like a mad man about it for three years, and you haven't bothered to find out anything that might be of use if you ever did go. You're still ignorant."

Tom drew back his hand from the packet that still lay untouched between them. Sister Molly lowered her voice to its even tone and went on.

"Listen. Six months ago that poor old Jew down on Huerfano went up the Leadville with a wagonload of fruit. Hay to feed his horses cost $200 a ton. He paid a dollar to sleep on the floor of a saloon. Even drinking water was bought by the barrel. But he sold every piece of his fruit and came back with enough money to buy himself a house and a little printin' shop downtown. I talked to him."

Tom opened his mouth. "Listen!" said Molly before he could speak. "I can't take no more chances. All I want is for you to make what money you can and come back to us. And this is how. I been down to the corral. Smithy is savin' us a good team of mules for a hundred dollars. You can buy a wagon, an outfit, and a big load of fresh apples, and have just enough to live on while you're gone with the rest of this $500." She picked up the packet and slid the bills out on the table before him.

"Oh, I see!" he ejaculated. "I'm supposed to drive up outside a saloon or on a street corner and get out on a box holdin' up a nice red apple. Shouting like the Kadles with their ducks. Playin' Jacob the Jew!"

"Yes, if necessary."

Tom roared. "What! Me do that? A great big fellow like me who maybe could spot a mine like the Robert E. Lee or the Chrysolite peddlin' apples? Chargin' a dollar apiece like a goddam Jew? They'd laugh me out of camp. Christ! I won't do it!"

"Are you sure?" she asked softly. Receiving no answer, she rose suddenly, overturning the chair. "Then get out! Get out!" she shrieked. "You've been nothing but a shiftless loafer ever since you been here. You've lived up all the land Joe gave you for a fresh start. You've borrowed and begged. And now you expect your wife to borrow to feed you. I won't, I tell you! Before I beg another loaf of bread from my sister, I'll see the boys starve cryin' before my eyes. You're worthless. You're no good. And I hope to God I never lay eyes on you again!"

She flung herself against the wall with outstretched arms and shaking shoulders, gasping for breath, but without a sob. Tom slid back his chair and crouched on its edge in an attitude of arrested flight. With one hand he pulled at his black hair in a futile endeavor to straighten out a kink. "Why sure, Molly," he stammered, "sure I'll go. I – I never knew you felt like this."

Sister Molly pushed herself away from the wall and sank upon the overturned chair which she righted as if it weighed a ton. She pushed back her own hair over her ears, and sat staring with dry fixed eyes across the table at him.

8

It was their last night together, and like their first, they spent it alone.

Bob and Hiney, making believe they were on the trip themselves, took their blankets outside and built a campfire. Sister Molly took them out two potatoes to bake, with bread and jam, and returned to the house. Standing at the window she could see their small forms humped over the tiny fire. The flames lit up the shapes of the sleepy mules tethered to a wheel of the wagon already loaded for the start in the early morning. Gradually the vision built up before her eyes a background of somber cliffs and pines. In the red glow appeared men sitting on the ground or leaning against rocks and wagons, pipes in mouth. Rifles, ore specimens, and liquor bottles passed from hand to hand. Always there was silver: silver ore, silver splinters of moonlight, their silvery words of hope — the moonlight metal ever-present in their thoughts and hers. Then a silvery mist before her eyes hid it all from sight, and Tom was beside her wiping away her tears.

"I love you so much I almost don't want to go, Molly," he

murmured huskily, arm around her waist.

"Oh, I love you so." Her deep tremulous voice welled up with all the anguish of the last few months, and cracking through her last reserve burst forth with a single word that shook him on his feet. "Tom!" It carried all that she could ever say. Turning in his arms, she clasped his head between her palms and bent it toward her. Every feature of his face, the wide careless mouth, the long tanned cheeks with their crescent seams, his dark round eyes, and boyish rumpled hair, she drank in with an eager vision as if to preserve them unaltered in the deep recesses of her lonely mind. And he, sensing their oneness, their perfect union for perhaps the first time in their life together, fell silent and ashamed before the moment's truth. He leaned sideways and blew out the lamp.

They sat together in darkness, looking out the window, then he drew her upon his lap.

"Those are our two kids out there, Molly. Can you believe it? We got two grown boys that'll soon be big enough to lick their dad. But it seems just like we were married this morning." His voice softened. He brushed back the hair from her temples. "And I been loving you all this time, Molly. There'll never be another woman for me."

She knew it. Whatever his many faults, he had given her his only love. She kept silent, running her fingers down his hard corded wrist to his long muscular fingers, firm-fleshed as wrapped steel.

" 'Member the first evening we were married?" he asked. "When we sat up in the hotel lookin' out at the lights and listenin' to the boats comin' up the river? And that little nigger's face what brought us up a bottle of port wine? You said it looked like a full brown moon when you give him a dollar. And say!" He squeezed her more tightly. "I'll bet you won't forget tryin' to get into your nightgown! I thought your fingers were clumsy because of all that wine – or maybe because you were ashamed. Then we lit the lamp and saw it was all sewed up across the bottom. And here we didn't think anybody knew we were goin' to get married. I won't forget that in a hundred years!"

In vivid phantasmagoria a hundred other scenes raced across her memory, too swift to be caught in a net of words. Lying relaxed in his arms she watched the moonlight thin, the night breeze grow colder. After a time even the tiny flames outside ceased writhing and lay curled redly asleep. "It's awful late, Tom. And you've got to be up early. Let's don't be late."

She rose and went outside. The night was still and gray. For a long moment she leaned with bent arms across the wagon-bed, staring at the two boys asleep on the ground. In the shadow of the wagon then she knelt on the cold ground in wordless prayer. She got up stiffly, passed a light hand over the necks of the two mules, and walked back to the house.

Tom was already in bed. She undressed in the darkness and crawled in beside him. Tom put his arm under her head and murmured sleepily in her ear. Then soon, as it comes only to a boy or to the damned, sound sleep came to him. A little while longer and moving in his sleep, he removed his arm, turned from her. Then tears came to her. She lay sobbing bitterly, biting her lips that she might not awaken him. Utterly worn out she finally reached up a hand to his high shoulder as if with the gesture of her lasting benediction, and bent her own wet face to the pillow beside him.

Soon after daybreak Bob and Hiney came in, cold and hungry, preferring their mother's kitchen stove to the trouble of making up their campfire. They found her already awake and dressed, making coffee at the stove. She kissed them as they came in, warmly as though they had been gone a long time, kneeling on the floor with her arms around them both. Then, almost brusquely, she rose and went back to the sink as if dismissing them instantly from her thoughts. They had never seen her more composed, more assured; and warming themselves at the stove, they stood watching her cutting thick slices of bread with unhurried capable hands.

Tom came in the door. "Why, there's ole Zeb Pike and Dan'l Boone!" he exclaimed jocularly. "Don't tell me you're goin' to eat under a roof! And standin' at a stove! Is there a blizzard blowin' outside?"

He was in a hearty, fun-loving mood. He put his arm around Sister Molly; but she, calm and unhurried, only turned her head with a resonant "Mornin', Tom!" and went on slicing bread without missing a stroke.

Before they had finished their bread and coffee the Rogiers pulled in the yard. They were all in a light spring wagon: Mrs. White,

Boné, and the girls sitting on planks laid across the sides behind Rogier and Martha, carrying Mary Ann. "All ready, Tom?" Rogier asked lightly. "Haven't forgotten a thing?"

"No, Joe," Sister Molly answered. "We're all ready the minute Tom hitches up."

"Sure," added Tom. "I'm all set to be gettin' off. I want to get me a place early in the line so there won't be so much dust from all the wagons in front. Come on out and I'll show you how my mules look. I been slickin' them up fine."

When they had gone out with the children, Sister Molly took down the kitchen curtains. They were the only ones remaining; and once down, folded, and placed upon the boxes of household goods, the room looked desolate in the gray light of early morning. Except for a few chairs and the things in the bedroom, all was ready to be moved to the Rogiers. Sister Molly turned for a last look at that crude home built for her simple needs. Mrs. White observed her glance with keen discernment. A woman inured to the faint but troublesome cry of life's appalling lonesomeness, with her own life broken to the fickle faithlessness of men's wayward ambitions, she stood silent with her two daughters as if engrossed in the mystery of her heritage falling with affliction upon but one.

Mrs. Rogier stepped up and put her arm around her sister. "I'm glad we're all going to be together again until Tom comes back." Sister Molly squared her heavy shoulders. Unlike her mother, and without the clinging tenaciousness of her sister, she might be broken but never bent. "Everything's all ready when Joe comes after them. The bed covers are folded up and put on top the mattress, and the breakfast dishes are stacked in the basket on the sink. Shall we be goin'?" She turned, and they followed her out the door.

It was a lovely morning for a ride. The air was dry and cold and exhilarating, so clear that the mountains seemed no more than a mile away. Tom, exultant, gave his mules a free rein. For a half-mile they flew along, the wagon bounding from bump to bump. Sister Molly hung on calmly with a straight face. Only once, hitting a rut with a terrific jolt, she murmured quietly, "I wouldn't bruise up all them apples, Tom. Nobody'll buy the squashy ones."

Rogier, driving behind him, watched Tom's crazy pace with annoyance. The mules would be blown and unfit to make the cruel grade up the Pass at such a rate. Deciding to get in front and force a slower pace, he increased the strides of his mares. There was about him a cold set calmness whenever he began anything he had once made up his mind to do. The mares drew down to the ground and spread their legs. Horses were Rogier's one acknowledged weakness. None of the family knew what he had paid for the team and would not have believed it had they known. Wiry and middle-sized, their looks did not betray their price or its complete justification. But Rogier knew, as did several other men who had tried to buy them with increasingly higher offers. Now, warmed up, the mares ran easily, smoothly, with ears laid back; and the wagon slipped up behind Tom in the swirling dust. Then Rogier lightly flipped the sorrel on the rump with the end of the rein and the mares passed Tom in a pattering flash. Rogier eased them down gradually and kept Tom behind them.

From Colorado City the road was crowded with teams and wagons, with men walking and on horseback. Manitou appeared at the base of the great blue barrier before them as though it had been dropped in a basket and burst open by the ridges of the canyons. Rogier, with Tom behind him, drove slowly up the rocky inclined road to the mouth of the Pass. There they turned off into an open meadow beside the trail, already spotted with a hundred wagons.

While Tom went for his place in line, the three women built a fire and prepared breakfast; the early ride had made them all hungry. Ona, gaining respite, had a moment to look around from the top of a nearby ridge. Incomparably beautiful it all spread out in the thin clear air: the great rocky meadow fringed with red sandstone cliffs; the white-hooded wagons reflecting the bright sunshine under a blue and cloudless sky; the Pass itself, winding narrow and steep above the stream that leapt down white and foaming to the little town below. And rising above them all, tier on tier, the great blue mountains majestic and serene. Ute Pass! Always to her at its sound returned the memory of that roadway as she saw it then. More than any roadway to a trackless sea with its crafts' set sails filling with the breeze, its name spoke to her with the wonder of things far off, sad as if muted by an incalculable distance, like the low voice of thunder echoed by the hills. For like the sea it was a land that slept in time and solitude – a vast realm raised high above the earth, close under the inscrutable eyes of a Heaven that attested the heroism of man's labor, his greed, his faithfulness, or his unfitness to the futile task of its subjection. Ute Pass led up to this domain through the narrow defile of its somber cliffs. A game trail centuries old, the historic pathway of the tribal Utes between mountain and plain, and now wagon wide for the new white breed – old as the hills themselves, it lay dusty in the glitter of the morning sun. And like a disjointed snake drawing its parts miraculously together, the long line of wagons formed round the curve.

Tom came back; he had his place in line. Rogier had gone over after him to satisfy himself that all was ready. There was nothing more to be done; the apples, sound and fresh, had been tied up tightly in gunny sacks to prevent them from rolling about and getting bruised; and over the sacks was thrown a protective tarpaulin lashed down with ropes. There was grain for the mules above timberline, grease for the wagon hubs, and plenty of bacon and blankets for Tom.

All about them as they sat eating, the smoke of other campfires rose unwavering in the still air like soft pillars upholding the vast canopy of the sky. Tom sat cross-legged on the ground, exultant and happy. To Bob and Hiney he was the gay and reckless adventurer of their boyish dreams, and he took every opportunity to strengthen their illusion. Sister Molly sat smiling beside him, staunchly upholding his jokes about the gold pieces to come back inside the gunny sacks. Only Rogier smoking a cigar, seemed to offer in silence the unexpressed faith of them all in one.

The clear trumpet of a bugle brought Tom to his feet, upsetting the coffee pot. Mrs. Rogier rose and stepped up beside him. In his shirt pocket she dropped a five-dollar gold piece wrapped in a piece of brown paper on which was scribbled a verse from the first epistle of John: " – let us not love in word, neither in tongue; but in deed and in truth." Tom laughed and caught up her frail body in one long arm. Then he grapped the children in turn, kissing them roughly and rumpling his boys' hair. "So long ever'body! I'll be seein' you all next spring with a brand new gold piece all around!" He put his arms around his wife. They stood for a long moment in silence before he released her, his eyes wet and shining. Then he turned running, waving one hand awkwardly. Sister Molly watched him go with a calm set face that did not betray the anguishing turmoil tearing at her heart.

Ona wandered back to the high ridge and stood staring fixedly at the long sinuous line of waiting wagons. For a long time it did not move; and then like a snake beginning its crawl, a ripple ran down the train. The first dozen wagons began to move forward. One by one they spread out, moving slowly along the single log railing that marked the edge of the steep precipice falling to the stream below. Against the high mountainside the frequent Conestogas stood out most plainly, their white hooded shapes filing past in the shadowless company of other benign ghosts. Between them heavy deep box wagons rolled cumbersomely behind their eight mules. There were other lighter wagons drawn by only six mules, or even one team like Tom's, but the crack of their skinners' whips echoed just as sharp and loud. And above all their reports, like the incessant shrilling of many insects, whined in a single strident voice the creaking of wagon wheels. It was a difficult grade.

Ona heard a sudden intake of breath beside her, and turned quickly to Sister Molly who had followed her up the draw. Sister Molly was kneeling, bent forward over the rim of rock. With a suppliant gesture of finality she had thrown out an arm. With her other hand she held her breast as if to still in a frenzied clutch the mechanism of pain that rent her. Her face was set in a rigid outline of despair and curious pride. Ona followed the direction of her gaze and out-stretched arm. Tom's light wagon, so small and shallow behind a large ore-box drawn by eight mules, crept up the grade. He sat upright in the exhuberant pride of his quest, waving his whip over his two mouse-mules – brave and foolish and futile, like a toy figure behind a toy team. Behind him the load of apples bumped over the rocks. In that far distance the light load, covered by a square of canvas, suggested a body under a grayish shroud.

Sister Molly breathed deeply again, the gasp of air whistling through her clenched teeth. She followed the hump under its dirty canvas with burning eyes. It was the body of her faith, her hope, her love, the love that giving everything demanded a subsistence that it might give still more. But also it was as if under that jolting tarp lay the corpse of her pride. And with the dull surfeit of her own intuitiveness, Ona watched the pain twisting her tearless cheeks as though Sister Molly sat grieving not for the irrevocable death of her pride, but because Tom believed it yet alive and jolting under the tight ropes that held it down.

At the top of the grade the Pass made a sudden turn around the cliffs. Clearly outlined in the bright glare the wagons seemed to halt a moment on the point. Then, as if admitted one by one through the narrow defile, they vanished suddenly from sight. Tom was almost there, one tiny joint in the gray reptile crawling through the Pass. Sister Molly stood up and grasped Ona by the arm. Curiously at that moment the girl felt as if the woman at her side was bequeathing to her the anguish of giving in bondage to the undying earth a beloved hostage for the preservation of their proud will.

"He's gone. God help me. Tom's gone," Sister Molly murmured helplessly, trying to remember that in the careless beneficence of man's enigmatic faith there always exists the possibility of their wildest, their most undeserved dreams coming true – the last and cruelest jest of all.

And with a last flicker of its gray, disjointed tail, the long reptilian line of wagons slid over the Pass, leaving the mountains like a deep blue curtain veiling their future from sight.

9

The house below Bijou Hill was as anomalous as its builder. Long, narrow, and three stories high, it rose from the flat prairie like an ungainly obelisk. To Ona, who often stared at it from Shook's Run where she went to gather watercress, it looked like a big wooden barn. Two protuberances relieved its stark shape: a small front porch and a balcony jutting out from the front second-story bedroom. The house would look better when provided with a long veranda, a glassed-in kitchen porch, gravelled driveway, and the trees and lilac bushes Rogier was setting out. If it bore the stamp of her father's outer simplicity, it also reminded Ona of the lean narrow faces of the smelly old Kadles, with its slanting roof of thin hair, the clapboard seams down it cheeks, and the long white beard straggling down the front steps.

The interior alone bore the marks of Rogier's taste and craftsmanship. The front hall and parlor were panelled in California hand-rubbed redwood, as were the sliding doors with their shiny brass fittings, and matched by a red brick fireplace. The three rooms on the ground floor – parlor, dining room, and kitchen, with a panelled china closet – were repeated on the second floor. The massive front bedroom with its balcony was also made of solid redwood as were its great bed, bureau, and dressing table. Provided with an open fireplace, three great windows, and clothes closet, this master bedroom was easily the best room in the house and comfortably held Sister Molly and her two boys who slept in an alcove. The middle bedroom was given to Mrs. White, the Rogiers using the back bedroom at the end of the hall, next to the bathroom.

The third floor was given over to Ona and the children. Immense, cold, and gloomy, it was the one area in the house that maintained through the years a passive and careless – and thus indestructible – sense of character. A half-story, its low sloping roof magnified the cavernous aspect of the long front room which extended more than half the length of the house. The only window was placed at the north under the gables, and the thin light diffused through its small panes only accentuated its gelid atmosphere. Here Ona, Sally Lee, and Mary Ann slept in beds pulled close to the fireplace Boné was given the small second room at the back, with a tiny south window looking out at Cheyenne Mountain. Between these two rooms was a dark landing with carved bannisters that terminated the stairway from the second floor. At the head of the stairs was a narrow west window looking out upon Pikes Peak.

Creeping upstairs to bed so as not to awaken the children, Ona blew out the lamp on the landing and undressed in darkness. She had just got into bed when an arm struck her in the side and a voice ejaculated, "Boo!"

"Boné! What are you doing here?"

The boy moved closer to her and murmured softly, "I like your bed best 'cause I can listen to so many things. Hearin' things is more fun. I bet I can hear more things than you!"

"Be quiet then." Ona pushed his head back upon the pillow. It was true; Boné had a peculiarly acute sense of hearing that made the other children deaf in comparison. His favorite game was to lie on the bank of Shook's Run and count on each finger a rippling sound made by the stream. Then one had to trace it up or down the stream to the particular eddy or shoal of rocks to prove his point. Boné invariably finished first. Unerringly too he could call the exact location whence came the cry of a prairie bird, and he was especially sensitive to voices.

"Who's talkin' now?" he whispered.

"Bob and Hiney are talking to Sister Molly."

"No. I mean downstairs in the parlor."

Ona concentrated with all her will upon the faintest hum of voices two flights down and ventured a guess. "Your grandmother."

The boy squeezed her hand. "Now let's try something else."

"You get to sleep."

"I'll tell you, Ona. The first one who hears a bird gets to poke the other."

For a long time Ona lay listening to the deep silence ebbing in the tiny window.

"Have you heard one yet?" whispered Boné.

"Yes," lied Ona, hoping he would go to sleep.

"You ought to have poked me." Then proud of his own forebearance he boasted, "I heard two, an owl down by the creek, and something in the leaves of the elm. I wondered how long it would take you to hear the owl; he's a long way off."

"What makes the steps squeak, Ona?"

"Ask Daddy. Something about the wood."

"Aunt Martha said it was the Kadles walking around. Who are they?"

Ona pinched his arm reassuringly. It was like her mother to say that, as if she believed the fantastic prophecy or threat that the Kadles would haunt the house built on their land! "Silly!" she told Boné. "The Kadles were two smelly old men with white beards who lived here before Daddy built the house. They're both dead now. You go to sleep now or back you go in your own bed!"

Long after he had gone to sleep Ona lay awake. The hoot of the owl sounded closer and down at the creek she heard the single strident voice of frogs and crickets. Then the night was still. There was only the light breathing of the boy beside her, and at long intervals the queer faint creak as of the Kadles, aged and rheumatic, prowling through the house.

Among the grownups in the parlor downstairs the talk was more disconcerting. As Ona had gone upstairs to bed Mrs. White had observed brusquely, "Looks like she's doin' most of the mothahing and work besides."

"Certainly not!" snapped Mrs. Rogier. "But it's good for her to learn such things."

Mrs. White turned to Rogier. "Too much work and no play for a girl goin' on seventeen, ain't it? She's lookin' peaked. Now music's restful. Why don't you give her some music lessons? If you can't afford a piano, I can. I'm goin' into business."

"Business! At your age! What kind?" demanded Mrs. Rogier.

"The only kind I know. A boahdin' house. I looked at a place today for sale on Cascade. I'll be down to your office tomorrow, Joe, to talk to you about it."

"I don't see any need for that," said Rogier. "We're all comfortable here, aren't we?"

"You can't teach an old dog new tricks," said Mrs. White. "Besides I like to be independent."

Sister Molly did not participate in the conversation. She sat in the corner as she sat outside under the elm all day, one hand at her breast, silently waiting for the weeks, the months, to pass. Thinking now how alike their two lives were: her mother, after three husbands, finishing her life alone, and herself with two husbands just as alone. She tried to think of a reason, a defect in their natures, that might have justified their similar fate. Her mother was honest, faithful, and had worked like a nigger. She too had always been honest with herself. Never in her life had she dodged an issue. It just wasn't in them to squirm and lie for the comfort of the moment. All that either of them had ever wanted was a home, somebody and something to work for. And what had it all come to, she wondered. Loneliness was her only answer. Loneliness! The unutterable cry of every human heart.

"I guess I'll be going up to bed," she said dully, rising and plodding upstairs.

"It's no use askin'," said Mrs. White. "She ain't heard from Tom yet?"

"No!" answered Mrs. Rogier sharply. "I don't know what he's thinking of, staying so long and never writing a word."

To this there was no answer.

There was to Mrs. Rogier something infinitely shocking, repulsively common, about her mother's business venture that menaced on her growing snobbishness now that Rogier was becoming so successful. Taking over Henry Haekel's place next to the livery stable! A rowdy boarding house for teamsters, roustabouts, and no-goods! For all her loyalty to her mother, she resolved never to set foot in the place. One couldn't afford to associate with such people if her husband was to become the town's most popular builder.

She urged him often to go in for the large ornate buildings that were marking Little London's growth as a resort. Two men in town who had struck it rich at Leadville had built an Opera House modelled after the Madison Square Theatre in New York. General Palmer, forced to abandon his railroad route to Mexico, had diverted his tracks west to tap the silver booms in Wet Mountain Valley, and at Leadville, Durango, and Silverton. Now he had just built a great new hotel at the end of Pike's Peak Avenue named The Antlers. Of English design, Queen Anne, its three lower stories were built of stone and the two upper stories of wood; it had gables, turrets, balconies, porches, and a round tower. Mrs. Rogier, taking Rogier to its opening, was even more impressed by its hydraulic elevator, gas lights, massive Gothic furniture, and fine rugs and linen.

"The finest hotel out West! A hundred and one feet high! Oh Daddy, if you could only get a contract for something like this!"

Rogier shook his head. "Let's don't get too big for our boots, Martha. The glass works doesn't look as well, but it'll do." The glass manufacturing plant he had just built in Colorado City was indeed no beauty but it was the largest of its kind in the West, turning out daily 19,000 green-glass bottles to hold Manitou's mineral water. The Antler's foreign air of charm and distinction aroused in him again a shame for his lack of education. Graciousness in architecture as graciousness in character implied the mellow strength of time. It would come, but for the present it was enough to continue constructing simple, stout churches, schools, business blocks, and houses.

If the Silver City in the Sea of Silver had brought to Little London an opera house with a Venetian drop curtain and a resort hotel with blue Wilton carpets, it also had drawn to the swiftly growing English spa a horde of ragamuffins on their way to or back from the mountains. Wagon trains creaking up Ute Pass were being replaced by coaches and narrow-gauge railroads crawling through canyons and over mountain passes, wherever sounded the cry of silver. Still, a straggle of wagons would come down the Pass bearing men ragged and unshaven, in boots split at the seams, demanding a cheap bed as the reward of their fruitless toil. It was a group of these Rogier noticed late that fall on the street corner. Drawing a match across the torso of a wooden Indian at the entrance of the tobacco shop and lighting his cigar, he strolled inside for information.

"Yes, Mr. Rogiér ," the man told him, "the last train this fall came down the Pass about noon. The town's full of freighters. The boys will be raisin' hell over in Colorado City tonight, won't they?"

Rogier nodded as he went out. Perhaps Tom had come down with them. It was his last chance before winter set in, and he wouldn't be spending another winter up in Leadville unless something had happened. Walking down the street in the twilight, he paused a moment in front of the old boarding house Mrs. White had taken over. The desicated wooden building needed painting, and the livery stable next door did not add to its appearance. He walked carefully up the steps of the ramshackle porch, avoiding the dunnage bestrewn all over, and went in the door.

Supper was being served. The long dining room table was loaded with food and crowded with men. There was only one woman, a young one, sitting next to Mrs. White's place at the head.

"Howdy, Joe. Set yourself in the parlor and I'll send in some coffee. Weah almost done."

Waiting in the small sitting room, Rogier watched Mrs. White with admiration. He never thought of her as his mother-in-law. He remembered her only as one who once had recalled him to the land of living in an upstairs garret; and he conceded her the homage due one who lived her life always with courage, often with regret, but never with shame. She moved with slow assurance behind the broad bent backs, stopping at the buffet to call out to the girl coming from the kitchen with another loaded tray. Then she sat down beside the young woman at the table. She was not eating, and answered with easy unconcern the rough jests called forth by the omission. She kept them in their place with a natural assumption of unmistakable authority without raising her voice above the drawling nigger-tone they all joked at between themselves. Then she talked quietly to the young woman, diverting her attention from the men in woolen shirts ravenously eating from the coarse dinnerware. A Southern gentlewoman who in her time had done grace to cut glass and silver gleaming in candlelight, she gave off an ineffable sense of good breeding without being aware that it always had been hers; she appeared common and she was never coarse.

In a few moments she rose. "Now boys, there's plenty of punkin pie. Y'all just tell Beth what you want." Then she led the young woman into the parlor.

"Joe, I want you to meet Miss Lilly Force. She's just come out West here and is figurin' on givin' music lessons."

Rogier bowed. His quick glance dropped from her black hair with its two-inch streak of premature gray to her small oval face, and then to her olive-tinged, swift-moving hands. He had the instant impression of a young woman sensitive and inexperienced, well-educated, and with more nervous force than she had learned to command.

"Mrs. White has been very considerate to sit through the meals with me. It's so much better than eating in my room." The girl smiled. "And I really don't mind the men, even when they joke. Anyway, it's all what I came out West for. I wanted something different."

Mrs. White gave the girl a key. "Well, I figgah theah's no account fo' you to be scairt while you're learnin' there's nothin' different heah from anywheah. You won't need this key, but take it anyway. They're all good boys. If you'd play them somethin' on that old piano, they'd be fetchin' you shirt buttons to sew on and offerin' to take you to church."

"I certainly shall," answered Miss Force, "and tonight too."

"Well, I got to be goin'. Joe will bring me back early so don't be gettin' figity."

As they walked out Rogier asked her, "You're not staying all night with us, then?"

"Jes' supper, Joe. A supper I don't have to think about gettin' always tastes pretty good. But the reason I wanted you to come by for me tonight was Lily Force." They walked slowly down the street. "Lily's got a lot to her," continued Mrs. White. "She's been over to Europe studyin' music for a year. Her father's a Methodist preacher in Illinois. He sent her. But she jes' had to come West like all the rest of us. Why don't you get her, Joe?"

"Always in a hurry, aren't you?"

"You better be, Joe. Somebody else will be grabbin' her and braggin' about fetchin' a music teacher from Europe. Lily would be jes' the one for Ona and maybe Sally Lee."

"We'll see."

"Anyway I'm goin' to fetch her down to the house some afternoon and have her stay for supper."

"That'll be fine," agreed Rogier.

From the top of Bijou hill they walked slowly down into the prairie lying flat and unbroken toward the straggle of trees along Shook's Run. Behind them rose the mountains, always familiarly near and never unheeded in Rogier's mind.

"Heard about the freighters that come down the Pass today?" asked Mrs. White. "The wagons were full of deer and ducks. The boys fetched me three bucks. I'm savin' one foh Martha till you come foh it in the buggy."

"She'll like that. Did you get any of the men down from Leadville?" he asked casually.

"The big fellah on the end and the red-whiskahed man alongside him. Been a lot of shootin' and jumpin' claims, they say. You can't leave a workin' to go after flour and beans, not unless somebody sits behind with a gun. An' the prices sky high. But I asked about Tom."

"Yes?"

"They nevah even heahed of him," she said casually.

The tall face of the house began to loom up in the darkness like the landmark it was. The place looked better now that its stark outlines were broken by shrubbery, the lilac and the lawn, and Sister Molly's big elm tree transplanted out in front. Again, as every night, Rogier felt a queer inquietude as he approached its shadow spread upon the earth like the dark halo of an invisible crown of pain worn so steadfastly by her who sat beneath it through the days.

Mrs. White moved closer to him and put her hand on his arm. "Joe," she asked in her low deep voice, "what can you be doin' about Tom?"

He bent his head and let down his arm. "Ask God and Sister Molly. It's up to them." He went on up the steps and opened the door before her.

10

As always when she got up, Sister Molly that morning had gone barefooted to the window for a look at the mountains before lighting the fire in the grate. Over them had hung the sign of a storm – a gathering of small clouds, low and puffy in the deep crevice between the Peak and Cameron's Cone. She dressed slowly and awakened the boys. Downstairs they ate breakfast with Rogier and Martha, the first buckwheat cakes of the season. Then Bob and Hiney left with Rogier, and Ona took Boné and the girls to school. Slow and lackadaisical, Sister Molly's gaunt body moved about with Mrs. Rogier doing up the work. At noon Mrs. Rogier left for town. "I'm goin' to ask Mother to come down for dinner tonight. Joe can call for her. You won't mind keepin' an eye on the children, will you?"

Sister Molly nodded. Already the day seemed weary and worn thin. She had hoped it might be warm enough to sit under the elm awhile; but true to the epiphanic clouds above the Peak the afternoon was gray and chill. So she sat in her rocker at the front window, gazing westward at the blue rampart that shut off the world of her conscious thought. Boné, Sally Lee, and Mary Ann came home from school. She could hear them playing up in the third floor.

Late that afternoon the clouds drew back from the sun, and Sister Molly sat staring out upon the gold and copper and brass of the fading Indian Summer.

She suddenly stiffened. Not a movement of her big-boned body was visible under the clean starched gingham; it seemed to have set in a cast of frigid shapelessness. Her face drained to the color of dried clay and hardened without a wrinkle. With effort she closed her eyes as though to beseech the powers of darkness for strength to free her from hopeless immobility. The moment passed. She opened her eyes and got to her feet. Clutching at her heart as though to maintain at precise equilibrium that mechanism of almost unbearable pain, she walked stiffly out of the house.

Under the branches of the elm, and hidden from the house by its trunk, Tom was waiting. She moved slowly to stand before him, unable to speak. Then as though still upholding the oppressive burden of those long months of anxious waiting, she slumped backward against the tree. Tom moved a step forward. "Molly – I'm back!" Sister Molly tore her hot bright eyes from his own. Slowly her gaze lowered from his bearded cheeks to his tattered jacket, down his shapeless trousers to boots covered with mud and split at the seams. He took off his hat, holding it against his leg as if to hide the rent in his trousers, and his uncut hair slid gently down over his eyes. Awkwardly he brushed it back. Yes! Tom was back! Without wagon and mules, even his duffle bag, he had begged his way down the Pass with the wagon train.

A fierce pride of possession burned through her as she stared at his hard rangy body, the thin brown face with its high cheek bones and careless twist to his large mouth. It was Tom. There was nothing – not pride or love, nor herself and the long empty years that stretched so interminably before them – nothing that could change Tom Hines. She opened her lips but could not speak. It all had been said before; there was nothing she could ever say.

Tom made an affectionate jump toward her and reached out a long arm as if dangling his battered hat like a trophy before her. Almost wearily Sister Molly leaned back her head to the elm and closed her eyes. It stopped him quicker than if her hand had struck him on the breast. A foolish look of anger drew his lips back from his gleaming teeth.

Suddenly conscious of the smell of his breath, Molly opened her eyes. She had thought it unlike him not to come swinging home, bursting in the door with a shout as if he owned the world and had it in his pocket like a prize. It was the bar whisky taken all afternoon to work up his courage to come sneaking behind the elm when all but herself were gone. But it had made him remember their last talk together. And it held him there, awkward, silent, and fumbling with his hat, like a shadowless vision ever between them. He remembered! And herself, remembering the worry, the anguish, the vain hopes of days passed, could only think of him drinking bar whisky in Levy's all afternoon instead of coming home to her, whatever had happened. It was the only thing Sister Molly could never have forgiven him, and the look in her eyes brought up a faint flush to his corded throat.

Defiantly he raised his head. "Well – I'm back," he said again.

Sister Molly pushed herself away from the supporting elm with a slight decisive inclination of her head. She stood, as if balanced precariously on stiff legs, one hand resting gently on her breast.

"Well, what're you goin' to say? Ain't you glad to see me?" demanded Tom.

"Yes," she spoke gently; and then as if recalled from a distant past soothing with faded memories to the unbearable contemplation of a world sharp with a living image, she repeated in a fierce whisper, "Yes!"

That was all. There was no surrender in her spoken assent. She stood tall and erect under the branches of the tree, and the last rays of sunlight gleaming through its shadows lit up for an instant her gray tense face. She raised her hand to a branch above. The dry twig snapped off with a sharp report. Tom started slightly. His mouth dropped open as though he had seen mirrored in her eyes a flash of lightning that might have split asunder the tree itself. Sister Molly did not move or speak. As with her hand raised in silent benediction, she watched him with a look of gentle understanding that flooded her whole face. Slowly she let her hand fall. It was as though she drew the curtains of the day dying in silence between them. The sunlight flickered and was gone, leaving the shadows dark and chill about their waiting figures. A sharp breeze ruffled the leaves at their feet; and shuffling suddenly in his boots, Tom turned to look back over his shoulder. When he turned around again, Sister Molly had let her head sink toward the hand still at her breast. As though facing a future so vast and unending that not the swiftest human hurry would ever hasten its interminable procession, she walked slowly toward the house. Tom watched her go with dark appealing eyes and an angry flush in his cheeks. He jammed his hat upon his head. "Goddamn it," he muttered in a low thick voice, his boots shuffling the brittle leaves that, falling gently, obliterated forever the trace of her footsteps underneath the elm.

Sister Molly went straight into the house and up to her room where she sat down facing the window. On the floor above, the children were still playing; she could hear their shouts and scampering feet. Suddenly aware that the need for maintaining her vigil out of the window was irrevocably past, she rose and wandered aimlessly about the big room. She could envision nothing that night or day might surprise her with, nothing that time could bring worth waiting for. Slowly the room began to chill and she lit a fire in the grate. From force of habit, she undressed, hanging her clothes carefully in the closet and throwing over her shoulders an old gray robe. With one hand pinching its buttonless sides together across her breast, she seated herself on a stool before the flames.

A little later Ona arrived and came in the room. "I didn't know you were here till Boné told me. Aren't you feeling well, Sister Molly?" When she did not answer, Ona patted her on the shoulder. "You just stay up here till supper time. Things are all started. I'll call you."

Mrs. Rogier arrived home late and bustled about getting supper. "Ona, you get the girls some mush and honey, and see they get up to bed. Mother's comin' with Daddy for supper. Where's Sister Molly?"

"She's not feelin' so good," answered the girl. "I told her I'd keep everybody quiet."

Going upstairs to change her dress, Mrs. Rogier called in to the front bedroom. "Hope you're feeling all right to come down, Molly. We've got a big supper. Mother's comin' home." She paused a moment, inclining her small head, bird-like, toward the room, but there was no answer.

When Rogier and Mrs. White arrived the house was quiet. Mrs. Rogier kissed her mother, then lit the big lamp in the dining room. "We've got a good supper, Mother. Let's don't wait or it'll spoil."

"Where's Sister Molly?" inquired Rogier.

"She won't be down. She's in bed," answered Ona.

"Reckon I'll run up and see her a minute," said Mrs. White.

They all went upstairs. Sister Molly was in bed, watching the dying flames across the room. Rogier stirred up the fire, and its ruddy glow lent warmth to her cold set face. With visible effort she answered their worried questions in a voice, cold and toneless, that expressed no interest in anything they might find to say.

"Anything happen today?" inquired Mrs. Rogier casually. "Seemed like there was a lot of people on the street uptown. Maybe because I don't get out too much. But I thought somebody might have dropped by."

A quick light flickered in Sister Molly's eyes, perhaps no more than the momentary reflection of an ember that burning through effused a spurt of sparks.

"Nobody except a man that stopped under the elm a minute," said Boné loitering in the doorway. "I heard him out of the window."

Mrs. Rogier turned, quick to remind him of his ready tongue, but he retreated up the third-floor stairs. Sister Molly seemed not to have heard him and even Mrs. White turned casually away. Rogier remained in the room after the women had gone downstairs. He idled about uncomfortably as if waiting for Sister Molly to speak, but she lay quiet, seemingly unaware of his anxious eyes. "Well, I'll be going down I guess," he said reluctantly. "Sure you don't want some supper?"

"Good night, Joe," she said dully.

Rogier closed the door behind him and followed Boné up to the third floor. The boy was already in bed at the head of the stairs. "Well, I didn't know you were sleeping here with Ona," he said, sitting down beside him.

"Just till she comes up. Then we play a bird-game and I go in to my own bed."

"Oh, I see."

"Yes, sir. Sometimes we can hear a long way off."

"Almost as far as the elm tree?"

"Aw, that's easy it's so close!" laughed the boy.

"So you think you really heard a man there this afternoon?"

"Sure. But when I looked out the window here he was standin' behind the tree. All I could see was Sister Molly."

Rogier drew the covers up over the boy. "You're a good one!

You probably heard a woodpecker. Now keep warm. Ona will be up in a few minutes." He rose and went downstairs.

All during dinner and afterward when they sat talking in front of the fire, he kept thinking of Boné's words and Sister Molly. Even while walking home with Mrs. White the thought engrossed him so that he did not speak. Mrs. White herself was silent, puffing from the climb up the hill. Suddenly she gripped his arm. "Don't look around," she said casually, "but get a hand on youah gun."

"You know I've never carried a gun in my life!" he answered sharply. "What's the trouble?"

"There's a man followin' us, Joe."

They crossed out into the middle of the road. "It's all right now," he said. "The lights are beginning to show up. Did you get enough dinner tonight?"

At the door of her boarding house, as she turned to go inside, Mrs. White reminded him to be careful walking home.

"I've got a couple of hours figurin' on that church front to do at the office first. Don't worry. I'll fetch that fine buck home tomorrow."

He kept a sharp eye along the street as he walked toward his office, but not until he stopped in the tobacco shop did he catch a glimpse of the figure behind him. With a cigar between his teeth, unlit, he sauntered out of the store and crossed the corner. He had the feeling that someone was still following behind. As the lights thinned out he increased his pace and swung rapidly along the dark block. At the entrance to his office he quickly stepped inside the doorway and turned around to face the street. Waiting for the steps rapidly approaching, he withdrew his right hand from his coat pocket. Then suddenly rasping into a burst of flame the match in his fingers, he thrust it forward face-high and stepped out upon the walk. The movement was timed exactly; the figure stopped before him with a grunt of surprise that betrayed the sharp smell of bar whisky on his breath. Rogier's quick glance played over the uncouth figure of the man revealed in the glow of his match. Imperturbably he lit his cigar and threw the match away. Still the man did not speak, but stood before him silently waiting.

"Come on upstairs with me, Tom," Rogier said quietly, and Tom slouched in behind him without a word.

11

For two days Sister Molly did not leave her room. Mrs. Rogier, unable to remember when she had been sick before, was worried by her curt refusals of every spoonful of medicine and kept wondering what was wrong with her. For breakfast Ona carried her the bowl of hot milk and fried toast the children called Bear Soup, and at supper sat with her until she ate something of what was brought. Sister Molly did not complain. All day and through the evening she sat in silence staring into the flames, her broad shoulders humped as if under an incalculable and invisible burden that could not quite crush her on the spot.

A light snow fell. And the land, absorbing the small flinty flakes, seemed to drain from the skies the dry gray chill, even the clouds that hung over the peaks. With the recrudescent sun the days turned bright and warm; and the long Indian Summer, mellowed by the touch of snow, glowed rich and golden till the year had almost passed. The good weather robbed Sister Molly of all excuses for sickness and drove her outside again. Yet she acted just the same, listless narcissistically bound up by her thoughts, as if emerging from a long illness that had drained her of interest in any living thing.

Even her two boys, lovingly attendant upon her wishes, moved about as though unnoticed under her dull surfeited look. But never did she return to the elm tree, nor did she ever stand staring out of the window again. When her work was done she went upstairs to her room, sitting in a catatonic stupor till supper time.

The months went by and Sister Molly did not change. An immobility of expression held frigid her broad freckled face. Even her big figure, growing gracious in contour as it thinned, gave an air of impenetrability through which none could divine the cause of her strange malady. Only Rogier knew. Often he made up his mind to talk to her of his meeting with Tom, but as if bound to silence by a casuistical passion for maintaining the integrity of his given word he said nothing.

Only once did Mrs. White voice her anxious surmise. "Somethin' has happened to Molly she won't tell." And she was too shrewd and human to say more. Mrs. Rogier became more worried. "She acts like she was just passing the time away until she died." Terrible phrase! Rogiér's conscience repeated it every night. But they all forebore to talk of Tom.

That winter Mrs. White's boarding house burned down. The hay rack of the livery stable next door caught fire, the flames spreading to the ramshackle building before an alarm could be given. Mrs. White and her boarders were eating supper when they were enveloped in a burst of smoke and rushed out before the entire side wall of the dining room collapsed, bringing down the roof. The fire burned almost everything Mrs. White owned and she moved back into the Rogier's middle bedroom with nothing left but a few clothes still hanging in the closet. The venture had taken all the money remaining from her father's estate.

For the first time since Rogier had known her, she seemed discouraged. Squinting at the memories she recalled, Mrs. White could see no pattern to her life. Yet over and over again there seemed repeated in her life and in Sister Molly's those similar happenings with which fate had marked their days. She remembered a night in her early married life. De Vinney was celebrating the christening of a river steamer. Six darkies had rowed her out to meet him. A hundred gentlemen with their ladies thronged the smooth decks and the salon, or danced sedately to music from Negroes whose eyes and teeth gleamed white in faces sweating black. De Vinney was not present to receive her and help her up the steps, although a dozen gentlemen crowded each other for the honor of her hand. He was at the roulette table in the main salon. From the doorway she saw him there under the brilliant crystals of the chandelier, his face flushed with wine, eyes bright for the whirl of the ivory ball, but not for her. And now, forty years later, she remembered that it was the same boat on which she had sent her son Ansil to New Orleans with all the money from his father's estate. She had believed it had been stolen from him as he lay dying of yellow fever in a hotel room at the end of his journey. But now, strangely after all the years, she seemed to see her son standing in his father's place in the same salon, his own face flushed, hands and heart eager with his father's full patrimony. A man like Tom. The vision passed to bring the memory of that fire long ago, burning the St. Louis warehouses that held her name and wealth. Queer that those flames of fate had followed her through all the years only to take from her at last a place as miserable as Henry Haekel's old boarding house. So Mrs. White sat with Sister Molly, facing a short and impoverished future after a long and malignant past.

Ona sat with them often. Herself big-boned and tall, she had become Sister Molly's constant companion. They never talked, yet the older woman's strange and pitiable infirmity preyed upon her mind. She could not keep away.

Late one afternoon Rogier saw all three of them sitting on the floor staring up at Sister Molly's graven mask of face. The dull bewilderment, the deep compassion in the girl's eyes, brought Rogier up short. For the first time he saw her as other than a child. She was his daughter; she had her own life to live; and he was damned if she wasn't beginning to look and act like both of them—as if all three were of a kind. The truth of that vagrant thought struck and clung quivering in his mind like a spent arrow that had reached its mark. Here she was when all her world should be unfolding with the bloom and fragrance of youth's spring. But instead of horseback rides, mountain picnics, and kisses in the moonlight, she chose to sit and share the insupportable burden of Sister Molly's hidden sorrow. That was no life for a girl. No one could help Sister Molly now. Resentment flooded his mind. This was a miserable house over which hovered like a black cloud a sense of stifling doom. There ought to be noise as in every other house – quarrels and laughter and the empty prattle of happy voices. But here only Boné seemed more than half alive.

Impetuously he called out, "Ona! go down and help your mother," as though work were something she had never known. But that night he told Mrs. Rogier that Ona was to do no more work around the house.

"But who'll take care of the children? And how will the work get done?

"Three grown women ought to be able to cook and sweep the floor," he answered gruffly. "Ona's done more than her share too long. It's time she was learning to play."

As he was getting ready to go back uptown he drew Mrs. White aside. "Whatever became of that music teacher, Lily Force?"

"I reckon she's boahdin' around, tryin' to give lessons."

"Suppose you bring her around. Ona's beginning to look seedy, worrying about things she can't help."

Mrs. White nodded. "This heah house needs a little music. It might keep you home of an evenin'."

Rogier went back to his office and his books without telling her she was probably right.

Stratton showed up at his office again. He looked not only more run-down-at-the-heels, but there was in his eyes the haunted look of a recluse. From Mrs. Rogier's gossip Rogier could understand why. He had married that young seventeen-year-old girl with whom he had been keeping company, Zeurah Stewart, and a few months later had sent her home to Illinois. There she gave birth to a child, a boy whom she claimed was Stratton's conceived before their marriage. Stratton asserted the child was not his and divorced her. To add to this unfortunate affair, it became known that Zeurah shortly after her marriage had received $3,000 from her family's estate which Stratton was believed to have spent on prospect trips. Wild conjectures and embittered gossip had changed the popular young carpenter and builder completely. He had left town to live like a recluse, still searching for silver. Now he was back, broke and friendless.

"I've got three jobs goin', Stratton. I can put you to work on any one of them." Rogier began to describe them, but Stratton interrupted.

"Never mind which. All I want is a good job as a journeyman carpenter to save up a grubstake for spring. Then I'm goin', hear!"

He launched immediately into an account of all the fabulous strikes made in the Sangre de Cristos, the San Juans, the Mosquito and Saguache ranges. He had seen them all, prospected every gulch and canyon, crossed every river, and from his solitary campfires had sprouted a dozen boom camps. Like Aspen on the Roaring Fork! Why, from the Mollie Gibson had been taken a single chunk of silver ore weighing 1,700 pounds and bringing $3,000. But Leadville, he insisted, was the daddy of them all. Tabor had sold the Chrysolite for $500,000. The Matchless was paying him $2,600 a day, and his Little Pittsburgh had brought him $1,000,000 more. What a mine that was! The crews of the Little Pittsburgh had raced those of the Robert E. Lee to determine which mine could produce the most ore in twenty-four hours. The Little Pittsburgh had won, producing $117,500 in silver for the day. Palmer's Denver and Rio Grande Railway had reached Leadville. Ulysses S. Grant was the guest of honor to ride the first train into town. Last year 6,000,000 ounces of silver worth nearly $10,000,000 had been taken out of its mines.

"Did you ever run into or hear of Tom Hines up there?" interrupted Rogier.

Stratton spread his hands emptily. "One man in thirty thousand, in fifty thousand. Who knows how many are up there running around, hunting for work?"

"What did you do to get along?" Rogier asked gently.

"Me? I was lucky. Tabor was building a bank with vaults to store his silver bullion. I got the job of building on top of it a big disc carved and painted like a silver dollar. 'Silver Dollar Tabor'!" He grinned sheepishly and then continued. "You know what he claims? That there's enough silver in these mountains to build a wall of solid silver four feet thick and forty feet high clear across the eastern boundary of Colorado. Colorado, the Silver State! These mountains are full of it, Joe. It makes no difference I haven't made a strike yet. That mountain I dreamed of as a boy is still holding it for me, and I'll recognize it when I see it!"

Yes, he had made the turn. He was wholly committed to his

obsessive search. Like Tom. But unlike Tom he would work. Rogier scribbled a note and handed it to him. "Take this down to Sample's. It'll get you bed and board till the first pay day. And listen, Stratton. You've got no tools. So you can use mine."

Stratton stood up. "Your own tools you brought with you?"

"I don't know of a better carpenter to use them," Rogier said gruffly.

Stratton went out without answering.

Mrs. White, Sister Molly, Ona, Tom, and Stratton—they all upset him. They brought back to him, stronger than ever, the sense of his own isolation on a strange and bitter earth. Strangers to each other, brought here by some indefinable magnetism to meet and part without knowing the hidden purpose of their lives. If there was an answer, that lofty snowy beacon rising before him held it with a face enigmatic and inscrutable as the day it had marked his own unplumbed fate.

Then lifting suddenly, the low clouds and chill mist that had clogged the days revealed a world awakened. The earth leapt forth to greet the sun. It was a time of carnival; green was its color; its song the ripple of water everywhere. Cottonwoods grew variolitic with buds. The lilac bloomed higher than the front window. Wedges of wild geese honked overhead. In soft, satiny twilight the stars gleamed like silver struck from the Chrysolite or Little Pittsburgh. Gaunt men in rags laughed along the bars in Colorado City, telling each other that silver bullion was selling for $1.29 an ounce – higher than ever before; and their whiskey, running freer in the warmth, certified their strength to tear out a fortune from the hills. Stratton threw up his job and struck out again. It was spring!—clear and rich and pure as virgin silver—and only Sister Molly did not awaken to new life. She was failing, the doctor said; there was nothing he could do to help her.

The family withheld the news from Ona and the children. Rogier began another desperate search for Tom, but he was gone as if vanished off the face of the earth—gone as Rogier had seen him last at the door of his office, with a bitter grin and eyes that snapped as he went out.

One evening when he arrived home, Mrs. Rogier met him at the door. Something was wrong with Sister Molly. He went upstairs.

She was propped up in bed, hiccoughing, with Mrs. White and Ona beside her. Several days earlier she had taken cold and developed a cough. This Mrs. Rogier had cured with honey, flax-seed, and lemon juice, but Sister Molly started hiccoughing instead. The attacks had become more frequent, and now since noon she had been unable to stop. The doctor had come and given her a sleeping powder, then left shaking his head. Rogier sent the others from the room and sat down on the bed beside her.

Sister Molly turned her face from the pillow, smiled faintly and hiccoughed, raising a pale hand to cover her mouth. Then, wordlessly, she transfixed upon him a beseeching look.

"Molly! Forgive me!" he confessed with pain and shame. "I've seen Tom."

With a resurgence of vital energy her eyes blazed forth upon him.

"It was last fall," Rogier went on. "He came up to my office one night. We talked till midnight. He promised to come home after one more chance. I gave him two hundred dollars—a crew's payroll in the safe."

The light in Sister Molly's eyes died out at his first sentence, leaving them gray and somber as if veiled by a fallen shadow.

"I know, Molly! Oh, I know. I knew it then, but I thought he'd soon come back. When he didn't I sent a man up to Leadville for a month to hunt for him. But I haven't heard a word. Not a word about him from any living man."

"Joe! That's all right! Don't say no more!" She hiccoughed, raising a hand again to her bloodless lips. "I just wanted to tell you I saw Tom that afternoon. It was me that sent him away, like I said I would." Her voice cracked. "He told you he'd seen me and that I kept my word, didn't he?"

Rogier lied, nodding his head.

"Joe, why did it seem like it was the thing to do? Why am I like I am!"

It was not a question, but a confession of that resolute integrity of self which for good or evil marks the essential—and lonely—independence of every human being.

"Tom's Tom too!" she cried out with broken pride. "He couldn't help himself any more'n I could. Tom will always be Tom!"

Again her voice broke and burst forth once more. "But don't you ever be thinkin' I've changed. I'll always be just Tom's."

Before the truth, clear yet indefinable, which found expression in the imperfect connotations of her common words, Rogier bent his head. How unspeakably mysterious is every human soul that it can never be wholly known, seldom approached with perception, and only partly understood with the priceless gift of vision.

Day and night Ona stayed with her, sleeping on a cot beside her bed. It was as if she, of them all, had been chosen to bear with strength and endurance the sinking burden none could support. It was not enough. When Sister Molly died she was buried in the pine-shadowed graveyard south of town. She lay with her head toward Pike's Peak; and the watchers at the funeral remembered how Sister Molly on a wager had scaled its lofty summit in the full strength of her big body—one of the first women to climb the precipitous Ruxton Trail. Now, benign and wrinkled, the Peak stared down upon her final resting place. And standing in the shadow of the enormous pine under which she was buried, none of her family spoke of Tom. Not then or afterward.

That night after the funeral Rogier sat alone in his office, staring out of the window at that high rocky selfhood which alone, of all the living, vibrating entities he had ever known, seemed great and enduring enough to serve as a repository for that human spirit which had escaped at last its small, fleshly and mortal frame.

PART II

GANGUE

1

A death is like a wound in the trunk of a tree; bark, roots, the sap within, all pour forth energy to heal and cover the hurt. So it was with the Rogier family after the death of Sister Molly. For the first time it took on an air of conscious unity, gave off a strength impersonal and fixed. If once its members had been exiles in a new strange land, they now formed one harmonious whole rooted to their earth like a single great pine.

Lamenting the barren outlook from the window, Mrs. Rogier demanded more trees; only the big elm stood between the house and Shook's Run. Rogier went to an old prospector who lived up on Wahsatch. "Maloney, the next time you come down from the mountains bring me a couple of young spruces for our yard. If you need any help I'll loan you a team."

A few weeks later Maloney returned with two half-grown blue spruce with long gnarled roots holding their burden of earth. They were exactly what Rogier wanted. One planted on each side of the walk would relieve the tall three-story face of the house of its gaunt aspect. As he idly kicked the crooked roots, a clump of earth was dislodged and split open on the ground. In it was a piece of rock as big as his two fists, grayish in color with a tinge of purple. A peculiar glint in the cleavage caught Rogier's eyes. Getting out his knife, he began to scrape it.

Calling Maloney off to one side, Rogier showed him the specimen. Maloney hefted it, squinted at it, gouged it with Rogier's knife. "I've done lots of work cause of worse samples," he said tentatively.

"What is it?"

"Could be a showin' of pay dirt."

"You're not sure?"

Maloney's face grew redder under his white hair as he expostulated all he knew. He was an old man, the common type of prospector who really knew little.

"I reckon you'd better take this piece to a good assayer," suggested Rogier. "Do you know of one who can keep his mouth shut? There's no need of going off half-cocked like everybody else."

Two days later the assayer reported that the specimen was an ore he did not know and hence was unable to test properly. Maloney, in Rogier's office, stamped back and forth in front of the window. "If it ain't silver, I'll bet it's gold!"

"Calm down, Maloney," said Rogier. "It's probably a false alarm. But it wouldn't hurt if you went back to where you took out those spruce and looked around. I'll give you a team with a grubstake and some tools."

After the old prospector had left, Rogier found himself unaccountably disturbed . Maloney had brought down the trees from the lower south slope of Pikes Peak. It seemed preposterous to believe that gold could be found there, so close to town, and on the very peak around which men had prospected for years and then gone on to distant ranges. But what if it were? He got up from his stool at the drafting board and began to walk back and forth himself.

For a century the currency system had been based on bimetallism, the unlimited coinage of both gold and silver. Then in the Crime of 1873, as he remembered, the government stopped the coinage of silver dollars and established gold as the standard of value. Five years later silver was discovered in Leadville and the increasing flow of silver from all Colorado began to cast a white shadow over the world at large. All loyal Coloradoans clamored for the right to have coined into dollars all the silver shipped to the mints, and demanded that the ratio of sixteen ounces of silver to one of gold be restored. A compromise was effected in the Bland-Allison Act, directing the purchase of from two to four million dollars worth of silver a year for coinage into dollars. Then, as Rogier knew, the political pot began to boil when Cleveland, opposed to free silver, was elected President in 1884. But the mountains still kept pouring forth a stream of silver – $20,000,000 worth a year now! Something was bound to happen when a country on the gold standard was being flooded with silver.

These considerations were only the surface strata of his perturbation. He kept pacing back and forth as if through a pale white shadow. How strange it was that of all the glistening peaks in every range of these Rockies only this massive mother-beacon for the tide of westward fortune-hunters – this instigator of the Pike's Peak Rush of Fifty-Eight – should have proved barren of its promise. Serene and majestic, beautiful and alluring as it seemed, Rogier knew how cruel it was. It had made fools and vagrants of a generation of men.

Rogier had not succumbed to the lure of silver. A man with ten mouths to feed couldn't afford that touch of moon-madness. Too, he prided himself upon being a rational man. He distrusted moonlight, with all that it always had implied. It had no primary source; it was simply sunlight reflected from a dead planetary body. And silver in turn was but its material reflection in the earth – insubstantial and comparatively worthless as it might prove to be.

But gold! That was something else! The very name held a magic that was unfathomable. Rogier brought up short at the window to stare out again at the enigmatic face of the Peak. What had led him to send Maloney off, hiding his own strange excitement? It wasn't the prospect of getting rich quick, he assured himself. In any case he should have kicked that ore specimen into the hole dug for the spruce. It had caused him only a lot of confounded worry.

Maloney, having exhausted his grubstake, came home disconsolate. He had found no signs on the bottom slope of the talus where he had uprooted the two spruce. As they were young trees, he believed they might have been uprooted and carried down by a landslide. But after packing up the slope and prospecting for days, he had been unable to find the ledge where the specimen had broken off or any trace of ore anywhere.

Rogier felt relieved, and flung himself back into his work with renewed vigor. Lily Force, who had been giving Ona piano lessons, was hunting for a new boarding house. "You come right down here and stay with us," Rogier insisted. "Sally Lee and Mary Ann need some music too." Shortly afterward Mrs. Rogier obtained a maid whom she had met through a peculiar incident.

The two women were kneeling in church one Sunday morning when the services were interrupted by the clanging of bells outside. The congregation kept on praying until the indisputable clamor of men dragging the fire-cart past the church door sounded. Mrs. Rogier raised her head from her arms to meet the gaze of the woman beside her who suddenly shrieked out, "Pray, brethen, let's pray! That's my house burnin'! I left the fire on to cook some beans!"

The woman's name was Lida Peck, and it really was her small shack that burned down. Mrs. Rogier brought her home and persuaded her to stay as a maid. She was enthusiastically religious, attending every church in town. Her yearly vacation of a week she spent attending the Free Methodist Camp Meeting on Fountain Creek outside of town. There would be dozens of tents pitched in a great ring around the rough tables and benches. After a hearty breakfast of wild game, smoked ham, and barbecued beef, the services began. At ten o'clock the songs started, and at three came testimonials from the converted. These daily sessions were attended only by converts and proselytes like Lida Peck. But in the evening people from town would visit; cowboys rode in from the ranches; and later men from the saloons and sporting women from the red-light district in Colorado City wandered over to get religion. They filled the back seats, and becoming hilarious, joined in the shouting. It was all very beautiful and touching to Lida Peck.

This year she conveyed an urgent invitation to the family, as Rogier had good-humoredly donated a tent and some supplies to her cause. With camping space reserved for them, the Rogiers drove over to the meadow between the creek and the red rock walls of the canyon. Mrs. Rogier, peeking out from the frill of her black bonnet, gave a sudden snort of alarm.

"Gypsies. Isn't that a gypsy camp pitched farther down? Right next to where there's a religious meetin' goin' on — even if it is a Shoutin' Methodist Revival. You children stay close to Ona now or they'll be stealin' you away!"

The revival bored Boné. Alone with Ona, he pleaded to spend the silver dollar Rogier had given him with a gypsy woman wearing big rings in her ears. So that evening when the services began they slipped away from the circle of tents and walked to the camp of the gypsies. There were any number of fortune-tellers sitting with their decks of Tarot cards spread out before their fires, or calling from their hooded wagons. Ona was for stopping at any one of them, but Boné walked on toward a thicket of willows.

In a clearing was a dirty canvas-topped schooner backed against a small fire. In it bending forward with her two bare arms crossed over red-stockinged legs, sat a big swart gypsy watching some men playing cards on the ground. "Ona. There she is. Look at the big gold rings in her ears," whispered Boné. "You ask her!"

"No, it's your dollar," she replied. The boy hesitated, then took her by the hand. Walking resolutely up to the gypsy, he laid down his dollar.

The woman grabbed him by the wrist. Rolling out his fingers, she examined both sides of his hand swiftly and intently. Then ringing the silver dollar on the floor of the wagon, she tossed it into the air, catching it in her lap and laughing. "Let a boy with such a hand sing for his own fortune, and not expect it from a gypsy queen with only a piece of silver!"

It had taken not half a minute; and walking back through the darkness Ona tried to console Boné. "These gypsies are sharper than horse-traders and won't be satisfied till they've got every penny on you. But maybe what she said meant more than we heard." Boné trudged beside her silent and sad because the gypsy woman had taken his dollar, not knowing that she had fitted the lasting truth to his long and slender hand.

Ona's own clumsy fingers often reminded her of that enigmatic prophecy. Boné's hands through a few stolen moments each day at the piano were far more adept than hers. Too, he had what Lily Force called perfect pitch. Standing beside Ona at the piano, back turned, he could call out "A", "G", "F-sharp" with astounding precision. Ona blamed Lily Force as well as her mother for the lamentable fact that Boné was not given lessons as well as herself and the two girls.

Though living with the Rogier , in return for which she gave music lessons to them, Lily Force insisted on strict punctuality. At ten o'clock she gave Ona her lesson, and at two o'clock went through the rudiments of music with Sally Lee and Mary Ann. On the evenings Rogier stayed home from work she played for him an hour on the piano. Invariably old Southern songs: "Old Folks at Home," "Old Black Joe," "Maryland, My Maryland." Rogier sat silent, chewing on his cigar. At the end of his favorite piece, "Carry Me Back to Old Virginny", he got up heavily, telling her that for all her technical training she would never know how to play it until she had heard it from Negroes singing.

This endlessly repeated remark infuriated her. She made up for it with her Sunday afternoon concerts to Mrs. Rogier's dinner guests and other invited visitors. It was a display of culture none of them forgot. Lily sat on the piano bench, slender and vivacious, her well-kept hands flitting faultlessly over the keys. Her favorite composer was Mozart, and his perfection of form and style suited her exactly. From time to time she paused to rest, turning to face her listeners. The sun, flooding the room, infused in her olive-tinged cheeks a spot of color like iodine. Her black hair with its two-inch strip of white was never smoother. After she had begun to die it black, the streak took on a greenish hue. No one noticed it, she spoke so prettily of the composers and their compositions. Often she prefaced her remarks with, "When I was in Leipzig" – "In Weimar I saw" – "Well do I remember that crooked little street in Vienna." Mrs. White sat with a smug air of "I-told-you-so," subtly attesting her discovery of Lily Force. Mrs. Rogier was deliriously proud of her and her growing reputation.

Lily Force played, talked on. She was as polyphonic as a Bach fugue. Were music cold and dead as a corpse, she would have excelled as one of its morticians. She knew composition, but not music. She understood the structural design of its skeleton, apprehended with skill the incredible intricacies of its strange texture; but never in her life was she to stand confounded before the profound mystery of the simplest melody. Sincere as her nature allowed, trained well and showing that education handsomely, she was a music expert but not a musician.

This was Ona's music teacher.

Promptly at ten o'clock Lily was always sitting primly at the piano waiting for Ona to come in. This morning, a little late, Ona halted in surprise. "Look here!" said Lily. A newspaper was spread across the piano covering all the music. It was opened at the "Personal" column and Lily's finger was pointing to an advertisement headed "Matrimonial." Lily read it out loud. " 'Wanted: A young blond lady of refinement and education to correspond with a professional, dark-complexioned gentleman with most honorable intentions.' What do you think of that, Ona?"

Ona stared at her with amazement. Lily read these foolish ads every week, but surely she would never dare to take one of them seriously!

"Well," said Lily with a smile, "I answered it anyway. Washington, D.C. it was. By the time he answers I ought to be able to bleach my hair. The pharmacist up on Tejon said it ought to come out well."

Suddenly changing tone, Lily folded up the newspaper and laid it aside. She was no longer frank and engagingly human, but academic, strictly impersonal. "I do wish you would get here on time, Ona. Every moment counts now. In church the other morning your fingers seemed quite stiff. Or were you a little frightened?"

"No," said Ona listlessly. What had it mattered? She merely had substituted for the regular organist to play four hymns.

"You should learn to play well enough to appear in church every Sunday. Then you might attract the attention of some nice young man. At your age you should be going out with one," went on Lily. "What I think the trouble is, is lack of interest in learning fundamentals. Keep on with our study of composition while we're learning to play. Don't you dear?"

"Yes," assented Ona in the same flat tone.

"All right, then. Let's begin."

Following a tedious dissection of the "Blue Danube," Ona started in on her third week's repetition of part of Chopin's Waltz in C-sharp Minor used for finger exercise. Neither of them were aware of Boné's presence in the doorway behind them until he interrupted.

"Why don't you make her play it right? She always gets her finger in the way halfway through and puts in the same wrong note every time. You never do tell her about it, either."

Lily whirled around as though unspun from the string of a top. Compressing her pretty lips she said nothing, but her hand, thrust back toward the piano, struck the keyboard to give out a blatant discord. Boné stood immersed in the sound, oblivious to her anger, and interested only in what his quick ears had detected.

"Don't bother us, Boné," said Ona. "Run out in the kitchen and ask Lida to give you one of her cookies."

Obediently the boy left the room. His small slight figure, with his black hair and blacker eyes, had grown to be the bane of Lily's musical existence. He was immune to her scoldings, unabashed by his daring and childish criticisms, and impregnable against her Sunday afternoon musicales.

Working away, Ona had to smile to herself at the amazing divination of Boné's remark. He would never know how exactly he had guessed her trouble! For the fourth time she flew through those first measures so pliant to her touch and then – she almost winced as her finger again sharped the note he had detected.

"Here," said Lily, "finger it this way." Following the score carefully, and trying to overcome her secret annoyance at Boné's perspicacity, she arched her wrists affectedly and skimmed through the passage.

Outside on the grass under the lilac where he lay munching cookies, Boné looked up at the open window with a childish look of intolerant disgust. Of them all – teacher, pupil, and casual listener, he was the only one in whom music fed a secret and unguessed want. To Lily music was a structure majestic, mysterious, and immense, to be inspected carefully and with caution. Ona liked to hear it and only hoped to learn to play the piano. With Boné it was immeasurably different. His craving for it was as natural as for meat and cookies; and he took it with as little concern. Music revealed to him its secret and subtle truths in audible symbols that all could hear but from which only he could read the meaning; polyphonic, it spoke to him with the wind, the rain upon the roof, the birds in the elm, the ripples of Shook's Run; it was his trumpet, his faith, a secret cancer in his soul, the knotted club for his self-flagellation, and the everlasting solace to his human – and thus lonely – heart. The gift of music was his – and the time was to come when he would offer himself upon its altar as proof of his unswerving devotion.

But now, flat on the grass, he heard through the window the rustle of a newspaper. The lesson was ended; and Lily's voice mused softly, "That's fine, Ona. How long do you think it will take a letter to come from Washington?" Boné rose, and stuffing the last cookie in his mouth moved languidly away.

2

It was Sunday morning and the Rogier family was getting ready for church. Pushed about helplessly, his toes trod on, his cigar knocked awry in his mouth, Rogier retreated to the china closet where seated on a tier of drawers he could watch with safety the confusion before him. Sally Lee and Mary Ann both wanted the same pink ribbon for their hair. In the front room Lily Force called out, "Ona, do you have your music ready?" Whereupon Ona got up from her knees before the two girls and jerked the pink ribbon from their hands to tie up her music – "and let that be a lesson to you both!" Out in the kitchen Lida Peck was finishing the dishes and muttering inculpabilities against all late risers. Her incriminations were softened by frequent looks at her new hat hanging on the cellar door. Bob Hines, already as big as his father, was stooping in front of the buffet mirror to adjust his cravat for the fourth time. "I do wish you'd come with us, Daddy," complained Mrs. Rogier again, hunting a pin for her small bonnet. "It's Palm Sunday." Rogier leaned back against the dark wainscoting listening to the bedlam, attesting with its rising crescendo that the Devil was doing his damndest to frustrate the heavenly design of Sunday morning.

He was no match for Mrs. Rogier. With the perfect composure of seasoned Christian soldiers the family marched out of the house. Rogier walked to the front window where he watched them up the street. Behind the two girls, sedate as white hens in starched muslin fluffing out in back like tail-feathers, followed Ona and Lida Peck. With them was Lily Force. Mrs. Rogier walked primly beside Bob, her hand on his arm. She carried herself erect, head up; and her frail figure garbed in black, with her indomitable, finely chiseled face, expressed all her heart-felt pretensions to Southern aristocracy. Boné loitered in back, straggling along the picket fence with his carved walking stick that Mrs. Rogier, five minutes before, had forbidden him to carry to church. He was discreetly silent, touching only gently with the end of the stick the slats that on week-days he rapped unmercifully with xylophonic glee.

Rogier turned from the window with a reflective puff on his cigar and strolled slowly through the house to the back yard. He had refused to be a deacon lest it might compel him to attend church, declined to act on the School Board because his bids for the school buildings were invariably accepted, and turned down an offer to get into politics without any reason at all. His aloofness created no adverse comment; all who knew him considered it a virtue that he minded strictly to his own business. It proved also to be his weakness. His large family, the prairie land from Bijou Hill to Shook's Run, and two store buildings uptown seemed to have come unbidden but not unwelcome to him. Yet none of them – his family, property, and profession – assuaged the secret conviction of his aloneless.

And the massive mountains rising tier on tier above the flat sunlit prairies refuted any sense of rooted security. He lacked something, he did not know what. Only his books, the evening hour listening to Lily Force at the piano, and the neigh of a horse in one of the stalls, soothed the strange longing that possessed him.

Mrs. White, too poorly for church, came out to sit on the back steps in the sun. She could see him wandering from stall to stall, the hay shed in the corner, the open buggy shed, and along the west side of the enclosure past a second row of stalls newly built and empty. Except for his mares, Lady and Lou – familiarly referred to by the family as Lady-Lou–all of Rogier's teams were draft horses for building work, yet he looked after them like children.

Seeing Mrs. White on the back steps, Rogier carefully closed the gate behind him and sauntered down the walk to sit beside her.

"Hiney ain't up yet," she remarked in a voice that did not conceal the suggestion that the time was nearly eleven o'clock.

"A good sleep won't hurt him any. He has to stay after the play's over to clear things up," answered Rogier, denying the implication of laziness. Hiney was a bright lad, apt at storytelling, and a lover of jokes. He had secured a job as stagehand at the new Opera House built by the two Little Londoners who had struck it rich in Leadville, and he was always coming home with amusing stories. One of Rogier's favorites was Hiney's account of the opening night performance starring Maude Granger in *Camille.* An invited guest asked one of the owners, old Ben, to translate the motto on the Venetian drop curtain, "*Nil sine numine.*" Old Ben, who had no idea what it meant, promptly replied, "No sign of a new mine."

"I allow you don't know what I mean," said Mrs. White. "But I ain't told nobody else."

"What do you mean?"

The old woman prodded the toe of her shoe with a broomstraw. "Well, one night las' month I come down the stairs to see a man from the Opera House standin' in the hall with Hiney. 'A prop fell down tonight and give your boy a rap,' he says. 'It didn't hurt him none, but I had to bring him home. He didn't remember the way.' And theah was Hiney grinnin' foolish-like and rubbin' the side of his head wheah the horse kicked him when he was a little tike. He didn't seem to know me, but followed me up to bed."

Rogier sat quietly beside her, one broad forearm resting on his knee. As if to rouse him from his lethargy, Mrs. White spoke sharply. "And that ain't all, Joe. The next mawnin' Hiney got up feelin' fine, but the othah day I saw somethin' else. It was along sundown, time fo' him to be gettin' to work. Yet he was sittin' right heah like a lost coon dog, and didn't remembah nothin' about it. Then in the middle of the evenin' up he starts up and off to the Opera House he goes. Like all of a sudden he'd jes' come to and remembahed all about himself. What do you reckon is wrong?"

"Nothing – probably nothing. He's been watching those actors and actresses so long, and play-acting like them, he's getting absent-minded.

"Go along!" Mrs. White answered testily.

Rogier looked up and grinned; they knew each other beyond the subterfuge of words. Tossing his cigar away, he rose and strolled down the back walk.

"I wouldn't want nothin' to happen to one of Sister Molly's boys," came a voice at his shoulder.

"I'll keep my eye on him" he promised, leaning upon the top of the gate.

Mrs. White stared over the fence. "What's the line of stalls fo' ovah theah? I ain't heahd of no new horses."

"Scrap lumber. Thought I might be needing some new work teams soon."

"Humm. Looks like the back yahd's full of them already. Now I remembah a bay gelding that De Vinney wanted down along the Mississippi. He used to say evah time he come up the rivah he'd give his eye-tooth fo' that horse. Well suh, he did! The day aftah he brought him home, he pitched cleah over his head, rolled into a stump, and come up spittin' that eye-tooth in his hand. A gelding, too. Only a ten-yeah-old niggah boy could do anything with him at all. But them shiny bay flanks of his would look mighty sweet in one of them new stalls, Joe."

Rogier kicked at a pebble on the walk, then ground it under his foot. "There's a race track being built north of town. Up along Monument Creek. They're getting up a Gentlemen's Pleasure and Driving Association to run it. Not that I'd go in for anything like that, but –" He hesitated, then confessed, "I've seen her several times. A sorrel mare just brought here from the east. She's fairly fast."

"A fast horse is fast in any company, Joe."

"Her name's Pet," said Rogier. "Gentle enough for the family to use her in the buggy."

"I wouldn't spoil her," said Mrs. White, watching him closely. He had perked up – considerable, she thought. A minute passed, then she said casually, "It ain't noon yet and the folks are still to church. You wasn't figurin' on goin' out fo' a look at that sorrel mare, was you?"

Rogier grinned: "Dom! You're right! Get your bonnet while I hook up."

She came out to the buggy carefully holding her bonnet in both hands. From it she removed a bottle, took out the cork with her teeth, and wiped off the neck with her long wrinkled fingers. "This heah bottle's been sittin' up in the china closet long enough. Don' you reckon we'd oughta do somethin' about it? De Vinney used to say a drop of brandy nevah spoiled the looks of a good horse."

Rogier waved his hand, grinning at the way she bent the bottle back. After his own turn he set her up in the seat, bonnet and bottle clutched in her lap, and shook Lady-Lou into a trot. She sat at ease as always, the breeze gently brushing her gray hair behind her ears.

"I wish that preachah could see us! A fingah of brandy and a ride behind a fast horse might help them sermons of his some. The smirkin' lil' dandy! Oh Lawdy! give me a good piece of horseflesh to a sermon every day. Don' you, Joe?"

Rogier threw up his head and laughed. "I'm going to buy that sorrel if I have to sell every piece of ground I own!"

Mrs. White was startled at his vehemence. She looked around, face flushed, then murmured complacently, "Sho' enough, Joe. I reckon that's what we're comin' out here for, ain't we?"

The outskirts of town had fallen behind; ahead swept the unbroken surge of prairies. Rogier tightened his grasp on the leather ribbons in his gloved hands, drew back the heads of his mares until their noses pointed at the line of mountains cut into the sky. "How about a little ride? Suppose you can hang on?" Mrs. White shifted her weight, sat on the empty bottle and her bonnet, and stuck out a hand for support. "I been heahin' you say these mares can run, but I ain't nevah see 'em yet!"

Rogier squashed the soft hat on his head, ruffled his sandy mustache. Then suddenly bending forward, he flung out the reins with a slap at Lady-Lou. With a leap the mares shot forward, ears back, and lay down to the road.

Pet was a welcome addition to the Rogier household. The family allowed her to do everything but eat at the table. She was a pretty thing, even-colored and even-tempered, swift and gentle as a rabbit. On week days while Rogier was gone the children often took her over to Manitou after iron and soda water, driving along the creek past thickets of willows, currants, and chokecherries. Sally Lee with her father's knack for handling horses did all the harnessing and driving.

Even Mrs. Rogier approved of the mare. The Little Londoners in the North End were always showing off their smart traps and spiders, their tandems and landaus. The sight of an elegant Park Four roused her to vociferous envy. She watched the wheelers swinging into line behind the two leaders, ebony black, with a crimson plume above each ear. "Gorgeous! And Daddy won't even get us a victoria!"

Rogier didn't give a damn for fancy rigs and tandems and the new Westcott speed wagons tearing along the Sunday streets. Nor could he subscribe to Mrs. Rogier's views. She was a singular woman. Outspoken, courageous to stubbornness, she stood out alone largely because of her false pride. She was dominated by a queer sense of superiority, an unshaken assurance that all the Rogiers had been born to the purple. None of the family could account for it and had long given up trying. But to quiet her, Rogier bought her a coach and horse called Colonel. The horse was slightly locoed but an excellent traveler. Sally Lee was delighted. It was going to be so much fun to care for four horses!

"You won't have any if Pet comes in with a tender mouth again! Were you afraid of her, the way you had to bit her all afternoon?" asked Rogier.

The purchase of a coach to take the family to church gave Rogier a free conscience and free Sunday mornings to take Pet out alone. He had not yet joined the Gentlemen's Pleasure and Driving Association which seemed too sociable for his simple tastes. But as it had leased the Pikes Peak Driving Park for trials of speed, Rogier thought he might see what Pet could do.

Early in the morning he would drive up the hill and turn north on Cascade. It was a wide street graveled smooth as a track. To the railroad north of town Rogier knew it like a line on his palm. When Pet warmed up, he shook her into pace and took out his watch. Then, a mile from the crossing, he let her out. It was a lively stretch. The full blown trees swept by him as on a moving belt. He sat upright, feet braced, head tilted slightly forward and to the left so that his cigar ashes swept past over his shoulder. The wind drove at his face, was parted by his narrowed gray eyes, and eddied about the wrinkles at their ends. Pet ran easily, smooth to the road. The muscles along her back eased and tightened like rubber bands under velvet. He listened to her stride, leaned down to catch a glimpse of her forefeet, and sat back to steal a look at his watch.

At the end of a mile he drew her up slowly. "Why, old girl, you don't mean to tell me you can't do better than 2:40 in this old buggy! We did that well last week!"

Yes, Pet was doing him a lot of good – and he needed a lot of encouragement with all that was going on.

Bob had come to his office one morning for a talk. He wanted to get married and needed Rogier to help him build a house. He was twenty-two, quite love-silly, but had a promising job in a store and was saving every dollar. Rogier helped him draw up his simple plans, and gave him a man and a team to help. Running short of lumber, Bob occasionally stopped at an empty hut on the outskirts of town and pried loose a plank to carry home. In a short time he had completely dismantled the old hut.

A few mornings later the sheriff entered Rogier's office and laid on the table a warrant for Bob's arrest. The boy had stolen the town's pest house. Rogier sent out a crew immediately to build a new pest house, and then finished Bob's house for his bride. It was a joke he never got over. Nor did Mrs. Rogier. The disgrace, the neighbors' laughing comments, and Bob's humiliation upset her for weeks.

And Lily Force! One night at dinner while Lida cleared the table for berries and cream, she looked up with a slight flush tinging her olive cheeks a rich orange. "I must tell you," she laughed with embarrassment. "I'm going to be married! At least I might!" And then, pell-mell, she gushed out the story of the want ad in the "Personal" column of the *Weekly Gazette*, the subsequent letters from the gentleman in Washington, D.C. who wanted to correspond with a light-haired lady of refinement, and the reason for bleaching her hair. Yes! He was coming out to Colorado. Immediately. A Judge Henry, some sort of government man.

Mrs. Rogier gasped. Ona and the children were thrilled. Rogier grinned. "You don't have to take him, Lily, unless you want to. Remember that."

After a half-hour of talking Lily felt better; she had got it out of her system. Mrs. Rogier had taken it better than Lily had expected. She only murmured vaguely, "I do hope, Lily, you and the judge won't repeat this to anyone. It's so – so unusual, you know."

Rogier was more upset than he could betray. Tom, Sister Molly, Bob, Hiney, Ona, failing Mrs. White, and now Lily – what was taking them, one by one, out of their ordered pattern of existence?" Let's have a little music tonight, Lily," he requested as usual. "You might start with a few old Southern tunes if you've a mind to."

Boné flashed Lily a sharp look and strode upstairs. New horses, new husbands – what were they to him? But with Lily gone, he might have more time to play on the piano.

3

Rogier sat on his long-legged stool, head bent over the drafting board. He was copying a page of Roman letters taken from the inscription on the monument to Leonardo Bruni in the church of Santa Croce in Florence. The letters were unusually light-faced, the width of stroke no more than one-tenth the height. Designed by Bernardo Rossellino, they were indeed considered his masterpiece.

Rogier worked hard. His right sleeve was rolled back to allow the free movement of his broad firm hand and muscular forearm across the board. From time to time he stopped to ponder upon the page before him. The force and simplicity, the endurable quality and sense of movement, the beauty of the lettering kept augmenting his admiration. Designed for the utmost ease of expression, of utility, not ornamentation. That was the key to their strength, their beauty. Simple rigid lines on stone.

He had a quick eye for lines, Rogier. The line of a building, the fractures in a stone, the lines of a horse. Yet his eye for line values was really an extraordinary sense of rhythm; a quality that so few men possess, and which an athlete, an artist must have. For some reason he was reminded of a queer incident that had recently happened. One evening at dusk he had gone to the mesa where the Utes were still allowed to encamp several months a year to dance, sing, and drop votive offerings in their sacred medicinal springs at the foot of the Peak. It was an old scene to Rogier. The circle of skin lodges. The orange-red flare of fires. Big-bellied squaws passing with loads of firewood. Bucks sitting around smoking. And a few white onlookers from town, bored to distraction, yet waiting to see the dance. It was for this Rogier himself came: to watch the lines of their naked bodies, the rhythmic steps, the ecstatic faces.

Suddenly he became aware of the beat of a drum. Like the heart of the earth suddenly beating with life. Not with the will to dominate, but softly, unvarying in tone, and insistent. A strange, magnetic rhythm that seemed to pull all within its own field.

Abruptly the big drum beat out stronger. In the same measure without increasing time. But stronger, more insistent and resistless, as if echoing the beat in his breast. One by one the Indians around the fires rose and threw off their blankets, walking within the circle of fires. They didn't walk chest out, belly in, as white men whose living center is in the head and chest. But in a slow shuffle, shoulders relaxed, belly out a little, as men whose center of gravity lies below. The dance step began. Eyes lowered, bodies doubled, they deliberately adjusted the ball of the foot to the ground. Pushing firmly to establish contact so that the earth-power might flow smoothly up their thighs. Then swiftly unbending, flinging up their heads. Lifting their dark faces, the sharp chiseled faces, eyes fixed upward in a blank stare, that the power might spark to the stars above and so complete the circuit to its unending source.

Rogier stirred uneasily. Something in him knew what he did not know. The secret that recoiled from his mind's grasp, that made of him an exile. The primordial power of the earth that must always be propitiated; never conquered, lest the victor be defeated by losing the integrity of his own being. To ally oneself with one's own mother-earth, to be at oneness with its great invisible forces, themselves obeying still greater laws, that one might feel within him the surge of its hidden strength. To seek always this truth of his own nature, acknowledging it above all temporal else. This was the only self-fulfillment, the only true success.

An Indian circling in the ring shouted suddenly. The cry was taken up in turn by those behind him. Then other smaller drums began, quick and reverberant, like the beat of rain. But the big hoarse drum, the belly drum, went on.

Then without warning it stopped. The sudden absence of sound created in Rogier a vacuum, the queer sensation of having descended too swiftly from a great height. His ears seemed to have stopped up; his blood beat at his temples and wrists. He stood foolishly irresolute, feeling lost in the darkness.

At that moment there sounded behind him a quick rustle of leaves in a dry ravine. Rogier stepped back. Believing he saw the form of a man, he spoke sharply, "Stand still!"

It was a boy crawling up out of the wash, Boné. His pale oval face was greenish-white in the moonlight, his lips were trembling. A faint electrical aura of nervous tension enveloped him. Rogier understood why. The beat of the drums, never changing, had worked powerfully upon his plastic childish will. The mesmeric quality of toneless rhythm invoked by the beat of an Indian drum! An ageless sound buried deep within the unconscious, re-emerging dark and mysterious like a dream-flow of things unrecognizable but still of that in us which reaffirms the everlasting mystery of our creation. Boné felt it. He knew! A boy like a violin string responding to the slightest touch. So Rogier had taken him home, his lips speaking comfortingly of common things.

Now, working at his drafting board on a clear spring morning, he methodically sharpened his soft drawing pencils. Placing the knife blade on the pencil and pushing it outward with his broad thumb. Then cupping the shavings and flinging them in a wastebasket. He had the air of seeming very busy. Yet at the moment he had little work on hand. He had just finished a new downtown building to house the *Gazette*. A brick four-story faced with red sandstone, widely pictured and advertised. Not much to look at really, but well constructed and clean-lined, built to last.

Glancing out the open window he noticed a crowd gathering on the corner. Two or three rigs went by at a rush. A queer excitement pervaded the air. Then steps rapidly crunched down the hall. A fist beat upon his door and a voice shouted, "Mr. Rogier! Come on down! They've found it behind the Peak. It's a strike!"

It was Maloney, the old prospector. Rogier accompanied him

downstairs and across the street to the newspaper office where the crowd was collecting. The news was compressed in a brief statement that a rich strike of gold had been made on the southwest slope of Pike's Peak in the Mount Pisgah district.

"That's the area I been workin', Joe!" cried Maloney. " 'Member those spruce! Now they've hit it sure! Gold!"

Once again a queer excitement, a strange foreboding, pervaded Rogier. He could not still it – not with Maloney dinning exhortations in his ears. Nor could he go back to his office to sit and wonder about it all day. "Well, if you're itching to go up there, I'll take you," he grumbled. "Might's well see what all the excitement's about, anyway."

Within an hour they had hitched up Lady-Lou, packed the buggy with blankets and supplies, and driven off. Despite his subterranean tremor of excitement it seemed preposterous to Rogier that gold could have been discovered on Pike's Peak. Why, the Pisgah district was only eighteen miles as the crow flies from the luxurious Antlers Hotel in the Saratoga of the West! But it lay directly behind Pike's Peak and a mile straight up. To reach it one had to spiral around three sides of the Peak, taking the Ute Pass road around it to the north and west as far as the divide, and then turning south. The Pass was crowded with buggies, buckboards, wagons, and groups of straggling men.

"Who made the strike?" Maloney cried to a bunch as they passed.

"Chicken Bill, I hear!" a man shouted back. "He's takin' nuggets out of the ground by the fistful!"

Impossible! thought Rogier, slowing his mares down on the steep grade. Since the Pike's Peak Rush of '58 thousands of men had prospected all around the peak. Not until 1874 had a trace of it been found, when a man named Theodore H. Lowe picked up some float along a crooked stream on the south slope. It was not rich enough to justify digging, and the place had been ignored until a Kentuckian, William H. Womack, had homesteaded a ranch along the stream. The high mountain meadow had good grass for cattle, but the steep-banked stream lamed so many of the animals that it was commonly known as Cripple Creek. A likely cow-pasture in which to find gold!

Reaching the divide, Rogier stopped to rest his mares. They were close to 10,000 feet high, he reckoned, and the whole area spread out in an immense panorama. It was all here, seen from above timberline – all the nobility of the wild and naked earth. A rugged, grassy meadow seamed with gulches and studded with bare, frost-shattered hills rising to an altitude of about 11,000 feet above sea-level. And surging in wave after wave, dark forested ranges rising toward the horizons on the north, west, and south to look down upon the Platte, Leadville, and the tips of the Sangre de Cristos. Only to the east did the mighty Peak itself rise like a wall to break the view. The hour was late and in the flare of the sinking sun its snowcap yellowed to the color of gold.

"Let's get goin'!" urged Maloney.

The road from now on was rough and rutty, the patches of corduroy giving way to bogs of mud. More and more men were strung along it, all heading toward a nipple looming out of the dusk toward the southwest. "Mount Pisgah!" said Maloney. Again he leaned out to shout. "What d'ya hear of Chicken Bill's strike?"

"Never heard of him!" a voice answered. "It's a fella called Butters that sunk a hole into the vein!"

It was dark and cold when they reached the base of Mount Pisgah. The enormous encampment was filled with two thousand men or more tending fires or huddled in tents and blankets. A lot of them were lined up at the back of a wagon where its enterprising owner was selling whisky out of two barrels. Rogier and Maloney pitched camp on the edge of the encampment, Rogier graining his team while Maloney cooked a bite to eat.

"You brought a gun?" asked Maloney.

"I never carry a gun!" replied Rogier.

"Well, I brought one. I figure with all that whisky goin' around, we'd better take turns keepin' watch."

"I'll stay up till midnight," said Rogier. "I wouldn't want anything to happen to my two mares. Then you can wake me if you hear anything."

Neither one of them could sleep. All night the sound of shouting, of still more men arriving, broke the silence of the hills. At daybreak they rushed with everyone over the goldfield, hunting for the site of the new strike. There was nothing: no outcroppings, no workings. There was only one hole about ten feet deep that obviously had been dug months or years before. It was barren of any sign of pay dirt.

"This is where Bútters said he took out those nuggets," a man insisted.

"He salted the damn hole, you fool! Look at it!"

A roar of indignation went up, followed by a roar of anger.

"Where's Butters?"

"Let's hang the son-of-a-bitch!"

But the perpetrator of the hoax could not be found. The Mount Pisgah fiasco was over. "Let's get out of here before the road's jammed," growled Rogier. "I'll hitch up while you stow the dunnage."

The two men drove steadily homeward. "Another Pike's Peak Bust," commented Rogier tersely. Whether he felt relieved or disappointed, he could not tell. But somehow he felt betrayed, either by himself or by that massive Peak rearing above him. It was seldom he saw it from this side and he studied it carefully. From down on the plains its face often seemed feminine and benignant. Here it showed its opposite side, a face masculine, sharp-featured, and cruel. With a start he realized the truth of its dual aspect. This androgynous great mother of mountains who forever watched down upon him with compassion, with menace, or with a strange and neuter aspect of passionless calm. And there swept over him the peculiar oppressive feeling that within the immutable depths of that majestic and enigmatic earth-being still remained hidden the ultimate destiny that was his to seek alone.

4

There was no doubt Rogier's house was haunted. Long before it had been built, Mrs. Rogier had taken just one look at the two Kadles who always camped on the spot, and made her prophecy. "Why, the ghosts of those two old men will be stompin' through the house in their smelly boots as long as it stands!"

And so they had – the Kadles. Late at night, lying asleep, you would be awakened by the creaking steps of those two old men prowling through the house. It was not at all scary to the girls. The sound came too regularly, night after night, until the Kadles' ghosts came to be as integral a part of the household as the horses Pet, Colonel, and Lady-Lou. But it kept them awake. Boné particularly could not go back to sleep until the Kadles had finished their nocturnal round of inspection.

Mrs. Rogier raised Cain without avail. The Kadles kept right on creeping up the third floor stairs. Rogier talked himself into a state of silent disgust trying to explain that the creaking was caused by a contraction of the old pine steps. To prove it he removed all the nails in the steps and replaced them with heavy screws. Two nights later she awakened him to see if Mrs. White or Lida Peck were walking in their sleep.

"A nice quiet house! Even the door jambs squeak!" she complained. "Boné told Mary Ann it was one of the Kadles leaning against the wall to hitch up his boots!"

The problem raised the old question of when she was to have her house in the North End. "This is a comfortable place," remonstrated Rogier. "Where would we find stalls and pasture for the horses? But I'll keep it in mind, Marthy. I promise."

To appease her, he did a refinishing job on the house. New furniture and rugs, and carpeting for both the second and third floor stairs. The noise of all the hammering had no more died away than that night up the carpeted stairway squeaked the Kadles investigating all the changes.

It was a very disheartening sound.

But at least the house had been refinished in time for Lily Force's wedding to Judge Henry. Mrs. Rogier so wanted him to think well of them. For at last he had come out to Colorado – a real judge attached to the Mexican minister's staff in Washington, D.C., and immediately becoming sincerely fond of Lily, even to the strip of white running through her hair which she had contritely confessed to bleaching.

This astounding romance – from the want ad in the *Gazette* to Judge Henry's own figure on the piano bench beside Lily – proved conclusively to the girls there might even be a Santa Claus. Mrs. Rogier herself was stunned with amazement, but she was soon won to the urbane and likable presence of Judge Henry. He was a genteel man with Spanish blood, a French childhood, and an American future. Although he was at least fifteen years older than Lily, they made a striking pair: the Judge grave and distinguished looking with black hair and dark complexion, and Lily with her olive-tinged cheeks and vivacious manner.

They left for Washington immediately after the wedding. Lily's departure put an end to Ona's music lessons, as Sister Molly's death had ended her schooldays. Although she had learned to play, her music lessons really had been a nuisance. Save for occasional Sunday mornings when she "officiated" at the church organ, Ona never touched a piano. Nor did Sally Lee; her one interest was hanging around the stalls of Pet, Colonel, and Lady-Lou. Mary Ann did better, occasionally pecking away at the piano in the front room though anyone could see it was more for amusement than from actual interest.

To Mrs. Rogier this was discouraging. Three daughters fated to become fashionable ladies – being Rogier – and not one of them interested in music! It was worse; it was out-and-out backsliding. But Boné, also freed of Lily Force, made hay while his sun was high. He simply couldn't stay away from the piano. He was at the keys every moment that Mrs. Rogier wasn't looking, and plaguing Ona with questions. It was amazing to her the way he soaked up her odd minutes of teaching so completely.

"Go on, Ona! Go on!" he would snap at her. "You said it. Now tell me why!"

There was no denying him. Sooner or later the truth or something they could not distinguish from it, would come out after a wearisome bout between them. It was easier and much more pleasant when Ona related to him the story, the idea, or picture behind the compositions. These had been the human things that had aroused her own imagination, and she remembered many of them vividly from Lily's wordy descriptions; like that of the symphonic poem the boy loved so well.

Boné sat still as death, as though he did not hear her. The vision leaped and remained before his eyes with such vividness he could not speak. A great black flood, viscous and dark, separating man and Hades. And in between, a white and spotless swan unmoving, singing its strange wild song.

Abruptly he rose and slouched out of the room. He walked out in back, through the gate to the stables, and climbed upon the haystack in the barn. Here he lay on his back, staring at the rafters spotted with sunlight overhead, seeing nothing, hearing nothing, but the song of the legendary swan of Tuonela. It revealed to him for the first time the meaning of music. How simple it was! He had heard through its accents the voice of many things speaking with authority to his deepest self. And now he saw in a flash what it meant not only to receive music, but to give it. One saw something: a ship on the sea, people dancing across a castle floor, or the beauty of the night – such a thing as that! – and gave it back in music for all to see and feel. A great accomplishment.

But to feel with profound disturbance something nonexistent yet real as the content of a dream which comes and comes again, indescribable, unspeakable, and impalpable. Like the invocation of an odd strain of melody which ran through him each time he saw the Peak risen above its morning mist like an island floating on a cloud. Like the vision in his mind of Der Schwan von Tuonela. And to give these things in music too, rendering into tangible form the phantoms and the beauties that plagued his secret soul. This was the greatest achievement.

He lay still in the hay, obsessed with his latent power to accomplish the impossible. Just by learning how to weave together those same old notes so long and carelessly misused into the ceaseless fabrics spinning through his mind. This was all he had to know!

School lessons were something else. The evening study hour was an ordeal for the whole family. Lida Peck would clear the dining room table and Sally Lee, Mary Ann, and Boné would gather around the lamp with their books. Mrs. Rogier would sit reading. Then Rogier, lighting a cigar, would offer to help the children with their arithmetic and algebra lessons.

"Now Daddy," Mrs. Rogier reminded him, "please remember to do their problems the way the teacher wants them solved. Not your way."

"Never mind," replied Rogier calmly. "The teacher is only trying to show them how to work problems. I'm trying to teach them to use their heads."

Rogier, feeling keenly his lack of education and at the same time despising the insistence of the teachers at solving all the problems in an orthodox manner, laid out his carpenter's steel square. On this he made his computations in a manner he had worked out alone in lieu of schooling; and though to others as intricate and confusing as a Chinese tangram, it enabled him to figure faster than any rival. But he could never explain its use. Meanwhile the smoke from his cigar rose into a blue cloud, causing the girls to cough and splutter, and their eyes to smart and burn. The evening usually ended in a row. Tired out, the girls went to bed without their lessons. Mrs. Rogier had to write them an excuse pleading "home duties." And more than often Sally Lee brought home her algebra teacher's request that she learn as she was taught and not to attempt improvements on the text-book.

"How about you, Boné? Don't you have any homework to

do?" Rogier would ask him.

"No sir; not tonight!" the boy would answer cheerfully, strolling off the the piano in the front room.

"Boné!"

Obediently he got up from the bench to wander through the house, hands in pockets, urbane, the master of his soul, and then slip upstairs to listen to the night.

When at the end of the school term he brought home a report of failing in his class, and a sealed letter from the professor, Mrs. Rogier was indignant. "Why, I had no idea! Even the letter says how smart he is. 'Exceptionally alert and receptive, but mentally lazy' – see?"

"I wouldn't worry none about that boy," drawled Mrs. White. "He appeahs to me like one of them high-strung horses you can lead to watah but you can't make him drink."

Rogier took the letter back uptown to read. Then he sent a doctor to see the boy, listened to the result of the examination, and promptly forgot the matter. It did not occur to him that he knew the capabilities and imperfections of his workmen and his horses, but not the members of his family.

But that summer Boné surprised them all. It was during the annual Sunflower Carnival when all the covered wagons, traps, and tandems, with Indians, cowboys, and miners trooping behind, paraded through the streets decorated with wildflowers. Boné had written a piece of music for the occasion. A music teacher, a former friend of Lily Force, had helped him with the orchestration and had made arrangements to have it printed. Boné came home thrilled with an armful of sheets. The Cowboy Riders Band of Colorado City was going to play his "Red Rock Garden March" at their night concert!

He was up early next morning to canvas every merchant with his music sheets. He even came to Rogier's office, insisting that he buy a copy, regular price. And during the parade Rogier could see him keeping it apace, selling copies to people bunched along the gutters. That night in Manitou at the pavilion by the iron spring the Cowboy Riders Band played the "Red Rock Garden March." The director, in high boots and higher Stetson, simply shouted out the title and Boné's name, and the band began playing. The piece was very short, but it was a great achievement of which even Mrs.

Rogier was duly proud.

A month later she handed Rogier a letter from the music company. Rogier opened it, glanced carelessly at the sheet inside, and stuffed it into his pocket.

"What is it? About Boné? Do they want him to write another march?" she queried.

"No. Nothing like that. Nothing at all," Rogier answered her carelessly and turned away. The letter enclosed a bill for ninety-three dollars for setting up in print the "Red Rock Garden March," credited with six dollars and forty cents which Boné had realized from his sales.

Ten days after school opened in the fall things came to a head. Mrs. Rogier happened to meet Boné's teacher on the street and she asked when he was going to start school. Mrs. Rogier was dumbfounded. Boné had left the house every morning with Sally Lee and Mary Ann. It was that music teacher friend of Lily's who had lured the boy away! Mrs. Rogier swept up the street holding her skirts high to make the utmost speed. Boné was there at the woman's home. Without a word she took the boy by the hand and marched him down to Rogier's office.

It was a hectic session. Boné denied nothing except that he had lied about going to school. Thin, taut, and white, he sat straight in his chair. "I won't go to school. I can't stand it any more. I hate it." It was all he had to say.

Mrs.Rogier wept.

Rogier sat silent, twiddling with a celluloid triangle while he watched Boné. The lad was stubborn as a mule; he meant what he said. But what was behind it? Indubitably there was something. He stared fixedly at Boné, as though he'd never seen him before. How thin and white he was, and nervously taut as a violin string! His own heavy silence kept pressing down upon woman and boy until Mrs. Rogier, fearful of his rare bursts of temper, cried out, "Daddy!"

Rogier stood up. "I'll think it over. You're both upset. Suppose you go home and we'll talk about it tonight."

After they had gone he sat for an hour, then went out. Boné was in bed when he arrived home. Mrs. Rogier, Mrs. White, and Ona were waiting at the dining room table. "I went to see the doctor again," he spoke without prelude. "The boy's too thin and nervous and highstrung. The doctor believes a year out of school and spent outdoors would help him."

"But what would he do around here, Daddy? It would be just as bad as school."

"Exactly. I though of that when I met the Vrain Girls on the street and walked home with them."

The Vrain Girls had been friends of the family for years. They were old maid sisters who had a house in the south part of town where they lived probably two months of the year. The rest of the time they lived in New Mexico among the Navajos, Lew serving as a government agent and Matie as a missionary. They were small, tanned dark, with graying hair, and their features seemed to be taking on the sharp chiseled aspect of the Indians with whom they already had spent so many unselfish years.

"But what about Boné?" insisted Mrs. Rogier.

"Just this," he said patiently. "The Vrain Girls are getting ready to go back to the Reservation. It was their own suggestion that they take Boné along."

"Livin' with Indians?" inquired Mrs.Rogier incredulously.

"Living with the Girls in a comfortable trading post, getting lots of good food, fresh air, and sunshine."

Next morning Rogier was sitting at the table when Boné came down for breakfast. He looked tired and nervous as he slid into his chair, and kept a wary eye on Rogier as he munched on a piece of toast.

"You look rather peaked, son. Did the Kadles keep you up all night?"

"I slept fine." The boy spoke obstinately, laying down his toast and withdrawing his hands into his lap.

"Well, eat a good breakfast. I'm going to drive Pet out to Templeton's Gap, and thought you might want to go along."

"Yes sir!" Boné relaxed instantly and ate a second piece of toast.

Ona, walking home that afternoon, saw them coming back. Rogier was looking straight ahead. Boné sat still, his eyes fixed on Rogier who turned to him and grinned as he pulled out a cigar. Boné laughed; and Ona knew that the matter was settled. Then Rogier shook up Pet and the buckboard dwindled away from her sight.

5

Time, the ageless and the sexless, the eunuch of all eunuchs. Time, the great builder, the great destroyer, life's great equation sign. The powerful and fickle ambassador of human fate. Time with its vigor and senility, its wisdom and capriciousness, and the infallibility to level with its own mistakes the greatest fruits of its handiwork. Linear flowing time, man's greatest and most persistent illusion in a world whose full-dimensional reality he cannot yet perceive.

Time, dom it! What had it been doing to them all these years? Rogier felt perplexed. Sister Molly had died, Tom had vanished. Boné and Lily Force had gone. Bob Hines was married and moved out of the house. Now Hiney was getting restless too. He arrived home later every night. Mrs. White and Rogier, sharing the secret of his affliction, lay listening for the sound of his cab. What if during another lapse of memory he might – what? The question kept growing in their minds, but Hiney was at the topside of his hour. He was forever regaling the girls with talk of the celebrities he had seen at the Opera House – Lillian Russell, Katherine Kidder, Frederic Ward, Nat Goodwin. One week he imitated Harry Webber from

"Nip and Tuck;" the next, Charlotte Thompson in "Phyllis Denhor." Barlow and Wilson's Mammoth Minstrels, the cast of George C. Miller's "Fool's Revenge"—his mimicry, like his colored cravats, seemed to stop at nothing. No one was surprised when he was asked to substitute as a stagehand for the run of Stanley Wood's opera "Brittle Silver" at the Tabor Grand Opera House in Denver. Think of that! The girls, seeing him off on the train with a new carpet bag and a new cravat flowery with red roses, thought of nothing else.

Held over for "Priscilla," Hiney came home with portentous news. He had not only worked behind the scenes in the Tabor Grand, Denver's million dollar opera house, the most beautiful in the country—in the whole wide world; now he had been offered a steady job, beginning next month, with a chance to work into the "profession." Tabor's great gesture, designed from the best theaters of London and Vienna, its carpets brought from Belgium, its brocades from France, its woodwork of cherry logs from Japan and mahogany from Honduras. And all of it derived from Colorado silver, Leadville silver, the outpouring silver stream flooding the world.

The "profession" was not quite up the highest social standards, but Mrs. Rogier was impressed. Everyone was delighted save Rogier who was troubled with anxious thoughts. Like his father Tom, Hiney was entranced with bright lights and make-believe, the glitter and tinsel of fame and fortune, with the moonlit gleam of silver. There was no stopping him.

"Hiney," he said, drawing him aside at the railroad depot on the morning he left, "I reckon I haven't paid as much mind to you as I ought to have, all these years. Putting up buildings — I don't know what else or why, son. It's not because I haven't thought of your mother every day since she's been gone, and your father too. I miss them, boy, and I'll miss you too. But remember" — his voice grew stern — "this is still your home! Never forget that, hear? If anything ever happens, come home. Anything! Understand?"

Hiney brushed the cowlick back under his new hat. "Yes sir. I know what you mean. But I only been troubled twice. I guess I just ate the wrong thing both times. I'll remember."

Time! If only time would deal gently with Sister Molly's youngest son!

Meanwhile Rogier let himself be swung in its illusionary flow.

There appeared in the Gazette a news item that pleased Mrs. Rogier immensely:

> Work on the new Lincoln and Garfield school houses in the fourth and second wards respectively, is being actively prosecuted. The rafters are in position on the Lincoln school and already it presents quite an imposing appearance when seen from the foothills west of town.
>
> Work on the Garfield school has been delayed somewhat on account of the limited supply of brick in the market, but the contractor and builder, Mr. Joseph Rogier, expects to have both buildings completed within the time specified in the contract.

In addition to these two schools, Rogier was getting ready to break ground for the construction of the new First Congregational Church. A rambling building of gray stone with a semi-circle of seven pillars upholding a triangular gable with an inset round window of stained glass. Its cost exceeded $35,000. If that triangular gable didn't look too squatty, too mashed-down on its curve of stone columns, it would be well worth the money – for a church.

Every night too he was working up an estimate on a new state institution, the Colorado School for the Deaf and Blind, a huge stone structure that for all his figuring he could not cut down to a less than $80,000 job.

His work did not interfere with his interest in his horses. Pet had produced her first colt, Dorothy, and could not be used. Instead he drove Colonel. Not a bad horse, but still a little loco and lazy. This combination of cussedness Rogiér took out of him on Sunday mornings. Meanwhile he kept hearing about a Maryland horse reputed to be very fast.

The excitement caused by the Mount Pisgah fiasco had died down. William H. Womack had sold his homestead on Cripple Creek; Bennett and Myers, two Denver real estate men, had picked it up for a trifling $7,500 and were running cattle on it. They employed Womack's nephew Bob as a cowboy. He was so careless and erratic, spending most of his time digging for gold, they called him "Crazy Bob." Nevertheless Bennett took a few samples of ore from one of his gopher holes to a pioneer Denver assayer. "There's no use wasting your money for an assay of this stuff, Mr. Bennett," reported the assayer after one look at the float. "There's no gold in it." Womack was not discouraged. He sunk a shaft in Poverty Gulch which he kept working, naming his claim the Chance. Periodically he rode into town, showing samples of ore in the Colorado City saloons. No one was interested. So year after year he relocated his claim without bothering to record it.

Again that winter Stratton came down from the mountains to work a few months for another stake—but not for prospecting this time. He was going to enroll in Professor Lamb's course in mineralogy at The Colorado College, held in Cutler Hall which Rogier had built.

"I've spent too many years chasing Lady Luck," he said straightforwardly. "I don't know anything about ores except hefting a sample in my hand and squinting at it in the sunlight. I'm going to find out!"

For a moment Rogier was surprised at his change in attitude. Stratton looked old and worn; there was the same haunted look in his eyes. Yet something about him, perhaps the leaner cut of his jaw, revealed that his frantic compulsion had set into a frigid determination fed by every cell in his mind and body.

"To start with," continued Stratton, "I got a job in the Nashold Mill up at Breckenridge. What I learned there about the amalgamation process of treating ores taught me how ignorant I am. So here I am. I tell you, Joe, when I finally hit it I'm going to know it – and what to do about it!"

Rogier nodded, remembering Siegerfries.

Like everyone else, the two men talked about the growing political issue of the time – silver. The Bland-Allison Act, authorizing the purchase of up to $4,000,000 worth of silver for coinage into dollars, had been insufficient. The production of silver was so great that the price kept declining. Throughout all the country demands by silver exponents increased. A Colorado Silver Alliance was formed, followed by a National Silver Convention in St. Louis. The result was the passage of the Sherman Act which provided for the purchase of 4,500,000 ounces of silver per month by the government. The price of silver had jumped to over a dollar an ounce, wildly acclaimed by almost two hundred silver clubs in

Colorado. But now the price was falling again.

"Figure it out for yourself," asserted Rogier. "There seems to be no end to the silver in these mountains. It's flooding the whole country. These Sherman purchases are just priming the economic pump. They can't go on – not as long as this country, and the rest of the world, is on the gold standard. Something's bound to happen."

"What?" demanded Stratton.

"I'm not a soothsayer, or a politician either," Rogier said bluntly.

Stratton looked at him a long time with a strange glint in his smoke-gray eyes. "I'm not pinning my hopes on silver any more. I'm going to find out about gold and every other ore the earth holds. That's why I'm going to Professor Lamb."

"Yes, gold," said Rogier quietly. "The sun of life in the earth."

They looked at each other without speaking, each thinking how strange it was that chance had not put him in the other's shoes. Then Stratton abruptly as usual rose and walked out.

If Stratton had been a little discomfited but not wholly surprised at Rogier's strange last remark, Rogier thought nothing about it. It reflected the texture of his thoughts as he spent night after night meditating on his books. They were strange books of which Mrs. Rogier and indeed few people in town would have approved, shipped directly to his office where he could study them without fear of detection and disturbance. Solid philosophy, Masonic ritual, medieval alchemy, the esoteric religions of the East, and treatises on what was becoming known as New Thought. What he first had hoped to find in them, as an uneducated man, was a simple explanation of the mystery that made him feel an exile on his earth. Whatever the mystery was, it was not simple. His loneliness had increased despite his prosperous business, his large family, and his horses. And so had his secret mounting need to find out who he was, and his relationship to this new wild earth to which he had been so unaccountably and irresistibly drawn by that high Peak which, year by year, focused all his hopes and his despair.

He found his own feelings duplicated by the reverence accorded other sacred mountains in the world – Popocatepetl in Mexico, Cotopaxi and Capac Urcu in the Andes of South America, Kilimanjaro of Africa, Fujiyama in Japan, Olympus in Greece, colossal upthrusts of the Himalayas in Asia. From time immemorial the root races of every continent, the black, the brown, the yellow, the red, and the white, had made pilgrimages to these great sacred mountains, as had the Indians to Pike's Peak, with votive offerings, prayer, song, and dance. Rogier had come to believe it was a matter of rhythm. For the inherent spirit-of-place of each continent, each land, vibrated to a different, indigenous rhythm. And only by attuning himself to this vibratory quality of his motherland could man release the dammed up power of creation within him. He had felt this years ago when he first heard the beat of Indian drums and the stamp of moccasined feet upon the earth. In the mountains you felt it best. They were like the swells of the sea, rising in wave after wave to crest in great peaks upthrust against the horizon – not immobile, as they might appear, but subtly vibrating as great repositories of power whose emanantions formed a magnetic field that could be felt for miles. This, Rogier was convinced, was what had drawn him here to this majestic Peak as it had drawn for centuries so many Indian tribes from the Great Plains and lesser forested ranges. It was alive as the whole earth was alive, each living stone, every breathing plant. And through the years he had come to recognize it as a homogenous entity, this androgenous mother of mountains which embraced the dual aspects of all creation. Yes, it was a living body like his own, the rock strata of its skeleton fleshed with earth, its veins watered by spring and stream, and in whose deep and hidden heart glowed the golden sun of life.

These reflections, which Rogier did not consider at all religious in nature as he was not a religious man, bore little resemblance to the tenets of the Shouting Methodists who perfervidly proclaimed the reality of harp-playing angels in Heaven and pitchfork-wielding devils in Hell. They did not coincide with the economic views of Free Silver advocates or the thousands of greedy white miners raping an inanimate earth of its natural resources. Nor, for that matter, would they have been acceptable to Little London businessmen and members of the Gentlemen's Driving and Pleasure Association. So Rogier kept them to himself. And if sometimes they seemed a little extravagant and frightening even to himself, he was again drawn back to them by his ever-growing need. And late at night, poring over his books, he would encounter a phrase, a thought, that swung open still another door to his intuition. There was something strange in him that knew what he did not know. It was as if it had known all this long before.

6

To Ona the days had become like beads on a string, separate yet indistinguishable, unending in their weary circle. No young man came to call on her; she was fast approaching the time when she would be regarded as an old maid. Without an interest, she seldom went out except for a walk uptown or a drive on Sunday afternoon. Once again she took up the lonely vigils of Sister Molly. On summer afternoons sitting alone under the elm or under the front window in the shade of the lilac; and in the winter rocking in the dark front room. Less than all the members of the family for being wholly theirs, she was a personality formed by the experience of their lives, out of the substance provided her by her own inheritance. Brooding alone through the months, she gradually assumed the placid, hard aspect of an idol cut in stone. Not with the unbroken repose of tranquility, but with the stillness of despair.

It became obvious to all the family that something had to be done about her, but it remained for Mrs. White to suggest what.

"That theah girl is jus' decayin' away. She ain't done nothin' but raise kids since she was eight yeahs old. You wouldn't wuk a horse that hahd, Joe. She needs a new pasture fo' awhile."

Rogier and Mrs. Rogier did not reply. Mrs. White continued. "I don' see why Ona can't go down to the Reservation and bring back Boné. He didn't come home with the Vrain Girls last yeah and he ain't writin' none. Like killin' two buhds with one stone."

"We'll think about it," said Rogier.

"A heap of thinkin' you need, with all the money youah makin' and horses eatin' it up by the bale. Ona's nevah had nothin'. I reckon you bettah be doin' that heap of thinkin' mighty fast!"

Rogier did, and wondered why he hadn't done it before.

Two weeks later the family saw her off on the Denver and Rio Grande for Durango, where the Girls were to meet her. She had a shiny new suitcase packed with new taffeta dresses, and a fifty-dollar bill pinned to her corset for an emergency.

The train finally pulled out; and when the Peak and the Devil's Horn were gone from sight, she leaned her head back and closed her eyes. For the first time in her life she was away from the family; a new world swung toward her as though the click of the wheels on the rails were the grind of subterranean machinery moving strange landscapes into view. Ona took no notice of them at all. She was utterly worn out. After a time she opened the little surprise packages given her by Sally Lee and Mary Ann, and put the trinkets away. She dozed, ate sparingly of the fried chicken in her lunch basket, and dozed again. Pueblo, Canyon City, the rushing Arkansas, and the frightening Royal Gorge it had carved, and always more mountains. The "Dirty, Ragged, and Greasy" little narrow-gauge kept climbing over them, going around and between them, heaving and jolting like a boat in a sea of tumultuous waves. The coach was crowded. Miners and prospectors. A sporting woman in a lace-trimmed hat. A group of Ute squaws huddled on the floor of the filthy aisle, blankets drawn up over their heads. Two drunken cowboys quarreling in the seat behind her. At dark the sputtering, hanging lamps were lit. Then when the spring night grew cold, the brakeman lighted a wood fire in the stove up front. Ona could not sleep for the clickety-clack of the wheels beneath her, the shrill whistle from the quill. Smoke was pouring from the straight-stacker now, seeping in every crack of the window. The patter of cinders on the roof sounded like rain. How horrible it was, alone and lost in a heaving sea of mountains in this frail and smelly toy train that never seemed to get anywhere at all.

But it did, late in the evening after a two-hour delay caused by a rock slide. Matie was waiting at the little wooden depot with a slim young Mexican. "Lew's off on a trip and so's Boné – they'll be back when we get home," she explained. "So Tony Lucero here drove me up in his wagon."

Lucero showed his teeth in what Ona supposed was meant to be a smile, and they got into a light spring wagon. "We'd better eat and sleep, then get an early start in the morning," said Matie decisively. Ona was disappointed in the appearance of Durango. The town was not yet ten years old and looked it: wooden buildings and shacks clustered around the yellow-painted railroad depot that had called it into being. There was no need to get out her new taffeta dresses when they arrived at the hotel. It looked more tawdry than Mrs. White's former boarding house. For a girl who had come from the celebrated and fashionable Saratoga of the West, everything looked raw and new. She chewed at an enormous steak and then went to bed on a hard and narrow mattress.

How different it was in the morning when they drove southward and downward toward the high plains of New Mexico! The very quality of the sunlight changed, mellowed and yellowed as if by time. Matie talked about her work at Farmington with the Women's Home Missionary Society. "How wonderful they are, '*The* People,' as they call themselves! Proud and arrogant, but so eager to learn!"

"Who are they?" asked Ona.

"The Navajos. The *Dineh, 'The* People.' They're the ones we work with mostly. But we have others. Utes from the north, and Jicarilla Apaches from the east. It's all Indian country, Ona."

"And they're not wild Indians?" asked Ona, remembering from childhood the Arapahoes and Cheyennes who had burned her bottom against the stove.

"Oh, there was a little trouble of sorts three or four years ago when Largo Pete – that means Big Pete – went on a rampage and troops from Fort Lewis were called out. But that's nothing to speak of."

Tony Lucero talked about the Stockton Gang of outlaws that hung around Bloomfield, twelve miles east of Farmington. "Port Stockton, Senorita, was the leader. He was killed, unfortunately, Senorita. But the Gang still prospers. It steals cattle from the white *rancheros* and sheep from the Navajos. That was their steak you ate last night, no? They run a butcher shop in Durango."

Indians, Mexicans, outlaws! Ona let herself be driven all day without protest down to a high, treeless plain where converged from the Colorado mountains three great rivers: the San Juan, La Plata, and Las Animas. Farmington. The main street was two blocks long. But a shady street, lined with fruit trees. It was filled with Utes, Apaches, and Navajos, Indian traders, cowboys, and cattle rustlers. A few miles away, along the San Juan that gleamed silver in the dusk, Lucero drew up beside a low and long trading post. Behind it stood an adobe in which Lew and Matie lived with the trader, Bert Bruce. Lucero unloaded their baggage and drove away.

"He works for Bert and lives with his wife down the road," explained Matie shortly, "He's a Mexican, but he speaks Navajo fluently and knows wool and hides." Without more ado she flung open the door of the adobe and pushed Ona inside.

There was Lew, small, sharp, and dark, giving her a hug; and the trader, Bruce, a taciturn man who didn't even rise when she was introduced, but whose swift appraising eyes stripped her bare, flung her on the scales, and calculated her intrinsic worth in one look. Yet it was the room itself that wrapped comfortingly about her. There was none of the stiff formality of the front room at home and other parlors in Little London. It was just a big mud hut, but it broke upon her with a burst of color mellowed by lamplight. Brilliant Navajo rugs covering the rude plank floor, beautiful weaving on the stiff chairs and wooden table, Indian rattles and silver bridles hanging on the walls, shelves of pottery. Ona felt at home immediately and after supper went to her small room to sleep dreamlessly at peace.

"Where's Boné?" she kept asking next morning. "Hasn't he come back yet?"

"Oh, he's off on another horseback trip. Maybe to Hon-Not-Klee, maybe to those old Aztec ruins. He likes to putter around, you know," answered Matie. "Why don't you walk down the trail to his room and see if he came in last night? It used to be Bert's rug room—where he stored his blankets, you know. But Boné fixed it up for his studio as he calls it."

Down the trail it stood, another adobe, stout-walled, with iron-barred windows. Ona hesitated, then lifted the latch and entered. With her first glance she recognized the room as Boné's all right. An old upright piano stood against the far wall. On the bench lay the scattered pages of a Kayser. Like the other house, it was full of Navajo rugs and weavings, pottery, and artifacts; and a handful of turquoise stones lay strewn over the top of a deal table, with a stack of loose music and a coffee cup full of cigarette stubs. But how untidy it was! A pair of denim trousers dangled from the back of a chair. Three socks were spread across a heap of firewood; and in the dry ashes of the fireplace lay a tumbled coffee pot. From a row of nails hung a dejected string of clothes. A colorful, untidy room whose inmate kept nothing he did not have a use for, and who kept it where his hand or eye could find it easiest.

With a sigh, Ona cleaned and straightened the room, made up the couch with fresh sheets. Then tired out, she lay down to rest. As she stared out the window a bluejay shot from a piñon like a burst of smoke. She closed her eyes as if anticipating the sound of a report. There was nothing but the deep yellow silence, and the sense of the infinite dryness of the barren plain stretching across the muddy San Juan.

She was awakened by the click of the latch. The door flung back and Boné stood in the doorway. "Ona! – Ona!" he cried joyously.

She jumped to her feet, conscious of his tall lean form and dark face, and was caught in his arms. Before she realized it, Boné had kissed her on the lips. She could have counted on her fingers the times she had been kissed by the undemonstrative Rogiers, and she too drew slightly away at this outward display of affection.

"Ona! Aren't you glad to see me!" shouted Boné, shaking her by the shoulders.

She stood with slightly misted eyes absorbing the sight of his rangy body, half a head taller than she. His cheap gray shirt was open at the throat, revealing a tan dark as the color of his face. An old pair of blue denim trousers clung tightly to his slim hips, and around his waist dangled a wide belt studded with silver conchos. There was about him a curious sense of freedom, a wildness almost.

"Why, Boné!" she murmured softly. "You've grown into a man."

He laughed as he sat down. "Now tell me quick: are the Kadles still creeping up steps every night?"

"Yes!"

"And is Uncle Joe all right?"

"Yes."

"Well then, you better start right down the list with Aunt Martha. I can't stand her a minute and I love her just the same, and if I live to be as old as Mrs. Black Kettle down the wash she'll still be able to make me jump!"

"Boné!"

"Oh, I know. Filial respect and all, but it doesn't mean we can't see them with our own eyes."

The same Boné of old, free from others' opinions, with the priceless faculty of never denying the truth of his own intuition.

"They're all fine, Bone, and want you home again. I have some presents for you from them. Now tell me what you've been doing."

"Working, Ona! Every minute! Look!" He strode to a packing crate behind the piano and began to lift out manuscript after manuscript, spreading them on the bench and table.

"Oh. Music scores!"

He sat down at the piano, rattled off a score, flung it aside. "A man nearby has been helping me with composition, orchestration, fingering, everything. Gene Lockhardt. A wonderful man. A great musician. He's coming over tonight to meet you."

Jumping up, he reached for an Indian rattle hanging on the wall. Giving it a shake, he said, "I've been learning to dance too." Humming softly he began to circle the room. Ona smiled at his serious face, the way he lifted his knees high and stuck out his behind. Suddenly catching his boot on a rug, Boné tripped and fell sprawling on the floor.

Ona laughed until the tears ran down her cheeks. Boné sat sheepishly on the floor, rubbing his elbow. "Right on the funny-bone," he muttered, standing up. "We'd better be going down to the house. We're giving you a party tonight."

Late that evening after the trading post had been locked and bolted against stragglers, they all gathered for supper in the house. Everybody: Bert Bruce, Tony Lucero and his fat pleasant wife, the two Vrain Girls, Boné and Ona, and Gene Lockhardt, the musician. They were simple people and they ate a hearty simple dinner and talked of simple things: a wagonload of supplies freighted down from

Durango, the Navajo sheep clip, and of neighbors named Spotted Horse and Mrs. Black Kettle. Only Lockhardt seemed out of place in this remote frontier region.

A middle-aged man, tall and gaunt with two telltale pink spots in his white cheeks, he had come in wearing a foreign-looking worsted coat over a fresh white shirt and blue brocaded tie. When introduced to Ona he murmured, "Pleased, I'm sure," and bowed. The gesture was so gracefully natural that she felt big and clumsy as an ox despite her new taffeta dress, the first occasion she'd had to wear it. All during dinner she kept staring at the immense diamond solitaire ring hanging loosely on his finger. He had the big knuckled, regular shaped hands of a pianist, and a sensitive face.

She had learned that afternoon Lockhardt was an Englishman, a somewhat famous pianist, who for many years had lived in San Francisco. He was an invalid – a consumptive or lunger as they were called in Little London – of course, and had moved way out here for his health. "But why here of all places?" she had asked. Bruce the trader had been the one to gruffly answer. "Bloomfield, that other straggle of buildings down the road, was settled by an Englishman named William B. Haines. I suppose Lockhardt learned about it through him or his folks." Still Ona kept wondering what kept such an immaculate, strange bird of passage here.

"Are you going to be here long Mr. Lockhardt?" she asked without thinking, wishing she had bitten off her tongue instead.

Lockhardt looked up with a blank stare. "Quite. You'll find me the next time you come out in the desert if the coyotes haven't dug me up. Or haven't you heard I came here to die? I assure you it's my only object."

She caught a glimpse of Boné's face. There was a look in his eyes no one save Lockhardt had the right to see. Ona was glad when supper was over and Tony and his wife left.

"Now," cried Boné, "we're all going to my studio for a party!"

Crowded in the one big room, sitting on the couch and on the floor, they watched Boné get out a pair of beautiful silver candlesticks which he lit and ceremoniously placed on the piano. Then, a little formally, he said in a hushed tone, "Gene's going to play for us." Lockhardt got up, grumbling, sat down at the piano. With his first touch on the keys Ona knew he was not only a pianist, but a musician. He played like an angel, a devil, a madman, a madonna. Lordy, how he could play! Why, Lily Force could never have imagined anybody could get so much out of an old piano.

Yet gradually Ona began to feel disturbed. Boné did not sit down with the rest of them. He stood or sat beside Lockhardt in a position of alert attendance and humble adoration; his eyes fixed on the pianist glowed in the candlelight with feverish devotion. Of course, Ona thought, he owed the older man the admiration of a novice for a master. But somehow it seemed more than that. She did not know what; it was something a woman feels about a man without knowing why. Lockhardt seemed oblivious to all but the magic he was conjuring. He was like a different man, alive, self-confident, joyous and sad and moody by turns. Nevertheless Ona began to mistrust him – this lonely, ill man who had come here to die. Suddenly he got up after a crashing crescendo, and bowed to Boné And now it was Boné playing, but not with the same concentration. No matter how well he played – and his execution was far beyond Ona's expectations – he seemed to be showing off. Showing off to Lockhardt, flashing him intimate looks of understanding after difficult passages.

At last Bruce rose. It was over. Ona went out feeling a little ashamed of her queer thoughts. But just the same she felt she knew what was keeping Boné here along the San Juan, if she didn't know what was keeping Lockhardt.

7

Day after day as summer drew on Ona could feel the strength rising within her. It was if she were recovering from a long illness, this joyful resurgence of interest in everything. Laughing deep inside her, she looked into the mirror surprised that she hadn't grown. Her broad square face with its firm set jaw and ample brow had lost its whiteness and was colored a creamy cinnamon. How cheerful and healthy it looked!

She loved to sit in the trading post watching Bruce or Lucero waiting on the Indians: weighing wool and sheep pelts, appraising silver and turquoise jewelry they brought to pawn, measuring out pinto beans, lard, or yards of velveteen and gingham. One day as she was sitting quietly behind the long counter, Bruce poked her in the side with his thumb. "Get off that stiff corset and them high button shoes! Here. Be comfortable." He flung her a purple velveteen blouse decorated with silver buttons and ten-cent coins, a bolt of flowered gingham to make a squaw skirt out of, and a pair of fawn-brown moccasins. Another time when she picked out a bracelet to take back home to Sally Lee, he grumbled, "Hell no, not that! Don't buy anything until you learn what it is." So she began to learn the values of shape, weight, and design of Najavo silver with its chunk turquoise.

Often she went to Matie's missionary headquarters in town. It was a ramshackle frame house with a bell hung over the door. Here Matie and another woman conducted both school and Methodist services for the Navajo families who drove in. Afterwards they distributed groceries and clothing as a reward for their attendance.

Her trips with Lew across the San Juan and into the Reservation were something else. How immense it was! A flat, treeless plain of 25,000 square miles without a town, a house, or a road except for the wagon wheel tracks winding through the dusty sage. Only Lew knew how to find her way to an isolated hut of logs and mud—a hogan—in which a Navajo family lived while grazing its flock of sheep for miles around.

Nominally Lew was a government agent entrusted to pick out the smartest children and to induce their families to let them be sent off to a government school. Acutally she did everything else. She was a good doctor, able to set a bone and break a fever. An excellent judge of sheep and wool; an expert on silver and turquoise, and Navajo blanket weaving and design. She could speak Navajo fluently and, more important, knew how to keep her mouth shut. Like the sparse traders in this immense empty wilderness, she was in effect one of the few human bridges between this proud, independent tribe and the alien race encroaching upon it. Lew justified their trust. Thin, taciturn, burnt brown, she looked and acted like one of The People themselves.

Often they stopped overnight at Hon-Not-Klee, Shallow Water, where Bruce maintained his most important trading post. The one near town he regarded as but a country store for the convenience of stray Utes, Apaches, Navajos, and whites alike. This one stood isolated in the sage, a great L-shaped adobe fortress with iron-barred windows and iron-studded doors. One wing, inside, was the immense trading room. It contained everything possible to supply the needs of The People. And in turn it held in a locked room a fortune in their fine blankets and pawned jewelry. The other wing was used as living quarters, and here Lew and Ona stayed.

It was here at Hon-Not-Klee that Ona saw The People as they were. Not the ragged town-loving Navajos nor the destitute families

Matie's missionary quarters tried to succor. But the hordes of Navajos riding in from the empty wilderness on quick-stepping ponies or in springless wagons. The men slim and erect, with bright headbands holding back their uncut hair. The women sitting fat and shapeless with their children in the wagonboxes, dressed in brilliant velveteen blouses and voluminous gingham skirts. And in all their dark Mongolian faces the same proud arrogance, the same wildness and nobility of the earth itself. All day they would hang around the post, slithering in to trade and bargain with soft voices and quick poetic hands. Ona could not keep her eyes off them. There came back to her again the memory of the band of Plains Indians which had surrounded the house when she was young. The face of the tall young brave who had burned her bottom against the hot stove. And once more she felt the strange admixture of pain and ecstasy and the mellow glow in her crotch creeping down the inner side of her leg in a warm trickle. She had forgotten it all; few people in Little London went over to the Ute encampment, it was so unfashionable to associate with Indians. But here it was different. This was Indian country; and she realized that strange as they were, they held her with a queer attraction.

Boné worked every morning at the piano in his studio, and usually in the evening rode horseback over to Lockhardt's house. Sometimes he stayed all night or for several days. Orchestrating the tunes he had composed, of course. At first this worried Ona, but gradually she accepted it like Bruce and the Vrain Girls.

The two men were always going on trips in a light wagon and they took Ona with them. To the lofty butte called Shiprock. To a vast complex of ruins said to have been anciently built by the Aztecs. To El Huerfano, a sheer peak rising out of the flat plain, sacred to the Navajos who allowed no one to climb it. And then, in the middle of the blistering summer, all the way to the Hopi Indian villages in Arizona. Lew and Matie went along too, so Lew who spoke Navajo could inquire the way and keep them out of trouble. Bruce gave them a team to pull the light wagon heavily loaded with camping equipment, and two riding horses on which they could take turns to save the team.

How wonderful it was! The tawny desert forever spreading out under a brassy sky. The clear sharp flicker of the stars above as they slept at night. And always, as if out of the empty earth itself, a Navajo appearing to lead them to his *hogan* for mutton ribs, fried bread, and cheap Arbuckle coffee sweetened with too much sugar. What a wonderful woman Lew was! They could not have done without her.

Eventually they reached the Hopi mesas. Three of them in the middle of the Navajo Reservation. With nine stone villages or pueblos perched on their lofty summits like eagle eyries, almost indistinguishable from the rock cliffs. What they had come to see, explained Boné, was a *kachina* dancc – a dance of masked men representing Hopi gods. There was a spring to camp by on one of the mesas; and while they waited for the day of the dance, they visited the pueblo where it was to be held. Ona was surprised that it looked no different than the ancient ruins she'd seen save that it was swarming with people. Rock and mud rising in terraces, one big honeycomb of tiny rooms.

"A thousand years old!" muttered Lockhardt. "And the people are still primitive as ever!"

Maybe so, thought Ona, but they looked so pleasant, these short, docile Hopis with their broad-faced, smiling faces. So different from the nomadic Navajos following their sheep from one waterhole to another.

The dance began at sunrise and lasted till sunset. They sat all day on a crowded housetop in the broiling sun, looking down into an archaic world populated only by dancing gods. Strange, anthropomorphic figures in their masks, part man, part beast, part bird, abstractly stylized as if they embodied the invisible powers of earth and sky. A long line of them, the *kachinas*, stretching across the cleared plaza. Curving into a circle, then forming into two lines with an old gray-headed priest between. Shaking their gourd rattles. Singing in deep voices that sounded like the wind through the spruce branches they carried. And always dancing, rhythmically, powerfully, calling up the potencies of the earth below and calling down the potencies of the brassy sky above. Ona stared hour after hour, mesmerized. It all seemed to exist in an invisible dimension her senses could not pierce.

Lockhardt broke the silence. "Ever see San Francisco, Boné? The most metropolitan city in the world. And the most beautiful.

The finest cuisine of every race. Opera. Symphonies, Music, boy! My apartment's on the Hill. Sitting at my Baby Grand I can look down upon the bay. The Golden Gate!"

No one answered, not even Boné. He sat as if he had not heard Lockhardt, staring down into that well-like plaza filled with sounds and sights old when the world was new. With one brown finger he was almost imperceptibly tapping out the rhythm.

The ride home was so long, so tedious! The feeling engendered by the mysterious ritual dance she had seen still lingered, but it began to be dissipated when she noticed that Boné and Lockhardt weren't as cosily familiar, as intimate, as usual. Nothing Ona could put her finger on, really, but it bothered her just the same.

When they arrived at Farmington, Boné remained at the post and in his own studio. A week wore on, and still he did not go over to Lockhardt's. Then again they resumed their companionship as if nothing had happened.

Late in September they evidently had another fuss, for Boné stayed home again. This time it was Lockhardt who came to make amends. He arrived in the evening as they were finishing supper and sat down to a cup of coffee. He had never looked so immaculate and distinguished, dressed in his loose, dark worsted jacket, white shirt, and flowing tie. But his gaunt pale face wore spots of deeper pink. When he emptied his cup he rose and said casually, "Well we must be off to Boné's room for a little work." The two men strolled up the trail.

Boné flung open the door of his studio and lit the lamp on the table. Lockhardt pulled out of his pocket a pint of whisky, the huge diamond solitaire on his finger sparkling as he opened the bottle. Taking a big swig, still standing, he resumed the conversation that had been broken off ten days before.

"Sweet mother nature – the great American foible! Look at Europe, its green meadows, its fertile fields, its peaceful rolling hills. Now look out there!" He waved a hand toward the window. "The American landscape. Jagged hills, monstrous mountains on every horizon. Or else a barren sun-struck desert without trees, without water. A devilish twist to every face it shows. It doesn't inspire me! I haven't been brought up to suckle a coyote's teat, and declare a holiday whenever it rains. This earth is malevolent, opposed and fatal to the white man. Every American hates it beneath his show-off sentimentality. There's so damned much of it here in America, heaped two miles or more high, that it exerts a gravity that drags one down. Like it has degraded the Indian and is still doing so. You can't argue against it, even with music."

Lockhardt took another hearty swig and when Boné did not answer, continued, "You're at the turn of your road, my dear boy. Get out of this primitive backwash into civilization. Absorb the rich culture of Europe, develop the traditions of classical music. Not tunes from the pipes of Pan!"

He hesitated, took another drink. "Rhythm, melody, symphonic orchestration. In that order. Those are the steps to the altar of art. But you must have a heart. Do you hear me? A heart! Like this!" He flung himself down on the piano bench. "Where's a light?"

Boné lit the silver candlesticks Lockhardt had given him, blew out the lamp, and sank upon the couch. The Englishman set the whiskey bottle on the floor beside him, closed his eyes. He brought both hands down, preluded brilliantly, then bent down to the keys. Wagner–Yes, *Tistan*. The music filled the dusky room, shook Boné like an ague. An hour passed. One of the candles, jarred loose in its holder, was dripping tallow down the long silver stick and building up slowly like a small stalagmite in the cavernous gloom. The other was out. Lockhardt kept on. At every momentary pause he reached for the bottle on the floor. Then he began again, reciting the different parts in a fervent, not unmusical voice. The moon rose, casting a tangent beam across his pale face. Keyed up by whiskey and drunk with emotion, almost ready to collapse, he began Isolde's Love-Death with shaking hands. It was almost more than Boné could bear.

That great mounting consumation, like surge after surge of moon-swung waves pounding against the sea-wall of man's resisting consciousness only to be flung back, to rise, and roll in once more. The most emotional music ever written but sexual surely, rising from the depths of instinct, of wildly passionate longing, that refused all sublimation and brooked no opposition. It would not let him still his heart nor catch his breath. And the angry tides kept pounding in, to triumphantly rise and crest and break at last in one great orgiastic climax of love and death.

"Gene!" The old man had collapsed over the keys. Boné ran to him, gathered the frail body in his arms, and laid him on the couch. Lighting the lamp on the table, he knelt beside him, watching him slowly come to with a gesture of one hand to the bottle on the floor. There was a drink left; and with it down, Lockhardt began to be himself.

"Oh, Gene! That's what I want! To write good music, big scores!"

Lockhardt, looking very old, turned on him a weary and shrewd look. "I don't know whether it's in you, dear boy. It takes more than I ever had. I rather believe you have more of a talent for lighter work." He was just drunk enough to be bluntly honest.

Boné flinched.

"Still you need to get to more congenial surroundings for professional work, Boné."

"Gene, I can't leave you! I need your help!" He leaned down and put his arms around the musician, staring imploringly into his eyes.

It was at this moment that Ona opened the door. Hearing the click of the latch and feeling the draft of cold air. Boné looked up defiantly.

All the Rogier undemonstrativeness in her rose to meet it. "Excuse me, Boné. I should have knocked. I only wanted to tell you the driver of the supply wagon brought me a letter. It's from Daddy. He's coming to take us back home."

Boné gave her an angry look. "Tell him I'm not going home!"

"Tell him yourself, Boné," she said quietly, and closed the door behind her.

8

The first sight of her father's heavy, powerful body and calm square face with its steady eyes and sandy mustache reminded Ona instantly of the mountains he had left behind. Rogier looked her over from head to toe, then turned to Bruce. "Been trying to make a squaw out of her, eh?" The trader did not crack a smile. "She'll make a good one for the right Indian."

"And what've you folks done to the boy all this time?"

"Boy? There's no boy around here," the trader replied just as gruffly. "There's a talented young man who might be dropping in."

"Maybe so. Maybe so."

Ona could tell they liked each other right off.

Rogier's reunion at supper with Ona, Boné, and the two Vrain Girls was warm and exciting. There was so much to talk about, what had happened here and back home. But it was Boné her father's eyes followed: every gesture, every emotion flitting across his sensitive face. "I reckon you have grown up, Boné," he admitted. "Have a cigar?"

"Not enough for that black a weed," cheerfully replied Boné rolling a cigarette.

All the trips they had taken that summer came up, and during the conversation Boné happened to mention another he was going to take next month—to see some remarkable cliff-dwellings just discovered on Mesa Verde by two cowboys hunting lost cattle.

"I thought you were coming home with Ona and me," Rogier said calmly.

"No sir." There was a stubborn defiance in Boné's voice that indicated he had not outgrown Rogier's hold upon him. His cheerful manner vanished instantly.

Rogier ignored the answer as if he had not heard it. It was consistent with Rogier's aloofness that he could not bear to discuss a personal or family affair in the presence of any outsider, even friends as old as the Vrain Girls.

After an awkward silence Matie suggested, "Boné, aren't you going to play for Joe and show him what a fine musician you've become in the last couple of years?"

They all filed up the trail to Boné's studio. Boné rather sullenly slumped upon the piano bench. "Give us a Southern tune or so, if you've a mind to," Rogier said as he used to say to Lily Force. The boy threw him a dark look of refutation and plunged instead into a difficult movement from Bach. Rogier had no developed ear for fine music, but at the boy's seemingly careless display of undeniable virtuosity his jaw dropped. "Dom! Sounds like you and that piano have got on more than speaking terms!"

"That lad's a born musician, Mr. Rogier," asserted Bruce. "You'll never make anything else out of him."

Rogier lit his cigar and leaned back for an hour's concert. Ona sat cracking pinon nuts between her teeth. The spectacle of Boné oppising Rogier with music, too proud and stubborn to confess openly the reason for his desire to stay and to ask Rogier's permission and aid, grew painful. Without Lockhardt at his elbow to criticize his slightest mistouch, determined to impress Rogier, and infused with excitement, Boné slurred a run, skipped a rest, and kept playing. The music rang out with an exultant challenge, with courageous sincerity, like a demand from Boné himself. If only her father would understand and avoid a quarrel!

Boné flung around. "What's the matter—don't you like my music?"

"It's getting late, Boné, and Daddy's had a long, hard ride," said Ona, getting up with Bruce and the Vrain Girls.

Rogier stamped around on one stiff leg, then sat down again. "You folks go on to bed. I'm going to listen to him out."

"That young fella's all right," Bruce whispered. "Just leave him alone. It'll work off like a dose of physic."

"The young jackass!"

Ona left with the others, but as she walked down the trail she couldn't hear any more playing.

Rogier stayed only a few days at the post. Lew had found an Indian boy to drive them to Durango, and he wanted to be off.

"I'll escort you by horseback to the top of the hill," said Boné.

The remark was Ona's first indication that Boné was not going home with them. She knew Rogier had talked to Lockhardt, Bruce, and the Vrain Girls about him, but still her curiosity prompted her to draw Boné aside. "Boné–I've got to know! Did you and Daddy really quarrel the other night about your not coming with us?"

"No, Ona. I've been ashamed ever since, the wonderful way he talked to me. He understands a lot more than he lets on, you know. And he's going to keep on sending me an allowance – a bigger one!"

The sudden realization that she had lost him as she had lost Hiney and Bob – he, this funny little boy whom she had loved best of all! – struck her like a blow. Tears leapt to her eyes. "Boné! You're one of us. You can't ever get clear away. Don't forget me, Boné!"

"Shoot, Ona. You'd know if I needed you if I were lost in Patagonia!"

Two mornings later at sun-up Rogier and Ona climbed on the wagon seat beside the Indian boy. Boné mounted his broomtail beside them. Lew and Matie came out with a going-away gift – a large and exquisitely woven Two-Gray-Hills blanket to throw over their laps. "Hold on!" cried Bruce, running up with a scooping handful of jewelry to thrust at Ona. A fortune in silver rings and bracelets set with chunk turquoise, a squash-blossom necklace, and a prize concho belt she had admired for six months! She began to weep, and Rogier drove off without a word.

Boné too jogged along in silence. What was there to say?

Perhaps all three of them were thinking of the jist of Rogier's talk to Boné that night. Rogier at least knew only too well to what a task the boy had set his hand with an urge as powerful as silver-madness. Like Tom, he was consecrating himself to the folly of extracting his meaning of life from a gangue that might not contain the silver ore of his dreams. But instead of force and luck, Boné was using a different approach: an elusive persuasiveness, more intangible, more heart-rendingly difficult, because there was no way to measure his success or failure. Rogier saw not the ready acclaim awarded to so few and lost so quickly, the deserved and final success attained perhaps by one man in his time, but only the toil and despair of the sincere who realize at the last the modicum they have been able to add to the work of those who have gone before. Never, after listening to Boné play, could he doubt his sincerity; but he could not measure whether the boy's strength would prove adequate to the task he had set himself.

At the top of the hill the wagon stopped. Boné dismounted, kissed Ona and squeezed Rogier's hand. Remounting, he trotted the old bay fifty feet into the trackless sage. Then standing in his stirrups, he raised his right arm aloft. The melodramatic, graceful gesture, as if unconsciously copied from a lurid print that hung on the kitchen door at home, brought a blur to Ona's eyes. Before she could wave, Boné turned back to his lifelong, lonely journey.

The wagon rolled on. Rogier settled himself on the seat, and with a face like flint, raised his eyes to the high steel-blue mountains before them.

Men, mere men, both of them, oblivious of the grandeur of their folly, blind to the futility of evoking an answer from an earth which but echoed back their questions in a voice hollow yet profound, and couched in terms neither could recognize for his own.

To Ona their long trip home was a miserable finale concluding a symphonic summer. It had seemed unusual that Rogier, busy as he was, had come merely to take her and Boné back. Now the real reason came out. Rogier wanted to look over some of the rich silver mines and boom towns. So now, following the Animas River north from Durango, they crept into the blue-ribbed Uncompahgre, San Juan, and Saguache ranges of the great male Rockies on the little D & RG narrow-gauge, by wagon, and by horseback. Silverton,

Ouray, Telluride, Ophir, Lake City – they all looked the same to Ona. Crude little towns and camps set in deep canyons or small mountain meadows. Squat one-story buildings with their false high "Leadville fronts." Miners with burros and pack horses crowding the narrow streets and thumping along the patches of wooden sidewalks. The sharp air was odorific with fresh-sawed pine and bar whisky. The noise of blasting echoed from the hills, picking up the clatter of a mechanical piano in a tinny minor melody.

Most of the time Ona stayed in the inevitable ramshackle hotel. She did not dare to walk about the streets in one of her still-new taffeta dresses for fear of being taken for a sporting woman; and her pride forbade that she go about in gingham or calico, ungloved. So she sat in her room, wondering if Tom had ever been here and why they'd never heard from him. Wondering too what had got into her father.

All day Rogier roamed mountainside and canyon, wherever there was a notable mine. In the evenings he talked in front of the stove in the hotel lobby, on the streets, and in the saloons, with mine-owners and workers. At night he sat in his room bending over maps and drawings in the light of a lamp.

Occasionally she visited mines with him. The difficult walks or horseback rides, with Rogier swinging along the trail ahead seemingly oblivious of her presence, tired her out completely. More exasperating were the hours she sat at the portal of a tunnel waiting for him to come up. When at last he did emerge, blinking at the sunlight, it was only to stand around talking, rapping his knuckles against the timbers. Or else he would pick at a piece of ore with his knife, and perhaps carry it into the assayer's office for another long palaver. Slow, methodical, never verbosely enthusiastic, he was not to be hurried.

"What's got into you, Daddy?" she asked bluntly. "You're not going into mining after all these years, are you?"

"Nothing like that at all!" he replied just as brusquely. "My trade's building – a process of addition, you might call it. Mining's subtraction, taking away. I just thought my education wouldn't be complete till I balanced the equation."

She looked at him sharply; he had a habit of speaking jocularly in such parables. "Why are you so interested in the composition of ore, then?"

"This is gangue! The country rock in which is imbedded mineral matter!" He thrust the specimen under her nose. "Dom it, Ona! A man ought to know what makes up the ground he walks on!"

It was October. Patches of aspen were turning deep yellow and pink among the forested blue mountainsides. The air was sharp with frost. An early snow might close the passes any night. But Rogier was not yet ready to head for home. They crept over Slumgullion Pass and turned south toward the headwaters of the Rio Grande where a fabulous new silver strike had been made.

Rogier recounted the details. The year before, a prospector named Nicholas C. Creede and his partner George Smith had worked north from Del Norte through Wagon Wheel Gap to the head of Willow Creek. Here they found float and sank a shaft. At the end of the day's work, Creede, examining the yellow quartz, had yelled, "Holy Moses!" thus naming the Holy Moses Mine.

The rush began. Two butchers at Wagon Wheel Gap, Granger and Buddenbock, grubstaked two prospectors, Haas and Renninger, who located the Last Chance. Creede, seeing the specimens, located another mine, the Amethyst. Shortly thereafter, Haas was bought off for $10,000 and returned to Germany. Renninger and Buddenbock each sold their shares for $70,000. Granger was offered and refused $100,000, and the Last Chance was now producing $180,000 per month. Creede had raked in $1,000,000 from the Holy Moses and Amethyst. And by the end of the first year the district around the camp of Creede had yielded $6,000,000.

Willow Gulch, when Rogier and Ona arrived, was jammed with people. For six miles up the creek every foot of ground had been staked out. Tents and shacks and cabins were crowded against the towering cliff walls between which crawled a corkscrew street barely wide enough for a wagon. There were a dozen hotels; one of them, a fresh pine shanty containing twenty cots in its single room, was named The Palace. Rogier finally obtained a room in another, the Cochetopa, for forty dollars a day. Here Ona huddled for three days, afraid to set foot outside, while Rogier prowled around.

Crêede was red-hot and chaotic. Its patron saints were Chance and Luck; its shrines the Keno, Little Delmonico, and the Holy Moses Saloon. Day and night the tortuous winding street below swarmed with prospectors and miners, speculators, gamblers, and dancehall girls. Ona could hear the sound of saws and hammers, the tinkle of pianos, the clink of silver on the gambling table below, the sharp bark of a six-shooter up the gulch. Years later it all came back to her in the words of the homey poet, Cy Warman:

> Here the meek-eyed burros
> On mineral mountains feed.
> It's day all day in the daytime,
> And there's no night in Creede.

What held Rogier here Ona did not know. A Rogier herself and peculiarly sensitive to her father, she sensed a vibrant excitement emanating from him that his air of deliberate unconcern, his steady voice, could not hide. The queer impending change in him was accentuated rather than subdued by his calm demeanor. The feeling carried her back to those terrible days of the Leadville boom when, high above the trail with Sister Molly, she had watched Tom ascending Ute Pass. And as if with an ear to the ground, she seemed to feel a subterranean tremor within him, the faintest rumble of a movement betokening a growing unrest that would uproot him from his ordered life. She was relieved no end when at last they turned toward home.

Mile after mile it all slid behind her: the months in Indian Country with Bruce, the Vrain Girls, and Boné; the weeks in the Rockies with Rogier. What did it all mean? Although she did not realize it, it was the gangue that imbedded for all of them the pay streaks of their future lives.

But she never forgot Creede. It was 1890 and Creede was the last of the great Colorado silver strikes. The silver moon was setting, and above the mountain-rimmed horizon the golden sun was rising.

PART III

GOLD

1

The following spring Rogier became fifty years old. Wide-shouldered, of medium height, with an easy swing to his gait, he looked solid as the hills. He had the accentuated upper-level forehead of a reflective thinker, the square firm jaw of a man who stood behind his decisions, and deep-sunk penetrative gray eyes. And his hands – big, strong, coarsened with early years of carpenter work, yet with fingers peculiarly sensitive – confirmed the impression of his face.

Aloof and reticent to an unwarranted degree, Rogier would have been amazed that even the Little Londoners in the North End regarded him with a respect tinged by a spot of fear. A respect inspired by his hard-earned success as a builder and his enviable possession of land and buildings throughout town. The fear a growing bewilderment because he did not flaunt them, never made a conciliatory move toward their society, and remained down in the ungainly house on Shook's Run – an attitude rightly judged as suspicious because he was different.

While he had been away unfavorable news had come of Hiney. Between theatrical engagements, he had taken the job of night watchman at the Brown Palace Hotel. One night he was caught crawling through the transom of a room. The guest was out, leaving money and some jeweled studs on the dresser, but Hiney had taken nothing. The next morning when he was questioned at the jail, Hiney could remember nothing. In desperation he sent his only friend, a girl named Margaret with whom he was in love, home to Rogier. And Rogier was away.

Rogier listened impatiently to Mrs. Rogier and Mrs. White. He could well imagine Martha receiving the girl with doubt and lifted eyebrows. Hiney, for all his upbringing, had strayed from the path of righteousness.

"Never mind," said Rogier. "What did you do?"

"I give that sweetheart of his some money to get him out of jail," answered Mrs. White. "She was done taken up with that boy, ridin' all night on the train to get back to Denver."

Mrs. Rogier sat upright, unsmiling. She too loved Hiney but she feared the Lord's wrath more, believing that forgiveness should be the fruit of repentance and not, like Atlanta's apples, tossed indiscriminately before swift feet racing to destruction.

Rogier and Mrs. White exchanged a quick, secret glance. They were the only ones who knew that Hiney was subject to lapses of memory. "I wouldn't worry none," finished Mrs. White. "That theah Mahgret of his sent us a postcard about his gettin' along fuhst rate now."

Pet's new colt, Silver Heels, looked as if she might be faster than Dorothy, her first. To break and train them both, Rogier moved them to Denman's ranch a few miles east of town. Denman was a fine old man whose only love and interest were horses. He had few of his own and made his living handling those given to his care. One afternoon his stable boy galloped furiously down to the Rogier house, then up to Rogier's office with the alarming news that Silver Heels was sick. Rogier rushed to the ranch and spent the night with Denman in the colt's stable. There was nothing either of them could do; Silver Heels died of a punctured bowel.

A few months later Rogier sent to Maryland for the papers of a filly he had been interested in for a long time. Finally he sent for her. Never in this life had any horse so aroused that inward glow, the tingle up the spine, which Rogier felt when he first saw her. Akeepee was a sleek little thing, dark bay, with a white diamond on her forehead and white stockings on the near front and hind feet. Even the family doted upon her. Stabled in back of the house, Akeepee was kind and gentle as a kitten, neighing across the fence, nosing all hands for a lump of sugar. Yet there was never any doubt what she was bred for, as she hardened and filled out.

Eventually Rogier took her to Judge Colton's excellent establishment near the track north of town. Not that he mistrusted Denman because of Silver Heel's unfortunate death, but he wanted Akeepee to have the best. The very best! "She's got the blood lines, the confirmation of a fine pacer," he kept insisting. "I want a horse that can run!"

A strange new passion for speed. None of the family could account for it.

There were a number of fine animals being trained at Colton's that winter. Even as early as March considerable excitement prevailed over the racing meeting to be held in the summer, and wagers were being made as to which of the horses would prove the fastest. Akeepee was considered one of the best. Her only rivals, in many an opinion, were Colton's big gray mare and a dun horse named Toller. Late one afternoon after Rogier had left, an impromptu race was held. Three starters dropped out halfaway around the course, leaving Akeepee and Toller running neck to neck. Cooped up inside for weeks waiting for the snow to clear from the track, neither was in the best of condition. And yet at the end of the mile they were whipped on for another stretch. Streaming wet, almost exhausted, their breaths enveloping them with frosty steam, the horses were led back to stable.

Whether Judge Colton was too drunk to care, or whether he did it to further the chances of his own gray mare, now warm and blanketed inside her box, no one ever knew. But Akeepee was left unblanketed and without being rubbed down. Providentially, an old handler who favored Akeepee sent for Rogier. With Sally Lee, Rogier hurried out in the buckboard and walked Akeepee home to his own stalls. A veterinary was waiting. All night he, Rogier, and Sally Lee worked her over with witch hazel and alcohol, drying her and wrapping her in blankets, then walking her around the yard. Akeepee almost died; it took weeks to get her back in shape; and from then on no one save Denman, Sally Lee, and Rogier touched her. No one ever knew what happened between Rogier and Judge Colton. Sally Lee insisted that Rogier horsewhipped him – perhaps a great exaggeration. But the incident drove Rogier away from the Gentleman's Pleasure and Driving Association he had finally joined; he didn't bother to submit a letter of withdrawal.

Soon afterward he bought a new Frazier sulky. Every evening as dusk clotted the prairie track, he sat in the low seat, legs outspread, leaning forward until his face was whipped with her silky tail, skimming the ground behind Akeepee. When she was warmed up he turned her into the straight-away, nose pointing at that lofty white Peak never even now out of his thoughts.

"See her, old girl?" he would ask in a rising voice. "Slam into her! Bust her wide open! Let's see what's inside!" And with a flick of his whip above her she would burst forward, leveling her stride into the path of projectile aimed at his heart's desire.

Embryonic in that high southern slope of Pike's Peak where the Pisgah excitement had ended in a miserable fiasco, a few disregarded but auspicious events were outcropping to surface. "Crazy Bob" Womack, the cowboy on the Broken Box Ranch, was still insisting there was gold along Cripple Creek. Having neglected to record his claim, the Chance, for six years, he finally relocated it as the El Paso. The samples he kept showing in town were ignored by everyone except a furniture store owner, E. M. de la Vergne, and his store manager, F. F. Frisbee. That January they had packed up to the Broken Box and staked claims. Not an experienced prospector in the area believed that gold could be found on that barren, high cow pasture on the slope of Pike's Peak. Yet by spring a hundred more tenderfeet and alfalfa miners were digging up the range along the meandering creek.

Bennett and Myers, the two Denver real estate men who owned the Broken Box, began to plat a townsite of eighty acres on the ranch, offering lots for fifty dollars apiece. The town was named Cripple Creek for mere convenience; the first purchasers of lots for cabin sites agreed to leave their timber to be used for patching fences after the town was abandoned.

In April Rogier met Stratton on the street. "Hunting for a job?"

he asked.

"Not this time, Joe I've already raised a grubstake. You know that plasterer, Leslie Popejoy? He's outfitting me. Maybe I'll take along another partner, Billy Fernay, so Popejoy can stay home and make more money."

Rogier did not reply. Billy Fernay was not too highly regarded in town. He seldom worked and was often carried home drunk on an ironing board which two friends kept handy for the purpose. The prognosis of success for the carpenter, plasterer, and town drunk was not too good, but Stratton seemed to know what he was after.

"Cryolite, Joe. Not well known but valuable. It's a fluoride used in making aluminum. I think there's a deposit somewhere near St. Peter's Dome or up Beaver Creek."

A few days later Rogier saw him and Fernay trying to pack their two burros in front of Stratton's boarding house. It was an unpleasant spectacle. The boarding house was near the corner of Pike's Peak Avenue and Cascade – almost directly in view of the luxurious Antlers Hotel, on whose porch laughed a group of ladies and gentlemen. Swiftly a crowd gathered around the prospectors. Rogier noticed that one of the Rocky Mountain Canaries had been cut on the back by barbed wire. The instant the pack touched the scab, the burro brayed and lashed out with both heels. Fernay stood back and swore. Stratton, with his quick temper, whacked the burro with a pick handle. Blood began to pour from the wound. A woman screamed, running to bring someone from the Humane Society. Hotel guests tittered. The crowd roared. Fernay finally wrapped a blanket over the burro's head and Stratton flung the pack on its back. As they ambled down the street the pack came off, spilling flour and beans. The two men did not wait to scrape up their supplies, but flinging the pack back on the beast, fled down the street.

Early in July the report came out that Stratton had struck a gold lode in Cripple Creek. Professor Lamb at the college had made the assays of the samples. They ran $380 to the ton! Most of the people in town were stunned. It seemed impossible to believe that a gold strike had been made scarcely twenty miles, as the crow flies, from the plush lobby of the Antlers Hotel. Why, the place was within picnic-distance of the Saratoga of the West! Moreover it had been passed over by prospectors since '58 – for thirty-three years! Self-important North Enders took it more seriously. They spoke of their duty to pronounce the fraud and nip the boom in the bud before the mining industry of Colorado was blackened with dishonor. Still something of a rush began – a slow, increasing influx into the region of men not wildly excited but taking no chances on losing out on a fortune.

Rogier was one of the many who kept his head. The secret nervousness, the repressed excitement, the sense of foreboding that had possessed him during the Leadville and Creede strikes, and all those between, did not trouble him now. It was as if all his life he had been preparing to meet the thing before him now. Sitting tight, he waited for the rumors to quiet down.

Late in the summer Stratton stopped in his office. He was dressed up, his mustache freshly trimmed, looking like a different man – a man who after seventeen years of fruitless searching had found what he sought. "It *was* a dream, Joe! Everything's settled now. I'll tell you about it."

For two months he and Fernay had hunted without finding any trace of the cryolite of which he had heard. They had then packed into the Cripple Creek district and prospected for another month. The region did not have the appearance of a mining country. Ordinarily veins of gold jutted boldly above the surface in outcrops known in Australia as reefs and in California as ledges. But here, except for a ledge of reddish granite at the foot of Battle Mountain which every prospector had passed by, the region was barren save for its innumerable hills. On the evening of July 3, on their way to make camp, he and Billy Fernay also passed this ledge.

Sitting at his campfire that night, listening to Fernay snore, Stratton remembered a scrap of geology Professor Lamb had taught him. The whole area once had been a monstrously huge volcano of which only Pike's Peak was now left. The country rock which composed it was granite of a pinkish tint that was now known as Pike's Peak Granite. Ages ago there had been a mighty eruption during which a complex of volcanic rock had burst through the granite. It was a purplish rock generally called porphyry: a name evolved from the Greek "porphyra" for purple, used to designate rock which the Romans had obtained from the quarries of Gebel

Dokhan on the shores of the Red Sea.

That night Stratton dreamed that there at that ledge where the granite and the porphyry met lay a vast deposit of mineral. "I could see a mine there, Joe. Right in that tangled briar patch on the slope of Battle Mountain, among the big boulders. A dream of gold on Pike's Peak! Just like the one I'd been carrying all these years!"

"And what did you do?" asked Rogier quietly.

"I woke up and rushed back there just as the sun was coming up. Some men far off were shooting off guns to celebrate the day – the Fourth of July. So I staked out a full lode claim on the spot and another beside it. Both named in honor of the holiday. The Independence and the Washington."

Three days later, Stratton went on, he had staked out two more claims, the Black Diamond and one named for Professor Lamb. There had followed the usual trouble: buying out Popejoy and Fernay, trying to develop all four claims. At last in desperation he had broken open the great boulders, some of them weighing over ten tons. Full of gold, they brought him $60,000 – enough money to sink a shaft on the site of the Independence.

"Then I hit it!" said Stratton. "That ore chute led directly into the main vein. Why, I never saw anything like it! Gold threads snarling up granite, porphyry, country rock, and grass roots, ore good enough to eat. Nine feet wide I figured and a hundred feet deep – $3,000,000 worth to start with, and more below!"

There he sat: forty-three years old, thin, stooped, and white-haired already, a lonely recluse. But a man who had found his dream. Winfield Scott Stratton, Colorado's new Gold King. He got up and the two men shook hands warmly.

"I've lost a good carpenter," said Rogier, grinning.

"I hope you're as lucky as I was," replied Stratton. "Don't wait too long."

2

During the few months of its first year the district produced $200,000 worth of gold. "Cripple Creek – the $200,000 Cow Pasture!"

Despite the general distrust of the district, the camp kept growing as a horde of tenderfoot Little Londoners, store clerks, bakers, and butchers scrambled up the Peak. Near as it was, the camp was difficult of access. Men had to pack up the mile-high Cheyenne Mountain trail; ride the Colorado Midland railroad train up Ute Pass to Florissant and thence eighteen miles south by stage or horseback; or leave the Denver and Rio Grande at Florence and ride thirty miles north in Concord stages drawn by six horses.

With the melting of the winter snows Rogier, never in a hurry, went up for a look around. Riding the Midland to the junction, he managed to get a seat in the stage. With the driver's whip cracking like pistol shots at the ears of the sixes, the boisterous shouts of the men inside, the dull thud of hoofs on the snowy road, the stage swung off into the thick gray silence of the hills.

Cripple Creek bore a distinct resemblance to the Broken Box which had given its name to the ranch on which the town had been built. Cabins, shacks, and lean-tos stood everywhere like the remnants of a wooden box. The town, built on the side of a steep hill, was divided by two streets: Bennett Avenue, trying to look something like a business street; and Myers Avenue, a block south, already being lined with false-front saloons, dancehalls, and cribs. Nearly 400 people crowded the camp. Water was selling for a nickel a bucket. Speculators were standing on the corners selling shares of stock in Frisbee's Gold King, the first mine to ship pay ore, and in the Buena Vista, the first mine on Bull Hill. Rogier waved them away. The town didn't interest him a whit. Nor did the reports of still more unbelievably true strikes.

His old druggist, A.D. Jones, had come up on his Sunday day-off. "I don't know anything about mining, boys!" he had shouted "Where'll I dig?"

"She's all good! Just throw your hat in the air!" they answered.

Jones without hesitation flung his hat in the air and dug where it fell, locating the Pharmacist, the second mine to ship ore in quantity.

The locator of the Elkton went broke and gave half-interest in it to pay off a grocery bill of $36.50. The two grocers let in a schoolteacher who during his vacation struck a vein that began producing $13,000,000. The Anaconda had been offered for $400; now the owners were considering $2,000,000 for a controlling interest. The first assay from the Rose Maud ran $2,800 to the ton.

Stopping in a saloon, Rogier listened to a bartender from Leadville who summed up the stories. "Hell! The tenderfeet are taking out gold where it is, and the miners are looking for it where it ought to be!" He mentioned a farmer from Missouri, A.G. White, who had laboriously dug through surface rock with no indication of mineral into a big ore chute that had yielded the Vindicator company $750,000. Professor Kimball was making gold discoveries by walking around with a willow branch. Another wizard, John Barbee, he claimed had located the vein of the El Paso with a forked stick.

Cy Warman, the home-spun poet, had arrived from Creede to inspect the Cripple Creek rush. His comparison was not entirely favorable: "People are rushing to Creede by the hundreds, and crawling to Cripple Creek by twos and fours."

To this he added the observation that "on the summit of Globe Hill in the camp of Cripple Creek they are prospecting with plows, mining with road-scrapers, and actually shipping the scenery." No man could deny it. The surface dirt on Globe Hill, specifically designated as that from the grass roots down six feet, was being contracted for by the wagon load.

Rogier, unlike the horde of hopefuls around him, did not feel bound to stake out a claim foolishly. He was not sure he wanted to stake one out at all. If he wanted anything, it was simply to know the district thoroughly. Learning it not only until its physiography was familiar to him at close hand, but geologically; and more than all, to feel out the indefinable strength of its will. It was like meeting a man for the first time. Rogier would have said he had to "size him up" before knowing how to deal with him.

The next morning after an uncomfortable night dozing on a chair in a saloon, he stretched his stiff legs in their stout boots, buttoned his overcoat, and holding a map in his gloved hands for ready reference, started out to encompass the district. Turning southeast past Poverty Gulch, he looked back at Mount Pisgah. It, like the town, was blurred in the gray mist. He walked on briskly, warming to his stride. Gradually the hills took shape around him, some bearing names consistent with the original cow pasture: Big Bull, Cow, Calf, Bull Cliffs, and Grassy Gulch. Others had sprouted newer names: Gold, Globe, Tenderfoot, Carbonate, Crystal, Mineral and Galena Hills, Beacon, Battle, Squaw and Straub Mountains. A maze of lumpish hills forested with spruce and pine and thin groves of aspens; and drained by Arequa, Squaw, and Eclipse gulches, crisscrossed with burro trails and the ruts of heavy wagons. A 10,000-foot-high shelf, as it seemed, on the south slope of that 14,000-foot Peak rising above him, aboe timberline, to stand nakedly white above the lifting mist. And silent with a queer silence that had in it the timelessness of an earth upthrust forever above the faintest murmur of the vast monotone of human misery far below.

Almost every hill bore signs of digging, open shafts, glory holes, new mines. In every gulch clustered a huddle of cabins and shanties already taking on names: Independence, Winfield, Strattonia, Anaconda, Goldfield, Arequa. Walking steadily southeast, Rogier began to notice that most of the new mines were not located in Poverty Gulch and around Cripple Creek to the west, but six miles east and southeast near the new camp of Victor. This was natural; Stratton's great strike on Battle Mountain had been made there. But still Rogier, constantly referring to his map, was inclined to believe that near here somewhere had occured the main eruption of porphyry through the granite walls of the now extinct volcano. How big was its diameter? Whatever was taking shape in his mind was too nebulous to see clearly, but he kept looking for it in the pinkish country rock and an occasional speck of purplish poryphry. There was little to see; a thin layer of snow still covered the ground.

Victor was a tawdry array of cabins, shacks, and tents. Men were cutting down trees to make way for streets: the pines for building and the aspens for firewood. Lots were being sold for $25 apiece. If a man did not have the cash he was asked merely to sign a paper as a future resident of the town, the signatures to be used in securing a postoffice.

Worn out, he turned back toward another sleepless night in Cripple Creek. Fortunately he met George Carr, the former foreman of the Broken Box Ranch and now being talked of for Cripple Creek's first mayor, who offered him a bed. That evening, dozing in front of the hot stove, Rogier learned of another strike on top of Battle Mountain that had been kept quiet.

"You know Jimmie Doyle, the carpenter, and Jimmie Burns, the plumber, down in town? They made it three months ago," began Carr.

"A carpenter and a plasterer, and now a carpenter and a plumber! Yes, I know them both."

"They filed a little claim of only one-sixth of an acre 700 feet above Stratton's full lode claim of ten acres, but didn't find much. So they took in another Irishman, Johnny Harnan, who had worked for Stratton. He hit it – thirty-two ounces to the ton!" Carr paused, then continued. "You can guess the trouble, even if they did lug out the ore on their backs by night. They couldn't follow their vein from its apex on top the mountain without running into the properties of other mines between them and the Independence, and vice versa. That meant lawsuits. The news got out and all the other mines went to court."

"I haven't heard anything about all this," commented Rogier.

"You will!" asserted Carr. "Stratton's no fool and he's learned how to keep his mouth shut. The case hasn't been settled, but he's given the Irishmen money to hire lawyers and to buy up the conflicting claims in exchange for stock. They'll win, all right! And when they do that little one-sixth of an acre will be forty acres big and Queen of the District controlled by and combined with Stratton's Independence as King of the District!"

Rogier went to sleep thinking how shrewd Stratton was, and how immensely rich and powerful he was becoming. But more than anything else of the importance of that eastern edge of the district around Victor.

He had encompassed the whole district, an area about ten miles square that contained every strike of note. He had looked at mines, shallow diggings, and prospects, talked with men of every age and type. The only mine he had not visited was the Independence; a stiff-necked pride had restrained him from looking up Stratton without an invitation.

Walking down the street in search of a geologist he wanted to talk with, Rogier reached for a cigar then suddenly stopped. He went through all his pockets. Their emptiness apprised him of the fact that he was also out of money. He looked down at his boots, hardly distinguishable in a pool of muddy water. His trousers too were splashed and torn at the cuffs. A queer looking customer to approach a consulting geologist without a cent! Abruptly he swung across the street to a general merchandise store and accosted the man behind the counter. "You're up from the Springs, aren't you?"

"Yes sir. On Huerfano Street. I sold out and moved my stock up here this spring.

"I thought I'd seen you down there. I'm out of cash. I want you to give me a hundred dollars. You can draw on me for that amount the next time you send down for supplies or I'll send you a draft. My name's Rogier."

The man met his steady gaze. "Why, I think I can let you have that much, Mr. Rogier." He went to the safe and came back with a wad of bills.

Rogier counted the notes carefully. "That's fine of you. I'll see you don't lose out."

As he walked out the door one of the men at the stove set up a guffaw. "God Almighty! Who's he think he is to come strollin' in and walk out with a hundred dollars?"

"I ain't worryin' none," the storekeeper replied quietly. "That there Mr. Rogier's name is as good as his bond. And if he gets to doin' anything up here this store's goin' to get a lot of hundreds rollin' in it wouldn't have got."

A chair overturned as one of the loungers leaped for the door. "Hey, Colonel!"

The shout stopped Rogier in the middle of the road. The man caught up with him, nervously heaving a deep breath. "Reynolds the name, Colonel. I'm plumb busted myself. Thirty dollars would grubstake me long enough to put down a ten-foot hole on a likely property I got my eyes set on."

Rogier's gaze went through him but the man did not flinch. Rogier drew out a ten-dollar bill. "The storekeeper will know you just got this from me. Tell him to give you twenty dollars more worth of goods on my account."

Reynolds grabbed his arm as he strode away. "What'll I call her, Colonel?"

"The 'Silver Heels' might do if you don't think of a better name," he said quietly and walked away.

When he finally arrived home, Mrs. Rogier and all the girls rushed into the hall to greet him.

"Daddy! Did you find a gold mine?" shouted Mary Ann. When he did not reply, she added, "Mr. Jones found one on his Sunday off – the Pharmacist he calls it!"

"No," Rogier answered good humoredly. "The hills were so full of holes I couldn't find enough solid ground to stand on to dig another."

"You look dirty enough to have dug out a dozen," Mrs. Rogier said testily, amazed that he of all men hadn't found a gold mine richer than any yet. "Look at those shoes! And you've probably ruined your good overcoat. The mud will never come out. I hope no one saw you walking from the depot."

"Well, draw me a hot bath and I'll get out of them. Mary Ann, find me a cigar. I haven't had a good smoke in a week!"

3

That year saw the turn. With the presidential re-election of Grover Cleveland, openly declaring himself a gold advocate, the free silver question came to a head. What could dam the flood of moonlit metal poring from the mountains – now $11,000,000 worth a year from Leadville alone? Eastern capitalists feared that the heavy purchases of silver under the Sherman Act would result in the replacement of the gold dollar by a depreciated silver dollar. Business tightened, commerical houses began to fail. A rush to redeem securities in gold brought down the national gold reserve to the danger point, $100,000,000. Then it dropped to $70,000,000.

Alarm spread throughout the world. Foreign governments stopped buying silver. The mints in far off India closed to silver. Within four days the price of silver plunged to sixty-two cents an ounce – less than half its set price – and then dropped to fifty cents. And when the Congress repealed the Sherman Act, Colorado's silver days were over. In Leadville, Creede, every silver camp in the Rockies, mines and smelters closed. Loose stones rattled down the dumps. Water filled the levels. The wind began to rip off planks from abandoned tool shanties and shaft houses. Silver Dollar

Tabor, multimillionaire and silver king, was toppled from his throne. All his vast holdings, his wild millions were swept away, leaving him a friendless, penniless man wandering the streets of Denver.

The silver reign was over; gold had come into its own; and the whole metallic West began to acclaim Stratton who had stepped upon Tabor's throne. "The King is dead! Long live the King!" And the thousands of men who were thrown out of work in the deserted silver camps swarmed to Cripple Creek to dig for gold. But prices were down, labor was cheap, and there were three men for every job. In the Mush and Milk House, the English Kitchen, and Monaco Buffet, at the bars of the Gold Dollar, Blue Bell, Becker and Nolan's, the Manitou Exchange, men tossed down their whisky straight and muttered surlily of shorter hours, more money, and a job for every man.

. . . Yet all this was but one facet of the problem confronting Rogier. There were other facts to be considered besides these of economics and politics, of climate and altitude, less discernible but subtly influencing the shape of his thought. Facts of geology, ore structure, and mine development. Facts of men, banking and finance. And of course there were his family, his horses, and his growing business.

"Ona," he asked one evening, drawing her aside, "how would you like a job? I'm so busy I never have time to make head or tail of those ledgers of mine. I can't stand to have Mooney or any other time-keeper messing in my business. Why don't you go down to the office every day and tend to them?"

"Why, all right, Daddy."

"I'll pay you a salary, of course. And you ought to have something to occupy your time," he added kindly.

Thereafter, with Ona trying to read his illegible great ledgers bursting with contracts and old check stubs, answering his mail, and keeping his accounts, Rogier went up to Cripple Creek more often. The family supposed he was prospecting for gold like everybody else. Rogier did not bother to deny it. A discovery was necessary to fulfill his purpose; that resolve born from his sense of alienation and directed against the implacable mystery of the Peak.

For the time at least he seemed like two different men. Day by day one of them went quietly, surely, about his work, visiting briefly with his family, pacing Akeepee in the evening; a man contemptuously indifferent to the craze for gold, the mad dreams of the riches and fame it might bring. The other sat alone in his office by night, his topographical maps and geological reports spread out on the drafting board, fingering a piece of ore. No one could have discerned if and where the two men fused. Yet at that contact between the logical, analytical man of his time, and that tormented spirit which knew no turning of the road to what he sought, but only the enigma formless and timeless that towered above him, might have been glimpsed the disturbing image at the end of his quest.

There was no hurry, none at all. He was as set to his course as a ship with rudder and sails lashed tight, waiting for the tide. Cripple Creek was having its share of labor troubles. Coxey's army was marching on Washington and 300 men from Cripple Creek commandeered a locomotive and a string of railroad cars to join them. The Strong Mine, just west of the Independence, was blown up. Fights and riots, and then a general strike called up the state militia.

Despite the strike – by which the miners won an eight-hour day – the production of the $200,000 Cow Pasture increased to $2,010,400 for the year, with the unheard-of average of more than three ounces of gold in every ton of rock shipped. Two railroads raced into Cripple Creek: the Midland Terminal connecting with the Colorado Midland at Divide to the north and the Florence and Cripple Creek connecting with the Denver and Rio Grande at Canyon City to the south. Dozens of mining companies were renting offices on Tejon Street in Little London. Every real-estator and land agent in town turned himself into a mining broker, and with hundreds of speculators and promoters stood along the sunny curbs of Pike's Peak Avenue in front of Rogier's office selling shares. The first thirty thousand shares of Virginia M were offered at ten cents each and sold out within an hour, Ona and Rogier hearing through the window the shouted announcement that the certificates hadn't been printed yet but would be as soon as possible. And men other than brokers swayed the price of shares as with a single wave of their hands, the stock of the Mutual instantly jumping from ten to twenty cents with the announcement that the noted wizard, Professor Kimball, had located the ore body. All day long Rogier and Ona were pestered with offerings until Rogier slammed the door behind a salesman and turned the key in the lock.

"But Daddy!" remonstrated Ona. "That was a nice young man with Anaconda stock. Yesterday when he came it was only a dime. Today it was thirty cents. Why —"

"Nonsense! Paper profits!" interrupted Rogier. "Keep those men out of here, Ona, or I'll throw you down the stairs with the next one who comes in here with a gold certificate!"

Shortly a Board of Trade and Colorado Springs Mining Stock Exchange was formed, with offices in his block, and was soon trading more shares than any other mining exchange in the world. This was more than Rogier could stand. "Ona, I won't have this business going on under my nose. If a man can't sit in peace in his own office he'd better get out!" He jammed his hat on his head and strutted out.

Ona sat staring at the closed door in shocked amazement; she had never known her father to betray such angry annoyance.

Rogier was as good as his word. Moving all his running horses to Denman's, he brought home a crew to wreck their stalls and build a huge two-story wooden shop in the barnyard. The upper story, with wide swing doors opening in back, was a loft for storing and seasoning green timber for use on his building jobs. The lower story, also one great room, served as a shop for his carpenters and cabinet makers. Along one side extended a work bench fitted with vises of all sizes, and supplemented with cabinets and racks to hold a vast collection of tools of all kinds. The north end, facing the house, he fitted up without a partition as his own office. The whole front was inset with glass panes slanted so there would be no glare. In front of this from wall to wall he constructed a high drafting table fully equipped with drawing boards, triangles, T-squares, scales, pencil racks, and blueprint cabinets. To the right were built his book-shelves, with a wood-stove near the corner for heat. Here was everything he needed: winches, reels, and concrete mixers stored under the wagon shed in the yard outside, spare lumber in the loft above, room for his carpenters and cabinet makers to work at the bench and a draftsman at the drafting table — and in the corner, close to his voluminous library, a private retreat where at night, undisturbed by the world outside, he could study his ore speci-mens, topographical maps, and geological reports of Pike's

Peak.

On the morning it was ready he went uptown to his office to make sure Ona knew how to instruct the packers and movers when they arrived. In silence he surveyed the room he had occupied for twenty years. From the window he had watched a frontier settlement grow into the famous Saratoga of the West with building after building of his own: Cutler Hall of The Colorado College, the Colorado Deaf and Blind School, the Elk Hotel, the downtown Gazette and Durkee buildings, churches, every school, houses galore. Down the wide, dirt avenue below he had watched covered wagons gathering to make up the trains which had crawled up Ute Pass on their way to Leadville. Here Sister Molly had come to him with a bunch of bluebells and worry about Tom; in the same chair, long afterward, Tom had sat in sullen defiance breathing whiskey fumes before vanishing forever from their sight. He remembered the boy Boné, white and shaking, but refusing obstinately to return to school; Mrs. White stopping by from Haekel's Boarding House; Bob coming to pay token installments on the Pest House; his own children playing with his pencils at the drafting board. This was the room in which he had heard the news of the Mount Pisgah Fiasco; the office young Stratton had given up to participate in the Yreteba Silver Lode bust, and to which he had returned seventeen years later with news of his discovery on Pike's Peak of the most fabulous gold mine in America. From his methodical, dedicated, simple work here he had fed a nest of hungry mouths – Martha and their three girls, Molly and Tom and their two boys, Mrs. White and Boné, to say nothing of Lida Peck, Lily Force, and his crews of workmen. A hundred trivial incidents leaped at him from the room, all impregnated with the smell of his innumerable cigars and with the one cloying dream that had held him there by night. To move away was like closing a door of his life behind him.

"Don't you hate to leave, Daddy, you've been here so long?" asked Ona.

"Places wear out like old clothes!" he answered brusquely. "Now be sure and have those movers pack those books carefully. I've had to send to Europe and India for some of them. Hear?"

"Daddy?"

"Yes?"

"Maybe I oughtn't to tell you now, but have you heard who's taking over your lease on this office? It's Mr. Stratton."

Rogier carefully bit the end off a cigar and lit it. "Sentimental nonsense, Ona! Haven't I just told you a man can't go back to old clothes he's outworn!" He turned on his heel and left without a backward look.

That night after everything had been unpacked and arranged to his satisfaction, Rogier settled down in what thereafter the family called "The Shop." It was indeed a workshop, an office, a *sanctum sanctorum*. But it was more than that. It was the cabin of a sea captain who from the charts on its wall piloted the course of his ship through an unknown sea. It was the tent of an army commander who laid out the strategy and tactics of a battle that was to be joined on a 10,000-foot-high field of a cloth of gold. And it was the dark interior of an unknown continent in which no explorer could find a trail marked by the milestones of the past. It was only by facing the infinite emptiness of the heavens above, and pinning his unshaken trust to that one star which in his despairing solitude he had chosen as his own, that a man could lay his path toward the destiny which was his alone. There could be no turning. And though he chose a star which glimmered and was gone, if it be lost behind the peak which undid his strength, still it remained for him to know that he had done what he had done – that his star had gleamed and faded, and rest in peace.

The lights in the house went out. Still Rogier sat there unstirring, staring at that massive granite-clothed adversary taking his measure in the darkness by timeless time. At last, curiously lightheaded, he blew out the lamp and went in to bed.

4

Hiney, ever since he had moved to Denver, came down occasionally to favor the family with his engaging presence. A tall, handsome Beau Brummel, he dressed nattily, spoke largely, and always carried crumbs of Sen-Sen in his pocket. In addition to moving stage props behind the curtain in the theater, it was understood that on due occasions he performed in front of it. His talents were many. He could mimic any noted actor, keep three balls in the air with one hand, and in the bathroom sang "She's Only a Bird in a Gilded Cage" to everyone's delight. Also in front of Nigger Bill, Rogier's stableman, he could dance with abandon – tap, soft shoe, and buck-and-wing. There was an air about him no one could deny.

He was a great favorite with Mary Ann, of course. In her teens and crazy after boys, she had learned how to overcome Mrs. Rogier's objections to her preposterous behavior. She had only to mention that a particular young man was a close friend of the well-known So-and-so in the North End, to secure permission to walk with him to church and to sit with him in the parlor that night till Mrs. Rogier's cough sounded from the head of the steps at ten o'clock. To the boys she alluded casually to "Colonel" Rogier, vaguely of a gold mine that was soon to erupt a fortune into the family's lap, and more specifically of cold chicken and a surreptitious drink of sherry after the family had gone to bed.

Ona could hardly blame either her or Sally Lee for catching at any straw that floated past the somber house on Shook's Run. They had been reared in that creaking structure as if it had been a house of glass through which any North Ender could observe their every move. Mrs. Rogier had watched over them like a hawk. There was no playing with ambiguous children down along the creek. They were too dirty, too illiterate, or just too "common" for a Rogier to be contaminated by their mere human frailities. Just what being a Rogier implied the girls never found out. It always enveloped them in a mysterious aura which they hardly dared to disturb with even a sudden sneeze. Restrained from participating in most school parties, they acted self-consciously their roles of lonely and miserable but perfect little snobs. Sometime the world would unfold to them like a flower, ripen into a fruit to be plucked only by her who was a Rogier and could prove it to high heaven with a pair of twin toes.

It seemed quite natural to Mary Ann then, giddy as she was, that Hiney wanted her to visit him for a few days. She was to come right away, tomorrow! His letter she did not read. It had been addressed to Rogier, as a matter of fact; but as he was up at Cripple Creek it had seemed appropriate for Mrs. Rogier and Ona to open it. The message was brief. Hiney was in trouble. He asked Rogier to send him a bank draft immediately, not by mail but by Mary Ann, in a sealed envelope. The two women debated the mystery at length. Mrs. Rogier was not one to send an innocent girl alone on her first train trip to a large city; Rogier could settle the matter when he returned.

"But Mother, Hiney can't wait. He's in trouble!" argued Ona.

"We have no money," wailed Mrs. Rogier.

"Get her ready," said Ona decisively. "I attend to Daddy's payroll and I'll make out the draft."

The next morning after breakfast Mrs. Rogier checked the contents of Mary Ann's suitcase, looked her over carefully to see that even her handkerchief was folded in place, and then mysteriously crooked her finger as she went upstairs. Mary Ann followed her into the bathroom and watched her mother lock the door.

Whenever Mrs. Rogier desired to lecture or impart important news to any member of the family, it was the bathroom that offered sanctuary. These "bathroom talks" were an institution holy and ceremonious as a talk with the pastor of the church or a meeting of a board of directors, and one emerged from them an enlightened and chastened spirit. Finally the door was unlocked and Mary Ann came out, a sealed envelope pinned to her underwear, like a messenger entrusted with all the secrets of state. Ona took her to the depot and put her on the train.

Had Mary Ann's been a mature mind able to look back through Hiney's life to his childhood fall from a horse, her reflections would have overshadowed every mile of the journey to Denver. But she had never heard of his queer lapses of memory, and was as blissfully ignorant of his last escapade as the rest of the family.

It had happened a couple of years before. Hiney and several of his cronies had emerged one night from the bar next to the Opera House. Strutting under silk top hats and holding themselves up with light Malacca canes, they hailed a cab. They were all quite drunk.

As he stepped into the cab, Hiney felt the thing happen as it had happened a dozen times before. His life, his whole past, seemed instantly obliterated. Sometimes a drink seemed to do the trick, a sudden jar, or more often nothing. It was as if an unseen hand reached into his head and jerked the switch that controlled his memory. He would find himself on a street car, in a barber's chair, or walking down a street not knowing who he was or where he was going. There was nothing to do but slink into a hotel and wait until time and mind again began to tick within him.

Now, adjusting the silk muffler around his throat, he hiccoughed and looked at the faces of his companions as if he had never seen them before. Beyond Hop Alley the cab drew up with a sudden halt as one of the men yelled and opened the door. A woman was crossing the road under the arc-light with a big bundle of washing. The men gathered around her, arguing who should carry the bundle home for her. The lot fell to Hiney. Heaving the bundle to his shoulder and leading the washwoman by the hand, Hiney set off with his companions shouting and trouping behind. Like a decrepit hearse the cab brought up the rear, the horse's hoofs breaking the spasmodic silence with steady clicks.

The woman lived in a wooden shack overflowing with children.

Once the lamp was lit, the gentlemen, hearts touched by the squalor, began another argument. Which one of them would oblige and become the widow washwomen's husband?" "Wantcher sh'd marry the lady?" queried Hiney, wavering on his long thin legs. "Sure, b'glad to!"

His companions howled approbation. "A perfect gemmleman – s'wat ch'ar Hiney!" The lady, nothing loath to secure a husband in a silk top-hat at a moment's notice in the dead of night, agreed heartily. The cab was dispatched for a preacher as fast as the horse could travel. In an hour Hiney was a married man. He was almost out; the men laid him on the bed with two small children, covering that miraculously grown family with a rag rug. It had been a perfect evening and they left singing an imperfect bridal chorus.

After spending two days in his bride's shack Hiney's memory returned. Neither he nor his companions had a single doubt that the marriage would be annulled the minute Hiney raised enough money to pay a lawyer's fee. The annulment was refused. Hiney was horrified. The girl Margaret who had got him out of jail after the Brown Palace episode was heartbroken; they had been planning to get married.

The washwoman was one of those queer oddities of human nature that could not be explained. Despite two grown sons who never worked and a small girl, she had a mania for adopting babies. When they had grown to be seven or eight years old she left them at an orphan's home or thrust them out upon the street. There were always two or three new ones in the squalorous shanty and for them she washed late into the nights. She was obdurate to Hiney's appeals for a divorce and had taken a six months' old baby to court, swearing that Hiney was its father and insisting on his support. She got it. For two years Hiney lived in a hell of despair, moving from one rooming house to another as fast as the family or the court learned his whereabouts. The woman's two grown sons followed him relentlessly. It took all the money Hiney earned to satisfy their insatiable demands. One night when he came home from his work at the theater he found that they had broken into his room. The next morning, after talking with Margaret, he had sent a letter home asking for a bank draft and Mary Ann.

This was the Beau Brummel Hiney with Sen-Sen in his pockets and "She Was Only a Bird in a Gilded Cage" on his lips Mary Ann was on her way to visit.

When she got off the train Hiney was not waiting on the platform. Instead, a woman came up to her smiling, and placing an arm across her shoulders, said, "I just know you're Mary Ann! My name's Margaret and I'm a friend of Hiney's. He's waiting for us across town."

Taking a street car, they rode to an ugly little street and went in an ugly little house. On the top floor Margaret got out a key and unlocked a door. The room was ugly too: it had a chipped iron bed and old dresser, even a hole in a threadbare carpet. "I've got to hurry to work now, but Hiney will be here in fifteen minutes," Margaret told her. "Tonight we're all going to the Opera House and eat supper in a fine restaurant. You're a big girl. You'll understand what Hiney tells you, I can see that. You're not afraid to wait here a little bit, are you?"

Mary Ann rubbed her new shoes together and nodded; a lump in her throat prevented her from speaking. For an hour after Margaret had gone she sat stiffly on the bed, thinking of the pretty dresses in her suitcase, listening for steps coming up the dark stairway, for a voice to tell her she was dreaming a tawdry dream.

At last it came: the clatter of a key in the lock, the bang of the opened door. It was Hiney all right – all dressed up like a Thanksgiving turkey, with a wide grin and a red flower in his buttonhole. "How-d'doodle!" he yelled, jumping on the bed to kiss her. Mary Ann felt better. They talked about the family, then she asked about Margaret and why they were here instead of in a nice big hotel like she expected. Hiney rose to draw down the window shades a bit more. Then suddenly he jumped up in the air and clicked the heels of his yellow shoes together three times before landing. It was a trick he had learned from actors in the theater, he said laughing fit to kill.

"You didn't think I lived in this dirty old house, did you? With this raggedy old carpet? Land sakes alive – look here!" He yanked open all the drawers in the tarnished dresser. "Empty, every one of them! Why? Because we're going to act parts in a mystery play all the time you're here. What do you think of that?" He paused dramatically. "No use of your coming up here just to sit and talk. That would be dull as Little London! The fun of it's the mystery. You can't ask questions. Just play your part."

"But what do I have to do, Hiney?"

"Practically nothing," he assured her, pulling a key out of his pocket with a tag on which was written the address of the rooming house they sat in. "Just suppose we're walking down the street and all of a sudden I run off and leave you. Or something like that. You just take this key, ask a man what streetcar to take and the conductor to let you off. Then you come here and unlock the door."

"What'll I do then?"

Hiney was suddenly very serious. "You brought something for me?"

"It's in an envelope pinned to my underwear, Hiney."

"The bathroom's down the hall. Take it out and bring it back to me."

When she came back he locked the door behind her and put his finger to his lips. "Here's the big secret!" He pulled back the covers on the bed, lifted the mattress. Underneath was a fat manilla envelope to which he added the envelope Mary Ann had brought. "Probably I won't ever come here again. But one of these times, when Margaret or I send you, you come here the way I told you and bring back these envelopes, both of them. Understand?" His face set in a hard gray mask as his eyes bored into her. "You'll remember? Don't say a word to anyone about it. And don't lose that key!"

Mary Ann was suddenly frightened. "It's all too mysterious and scary, Hiney. I brought my Sunday dress and new shoes, and I'd rather go to the Opera House and eat supper at a restaurant and all that."

Immediately he put his arms around her. "You little goose! Afraid to have a single adventure without Ona holding you by the hand!"

"I'm not either, Hiney!"

Lying on the bed together, they talked about Akeepee and the gold mine Rogier was going to find while Hiney blew smoke rings from his cigarette. Then the room began to get dark and it was time to go after Margaret.

All her life Mary Ann was to remember every detail of her strange visit to Hiney. The first night was a glorious celebration of her arrival. They had supper in the Manhattan Restaurant on Larimer Street where Hiney ordered her a lobster which she had never tasted before and everything else she wanted. Margaret was dressed up her prettiest in white, wearing long amethyst earrings, watching every man who came in through the frosted glass doors. "I wonder if we've been wise to come here tonight," she asked quietly. Hiney patted her hand. "Of course. They'd never expect me here of all places. And we may never see it again."

In the Tabor Grand afterward they sat way back in a box where Hiney could tell Mary Ann about the actors and actresses, all of whom he knew by their first names. Walking out, Hiney stopped short as if he saw a ghost in the lobby. Immediately they turned around, going backstage where he introduced Mary Ann to the actors in their dressing rooms. Then they slipped out into the alley and up the street to Mary Ann's hotel room. It was a wonderful room with pictures of stage people, wine lists and menus tacked on the walls. Hiney's clothes were in it, but a few minutes after Margaret left he went to sleep somewhere else. It was a glorious nght, but it was not repeated.

The following two nights Hiney put her in different hotels as Margaret insisted. "I wish I could have her with me, but we can't take chances," she told Hiney. "We've got to make it Saturday morning."

In the daytime Hiney took her to a matinee or out to the park, or Margaret to stores and museums. But never together. And each one of them was always nervously watching everyone around them. The nights alone made her nervous too. She thought longingly of her bed at home. The squeaky steps of the Kadles would never seem mysterious after Hiney's and Margaret's queer behavior: taking her to a different hotel every night and suddenly leaving her as they walked along the street, only to show up later without a word.

Mary Ann was relieved when on Saturday morning Hiney took her to the depot. He carried two suitcases besides her own. It was long before train time, but he was on pins and needles and kept looking at his watch so often Mary Ann was afraid he'd wear it out. At last a woman in a big hat and veil sat down beside them. Hiney without a word got up and left.

"Don't be nervous and don't turn around," the woman said after a time, raising her veil a trifle. Mary Ann recognized Margaret's voice. "That big man in a derby hat is looking for Hiney," she went on. "Now do just as I say. Ride on the street car to that rooming house I first took you to. Remember the big secret? You have the key to the room. Get the envelopes under the mattress and hurry back. If we don't happen to be here, take the train and give the envelopes to your father at home. Are you sure you understand? Sure, Mary Ann? Now get up and buy a package of chewing gum. And then walk out very slowly. And don't say a word to anyone till you get back. Go on now, dear!"

Mary Ann did as she was told. On the street car she sat looking from the tag on her key to every street she passed. She had not returned to that tawdry rooming house since, and was afraid she had taken the wrong car. Finally the conductor called out the street. A few doors from the corner she recognized the house. Running up the stairs she opened the door to the barren room. Queerly frightened, she lifted the mattress, took out the fat and slim manilla envelopes, and hid them in her dress. Then she ran out of the room and down the steps.

On the street car a new fear attacked her – Hiney and Margaret wouldn't be at the depot and her train would go off without her. When she arrived in the big waiting room, a man was calling out her train and Margaret was standing at the gate. "Did you get it?" she asked anxiously.

"Yes," said Mary Ann, pulling the envelopes out from her bosom and giving them to her.

Margaret let out a sigh. "Oh, if Hiney only comes in time!"

A minute later he sauntered up. His sleeve was torn and he had a bruise on his cheek, but he was grinning like a cat. "How do you do, folks! Taking a little train ride this morning?"

"Thank God!" breathed Margaret. "Mary Ann got the money and the papers. How lucky you showed her where they were. Neither one of us could have got back for them."

The conductor was yelling "All aboard!" now. Hiney and Margaret took her to the train and boosted her suitcase to the vestibule, but they kept standing there with the other suitcases Hiney had brought. He kissed her. "Remember me, Mary Ann. I'll thank you all my life. And give this letter to your father. He'll understand."

There were tears in Margaret's eyes as she kissed her too. "I love you too, Mary Ann. Almost as much as Hiney."

As the train pulled out Mary Ann could see them crossing the platform to another train. Where it went she never knew.

5

Hiney's strange disappearance or elopement with Margaret was a mystery to the family, compounded by Mary Ann's exorbitant and melodramatic tales. Still he was one of the family even if he were a little strange, and Ona missed him. Not as much as she missed Boné who had gone to San Francisco with Lockhardt. She thought of Lockhardt impeccably dressed in his white shirt and dark worsted jacket, the yellow candlelight striking white fire from the big diamond on his finger as he pounded the piano keys so forcibly that it set atremble the tumbler of whisky above his bent head. Now he had left Indian Country despite his health, as he had to; for in the end we reject everything we are unsuited to assimilate, however much we may admire it. Back to sit at his Baby Grand, looking down at the misty gray bay, eating the best euisine of every race in the world, and attending operas and symphonies. But what was Boné doing with him? Writing music that Lockhardt was going to have published. Still Ona worried about him as she did not worry about Hiney.

Rooted in the passionless stability of the big house and the irritating confusion of Rogier's business records, Ona often looked back with nostalgia to her stay on the Reservation. Shadows of clouds in the sunshine, distant jutting mesas flaming red at dawn, dark faces and soft voices, the sound of drums across the San Juan – it all came back to her with that remote and inconsequential trading post maintained in austere dignity by Bruce and the Vrain Girls.

She was reminded of it, curiously, by her first sight of the family's new roomer. Or rather Sally Lee's, for she had persuaded Rogier to let her rent her room when he had refused to increase her allowance. The new roomer had moved in last night, and Mrs. Rogier had invited him for supper this evening. Both Sally Lee and Mary Ann were in the kitchen helping Lida when Ona came in from the shop. In the dining room they had set the table, lit candles and lamps. How exciting it was! A new man in the house! Ona walked on out to the front porch and sat down beside ailing Mrs. White.

"Has the roomer come home yet?" she asked.

"Reckon not or Marthy would be buzzin' around him like a fly over a sorghum barrel."

"You don't like him?"

"Humph. One look was enough to tell me he's a Jew or a foreigner of some kind. Different."

In a few moments Mrs. Rogier came out and seated herself primly. "I do hope Mr. Cable comes soon and that Daddy's not late again. Baked ham dries out fast, and I allowed Lida to use brandy in the cider."

The sun had dropped behind Pike's Peak and dusk was blurring the branches of the lilac. Down along Shook's Run the crickets were beginning a faint but strident chorus only to be interrupted by the sound of soft footsteps coming down the walk. "Here he comes," murmured Mrs. Rogier.

Ona turned her head to see the figure of Jonathan Cable turning in the yard. What struck her immediately, before she could clearly distinguish his face, was the sinuous litheness of his walk. An inch under six feet, his slender body gave out the impression of a soft sensuousness wrapped in iron nerves. Before she could rise, his foot was on the step and she was looking up at a pair of large brown eyes and an arching Roman nose set into a high-cheekboned swarthy face.

For fifteen minutes Mrs. Rogier kept him on the porch. She had put on her Sunday dress of gray and black and chatted aimlessly. Cable was pleasant but silent, and Ona was relieved when they went in to table. In the light she was impressed by the red-brown color of his face, a swarthiness deeper than weather exposure. Even his wrists showed an even sepia whenever his starched white cuffs crawled up his coat sleeves. From his big nose one might admit Mrs. White's implication of Jewish blood. But to Ona his hair, every separate strand, gave him away. It was Indian, straight and black, without kink or sheen, as heavy and coarse as a horse's mane.

Rogier strode in and sat down. "Hello Cable! How did the first night go in your new room?"

"It's going to be fine, I'm sure," replied Cable cheerfully.

"I just wondered if the Kadles walking around all night kept you awake." Rogier grinned at the girls, avoiding Mrs. Rogier's face.

"I did hear someone walking up and down the stairs. I hope none of you was sick." He looked from face to face as a restrained titter ran around the table.

"No indeed," went on Rogier, ignoring Mrs. Rogier's pinch under the table. "It was just a couple of white-bearded old fellows who have been dead for fifteen years or so, but who had to investigate the new occupant of your room. The girls will tell you about them. They're old friends by now."

Cable's face had set darkly as if he were being made fun of, but with the girls' giggling explanations he grinned humorously.

"And how was Little Man, Daddy?" asked Mrs. Rogier, watching him slice the ham. "Do you think he'll ever beat his mother's time of – wasn't it three minutes?"

"Three minutes!" ejaculated Sally Lee with horrified amazement. "Why, Akeepee could pull that old lumber wagon of Daddy's around the track in less than three minutes! Two-sixteen for the mile is more like it!"

Mrs. Rogier smiled apologetically at Cable. "We have so many lovely race horses I just can't remember all the times they make."

"Maybe you can give me some information about Cripple Creek, Mr. Rogier?" asked Cable. "I hear you're a mine owner."

"I'm not," Rogier answered curtly," but tomorrow I'll give you what information I have. Is that what brought you here?"

"I've got a third interest in a claim on Big Bull."

Mary Ann exploded a giggle into her napkin.

"Mary Ann! The very idea! Get up this minute!" ordered Mrs. Rogier.

Mary Ann, shamefacedly rising, confessed the plausible cause of her guilt. "The very minute Mr. Cable mentioned Bull Hill, why Bull Hill pinched me on the leg!" She stooped and lifted up a puppy.

"Well, you just take him out of here and don't come back till you can sit up in your chair quiet like a lady!" Turning to Cable, Mrs. Rogier explained with profuse apologies. "You see, Daddy found that little puppy near Bull Hill and brought him home. That's why we named him Bull Hill. Once Daddy brought the children down a fawn – when everybody had a pet fawn in the yard."

Rogier interrupted. "Big Bull and Bull Hill aren't the same at all. I can't say I'm too impressed with the showings around you, Cable, however highly they're touted. But I'm no mining man."

Cable spread his hands and smiled. "The claim's only a ten-foot hole yet. I hope there's something in it or I'll be stone broke."

The almost childish simplicity and outspoken honesty of this dark and stern looking man nonplussed every Rogier around the table, yet instantly drew them to him.

"You have no experience in mining?" asked Rogier with a sympathetic grin.

"None. A bit of Indian blood has always kept me out on the long grass plains and prairies. I know nothing about these mountains."

This confirmation of her intuition aroused in Ona a quick glow of satisfaction. It was broken by Mrs. White who flung down her napkin and pushed back her chair.

"Mother! Wait for dessert," remonstrated Mrs. Rogier. "It's tapioca and pineapple with whipped cream."

"It's always tapioca!" With a sharp look at Cable, she left the room.

The two men, with Ona listening beside them, continued to sit over their coffee long after the others had left the table. Mrs. Rogier, peering from the china closet, was infuriated by the sight of Rogier, left arm resting on the table where he had pushed back his dishes, calmly smoking his cigar, and holding Cable like a fly in a web. Mining was all very well if it would bring a gold mine into the family, but to hear talk of it night and day, at every meal, was more than she could stand.

In a few minutes Ona silently left the two men and went out on the porch. Cable's glance followed her as she left the room, and after awhile he followed her. In the darkness her white dress was a pale splotch on the front steps. The scratch of a match and its quick yellow flare illumining his face as he lit his pipe aroused her. "Oh, hello. Sit down if you want to."

"Don't you want me to bring you a wrap? This mountain air gets cold the minute the sun goes down. Maybe I should have said 'fetch'. All the family says that."

Ona laughed. "Well, go fetch my scarf then if that makes you feel better!" How observant and sensitive was this man who looked so sharp and stubborn!

Cable returned, sprawling down on the steps beside her.

"What do you think of our town by now?" she asked.

Cable inclined his head toward the pale splotch of Pike's Peak's snowy cone against the sky. "Can't get used to these mountains sticking up like a wall. I like open country. Prairie country with the grass bending in the wind as far as you can see. Makes me feel free."

How much Indian blood he had, what tribe it had come from, and how, he did not say. But it was there: in his appearance, his small feet which she now noticed for the first time, his reactions – and his reticence. He had been born in a large family which lived on a wooded quarter-section of land on the Iowa-Missouri border. Poor farmers, none of them had obtained much of an education. Cable had made the most of his opportunities in the small village nearby. Beginning work after school as a printer's devil on the weekly newspaper, he had learned with stubborn thoroughness to set type, write simple accounts of the happenings for miles around, and to balance the books – a literacy, interest in people, and rudimentary business education he could not have obtained had he remained in school. When his step-father died Cable struck out on his own, falling in with an Indian trader on the Great Plains. Here he came into his own. Chivington's massacre had broken the power of the two tribes which had claimed by right of treaty most of the plains west of the Rockies. Sent to a Reservation in Oklahoma, bands of them still kept coming back to hunt, trade, and conduct their ceremonies – the same bands, thought Ona, that she had seen as a child. From the trader, Cable learned to speak Cheyenne fluently and Arapaho haltingly, and often stayed in their encampment of tepees. If something in his nature rose up to meet them, it also set him apart from the increasing settlers and homesteaders who still held that the only good Indian was a dead Indian. As the bands stopped coming, Cable and a man named Grimes opened a general merchandising store on the Colorado-Kansas line. It was here that the Cripple Creek tide had caught him up. Grimes' brother had staked a claim on Big Bull, but needed a stake to develop it. So Cable and his partner had sold their store and come to work the mine with him.

"It looks like mining will be an expensive business," ended Cable. "We're thinking of opening a store here in town so we can take turns running it while the other two work the mine."

"What kind of a store?" asked Ona.

"My partners want a men's clothing store."

Ona could not imagine Cable selling neckties behind a counter. "Well, Little London's an unusual town. You should learn what it's like before you make up your mind."

Cable puffed silently at his pipe before answering. "I wonder – if I get a horse and rig from uptown will you drive around with me sometime?"

"Some afternoon when I don't have too much work I will." In the darkness she smiled. With a stable of horses out at Denman's, she was going in a rented rig. What would her mother think of that?

As she went upstairs to bed, she met Mrs. White in the hall wearing a sulky frown. "What's the trouble?" Ona asked.

"A red niggah in the house!"

Ona shrugged and went into her room. How old and cantankerous her grandmother was getting!

A few days later Ona went on a drive with Cable. She enjoyed it; she had not realized how Little London had blossomed under the influx of Cripple Creek gold. The electric street cars which had replaced the horse cars ran in all directions and were crowded with people. "Fifteen thousand people in town now," Ona told him "and three railroad lines bringing more every day. The widest streets of any town in the country. Here. Turn up Cascade." The wide avenue was lovely, lined with shade trees on each side, and another double line flanking the bridle path in the center. Big brownstone houses stood on each side, set back in wide lawns smooth as velvet. A block west, beginning at the campus of The Colorado College and running north, ran Millionaires' Row.

"It's called that because here's where all the Cripple Creek millionaires are building their mansions. Its real name is Wood Avenue. I suppose it's named for somebody in the Woods family – the three Woods brothers who've got control of about sixty mines in the district, established the town of Victor, and now are building a big hotel in the middle of it. Now stop a minute!" Cable obediently pulled back his reins. "Here you are," went on Ona. "The show-place of all the mansions: 1315 Wood Avenue. That's all you have to say in town. Everybody knows it belongs to James Burns the plumber, one of the three men who discovered the Portland, the Queen of the district, just above the Independence, the King. Stratton helped them settle twenty-seven lawsuits and consolidated all the thirty-seven mines into one company. Lordy knows how many millions it'll produce!"

"I don't know that a big mansion like this can come out of the little hole we've got," said Cable dubiously, turning back.

Ona laughed. "You can see how foolish Mother is for wanting a house up here in the North End. Poor thing! She just doesn't realize how much money it would cost. So we just let her talk."

They drove west to the mesa and up to the mouth of Queen's Canyon where Ona pointed out the solitary munificence of Palmer's castle, Glen Eyrie. "General Palmer, the one who founded Little London and built the Denver and Rio Grande Railroad. Just to show you a man can become rich on something besides Cripple Creek gold. But nobody envies him. His wife left him and he lives there all alone – always riding around on his horse in an English tweed jacket and boots. A stone man on a stone horse."

Cable and his two partners found a likely space on Tejon Street for their new store, which Cable showed to Ona. The location, she thought, was good; but the narrow room seemed too small, squeezed between two office buildings. Nevertheless Cable, with the help of two carpenters, was busy at work putting up a partition between a salesroom and a storeroom. Often after work in the late fall afternoons he took Ona for more drives.

One afternoon they drove to the lower slopes of Cheyenne Mountain southwest of town. Here in front of Cheyenne Lake rose an elegantly beautiful, three-storied building with long verandas flanked by gracious white pillars. "The Broadmoore Casino!" explained Ona proudly. "Built by Count Pourtales of Prussia. They say the dining rooms are elegant and the French chef who prepares the meals was brought from Delmonico's in New York. I've seen Rosner's Band which plays there. Hungarians and Austrians dressed up in gorgeous uniforms – white trousers and blue coats trimmed with gold. Up till a few years ago one out of every ten people here was a Britisher. But now Little London's becoming a cosmopolitan spa, the Saratoga of the West, with Cripple Creek just around the corner!"

"And a mile straight up!" Cable reminded her, glancing up at the wall of mountains rising above them.

How pleasant it was to drive in a rented rig with this dark, silent, and unaffected man. Over to the mineral springs in Manitou, through the queerly eroded red sandstone and white limestone area known as the Garden of the Gods, and up North and South Cheyenne Canyon along winding carriage roads beside tumbling white-water streams.

Early in December, Cable showed Ona the new haberdashery shop. The partition between storeroom and salesroom had been erected. Furnishings and display cases had been installed and sales goods were coming in.

"We've opened the New Moon in Cripple Creek," he explained. "It's not much shakes as a curb mine and our stake is exhausted. But its first showings are good. Let's hope the shop will carry the mine through the winter."

Then, without telling Ona where he was going, he swung over the mesa to the encampment of the Utes who were still permitted to pitch their lodges here for a few months each year. Leaving the rig, they walked slowly into the ring of smoke-gray tepees. How tawdry it seemed after Glen Eyrie, the Broadmoore Casino, and Burns' mansion. Old men with faces of dark wrinkled leather were squatting silently in front of their lodges. Half-naked children crawled about in the dirt. Boys were trying to mount shaggy, broomtailed ponies and being pitched to the ground. An old woman was hacking at a fresh red carcass covered with flies. The whole place seemed permeated with a smell compounded of smoke, refuse, and urine-soaked earth.

Cable seemed not to mind at all. In his derby hat and halfboots, always carefully polished although he sometimes neglected his well-worn suit, he was walking down the lanes thoroughly enjoying himself. Abruptly he halted. An old Ute woman with a maimed arm had burst out of a tepee rubbing the tears out of her smoke-filled eyes. Cable, without a word, walked around to the side. Ona was casually familiar with these lodges or tepees, simply skins stretched over a conical framework of poles with an opening at the high, pointed apex for the smoke to escape. She had never noticed on the outside an inclined pole attached at the top to a protruding, triangular wing or fin. As she watched him, Cable jerked loose the bottom end of the pole imbedded in the ground and moved it several feet around the circular edge. As he did so, the triangular wing swung with him like a rudder. For a moment he stood looking up at it, testing the wind. Then he imbedded the end of the pole firmly in the ground again.

The actions of this white man in a derby and shined boots drew the lounging Utes around him. Cable got up, dusted his knees, and looked through the doorway. Ona and the old woman peeked in beside him. The smoke from the open fire was rising in an unbroken column through the opening at the top. All the Utes were now jabbering and gesticulating, talking to Cable. Unable to understand them, he simply grinned and with the forefinger and middle finger of his right hand made the rapid gesture of slashing the inside of his left wrist. The old men's leathery faces broke into grins of surprise and approbation. The woman patted him with her maimed arm.

In a few minutes Cable took Ona by the arm and they walked back to the rig. "That dew-flap had to be adjusted to catch the draft," he said casually.

"What did that funny movement of your hand mean?"

"Oh, just Cheyenne in sign language."

His casual, terse comments, the whole incident, momentarily

confused her. She had got so used to him she had forgotten how different he was. And now suddenly he had slipped away from her, like a cake of soap, into a different world.

"You know, I don't think I'd mention to grandmother tonight that we drove out to see those Utes. She – "

Instantly she wished she'd bitten off her tongue instead. But Cable did not reply. As they drove into town he said quietly, "I'm leaving for the mountains tomorrow. I've been lucky, staying here to work on the shop so long. But now it's my turn to work in the mine for awhile."

"Be sure to come down for Christmas," replied Ona warmly. "There'll be room for you here, though not for the Grimes."

Cable, a few weeks before, had brought his two partners to meet the family. They were big men, gruff and hearty and good-natured, but somehow they did not seem to fit into the household. Although neither requested it, Ona rather suspected that they wanted to occupy Cable's room during their turns of work in Little London. Logical as was her assumption, Mrs. Rogier scotched the idea the minute they walked out the door. "I do hope they don't think we're running a boarding house for every Tom, Dick, and Harry. Jonathan is all right, but – "

"No, of course," answered Cable. "As a matter of fact they have a good friend in Colorado City who's going to bunk them whenever they're in town. I'm the lucky one. Both your mother and Sally Lee said they'd save my room so I'd have a place to come back to anytime."

Ona felt relieved, a little glad really.

6

Two miles above tidewater in its amphitheater of innumerable hills, Cripple Creek blinked through the snow-flecked dusk of a late December storm.

Since early morning the gaunt ridges had lain beclouded in gloom as if the wind had snuffed out the lighted taper behind the leaden skies. Dropping heavily, filling the canyons with a warm wet mist, and trailing albuminous streamers through the somber pine slopes, the clouds just past noon had snagged upon the rocks. At first slowly fluttering to earth like the feathers of a wild goose, the snow fell faster until the skies were driving white. The dark forested ridges, the bare mountain tops were enwrapped steadily until all the hills were as anonymous as a group of women in white furs. And still the storm rushed slantwise, smothering the earth with snow. Seen from one of the hills at dusk the yellow lights along Bennett Avenue looked like a row of portholes in a ship laboring through a heavy sea. The whole town wallowed in a trough of drifts. For a moment the storm subsided, and the windows of Becker and Nolan's, the Gold Dollar, and other saloons glowed steamy yellow behind the frosted spume sticking to the panes. Then the wind began again, and like a ship resuming its crawl between the foamy crests of two waves, the town appeared to move forward through its white drifts as if uneasy of coming to grief on Pike's Peak's granite reefs.

Near ten o'clock the wind let up. Within an hour the skies were drained of snow. A silver moon polished smooth as ivory by the storm wore through the sky above Gold Hill. In the luminescence of a new white world Cripple Creek stirred and unbuttoned. Men got busy and shoveled their way to freedom – at least to the nearest saloon. The Pueblo House, the Red Elk, and the Palace Hotel, the English Kitchen and the Mush and Milk House, every store opened its doors.

Towards midnight the skies hardened to the ashy gray of new-cut steel. The night grew so clear and cold a man could hear across town the squeak of his partner's boots in the snow. A mile down on the plains it was still snowing. But here above timberline and close to the gritty brilliant stars, men felt the stir of a new day as the world clicked on its hinges. In a ravine on Crystal Hill a wolf howled waveringly. A group of men, tipsy on the walk, yowled back before turning into the Mint Saloon. Inside, the bar was wild with shouts. It was twelve o'clock, December 31, and Cripple Creek had finished, was beginning, another year.

That area of barren hills which had jumped upon the map in a scant six months as a $200,000 Cow Pasture, had increased its production of gold tenfold to $2,010,400, tripled this, and then doubled it until in the year just ended the production had reached the colossal amount of $12,000,000. And that was nothing compared to what it would do! Sir Morton Frewer, the English bimetallist, said so in an article in the *Great Divide*. He stated that in 1887 when gold was discovered in Johannesburg, South Africa, London experts reported that the formation at the Witwatersrandt gold field was unfavorable for gold production. The Rothschilds refused to pay £20,000 sterling for the Randt gold quartz reef. Yet its production had increased from 13,000 ounces of gold per month in 1887 to 140,000 ounces per month in 1894 – in six years placing the Dutch republic at the head of the gold producing countries of the world. But at the rate Cripple Creek was developing, Sir Frewer believed it would catch up and surpass the record of Johannesburg.

"Hell, yes!" the talk ran in the saloons. "The Independence is already the marvel of the mining world. It's not a mine. It's a blooming bank. You heard about that chamber Stratton hit and called the Bull Pen? The stuff assayed as high as $100 a pound. Why, the ore they're shipping out of it without sorting returns $450 to the ton. And that mineral bank is yielding over $120,000 a month!"

A mile below, Rogier sat in his shop in Little London. There was some kind of a New Year's Eve party going on in the house, with Ona and Cable chaperoning the girls and their guests. Every light in the house was on, the whole place vibrated with noise. To escape the confusion Rogier had fled to his shop out in back. Here, seated at the long drafting table with his back to the hot stove, he bent over his maps and reports of the Cripple Creek district.

There had been another one of those unbelievable strikes that was spreading the fame of the Pike's Peak district. The three Woods brothers who had laid out the new town of Victor, east of Cripple Creek, had drawn elaborate plans for their Victor Hotel to be located in the center of town. Contracts were let and excavations were being made for the foundations when a curious assayer scooped up a few samples of loose dirt. They assayed rich in gold. The blueprints for the hotel were jubilantly town up and a large shaft house was erected on the spot instead, the gallows frame being sixty-five feet high on a stone base. Below it the vein, eight feet wide and averaging $46 to the ton, ran under the town itself. Victor was no longer merely a town of 6,000 people, but the surface of an immense mine with a mile of underground workings already, and beginning its average production of $1,000,000 a year. The Gold Coin!

Its location pleased Rogier. For months on end he had been patiently marking on his map the locations of new mines as they were reported. It was a large map thumbtacked to a soft pine drawing board propped up before him. Embracing the area from the western edge of Long Hungry Gulch to Cow Mountain on the east, and from Tenderfoot Hill southward to Big Bull, it topographically outlined with their elevations every hill, gulch, and stream. The map had become fly-specked with dots which, scrutinized more closely, resolved into fine inked squares which located shafts, triangular wedges which designated tunnels, and tiny bars with vertical cross-cuts to mark the locations of steam hoists. With this map before him, and remembering the topography of the district more clearly than any face in his family, Rogier was beginning to arrive at the conclusion on which he was to base his secret plans.

The Cripple Creek gold belt, as it was first known, comprised an area about eleven miles square. Gradually the thousands of men prospecting the hills and gulches drew in to a section roughly seven by eight miles in extent. Then it became evident that most of the gold deposits lay in a small area of some six square miles. Nothing like it had ever been known: an area so small and so confoundingly rich. Geologists could explain it only by the theory that the district occupied the floor of an extinct volcano whose superstructure had been removed by erosion, leaving Pike's Peak as its culminating point. The basic country rock was Pike's Peak Granite whose pinkish color was imparted to it by feldspar, and which was assumed to have formed the bed of an ancient sea which received the sediments now composing the sandstones of the Garden of the Gods a mile below.

During the great eruption a mass of volcanic material had burst through the granite in an aqueo-igneous condition. Cooling, solidification, and contraction followed, resulting in the formation of fissures. Hot water ascended with great velocity from the depths of the volcano, and nearing the surface spread slowly through the fissures. As it stagnated, deposition and chemical action changed the composition of the solution and gold ore was precipitated. The principal volcanic rock was andesite breccia, more commonly known as porphyry from its deep purple color.

The ore itself was something of an enigma. As Rogier remembered, one of the first carloads which Stratton had shipped to a Denver smelter had been held as waste, the officials believing a load of ballast had been sent by mistake. The ores were tellurides, calaverite, and sylvanite, which had been found in Transylvania but which were little known in America – the reason, of course, why prospectors had passed over the district for so many years without recognizing it.

This deposition theory, held by the most noted Geological Survey engineers and generally accepted, had bothered Rogier. It maintained that precipitation had taken place abundantly near the surface but very sparsely at depth. Free gold, the engineers asserted, did not occur except when set free by oxidation; and this zone of oxidation did not exceed a depth of 1,000 feet, the depth to which oxygen could penetrate in water or through fissures. The extremely large number of surface strikes first made by tenderfoot and alfalfa miners, especially on Globe and Gold Hill, bore out this assumption. Indeed, half of the sixty most important pay chutes were still less than 500 feet down.

It was this that for so long had held Rogier back. Only to the extent and depth that the layer of porphyry with its interlaced veins of gold held out would Cripple Creek exist – a short-lived grass roots mining district.

Then gold had been found in the granite. All over the gold-bearing area the underlying granite showed evidence of disturbance. It was penetrated and traversed by vertical sheets of phonolite called dikes – a dike being easily seen where the softer rock had scored away. During the vein deposition the phonolite had been disintegrated and replaced by equivalent volumes of ore in fissure veins carried up by hot waters and heated gases. These fissure veins were vertical or inclined, varying in width from a few inches to several feet. The one fact that stood out clearly in Rogier's mind at last was that the deposition of gold had taken place in fissures after the eruption and solidification of the volcanic breccia, and was not restricted to its confines. Gold could be found in the granite depths of the Peak!

Now, hunched over his midnight lamp, he began to mark his map in a peculiar way: tracing the brecciation in the three central hills, Gold, Raven, and Bull Hill; then from Tenderfoot Hill south to Squaw Mountain; and down the eastern boundary from Trachyte Mountain to Big Bull, where the phonolite capped the granite hills. There were five general ore zones, trending from south to north. In these zones he plotted the trends of the veins of their most important mines. The Lillie-Vindicator zone system on the east swung to the northwest; the Independence-Portland system had a northward trend as had the Gold Coin zone; the Elkton vein swung to the northeast; while the two westerly zones, the Raven and the Mary McKinney-Anaconda, swung to the northeast. Sticking out on the map like the rude outline of a pear, the blue-penciled lines disclosed that the ore-producing area was broad at the south and narrow at the north. A bulbous pear-shaped region of mineralization, as if the veins had risen from the depths of the earth at the southern base of the pear and run together toward the north – into the very summit of the Peak itself.

Other men, he knew, had been studying the district assiduously. Like Stratton, who believed Gold and Globe Hills were the primal sources of mineralization, and who was buying up all the patented claims he could get.

The lights up front had gone out. The house was dark and still. Rogier was unaware of it. Profoundly disturbed, he sat staring at his map. He could see the Peak as clearly as if its hills and gulches stood before him. It was like that legendary lodestone imbedded in a sea-girt cliff against whose pull ancient mariners fought their ships, but which drew out even the iron bolts from the planks. Through the long years of his exile he had sought the key that would unlock the secret of its hold upon him and free him from its bondage. And now, having marked the course of its veins upon his map, he saw with revealing clarity the way to his fulfillment. He knew now where to search for the bloodstream of its living flesh, where to sink a shaft to tap that great arterial fountain whose viscuous veins ran through pulsing stone. Life! And yet it was also death. A gate and a tomb. The final oubliette.

The fire in the stove behind him had gone out. Shuddering with the cold, he turned over the page of the calendar on the desk. Then blowing out the lamp, he went into the house and up the creaking stairs to bed.

7

A family is a peculiar entity. Its members are like islands in the same archipelago. Sometimes the constantly changing stream of life tears a new channel through the group. Internal ruptures break away reefs. Old atolls sink and new ones rise from the placid blue depths. The eternal palingenesis goes on, but the island group remains a whole. Far down in the impenetrable bloodstream they remain fixed together, adjusted to the same internal vibration, knowing one communion in the deep unseen currents that wash between them.

So it was with Ona and Rogier. The indecencies of family "heart-to-heart" exposures were not, thank God, vices of the Rogiers. Yet a silent understanding always had held them together. Now, as she worked daily on his books and papers, she began to see him not only as her father but as man whom no one had ever known before.

The job of looking after his affairs while he was in the mountains was the worst Ona had ever attempted. She would have preferred the Herculean task of cleaning up the barny third floor in the house to spending the day puzzling over Rogier's ledgers. There were a dozen of the big volumes crammed with old letters and scrawled in his handwriting, records of every job he had figured on, copies of bids he had submitted with their detailed supporting data, and periodic records as the construction progressed, together with monthly bills for material used and deposit slips for money deposited in the bank to his various expense accounts. Rogier always wrote in his ledgers with ink but seldom bothered to use a blotter. Many pages looked as if he had closed the book with a bang,imprisoning ink like a crushed fly.

It seemed paradoxical that he could be so methodical, sure, and accurate in his work, and so sloppy even with his time sheets and payrolls. Mooney the timekeeper sent him impeccable records each week, and Rogier invariably spoiled the neat rows of figures with scrawled comments. He knew every man who worked for him. Ona had often seen him on the job talking to a stonemason, holding a plumb line for a bricklayer, or looking over a mule with a teamster. He could take off his coat and square a timber with any carpenter on the job; one who worked for him more than once had to be jim-dandy at his trade. He was hardly ever in the shanty that served as a field office, and Ona could see the results of his observations – a random comment on a laborer and a note on Diston saws, but interspersed with a statement that Akeepee needed more grain.

But when she balanced his books and bank accounts she was stunned. All the pasture land along Shook's Run he had not sold had been subdivided into lots which were selling at nice prices indeed. He owned houses on Wahsatch, and several pieces of valuable property and store buildings in the business district uptown. Receiving the evaluation on each that he had requested, together with statements from the banks, and making an approximate conversion evaluation of his construction machinery, winches, cement mixers, drays and work teams, tools, timber, finished lumber, and supplies, Ona stared open-mouthed at the sum of her father's holdings. Why, he was rich as a North Ender!

Naturally he had made money on contracts that ran as high as $80,000. But it was necessary to post big bonds and expend a great deal before the job was entirely paid for. Still he was a peculiar man. There were many things he did not tell her or entrust to his records. He might walk in and mention a piece of property he had owned for years that none of the family had ever heard of, or give her a check on an account for which she had never seen the pass book. Some time ago a man from Cripple Creek had called, telling her he had come for $120. While they were talking Rogier walked in.

"Why, of course, Ona, write out a check." The two men shook hands. "I hope you haven't been put out any."

Then one day a tacky man named Reynolds came in to see Rogier. For an hour they talked quietly in the corner. "I tell you, Colonel, this here Silver Heels is goin' to pan out. The assay says so."

Ona pricked up her ears at the name, and heard the rustle of Rogier's big map. "Open her up then. But not until you take a hard look where I told you. Up the gulch, Reynolds. Up, not down. And mind you, keep my name out of it if you have to sign any papers. Use your own."

When Reynolds was ready to leave, Rogier directed Ona to walk up town with him and draw for him from the bank $1,000 in currency.

"Silver Heels—isn't that nice to remember her! Have you got a gold mine, Daddy?"

"I wouldn't call it that," he answered tersely.

"It will be, Ma'am, and we're partners," spoke up Reynolds.

Rogier didn't try to dodge out of it. "Your wife's in town, isn't she? Bring her down for supper tonight." Then turning to Ona he ordered, "On your way through the house tell your mother and Lida to cook up a good one. If a man's my partner he's got a place at my table."

The news that Daddy had a gold mine and his partner and wife were coming to dinner threw Mrs. Rogier into a turmoil of excitement that was transmitted to the whole family. Out came the Sunday china, on went party clothes, in went a huge turkey to brown. What she expected, of course, was a prosperous mine-owner cut to the cloth of Millionaire Row. Reynolds, however, had come down from his shack in the gulch dressed in an old suit covered with fly specks and moth holes. His lady did better, this first time in town for nearly a year. Her get-up was astonishing from her red and purple petticoats to her enormous fruit-and-flower-trimmed hat, large as the bottom of a hogshead, which she refused to take off at the table. Rogier alone seemed to enjoy the occasion. Overlooking

Mrs. Rogier's shocked amazement and the girls' sly smiles, he kept refilling Reynolds' plate until he had to unbutton his vest and stretch out his legs sideways.

Speculating on how their first million dollars from the Silver Heels was to be spent, Reynolds suddenly slapped his lady on the knee and said lustily, "And Old Girl, we'll get us married too! We'll ride to church behind a team of big gray horses wearin' red plumes, and have a little tike throwin' red roses along the aisle!"

The lady snorted. "It's just like my Old Man to be throwin' away good money fer nothin'! With them front teeth of his'n out, I ain't afraid of any other female gettin' him even if we ain't hitched!"

Mrs. Rogier stiffened and became polite as a cold oyster. Rogier had forgotten to mention that no marriage certificate had ever been drawn up between these two faithful weather-beaten cronies of thirty years. Rogier looked at her with sudden admiration. Not the devil nor the prospect of Cripple Creek gold could quench the fire of her righteous indignation.

Yet now, with a gold mine in the family, there was no reason why she shouldn't have at last her mansion in the North End among the divine gentility of Little London. During her evening drives with Sally Lee or Jonathan Cable when he was in town, she would stare longingly at the great houses set back in their close-cropped lawns as if fearful of contact with the vulgar stream of life, peering over a wall or through the iron grillwork of a huge gate. Sometimes as a door opened there would be a momentary glimpse of a marble Apollo or a plaster cast of Venus de Milo behind a liveried servant. But even through the orange-lit windows her penetrating eyes seemed able to discern those ornate manifestations of wealth and culture destined to be hers someday. She knew every house; the driveway that boasted a Park Four or a spike team of three grays; whether this lawn had a circular fountain or that one a cast iron deer peering toward the shrubbery surrounding the summer pavilion; and on every vacant lot she recreated those parts of each that she meant to fuse into the Rogier mansion.

"Not yet, Martha," Rogier said decisively. "I'm too poor and too busy to throw up one of those big barns. You'll just have to wait. What's wrong with this place, anyway?"

It did look comfortable enough and very tidy, now that the big.

pasture had been cut through with shady streets and houses were going up, and a new bridge had been thrown over Shook's Run. The driveway of the house had been graveled, and in front stood as a hitching post a little cast iron nigger boy whose riding silks were painted red, yellow and blue. A large open porch had been added in back. The walk leading to the shop was flanked on each side with purple flags, the garden filled with currant bushes.

"It's all in your name, Martha," Rogier assured her again. "I can never touch it for any reason."

A few weeks later Rogier had another caller. Working with Ona in the shop, he saw him coming down the walk from the house.

"Stratton! Mr. Stratton, my daughter Ona! I'm glad to see you again!"

The Croesus of Cripple Creek, the Midas of the Rockies, with an income of $3,000 a day, more than $1,000,000 a year, resembled little the $3-a-day carpenter of a few years ago. He was dressed neatly in a gray tailored suit and handmade boots, and wore an air of importance and authority. Yet his tall thin body was frail and stooped, his hair thin and white as silk. He looked like a man bent under a burden too heavy to bear. There was little the town did not know about his peculiarities. Instead of building a mansion on Millionaire Row he had moved into a house on Weber Street, a few blocks from the Rogier's; a simple, two-story frame house he once had worked on as a carpenter. Aloof and lonely, he ignored Little London society in a futile effort to spend the wealth remorselessly pouring into his lap. Not only was he buying up hundreds of claims in Cripple Creek, smelters and stock control of other companies, but business blocks in downtown Denver. In Little London he had acquired his old office building which he converted into a modern Mining Exchange Building, the electric streetcar system which he extended to the Stratton Park he was establishing, and downtown corners which he was donating as sites for a new post office, city hall, and courthouse. His generosity was already legendary: money to ruined Tabor and to penniless Bob Womack who first had discovered gold in Cripple Creek, meal tickets to the hungry, donations right and left. All this was not enough to assuage the nameless hunger gnawing at his mind and bowels. Tales of his Satanic revels, of his Bluebeard stable of kept women, enraged every housewife in town. And he had begun to drink heavily, a quart of whiskey a day. A man from whom seventeen years of privation and despair were now taking their frightful toll.

What had brought him here Rogier could not imagine. Nor did Stratton have a chance to tell him. For down the walk behind him came Mrs. Rogier, head up, eyes blazing. Sweeping in the door, she thrust a handful of gold coins into Stratton's lap. "What do you mean giving my girls and maid these, Mr. Stratton? I will have you distinctly understand we do not need your charity!"

Ona jumped to her feet. "A gold piece from Mr. Stratton's a souvenir anybody'd be glad to have! And I've heard about your giving a bicycle to every laundry girl in town so she wouldn't have to walk to work. That's kind of you, Mr. Stratton!"

Mrs. Rogier took her by the hand and marched out the door.

"Damned women! I hate them all!" Stratton shouted after them.

Rogier shrugged his heavy shoulders. "They're a queer breed, Stratton. I can never make them out."

Stratton stalked out the back door.

Never again did he come to the house, but a few days later and several times thereafter he came down the alley and through the back door of the shop. Each time he came Rogier sent Ona into the house, ostensibly to avoid any more scenes. The purpose of Stratton's calls was simple.

"You haven't been up to the Independence," he said. "Strange for an old friend and a man who's getting interested in the district."

"You're bothered too much and I'm busy myself."

"You must be. I hear you've leased the Garnet and Fleur-de-Lis."

How astute he was! He knew everything going on up there, and this arrangement had been kept quiet. Two businessmen, Diggs and Handel, had been working the Garnet profitably until a horse in the vein had cut down their returns. Indications were that the main chute would be picked up again on the adjacent claim, the Fleur-de-Lis, and they proposed that Rogier go into partnership with them to open up the new mine. Rogier, despite abhorring partnerships, had agreed.

The properties were no good, insisted Stratton. They lay just outside the rim of that great porphry-filled granite bowl in which sat the Independence and the Portland. He proposed instead that Rogier develop for him a new property, the American Eagles, as he felt ill and was going away to recuperate.

Rogier declined; he had a different opinion of the Garnet and Fleur-de-Lis location.

"It's no good, whatever it is!" angrily declaimed Stratton. "And Diggs and Handel are no better!" But he made another offer. If Rogier would develop the American Eagles, Stratton for a share would guarantee to develop the Fleur-de-Lis to the extent of Rogier's one-third interest, insuring him against total loss of his investment.

Rogier gladly accepted. Both men agreed no contract should be drawn as Stratton wanted to avoid publicity and they were old, trusted friends. "Come up to the Independence on Monday and I'll show you through. Then we can look over the Eagles," said Stratton. The two men shook hands on the agreement, and Stratton left by the alley door.

Not only Rogier was amazed at the Independence. An investigating committee comprised of members from the Colorado Scientific Society, American Institute of Mechanical Engineers, the United States Department of Mining, and several other civil and mining engineers, had reported it to be the most noteworthy gold mine in the Western Hemisphere if not in the world. It now embraced fourteen claims covering more than a hundred acres. The main shaft was down 415 feet and its underground workings aggregated more than six miles. The principal veins were so rich that they had been named like other complete mines: the Independence, Bobtail, and Emerson. "Now I'll show you the Bull Pen," said Stratton, signalling for the third level. The gold depository was a chamber from eight to thirty feet wide of sylvanite that ran from hundreds to thousands of dollars a ton. "I don't mine it," explained Stratton. "I just dip in it, like a bank, when I need ready cash. I'm trying to curtail the Independence production to $120,000 a month." Turning to Rogier with one of his rare smiles, he added, "You know, gold is worth more in the ground than out of it."

Shooting up to surface the two men climbed up to the American Eagles which when opened up for production would be the highest mine in the district. "The showing is good and I want no expense spared," ordered Stratton. "I've got two good mining men to lay out the levels, drifts, and crosscuts as we follow the vein. What I want you for is to sink the shaft and put in the surface plant. And manage the men. I don't want any labor troubles." He paused. "Stop fooling around with those rat holes like the Silver Heels. And don't waste your money on that Fleur-de-Lis. They're no good!"

"I'll do your job," Rogier answered quietly. "But don't you interfere with my affairs. I've got my own ideas."

"You're a fool!" Nevertheless he stuck out his hand before turning back down the slope.

8

The news came out, of course, that Rogier had thrown in his resources with Diggs and Handel to develop their sister mines, the Garnet and Fleur-de-Lis. It not only raised the sagging price of the stock on the exchange and reestablished the two men on a footing with their bankers and neighbors, but it briefly focused attention on the aloof and retiring contractor. Rogier was invited to a banquet given by the mine owners of Cripple Creek. Swearing that it was nothing but a back-slapping orgy, he protested against going until Mrs. Rogier cornered him for one of her bathroom talks.

"They've invited you, Daddy! Your place at the table is marked with 'Colonel Rogier.' The *Gazette* said so. You've got to go!"

With the three girls she got him ready in his broadcloth suit and starched white shirts. Then another argument started. He wouldn't wear a tie. Always he wore a stiff collar fastened by his only piece of jewelry, a diamond collar button. This was the way he finally went despite their protestations. Yet when he stepped out to the carriage waiting with Nigger Bill in the front seat, the fine texture of his coat revealing his wide muscular shoulders, his graying hair gleaming above the diamond at his throat, none of the family but admitted that, however he detested the false appellation, he was indeed Little London's Colonel Rogier.

To Ona there was no doubt left that Rogier was committed to Cripple Creek. He was letting his work slide, neglecting to bid on several promising jobs. For days on end he would be up in the district. She was stunned by the checks she made out, the money he so casually commanded. Just what he was doing up there she did not know, but it often seemed to her that his interests and money were being expended on something besides the Fleur-de-Lis and the Silver Heels.

It was his ledgers that gave him away. Stuck in one of the dusty volumes she happened by chance to find a cryptic note scrawled on a scrap of crumpled paper. Spreading out the paper to decipher the cramped writing, she felt leap out at her those terse phrases oddly turned of wording and impulsively expressing an inner thought of the writer, sublime and yet pathetic, that was not meant to be read by any man. Abashed like any Rogier by the candor of a heart that had so forgotten itself to reveal without repression its most secret treasure, Ona tore the page across and dropped the fragments into the waste basket. For the first time she had an intimation of what Rogier might be seeking in Cripple Creek.

A few weeks later she drove up to the district in the family buggy with Jonathan Cable; next day Rogier would drive her back. The Cheyenne Mountain Trail had been widened to a four-horse stage road to give shorter access into the district, and it was beautiful: climbing up through deep canyons thickly forested with pine and spruce, and winding through high mountain meadows ablaze with wildflowers. It was always good to be with Cable. Despite his absences this Red Niggah, as her cantankerous grandmother still called him, had come to be accepted as part of the family.

They talked little all day as he drove her around the district. Victor, the City of Mines, was booming above the Gold Coin. Cripple Creek she did not recognize. Jennie Larue, a dancehall girl in a den of vice, and her lover had knocked over a gasoline stove while quarreling, and the ensuing fire had wiped out most of the wooden buildings of the camp. Now it was being rebuilt into a modern city with stone and red brick buildings glowing on the dull gray granite hillsides. A town of 10,000 people without a tree. Everywhere they drove stood other huddles of shacks growing into more new towns. Everywhere she looked, she could see the gallows frames of great mines, gaping holes blasted out of the hillsides, shanties and tool houses, litters of machinery, swarms of toiling men. And rising above them all the pyramidal bare summit of the Peak itself.

The Silver Heels was not up to her expectations. A dark vertical shaft surmounted by a hoist house and nearby, Reynolds' squat board shanty. His wife had taken off her hat, Ona thought grimly, and was dishing up beans and salt pork to Reynolds.

"Where's father?" she asked.

"Oh, he's over the hill and up the gulch, Miss Ona." He thumbed toward the Peak. "I wouldn't go up there, he's mighty touchy – if you could get up there in them nice clothes."

Glad as he was to see them, he seemed reluctant to answer questions and Ona left them to their cold beans.

"Now I want to see your mine, Jonathan. That's what I came up here for."

Cable grinned as he drove her to Big Bull Mountain. "The New Moon's not the sliver it was," he said humorously, "but it doesn't seem to fill out too fast. But we're getting along."

The best that could be said of it was that it was a working mine like hundreds of others in the district. The three partners now had a crew of three more men, and Cable showed her the inclined tunnel down which they went to work. They were underground now, hacking away and filling a little metal cart with ore which from time to time a burro pulled out. There was a large log cabin with tiers of bunks in which they slept, and an adjoining plank kitchen in which they took turns cooking. It all looked very dull to Ona and she was glad to go out on the dump to sit in the late afternoon sunlight. Picking up a grayish, damp piece of rock, she asked, "So this is ore, gangue, whatever you call it?"

He nodded. "Calaverite, a telluride. We had a hard time at first. Ore containing less than an ounce of gold to the ton didn't leave us much profit. But now we're shipping to a new mill in Florence that uses cynanide instead of chlorine as a solvent, we're making money even on half-ounce ore."

"You mean to say all these hundreds of mines and thousands of men have to blast and dig out a ton of rock to get a tiny ounce or less of gold!"

"Doesn't the place look dug up enough to produce $19,000,000 worth a year?" There was a somber tone to his voice and a far-away look in his eyes as she followed his gaze across the gutted hillsides and torn up gulches. This was not a man, with his love for open prairies, to devote himself to mining. Yet tomorrow he would be down there in the clammy blackness, hacking away with the rest of them.

Not too surprisingly Rogier drove up in a buckboard. "I've been expecting you. Reynolds said you were here." He flung a quick look around. "Still at the grass roots, eh Cable? You've got to get down, way down!"

They all drove to Cripple Creek and had dinner at the National Hotel where Ona was to stay that night. Rogier was no more talkative than Cable, but Ona detected in him a nervous excitement, a keyed up expectancy, that he had never betrayed during his work in Little London. Cable was a reassuring presence; a simple man, sensitive to his surroundings, without a driving ambition perhaps, but living fully in the moment.

"Did you register for a room?" Rogier asked her. "Make it for two nights, I can't drive you back tomorrow. But I'll show you some of the big mines."

"No," she answered decisively. "I'll take the Midland back tonight. I want to see the new resorts at Cascade and Green Mountain Falls. This is no place for women – or trees."

Rogier gave her a sharp look but did not answer.

When he returned to town, Ona gave him the clippings of statistics she had been saving for him. He thumbed through them rapidly, then reached for his big steel square. "Humm. That's interesting. The district producing almost $20,000,000, Colorado $26,000,000, the United States $70,000,000, and the world about $300,000,000. That means Cripple Creek is accounting for four-fifths of the annual gold production in Colorado, nearly a third of the country's, and one-fifteenth of the gold mined in the world. Already! And most of that is coming from a little block of six square miles. Now figure that per square foot and you'll see – "

"I hate figures! Copying them all day long!"

Holding the square on his knee, he said quietly, "You don't dislike figures as much as you think you do. What marks the time you get up in the morning and every second of the day? Figures. Why, astrologers claim that the moment you're born is no more than an astronomical juxtaposition of universal figures which determine your future, and that your life vibrates to one primary number just as a thin wine-glass vibrates to a certain pitch. Your mother will tell you from her Bible that even the hairs of your head are numbered. But she won't be able to tell you why the Book of Revelation is composed almost entirely of numbers whose significance is unknown. What locates a ship on the boundless seas but figures!"

"But Daddy!" She wanted to ask him how he expected her to balance his own figures when he was spending more than his income – and without knowing where it all went. But Rogier could not be stopped.

"How good is Little Man? Only figures can tell us. Jot them down – 5,280 feet in a mile, and you can figure a good horse can pace it in 2:15. That's 135 seconds – say forty feet a second. How long is a horse's body, Ona? Say six feet. A good trotter or pacer to do that time will have to move forward about six times the length of his body every second." Taking the scratch pad from her, he went on. "But how does he do it? You've got to breed a good horse for spirit, feed him for stamina, and work him for wind. Then you've got to train him. Every stride just so long to give him the most drive forward for what he's got. Stretch him out! Every hair in place, by Jove! Just to get him ahead six lengths every second. But it's the horse – and his mammy and his sire, and his mammy before that – who has to win his own race. Breeding, evolution, the time comes when every living soul has to run his race against the past!"

Ona quietly put away her pencil and paper, closed her ledgers. "It's getting late. You'll be wanting to see Little Man before suppertime."

Not even Cripple Creek had lessened Rogier's love for his horses; a love, fascination, queer in a man so slow and methodical, of seeing the speed he could get out of them. There had been so many of them: Lady-Lou, Pet and her fillies Dorothy and Silver Heels, old blind Colonel, and that great Maryland lady, Akeepee, each a little faster than the others. He had been sure that Akeepee, a pacer, would fulfill his hopes. But Judge Colton had ruined her, and he had let her foal two colts, first Little Man and then Aralee, still a spindling brat.

Rogier rode out with Ona and Sally Lee to visit Little Man at the ranch. This horse had taken the cake for orneryness from the day he was foaled. Nigger Bill said he was brimmin' with hell-fire. And after the only occasion he was sent out on the streets with a buggy, the *Gazette* reported he had tried to climb the telegraph poles. He was not high-spirited; he was a long-legged devil in a smooth satin skin, a chicken-killer who delighted in nipping any arm or leg within his reach. Fearless and excellent a hand with horses as she was, Sally Lee could never acquire Rogier's persuasive touch. Little Man was no exception. Whenever anyone approached, he would rear up on hind feet, pawing with his forefeet. Denman could handle him with care, but only for Rogier would he stretch out his muzzle with a rumble of welcome.

Arriving at Denman's ranch, Rogier wandered from stall to stall, having a look at every horse. He greeted them as old friends; scrutinized them like delicately chiseled stone statues; went over them like a physician. By this time the handlers had made ready his sulky and brought out Little Man. Rogier settled himself firmly in the low seat, legs outspread, and drove slowly to the track. The sun, settling in its crotch in the blue mountain wall, flooded the prairie with a light coppery sheen. Cut into the dry level expanse of buffalo grass and tumbleweed, the circular track looked black, fresh, and inviting. Waiting on the course until the men were ready at their posts and the girls had come up, he held Little Man while Denman inspected his leg wrappings for the last time and then stepped back with his watch. Then suddenly they were away, Little Man lunging viciously into his stride and Rogier settling down to his one invigorating relaxation.

The wind streaked past whining softly, but too weak to extinguish the blur of dust that followed him like the smoke of a burning fuse. He could hear the rhythmic concatenation of the hoofs before him and glimpse the twinkle of the white wrappings, could watch Little Man's breathing as his sides swelled and receded regularly against the trembling shafts. Timing his pace, he watched for the first man's hand to fall exactly as he passed the two-furlong mark. Alive to every stride, it was as if his own self had died and had been born anew. His worries and troubles dropped from him and were trampled into the fine dry dust. An elixir electric as a current swept through his veins. The track curved northward in its turn; Little Man was a length behind at the half-mile. Rogier leaned forward, let out the reins. Little Man ran smoothly, every stride in time. Slowly the high blue mountains swung across the course like a dark and menacing wall of rock. And far down the track, like a pigmy at its foot, Denman stood with his arm upraised as with solemn warning. Rogier compressed his lips as he took a tighter hold of the reins. Always that Peak forbiddingly blocking his path! But sensing the splendid power leaping into his fingers and flowing up his arms, he felt that with one plunge he might hurtle over it into the waiting blood-red sun. With a quick slap he threw out the reins, and Little Man lunged forward.

Everybody was shouting and grinning when he eased Little Man back. "Man. I was sho you was goin' to jump that theah chah'iot ovah the sun and moon!" yelled Nigger Bill. "He's the one, Daddy!" cried Sally Lee, eyes shining. "You *have* entered him in the meeting, haven't you?"

"Maybe so, maybe so. We'll see," replied Rogier.

Comparing observations and the time of each quarter-mile, Rogier and Denman walked back to the ranch with the girls while the men followed with Little Man. That evening at home Rogier made up his mind to enter him in the race meeting. "You better," said Mrs. White, old and poorly as she was. "What you keepin' all them horses for if it ain't to race? Buyin' enough hay and grain every month to feed us a year! If you're doin' it jes for an evenin' ride, it's better you tuk Akeepee out in the buggy!"

The meeting was a great event to which every member of the family went. Cable was along, and so was Lida Peck who wanted to see how her former barnyard enemy, the chicken killer, would behave in company. There were five harness events, trotting, pacing, a free-for-all, a six furlong running event, and the last a mile pace for which Rogier had registered. During all the races the rest of the family kept their eyes on Rogier talking quietly to Denman and Nigger Bill as if he had no concern at all. When the last race was called, Cable walked Ona and Sally Lee down to the finishing line, leaving the rest of the family in the coach fronting the track.

Mrs. Rogier swelled with pride when Rogier drove up to the starting line, his sulky polished until its frail outline reflected the sun. Little Man was too docile for words, arching his neck and glancing demurely at the crowd.

"That chicken killer!" spat out Lida under another new hat. "He's actin' too good to be true. Showin' off!"

Mrs. Rogier sat back, folding her hands. "Blood will tell, Lida. He knows when to be on his good behavior."

Almost before they knew it the horses were off, streaking for the inside. It was a fair field, and two entries beside Rogier bunched at the turn with the others strung out obliquely behind. Little Man held his stride beautifully, running smoothly as if he were alone at dusk on Denman's track. At the half-mile he was leading by half a length with a young black gelding just behind and a little sorrel mare coming up fast. Rogier paid no attention to the black but glanced back once at the sorrel. He was running Little Man at the pace agreed upon with Denman, but it was obvious his race was with the little mare. At the fifth furlong the gelding burst ahead, lost his stride and began to drop behind. In an instant the little sorrel took her position beside Rogier. Then she and Little Man went at it neck to neck. Rogier never took his eyes from the finish line.

Quick as a wink it happened. The sorrel lengthened her stride and was a good head beyond Little Man when that beautifully behaving colt saw her at the corner of his blinders. He twisted his head, let out a squeal. Before Rogier could pull him back Little Man bared his teeth and made a grab for the mare's ear. The two sulkies met with a bump that almost overturned them both. Then Little Man stretched out his nose, broke away, and streaked for the finish. Running wild, his stride broken and ragged, he finished four lengths in front of the field.

The fiasco set the crowd wild, whooping and hollering for the horse from Shook's Run. Lida sat screaming, "Chicken killer! Look at that ornery horse run!" Mrs. Rogier did not answer. She sat stiff as a corpse, feeling her ears slowly burning off.

Little Man was disqualified and the purse awarded the sorrel mare. As it had been a selling race, Little Man was offered for sale according to the rules and Rogier had to buy him back for three hundred dollars. It was the last straw Mrs. Rogier's dignity could uphold. She drove home in a silent coach.

Rogier was put out at Little Man's action, particularly because the colt had shown up so well in training. Speed and power were no good without complete control. He let Nigger Bill blanket and walk the horse home alone. That evening he drove out to Denman's ranch. It was dusk when he approached the stable. The door was open, and Little Man unhaltered heard him talking to Denman. At the sound of a squeal Rogier looked up. There was Little Man uprisen on his hind legs, pawing the air as he walked toward them. Then he dropped to all four feet, whisked his tail mischievously, and stretched out his muzzle toward Rogier. Suddenly Rogier grinned. "You ornery colt, you!" he said, putting out both hands.

Little Man should have had twin toes.

9

Rogier was up at the Silver Heels when the results of the assays came in. "It's a strike, Colonel," Reynolds said solemnly. "Sixty dollars to the ton." He acted little like a man who had hit his mark after years of toil and privation.

Nor did Rogier betray any elation. "I've told you before to stop calling me 'Colonel!' Have you hit a defined vein or is it still grass roots gangue?"

"Three ounces a ton at a hundred feet's good enough for me, Colonel! When can we start shipping?"

Mrs. Reynolds was in town for groceries. They sat down to a cup of muddy coffee undisturbed. Reynolds was a born miner. He knew the earth as a bookbinder knows a book. The strata unfolding beneath him, leaf after leaf; its type the hieroglyphic marks of fossil and geological change; its bindings the tunnels, shafts, and gallows frames that rose about him. Rogier trusted him completely. And yet – what was the meaning of the text?

The argument began – a queer time for an argument! Rogier of course would bring in machinery, men, and supplies. But only on the condition that if the vein pinched out, or could not be found,

Reynolds would move with the equipment to a new working he had in mind.

Reynolds looked at him as if he were staring at a mad man. "Colonel! We've made the strike we been after! We're goin' to get rich! And here you're talkin' about leavin' it for a no-account prospect already."

Rogier appeared unconvinced. "Reynolds, the Silver Heels is a step in the right direction, that's all. We're going after something better!"

"But Colonel!" Reynolds grasped at a last straw. "What are you going to use for money, buyin' all that machinery for the Fleur-de-Lis, bringin' more here, payin' all the crews? You got to get the gold right here in the Silver Heels to keep you goin'! I'm your partner, Colonel! I'll sink or swim with you. But haven't I hit it for you like I said I would?"

Rogier got up, flung his arm around him in a hearty hug. "Get some muckers up here! I'll move in some machinery. Let's go down!"

"Hooray!" shouted Reynolds. "Wait'll the Old Girl hears of this!"

Now at sunset Rogier sat on a spur of that high saddle between Bull Hill and Bull Cliffs where perched a conglomeration of shacks growing into the highest incorporated town in the world and named after another lucky carpenter, Sam Altman; sitting alone in a rock cleft, letting its full meaning sink into his mind and heart. He had drawn blood at last! And just where he'd known he would – at the mouth of that grassy gulch running northward like a heart line directly up into the bare snowy summit of the Peak itself. Sitting 11,000 feet high, he could see it looming another three thousand feet above him. Like a great snow-goose halted a split instant in flight for his arrow to strike home, like an uprisen saurian beast baring its heart, like a monstrous fish breaking water – like nothing but that massive anthropomorphous Peak of heart's desire itself. The showing in the Silver Heels was not a vein, merely a capillary indication of its living flesh that confirmed the truth of his aim. When it petered out he would move up the gulch and sink deeper at a location he already had staked out. And with the gold shipped from it he would ascend the steadily narrowing cut to its last granite crack and at last strike deep into that hot beating heart within the stone of all stones, the self of all selves.

It was a pear-shaped pattern of conquest that had formed on his maps and in his mind long ago, a strategy he had followed in taking a job on the American Eagles on top of Bull Hill and developing the Garnet and Fleur-de-Lis on the Altman saddle. They were all in line with the arrow course of his secret hope. But not until he had drawn blood from the Silver Heels had he realized how close his triumph was. And it was Reynolds, that profane and ratty miner, who had jerked him down to earth. Dom! How much money it would take, all he could raise! Rogier rose, his mind clear, to begin the tactics of his campaign.

With the first shipment of ore from the Silver Heels, Reynolds and his wife went on a spree that rocked Myers Avenue on its own silver and gold heels. Rogier gave his share from the first carloads to Mrs. Rogier. It was enough pin money to go around handsomely for new frocks and to justify all the time he spent in Cripple Creek. Even Nigger Bill's little son, George Washington, age seven, came in for a brand new suit – candy-striped red, blue and white just like the cast-iron blackamore hitching post in front. The whole family blossomed out like an anemone breaking through the snow. Daddy, doing no more than what everyone expected of him, finally had discovered a gold mine.

Mrs. Rogier, thin and electric, was a Frenchwoman from her sharp aristocratic nose, upraised to cut the air before her. In church she obeyed the divine necessity of maintaining an irreproachable front. Devoutly conscious of the eyes upon her—with her solid entrenchment in that House of the Lord whose pillar she had been longer than most of the congregation could remember—and of the full weight of that carload of ore from the Silver Heels, she sat like a stone carved from pride into an image of humility.

There was much to be proud of. Boné from San Francisco had sent the first copy of his Indian Suite "Manitou" for which Lockhardt had found a publisher, and all the clippings about it. The four songs were catching on. During the evening concerts in Acacia Park, even at the Broadmoore Casino, his "Song of the Corn," "The Wolf Song," "Fire Dance," and "Song of the Willows" were played. With a composer in the family – despite it – Mrs. Rogier felt it incumbent to produce at least one member of the household who could perform gracefully at the piano.

Ona was too old and dull. Mary Ann too young and giddy, and thought only of eating. Perhaps because she had a new beau, whose father owned a delicatessen store catering to the North End trade. To impress him and the young gentlemen who called with him, she jumped to the telephone a half-dozen times a day to call for special dainties. And to placate Rogier in case he might notice the growing bills she ordered oysters and mackerel shipped all the way from his beloved Maryland.

Only Sally Lee could do. Horsey as she was, she had a good ear and a deep rich contralto that enabled her to sing "The Dawn" by D'Hardelot, Stuart's "Bandolero," "L'Esclave" by Lalo, and a group of selected nursery songs of Geibel, Neidlinger, and Riley whenever called upon. To develop her, Rogier obtained Professor Albert E. Dearson. He was a talented man of German and Russian extraction who once had conducted an orchestra in Leipzig, and was now in Colorado for his health. For awhile he was in great demand in the North End. Then the man militated against the musician. He went around in brown leather leggings, neglected to trim his stubble of reddish gray whiskers, and never accepted an invitation to a social function as an unpaid guest. Above all, he had a violent temper. Soon, with one accord, the whole North End raised hands and exclaimed over teacups, "The Master of Musicians, but – !"

Even Rogier met his match the day Professor Dearson came down to audition Sally Lee. The big sliding doors were pulled shut upon professor and pupil, her father and mother. There was not a word spoken until she had finished. "Well," asked Rogier, "do you want to take her?"

Professor Dearson was as blunt. "What! With that old box! It sounds like a street organ!"

"Appears to me it's not the shoes that count but the man who fills them" Rogier answered calmly.

Nevertheless a new piano was installed before Professor Dearson returned. Despite his social setback it was a feather in one's cap to have captured him, and Mrs. Rogier made the most of the opportunity. With Sally Lee driving up to his house with a hundred dollars every whip-stitch, it behooved her to see that Sally Lee learned her lessons. The sanctimonious hours when she was entombed to practice were very well, but let her give vent to her predeliction for the new ragtime and Mrs. Rogier was on her before you could say "Jack Robinson!" The first bar of the "Yama Yama Man" or the "Black Hand Rag" was sufficient to start a row. Still, in due time Sally Lee was admitted into the Musical Club, and even Professor Dearson appeared satisfied that he had wrung the last ounce of gold out of the ore given him to refine.

By summer Cable's position in the house was secure. For weeks he would be away, working up in Cripple Creek. Then he would come down to work in the haberdashery store, sliding into his room and niche in the Rogier household as if he'd never been away. The New Moon apparently had hit a good pocket. "None of us think it's more than that," admitted Cable. "But it has enabled us to lay in a stock of the most fashionable cravats and waistcoats in town. The sale of these should carry us through the summer and give me more time in town."

Everyone of the Rogiers liked the Red Niggah, except Mrs. White; and, as the only man in the house while Rogier was away, he was relied on more and more. Sally Lee and Mary Ann conjectured privately when Ona would marry him. Their conjectures were without the warmth of conviction, however, for there was no sign of romance between them. Besides, they were too old: Ona, an old maid of thirty, and Cable nearing forty.

For Ona herself Cable's friendly companionship seemed quite sufficient. Big-boned and resolute as Rogier, she too repressed within her granite shell any indication of volcanic porphyry within. Cable made no attempt to draw her out. Fluid as he was, sensitive and responsive, Ona felt within him a hard and secret quality that frightened her a little. She no longer thought of his Indian blood, but sometimes she was aware of a peculiar difference in him that for an instant set him apart from everyone else. For one thing, his small feet for a man his size and the care he took to keep them well shod. Shoes were his one extravagance; he always had them handmade from his last at the bootmaker. And the way he walked in them, so softly and lithely that you never heard him coming until he was up to you!

That midsummer evening they drove Akeepee to a place unusual for them both, the Broadmoore Casino. It was still early. Cheyenne Mountain, blue, soft, and benign, loomed up like a backdrop to a prairie stage of flaming Indian paintbrush, bluebells, and wild onions screaming patriotically with vivid colors.

"Isn't the Casino extravagantly expensive?" asked Ona. "Are you celebrating something?"

"Oh, nothing special. But things look pretty good all the way around. The New Moon and the haberdashery shop are each paying their own way, though we're not making much money. And my partners would rather work in the mine than down there, which is good for me."

"And good for me too, Jonathan!" she replied warmly. Nevertheless Ona could not repress her qualms. If she could not envision Cable mucking underground in Cripple Creek with the two husky Grimes, her every glimpse of him in the haberdashery shop showing cravats and waistcoats to genteel New Londoners was more foreboding. A strange dark man whom she could never quite place in his proper setting.

Slapping out the reins, Cable shook Akeepee into a smooth, fast pace. The wind flapped the ends of Ona's scarf about her head and brought the blood to her cheeks, as they flew up the mesa and rounded the curve toward a blazing diamond set in an emerald park.

The long two-storied temple of pleasure, girdled by broad piazzas, its gabled roof upheld by four high, spotless white pillars, was as elegant inside as out. Bar and game and reading rooms were crowded; in the ladies' salon Ona could hear the discreet murmur of Rosner's Hungarian Orchestra reflected from the polished floor of the immense ballroom. A table in the great dining room was reserved for them and Ona sat down with some trepidation among the fashionable, distinguished, and wealthy guests. She would have been distinctly uncomfortable had Mrs. Rogier been present with that air of superiority which masked a lack of the cultural and financial habiliments she had not yet attained. Cable was not impressed. He was not a drinking man, as Mrs. Rogier said, but he loved wine; and he was not too proud to ask for advice in the selection of something appropriate to their taste. He ate hungrily, enjoying the novelty of the food and surroundings. Sitting there he had something of a foreign look about him, with his dark face and Roman nose, his straight black hair, and sensitive brown hands protruding from his starched white cuffs. A simple unaffected man, he knew exactly what he was. Ona was reassured by his presence.

After dinner they rowed across the lake to sit in the little pavilion, staring at the reflection of the Casino lights in the water and listening to the strains of the Hungarian orchestra.

"Why, that's Boné's 'Song of the Willows'," she said suddenly.

"They're all good tunes, that suite of his," Cable replied casually, "but there's nothing Indian about them. They all seem to come from the nose and not the belly."

This extremely acute observation mentioned with such casualness struck her with singular force. She too had been a little disappointed with Boné's Indian suite, expecting something more serious and with a fuller texture than these light melodies. At times she secretly suspected Lockhardt's touch, for had he not prophesied one that Boné's future lay in lighter work?

"You can't very well put a belly-drum in the middle of a piano score," she said defensively. "And of all his songs I like this one best." It was indeed the only one heard often of late. It reminded her not of summer's lush weeping willows drooping over the stream, but of those stark bare branches glowing pink and red against the snow.

Returning to the Casino they watched the dancing in the ballroom awhile, then drove slowly back home in the moonlight. It had been a perfect evening; she felt relaxed and content. Cable acted so too. She could hear him talking to Akeepee as he put her in the stall next to the carriage house, and whistling lowly to the pigeons in their loft.

She was not aware when he came out, so quiet were his steps. Then abruptly, without warning, she felt caught in his arms. It was as if a brutal, engulfing passion had leapt upon her from a darkness where it long had been lurking. Everything struck her at once. The peculiar odor of his body as he bent over her; his hot breath in the instant he kissed her full upon the mouth; the pressure of his knee between her thighs. And suddenly it all came back to her from childhood: that other dark aquiline face with the steady fixed stare of its black eyes into her own, the sharp pain of her burned behind creeping down like a slow mellow glow to her crotch, and the feeling of a warm wet trickle down the inner side of one leg. Here it was again, all of it – the pain and the ecstasy, the fright and sweetness and strange familiarity, all blended together in one incomprehensible whole.

At her cry he released her at once, stepping back into the shadow like an animal withdrawing from its prey. "What's the matter?" he asked in a far-off, strange voice.

And she could hear herself answering in a tremulous voice not her own. "Nothing! Oh Jonathan! Just kiss me again! Now!"

They were married a month later, on a late Sunday morning, in the front room of the house. Only the family and friends were present, yet there was quite a crowd: Professor Dearson, Cable's two partners and the Reynolds couple from Cripple Creek, Denman, Lida of course, Nigger Bill who was to drive them to the depot to catch the train to Denver where they were going to honeymoon in the Brown Palace, and close neighbors.

The news had been calmly accepted in the family. Mrs. Rogier had proposed at once they live in the big master bedroom on the second floor. Ona was delighted with the prospect.

"No!" Cable replied firmly. "We'll have our own home!"

"Not too far away for her to walk here every day. I need her to look after my affairs," Rogier cautioned him.

Now again, as the couple was ready to go out to the waiting carriage, Rogier said gruffly, "Now look, Cable, don't you be staying too long up in Denver. Ona's got a lot of thinking to do about all the work I need done."

Cable's dark face set. "She won't do a bit of thinking about all that if I can help it."

There was a look in Ona's eyes as she ran out to the carriage that remained stamped on all the hearts of the family long after the wheels had rolled away. The look of a woman from whom the curse of an eldest daughter had been suddenly lifted and who at last had found her heart's home. It wasn't as if she had been the family drudge. Hadn't Lida been hired to do most of the work, and didn't the younger girls do their share of chores? But still into the suddenly gaping vacuum created by her absence rushed memories of the quiet, capable, and generally ignored girl who from childhood had borne uncomplainingly the brunt of their pain and worry; who had helped to raise Sally Lee and Mary Ann, Bob, Hiney, and Bone;

who had shared the fatal burden of Sister Molly; who had endured the foibles of Mrs. Rogier and Mrs. White; whom Rogier now depended upon to look after his affairs; this simple, untalented girl who had never had time to finish school, had never been kissed. Ona!

A long keening cry burst from Mrs. Rogier. And suddenly, unaccountably, they all broke into tears. Behind them in the dining room, table and buffet were loaded with everything appropriate to the occasion: the meats and sweets, pickles and pastries, the rolls and hot biscuits and honey, the wine and raw whiskey, a box of Rogier's cigars. No one noticed the spread. They sat weeping because Ona had got married.

Rogier brushed a furtive tear out of his eye with his fist. "Well, I hope she stays as long as she has a mind to!" Then he strode out to sit alone in his shop.

10

These were the days they all remembered! Days lengthening and shortening with the seasons like the rhythmic strokes of Time's accordion. Everywhere, high in the mountains, wide upon the plains, the wine of life rose brimming in its cup; the days shone bright with promise; and ever the song ran on.

In its first decade Cripple Creek had produced $100,000,000 worth of gold. With the closing of the Transvaal mines during the South African War it was leading the world in gold production, and had enabled the United States to acquire $118,435,562 of the world's $255,954,654 worth of gold. The population of Little London, a mile below this greatest gold camp on earth, had increased to 35,000. In the North End there were forty millionaires; on Tejon Street more than 400 mining company offices. No one in the family cared about these statistics – or about those other phenomenal figures on the monthly bills which Rogier casually tossed to Ona to pay. Like a shield bright against the day, tempered to withstand the world, the family stood waiting to receive the heraldic crest of its own Cripple Creek gold. Rogier, as a matter of fact, had given Cable as a wedding token a set of shirt studs fashioned by the jeweler from

Silver Heels gold in the shape of small acorns in which was set a tiny pearl.

Not that Cable had frequent occasions to wear them, selling haberdashery in his and his partners' store the months he was in town, and mucking ore in Cripple Creek the rest of the time. Ona was busy too. They had moved into a little frame house along the creek, just past the Santa Fe Railroad underpass; close enough to walk to the shop every day where she worked for Rogier.

What did it matter? These were the days they all remembered! Days woven into a tapestry of bright promise with threads of Cripple Creek gold.

September came; and as if to end that Indian Summer of a glorious decade with a pageant of praise, Little London held its Sunflower Carnival. No expense was spared to make it the greatest festival the mountains and plains had evern witnessed. All the Utes had come down to their annual encampment to hold their Shan Kive: Chief Ouray, for whom a mountain, town, and county had been named; his wife, the venerated sage, Chipeta; the lesser chiefs, Colorow, Red Shirt, and Little Mound; and little Dripping Spring and Charley Horse. Day and night the drums beat while onlookers, forgetting their prejudices, clapped and yelled. Charley Horse rode a pony to death before a crowd that laughed at the boy's indomitable pride and cold brutality. At a free Cowboy Barbecue booted cooks handed out steaming chunks of beef from a pit six feet wide and thirty feet long. Manitou Day and Pike's Peak Day were tooted in and out with the Colorado Midland Band, the Cowboy Band from Pueblo, and the Rough Riders Band of Colorado City, Past, present, and future paraded by in an endless procession of feathered Utes, cowboys, miners, covered wagons, ore wagons, buckboards, carriages and a horseless Locomobile steam carriage spouting black smoke.

Then came the Flower Parade, arranged by the flower of Little London's aristocracy. From the roof of Cable's store the Rogiers watched the gorgeous display of pride and wealth. Pony traps, spiders, four-wheelers, surreys, tandems, and four-in-hands followed each other down the wide avenues. There was a trap of clematis and oak leaves, another trimmed with holly and evergreen, a spider phaeton smothered in chrysanthemums. Behind this a liveried groom sat enthroned on a seat covered with light blue hollyhocks, proudly driving a chestnut stallion decorated with blue ribbons. Then came Donaldson's brake drawn by a spike team of three grays. Mrs. Rogier gasped. Four thousand! – as the *Gazette* said – 4,000 Jacquinot roses bordered by kinnikinnick! Only to be followed by a team of white mares sporting white snowballs and white silver-willow branches. And still another all red and black: red and black poppies, black horses with red satin blankets, and with harness and hoofs painted red.

The celebrations were climaxed with a four-day meeting of the racing association which had reorganized with an eye toward membership in the Grand Western Circuit. The meeting was held north of town at the new Roswell track built and donated by Stratton. Restrictions were imposed on local horses and no expense was spared to bring for show the finest horseflesh in the West. Ensconsed in a grandstand box, the whole Rogier family watched the first day's exhibitions. Lena N who had come within a second of the track record of 2:14 showed off beautifully as did Asbrook's high stepper Jean Valjean and Roberts' trotter Trilby with a record of 2:13½. A sulky was displayed weighing only twenty-four pounds. Drawn by Star Pointer when he made a world record of 1:59¼, it was the only sulky drawn by a harness horse in less than two minutes.

Sally Lee sat disconsolately, chin in hand. "Daddy, I'm just sick you haven't entered Aralee! Why not?"

"A green horse that's never run? In company like this? You must be crazy!"

There were thirteen harness events with $7,500 for purses, running races with $250 purses, and innumerable heats. Monday passed and Tuesday, each complete with thrills. The crowd was settling down. Elimination heats had weeded out many entries and the time was beginning to drop. Ariel in the 2:16 trotting class made 2:22. Torsion in 1:03½ ran the three-quarter mile with lots to spare.

Rogier had begun to look tense and moody. Quitting the grandstand, he spent his time with Denman in the paddock. In the evenings he did not come home for supper, but stayed at Denman's ranch. There he went over Aralee as though she were a fragile piece of amber glass. Aralee, following Little Man, was Akeepee's second colt. A liver-colored chestnut with the same markings – a diamond in her forehead, and white stockings on her near fore and off hind feet, she was in appearance, size, and temperament exactly like her mother. An inch under fifteen hands high, with long sloping shoulders, hocks well down, Aralee showed in her breeding Akeepee's Maryland blue-blood. Just three years old, she paced like a veteran. Gentle and unexcitable as her mother, she ran as if she were alone in all the world. Another Akeepee with the strength of youth, a dream come true at last!

Darkness settled. The stars popped out. Out on the prairies a coyote yapped. "Well, what do you think? It's a terrible chance to take," said Rogier.

Denman lit his pipe. "Damn that Judge! Did you really horsewhip him that time?"

"I said what do you think?"

Denman gave him a curious look. "There never was a horse any righter."

"Then take her down tonight. Late. And be careful." He turned and walked away.

At breakfast on the last day of the meeting Rogier announced curtly, "Everybody be at the track today! I want you to see what a good horse can do!"

"Which one? Taffy Lass?" Sally Lee asked morosely.

"Keep the bit between your teeth and you'll find out."

The big race of the day was a mile for three-year-olds and up, the winners of the previous elimination heats. The four leaders were Priam, a big gray from the North End; Cheyenne Annie, a Wyoming horse; a beautiful bay mare Ilena II, from Denver; and a nervous little buckskin from New Mexico called Mazie. To compete against these winners the Association had brought one of the finest pacers on the Grand Western Circuit, a foreign chestnut named Taffy Lass, the much touted favorite. Just before the horses were led out, Rogier left the family's box and walked down to the track. They could see his wide shoulders holding back the crowd, legs wide apart, a wisp of smoke from his cigar ruffling in the wind which was to prevent fast time. Denman and Nigger Bill were not in sight.

The long string filed out, followed by the chestnut, fashionably late but not enough to irk the waiting judges. The crowd set up a yell. Taffy Lass, the favorite! The liver-colored chestnut stood in a tremble hardly visible, head down like a thoroughbred in a pasture, wholly unconcerned over the noise, the flutter of ribbons, and the trouble in keeping Mazie still.

"What's the matter with Taffy Lass today?" asked Sally Lee. "Every time she's showed off she keeps arching her neck like she was taking a bow." She kept intently staring at Taffy Lass. "Seems to me she had white stockings on one forefoot and both hindfeet. Do you remember?"

"It's the wrappings. I can't tell," answered Cable.

Then Taffy Lass turned around, stretching out her long neck. Sally Lee caught her breath. The line of those long sloping shoulders, the white diamond on her forehead! Abruptly they broke away, lunged forward, and were off. Sally Lee jumped to her feet. "Aralee! Aralee! It's Aralee!" she kept screaming. A hundred times she had watched that awkward first plunge as the mare settled into her gait, the level head, nose forward, the deceptive long stride. "Aralee! Watch our Aralee!"

The gray beat her at the start, the nervous Mazie jerking at the reins and setting up the dust beside her; but Sally Lee's gaze hung on Aralee. She couldn't tell who was driving, but it wasn't Denman. Ilena II broke from the field with Cheyenne Annie close behind. At the first turn six sulkies were spread out across the track. The little buckskin was too eager and lost her place to the big gray. Ilena II kept her stride like a lady and fought it out with Cheyenne Annie for second place. A length behind, Aralee drew away from the field and slowly crept up on the leaders. With her long even stride she seemed to be moving slowly but unconcernedly, nose out and slightly up, running without effort. Sally Lee shifted her gaze to the man in the sulky. "Oh, if only he doesn't give her her head! I hope Daddy told him what to do till the half!"

As the field swept into the far turn, Sally Lee glanced from the track to steal a look at Rogier down at the finish line. He had thrown away his cigar and stood as if alone and lonely, twisting the hat in his hands. Denman in overalls stood silently beside him. In the box with her, Mrs. Rogier was shrilly screaming at old Mrs. White, wrapped in blankets. Lida Peck and Cable sat with wide eyes, watching a lady of the family run her race. Ona breathed deeply as if at the end of a silent prayer and clasped her hands. And only that great seamed face of Pike's Peak rising majestic and unmoved above the cottonwoods along the creek, stared down at the crowd clamoring for Taffy Lass to lead into the stretch.

It was very close. Aralee and Ilena II, both ladies, were neck and neck with their respective partners, Mazie and Cheyenne Annie. Priam, the gray Beau Brummel, was back with the field. The little buckskin, still nervous, shied at the fluttering ribbons ahead of her at the finish just enough to let Aralee cut ahead into the stretch. Cheyenne Annie who, unharnessed, might have run the legs off any horse on open prairie, gave way to Ilena II. The two ladies swept evenly into the long straight stretch.

Ilena II was fighting beautifully, reins limp on her back, every tremendous stride seeming likely to tear apart her slender body. But Aralee! – in the sunlight she was dark with sweat, her nostrils flaming pink, and still she ran smoothly true in every paced stride, like a machine whirring in perfect time. She had her head and kept her course like an arrow.

Sally Lee jumped up, a flood of tears bursting from her eyes until she could hardly see. Aralee's driver had lifted his whip. "Goddamim" she screamed through her tears. "Don't let him whip her, God! Now now!"

But he did. Yet of Sally Lee, Denman clawing his lower lip, immobile Rogier, of all the crowd, Aralee was the only one who did not seem to notice the whiplash laid on her flank.

Sally Lee let out a single, sobbing scream. "Akeepee!" It was the one perfect tribute. Aralee swept in a nose ahead.

The crowd went wild. Much as it would have liked to see its own horse win, a champion and a favorite had demonstrated her right to their acclaim. The Rogiers stood watching people pouring down from the stands, filling the winning sulky with flowers, and throwing a garland upon a liver-colored chestnut dark with sweat. A few days ago they had stood on the street, a mere family up from Shook's Run, marveling at all the gorgeous flowers displayed by the North End. And now look! Look at those same flowers being thrown at a horse raised in their own back yard, a spindling colt begging cookies at the kitchen door. Aralee! Not Taffy Lass, but Aralee!

Rogier, down on the track, had his hands full pushing back the crowd while Denman hurriedly blanketed Aralee and Nigger Bill unhitched her from the sulky, so they could lead her to the tents. A man in a top hat walked up with the judges. "A beautiful run, Rogier. We just can't thank you. You'll be in your office tomorrow?" Shaking Rogier's hand, he helped to keep back the crowd.

In a dusky stall in the big tent they were alone now. Rogier removed the garland from Aralee's long wet neck. Unobtrusively he tore out a rose and thrust it into his coat pocket. Then he stood at her head, swabbing her nostrils with a wet sponge while Denman and Nigger Bill rubbed her down. Two stalls down, some hostlers were dousing Taffy Lass with warm water to stain her coat darker. Finally Denman and Nigger Bill blanketed Aralee and fastened the straps.

"Is she all right?" asked Rogier.

Denman grinned back. "All right? There never was a horse any righter!"

Rogier thrust a roll of bills into Nigger Bill's hand.

"No, suh!" remonstrated Nigger Bill. "Ah put mah wad on huh nose! I'se all fixed good!"

"Well it won't hurt none if George Washington collects his little bet too, will it?"

They slapped each other on the back, then Rogier turned to Denman. "When it gets dark hitch her to the buckboard and walk her back slowly. I'll see you later."

As he drove down Bijou Hill on his way home, Rogier could see the house ablaze with lights. He pushed open the door, crossed the hall into the dining room. The table was set with a fancy lace cloth and the buffet was stacked with china and polished silver. In the front room all the family were waiting in their Sunday best. Mrs. Rogier was wearing her black silk dress, at her breast a silver brooch given her by Hiney who had lifted it from the boudoir of a famous actress.

"Daddy! I knew she could do it!" yelled Sally Lee.

"I reckon she did come in first," Rogier said shyly.

"I'm just dying to have it!" began Mrs. Rogier. "We could see it from the stand. Isn't it lovely? It'll hang right over the mantel. Then we'll save it in the trunk with the Confederate flag."

"What's that, Martha?" he asked.

Switching around on her chair like a duchess assuming imperial sway, she stuck out her foot for Rogier to tie a black ribbon shoe-lace. While he knelt awkwardly before her, she went on. "That big horseshoe of roses they put over Aralee's head. And that sulky-full of flowers. Why, we'll have enough to smell up the whole house! I told Mary Ann I'd give her a switching if she didn't fill every vase in the house with water. And you better hurry to get fixed up before they come, too!"

Rogier rose slowly and backed against the fireplace. "Who's that coming, you say?"

Mrs. Rogier got up and stamped her foot. "Why, the men with the flowers if you didn't fetch them! And all the people who'll be coming down to congratulate us now they know it was Aralee instead of Taffy Lass. We're all ready to give them wine and coffee. And Mary Ann had some of Durgess' finest cakes sent down." Something in Rogier's face kindled her to sudden anger. "Of course they will! Even the North Enders aren't that stuck up! Why, if Aralee was a nigger's horse you know we'd go down to congratulate him!"

Rogier looked hard and grim. "Sit down and keep quiet. And you, Mary Ann, bring Lida in here too. I've got something to say to all of you that's not to be repeated outside of this house."

He stated the facts briefly and methodically. He and Judge Colton, as they remembered, had had a little trouble after the Judge had ruined Akeepee. That's why he had walked out of the Gentlemen's Driving Association, but without submitting his resignation. All these years the Judge had nursed his grudge, and he had finally got even by not allowing Rogier to enter Aralee. Maybe he was right. By Rogier's failure to submit his resignation, he had been carried on the books as a member who had never paid his dues and was therefore ineligible to enter a horse as a member of the new racing association formed from it. Nor could Rogier enter Aralee as a visiting horse.

But as the meeting got under way, something happened. Taffy Lass had been brought at great expense in order to insure the racing association's admittance into the Grand Western Circuit. She had been exhibited the first day with state-wide publicity, drawing a great crowd to see her run. But the next morning after a workout she had come in weak and trembling like a foaled colt. Off her feed, the altitude, nobody knew what. The owners refused to let her run lest she be injured irreparably. Think what happened to Akeepee. In this devil of a fix the officials themselves had appealed to Rogier to benefit the association, the great crowd, the town itself with a harmless subterfuge. Aralee, an unknown horse, was the same size, color, and build as Taffy Lass, and her clocking on Denman's track warranted her substitution for Taffy Lass. Who could tell the difference in the excitement? In return for this favor, Rogier would be reinstated as a member of the racing association, permitting him to run Aralee under her own name thereafter. What would be the harm? Rogier had been undecided. But Denman had swung him over with a single remark. "Let's see her run. We've waited and worked long enough, Joe." Didn't he owe Denman that, and Nigger Bill, and Akeepee herself? So he assented.

"Poppycock! Monkey business! They've pulled the wool over your eyes!" Mrs. Rogier stood up, her frail body shaking until the black beads trembled on her throat. "Aralee won! That's all there is to it! And me and the girls will see to it everybody in town knows it, if we have to go door to door!"

"Nobody would believe you, Martha. Taffy Lass' name is posted on the records. Not even her owners could do anything about it now. Everybody would think you were just bragging."

There was a deathly silence in the room. Word by word he had stripped away every possibility of flowers, of congratulatory guests, of even confiding the secret to neighbors. Now after twenty years of raising horses, the betrayal of Akeepee, and Little Man's disgrace, Aralee had justified their faith only to have Rogier reduce their one great triumph to the taste of ashes on every tongue.

Sally Lee flung over on the sofa, head down, hands clenched, and began to sob. Rogier walked over to her. "Don't take it like that, girl," he said in a low, halting voice. "When the *Gazette* comes out with a picture of Aralee and Taffy Lass's name under it, let's just sit back and chuckle. It's not the talk and the flowers that count. Akeepee's finally run her race, and Aralee. So've all of us too, I reckon. We all know that, and it's enough." His hand suddenly encountered the crushed rose in his coat pocket. He brought it out and bashfully entwined its stem in Sally Lee's hair. "Dom! It was just a horse race, wasn't it?"

11

The track meeting with Aralee was the straw that indicated how the wind was shifting. Rogier was in trouble in Cripple Creek.

The dip of the original Garnet vein ran northwest and the working shaft had been sunk in a parallel incline in the footwall in order to obtain minimum cost and maximum stability. Diggs and Handel had come to grief at a fault in the vein. It appeared to have been displaced some distance westward, then continuing at the same angle into the leased Fleur-de-Lis property. At this time Rogier, becoming a partner, took over the development. In order to avoid excessive drifting and long tramming by cars to the chutes, it was decided that it would be cheaper to sink another shaft westward at a site suitable for the surface plant. Accordingly Rogier sank a vertical shaft cutting the inclined vein at the second level – two hundred feet. It was continued another hundred feet and the levels connected by a winze, an interior shaft driven at an angle downward in the ore body from a drift and used for ventilation. A new shaft house and boiler room were built, and a small electric light plant installed. Then again the vein had faulted just before the lease was up. Rogier had wired Diggs and Handel to come up on the noon train and was now waiting for them.

It was early fall and the air was chill. Across the gulch he could see a few hirsute aspens quaking in the breeze. A muffled sound as of blasting rolled in upon him, immediately dispelled by the shrill scream of a whistle. It was one o'clock; and exactly on time, like men who thought little of keeping their word but who kept their working hours punctiliously as slaves, Diggs and Handel walked in the door.

Diggs with his bald head, sharp nose, and chamois gloves reminded Rogier of a Thanksgiving turkey. Handel had small feral eyes and a dead white face so smoothly shaven that the bluish tint of his whiskers underneath made his fleshy cheeks appear bloated and decomposed.

Rogier stated the conditions tersely. The assays had been decreasing alarmingly; again the vein had faulted; the lease on the Fleur-de-Lis was almost up. If it were not renewed all the development expense would be lost. If it were renewed there was no guarantee they would not be throwing good money after bad. However he believed that with a crosscut they would pick up the vein again; the Fleur-de-Lis was within the curve of the prophyry limits. He wanted their concurrence and money to proceed.

The two men settled back, Diggs drawing his chamois gloves between his fingers; Handel, poker-faced, eyeing him steadily across the table. They had already discussed the matter, Diggs said, and were ready to abandon the disappointing venture. They both hoped the partnership could be dissolved amicably, and that next time with better luck – his voice spun out into silence.

Something in their ready acquiescence to defeat sounded a warning Rogier could not ignore. "All right. We have only to balance the books and allocate your shares of the cost of the development to you for payment. Also the whole of last month's running expenses which I've paid without holding things up to locate you."

The two men droned their rebuttal in oily tones, Handel murmuring apologetically about poor business in their trucking business, the unpaid loans at the bank. Diggs finally came to the point, explaining that the two mines were not separated specifically in the partnership agreement, and that as he and Handel had done their share on the Garnet, it had been up to Rogier to develop the Fleur-de-Lis.

"Preposterous!" Rogier said gruffly. "The Garnet was your own sole venture long before I came in. The development of the Fleur-de-Lis was undertaken by the three of us as partners, bearing equal shares of the cost!"

"As I say, the agreement does not separate the two interlocked mines. We've had it carefully gone over by legal counsel."

"Poppycock, and you know it!" snorted Rogier. "Personally I believe enough in the Fleur-de-Lis to renew the lease by myself if you're backing out."

"But the lease is in our three names. It can't be renewed by one separately," answered Diggs softly.

"All I want from you now is the statement you're through! Are you or aren't you?"

The now heated conference ended fifteen minutes before train-time with the verbal agreement that Diggs and Handel, through their lawyer who had drawn up the partnership agreement, would renew the lease in all their names for another six months, and that operations should be continued. They shook hands formally, and the two men rushed for their train.

The months dragged by. Rogier's suspicions increased. The noncommittal lawyer, Nicholas, who had drawn up the original agreement, stated he had received no instructions to draw up an extension of the lease. Diggs and Handel could not be found; whenever Rogier called at their office, they were out of town. Rogier accepted this as plausible, for they owned a trucking business that covered a large area. Curtailing expenses was not enough; Rogier was running short of cash with the heavy drain upon him. Reason and suspicion counseled him to shut down the working and sit tight. Yet some perverse compulsion kept him driving down the shaft.

Then he happened to think of Stratton who had agreed to guarantee him against loss in return for a one-sixth share of the Fleur-de-Lis if Rogier would develop his American Eagles.

This Rogier had done. The American Eagle No. 1 and Number 2 on top of Bull Hill were great mines in the Stratton tradition and with Stratton's millions behind them to provide a great shaft house containing the best surface plant money could buy, deep shafts, tunnels well timbered with seasoned pine stulls and props, and a triple expansion pumping engine with a capacity of one thousand gallons a minute. The work had been little trouble, and Rogier had taken the precaution of installing change rooms to prevent high-grading.

The practice was becoming profitable in the district. Selected high-grade ore worth from $10 to $30 a pound could be slipped out by miners wearing high-graders' belts under their clothes. Change rooms prevented these thefts. The arrangement provided two rooms, one for working clothes and the other for street clothes, miners being obliged to walk naked between them so that concealed ore could be detected.

Stratton meanwhile had sailed to Europe in an effort to recuperate from the strain of worry over his mounting millions, and his excessive drinking. None of the spas did him any good – Aix-les-Bains in southern France, Constance in Switzerland, Carlsbad, Vienna, Brighton on the south coast of England. Suddenly from London came the electrifying news that in a fit of despair he had sold his Independence for $10,000,000.

Now, in the midst of Rogier's worries, he returned home and shortly walked down the alley to Rogier's shop. Rogier was frightened at the change in him. Frail and wasted, moody and irritable, Stratton had begun to die. He seemed pleased enough with the work done at the American Eagles, but with his hands twitching he demanded abruptly why Rogier had fired a man called Bert Jensen.

"He's a high-grader and an agitator. I kicked him out the minute I recognized him," Rogier replied.

Stratton's gray-blue eyes chilled. "You're working for me now and don't you forget it! When I send a man up to work for me he stays!"

They faced each other for the last time: Rogier who first had worked for Stratton, Stratton who then worked for Rogier, and now Rogier who again had worked for Stratton.

"Not with me around, Stratton!"

Stratton flew into a rage. "This is the last time I'll have any dealing with you! I'm through with you for good!" He yanked out his check book. "I'm going to pay you off for everything! How much?"

Rogier was about to mention the large sum representing Stratton's private one-sixth share in the Fleur-de-Lis and for which he was now in debt. Before he could speak, Stratton, who perhaps had forgotten the matter, resumed his tirade while scribbling his name on a blank check. "Everybody I know is trying to get something out of me, trumping up verbal promises, filing fake lawsuits, foisting off on me dry holes! Here! Fill out the amount yourself and be damned to you!"

Rogier looked at the check after Stratton had stalked out the alley door. It had been signed, but the amount left blank. How shrewd his old carpenter had become! Had he really trusted his old friend to fill out a modest amount? Or was he already on his way to the bank to stop payment? Or was this merely a grand gesture to shame him? Angry himself, Rogier thrust the check in a book on the shelf.

The agonizing months wore on. Distrusting lawyers whom he had never used as an honest builder, and trying to conceal his affairs from Ona, he depended on himself to weather the storm: borrowing money from the bank, transferring his accounts back and forth, selling one of his downtown store buildings. When this was not sufficient, he bid on two new construction jobs – one for rebuilding the Broadmoore Casino which had burned down, a lucrative job which he lost; and the other a four-story addition to one of the town's hotels which was awarded to him. With this to supervise as well as the Silver Heels and Fleur-de-Lis, he was seldom in the shop.

"What's this bill for pumping equipment marked Gloriana?" Ona asked him one day when he came in. "Don't tell me you've opened another new working, Daddy?"

"Pay it and forget it! I know what I'm doing if you don't!"

It was soon evident that he didn't. He was too frantically busy, in fact, to follow the rumors of Stratton's activities until the official reports made front-page news. The Midas of the Rockies, Colorado's Count of Monte Cristo, the Croesus of Cripple Creek was dying of a cirrhotic liver and diabetes, and drinking more than ever. But the other fatal disease he had contracted years before was spreading at a more alarming pace. Through his veins raced liquid gold; from his inflamed mind rose fantasies of greater wealth – no less than all the gold in Cripple Creek. To obtain it he already had bought hundreds of claims and acres, one-fifth of all the gold producing area, and was still buying every mine and working he could get his hands on. Nor was this enough. The Klondike gold rush in Alaska was under way; and Stratton, outfitting an expedition, had sent two boats, the *W.S. Stratton* and the *Florence,* up the Yukon to Dawson.

If this tragic display of the last ravages of gold fever shocked Rogier, he was stunned by the impertinent assumption on which Stratton had based his Cripple Creek purchases. Why, he believed that the convergence of all the veins and ore chutes criss-crossing the district was somewhere in the triangle marked by Gold, Globe and Ironclad Hill. What a monstrous fantasy!

Rogier's own intuition had guided him slowly and surely up into the neck of that heart-like, pear-shaped, porphyritic area of mineralization; over the Altman saddle; up the narrowing gulch beyond the Silver Heels to the root-stem of the fruit – that deep crack high on the slope of the Peak itself into which he would strike into its golden heart. But to prove it, he would have to strike a showing in the Fleur-de-Lis; and Stratton's announced assumption only committed him further to the folly of pouring down its shaft all the profits from his job in town.

The assays increased in value, but pay ore had not been reached and the renewed lease ran out. Rogier knew he had reached the end of his rope. He dismissed the crew, closed the mine, and notified Diggs and Handel he was through. This time they were in their office with Nicholas when he arrived for the meeting.

"I'm sorry we were not advised of your action in closing the mine," said Diggs. "Handel and I had just persuaded Mr. Nicholas here to extend the lease again. Now you have made it worthless. But as long as termination papers have drawn, you might as well sign your release so we can wind things up legally."

Rogier gave each of the three men a look of unutterable scorn. "You heard what I said, didn't you? I'm through!" He turned and walked out the door with the same ingrained integrity and foolish pride with which his father before him had relinquished his rice plantation.

In despair he went to one of the best mining lawyers in town in an effort to obtain reimbursement of expenses for his development of the working. The lawyer, Brooks, listened to him carefully. "Leave your papers with me, Mr. Rogier, and come back a week from today. My secretary will give you an appointment."

A week later Brooks received him with a dour face. "I have reviewed your matter fully, Mr. Rogier. I find this agreement highly irregular. May I be presumptious enough to ask why, before entering into such a partnership and spending such considerable sums of money, you did not come to me or another reputable mining attorney?"

"Diggs and Handel assured me that Nicholas would handle the matter to all our best interests."

"Mr. Nicholas is retained to look after the best interest of Mr. Diggs and Mr. Handel and their freight truckage business. Apparently he has done so."

"I'm not in the habit of questioning any man's integrity! My own word's as good as my bond. Ask any man!"

"I have," replied Brooks softly. Then after looking at Rogier a long time he said sternly, "Mr. Rogier. Business is growing more and more complicated. Each type has its own peculiarities. That's why there are professional attorneys in every field. No one should hesitate to take advantage of them." He drummed on the table with his fingers. "You might take the case to court, but I couldn't handle it. There are holes in this agreement you could drive an elephant through."

Rogier jumped up from his chair. "You're trying to tell me I've been hoodwinked and hornswaggled by those mountebanks, thieves, and downright crooks!"

Brooks' only reply was to open his hands emptily.

Ona, entering the shop a short time later, saw Rogier bending over a roaring fire in the stove. "What are you burning on such a warm morning, Daddy?"

Rogier snorted. "All that stock in the Garnet and Fleur-de-Lis I bought out of courtesy to those two mountebanks!"

Ona looked at him a long time. Then she said quietly, "That stock went up this morning seventeen points on the announcement that Diggs and Handel had sold the properties to Stratton."

The look in his eyes was frightening. She went back to the house.

Diggs and Handel had sold out just in time. That September Stratton died – just over ten years since he, as an obscure carpenter and penniless prospector, had discovered the Independence and opened up the greatest gold camp on earth.

The fame and the glory of success, the thunderous roar of world acclaim, the glowing wealth of Cripple Creek gold – what did it matter to a man who like Silver Dollar Tabor before him now lay entombed in pinkish Pike's Peak granite, while down a hundred gulches the sparse aspens quaked in the breeze, and wisps of clouds gathered languidly above the Peak to presage the first snowfall?

Rogier released the end of his T-square to slap decisively on the drafting table and stared out the window. The sun was rising but a few stars still shone brightly in the sky. Once again it loomed before him as it had the first time he had glimpsed it a quarter of a century ago; like something risen from the depths of dreamless sleep to the horizon of wakeful consciousness, without clear outline yet embodying the substance of a hope and meaning that seemed as vaguely familiar as it was ineffable. The clouds lifted. Shadows, seams, and wrinkles smoothed out. Under the rising sun it lifted a face, serene, majectic, and suffused a glowing pink, yet wearing a look benign, compassionate, and divine that he had never recognized before. Oh great mother of mountains, womb of all creation, Self of all selves, how he had misjudged her! She was not an adversary but an ally in his quest. Men had lived and died, never knowing what they sought while she had waited to clasp them to her granite breast, to take them into the prophyric womb from which they had been born, and to welcome them home again into the one vast golden heart of which they had been a single beat. There she stood as she had stood for aeons immeasurable and would still stand, rearing solidly aloft until the stars themselves were pulled from their sockets by the hand of Time. But he himself was Time! He could feel the ages born within him hardening his bones as they had hardened the sharks' teeth imbedded in the limestone cliffs, running through his veins with their ebbs and tides, evolving the brain cells that had envisioned the image of the goal now clear before him. Time! Eternity would give him all the time he needed to achieve it.

Mrs. Rogier pushed open the door. "Daddy! Haven't you been to bed all night! You wanted to catch the first train to Cripple Creek, so I came down."

He patted her clumsily on the back. Good women, like bright blades, shine best in adversity. "Just doing a little figuring, Martha. That's all."

"It's going to snow up there. I've laid out your winter coat and packed your bag. You better get ready. Ona and Jonathon will be coming after you."

"I'm ready, Martha! Been ready a long time!" he answered cheerfully.

BOOK TWO

Below Grass Roots

PART I

GRANITE

1

To glimpse again, after an absence of only months, that great Peak rising over the ears of his team; to watch it take shape above the forested slopes of pine and spruce and sparse aspen, above the frost-shattered granite of timberline; to see it stand at last an imperturbable sentinel on the crest of that Great Divide which separates earth and heaven as it does dreamless sleep and wakeful consciousness – to meet it thus, face to face, was to arouse in Rogier a resurgence of those inexpressible thoughts and conflicting emotions provoked always in a man who returns to a realm which destiny has marked for his own.

He drove steadily up the steep winding road, reins held loosely in his hands, the wind stirring gently the wisps of white hair sticking out from his hat. Ahead of him two men on foot were puffing up the grade. Rogier pulled up beside them. "Figurin' on a ride, boys?"

"We wasn't figurin' on it," spoke up one, stowing his blanket roll in back, "but we ain't objectin' any."

The two men climbed in beside him, both giants, middle-aged, red-faced, and dressed in corduroys and flannel shirts. For a time none of them spoke. "We're getting along," Rogier said at last. "You're just coming to the district?"

The two men looked him over again before replying: his black broadcloth coat stretched over his wide shoulders, the excellent but dust-covered hat, and beneath it the calm forceful face of a man with its graying mustache and white wisps of hair who looked as if he had long known the vagaries of men and mines alike.

"We had us a job in the mill in the Springs," said one. "To get it we had to take out a union card, and then the Standard let us out because we had one."

"What's the trouble?"

"Not enough pay. $1.80 a day less'n five cents insurance and one percent discount. So the Western Federation of Miners is organizin' the mill workers to get $2.50."

"Anyway we lost our jobs and have come up to Cripple to hunt for another. You got somethin'?" asked the other.

"Not a thing, sorry to say," answered Rogier.

"Saw an outfit in back, beggin' pardon," the other refuted calmly. "We ain't scabs or union men neither. Jes' two hungry men huntin' for bed and board."

For a moment the men were silent. Then one said, "I tell you, Colonel, if you're figurin' on somethin, we can keep our mouths shut and are tolerable hard-rock miners – leastways we get up our appetites. You might be keepin' us in mind. Zebbelin's the name. Jake here and me, Abe."

"I'll remember you, boys."

"And what do you call yourself, Colonel?"

"Rogier. Joseph Rogier. Plain Mister, boys."

"That's all right," spoke up Jake, drawing his finger under his woolen collar protruding an inch from his creased brown neck. "Somethin's liable to pop up any time. You can't ship scenery no more. You got to go down below grass roots. But mines are just like ladies. Stubborn as all get-out, not a welcomin' smile for months. And then first thing you know, like spring had got under their hides, there they be just beamin' at you all over! Take that old workin' we had once. Refusin' to show a color all winter. Then when Abe got mad and heaved his pick into her fer the last time – what do you reckon he saw! In a piece of quartz no bigger'n a fist, four leaders of wire gold you could pick out with a nail! Yes, sir! If you got a flighty workin' in mind, me and Abe's the men for you!"

Garrulous old men! Rogier shut his ears to their steady flow; and when they reached the Gold Coin shaft house on Diamond Avenue in Victor, he was glad to slip them a bill for eats and drive on alone. It was a steep cruel grade up to Altman on the high saddle between Bull Hill and Bull Cliffs. Putting up his team, he walked along the street and sat down on the rickety porch of Smith and Peters' saloon. Sam's highest city in the world was an eyrie of unpainted shacks overlooking the richest producing area in the district. Nearby rose the great shaft house Rogier had built for the American Eagles, and the Garnet and Fleur-de-Lis he had given up. Directly below him lay the Independence and Portland, and three other great producers – the Buena Vista, Victor, and Jones' Pharmacist. To the south lay Victor and Goldfield surrounded by the portals and gallows frames of a hundred more mines, thinning out toward Cable's New Moon on Big Bull. None of them mattered to Rogier. For to the north spread out his own garden of dreams pasturing the immemorial cow and her calf.

Directly below him, inclining west to east, stretched a grassy alpine valley watered by a meandering creek. From it now rose a small puff of smoke followed by the faint screech of a whistle. He watched a toy train emerge to view, running over a spindly straw trestle, chugging up Grassy Gulch and vanishing on its climb into the district. Across the meadow to the northeast rose Cow Mountain and her Calf, a thousand feet lower and sucking at a teat of granite protruding from her aspen covered flanks. Between them, entering this grassy trough from the north, lay a steeply rising gulch down which wound Beaver Creek and an old wagon road. Near its mouth Rogier could make out the shaft house of the Silver Heels and Reynolds' enlarged shanty. Above it, the right fork of the gulch narrowed and deepened, rising past a thin grove of aspens beyond which lay the Gloriana. Still it rose upward like a deep cleft in the granite cliffs. And above it, sheer and shaven, stood the pink face of the summit of the Peak itself. It looked, from where he sat at 11,000 feet, as close as a face in a mirror, one whose features he knew better than his own. But he could not see its deep gorges and rugged cliffs for the thing itself. As he stared back at it the sun sank with a livid blood red flare that deepened the pink of the granite hills and filled the shadowy gulches with pools of porphyry. Then suddenly it was dark. Worn out, he had a drink inside and a hearty supper before turning into bed.

Next morning at the Silver Heels he and Reynolds got down to business. Months before, when the vein began to splay out, Rogier had reminded Reynolds of his agreement to close the mine and move up the gulch to the Gloriana. Reynolds had bucked; he was sure they would pick up the vein again. But Rogier was obstinate and Reynolds had moved his crew to open the new working.

Everything had gone wrong from the start. The Gloriana ran into water. Cripple Creek from the beginning had been known as a wet mining district. Annual precipitation of from fifteen to eighteen inches accumulated water which had no outlet from this big granite bowl of porphyry. Hence the depth limit of all mines was restricted by the underground water that filled the shafts faster than it could be pumped out. As the average altitude of the top of the bowl was about 9,200 feet, and the average altitude of the mine portals was 10,000 feet, the depth limit of the shafts was 800 feet. But when Reynolds began to drill into clammy gangue below the first level he protested to Rogier with a common-sense observation. The Gloriana lay in a steep gulch that received the runoff of the snowpacks on the very summit of the Peak. There was no use going deeper.

Rogier was stubborn. He argued that its portal elevation was not too much higher than that of the Strong Mine on Battle Mountain at 9,756 feet, and the depth of the first water level would not be far short of the 700 feet of the Strong. "What if it's only half that?" he demanded. "Keep going down!"

They resumed drilling – at $36 a foot through hard granite. Two hundred feet down Reynolds struck water. Indomitably Rogier snaked in and installed pumps. Still the Gloriana, water-logged as an old ship weary for its inevitable grave, wallowed in a sea of eruptive porous rock that soaked up water like a sponge. The men, in slimy clothes that never dried out, began to grumble. Reynolds, who never swore, swore. Only Rogier kept silent. By day he would stand there, worrying about the huge sum he had sunk into the Garnet and Fleur-de-Lis for the benefit of Diggs and Handel, the loss of income from the abandoned Silver Heels and abandoned construction work in Little London, and watching pour out in a muddy stream one of his downtown store buildings and a house in town. In the evening after the crew had left he would still be there staring up the gulch. The clouds rolled in and all became a billowing sea of white upon which floated, high above, an iceberg of stainless purity, its smooth sides unscored by any mark of mortal earth. A little light-headed from the thin rarefied air perhaps, Rogier was discomfited by its metamorphosis from the intimately personal to the monstrously impersonal. It was as if that great living entity had withdrawn into a sheath of ice which it was melting, day and night, to flood his world with water.

The rains began, confirming the illusion. Water poured down the gulch in an angry flood. Patches of soggy earth on the hillsides gave way, carrying down trees and boulders. The few aspens, dripping rain, provided little firewood. The men, already slimy from manning the pumps, became soggy under the onslaught of water from above and below. Rogier could not break the spell cast upon him. Every time he went down the shaft, feeling the dank walls closing about him and hearing the gurgle of water below, he felt like a foetus still immersed in its prenatal fluid darkness, struggling vainly to be released to a world of air and earth.

"We'll empty her!" he kept insisting, reminding Reynolds that the new El Paso drainage tunnel, a mile long and built at a cost of $80,000, had lowered the water level to 8,800 feet.

Reynolds had become strangely quiet and solicitous. "But we're above that, Colonel," he said gently. "This ain't no mine. It's a well."

"Keep on pumping, man. I'll foot the bills."

Just how, Rogier did not know. But with great effort he tore himself away, and went down to Little London to find out. A week later when he returned, Rogier found the Gloriana boarded up and abandoned. Reynolds had taken the men back to the Silver Heels and was driving a new tunnel. It had saved him, despite his shocked amazement at the unspoken firmness of his uncouth partner. Not only had Reynolds immediately stopped his frightful expenditures, enabling him that winter to finish two construction jobs in Little London which restored his credit at the banks, but he had struck pay ore again.

But now again that mounting frantic urge had driven him to face Reynolds across the long kitchen table in his quarters at the Silver Heels. "Look, man!" He laid the results of the last assays before him. "Down to a half-ounce again. I told you at the beginning this was not a blanket vein or a chimney. Just gash veins always petering out. We've got to go down. Way down. And way up the gulch. There's where we'll strike the sheer wall of the granite dropping into the prophyry heart."

Mrs. Reynolds came in with a pot of coffee and two mugs. "Colonel, you hadn't ought to be movin' us again. Not when we're so comfortable like." She waved a hand toward the chinked walls plastered with the warm pink front pages of the *Denver Post,* the little bedroom adjoining, where they slept, the room beyond with bunks for the unmarried men of the crew who lived with them, and the opposite kitchen with its big wood stove and stocked shelves. "Why, this has been home for us nigh on ten years, Colonel! The boys and us are jes' one happy family!" She flounced out to her interminably dirty pots and pans.

"He's not movin' me!" Reynolds called to her departing footsteps with the voice of a new and unwarranted independence. "I'm rememberin' that day when I staked her out – the Silver Heels. And I reckon you ain't forgot the day you grubstaked me either, Colonel. There was gold here, like I told you. Not too much or too little, but enough. Sure we've had our ups and downs. But through thick and thin I've stuck by you. And so has the Silver Heels."

Yes, Rogier remembered it and more too – the humbleness and faithfulness of these two stout souls who had become like members of his own family. What could he have done without them? Still he knew how a man got attached to a mine, the great fallacy of every mining camp.

"That's true," he admitted. "But every mine, even the best one, has its day. Let's go on to a better one, Reynolds!"

"The Magpie, eh?"

Rogier grinned like a boy caught stealing cookies. "I did use that name when I filed papers on her," he confessed.

"Well, I don't know of a better one. The second bird in the bush worth less'n the one in hand!"

Rogier resumed his attack. "Look at its showin'. Here!"

Reynolds ignored the assays spread out before him, looking at Rogier as if he had heard all this an incalculable number of times. "We been all through this with the Gloriana. She's waterlogged, watersoaked, a bloomin' well."

Rogier leaned forward and as if imparting a great secret said solemnly, "But we're going above water."

Reynolds, so often childish, answered as if speaking to a still younger child. "Above water? Colonel, above gold."

"Why, man – " Rogier suddenly halted. There were some things he could not say to any man.

Reynolds' long narrow face with its walrus mustaches softened with the trace of a benign smile. "Now here's the Silver Heels. A producin' gold mine. Payin' the boys a livin' wage, providin' me and the Old Girl a mite against rheumatism and a rainy day, payin' your own bills, Colonel! And here you want to desert her again for a no-account claim outside the prophyry, way up the Peak itself! Partner, I believe in our mine. I'll stick by her!"

Nevertheless two weeks later men and mules began hauling the machinery salvaged from the Gloriana up the gulch to the Magpie, and cutting timber for a cabin to house Reynolds and his crew. Rogier was elated as he drove back to Little London. Not for a minute did he regret the money out of which he had been cheated by those mountebanks, Diggs and Handel. What if he had gained control of the Garnet and Fleur-de-Lis, or any of the big leases and million dollar producers with their splendid surface plants, the double-cage steam hoists, well timbered tunnels and tidy drifts, the ore blocked out and removed with mathematical precision? Then he would be facing the economics of illumination, transportation, and hoisting: estimating the tractive power of a burro on a two percent grade and deciding if the cars could be more cheaply trammed by hand, figuring the shipping and treatment cost of $30 ore – a mundane business like running a bank! But he had been saved from this by the Silver Heels and the Gloriana, each representing not only fundamentals in mining but elemental approaches to the elusive truth of his secret quest.

As he swung out of the steep-walled canyon the Peak rose to sight again. Once more it looked down upon him with a face calm and unperturbed as his own. He was free of the spell it had cast upon him. He felt born out of its gelid, watery womb into the light and air of the world outside. A deer stepped daintily across the road. A huge magpie, glistening white and blue-black, accompanied him from pine to pine. As it flew overhead one of its feathers settled on the seat beside him. An augury of good fortune! Rogier proudly fastened it in his coat lapel. The Magpie! That now was the step ahead and upward. And he was taking it resolutely, with a joyful quickening of his heart that convinced him he was nearing his goal.

2

Ona, in the last days of her pregnancy, left her little frame house to go home for confinement. Cable had wanted her to go to a hospital, but she refused. Home was home; she wouldn't think of having their baby born anywhere but in the great redwood bed in the master bedroom on the second floor. Cable's face was grim, but he said nothing. So this morning after he had gone to work, lest she hurt his feelings, she had laid out on the bed everything she wanted him to bring her and latched the door behind her.

The hour was almost nine o'clock. The sun was high in the summer sky, and she could feel its warm rays taking possession of her langorous big body as she walked slowly along the creek. It was July. The birds hopped busily through Mrs. Cullen's apple trees; the bees hummed their monotonous drone of summer; even the sand daisies and tall sunflowers in the patch of prairie beyond the Santa Fe underpass seemed to be smiling at the morning. A long block farther she reached Shook's Run and sat down weakly on the planks of the bridge, unmindful of the sun and dust.

Never in her life had she felt so secure and relaxed. It was as if her mind had been disjointed from her body, her thoughts wandering at random like clouds in the sky. Something mysterious was taking place within her body, so swollen now she could not recognize it as her own, but over it she had no control. She belonged to nature, something nebulous that had no time nor bounds but to which for the first time she felt intimately connected. As though she had never noticed them before, she watched the green leaves turning up with the breeze, their undersides coated gray with dust. Preternaturally alert, she noticed the sound of a woodpecker's hammering far up the lane of trees, the flicker of sunshine through willow branches, the murmurous undertone of Shook's Run below the iron-girded bridge. With difficulty she withdrew herself out of this vast anonymity, managed to get to her feet, and walked sedately to the tall gaunt house across the street.

Mrs. Rogier met her at the door with loud disapproval. "Of all things! Walking down alone! Jonathan come by and said he'd fetch you home 'round midday. What—you wasn't in a hurry, Ona?" she asked anxiously.

Ona laughed. "It was time to come and an awfully nice morning for a walk."

"You get up those stairs then. The room's all ready. We'll fetch the doctor just in case."

Soon the doctor came down in his buggy, joked, and said he'd look in again after supper. At noon Jonathan brought down her things. Then after a nap she put on her best nightgown and old robe, and sat resting in a big armchair drawn up in front of the windows. How wonderful to be home in this great room with its hand-burnished redwood bed, dresser, bureau, and panelling, its alcove and balcony! Methodically brushing her long hair and staring out upon the wall of mountains, cool blue in the dusty afternoon, she felt oddly detached from that complex world of the Rogiers bounded by Shook's Run and Bijou Hill. It was as if always she had been sitting here at life's window, watching like Sister Molly the intricate interplay of their human hopes and endeavors, forgiving with compassion the folly of those who lived courageously their thoughtless lives. Rogier and her mother, Sister Molly, Tom and Bob and Hiney, Mrs. White and Boné, Sally Lee and Mary Ann, Jonathan too! What a patternless fabric of continuity their lives wove, that neither ambition nor humility, nor hope and fear, courage and folly, could ever alter.

She dozed, slept. The doctor came and went. Mrs. Rogier poked her head in the door every whipstitch. "How do you feel now?" Sally Lee and Mary Ann came in. Lida brought bear soup and delicacies. Jonathan, sleeping in the alcove, was attentive. "Do you have everything you want?" She smiled. "Bring me that Two Gray Hills blanket from Shallow Water Bruce gave me. I miss it across the foot of the bed." One afternoon Rogier looked in the door. For a moment he stood motionless as if arrested by the specter of a woman wrapped in an old gray robe so like Sister Molly he stared transfixed.

"Well!" he said at last. "You're here."

Ona smiled. "It won't be long, Daddy. I'm glad that even the Kadles will be coming up the steps tonight. I wouldn't be anywhere else."

That night it happened. At five minutes till midnight. The doctor arrived in plenty of time. He could see the house blazing with lights from the top of Bijou Hill; and when he entered the house, satchel in hand, everybody in the household was crowded in the hall except Rogier who was still sitting in the shop. Yet he too came pounding up the steps when it was all over and the doctor, pen in hand, was bent over the birth certificate. "What name have you selected for this July baby, Mr. Cable?" he was inquiring.

Cable looked confused as all husbands, especially over forty, at such a time. Mrs. White, failing and irascible, stood at the foot of the bed, amazingly surprised and completely scandalized at the inevitable result of such a miscegenation of a Rogier and a De Vinney with a red niggah. Rogier flipped up the blanket, discovered that the infant had the Rogier twin toes. Yet even this apparently did not seem sufficient to allay a reasonable doubt engendered by Mrs. White's decidedly unforgiving stare.

"A July baby, nothing!" he said humorously. "The boy's going to be wild as a March wind! Eh, Cable?"

Cable's dark face set. Brushing back his straight black hair from a wet forehead, he took the pen from the Doctor with his slim brown hand, and swiftly inscribed on the certificate the name "March."

Important as a baby in the family was – and his own first grandchild – Rogier had his mind on other wild winds. There had been a fire at Altman. A block of cabins was wiped out, the gallows frames of the Pinto and Mercer mines just off the street were weakened, and all the timbering holding the dumps above the road had given way. It was necessary to clear the road for the steep climb up to the saddle and to reset the timber frames. Rogier was given the job. Hardly had he put a crew to work than he contracted to build a big mess hall and a dozen cabins on Bull Hill to house and feed those made homeless by the fire. The buildings were crude and cheap. and their construction gave him time to push work on the Magpie.

Then came another interruption far more serious. The trouble down in the ore reduction mills in Colorado City came to a sudden head early in August. The Western Federation of Miners called out all the mill workers in a general strike. Then, to make sure the mills could not receive ore shipments and reopen with scab labor, all the mines in Cripple Creek were ordered closed. Rogier could hardly believe it. The district was at its zenith with 475 shipping mines. In its ten towns and camps there was a floating population of some 43,000, with more than 6,000 men working in the mines. Yet within three days 3,500 men were out and the *Cripple Creek Times* ran the headline:

ALL THE MEN ARE NOW OUT
ALL THE FIRES ARE BANKED
GOD PROTECT THE DISTRICT!

The Mine Owners Association met and agreed to operate with scabs, opening several mines. The strikers retailiated with acts of violence. Governor Peabody ordered out the state militia with Brigadier Generals Chase and Bell in command. One thousand troopers arrived with 600,000 rounds of ammunition and a Gatling gun, establishing camp on Battle Mountain between the Portland and the Independence. The strikers derisively called it "Camp Peabody" or "Camp Goldfield," hooted at the soldiers, and on Labor Day marched throught the streets in a parade 5,000 strong. General Chase seized editor George Kyner and four members of the office force of the *Victor Record* for publishing editorials sympathetic to the strikers, and imprisoned them in a bull pen at the camp. The case brought up the question of *habeas corpus*.The prisoners asserted that as martial law had not been declared they could not be held. General Chase continued to hold them until the district judge ordered a hearing, whereupon Chase and his troop marched the prisoners to Cripple Creek. By the time they arrived at the courthouse, Bennett Avenue was lined with cavalrymen and the Gatling gun was mounted on the corner at Fourth Street. Judge Seeds imperturbably ordered Kyner and his employees released. Then followed a court-martial of the officers. General Chase was found guilty of disobedience, but Governor Peabody remitted punishment.

Rogier in his eyrie on the saddle – a one-room cabin – looked down upon crowds gathering in the streets of the camps, groups outside portals and shaft houses being harangued by shouting speakers, men walking furtively as criminals past his own door. His work held up, he remained in the district despite Mrs. Rogier's frantic letters. A cold September rain made the camp miserable. Water ran in the door of the unfinished messhall, the roofs of the cabins leaked. He was threatened with a suit for defaulting on his contract, damned by Union and scab workers whenever he tried to resume work with either. At night he slept little, watching his material. By day he stewed and fretted.

Snow and cold set in. The miners began to feel the pinch of coming winter. The troopers, unable to stand the high altitude, came down with mountain sickness and were ordered to forego coffee. Eleven hundred men were now working. A hundred more were imported from Idaho.

Then late in November it happened just below Rogier. At mid-morning in the sixth level of the Vindicator an infernal machine containing twenty-five pounds of dynamite was exploded, killing Superintendent Charles McCormick and Shift Boss Melvin Beck.

The camp went wild. More troops were rushed in under General Bell, the mine owners agreeing to loan the state enough money to pay the militia's expenses. Martial law was proclaimed. Wholesale arrests were made and the bull pen filled with men. Rogier that evening, hurriedly walking through the crowd on Diamond Avenue in Victor, suddenly felt the grip of a huge iron paw on his shoulder. Spun about, he recognized one of the giant workers to whom he had given a lift months before.

"Colonel! It's me, Jake. We wasn't doin' a thing. Just walkin' down the street when they up and grabbed Abe. That quick he was down on the ground, bleedin' from a cut on the head, and they was measurin' his foot. Just because he looked like he wore a number eight. Dammit, Colonel! You know he don't wear no number eight." He stuck out his own muck-smeared eleven.

Rogier had no opportunity to listen further to his explanation. Both of them, like flotsam on a mounting tide, were shoved inside a saloon. The place was jammed with strikers listening to a derbied figure haranguing them from on top the bar.

"Brothers! Are we going to let our lives be dictated by a capitalistic slave in striped pants planted in an armchair down in Denver?Fathers! Are we going to take the bread from our children's mouths to fill the pork barrels of mine owners with their millions? See their little hands outstretched – not for pearls and diamonds, my fathers! Not for silks and satins. For bread, fathers! Dry crusts. Dry as snow crusts in winter!"

The speaker let down his arms, fumbled the watch chain slung across his vest, and waited for the yells and stamping to subside. Rogier, with a knee at his behind, was shoved closer to him. "Men!" the speaker began again. "Workers of the soil, workers in mill and factory, workers of hard rock. The best hard-rock miners in the greatest gold camp on earth – and the least paid, by God! Listen!"

He cursed mine owners – the dirty rich; Governor Peabody – the dirty capitalistic slave; General Bell – the dirty military; and the dirty scabs. Rogier could feel the dirt sifting through his clothes. He felt intolerably smirched with profanity, his common sense insulted, and his inborn aloofness unforgivably violated. He reached up and caught the speaker by the ankle, with one quick pull bringing him down off the bar, head over heels, into a spittoon. Then quite spryly for his sixty years, he scrambled on top the bar.

"Gentlemen! A little less noise and confusion! Let's don't lose our heads!"

Jake, awakened from the spell cast upon him by the grandiloquent delivery of the moment before, stood, big and brawny, peering up at Rogier with a look of stunned amazement on his simple unlined face – like a child who had suddenly seen Cinderella jump off the page of a fairytale. The speaker on the floor beside him had just extricated his bony elbow from the brass spittoon; he got up, cursing and exhorting his companions to get that damned capitalistic spy off the bar. Jake reached out a long muscular arm and thrust him down again like a jack-in-the-box, and continued staring fixedly at Rogier. He had not even looked down. The room behind him shook with stamping and shouting. "You up front! Out with the old fool!" – "Give the Colonel a chance!" – "Look at that rock! Who said he was a scab?"

Rogier, meanwhile, looked like a man shouting at Niagra Falls. He gestured, leaned forward. His mouth opened, his lips moved. He had lost his hat; and his hair, reflecting the bar lights, shone like a silver halo. To all those figures below him, to their shouts and curses, their slow eyes burning upon him like the fires in their pipe-bowls, the wool-clad arms and stubby fingers that shot out to transfix him, he continued to deliver the unalterable convictions of an outraged man: flouting their follies with courageous sincerity, condoning their faults and condemning their injustices, and imploring their common sense. Of all this not a word was heard.

There was a sudden crash. Some troopers, riding to break up the crowd, had spurred up on the sidewalk to the door. One of the horses, rearing on its back legs, had kicked out the front window. The beast screamed, more from fright than cuts; and this shrill and frantic sound rose above the splintering of broken glass. The cavalrymen, dismounting, began to beat at the crowd. For a few moments a few lusty fellows resisted. Fists and boots beat against gun stocks, with stones, jiggers, and a bottle flying overhead. Then suddenly the trickle through the door became a cataract. In a jiffy the place was cleared. Jake, on his back in the gutter, looked back inside to see a trooper jerking Rogier to his feet from off the floor.

"Damn me! The old gent that was raisin' all the rumpus up on the bar!"

A stray missile had caught Rogier on the side of the head and a thin trickle of blood was seeping down his collar. He tried to raise his head and transfix his captor with an indignant stare. Instead it slumped down on his chest; his knees buckled. The trooper caught him by the back of the collar before he fell, cheerfully dragged him outside, and threw him over his horse.

Just outside of town Rogier was awakened by a volley of shots from behind. "By Jove, man! I won't be carted like this – a sack of meal!" It was a weak voice: the trooper could hardly catch it.

"Cheer up! Ain't I goin' easy as I can?"

As if to answer his question, the horse stumbled in the loose granite. " – fool – weight on her withers – " The trooper pulled up, catching a glimpse of his prisoner's white hair, the diamond collar button at his throat. "Can you sit up if I let you get in back? Put your arms around me. I ain't going to have you fall off and bust your head open!"

The transfer was made in silence. Reaching Camp Peabody at last, Rogier weakly slid off the rump into his captor's arms and was pushed inside the bull pen.

The inside of the tent to which he was taken was lit by a single guttering candle. On one side stretched a long plank bench. Four men were huddled on it, staring half asleep at the dying embers of a small fire on the earth floor. Beside it, on a mud-smirched blanket, lay a man who got up and stared at Rogier who had fallen to the ground. It was Abe. He knelt, lifted Rogier like a child, and laid him on the blanket. The night was bitterly cold. He turned up Rogier's coat collar against the gusts of wind blowing through the tent flap, and began to putter about the floor.

"Goddamn it!" came a voice from across the room. "You know they ain't no more sticks. Or any matches either."

Abe got up, peering out the flap at the sentry pacing by outside, and beyond him at the granite slope black against the night.

Down the draw sat Jake. He was staring at the few lights of the camp with a look of dull bewilderment. A coyote howled. And still he sat there, patient and enduring, completely bewildered by the night's happenings.

3

It was two days before Rogier received a hearing and was allowed to present his credentials and identification papers proving he was not a striker nor an agitator. But as a mine owner registered with the association, why was he continuing to employ union workers?

Rogier summoned what dignity he had left to explain that as a contractor and builder in the Springs, he hired without prejudice both union and non-union men, paying both the same scale – three dollars for an eight-hour day; that in Altman, with the present difficulty of meeting the terms of his contract, he was following the same procedure.

That was not the question, he was reminded. Rogier was employing miners at the Silver Heels who had not been issued work permits by the Mine Owners Association showing that they were not members of the Western Federation of Miners.

The statement hit Rogier like a blow in the belly. Reynolds and his men, as far as he knew, were not working at the Silver Heels but at the Magpie. He had sense enough to reply only that the greatest mine in the district, Jimmie Burn's Portland, had not closed a single day and was still working W.F.M. men.

"That is unfortunately true, Mr. Rogier," his military questioner replied sharply. "If it continues steps will be taken to close the mine. You may take the warning yourself."

Finally let out of the bull pen, Rogier trudged up to his cabin in blood-stained linen, a suit that had been slept in for three nights, and in a mood more black and somber than the cold winter night. That he could have been taken for a cheap agitator, penned up like a criminal, his very integrity questioned – these, the inexcusable, rankled in his mind, pricked his self-assurance, made him out a fool. Yet all this was nothing compared to the devouring suspicion that Reynolds and his men had given up working on the Magpie.

It was dark when he reached his cabin on the saddle; the wind was shrieking like a mountain cat. But through the window gleamed the light of a lamp. He flung open the door. Jake was squatting beside the stove, intently reading a newspaper line by line with a stubby finger. Abe stood at the table, laying out plates and cups.

"Come in, Colonel!" Jake looked up and grinned.

"I see you found the place all right," Rogier said.

"You're just in time. Set and eat."

The three men ate in silence. Then Jake got up to wash the dishes. Abe pulled off his coat and shirt, laid them carefully on a chair. "Let's have your coat first, Colonel."

Rogier silently peeled off his coat and slumped down on a chair by the stove. Abe spread it over the table and took up needle and thread. The lamplight shimmered on his dead white arms and shoulders; underneath, the great muscles crawled like snakes under satin. His bald head never lifted as steadily, with a big coarse hand, he plied needle and thread in small stitches that would have shamed any woman's. When he had sewed up the tear, he gave the coat a good brushing and handed it back to Rogier. "There, Colonel. Reckon it will hold."

Rogier slipped it on. "Much obliged," he said gruffly, deeply grateful.

"Well, we got a job!" Jake said cheerfully. "I knowed you'd find us one, Colonel!"

Rogier sat there, cooked and sewed for, and protected by these brawny giants who had moved in with him with never a word, feeling as though he had adopted, with all his own worries, two helpless children. "I suppose you boys can finish those cabins. All the logs are there, and here's the keys to the tool house. You won't be troubled about work permits till you finish 'em anyway."

"We ain't carpenters. We're hard-rock miners," Abe said quietly.

"You can drive nails as well as I can while all this trouble's going on!" snapped Rogier. Worn out, he flung himself down on a cot and dropped into a troubled sleep.

Next morning he trudged to the Silver Heels. They were there as he expected: Mrs. Reynolds cooking pancakes for Reynolds and two of the men, comfy and cheerful as a family at Sunday breakfast. Rogier sat down to a high stack set out before him without asking questions. Reynolds as usual had obeyed the dictate of common sense. He and his crew had sunk the shaft of the Magpie into hard granite without a sign of paying ore. Their makeshift quarters would never do through winter, nor could they trudge back and forth through snow to the Silver Heels. So they had simply boarded up the mine and returned home here, where with a skeleton crew Reynolds intended to open up a new drift.

"Skeleton crew?" asked Rogier, peering in the empty bunk-room.

"Yep. Us three boys are all that's left."

"What about McGee and Carson?" asked Rogier, referring to the two married men who lived with their families in Altman.

Reynolds patiently explained. Rioting strikers had threatened both families unless the two men joined the W.F.M. and went on strike. Carson had joined and moved to Cripple Creek, hoping to pick up odd jobs to carry him through the strike. McGee was living with his family in a shack at Goldfield to protect them from possible harm. Reynolds and the two single men did not have work permits, but hell, they weren't workin', was they? They were simply wintering at a resort 10,000 feet high and fattening up on Mrs. Reynolds' pancakes. Money was not forthcoming too regularly, Reynolds added mildly, but when some did come in they might open up that drift. It wasn't likely they'd be bothered by any more nosey members of the military, W.F.M., M.W.A., or mine inspectors till spring.

"Money'll be coming! Haven't I always got it for you!" growled

Rogier. "But not one cent for timbering any more new cuts in this worked-out old mine! Come spring, we're going back down into the Magpie. I'll get McGee back. He's a good man with powder. You need him!"

A one-room, unpainted board shack on the outskirts of Goldfield held the McGees and their two small children. When Rogier arrived, McGee was covering the cracks in the wall with newspapers to keep out the cold. Mrs. McGee, who was taking in washing to support the family, was bent over a tub in the middle of the room. The two children were in school. McGee, who had worked at the Silver Heels for a long time, was embarrassed at having left but firm in his refusal to return to work. He could not join the W.F.M. because they couldn't give him a job to pay his dues and assessments. But neither could he scab for fear for his family. So like many hundreds of others he was trying to wait out the strike.

"I just can't figure it out," he said in a patiently suffering voice. "Gold worth a hundred million dollars or more comin' out of Cripple, and here we are with no more than a leaky roof over our heads. We're not standing in the bread line for something for the kids like hundreds of others around us. Alice takes care of that, washing all day and late into the night. But the strike's spread to the coal mines down south. Near Trinidad there's been a battle with thirty Italian strikers and two of them were killed. I can't see no reason for it at all."

Discouraged and balked at every turn, Rogier finally returned to Little London a week before Christmas. The holiday season always had been a big time for the family, and this year, despite an obvious turn in its fortune, everyone seemed to be heading into the stretch for a better one. The blue spruce tree in the front room just tipped the ceiling. Underneath it Sally Lee and Mary Ann kept piling more and more beautifully wrapped presents. Lida was busy all day in the kitchen. The fruit cake had to be prepared two weeks before New Year's Day and set aside to soak up the brandy. Then there were mince pies and chocolate cakes to bake, loaves of bread with crusts browned with butter. Two fifty-pound cans of honey arrived: one of strained honey, and one of hard sugared honey to spread on buckwheat cakes. Then there was cranberry sauce to make, jellies and jams and sauces to be brought up from the basement. And finally, as the tension mounted, the goose and the turkey to be bought and plucked. To all this confounded extravagance everyone in the family from Mrs. Rogier down had only one incontrovertible answer. What was Christmas for, except for children! Now there was a baby in the family, March, and this was his first Christmas!

Two days before Christmas, Cable, Ona, and March came down to stay in Sister Molly's big room upstairs. Cable looked glum. He had bought a tree for their own house, expecting to celebrate Christmas in his own home like any man. But this, he was finding out, was a false assumption. Home to Ona, who belonged with every entegument, ligament, and cell of her body to the Rogier tribal entity, was the big house down on Bijou. Here she had lived, been married, given birth to her son; and here, for every holiday, she had to return.

"Why of course, Jonathan! How could we sit here alone, when not a half-mile away everyone is waiting for us! It's your family too, Jonathan! Don't you realize that?"

The red niggah didn't. Familiarly acceptable to all the family as he was, one member still raised between her and him that strange and intangible barrier which in the South of her own girlhood had constituted an unbreakable color line. Nor could one impute to her an individual prejudice. Black niggers in the South, red niggers in the West, what was the difference? They both menaced by the color of their skins, which soaked through to their hearts and minds, the unstained purity of the superior white Anglo-Saxon race to which, by divine Providence, she had been born. Mrs. White, for all her outward vulgarity of speech, was a lady of breeding. Never by word of mouth had she ever insulted Cable in the presence of the family so devoted to him. She simply found it expedient to retire to her room. But since the night March had been born—that outright result of miscegenation between the Rogier and De Vinney aristocracy and a primitive race of savages condemned by the nation to extinction—Mrs. White had refused to speak to Cable. The rest of the family was at first embarrassed and then amused. They joked about it to Cable, a sure sign of their complete loyalty. But to Cable, a sensitive man, the hurt rankled. It made it more difficult for him to move down to the Rogiers' for Christmas. But of course he did.

The New Moon had been forced to close down by the strike, and Cable and both of his partners were making out in their haberdashery store. Coming home from work, he would go out to the shop to visit with Rogier. The older man was always tacking up clippings and quotations on the walls, the pillars, the window sills.

> The earth neither lags nor hastens, does not withhold, is generous enough, the truths of the earth continually wait, they are not so concealed either, they are calm, subtle, untransmissable by print.

> As the ox ought he to do; and his happiness should smell of the earth and not of contempt of the earth.

> The subterranean miner that works in us all, how can one tell whither leads his shaft by the ever shifting, muffled sound of his pick?

If to Cable they all seemed very much alike, they also reflected for Rogier the one dominating thought never out of his mind. He was worried by the prolonged strike. It was like a curtain upon which men and events moved dimly. He sat before it, striving to see the thing behind. Years before, when he had come West, it had been the familiar song of America he had tried to understand. The creak of canvas-topped wagons, the snap of flames burning off the prairie grass, the bite of double-bladed axes hewing down the thick sprawled forests, the rumble of buffalo driven over the last horizon, the whir of a million wings frightened from the drying water holes by gun blasts. It was the creak of ore trains crawling down the Pass, the sound of steel driven into granite, the steady beat of spikes as rail-ends crossed the plains and crept into the mountains. It was the voice of a hundred-tongued race of intruders stealing a continent with strong laughter and six-syllable Colts.

And now the song was sung. There was still a song of sorts, but it had a mechanical sound. It was no longer spontaneous, many-voiced, crude and strong. It was measured and metallic. You could hear in it the wheels go round. And the men who sang it sat in cushioned directors' chairs and counted every beat.

But the earth, the mute unresistant earth of a continent that had been burnt over, mutilated, dug into, disfigured, and reshaped, it too had a song, sung darkly like a rhythm in the blood.

> I am of today and heretofore, but something is in me that is of the morrow and the day after and the hereafter.
>
> To blaspheme the earth is now the dreadfullest sin, and to rate the heart of the unknowable higher than the meaning of the earth.
>
> The gold, however, and the laughter – these doth he take out of the heart of the earth: for, that thou mayest know it, the heart of the earth is of gold.

As if through a veil Rogier seemed now to glimpse a meaning in the blind, restless greed of men who had thought to rape and gut a continent without reckoning that the earth must have its due. They had creamed the top, had skimmed the grass roots. And now, down in granite, they were come up against the sterner stuff.

This was the new continent, this virgin America with rich long-grass prairies unmapped, and short-grass buffalo plains boundless as tawny seas; with dark, green forests primeval; a land of great slow rivers, brown and red, and countless white-water beaver streams; where one man's range would have made a royal realm overseas, his longhorn subjects more numerous than many a king's; it was a land watched over by great stone prophets lifting their white heads into the sky; a land where distance was measured in days; a vast unexplored treasure chest, halfburied, whose hinges a man's burro might accidentally kick off and reveal the hidden gold; an Ophir of mines thicker than prairie dog holes and scarcely deeper than topsoil. A land whose high snowy beacon was known from sea to sea. A land whose mother was the great mother of them all, the rain and the rivers, the thunder and the forests; the chief spokesman for every living stone and seed; the vessel of all life, the underworld womb of the unborn sun, the one great mother of the one great song. A scaly monstrous earth-mother of disillusionment, destruction, and death too, whom men had thought to bleed and carve and proportion in their bank ledgers. And now, unhurried, she was idly watching them grow mad over her mere surface wealth.

Rogier sat thinking of the hordes of strikers crowding the streets of camp, the women lined up with pennies for bread and soup, the troopers sick with fear yet riding up and down, dodging stones. He remembered a child walking barefoot in the snow and thumbing his nose at the sheriff, the bodies of McCormick and Beck too mutilated to be recognized at their funeral, a brick crashing through a restaurant window into his own soup. He thought of the inconceivable bitterness, the hopeless folly and fury of men fighting like mad dogs over a bone big enough for all.

The Peak, showing granite, had turned their picks and powder upon themselves. In the cry of Labor he heard the whine of machines dissonant with the forgotten earth.

"Daddy!" Mrs. Rogier pushed open the door. "Jonathan said he'd left you out here alone. Why, for goodness sakes, it's Christmas Eve! The candles on the tree are lit. Jonathan invited the Grimes down, and Mr. Denman's on the way. Professor Dearson's already here to play the carols the girls are going to sing. Land sakes alive! What can you be thinking of to be so late getting ready?"

It was never out of Rogier's mind, even during the confusion of Christmas morning with everyone tearing open packages, whooping and hollering, drinking egg nogs with every visiting neighbor, watching the baby. The big two o'clock dinner was no relief. He could hardly eat for thinking of Abe and Jake up in their cabin. Why, indeed, hadn't he brought them down if it was going to spoil his whole Christmas, asked Mrs. Rogier. Rogier abruptly gulped down his glass of after-dinner port, flung aside his lace-trimmed napkin, and called Mrs. Rogier into the kitchen.

That little frail woman no doubt had her faults, but she possessed that supreme virtue which permitted the girls to concede her to be what they called a "good sport." Within minutes she had commandeered the help and approbation of the whole family. While Mary Ann ran for a big striped box, she laid out plenty of turkey, cranberry sauce, rolls, mince pie, candy, nuts—"but Jake hasn't got teeth for" interrupted Rogier. Ona pulled him away. "Daddy, this is going to be a real Christmas box. We're not going to leave out a thing. And we're going to tie it with red and green ribbon!" Mary Ann came whooping in from the front room. She had heard of those two big raw-bones and had stolen off the tree two of March's trinkets to put in the box for them—a monkey on a stick and a small jack-in-the-box.

Rogier, elated, ran with many kisses to catch the late afternoon train. By nightfall he was trudging the steep trail up to Altman, the big box under his arm. The cabin was dark and cold. He lit a fire, adjusted the lamp, and sat down in his overcoat to wait for Abe and Jake.

They came in two hours later, both half-drunk and hilarious, too full to eat a bite. One of General Booth's "Blood and Fire Warriors" had squeezed them into a Salvation Army Christmas Dinner for destitute strikers.

Rogier felt so angry and ashamed that he pitched the box out the back door and went to bed in a huff. Rogier sentimentality! What a fool he had been to miss Christmas night at home with his family!

He was awakened by a stealthy whispering. He rolled over. Abe and Jake were bent over their bunk with lighted matches; they had crawled down the snowy draw and brought back the box. The bottle of port had not been broken, and they were trying to finish it without waking him.

"Hold on!" he cried, jumping out of bed and lighting the lamp. He had suddenly thought of the toys inside. "You two boys have had your Christmas dinner and so have I. But what about the McGees down below? What about them, hey?"

Abe with a shout had discovered the monkey on a stick inside and was trying to trade the jack-in-the-box to Jake for another swig of port. Good-natured and hilarious, they passed the bottle to Rogier and helped him into his boots. Then shortly before midnight, the three men left the cabin and set out. Abe, in front, held up a lantern and the little furred monkey on his stick. Jake, behind, carried the jack-in-the-box and a pick handle. In the middle, surreptitiously sipping port to keep warm, Rogier plunged through the drifts with the huge box.

The trail, greenish white in moonlight, dipped into the shadow of the cliffs. The stars hung low, cold, and brilliant as bottle glass. Down below glittered the few lights of Independence; at the bottom of the gulch on Wilson Creek loomed the larger splotch of Goldfield. The trail curved again. A thin wisp of smoke was rising out of McGee's chimney; the fire was not yet out.

Dom! It felt like Christmas night after all!

4

The second year of the strike began auspiciously. The mine owners had taken a resolute stand. A "vag" law was passed which in effect ordered every man in the district to work or get out. About 1,700 men were now working: imported scabs and workers who had given up their union cards. On the other side, the strikers were cheered by the news that their quarrel had been taken up by the United Mine Workers of America and a strike of coal miners was being called throughout Colorado. Las Animas County, following the battle at Trinidad, was declared to be in a state of insurrection; and militia had been sent into San Miguel County, where outbreaks had occurred in Telluride.

Late in January, after someone had greased the brakes, the big double-deck cage of the Independence failed to stop when coming up with a load of men. It shot up to the top of the frame, crashed against the timbers, and fell 1,400 feet back down the shaft, killing fifteen men. This was followed by a shooting affray at Anaconda in Squaw Gulch over the flag posted outside the Miners Union Store, setting off more outbreaks.

Rogier returned to Little London: he had been awarded a

contract for a new school, a fair-sized job whose proceeds he desperately needed. Leaving Rawlings, his construction foreman of many years, in charge, he hurried back to Altman. Abe and Jake were taking longer to put up a miserable log cabin with twenty bunks than would have been allowed him to construct a four-story hotel. The owners were in no hurry. Conditions were so bad and so many men out that the mess hall, built for over a hundred, was lucky to have a dozen men at meals. "Good God, Rogier!" they told him. "Why finish that last cabin? Haven't we paid off on the whole job, anyway? A pretty penny to spend in a hell-hole so torn up they ought to blow the whole thing to blazes and be done with it!" Still Rogier persisted in finishing it, not only to clear his contract, but to give Abe and Jake something to do.

Early that spring he drove Reynolds and his skeleton crew back to the Magpie. His whip was simple and effective. Money was coming in again, but he wouldn't spend one red cent to timber up any new cuts in the Silver Heels. If the men wanted to work and be paid for it, they could go to the Magpie. Like the earth, he would not lag nor hasten; strike or no strike, he was going down.

They had not gone very far down when they encountered trouble—bad air. Rogier went down the shaft with Reynolds and turned into a long tunnel. From habit he kept stopping to inspect the trapezoidal sections of timber sets, stamping on the sills, sounding the props and stulls, and peering up at the top lagging boards above him to see if any were bent, the first sign of pressure. Then Reynolds turned into a small crosscut leading off at right angles and stopped. Lighting a candle, he walked in a few feet. The candle went out.

"You see how it is," Reynolds explained. "It ain't got no color a man can see, and you can't taste it or smell it either. All you know is it's thick and wavy and lays down low. We always lower a bottle with water, empty it, and see if it fills up with gas. But it don't always work. One day it will be there and the next day it won't."

They returned to surface with a sample which Rogier took to have analyzed. The air of the Conundrum Mine, carefully analyzed by volume not long ago, had been found to contain 79.6% nitrogen with 10.2% oxygen and only .03% carbon dioxide. Yet Reynolds was encountering in the Magpie an air with 20% carbon dioxide — worse than ever the Elkton had, with over fifty times the amount of carbon dioxide than normal air.

"It's just a pocket. We'll ventilate," insisted Rogier.

So they connected the two levels with a winze driven through the orebody for ventilation. Then they encountered another gas pocket and another, driving more air shafts. It was expensive, and Rogier impatiently sold his remaining downtown store building in Little London to keep up the work. There was a showing of ore, of course. And he could not but believe that soon—soon!—they would exhaust all bad vapors. Yet every rock seemed to mechanically enclose gasses.

One bright spring morning Reynolds pointed toward one of the muckers sitting in the sunlight. His hat was off; his face was tinged greenish yellow from vomiting; he was rubbing his back. Rogier nodded. He knew the effects: first oppression and heaviness, perhaps a headache, then rapid pulse and breathing; the after-effects, nausea, vomiting, and pains in the back.

"This ain't no mine, Colonel," Reynolds said quietly. "You're spending all your money letting air in, not takin' ore out."

Rogier was not to be balked. Not here, high up on the shaft of that arrow pointed to his secret goal. Not yet!

"Keep at it, Reynolds, Once more is all I ask. Time and a half. And tell the men to take no chances."

He left them to go down to Little London in response to a telegram from Mrs. Rogier. She met him at the door and without preamble broke the news at once. Mary Ann had run off to Chicago with the Durgess boy and got married.

"That jackass? How can a man go through life pulling taffy and frosting doughnuts!"

"You forget Durgess Caterers is the best in town. But it does seem she might have had a dignified wedding in her own home!"

Rogier, as a matter of fact, was a little relieved; an expensive wedding now would have been impossible. "Well, what's the trouble you called me down here for?"

She looked at him with indignant amazement. "Trouble! Mary Ann! Daddy, what can we do about it?"

"Just stop worrying about bills from the caterers from now on!" He brushed past her and walked out to the shop.

There was trouble enough, although he did not know it. Ona,

now that March was big enough to trundle home in a baby carriage or little wagon, had resumed coming to the shop every day to help look after Rogier's work. Her absence had given Rogier plenty of time to thoroughly muddle his affairs. Property had been sold, money spent, mines opened and closed, construction jobs bid on and forgotten, accounts transferred – what a mess it was! Apparently he did nothing here in the shop but tack up clippings and quotations until the walls and pillars were covered. What in the world was happening to him, usually so methodical and constantly lecturing to her about figures? Figures!

Rawlings, his old construction foreman, had come down one afternoon soon after work on the new school had started. Rogier was in Cripple Creek. "You can sit awhile, can't you?" she asked. "It's been a long time since we used to eat ice cream up in Daddy's office."

"Don't mind if I do," he said, sliding into a chair. He was a small, blue-eyed man with a weak voice and shy manner that disguised, off the job, his knack of pushing things along. Rogier often declared that without him he'd have gone out of business. After awhile he undid a roll of blueprints. "I came down to see about this foundation, Miss Ona. He told me this ought to be twelve feet six. But look, the plans are marked twelve."

"You've scaled it?"

Rawlings looked embarrassed. "He added all them figures up according to numerology or something and they didn't fit in with the moon – something of the sort. So he said just to add the half all the way around. But that'll throw it off plumb. Do you reckon he was jokin'?"

"Of course, Mr. Rawlings. You just stick to the prints. Daddy doesn't go wrong on figures very often."

"That's the trouble." He hesitated. "Between you and me, Miss Ona, your Dad's got somethin' on his mind. He –"

Ona put her hand on his arm. "Mr. Rawlings, you were working for Daddy when I was in short dresses. He depends on you. You know what to do. Do it and don't let him bother you." For a moment she was silent and then courageously blurted out, "Rawlings, that spell of bad luck didn't do Daddy any good. He's having a hard time keeping in harness."

"Sure, oh sure," said Rawlings, rising. "I ain't criticizin' the likes of a man like Rogier. There's not another builder in town I wouldn't throw over to work for him. I'll push it along. Don't worry."

He had pushed it along, poured concrete, cut stone, and ordered brick. Rogier when he saw the work was pleased enough to slap him on the back. "Rawlings, when are you going to get off my back and stand on your own feet? I've been telling you for years you ought to get in business for yourself! You'd make us all hump!"

"I was just talking to Charlie about that," Rawlings said somberly. "Here he comes now." They were standing in front of the timekeeper's shanty when one of Rogier's rival contractors walked over from the new brick wall of the school.

"Charlie Geysling!" exclaimed Rogier, grabbing at the man's outstretched hand and looking into his worn, lined face. They stood exchanging the trivialities common to men of a kind and friends for many years. "I was just telling Rawlings he's too good a man to be working for another one. He ought to be making money on his own. Putting up something as tolerable looking as that new church of yours, eh?"

Geysling smiled a bit wanly, then let out a chuckle. "Between us and the gatepost, do you know what I got out of it?" He stepped aside and turned around. "This thirteen dollar suit of clothes! They figured me so close I was lucky to come out with a pair of pants!"

Rogier grinned; they understood each other. Yet the remark struck home. A suit of clothes for a good six months' work, and one that hardly covered his frayed shirt! And the man was actually getting old; his left leg had never dragged so noticeably before.

"Times are changing, Rogier," went on Geysling. "It isn't a clean-cut job of putting up a building anymore. There's a building permit, a heavy bond at the bank, a collateral assignment for material, union labor, everything else. A fellow has to figure down to the last piece of scrap lumber. You were always good at that, Joe."

"Yes. Figuring is the trick, not the building, eh Rawlings?" Rogier replied somberly. "Accurate figuring. Long hours. You've got to put your heart in it."

Rawlings bit off a chew without replying.

Back home in his shop, Rogier sat at his drawing board, chin in hand, staring out the window. He had looked forward to resuming business, to bidding on a couple of new jobs. Only to find himself caught in a boredom of unexpressive effort that left him no peace of mind. The school was taking shape under Rawlings' quiet and unassuming direction. All morning Rogier would spend with him on the ground, jacking up the men, turning back a load of brick, giving the assurance of a blunt and resolute man who knew what he wanted and expected it done without quibbling. Then all these details of construction would turn stale and unbearable. And he would return to his shop – to Ona working on his books, his ledgers, his cluttered files.

"Daddy!" Her voice was sharp. "You simply have to give me a full afternoon. Everything is in such a mess I can't make head or tail out of it. Take this invoice –"

"Now Ona!" he replied in a sharper voice. "If you haven't learned how to figure out those papers after all this time, there's nothing to be done about it now. Can't you see I'm too busy?"

Shortly afterward, on the fourth of June, he returned to Altman.

5

That night the moon rode clear, shining through the open door of his cabin. He got up and closed the door. Still it glimmered through the window over his bunk, keeping him awake. Abe was snoring like an angry cougar caught in a trap. Restlessly, Rogier kept turning over and over. Then abruptly, about two o'clock, he found himself sitting upright, holding with both hands to the framework of the bunk. A dull resonant roar, like a clap of thunder, had almost shaken him to the floor and was dying away.

"God Almighty! Is it the Independence—or what?" shouted Abe, bounding from his bunk and throwing open the door.

Rogier, with Jake, leaped across the room and looked down. The hillsides were alive with twinkling lights as men hurried down the trails with lanterns and torches. The lights of Goldfield and Victor farther down flared up from every window. Rogier flung on his own clothes and with Abe and Jake hurried down the gulch. Flares were leaping from the hilltops. Every mine had put on its lights, showing men hurrying down the gulch. They were converging at the camp of Independence below Bull Hill.

The three men followed the crowd to the Florence and Cripple

Creek Railroad depot which stood near the Findley, Delmonico, Orpha May, and Lucky Cuss mines. Here they stopped: Rogier, with a stomach that suddenly turned over inside him, and Abe with a hoarse, "God A'mighty – they done it now!" The 2:15 A.M. train stood a hundred feet away, its headlights glaring upon an uprooted platform, lengths of rails sticking upright in the air, dead and mangled bodies, and directly in front of them a leg with the boot still on.

The explosion of the load of dynamite had been timed for the arrival of the train filled with non-union miners to replace the night crew of the Findley Mine waiting on the platform. It had gone off just before the train had stopped, killing thirteen of the men waiting to go home and blowing their bodies up the hillside as far as the Delmonico. Nobody knew how many others were injured. Miners were stretching them out beside the tracks, waiting for a switch engine to bring doctors and nurses from Cripple Creek. By daylight the place looked like the scene of the monstrous crime it was. People from every camp in the district milled around like mad cattle. Women weeping as they dug into the wreckage, and shrieking when they found a piece of flesh. Men hunting for a bit of wire, a contact plug, of the infernal machine.

No one knew who had set off the explosion. The Mine Owners Association blamed it on the Western Federation of Miners; it in turn condemned the crime as the work of a hired criminal and offered a reward for his arrest. The sheriff, marshal, and coroner were forced to resign. At Goldfield, six aldermen, the commissioners, and treasurer were placed under military arrest.

By three o'clock in the afternoon thousands were gathered for a mass meeting at Fourth and Victor Avenue in Victor. A special train had arrived with C. C. Hamlin, secretary of the Mine Owners Association, who faced the crowd as chief speaker. It was a time and situation which demanded a man of courage and coolness – above all, tact. Small, excitable Hamlin, justly outraged, was not the man. He shouted, flung up his arms, damning the strikers as murderers, exhorting every decent man to drive them from the district and stamp out unionism like a snake.

Rogier, standing in the crowd, let out a groan at the folly. He saw the accusing finger of the speaker sweeping over the crowd, pointing unintentionally at someone on his right as at hundreds of others. The someone's neighbor mumbled a word or two. There was a scuffle. Fists flew. Shots rang out. In less than a minute a riot was under way.

Rogier ducked and ran for cover, watching from a doorway the troopers clearing the lot and carrying off the two men killed and the five wounded. Then slowly he walked back up to his cabin. About midnight the Zebbelins arrived, telling him they had been among 1,300 men suspected and questioned, 200 being put under arrest.

At two o'clock next morning 200 men were assaulted at the Miners Union Hall and for three days violence was unabated. Union stores at Victor, Goldfield, Anaconda, and Cripple Creek were destroyed. The W.F.M. headquarters in Engineers Hall was broken into, flags and pictures torn down, furniture smashed. The *Victor Daily Record* plant was destroyed. James Murphy, superintendent of the Findley Mine, met a woman walking down the street whom he recognized as the wife of a union sympathizer. He tore her clothes off, kicked her until she was half-dead, and left her lying in the gutter.

General Bell, declaring martial law, issued a proclamation closing the Portland Mine for harboring dangerous and lawless men. Its entire force of 500 men were arrested because they were members of the Miners Union which had not taken out cards in the Mine Owners Association. The Portland directors then voted the mine's discoverer and president, Jimmie Burns, out of office. Deportation began of all men who refused to renounce the union.

Rogier's very entrails writhed in agony. The great Portland and Independence, King and Queen of the District, closed; hundreds of others. Production almost cut in half from its peak year—a gold camp that already had produced more than $126,000,000 and had three times that much more to give. The bloodshed. The savage violence. The corrosive bitterness that had preternaturally oozed in poisonous vapors from every stone in the Magpie! A raped and gutted earth that finally had turned on those who thought themselves its masters.

It was all there in the great Peak that loomed above him. Enveloped by black clouds through which protruded only its pale summit, it looked like a ghastly spider waiting in its web. Rather it looked like the bloodless face of a giant underwater squib spewing out its inkish black fluid to poison all it touched. Then fangs of lightning shot from it into a rainless June sky, and it took on the inimical aspect of the great devouring cosmic serpent itself.

There was no use going up to the Magpie. He knew that it already had succumbed to its poisonous vapors. Sick and shaken, he returned to Little London, leaving Abe and Jake to close the cabin and to find a room in Cripple Creek until things quieted down.

Sally Lee, slowly and unwittingly, had been caught in another kind of a web. Tall, big-breasted, with dark hair, she was by nature an energetic, outgoing girl whose one great love was horses. This activity had been denied her since Rogier unaccountably had lost his interest in them. It was as if in Aralee his strange mania for speed had been fulfilled. He had never raced her since, although he had let Denman take her on the Grand Western Circuit. Akeepee was still loved, but she was in foal again. So Sally Lee had given up going out to Denman's track and had resumed her music lessons with Professor Dearson.

This Master of Musicians was more of a chronic grouch, sarcastic and eccentric, than ever. He still drove around town in a rusty brown coat and leather puttees to match his reddish gray whiskers. Also he had picked up an Airdale dog, Dan, who accompanied him wherever he went, lying down under the piano while the old man played. Like many musicians, Dearson had the habit of humming while he played; and at a certain pitch in his voice, Dan would raise his nose and howl. The Professor's services at the College Conservatory had been abruptly terminated, and he had moved his specially built concert grand to his apartment; Rogier had been forced to tear out the two front windows to admit it. Here Sally Lee went to her lessons.

It soon became evident to Mrs. Rogier that she was at Dearson's every day on non-paying visits. "Of course!" Sally Lee replied. "He's helping us to arrange our program for the Trio. Oh, he's the gentlest, kindest, and most talented man in the world!"

The Freolich Trio, as Mrs. Rogier soon found out, was work the Devil had found for her idle hands. Sally Lee, oppressed by the dreary solidarity of the family and the big house so gloomy with a sense of impending change, wanted to get away from home. Her subterfuge was the Freolich Trio she was organizing to make a recital tour. Her willing accomplices were a German girl named Gussie who gave excellent humorous readings like a rags-bottles-and sacks man sing-songing through an alley, and a fair pianist named Alice. Sally Lee's voice, a deep contralto, they relied upon as the mainstay of the program. Before long Sally Lee showed her mother several letters from music clubs back east which expressed great interest in the coming recitals—letters which Gussie had composed and sent to friends to mail. Fortified by this sign of public encouragement, Sally Lee enlisted Professor Dearson's help in arranging a program and began going to his apartment daily.

Dearson's attitude toward his pupils was a mixture of hopeful patience, tenderness, and violently stimulating criticism. To sit through a lesson with him was an unforgettable experience. He had the magic of music. He became to Sally Lee no longer a cantankerous and uncouth old man, but a bright and luminous spirit that fanned into flame all the longings within her. She fell wholly, romantically, in love with him. Irascible as he was, there were depths in him that could be touched. And something about this big breasted, outgoing girl with a tragic innocence far beyond her years touched him. At least enough to let him bask without resistance in the warm halo of her homage.

It was only by chance that Mrs. Rogier stumbled into this compromising state of affairs when she stopped in at Professor Dearson's apartment. The afternoon was late, the window open. Pausing a moment on the front steps she peeked inside and gave one gasp of horror. Then, without a word, she swept inside, grabbed Sally Lee by one ear, and marched her home.

Now for a week Sally Lee had been weeping and pining in her room upstairs while Mrs. Rogier downstairs went about with a look of grim determination. When Rogier came down from Cripple Creek she explained things in no uncertain terms. Just exactly in what compromising situation she had discovered Sally Lee and that old reprobate she did not describe, but certainly the honor of the house was at stake. "And look at this!" She flaunted a paper in his face. "A bill from him for her music lessons! The effrontery! Wanting us to pay for his kisses! Daddy, there is only one thing for you to do."

"What's that?"

"Drive right up to Professor Dearson's. And take your horsewhip."

If Rogier was inclined to believe her zeal slightly excessive, he was mystified by Sally Lee's attitude. Through her tears she proclaimed her love for the Professor and talked wildly of running away with him. There had been considerable gossip of the sort about Dearson, as a matter of fact. Shortly after arriving in town, he had married a prominent widow named Mrs. Burke. They had left after the wedding for a tour around the world. On the second day from home they had had a lively quarrel. The Professor had torn up her ticket and continued his travels alone. While in Egypt he composed a piece while listening to a native orchestra. It was published and dedicated to his wife, he said, because the frantic antics and shouts of the dancers had reminded him of Mrs. Burke's quarreling.

That afternoon Rogier drove up to Dearson's apartment. The door was open and Dearson was stretched out on the couch. He jumped up and grabbed Rogier's hand warmly. "Well! You boys have certainly been orchestrating a symphony up there in the district! A Cripple Creek Suite for Gallow Strings! Sit down and have a glass of sherry and some biscuits!"

Rogier sat down stiffly and said in a quiet voice, "Dearson, I've come here on a deeply personal matter. Shall we speak frankly?"

Dearson rubbed his graying whiskers reflectively. "These damned women. They always cause trouble. But I must say that at your age you don't act the role of an avenging angel very convincingly. You should have a marriage license in one hand and a shotgun in the other. Eh? Is that the trouble?"

"You're an old fool yourself, Dearson. Far too old to let your back be scratched by a young girl."

"Oh Christ! What a mess you've got me into. Keeping all those girls penned up like animals in a zoo. While you go traipsing off to the mountains on a wild gold chase. Little wonder they all fall in love with the first thing in pants who shows them a little kindness."

Rogier relaxed and poured himself some sherry. "You got yourself into it, Dearson. How are you going to get yourself out?"

The Professor jumped up in his old scuffed puttees, took away Rogier's sherry, and poured them each a stiff drink of scotch. "I'll be damned if I know, Rogier, and I've been thinking about it a long time. She's a good girl. I'm too fond of her to hurt her – although I know that's the way to do it. Just get rid of her. Painful but quick."

Rogier was beginning to feel pleasantly amused. "What did you have in mind, cyanide or arsenic?"

"Well, if you insist on giving us a champagne wedding, a trip to Europe, and a dowry of a Cripple Creek gold mine, I suppose I can buckle down to it."

The two men stared at each other a long time, then both broke out into chuckles. Dearson jumped to the piano, rattled off a few bars of Chopin, then flung around. "I'll tell you what'll be cheaper, old man. Pack her off on that recital tour she's so anxious for. God knows, she needs to get away from that zoo down on Shook's Run as well as from me!" He paused. "I'm serious. Sally Lee's voice is not dependable enough for concert work. Nothing that grueling. But it's quite presentable for music clubs anywhere, perhaps small halls. They'll get along if you give them a chance."

The two men had another drink, shook hands, and as Rogier left he could hear Dearson pounding away at the piano his triumphant release from all worry. What an odd, kindly old man he was!

Sally Lee, upon hearing that the Trio was to be allowed to go on tour, showed immediate signs of recovering from the blow dealt her. She could see herself returning in triumph to kneel at the puttees of that grizzled knight who had refused her heart only that she might give it to an applauding world. Mrs. Rogier's assent was practical. From her cookie jar she miraculously withdrew enough money for two new frocks and a traveling suit.

Elated, the three girls who called themselves the Freolich Trio, unaware of the misspelled name, had some programs printed. Gussie, now named Augusta von Hering, was named the reader, with Sally Lee as soloist and Alice as pianist. Dearson fortunately never knew what they did to his carefully suggested program. It started out well enough with a Chopin prelude, followed by two vocal selections: "The Dawn" by D'Hardelot, and Fisher's "Noon and Night." Between them and the "Funeral March" was stuck, of all things, a reading by Gussie of "The Uncut Diamond"—that cowboy with a rough exterior and heart of gold. Sally Lee was to remove any lingering jocularity with her best group of songs: "The Bandolero," "The Prince," and Lalo's "L'Esclave." These did not ward off the inevitable "Dooley on the Grip" and "A Puzzled Dutchman," in which Gussie could not restrain an unaccountable emotion. After two short nursery songs by Geibel and Neidlinger, Alice appropriately ended the concert with Ethelbert Nevins' "Buono Notte."

Rogier drove them to the depot to catch the train. Amusing as the whole incident had been, there was a catch in his throat. Dearson's accusations had hurt. The girls had been penned up too strictly at home and he had never given enough attention to the family. Now all the children were gone except Sally Lee who was waving a last goodbye from the receding train. And where was she going – this last one, who from the time she was a gangling, freckle-faced youngster could sit a horse and handle the reins of a trotter or a pacer better than most men? He could feel again her skinny little arms around his neck, and shuddered as he thought of them lovingly entwined about the soiled, wrinkled collar of that damned weak-kneed piano professor. No harm had been done, but why had it happened? The heart of a young girl, who ever knew what it held? For a moment, as the train swung out of sight around the bend, it seemed as implacably mysterious and profound as that other golden heart imbedded in a cloud of granite rearing in the western sky.

6

The district had quieted down when Rogier returned. Ninety-seven members of the Western Federation of Miners had been rounded up for deportation. Some of them were bundled into trains under guard and carried across the state line into Kansas, others being carried south and dumped into New Mexico. Two hundred more names were now posted under the proclamation that every striker was to be driven out to the tune of Cripple Creek's "Liberty Anthem:"

> You can never come back, boys, never.
> The game's all up with you forever.
> We trusted you square, and the pay was fair,
> And all would be yours yet, but now you'll beware.
> The W.F.M. is fated, and you'll stay there, you bet!

Rogier like everyone else – mine owners, strikers, and noncombatants – knew that the disastrous strike and the power and right of union labor was ended. He knew too that the district was entering a new era. The days of independent mining development by men like Stratton, Burns, and a hundred lucky butchers, bakers, and candlestick makers were over. From now on mining was to be carried on by big business operators, syndicates, and boards of directors.

Abe and Jake had disappeared into the obscurity of a Cripple Creek rooming house out of fear of being deported. Reynolds, as Rogier had known, had deserted the Magpie and gone back to the Silver Heels. Rounding the curve of the road, he could see Mrs. Reynolds hanging out her wash outside the cabin. He did not go down to talk to her, but struck off to the mine and sat down on the slope in the bright June sunlight.

He could not blame Reynolds; the Magpie like the Gloriana had been too much for him, and for quite sensible reasons. Still Rogier was disturbed by an unaccountable feeling, almost of resentment, against the mine below him. The Silver Heels was very tidy indeed: a passably large shaft house containing a good hoist, a vertical shaft, levels well marked, dry tunnels needing little pumping, well ventilated, and easy to work in; and off to the right the enlarged cabin with its bunkhouse and well-stocked kitchen. A far cry from that first crude, inclined shaft into the original working, and the single-room log cabin Reynolds and his wife had lived in so long. They had not struck a rich chute of telluride. The ore lay in gash veins soon exhausted. It had not made them rich but through the years, by dint of Reynolds' persistence, it had been a paying proposition. The Silver Heels, in short, was a good working mine of which its discoverer was justly proud and to which he had prudently returned after successive and futile flings at fortune up the gulch.

If Rogier could admit its unspectacular and persistent virtues, like those of his partner, he also had to admit that the Silver Heels had served his purpose. That purpose was emphatically not to make a mint of money by grubbing for gold like any businessman! No! He had something else in mind that Reynolds wouldn't understand.

Two men came out of the old inclined shaft to the left with a small tram car of ore dragged by burros. They emptied it and began sorting the ore. Reynolds came out, and seeing Rogier came up to sit with him. They shook hands warmly as usual, neither man alluding to Reynold's abandonment of the Magpie. Reynolds briefly explained what he was doing. As there was no money available to go down another level in the Silver Heels, he had gone back into the original working on a hunch. He had broken into a cavernous chamber, encountering gash veins frozen to the wall but extending only a short distance until they gave out. Here in the stope he was bulldozing, exploding sticks of fifty per cent dynamite. Then, when the dust had settled, the two men helping him would tram out the ore for sorting.

Rogier nodded. It was the same old story. Gash veins. Low grade ore. Laborious work. And dangerous, for the timber sets in that old working were growing weak and wormy, the lagging boards arched with rock and gravel that trickled between them and rolled down into the darkness.

Reynolds did not request that new timbering be provided. Rogier did not suggest he continue development of the mine down the new vertical shaft. They simply sat there together, Reynolds biting off a wad from his plug, Rogier chewing on the end of a smoked out cigar. The silence held between them. What was there to say? It had all been said on the Gloriana and the Magpie, over and over again. Friends and partners for years, they knew each other beyond words.

Finally Reynolds got up. "I'll be goin' now. Got to keep the boys busy."

Rogier watched him saunter back down the inclined tunnel. The two men continued to sort ore. Mrs. Reynolds came out with another tub of washing. After a time he ground out his cigar, stiffly got to his feet, and walked down toward the road. Just as he reached the brow of the hill he slipped on the loose granite and fell forward with arms outspread. At that instant he had the momentary and peculiar sensation as of the earth lifting gently to meet him. Concurrently a faint rumble sounded from the ground. Before he could sit up, the muffled roar of an explosion reached him from the mouth of the shaft on the slope below. It was immediately followed by a faint but sharp crackling as of timbers, then the loud rumble of sliding, shattered rock.

His face paling gray as a piece of rock clenched in his hand, Rogier leaped to his feet and rushed wildly down the slope. The two ore sorters were wildly gesticulating as he plunged into the mouth of the shaft. One of them grabbed at his coat tail, was flung aside, and followed him with a carbide lamp.

The tunnel was so full of dust they could hardly see or breathe.

The top and side lagging boards were squeaking with sudden pressure. Then came the ominous splintering of props and stulls. A hand jerked Rogier back. A voice screamed in his ear. "It's comin' down! – On the magazine! – Back!" As they reached the crosscut the timber sets behind them gave way with a crash. They heard the beginning of a terrific roar of splintering rock, a sudden concussion that enwrapped them in a blast of sound. Rogier felt himself hurled against the wall. A sudden splatter of blood warmed his face. Then a hand got him by the collar, jerked him erect. Revived by a blast of air at the mouth of the shaft, he leaned against the cribbing, weakly clasping a big-bosomed woman who smelled of soap. With a face so covered with blood and rock dust that he seemed to be staring over her shoulder from a grotesque mask, he kept screaming back into the dusty chute, "Reynolds! Hey, Reynolds! Reynolds, come out!"

Reynolds never did.

From somewhere he raised $1,000 cash and took Reynolds' wife to her folks in Leadville, saying the money was a state compensation. From there he returned to the Silver Heels. The two men had been released, the burros set free to roam the gulch like dozens of others. He slept on a cot in the tool house, unable to enter the big cabin which had been the home of those two faithful cronies of many years. Occasionally he peeked in the window. The grimy blankets of their bed were thrown back as if they had just climbed out. One of the old man's trousers was hanging on a nail; one of her big hats lay on the floor. In the kitchen a pot of beans was molding on the stove. A tub of washed clothes sat on a bench. Cobwebs were beginning to form in the corners of the ceiling. It was impossible to believe that they had gone – so suddenly and without warning! – never to come back.

On the perimeter of his thoughts, like a wolf at the edge of firelight, there prowled the specter of an accusation that he might have replaced those old timber sets. Or better yet, raised money to sink the newer shaft still another level by organizing the mine as a company and selling shares in it on the exchange. Such a thought had never entered his head. He was a man who all his life owned outright whatever he owned and conducted his business as he saw fit. He could no more change now than Reynolds could have changed. With such rationalizations he drove back the guilt that kept haunting him, ignoring the greater specter that flooded his mind from depths deeper than the Silver Heels.

Mostly he puttered around the dump and the ore bins, selecting the best samples. These he ground with mortar and pestle, pouring the pulverized ore into a white saucer and adding three or four drops of sulphuric acid. Heating this over a lamp, he watched the tellurium in composition with the mineral slowly turn the acid purple. Or sometimes towards evening, building a fire in the blacksmith's forge to cook his beans and salt pork, he would roast a bit of the ore. The process was known as "sweating," the telluride passing off in white fumes and leaving a few tiny globules to muse over while the flames died and the moon rose full and golden as if beaten out from the specks in his palm.

Gold. The most treasured, valuable, and sought after of all metals, it occurred everywhere: in almost all rocks, in vegetation, in sea water. The most malleable, it could be hammered into a leaf so thin that one ounce of it could be spread over 150 square feet. The most ductile, it could be drawn into a wire so fragile that two miles of it would weigh but a single gram. The softest too, yet indestructible: permanent in water and air under all pressures and temperatures, indissoluble except by selenic acid. Like the spectrum it contained all colors, yellow, pink, red, blue, purple, and even black; and when beaten thin it was translucent, transmitting a greenish light. The first metal known to man, and still the strangest and most perfect. The one irreducible element in the earth. The standard of value, it was a synonym for purity, trueness, and generosity, as it was for selfishness, miserliness, and betrayal. The one great mystery of nature, equated since earliest times with the sun, the divinity Himself. Who knew what it really was?

Rogier stared time and again at the miniscule specks in his horny hand as if mesmerized. Whatever they were, they were drops of blood drawn from an arterial stream he had not yet tapped, from a heart he meant to find, come what may. Deep down in granite flesh it pulsed, giving forth life to plant and bird and beast. In the congealed tracery of the veins, the suppurating wounds of a pick, he read a life that gave heat to the walls. He could feel it when he walked into the sweaty darkness of the shaft, in the eagerness with which he climbed deeper and deeper until his very flesh seemed one with the granite that shut off his sight, constructed his breath, and enclosed him like a tomb in which he felt himself mysteriously living a life unknown.

Reaching the edge of the stope where Reynolds had been buried by an avalanche of rock, he would lift high his candle or one of the mucker's lamps and bend down into the darkness. By degrees the far rock wall emerged in the dim light. He could see the narrow contact vein arched like a broken rib above him, could turn and hold his light against the wall until every inch of rock seemed revealed with the clarity of a petrified instant of eternity. Sometimes he half-expected the Acheronic figure of old man Reynolds to climb tranquilly from the depths. Instead, there stared back at him with vague eternal features the face of Time itself. Then, standing as within a circumvallation of precious metals, where even the granite walls held radioactive substances expending life for ages uncounted, he abhorently refuted death. For men, being part of universal life, do not die. Like a speck of radium they send out their vibrations to be caught and transmitted again from other dynamic bodies long after they themselves have expended their individual force.

Then he would blow out his light; and pressed hard against the hanging wall he stared down into a blackness blacker and more infinitely remote than interstellar space. Sometimes he believed he could hear, like the sound of water, the slow pulse of vein matter; could see lights like the recrudescence of stars when he emerged from the shaft. He heard his own breathing, the beat of his heart slowing, felt his body stealthily and infinitesimally sinking into the wall, as if it were the heart of the rock that pulsed rhythmically in the silence that enwrapped him –

Coming out of the shaft one morning he saw Ona and Cable standing on the dump, a suitcase at their feet. He walked up to them slowly, knowing why they were there.

"We've come after you, Daddy," Ona said as cheerfully as she could. "I've already packed your things."

Cable said nothing.

Rogier stared past him with a dull surfeited look at a couple of long-eared burros watching them. Suddenly, decisvely, he flung wide his arms to frighten them away, and then threw a piece of ore to hasten them up the hill. "Wait for me down the gulch."

Ona with a warning glance at Cable turned and walked down the trail.

"I'll wait," Cable said obstinately, a grim look on his face.

Rogier turned on him the full force of his unsheathed gaze. "Get off this property!"

Cable stalked away without a word. Rogier hurried to a shallow pit near the mouth of the shaft. With a short-handled shovel he dug up a box of dynamite that had been frozen and which Reynolds had been thawing out by imbedding it in burro manure. He worked quickly, wedging the sticks in the loose rock at the portal, the cribbing, and in the wall of the shaft house. Then he ran to place the last sticks under the door of Reynolds' cabin. Cable, rebuked by Ona and nervous at the delay, was running back up the trail. Rogier yelled, waved him back, and struck a match to the fuse. Deliberately he waited to be sure the breeze was not too strong, then turned and walked swiftly down the trail.

Cable, panting with exertion, met him and turned to walk at his side. Rogier did not turn his head. Nor did he lift his eyes to Ona, anxiously waiting at the turn. Head up and twisted slightly to one side, his right arm swinging rhythmically with his long stride, he walked past them without a word.

It was then Ona felt a slight and sudden jar. She looked up. The slope above the Silver Heels was expanding like an immense pie dough puffing up from inside. Suddenly it burst, rent with cracks, and throwing up puffs of dirt like flour. Concurrently Reynolds' cabin hopped up from its foundations. As it split apart in mid-air, there came the roar of a terrific explosion. For a single instant the shaft gaped open. Then an avalanche of rock swept over it, obliterating shaft, surface plant, corral, and the splinters of Reynolds' cabin.

Ona clung to Cable's arm, staring at the ruin. The roar subsided. The dust began to settle. Far up the slope the two burros stuck their heads inquisitively forward, ears up, and above them a hawk swooped leisurely out of its circle. And the hill, already immemorially old and disturbed but for that evanescent instant of one man's futile pecking at the enigmatic secret of its enduring strength, lay again supinely resistant to the wind and the rain, the glitter of the sun, and the ever-virginal snow that was soon to obliterate its trivial scar.

Rogier, almost out of sight, had never once looked back.

7

Mrs. Rogier for some weeks had been growing suspicious of Sally Lee's continued absence. The Freolich Trio's first stop had been Rogers, Arkansas where the girls appeared in the town hall and left on the midnight train for Springfield, Missouri. Here they performed at a cantata sponsored by a women's Christian association in return for their dinners and two nights lodging. Already short of money, Sally Lee telegraphed a kissing cousin in Memphis, Tennessee, whose name old Mrs. White had given her. A prompt and satisfactory reply was forthcoming; money for railroad fare and an invitation to visit the family, a branch of the De Vinneys.

In Tennessee, life for the Freolich Trio began to brighten, according to Sally Lee's letters. Under the auspices of the Confederate Veterans they gave programs at Ripley, Covington, and Lauderdale, with a trip to Fulton, Kentucky. To make the programs more palatable to their Southern audiences, Gussie's readings of "An Uncut Diamond" and "A Puzzled Dutchman" were eliminated, and the finger gymnastics of Alice on the piano were replaced by Dixie melodies. Apparently they were making innumerable friends and little money – a pleasant tour whose worry was borne by Mrs. Rogier and whose expenses were evidently footed by their Memphis hosts.

The phlegmatic Gussie returned home with Alice, dutifully reporting to Mrs. Rogier that Sally Lee was extending her visit with the De Vinneys, a most hospitable family. The information lacked specifics. And when Sally Lee's letters became more and more general, Mrs. Rogier's suspicions were aroused. A discreet phrase, a lady-like remark, a modest assurance – over and over Mrs. Rogier read them to Ona, wondering what lay behind them. Finally exasperated she had summoned Sally Lee home, emptying her sugar bowl for the necessary railroad fare.

Sally Lee arrived. Her trip had been the one episode during that dire period of the family's fortunes which attested, as if prophetically, that though the Rogiers had lost everything else, they still retained their capacity for propagating witless follies.

Her first evening home was something of a family reunion. Rogier had been brought back from Cripple Creek, and sat stolidly smoking. Mary Ann and her husband, Cecil Durgess, had returned home disillusioned. Young Durgess because Colonel Rogier's gold mines were not erupting a stream of wealth in everyone's lap. Mary Ann because the Durgess family expected her bridegroom to work for a living. Hence both of them were helping out in the catering shop. They were living in the North End, of course, but only in a cottage. They were an ill-matched pair but on this evening at least showed no marks of friction. Ona and Cable had brought down March as usual, and old Mrs. White sat in the corner gnawing at a wart. The focus of all their attention was Sally Lee singing beside Mary Ann who was accompanying her at the piano.

Mrs. Rogier, sitting erect on the sofa, watched her with the eyes of a mother hawk. The chick had hatched; there was no doubt of it. Tall, deep-chested, and full-throated, she sang with the aplomb of a professional just back from a successful tour. But at the end of a piece Mary Ann would whisper something to her with a giggle, and Sally Lee would smile back mysteriously. Something was in the wind. Then, when Sally Lee raised her left hand to brush back her dark brown hair, Mrs. Rogier caught the sparkle on her finger. That was enough. Waiting until everyone had risen to group around the piano for a family sing, she crooked her finger at Sally Lee and went upstairs.

Sally Lee obediently followed her to the bathroom. She closed and latched the door, then turned around to face her mother. Mrs. Rogier, as of old, was sitting on the closet seat, her left arm resting on the wash basin, and leaning forward. "Hasn't my girl something to tell me of her own free will before bedtime?"

A tremble of nervousness shook the girl. She took a deep breath, then suddenly burst into tears. Mrs. Rogier rose and put her arms around her; she was just short enough to support Sally Lee's head on her shoulder.

"I was going to tell you first off, Mother, before anybody. Really I was!"

"I know. I know," Mrs. Rogier said soothingly, raising the girl's head and wiping away her tears with a hanky.

"He's a wonderful man, Mother! Oh, he's the best man in the whole world – except Daddy, maybe," Sally Lee dutifully amended between sniffles.

Mrs. Rogier reseated herself to receive a full confession. "Now tell me about it," she said briskly.

Sally Lee sat down on the rim of the bathtub. "I didn't see him until that evening when he stepped out from behind that big cypress near the house. It was the very first time I ever saw him! He took off his hat, and with his hat off he looked just like –"

In twenty minutes she had come to the fox fur Mrs. Rogier had glimpsed in her bag. "But not until after – till I had my ring. Mother, really! I said a fur in Memphis! you know, but he said with the cold and snow here –"

"Nevertheless when he comes, if he does come, I think it should be mentioned. If only to assure him your father and I at least are aware of certain proprieties. But now I think you owe it to everyone to tell them too." She rose and unlatched the door, and Sally Lee dutifully followed her down the stairs to announce her engagement to Aurand De Vinney of Memphis, Tennessee.

He arrived one evening when they were all sitting on the porch, and presented his credentials by jumping out of the station hack and running up and kissing Sally Lee in front of all the family and neighbors – a courageous assault on Rogier undemonstrativeness that endeared him from the start. He was a big, black-haired, and goodnatured, with three suits of clothes and a careless manner of stuffing a wad of banknotes in Sally Lee's pocket whenever she went to town. Just where it came from the family did not learn, save that he ran a wholesale business of some sort and dealt in raw cotton. His parents had died, leaving him a rather large house looked after by an old maid aunt – a woman whom Mrs. White remembered vaguely as a charming debutante.

It was a trying week. Sally Lee spent most of the time upstairs with a dressmaker cutting corners on expenses at Mrs. Rogier's instruction. De Vinney took Mrs. Rogier to call on two New Orleans ladies visiting Mrs. James Slowe Puffer in the North End. Their visit had been prominently heralded on the society page of the *Gazette,* and Mrs. Rogier recalled their names instantly. The two ladies were in fact wilting flowers of the Old South, obscure relatives of Jeff Davis. Mrs. Rogier took for granted it was her duty as a Rogier and a De Vinney to reassure them that though the old mold of Southern aristocracy had been broken, its strength still ran true in every vein. In this high mood she was ushered with De Vinney into the drawing room of the Slowe Puffer mansion on Cascade Avenue she had stared at for years.

De Vinney was taken into the study for a drink with a few men. Mrs. Rogier was seated in the great drawing room on the edge of a circle of women whose names and backgrounds she knew well – women who had risen in grace to the exact level that their men folk had dug into Cripple Creek hillsides. In silk and lace and jewels they sat chattering with empty-headed abandon, giving sly looks at the little woman in black silk and black bonnet sipping her tea. The two guests of honor were decidedly not impressive. They were painted and overdressed, and looked sharp and cold. Mrs Rogier sat dumbfounded, listening to these gentlewomen of the Old South repudiating their birthright by talking of a New South – of the profit to be made by picking up old plantations at a song and splitting them up into small farms and land development areas, of cotton futures, of rising corn prices. One of them kept nudging the other to look at the pin on Mrs. Rogier's breast, a full-color enamel Confederate flag.

The climax came when one of them asked in a quite audible whisper, "Who's that Mrs. Rip Van Winkle? Doesn't she know the war's over?" At this moment Aurand De Vinney walked in and, hearing her, rose gallantly to the occasion. Flashing an engaging smile at the whisperer, he walked over and put his arm around Mrs. Rogier's shoulder, and led her straight across to the woman.

"Beggin' pahdon, Ma'am, I reckon you wasn't introduced properly. I have the honoh, Ma'am, of presenting my mothah-in-law of next Saturday mawnin'." Unbending his tall and handsome body from a slight bow, he then said in a direct and challenging voice, "All of us De Vinneys, my whole family Ma'am, will take it to heaht if you do not do us the honah of attending a De Vinney wedding,"

The hoyden! She *was* sharp! "And in what church will the wedding be held?"

Mrs. Rogier's heart sank in her boots and, as if grasping for support, she weakly reached up to finger her Confederate pin. Poor as the family was now, she had intended to have Sally Lee and De Vinney married in a simple ceremony in their own home. But now with this challenge flung back at her across the great room with its crystal chandelier and statuary, she too rose to the occasion. "The church which we have helped to establish and maintain for twenty years, whose pews my husband made at his own workbench, the only church we have ever and will ever attend! The Southern Methodist!"

A snicker went up and was suddenly stilled when De Vinney flung around a cold, appraising look. Then, with a bow, he offered his arm to Mrs. Rogier and they walked to their carriage.

Once inside, her fortitude gave way. She began to sniffle with shame and mortification. De Vinney gently laid his hand on her black silk glove. "They'll be theah! They know I'll blackball them from Natchez to New Orleans if they aren't. Yes Ma'am, they know which side theah cohn and cotton's buttahed on!"

"Oh, I knew you were a gentleman!"

"That, Mothah, is very neah the highest compliment evah paid me." He bent and kissed her glove.

Mrs. Rogier's sniffles were over before they reached home. She got out and in a cold fury began preparations to take over the little Southern Methodist Church and to transform it completely. Her extravagance knew no bounds; she never glanced at the florists' bills.

During all this hue and cry Rogier was nowhere to be seen.

What he thought of his coming new son-in-law no one knew; nor what De Vinney thought of the older man so dignified and so hazy of manner whom he had never talked to. Finally on the day before the wedding De Vinney walked out to the shop carrying a bottle of brandy. Rogier was seated at his drafting board staring out of the window, wisps of white hair sticking out from his hat. "Come in, sir! Yes! Come in!"

De Vinney for once had lost his casual ease. He set the bottle before Rogier and stepped back to watch him read the label. "From New Orleans, suh. I meant to get it out of my trunk for you before this."

"Humm. Reckon a nip would take the bad taste out of your mouth right now, wouldn't it? Supposin' you latch that door before you sit down."

Rogier wiped out two glasses with a handful of waste while De Vinney opened the bottle. Then, over their drinks, De Vinney began his efforts to get acquainted. "I don't know anything about gold, suh. Cohn, cotton, and maybe a lil' sugah, is my line. But youah gold mines, suh, must be a mighty fascinatin' business!"

Rogier did not reply.

De Vinney tried again. "Goin' to be a good day for a weddin'! My lucky day, suh! Why, I tumbled fo' that girl of youah's the fust time I laid eyes on her! I wondah what she was like when she was little."

This didn't work either. Desperately De Vinney launched into the background of the De Vinney family in an effort to convince this difficult old gentleman that his daughter would remain in a family distantly related to his own and highly respected still. Beginning with the appeal to the English government in 1629 by Antoine de Ridouet, Baron de Seance, in behalf of French Huguenots asking encouragement to settle in Virginia; the first settlement made near Appalachee Bay, on Nansemond River near Dismal Swamp; the influx of De Vinneys to Queen Anne County, and thence into Louisiana, Tennessee, and Kentucky; reviewing the De Vinney pedigree through General Marion, the Lee and Rogier ramifications; and ending with an ample discourse on everything that Robert E. Lee and Jeff Davis had fought and bled for, De Vinney left out nothing.

Rogier finished his glass and then another. He listened quietly without interrupting, staring a little dreamily out the window. When De Vinney finally finished, he remarked, "You've got it down pat, son. Good blood lines. A fine family. I'm proud Sally Lee's getting into it." He paused. "Fact is, my boy, I don't know of another pedigree that can quite match it – except maybe –"

De Vinney flashed him an engaging smile and leaned forward with anticipation. "I know, suh! That's one reason I'm marryin' her, suh. Not the main reason, bein' in love with huh. But I know the Rogiers –"

Rogier seemed not to hear him. Standing up on the rungs of his stool, he was pawing through his files of ledgers. From one he took out a thick sheaf of papers, the pedigree of the finest and purest bred lady –

"Amen, suh!" De Vinney loudly slapped his leg.

Rogier began reading through the pedigree of Akeepee –

The wedding next morning was quite satisfactory. The church was full of flowers. Cable had taken a day off to drive to the mountains with Ona and bring back a carriage full of wild flowers to shame those brought by the florist. The church was not so full of people, of course, but conspicuous in the front pew were Mrs. James Slowe Puffer and the ladies from New Orleans to whom De Vinney had extended such a cordial invitation.

At last all was ready. The preacher up front was waiting with his Bible. Mary Ann was at the organ beginning to play the wedding march. And Rogier, with a bleak look on his face, was standing in back with Sally Lee on his arm – When in the front door strode Professor Dearson in his greasy leggings, with Dan at his heels. Without greeting, he stopped Rogier by the arm and plucked a rose from Sally Lees' bouquet to put in his coat. Then he strode down the aisle to the organ.

"Get up, child. Ge-TUP!"

Mary Ann rose, walked back against the window. Professor Dearson threw back his long coat tails and sat down in her place, pulling up one of his leggings. Dan settled at his feet. At last, with a gentle smile, the old man reached out his hands to the keys. Rogier, still in a daze, did not stir. The Professor nodded at him, played more loudly, then began to hum. It was the pitch Dan knew as his cue. The dog rose deliberately, stretched, and let out a mournful howl. And with this prologue to Mendelssohn's march Rogier and Sally Lee walked down the aisle.

That night when it was all over – bride and bridegroom on the train, guests departed, Professor Dearson lurching home full of bourbon, brandy, and port, the family up in bed – Mrs. Rogier, worn out, slumped down on the sofa beside Rogier and clasped both his hands. When had they been like this before, alone, just they two, confronting a frightening future? "That's the last one, Daddy. The very last one of them all! Oh, what have we done for them? What'll we do now?" She had no tears now. Her anguish was deeper than that.

Rogier caressingly stroked the head on his shoulder, but as if to avoid a full demonstration of his own concern, answered in a gruff voice.

"Yes, Martha. And we got rid of her just in time, too!"

She knew what he meant behind the words. "It's not that bad, is it Daddy?"

"I'm broke. Busted, by gosh! There's no use beatin' around the bush."

8

The wedding bills kept comin in: from the florists, the dressmaker, the caterers; for food, liquor, and nonsense galore. To these were added the normal household bills and feed bills for the horses at Denman's ranch that had been accumulating. And yet all these were but the last embroidery on the immense tapestry of Cripple Creek debt Rogier had woven: pumping equipment for the Gloriana, hoist machinery shipped to the Magpie, supplies drawn by Reynolds from an Altman store, and an overdrawn account on a Victor bank. Ona, ruthlessly meticulous, had unwound all the threads.

"I thought I'd paid all those," muttered Rogier.

"They're still coming in," Ona answered quietly. "It seems that mining is an expensive business."

He fixed on her a level look without rancor. "What do you know about it?"

There was only one thing to do and Rogier did it. He went out to Denman's and told him to sell his entire stable. "I'm washing my hands of the whole kabosh! I can't be buying any more bales of hay."

There was something incongruously pathetic, revoltingly funny, about Tolar and Dorothy going to pay the milk man and the grocer, and that incorrigible chicken-killer Little Man being taken by the owner of the biggest women's clothing store. Aralee was something else. Rogier gave her to Denman in payment for the big feed bill due him, but Denman could not afford to race her. So she was sold to the owner of the hotel Rogier had built who got his money back by periodically racing her in Canada. There remained only Akeepee who had foaled her third and last colt.

"What are you going to call her?" asked Denman.

"Name her yourself. Here." Rogier passed him a bill of sale for both Akeepee and the colt.

The two men seemed suddenly abashed by each other's presence. Denman stood on one leg and then the other. "You better take her home, she's a good carriage horse," he said at last.

"The colt needs looking after. Keep her here."

Denman took his hands out of his pockets where they dangled helplessly as his tongue. "Look here, Joe!" he blurted. "I'll put that little filly in shape. But I reckon we know who Akeepee belongs to. She can't never belong to nobody else!"

It stood at that. No one ever knew whether Akeepee belonged to or was loaned to Denman. She was always only Akeepee and continued to accept Rogier's and Denman's common fealty as her rightful due.

To give up her last lingering hope of moving into a mansion in the North End was for Mrs. Rogier a feat of renunciation accomplished without bitterness or regret. She sat rocking in front of the window, counting off on her fingers the ragtag and bobtail of town who had struck it rich in Cripple Creek. George and Sam Bernard the grocers, the druggists Jones and Miller, the butcher Stark, Peck the cigar store man and Sam Strong the roustabout, the carpenters Stratton and Altman, Burns the plumber, Doyle the handyman, Reed, whose father ran a livery stable – more than forty who had become millionaires and were now the cream of North End society! Why it was that Lady Luck had led these men to fame and fortune instead of Rogier, so much smarter and more deserving, she could not imagine unless the Lord in His divine wisdom had taken a hand in the matter. Mrs. Rogier did not question it. She was content to sit rocking within that gaunt old house haunted by the Kadles which to her now had become a fortress of faith she meant to defend at all costs.

Rogier wandered about town, wondering where he could find a job of work to do. Never a good mixer, he went to the courthouse and the city hall, more diffident inwardly and more crusty of manner than ever before. Rumors of a projected large downtown building, a new steel bridge, threw him into a turmoil. He was profoundly relieved when nothing came of either. In the park he found himself scanning the construction news for small store buildings and residences which once he had refused to bother with. There was no doubt about it; he was out of touch with the times. Even Little London had changed so much he could hardly recognize it, with all its new large buildings and streetcars whizzing by full of people.

Late one afternoon he fetched up on the Busy Corner, leaning against a lamp post and staring at the Peak rising above the Antlers Hotel at the end of Pike's Peak Avenue. It was no longer a clear-cut living entity. It had subtly withdrawn into itself and floated remote and nebulous as a cloud in the sky—as he had first seen it more than a quarter of a century ago from out on the plains. As if he had never known the divinity of its everlasting promise of fulfillment, the diabolic cruelty with which it had blocked his every attempt to plumb its mystery!

Yet never for an instant, even now, did it occur to him to give up his search. Dazed and discouraged as he was, he still dimly knew that there comes to every man in that one long evolutionary life no more interrupted by death than by sleep the time when he must fight through to the life of his own inner being and so make the turn into the greater life of which he was an ultimate part. For him that time had come. Everything else – the whizzing streetcars, the passing people, his own financial worries – seemed a fantastic illusion of insubstantial reality.

"Rogier, Old Man! Where've you been all this time?"

Almost knocked down by the slap on his back, Rogier spun around to stare at an apparition in brown derby and spats and sporting a carnation in his buttonhole. Timothy: that was the name. But where he had seen him Rogier could not remember. On the school board, at the racing association?

Timothy seemed to have no doubt of his long familiarity.

"Anybody gone as long as you up in the district must have something up his sleeve. Come along now. Just time for a drink before dinner. Right out of George's new shipment from London, he told me yesterday."

Rogier, still in a daze, let himself be propelled up the street to the Ruxton Club. As the frosted glass doors swung behind them he felt immediately soothed by the quiet gentility of the place. He was conscious of the paneled woodwork and heavy beams, felt the balance of joists and pillars, was comforted by the gleams of light palely spotting the mellow ripeness of the room. Timothy at the bar, still loquacious, recommended both him and the Scotch in the same breath, then led him into the lounge to wait for their drinks. In a corner two men were playing chess; on the window seat two others sat watching as if asleep. The game ended as Rogier and Timothy walked up, the players pushing aside the small mahogany table as they stood up to shake hands. Drinks arrived and they all sat listening to Timothy animatedly talking about nothing at all. None of them seemed to mind him; and to Rogier he now appeared harmless as a buzzing fly.

"Been trying to get Rogier to tell me what's going on up in the district now that the strike's over. He must have something up his sleeve, being gone so long."

"Don't know a thing!" insisted Rogier. "I've wound up my small affairs up there."

"Righto!" applauded a heavy set man named Nelson, polishing his nose glasses. "The place is on its last legs."

"I'm not so sure about that," said the man called McHugh. "What about going deeper? They've struck four-ounce ore in the American Eagles at fifteen hundred feet. You can't expect to dig it up with shovels forever."

"The eternal optimist!" Nelson winked at Rogier. "Even at the Wild Horse the oxidation goes down only one thousand feet. Why spend good money to bring up dirt. Like you, I'm keeping out."

Rogier frowned. "I'm keeping out myself, as I said. But I'm not giving anybody else the same advice. I wouldn't be surprised to see the best discoveries made at depth – if you've got the money to go down."

Apparently few people made it a habit to contradict Nelson,

and Timothy kept his eye on Rogier as he continued talking. In his broadcloth, out of style but well cut, with his white hair and diamond collar-button both catching the light from the wall bracket, Rogier seemed quite assured. "Yes, by Jove! Nelson, you're a corporation lawyer and you've got the figures pat. You can block out ore on paper, but it's never anywhere for certain till it's at the end of a pick. So with all your facts and precedents, you're always a jump behind – a mathematical historian!"

Somebody let out a laugh. "Put that on your door, Nelson!"

During the chafing a tall sandy-haired man had come up and sat down. Timothy leaned over, presented Rogier. "This is the one I told you about, Mr. Andrews. Mr. Rogier, one of the oldest architects and builders in town. The first courthouse, the old college academy, Gazette building, churches, schools –"

"And many an outhouse you can add to that, Timothy!" interrupted Rogier.

Andrews smiled and drew him aside. "Perhaps you're just the man I should see. I'm thinking of building a summer home here. A Queen Ann cottage. Twelve rooms. Do you think you might look over the plans? They're upstairs."

"Don't mind me!" said Timothy. "Must dress for dinner. The McBurney's. She can't abide a moment's tardiness. Last time, she kept me waiting till the rest were through souping. Must off, really. Drop in again, Rogier!"

"Jackass!" somebody flung after him. "Don't know why I like him – and everybody else!"

Rogier followed Andrew up to his room and looked at his plans.

"I'm really thick on it, sir," explained Andrews, "but with building so expensive these days it's a little too dear for me. Still, with a few changes, perhaps – will you look them over?"

Rogier rolled up the blueprints and stuck them under his arm. "I'll let you know, Mr. Andrews."

Arriving back home, he chucked the roll on the sofa and wearily sat down before the fire beside Mrs. Rogier. "A lead on a job, Daddy?"

"A house for a man named Andres. Maybe."

"The Englishman? Why, he's a rich man come out here to get well. There was an article about him in the paper. He's staying at the

Ruxton Club."

"That's where I ran into him. I was up there wasting my time with that fop Timothy and a lawyer Nelson, an obstinate encyclopedia."

"Mr. Nelson—the biggest and smartest lawyer in town! And Mr. Andrews wants you to build for him, really?"

Rogier snorted. "A Queen Anne cottage speckled with gables and dormers thick as warts. Another dome bit of superficiality to disfigure a landscape that any fool could see was meant for native sandstone. Why, before I stoop to the level of contractors who kiss the behind of the North End for a living, I'll build outhouses for mill workers at Colorado City!"

She jumped up, eyes blazing. "Yes, you would! With twenty Charlie Geyslings waiting to grab such a chance!"

He grabbed up the blueprints and stalked out to the shop.

Mrs. Rogier sat trying to rock to sleep her awakened mistrust of this blunt and obstinate, proud and humble paradox of unpremeditated decisions. She knew him insecurely enough to fear the implications of his visit to the club. The fashionable Ruxton too, with its marble statuary, painting, and its monogram on all window panes, silver, linens, and stationery; the sanctum of North End society. All his life he had been independent, aloof, solitary as a relic of a vanished generation. To what end! – that now, broke and in debt, he should casually stroll inside, pick up a job with the right people, and make himself at home. Clasping her hands, she recognized it as a miracle. This was the turn! She was profoundly relieved that he had had on his best suit, and she was profoundly dubious that nothing untoward had happened – he was that careless of what he said. She could only sit rocking before the fire the hope that Rogier at last had awakened to the world about him.

9

Mr. Andrews was comfortably settled in the card room of the club when Rogier entered promptly at ten o'clock. "I felt so chipper yesterday I took a ride, Mr. Rogier. Had my man drive past some of your buildings. Hope you don't mind my looking at your credentials?"

"All public, Mr. Andrews. You saw I don't do much fancy work."

"Solid construction. Simple taste. I liked them."

He rang for coffee and cigars while Rogier unrolled the blueprints and got out a pencil. In coarse tweeds that did not hide the bony structure on which they hung, he leaned forward.

"I took these to an architect – a boy who used to work for me as a draughtsman. Then I did some figuring. You might knock off these two dormers, eliminate a room, and straighten the lines." Rogier marked the print. "That'll cut the cost down considerably."

"You don't like those – outcrops, as one might say here? Do you, Mr. Rogier?" He smiled.

Rogier looked up. "Look. You're overhanging the creek, set against the rise of the mesa and the mountains. Why not blend in the lines of your place with the background?"

Andrews coughed, then laughed discreetly. "You have me there, man! The architect did draw up these plans for a greensward back east. But this cough. Had to change sites. What will the change in plans amount to financially?"

Rogier drew out from his pocket a sheaf of figures.

So it continued: a new sketch submitted to Andrews, his inventory and estimate to prepare, a building permit obtained, the lien taken on the property to protect his work, and finally a trip down to Sawyer's Lumber Company to see about a collateral assignment. It was that or crawling to a bank for a heavy bond.

One would never have known from his manner when he stood in the doorway of Thompson's office that the very cigars in his pocket had been borrowed from Mrs. Rogier's sugar bowl. Thompson, full cheeked as a squirrel, looked up from the invoices for the first order Rogier had placed with the foreman. "Sit down. Let's talk things over. You've been away a long time."

Rogier pushed back his hat an inch. "No time to talk today. I've got a crew starting work."

Thompson leaned back and put one thumb in his vest. "Seven or eight thousand dollars this might run. Without any security—the Old Man—you know—"

"No, I don't," drawled Rogier. "All I know is that for over twenty-five years I've been giving Sawyer my business when at times any Denver mill would have done better. Now here's another job. You can have all but the plumbing. But I want a good competitive price. And Thompson, no beatin' around the bush."

Despite — or due to — his high-handed manner, the thing went through. Teamsters and a crew, stone and brick had been secured; subcontracts let, excavation begun under Rawlings. All these details were no longer incidentals. They were worms of worry that ate inside him, leaving him depleted each night. They bored him so! The whole job, the work itself, no longer held for him a meaning.

He took to dropping in the Ruxton to which he had been given a guest card, thanks to that fop Timothy. It was usually in the afternoon before most of the members gathered for drinks. For if the quiet luxury of the club rooms always appeased him, its members too often riled him to a nervous pitch. Indeed, he had come to be regarded as agreeable and well liked, but an eccentric old-timer who could be baited.

"Well, Rogier," Nelson would greet him cheerfully, "what do you say to the Golden CycleMill in Colorado City burning down?"

"It'll be built up again," Rogier would answer.

"What for? Everybody knows the district's on the downgrade!"

Or Nelson would saunter in and shout for the boy to bring the cigar tray. "Get a good one, boys. The First Chance on Mineral Hill has finally closed down. A good hundred-thousand sunk in that hole. Did they ever get anything out, Rogier?"

"The First Chance you say?" Rogier paused. "Met Perrault once – Louis, I think. Seemed to know what he was doing. Sank three shafts and got some forty-dollar ore, but never enough to ship. Well –" And he would launch out in defense, not of the unfortunate Perrault, but of those hills so full of tragic holes.

"A jolly queer one!" one would exclaim when he left in a huff. "But on my soul I do believe he knows minin'."

"Sure," Nelson would answer. "Had a couple of good ones, too. Don't know why he let them go. There's a story, though, that he blew up one for another worthless hole. But a smart man on building. None better."

Rogier, for his part, had grown to dislike the fat and jovial lawyer who had given up his mining clients to manage estates of the retired wealthy. And he resented the growing attitude toward Cripple Creek. Sitting there in the comfortable lounge he could hear the declamations against the strike, the workers, the mines themselves. Usually they were politely hushed, well bred, bitter voices, always with an expression of aloofness from contact with the thing itself. Insulated – they, voices and men, against the very earth whose richness had brought them hence.

Nor did the town itself assuage his sense of exile. It had been conceived at the start by a Philadelphian born with the strange compulsion to ape English life and manners; and as Little London it had grown up as a genteel English spa in the midst of the crude American West. Its architecture, life, and thought showed no homogeneity with the land. The outpouring of native gold from its signal peak had increased not its culture but its vulgarity. And now substituting scenic attractions for natural beauty, luxurious accommodations for simple hospitality, petty chicanery for honesty, it was becoming a prostitute pampering to rich visitors, one which did not have even the brazen honesty of her calling, a tourist town.

Yet, he thought, trudging home, his town had always had a life of which it was now ashamed, to keep it breathing today. It had had men like Tom who dreamed and were defeated; men crazed with the same avarice that made heroes of their more lucky neighbors; men who swarmed up the mountains and died a hundred deaths. Men hardworking, simple, and unsung, the great average of men everywhere whose lives like reefs of coral build up only for others to build upon. And among all of Little London's ladies there had been women in faded gingham standing at their kitchen sinks and reading the clouds above the Peak; women like Sister Molly watching the Pass day after day with hopeless incertitude; mothers grown old upon the trail with nothing but memories of an unremitting bondage for their faithfulness; women courageous and vulgar, the indolent and the damned, like women everywhere. And there must still be children in whom all this beauty roused inquietude and unrest, and disturbed with dreams impossible, as it had the children who bore them. Children tinged with the bitterness of the wealth and luxury at their hands' reach but forever beyond their grasp, and touched by its splendor too. Children of that soil who hated it and yet were bound to it forever. Who loved it and were driven from it by the same blind fury that had brought their fathers. Men, women, and children all—they were the voiceless, and their expressive silence would confound the ears long after all others' words had died away and were forgotten. They were the poor and their lives would enrich the earth. They achieved no dreams, but the dreams they made possible for others would confute the most fantastic. In their anguish and despair and folly were nourished all seeds of truth, their exultation, and their moment of success. They were Little London's only hard-rock integrity.

So Rogier, irritated with his work, bored by the club, and out of step with the town itself, trudged home to sit brooding in his shop. It was all a fantasy, like a child's game he had long outgrown. The reality lay deep within him, as if locked in hard granite to which he had no key.

One fall morning before he had left the shop, the two raw-boned

Zebbelins came swinging down the back walk and pounded on the door. They were in trouble. The last bunch of strikers was being rounded up and the mines were being reopened. But for some reason Abe had been unable to get a new work card from the Association and both men were afraid they might be posted for deportation. "Durn it, Colonel! We got to stay in the district. We ain't harvest hands. We're hard-rock men. And they ain't nowhere else to go if we had money to get there. Ain't you got somethin' in mind? Just beans and bacon is all we ask. And if there's an ounce of color we'll hit it for you!"

It was a magnificent appeal. Rogier had never suspected there were that many words in the two of them. "Now boys," he began resolutely, then stopped. Their clear gray-blue eyes, set in faces brown and rugged as the hills, stared at him with an appeal at once childish and profound. In their insistence he still had something in mind, he lost all qualms that they might be foisting themselves on him again like a couple of no-account loafers. For an instant he believed they had seen into him from the day he met them. It was inexplicable, profound, weirdly prophetic that they called up now from the hidden recesses within him that one thought he believed buried and locked. The spark they struck inflamed him, swept through him with a roar. He controlled himself, turning away his face and gripping the seat of his stool. Finally he turned around, jamming his trembling hands into his coat pockets.

"Now listen here, you boys. I haven't a thing for you. I'm broke and out of the district. There's only one thing I've got left. Straight off and no fooling. You can take it or leave it."

Jake grinned at Abe. "Ain't I told you!"

Rogier continued. "A long time ago I had papers on an old working up there. Got down a level, inclined shaft, hand tramming and burros. A showing of sylvanite, but not enough to ship. So I left her."

Abe was watching Rogier's face. "She wasn't that bad, was she? They ain't no mine plumb bad, if you know what's ailing her."

"It's a poor bet," Rogier said resolutely. "It would have to be refiled. There's not been any work done to hold it. You'd have to put up a cabin and get along on a grubstake. The only good thing about it is that you could lay low up there through the winter. It might be the end of the world as far as everybody else is concerned. Then by spring this trouble should be over and you can get a regular job."

Jake was jubilant. "When we know a man that's got the looks of somebody and says out fair and square, 'Boys, here's a proposition,' we're for him. Ain't it so, Abe?"

Again Abe asked, "What was so cantankerous about her, Colonel, you not doin' enough work to see she really was a mine?"

Rogier jerked erect. "What do you reckon I was throwing money into her for if not to find that out!"

Abe grinned knowingly. "What do you say we have a look at her, Colonel?"

As Rogier walked out the door with them, he met Ona coming to work on his books. "Tell Martha I'll not be home tonight. Back tomorrow."

She looked over the Zebbelins coldly, then gave him a level stare. "Daddy, you're not – it's not Cripple Creek!"

"I'm tryin' to find two men work!" He turned on his heel and walked up the alley with Abe and Jake.

By late that afternoon the three men on horseback were behind the Calf and skirting the base of the Cow. Before them rose the gulch as it had always been and would be always. The ruts in the road were overgrown with weeds. Not a soul had passed since that day, when touching match to fuse, he had walked resolutely away forever. There to the left lay what was left of the Silver Heels: strewn planks, decaying scraps of bedding, rusty pieces of iron, a few splintered timbers, all half-covered by the sheered-off side of the hill. Reynolds' unmarked tomb.

Callously they rode on without stopping. The canyon grew darker, narrower. The little stream, blocked by beavers, murmured at the bulwark of logs, trickled over the rocks. Jake nudged Abe, pointing to an old dump, yellow with oxidation, and a gaping shaft – the Gloriana. Aspens appeared, the quaking brittle leaves already turned yellow. A red-tailed hawk shot up from the cliffs, hung a moment at the tip of its flight, and floated across another abandoned working – the Magpie. The two men looked inquiringly at Rogier, but he gave no sign of having noticed it. The wagon road ended here. From now on, climbing still higher, there was only a faint trail. Beside it bristled a porcupine, immovable as bunch grass.

After a time Rogier reined up his mare. "Whoa-up! Whoa, girl!" He took off his hat and ran his fingers through his white hair. Straight ahead and upward the gulch ended in a narrow slit in the bare, frost-shattered, granite slope on whose lofty summit fat white cloud-stallions were lazily nibbling. A great stone face that looked down with neither compassion nor defiance, with no sign of recognition.

"There she is, boys. You get what I mean, don't you?"

There was little to see. A landslide had covered the old portal. Only the outline of a corral remained, the thin aspen poles turned grayish-black. Jake and Abe did not reply. They noted the growth of spruce and pine that could be cut for cabin logs, stulls, and props; reckoned the length of haul for aspen poles for a new corral; pointed to the changing formation of the cliffs. They dismounted, tied up their horses, and began to prowl around; then climbed up the ridge and chipped off samples at different points directed by Rogier below.

"See how we followed this ridge around hunting for values? Then this outcrop. Not a speck of color—even the dullest, in that oxidized streak. It was the unoxidized stuff we went down on. Sylvanite. Not a bad showing, but it didn't last."

"You and Reynolds didn't hunt long enough for the right lead," Abe said tersely.

This was the first time Reynolds' name had been mentioned. Rogier flinched. "That was long ago and this was a long way to bring a woman!" he said irritably. "I told you this was no picnic ground!"

Abe continued to peck around, finally coming back with a piece of gangue which he held up in the fading sunlight. "Maybe it is and maybe it ain't. But if they's a thing here, we'll find it."

Rogier drew a deep breath. "I've got no promises to make. As I say, it's a poor bet."

"Gold is where you find it." Abe quoted the saying with an air of incontrovertible wisdom.

They rode back to Victor in silence. But as Rogier got on the train next day they wrung his hand till the knuckles cracked; their blue eyes gleamed; they ran beside the coach, brown faces uplifted, their long muscular arms clumsily waving in the air as if knotting anew the threads that bound him to them.

10

There was no keeping it a secret that Rogier was grubstaking those two giant rawbones on another wild goose chase in Cripple Creek. Mrs. Rogier wearily acknowledged it in her prayers: "Dear Lord, keep Daddy from getting back into it again!" Ona, thin lipped, made out the monthly checks for the Zebbelins' supplies without a word. But she needed a name under which to list the account in her books; and Rogier, required to supply one when he filed relocation papers on the old working, had simply filled in the name of the ore – sylvanite.

So as the Sylvanite it became known even to doddering old Mrs. White. She was sitting in her corner, chewing on her wart, when Denman came in from his ranch. He could no longer wait for a name under which to register Akeepee's last colt. "Silvah Night would be a fetchin' name. Ain't that what Joe calls that theah new mine of his?" Mrs. White suggested.

"Suits her fine!" Denman agreed and hurried off.

That evening when Rogier went out to the ranch, Denman showed him the papers made out in the name of Silver Night. Rogier frowned. "Sylvanite's the name. God Almighty, man, can't you spell?"

Denman blinked his eyes, then slapped his leg and let out a roar of laughter. "God Almighty yourself, Joe! With a Confederate veteran in the house with a Southern brogue thicker'n cotton, how do you folks keep anything straight!"

Silver Night, however, fitted the filly exactly. Even Rogier agreed. Possibly there was something intangibly connecting her to the Sylvanite, as there had been between Silver Heels and the mine named after her. Rogier went out to the stall with Denman to see her for the last time. Certainly she was Akeepee's colt with every toss of her head. But where Akeepee was small and compact, with round hips, perfectly shaped as a picture horse, Silver Night was certain to be over sixteen hands high and always lean. One might suppose that with her big feet and a heavy head carried almost even with her withers she would be only a fair to middling pacer. Rogier recognized her as the epitome of his, Denman's, and Akeepee's combined efforts. As a horseman he saw how well she was let down behind, with a deep chest though light in the body. He observed how closely she was coupled, the long sloping shoulders, the sinewy legs. And he knew that if she had a heart as strong as her body they had produced a horse.

"Sure you want to sell her?" asked Denman.

"She's the last one. Let her go," Rogier said imperturbably.

But as he watched her being led away, and ever after, he maintained that Silver Night would be the fastest horse he had ever owned.

All winter, despite himself, he was kept busy. He worried, fretted, fumed; he dreamed of failures and rejected bids; he imagined himself forgotten, ignored, tolerated at best. There was always another job before him—a small residence, a hotel annex, another schoolhouse. The only one in which he took an interest was a mill job in Colorado City. Cripple Creek ore reduction had been a problem since the first stamp mill had been built along Cripple Creek, posing the difficulties of amalgamation. A chlorination plant had been built later at Gillette, but most of the ore had been shipped to the two mills in Florence. Colorado City then had put in its bid for the thousands of tons of rich ore ripped from the grass roots by erecting two chlorination plants, the Portland and the Standard.

These were followed by the Telluride, using bromide instead of chlorine as the solvent for gold. This had been taken over by the Golden Cycle, putting in a roast amalgamation – cyanide plant instead of using bromide and hot chlorine. Despite its fire, the mill was now running three shifts and expanding. The strike was over, mines were reopening, and long trains of ore were coming down. Vast new bins were needed, and Rogier was building them. This was his one touch with the district. What the Zebbelins were doing he didn't know. A monthly postcard, scrawled in a handwriting he sometimes couldn't read, was his only news.

Family events too ensnared his casual interest, if only temporarily. Although Mrs. Rogier hardly admitted it to herself, Mary Ann's baby had been born after an unusually short pregnancy. Now it was quite apparent that she and young Durgess were not wholly compatible. They both worked in the elder Durgess' catering shop where Mary Ann was avidly learning to make candy, dip chocolates, decorate cakes, make English-style muffins and other arts of the trade, as well as the value of money. All this came out during the frequent occasions Mary Ann brought down the baby, a girl named Nancy, to stay for a few days or a week at a time.

"I simply can't stand a man all day and night too!" she would complain. So leaving the baby at home, she would go to the store to work with him all day and return at night. It was obvious that trouble of a disgraceful sort was in the making, as well as blueberry muffins.

Ona had a new baby too, a girl named Leona. Once again she moved down into the old house on Shook's Run so the baby could be born "at home" like March. During the month she was there, Cable stayed too, more grim of manner than the first time. So with two daughters back home temporarily, and with three grandchildren, Mrs. Rogier was delighted. Rogier seemed too busy to do more than take their presence for granted.

Divine Providence, having supplied two new additions to the family, now exercised its prerogative of subtraction. Late in January, during a severe blizzard, Mrs. White died. They all trudged knee deep in snow from the waiting carriages to her grave in the pine-grown cemetery southeast of town. The Red Niggah, to whom she had not spoken one direct word since the midnight March was born, helped to carry her coffin.

Her death did not upset Rogier; the indomitable old lady had been ready to go for some time. But seeing her lowered into the grave beside Sister Molly under the big pine gave him a bad turn. Those two women, so alike, and caught in the same pattern of helpless futility as if it had been ordained for them from birth! Indeed the whole Hines family seemed woven from the same tribal propensities. Tom, after all these years, had never been heard of. Hiney too had vanished. Bob had moved to San Francisco and while there had been informed by an insurance company examiner that Hiney and Margaret had been traced to Shanghai, China where his trail had been lost. Bob also had visited Boné. Lockhardt had died, leaving him his money. Boné was quite a gay dog, playing the piano down on the Barbary Coast and writing popular songs. Enclosed in Bob's letter was a sample piece of sheet music, "Ching, Ching, Chinaman."

Ona, when Mary Ann played it, was shocked. "That awful bang, bang! That tin-panny ragtime song! Stop it! I hate it!"

"Hold on!" Rogier had said. "You're getting yourself all riled up for nothing. Like as not Boné's got to make a living like the rest of us."

Yet there was something infinitely repugnant to them all in the thought of Boné living in that sinister area of San Francisco's waterfront known as the Barbary Coast. Mrs. Rogier more than once had echoed the preacher's prophecy that the Lord would destroy it in its wickedness as He had Sodom and Gomorrah.

Meanwhile Rogier, who had sat brooding in the shop day and night, showed signs of rejuvenated life and interest. He had three crews working. Money was coming in: not enough to pay off all his monstrous debt, but to re-open his accounts, re-establish his credit, replenish Mrs. Rogier's sugar bowl, and to keep the Zebbelins in bacon and beans and a few unspecified items. What they were doing he didn't know; it had been two months now since he had received their last postcard. This did not worry him. Something was happening he was not fully aware of and which he could not account for. It was as if something deep inside him was rising to surface, just as the Peak once more was slowly emerging with all the clarity of its first purity and promise. He felt himself becalmed in an interregnum that could not be broken or shortened, a period of gestation for immeasurable and unpredictable events.

11

Calendar pages kept turning. Events outcropped above the sensory horizon and sank back down. Buildings were going up; bills were being paid. But time stayed still. Rogier, however else anyone knew him, was a man for whom time had stopped. The flowing linear stream of time – what an illusion it really was! Time was a great still pool, an element as basic as earth and air, water and fire, in which life developed at its own immeasurable pace to its own degree of fulfillment. Time! What did it mean to him now! In that invisible, immeasurable, impalpable pool both he and the Peak had been rooted for aeons to confront at last the meaning of their inner selves. Rogier kept staring at it in moonlight and in sunlight, at its dual faces of benign motherliness and masculine malignity, combined into an enigmatic mask which now he recognized for what it was. In geologic time it had stood there, a monstrous volcano belching fire and smoke upon a world that had sunk beneath forgotten seas. It had stood there in orogenic time, a lofty snow-crowned peak looking down upon a virgin continent yet unraped by greedy man. Through the quick gasp of a century it had remained inviolable while lesser prophets, robed in silver, had been gutted of their riches. And now it had come to its moment of revelation. He could see it at dawn when the rising sun flushed its snowcap pale gold, when the setting sun brought out the pinkish-red glow of its granite walls, when its dark red porphyry stood purple as blood against the melting snowpack. Gold, in all its shades and tints! And what was that? Let other greedy fools scratch the grass roots of its rocky epidermis for a modicum of pay dirt to make them rich and famous! Not he! For he also was a growth within that immovable, immeasurable, deep still pool of time, as old as the Peak itself. And now at last in their moment of truth and fruition they faced each other like two adversaries bound together in a common selfhood. Over them both a common golden sun rose and set. Through both their flesh ran the veins of liquid golden life, pulsating to the same diastolic and systolic beat. And in each of them glowed the reflection of the one great sun, the golden sun that was the heart of all. Gold! A great gold heart embodied in the depths of that extinct volcano whose remnant was the puny Peak. A heart whose beat was in rhythm with his own; whose meaning, if he could but fathom it, would illumine for him the secret of his existence which had seemed so alien to this mortal earth. Of course he would reach it, if he had to blast the whole dom top off the Peak and dig by hand down to the convergence of its golden veins in the heart that lay beneath! For time, the human illusion of flowing time, no longer existed. He had been born for this, geological eras, biological ages ago. Born as an incipient mammal to grow into an individual egohood only to seek and to find at last that universal self which combined within it both himself and the massive Peak whose granite armor he was meant to pierce.

To even the rational shell of the man who sat staring at that numinous specter it was evident that its future lay in depth. The disastrous strike was over. The population of the Cripple Creek district had been reduced from 43,237 to 28,050; the number of shipping mines had decreased from 475 to 200. Never again was their annual production to equal the high peak of $19,000,000. Still, $15,000,000 worth of ore a year was being taken out – 99½% gold to only ½% silver. And to date more than $153,000,000 had been produced from an area of only six square miles.

The statistics reassured Rogier. For all its setbacks, Cripple Creek was doing better than the Mother Lode of California, the Klondike in Alaska, the Comstock Lode in Nevada, and the gold camps of Kalgoorlie, Australia, Kolar, British India, and the Yenisei region of Siberia. What was wrong with that!

Underground water still posed a problem. The mile-long El Paso drainage tunnel had punctured the gold-filled granite bowl at 8,800 feet, releasing the water into Cripple Creek and allowing the mines to go deeper than 800 feet without pumping. Now work was beginning to drive another, the Roosevelt deep drainage tunnel, into the Peak at 8,000 feet altitude. This would drain off all water above the 2,100 foot depth reached by the deepest mine, the American Eagles, whose portal was just over 10,000 feet high, permitting other large producers to sink their shafts still deeper. Gold would be found at depth; it was not restricted to the volcanic porphyry, but lay in the granite below, as well.

To Rogier this had been a momentous discovery. It had given him a perspective of the vast subterranean world whose life went on unceasing and unhurried beneath his feet. An earth that like the sea flowed in rhythm to the moon and stars, obeying the same universal laws that kept the sun in place, maintaining an isotatic equilibrium by which mountains crumbled and washed away, old sea floors subsided under the weight of their conglomerate ooze, and new mountain peaks arose with sea shells on their summits. He could almost feel beneath him that great arterial fountain bursting from the hot, mysterious heart of the Peak.

Many pools of eruption had broken through the granite and left their gold deposits near the surface, at the very grass roots. No wonder they had been so easily found and were now being exhausted. The last and greatest pool of all still lay beneath the solid granite it had not been able to break through. For this it would be necessary to sink to depth. The fact substantiated Rogier's wildest dreams, and left him with a mind cold and clear as ice. It seemed inconceivable no one had thought of it years before. For of all that superimposed granite where was it thicker, deeper, and more resistant than the culminating point, the highest and only remnant of that ancient volcano which had towered even higher in the skies! The height that counter-balanced the depth of its hidden pool.

Instinct, intuition, foreknowledge — something, whatever it was, had pointed the way long ago. Now the light of cold reason thrown on factual statistics was substantiating it. He could feel the opposite polarities within himself coming to a verge; every thought and feeling converging, like the veins in the Peak, to a center. There was no hastening it nor retarding it; it would come when it would.

It came late one afternoon when Rogier in the shop glanced out the window to see the Zebbelins plodding down the driveway. They opened the gate, crossed the barnyard, and knocked on the door. Rogier unlatched it. "Well! Thought I told you to come in the back!"

Neither answered. They walked in, grinning like apes. Abe took off his battered hat, revealing a head brown and smooth as an acorn. Jake stood in overalls, that bulged from both pockets.

"You ain't taken up with business, are you, Colonel?" he asked.

"No," answered Rogier. "Not till you boys give an account of yourselves. Haven't got one of those postcards from you for three months."

Jake's grin spread over his face. "We was running short of money so we worked in the Mary McKinney and saved part of our wages."

Abe nudged his brother. "We ain't forgot you. We got somethin' for you." Again he poked Jake who hauled a specimen out of his pocket. Another came out of the second pocket. Two pieces of grayish ore the size of both fists, which he laid in Rogier's lap.

"Workin' in the McKinney we found out what forms the tellurides took. And lookin' for it we run into this sylvanite," Abe said slowly.

"Not a hundred yards from the old tunnel!" shouted Jake. "It was there all the time, covered up by a slide."

"A defined vein, Colonel. We followed it. The assays say it's shipping ore. What you were lookin' for."

What could be more natural? The old abandoned working had been a name and a mine to all the family for months, worthless as it might have proved to be. He thought of those other false hopes and abandoned workings—the Garnet and Fleur-de-Lis, the Silver Heels, Gloriana, and the Magpie. But now here it was, sylvanite from the Sylvanite.

"Look at that stuff! Look at it, man! We got somethin', sure as Moses!"

Rogier sat, a specimen in each hand, listening with an inscrutable face to the alternately rising voices of Abe and Jake driving like iron into the granite recesses of his being where lay the hope hidden from all but his secret self. He spun around on his stool, swept papers aside, and laid the specimens on the board. With a glass he examined minutely the fine silver-clear crystals imbedded in the rock. This was it! It was! The old voice that had shouted to him years ago when Reynolds first had run into the formation now again began to cry out.

"Crystals? Hummn. Crystals!" he muttered softly.

"One piece ran thirty-two dollars!" Jake was at his elbow, poking his finger under the glass. "We told you we'd find out if it was a mine or not!"

Rogier turned around at Abe's slow voice.

"It won't all be this good. But I figure there's enough to go down on if you've a mind to, Colonel. It'll take a piece of money to sink a shaft. Do you reckon you want to – "

"Want to!" He tried to control his voice. "There'll be money to go down! Way down!" He trembled like the last brittle leaf on a tree; and his nervous hand running through his thin white hair left wisps sticking up as though blown upright by the tempest within him. It had come at last, at the end of a lifetime of mocking toil, at the end of a boredom which had almost driven him mad. There had been other strikes before. Each time the Peak had defeated him – through the chicanery of rich men's greed, by organized labor's demand for a living wage, by the elements themselves – earth, air, and water. Now only the Peak itself offered the last barrier. He swept off a high shelf and on it placed the specimens to catch the light from the window. "Look at 'em boys! That's what we're after. We're going to drive a shaft through country rock and gangue, through breccia and sylvanite, into the granite of the old Peak herself!"

Perhaps for an instant his impassioned intensity of purpose illumined in awful splendor the depths within him. "It's just a mine, Colonel," said Abe quietly, "and she ain't even that yet. And we can only go as far as shipping ore holds out."

"A mine!" Rogier shouted irritably. "God Almighty!" He pointed out over the roof of the shed at the lofty white peak rising palely above the rampart of blue mountains. "There's your mine! We're going down into her rock bottom if we have to blow off her whole top! I won't be stopped again. Not by God or granite or human flesh. We're going down below grass roots this time. Way down!"

PART II

ADOBE

1

It was late Sunday morning, and Ona, washing the breakfast dishes, parted the muslin curtains with a soapy hand to stare past Mrs. Cullen's apple trees at the blue mountains beyond. The October day was clear and bright, not a cloud hanging over the Peak. There was something about Sundays that made them all alike. An intangible sense of laxity seemed to permeate the very air. Cable had got out of bed, thrown off his pajama top, and stood breathing deeply at the open widow. Tall and thin but muscular, his smooth brown skin glowed in the sunlight. The outline of his Roman nose reminded her of a laughable occurrence shortly after their marriage. He had been walking down the street when a visiting Rabbi had silently taken his arm and turned him into a nearby house to attend a Jewish wake. Cable, simple as he was, had not suspected that he had been taken for a Jew and had sat through the affair without comment.

Now he was sitting out on the porch with March on his lap. The boy as usual was bitterly disappointed because there was no funny paper to read. The preachers of Little London, bent on making it a "City of Churches," had been successful in forcing the *Gazette* to discontinue the weekly comic page because it kept the children from studying their Sunday School lessons. Cable had laid aside his paper to make up stories about bears and Indians for the boy.

In a little while he came in the kitchen. "What! Through already? Why didn't you call?"

"It's such a nice day for a picnic I thought we'd go by home and all of us go up Cheyenne Canyon."

"We'll do it some other time. I've already ordered a buggy so we can drive out and look at the lot."

Ona bit her lip, then blurted out, "It'll still be there!"

While Cable and March walked to the livery stable, she dressed and got the baby ready. Neither March nor Leona had their father's coarse black hair. But if March had his father's build and high cheek bones, little Leona had his dark skin. She was a great favorite with Mrs. Rogier who always hugged her, exclaiming, "The only Rogier in the bunch!" To this she always added, "The stork didn't bring you, honey. An old Nigger man left you on the doorstep." And she would hold up a dark leg or arm in proof.

When Cable and March returned with the buggy, they all drove out on the prairie past Nob Hill to look at the few acres Cable had bought with his savings. Waiting in the buggy, she watched him pace off a patch of tall grass and tumbleweeds, bending down to see that the stakes were set. "It'll be a fine place someday!" he said, coming back. "Look! Not a house for miles around!"

Ona nodded. She could see well enough the dry prairies stretching eastward, brown and unfenced; the rough dirt road crawling so far back to town; the glimmer of sunlight on white alkalai patches.

"We'll have us a house of our own out here," he promised. "Not a fancy place like those in the North End with an iron fence all around and statues on the lawn. But open to the wind."

Ona covered her mouth with a handkerchief and snuggled Leona against her breast to protect her from a dust devil that came whirling across the plains. "You'll get plenty of it, all right," she said when it had passed. "But I should think, Jonathan, we ought to be in town, closer to water and trees and where the children can get to school. I want March to make something of himself."

Cable slapped the boy on the back. "Ah! A line of cottonwoods will stop that little wind, all right. And how'd you like a horse to ride to school on, eh March?"

All the way back he prattled on. Only that stretch of desolate prairie aroused in him such enthusiasm. Hardly a week passed that he did not have to drive out to see it—as if, like a patch of kelp, it might float away on that vast pelagic plain. He was so simple and straightforward, so easily satisfied with her and the children, naive as a child. He seemed to live by feeling instead of by reasoning. A sensuous and sensitive man, the kindest she had ever known, and also the most violent when aroused. From the very first he had accepted her wholly and irrationally; and this was exactly what still held her to him. Yet she found herself beginning to resent his mindless absorption in their simple life.

Early that evening she suggested casually, "If we're going to church we ought to get started, so we can go by home."

"Home?" Cable paused. "I didn't borrow you from the family, you know. I married you."

"Oh Jonathan!"

She loved him, their children, their home. Yet it was that ramshackle old domain on Shook's Run she still unconsciously called home. A family worm-eaten with false pride, an aristocratic plant gone to seed, a box full of trinkets covered by a Confederate flag, a ghost-ridden house—whatever it was, no member of the family ever permanently left it; sometime he always snapped back. Ona, like Mary Ann, could return, take her accustomed place at table and go to bed upstairs as if she had never been away. And she did so often, every holiday and birthday, whenever anything unusual came up.

So of course they went, Cable pushing Leona in her baby-buggy: past Mrs. Cullen's apple orchard, following the creek west, passing under the railway trestle, and thence a quarter-mile up Bijou to the old bridge over Shook's Run. The big house was empty. Apparently Rogier was up in Cripple Creek and Mary Ann had taken Mrs. Rogier to church.

The small Southern Methodist Church was full when they arrived, the first hymn resounding from rafter to rafter. They were lucky to get seats in the back row. Up in a front pew sat Mary Ann and Mrs. Rogier, head turned to one side to favor her poor ear. During the sermon Ona noticed a man to her left staring intently at her. He nudged his wife and she too turned to stare. Ona lifted her head disdainfully but began to figit, wondering if her collar was askew or her hair messed.

Cable, with March asleep on his lap, leaned over. "What's that fellow Bennett staring at you for?" he whispered.

Ona shook her head, her eyes fixed steadily at the shouting preacher. Cable sat quietly, his dark face immobile, but keeping watch on Bennett. Ona began to worry. There was no telling what Cable might do when the services were over. She rose immediately after the last hymn, hurrying him out ahead of the crowd without stopping to see her mother and Mary Ann.

The walk home seemed long. The night was beginning to get cold; wind rattled the dry leaves on the trees. March grew tired and Cable lifted him into the buggy with his little sister. Then as Ona and Cable walked down the narrow sidewalk in front of the house next door to their own, their figures obscuring the faint glimmer of the arc-light on the corner behind them, it happened: a sudden bump and crash, a frightened scream from March, and a wail from awakened Leona. Cable, pushing the baby carriage in the darkness, had run into the iron front gate of the Franklin house. The childless, middle-aged couple was always leaving it open, blocking the sidewalk. Cable had barked his shins on it before, and several times had requested Franklin to keep it closed at night. Ona, annoyed at the mishap blurted out, "Those durn Franklins!"

Cable did not reply. In deathly silence he pushed the buggy to one side. Then in the darkness he wrenched the iron-lattice gate from its hinges, lifted it over his head, and walked deliberately down the front walk to the porch of Franklin's house. Here, with a heave of his muscular shoulders, he threw the gate at the front door. There was the sound of shattering glass and splintering wood, the crash of the gate on the floor of the porch, a woman's screams from inside. The lights flicked on and Mr. and Mrs. Franklin rushed out to confront Cable standing wordlessly in front of them.

Something in his quiet, expectant, and challenging appearance held Franklin silent and immobile. Cable turned, walked slowly back to the sidewalk, and pushing the baby carriage went on to his own house, followed by Ona.

The next evening Cable returned home from work in good

humor. "This morning first thing I stopped in Bennett's real estate office – you know, the man who kept staring at you in church last night."

Ona sat down on a chair beside the kitchen stove, entwined her fingers, and slowly looked up into his dark face. She suspected by his voice and manner what a disgraceful scene had occurred. Cable went on.

"Before I could say a word, Bennett stepped back of the counter and put up his hand. 'Please, Mr. Cable! Do you have a silver dollar in your pocket? Lay it down on the counter and look at it.' I thought he was crazy but I did it. 'Take a good look at that woman's face on it. Mrs. Bennett and I say it's an exact outline of your wife's. We couldn't help staring at her all evening. Perhaps you both noticed it. We apologize, but you must show it to your wife.' "

Cable dug out a silver dollar and passed it to Ona. "Bennett said a funny thing to me just before I left. 'If you ever leave your haberdashery store, Cable, come over and see me. I think we could get along.' Now how the devil did he know we were just about broke and ready to close doors?"

"Oh but you're not, Jonathan!"

"The store kept the New Moon going too long. We ought to have closed up that old mine long ago. Now the mortgages on the store are weighing us down. If we can get rid of it we figure we'll each have a little left to start over fresh and not be saddled with debts and heavy interest. That's why Bennett gave me an idea."

"It might be", said Ona thoughtfully, getting up and putting supper on the table. There was always something incongruous about Cable selling neckties and colored waistcoats in a haberdashery store – although, for that matter, she was never comfortable thinking of him mucking ore up in Cripple Creek. Sitting down at table she resumed the conversation. "All along I've been hoping you could get into something where you'd be happier and better known. If you could get to selling property in the North End to all the retired Easterners coming out it might be all right. But – " she paused. "Mr. Bennett might like my profile, but I don't think much of his. It's too sly and cunning. You couldn't keep up with him, Jonathan."

"I'll think about it," he said quietly.

A few evenings later when they went down for supper with the

Rogiers it was evident to Ona that Cable and his two partners, the Grimes, had been doing more thinking about their store. Rogier had returned from Cripple Creek. As if none of them knew what he was up to, he said casually, "Yes, the boys struck a lead in the old Sylvanite. Wouldn't be surprised if we opened her up – if it isn't too expensive. That's why I want those specifications, Ona. I had them all laid out."

"After supper," Ona said firmly.

Rogier reached for a spoon. "Tapioca and pineapple again. Humm. Oh say, Cable. I ran into Johnny Grimes up there. Said you were finally giving up that old hole of yours on Big Bull and trying to salvage something. I looked at the machinery, thinking I might help you out, but it wasn't worth a song. What's going on?"

Cable grinned. "The strike finished the New Moon. But we've just decided what to do at a directors' meeting of the President, Vice-President, and Secretary-Treasurer – me and the two Grimes. The current price for our one-dollar par value shares was one cent, and our last sale was four dollars for one thousand shares. So we decided to empty the treasury of its fifty-seven dollars cash and split the shares – a trunk load apiece to paper our houses!"

Rogier's eyes twinkled. "A wise move, you directors. But say!" He thrust his tapioca aside and leaned forward. "If you all quit, you might throw in with us on a real mine. We've got something. There's no telling how big it'll be. But I'll say this: we're going down. Below grass roots this time!" His booming voice lowered. He leaned back and lit a cigar. "Cable, you come out to the shop and talk with me. You won't regret it."

"No!" Ona said decisively. "Jonathan will have no time to work with you on another mine. He didn't have a chance to tell you he and the Grimes are closing down the store too. Jonathan is going in with Mr. Bennett – real estate. A fine thing for him, too."

Cable sat back, his long brown fingers toying with his silver.

Rogier got up. "Well, I'll give you the chance anyway. I'm finishing up things here, myself. Now Ona, I want those specifications. You're always hiding my papers where even a pack rat couldn't find them." Still grumbling, he walked out to the shop.

"Daddy's in it again, for sure!" Mary Ann said lightly. "We're likely to be praying even for tapioca!"

"You take March upstairs, and see if the two girls are sleeping," ordered Mrs. Rogier sternly. "Your father can take care of himself – and us – without your criticism."

Ona, still stiff and upright in her chair, watched Cable fill his pipe. His long fingers swept the cloth clean of a few flakes of tobacco, pressed them firmly into the bowl; his face was dark and expressionless as a wooden Indian's. Then she got up and followed Rogier out to the shop.

It took her but a few moments to find the papers. Now she stood with them clasped to her breast.

"Here. Give 'em here," Rogier demanded, looking up from his stool at the drafting table.

Ona did not move or reply. Her face was pale; there was an unnatural gleam in her clear eyes.

Rogier stood up. "What's the matter, girl?" he asked kindly.

The matter – dear God! The simple question illuminated the enormity of his folly and held her spellbound. How well she knew him now, this man who always had been more than her father; with whom she had worked for years; her one confidant, as she was his. He didn't know what he was doing. And to tell him would be to betray him for the first time in her life, and forever.

"Out with it, Ona!"

She stepped back a pace, clutching the sheaf of papers as if it were a treasure to be bargained between them. "You're getting back into mining again," she stated weakly.

"Dom! Haven't we been in it for years? What's itching you?"

"You're trying to pull Jonathan into the hole too!"

It was out! There was no more to be said. In that one simple statement was implied her distrust of his power, her loyalty to Cable. She could see the almost imperceptible change in his face. It struck at her heart; she knew that henceforth it was always to be between them.

In the awkward silence neither spoke. Both peas in a pod, with Rogier undemonstrativeness, they fought to get back to the casual.

"Now Daddy," she went on, "we know your luck might change. But mining is a risky and expensive venture. I really wish you'd keep out of it. What I do mean is that Jonathan hasn't any business in it, even with you. He knows nothing about it. He's got me and the children to look after. He can't afford to take any chances."

"Fol-de-rol, girl! You're getting worse than your mother. You don't have to worry. I'm letting him in just for your sake."

She could tell that now he too was merely talking.

"Come on, the papers now," he demanded. "And stop your worrying."

Ona clasped them tighter. "Daddy," she said with a resolute voice, "I don't want Jonathan mixed up with your mining."

Two chips off the same granite, they stood eyeing each other.

"Ona! A man's a man, whether he's your husband or not. Don't you try to run Cable's life."

"Or you!"

He turned abruptly and flung himself on his stool. They understood each other. The tears jumped to her eyes. But oh, if he would only remember that she meant what she had said!

"Here're your papers," she said softly, laying them down before him. "I'm going to help you all I can, like I always have. But please, Daddy! Don't bring Jonathan into it. Promise!"

He did not reply. And in his silence she felt impending a disaster that would rend her apart. It was to be a long, hard fight; to it she would have to give her best.

2

Already by five o'clock it was almost dark – these cold fall days when the trees were stark skeletons and the withered squash vines glistened with rime, when the brittle corn stalks crackled faintly in the wind and the little creek flowing into Shook's Run was covered each morning with paper ice. Ona, sitting at the window, watched for Cable. When he first appeared, emerging from under the railway trestle into the glow of the arc-light, she would get up and put the biscuits in the oven. Then she would return to her seat and watch his lanky body striding up the road. Now, with Leona in bed and March whining for supper, she still waited patiently. The tea kettle began to sing.

"Is there a genie in the kettle, Mother – like the picture in the book?"

"No, Sonny. That's just a fairy tale."

"Tell me a story about Indians. And bears and wolves. I like them better."

"Those are all fairy tales too. But I'll tell you a true story about Indians and your uncle Boné – the one who writes nice music for people to play and sing."

The boy climbed into her lap and snuggled against her shoulder.

"March! You're not going to sleep? Here, let's go get some supper if you don't want to wait for Daddy. Then you can go to bed."

Again she sat alone in front of the window. Seven o'clock and still Jonathan had not come home. Since he had started working for Bennett there was no telling how late he'd be. Out in his buggy all day and at his desk later every evening—a shame, the way Bennett treated him! She'd known from his coyote-sharp face that Bennett wouldn't stick to his promise and let Cable handle the North End properties. It was only the prairie land east of town and down along the Fontaine-qui-Bouille that had been given him. Not that Cable minded. He was like the land he sold—not barren but devoid of artificialities; not wild but forever to remain untamable completely; and whose subtle charm, once known, could never be replaced with a softer or more striking beauty.

One afternoon Ona had driven out with him and a manufacturer from New Jersey to look at a tract east of his own little piece. "Yes, sir!" said Cable, reining the horse to point out his own property. "I bought it long before I started selling land. My wife and I are going to build pretty soon. People are coming in fast, like yourself, Mr. Hichens."

"Hadn't we better drive on?" suggested Ona. "Mr. Hichens would rather see the tract. And it's getting late."

The fall rains were over; now the warm air suggested snow. The mountain tops were obscured by clouds that looked like a canopy let down from the sky. Ona could see Mr. Hichens flashing an apprehensive look back from time to time. Still the road crawled ahead into what seemed a vast brown undulating sea. Cable had taken off his hat. The wind never ruffled his straight black hair. She could see his dark face in gentle repose, knew he was thinking of his years on the plains. Again a quick momentary vision of his birthright came to her. For an instant she seemed to see it all through his eyes: the long stalk of a lone sunflower, the tumbleweeds rolling and bounding, the imperceptible movement of the wind through the grass, like breath blown over fur.

"Here we are!" said Cable, reining up the horse. "Get down so you can see exactly what we're talking about."

Mr. Hichens face betrayed what he thought about it. Indeed, how anyone could have distinguished it from any other spot in any direction was to Ona a mystery. Nevertheless he got out, stretched his legs while looking back disconsolately toward town, and politely offered her his arm.

Cable began pacing off his steps, hunting dutifully for a stake. The sod was damp and sticky; between humps of bunch grass and tumbleweed there were patches of alkalai and an occasional streak of water. Suddenly Mr. Hichens bogged down over his ankles. Ona, grabbing his arm, found herself mired. The mud was slippery, reddish adobe; the more they struggled the deeper they became entrenched. Water began to soak in over their shoetops.

"Quicksand!" yelled Mr. Hichens with the vision of sinking over his head. His legs began to work like pump handles; his feet never left the ground. Ona, herself stuck, quieted him and called for Cable. He came up behind them with an arm-load of tumbleweeds and without a word threw them at their feet. In a moment they were out: Mr. Hichens red-faced and angry, and Ona plodding to the buggy in a pair of ruined shoes and stockings.

"Adobe. Nothin' but a bit of adobe," said Cable quietly, bending down to scrape off her shoes and partially dry her feet with his handkerchief. "It don't look like much, but it takes a hold."

The episode had spoiled a sale as well as Mr. Hichens' new boots, trousers, and temper. He had sat pouting in the buggy all the way home. Too, it had occasioned a lively quarrel between her and Cable. And though all this already had almost faded from her mind, she remembered Cable's head bent before her as he methodically scraped with long gentle fingers the thick reddish adobe from her shoes. He didn't look like much either, simple and taciturn Jonathan; but dear God, she did love him so!

It was too dark now to see him from the window. Nor did she hear his light step on the porch until he flung open the door. "Jonathan! I was getting worried. Never mind. I'll put the biscuits in right now."

"Do we have to wait till you make biscuits? I'm hungry!"

"It won't take a minute. Hot biscuits and honey! How late you are. March is in bed already."

Not until they had eaten did he venture the cause of his delay.

Then, leaning back to fill his pipe, he remarked casually, "That prairie tract east of Nob Hill—it isn't going at all. Bennett's about ready to give it up. Says he's twenty years too soon." He scratched a match, lit his pipe. "It's too far out for a residential district, and the city doesn't want any manufacturing out there. In fact, Bennett's going to given up his option on it tomorrow morning."

"So you get to handle the North End properties?"

"No. I told him that didn't appeal to me. Chasing after the coattails of stuck-up toads and waiting in hotel lobbies for fat old dowagers is more than I can stand. He wants to give me some property south to get rid of. Why anybody wouldn't jump at the chance to get hold of that prairie land is beyond me!"

Unable to restrain her disappointment, Ona burst out, "I thought you had more sense! The big chance you've been waiting for, and you turn it down. The opportunity to meet important business men, to handle the most expensive property at handsome commissions, and to make something of yourself—something March can be proud of. For what! To ride outdoors in a buggy and look at barren prairie land that hardly supports jack rabbits and prairie dogs, to get stuck in adobe—"

"My mother's people always found enough there for their needs," he replied softly.

This direct acknowledgment of his Indian heritage made her bite her lip. It abruptly tumbled to a common level the imagined magnificent structure of the Rogiers. For the moment she unconsciously admitted the unconquerable force and proud humility of a race too secure in its heritage of strength and pride to defame it by casual boasts.

"But Jonathan," she said in a subdued tone, "you've outgrown that. Times have changed. And this new deal of Bennett's won't last through the winter at best."

His big brown eyes grew bigger, softer. He took out his pipe and grinned. "That's what I thought — As a matter of fact, I stopped by Shook's Run on the way home and Joe cornered me in the shop. That's where I was for two hours."

Ona drew a deep breath.

"He wants me to go in with him on the Sylvanite. The two Zebbelins won't be enough. They'll be underground and I'll be top man. Joe will have to be down here part time—till we get to shipping regularly. It'll be opened early next spring. Your father knows mining, Ona."

"If he knows mining why didn't he make a go of it years ago, when Cripple Creek was first discovered? Why did he lose the opportunity of becoming one of Stratton's partners when he developed the American Eagles, Number One and Number Two? Why did he allow himself to be cheated out of the Garnet and the Fleur-de-Lis? Sunk his downtown store buildings in the Gloriana and the Magpie? And the Silver Heels! You watched him blow it up with dynamite after Reynolds was killed in it. And look what those cursed mines did to Daddy, to Mother, to all of us. They took his business, his downtown properties and residential lots, most of the land around Shook's Run, his stable of horses, the home up in the North End he'd promised Mother, his children's chances for success!"

Her voice had risen to a shriek of outraged injustice that carried in it the frustrations of all the Rogiers. Gulping another breath, she continued. "Yes! They made an old man out of Daddy. He is! Look at his hair. Hear him talk. I know how much trouble he has with his accounts and ledgers. With buildings, with Rawlings. And now he wants to drag you into another damned mine. I won't let him ruin you and March, Jonathan. I tell you, I won't! My boy's going to have all he ought to have—a nice home, a good education, all that. You're not going in on the Sylvanite. You're not!"

Cable had laid down his pipe and arm on the table and sat watching her with an impassive face. She had learned long ago that against any emotional displays he was resistant as slick adobe. Like an Indian, he did not fight against the unbeautiful; he simply ignored it as if it did not exist. "You're getting yourself all riled up," he said shortly, rising and walking into the front room. "You better get to bed."

She lay there, restless and tormented. How easily in her outburst it all had come out—the secret, stifled resentment of the family that Rogier had not gained for them the wealth and acclaim they deserved. In a sane moment she realized its untruth. Born and brought up during those years of the great unrest, familiar with mines since childhood, she knew the vagaries of chance that led fools and tenderfeet to the great discoveries more often than the deserving. In those days luck had dealt out fortunes impartially to all. She had been her father's secretary, clerk, banker; she knew the sane judgment on which he, the methodical, had based his decisions and suspected the hazy motive that inspired his decisions.

Until now she had condoned his faults, excused his idiocyncrasies. Herself a Rogier and his daughter, she found him flawless. But now, a mother, she awoke to a life apart from his. His weaknesses, his peculiarities and appearance presented to her with preternatural clearness a loved but pathetic figure with whom she could no longer stand undivided. For the first time she was stunned by the appalling uniqueness of her marriage outside the family ties. Lying there, tossing on the bed or staring dully at the dim pattern of light on the ceiling, she realized that nothing could stop Rogier now. Neither she nor Mrs. Rogier, the consensus of many old-timers in Cripple Creek that the Sylvanite was out of the producing area, nor the joshing at the Ruxton Club, could deter him from his purpose.

From the other room came the faint rustle of Cable's newspaper, the dull clack of his pipe against his shoe. The homely sounds roused a phantom within her mind. She loved her father, but to him and the Sylvanite she would never give as hostages Jonathan and her boy. She gritted her teeth and lay waiting for Cable to come in.

"Jonathan, you won't go?" she asked from the darkness as he stood unbuttoning his collar.

"Aren't you asleep yet?" he asked quietly. "I'm going down to stoke the furnace."

3

Rogier was still in the shop where Cable had left him. Musing for an hour or more, he had let the stove fire go out. With cold hands he rebuilt it. On a chair lay a plate of sandwiches Mary Ann had brought out when he did not come in to supper. Munching on one of these, he backed up to the stove, waiting for it to warm up a pot of stale coffee. Before it came to a boil he poured a cup and sat down.

With the heat from the crackling stove and the black sugarless coffee, Rogier began to come to life. His mind, deadened by prolonged concentration, awoke like a sleeping conscience. Unable to remember just how much he had done of all that had to be done, he quickly ran through his work: specifications for hoist and cable; cost estimates for shaft sinking per foot through different rock; preliminary sketches for two level workings; the timbering required for gallows frame, cribbing, and stulls; figures on tramming, assays, and ore treatment – all to be done and checked this winter while Abe and Jake were putting down another shaft and cutting timber for the shaft house and two bridges across the creek . . . And on top of all this, a revision of his bid for a new group of school buildings, an annoying interruption. But it would all be done, by Jove!

Again he added up in his mind the astounding costs, tried to balance the amount against his accounts. The profits from his current and next job, with a few thousand dollars from somewhere else, would get him started. None of this capitalizing and issuing shares at a par value of a dollar and getting one cent for them, like the Butcher Boy and the Nameless mines. Too much publicity, too much red tape, and too many stockholders coming up to see "their" mine. Damn the expense! He knew what he wanted: the Sylvanite, unknown and stuck up in a remote canyon where he and the Zebbelins could work as they pleased, safe from prying eyes.

But what was wrong with Cable? Given the chance of a lifetime, he had sat there dark-faced and noncommittal as a wooden Indian. His own son-in-law, to thus refuse him. But he would win him over from this crazy real estate business, stepping off the surface of the earth, unmindful of the dark profundity, the unceasing hidden life below. A little more persuasion and Cable would sell his prairie land. The proceeds, with the $1,000 he had realized from dissolving partnership with the Grimes, would come in handy for running expenses. And he needed Cable's help—a man in the family who could stay up at the Sylvanite and keep his mouth shut. And Ona! What had got into her, of all persons? Patience! A little patience!

It was a word whose meaning he had forgotten; a sluggish drag that the fire in his veins had consumed utterly. His mind jumped the months of work ahead to the completed plant: the big shaft house, the rapid unrolling of the hoist drums, the spinning cable letting him down, down below grass roots, down into granite, down into the great Peak whose inner life he meant to make his. Let Abe and Jake worry about following the vein. Let Cable worry about ore shipments and treatment charges. Let Ona worry about paying the bills. But for him alone the quest he meant this time to follow to the end.

He ambled around the room, looking at his shelves of ore specimens and reading the clippings tacked up everywhere.

> Whence cometh the highest mountains? So did I once ask. Then did I learn that they came out of the sea. That testimony is inscribed on their stones and on the walls of their summits. Out of the deepest must the highest come to

its height.
The gold, however, and the laughter—these doth he take out of the heart of the earth: for that thou mayest know it—the heart of the earth is of gold.

Worn out at last, he turned off the light and trudged through the yard to the house. Long after he had climbed the stairs to bed the sound of the Kadles' steps followed him, squeaking in the cold eerie silence. Rogier, as usual, had kept those faithful family ghosts up late.

Next morning he was awakened by Mrs. Rogier, Mary Ann, and Ona trooping in with a cup of coffee and the *Gazette*. "Boné's coming home," announced Mrs. Rogier. "It is in the newspaper!"

It was true. The eminent composer of several piano sonatas but better known for his popular songs was expected for a brief visit. "Late of San Francisco, but evicted since the burning of his studio during the great earthquake, he has been on a successful tour of the East, where he appeared on many concert stages. It was reported he is on the verge of a nervous breakdown, and may choose to linger on the scene of his boyhood days. His first published piece, 'The Red Rock Garden March,' was written here; and 'The Song of the Willows' from his 'Indian Suite,' the piece which brought him success, was composed shortly after his leaving for the Territory of New Mexico. In addition to his family, the Joseph Rogiers of this city, his many friends and members of musical circles —"

This, then, was the small, saucy boy Mrs. Rogier had reared from childhood; the eminent composer whose hands she had continually slapped for fooling with the piano; the pianist she had yanked by the ear down to Rogier's office for refusing to go to school. No wonder he hadn't let them know he was coming.

He was still a Rogier, however, for an hour later a telegram came from him. It read simply: "Inform the Kadles to stop by the third floor cot on their rounds tonight. Arriving two o'clock."

Ona went alone to the station that afternoon to meet him, leaving March and Leona and Mary Ann's Nancy with Mrs. Rogier. Waiting on the platform as the train whistled round the bend, she remembered the last time she had seen him: down in New Mexico, standing in the stirrups on Lew's old bay nag, right arm aloft in a graceful melodramatic gesture of farewell. And there in the vestibule as the train swept in, he stood again, right arm raised in greeting, as if the years between had never been. She gulped down a catch in her throat, rushed to the coach, and was caught in his hearty hug.

"Boné! After all this time! We've missed you so!"

Tipping the porter, turning over his bags to a hack driver, suggesting they walk home—he was still the same, nervous and changeable as light on water. Still there were slight changes. He seemed a trifle shorter and his black hair showed faintly gray at the temples. With a woman's eyes she noticed the excellent cut of his soft gray worsted, the careless knot of his tie, the expensive fresh-shined shoes.

"A damned nuisance jumping around the country and hopping up and down stage platforms," he was saying, plunging along beside her. "I'm not an acrobat. I'm a composer and I can't do any work trying to show off. Besides my nose isn't built right and my shanks are too thin. But you should see New York! 'Member Shiprock sticking up out of the desert at sunup? That's Manhattan from the harbor – a pin cushion of Shiprocks!"

Ona stole a look at his face. It was a little too pale and drawn, and his talk showed he was keyed up higher than an E-string. "But Boné – the paper said you were about to have a nervous breakdown."

"Why, look!" He stopped in his tracks. "A new bridge over Shook's Run. Iron girders, too. No, that nervous breakdown story is a good excuse. It gets me a good night's sleep right often. I tell you, Ona, it wouldn't be so bad if they liked my best. That Sonata in B, now. But all they seem to like are my songs, the worse the better. My God, and haven't I written some awful ones! Ah, that lovely, lyrical 'Ching, Ching, Chinaman!' " He put his thumbs in his ears, wriggled his fingers. And Ona, still laughing, followed him across the street.

Throwing open the front door, Boné gave Mrs. Rogier no time for a hesitant though warm reception. He lifted her up for a kiss that took her breath, set her down, and was out prowling in the pantry before she could utter a word. He came back with his mouth and hands full of cookies. "The same old piano and the same old cookies!" he mumbled, spilling crumbs all over the carpet. "Dear Aunt Marthy! The loveliest mother a boy ever had even if you did used to drive me away from the piano. Still I gained in cookies. And I know you made these just for me this morning!"

Mrs. Rogier listened to him running up the stairs to wash. Then she slowly walked into the kitchen pantry. In the darkness she removed the lid from the cookie jar and felt within. It was empty. Boné had eaten the last of the batch she had baked, not this morning, but three days ago. Then, folding her hands on top, she bent her head and wept.

For two weeks Boné was hardly ever home. A second article in the *Gazette* embroidered his career, claimed him as the town's, and heralded his arrival like important news. It did not take "the members of our own musical circles" long to launch their attack. Feminine, flattering notes on scented stationery were followed by their writers. They needed no introduction nor invitation. At any afternoon hour one might descend from her carriage, adjust her hat and muff, and trip daintily to the door.

"My dear Mrs. Rogier! It has been so long since we have seen you! How lovely – oh, can I come in a minute, just a teeny, weeny minute! – to have the composer of 'Ching, Ching, Chinaman' home again. Don't you love that tune? So truly Oriental! Is he home?"

Mrs. Rogier, exceedingly polite, would seat the caller with a cup of tea and call Boné. Or the visitor, on being informed Boné was absent, would gulp her tea, get up and exclaim, "Such a disappointment! I just wanted to remind him of the twenty-eighth.
Eight o'clock. We have so many guests coming only to hear him play. We won't let him forget, will we, you and I?" And pinching Mrs. Rogier on the arm, she would trip back out to her carriage.

Boné, with astounding cheerfulness, complied with every request. He went to afternoon teas and late suppers, "kindly obliged" at private parties, and played for all three musical clubs. As often as possible he took Mrs. Rogier. She enjoyed getting out, but was no longer impressed by these estimable ladies who a month before had not known her from a lamp post – and would not, a month hence.

In all the hullabaloo Boné had not yet met Professor Dearson. Mrs. Rogier, Mary Ann, and Ona recognized the need. What the

Professor would think of this young man so widely heralded, they trembled to contemplate, he was such a bear on the classics. But Boné too had a mind of his own behind his pleasant, jumpy manner. In many respects they were appallingly alike – not quite normal – and to arrange a formal meeting seemed impossible.

As might have been expected, the meeting came about quite naturally, too naturally, it seemed to Mrs. Rogier and Ona who happened to see it out the window. It was early afternoon; snow had fallen all morning and Boné was cleaning off the walk when the familiar pop! pop! of Professor Dearson's motorcycle was heard coming down Bijou Hill. Boné, head swathed in a muffler, paid no attention to the visitor who turned into the driveway and cut across the lawn. When Dearson was not a half-dozen steps away Boné gave a lusty heave. The shovelful of snow splattered the Professor from head to foot.

"You young blatherskite! Why don't you look what you're doing!"

Boné looked up, leaning on his shovel. "And why don't you tie up that gasoline nag of yours at the Nigger Boy and walk in from the front!"

Dan had stopped barking and now crouched growling at Boné's feet. Boné took off his glove and without hesitation reached down to scratch the airedale behind the ears. Dan immediately stopped growling and began a delighted whimpering, rubbing against his leg.

Prefessor Dearson snorted and stamped into the house, followed by Boné. Ona, horrified, managed an embarrassed introduction. "Professor Dearson, this is Boné. You know –"

"Why shouldn't I know! I read the newspapers!" growled Dearson. "And from his music I can tell he doesn't use his left hand enough!"

"Haven't learned to use my right yet!" Boné answered cheerfully.

Over his tea the Professor began to berate the weather. He had lost his umbrella from the motorcycle and –

"Professor Dearson would like a glass of port instead of tea," suggested Boné. "At least I would."

An hour or more later they had reached the subject of music. "Damn Wagner!" exclaimed Dearson. "A sensualist if ever a butcher was one!"

"And if he had changed a note in those first fourteen bars – "

At this moment they both looked up to see standing in the hall doorway an apparition wrapped in an ankle-length fur coat from which protruded a rosy benign countenance. It was Mr. Timothy who had unaccountably driven up in a carriage and had been admitted by a confused Mrs. Rogier.

"You, sir," greeted Professor Dearson, "are interrupting a conference between myself and my young friend here – who despite some talent and an indisputably better left hand than he is given credit for – yet persists in claiming for Wagner – "

Timothy was not intimidated. He strode in, clapped Boné on the shoulder, "Been after Joe to bring you around, Boné!" Then he reached over to grip Professor Dearson's arm. "You yourself, sir. Have you ever got rid of me till I was satisfied? You incorrigible genius!" Turning to Mrs. Rogier he said, "Madame, this is a great honor to be admitted to your home for the first time. I came only to inquire of Mr. Rogier about this notice in the *Cripple Creek Times* of a new mine he is opening."

Ona, who had come up behind her, answered quickly, "Mines are unpredictable, Mr. Timothy."

"That's why they fascinate us – both Mr. Rogier and myself," he answered quickly. Stripping off his coat to hand to Lida Peck, he added, "A Scotch and soda will do."

"Scotch after port?" Mrs. Rogier was confused. "Lida, is there any Scotch in the house?"

"In the cellar, for them as has a mind to drink it," answered Lida.

"I'll have one," said Boné.

"Me too!" added Professor Dearson.

By five o'clock Mr. Timothy had come to the point. "I'm going to give a party in honor of the sharps and flats. Been left out of everything since Boné's been in town. Won't have it! Friday night when Joe returns from Cripple Creek. The Ruxton Club. Eight o'clock.

"Count me out!" said the Professor. "I haven't entered the portals of that *sanctum sanctorum* of conservatism for years."

"This is my home. My mother would be honored to have you all," said Boné.

"Nonsense! The Deer Horn Lodge then."

"Every time you come around it means fuss and dinner," growled the Professor.

"I shall call for each of you promptly at six," added Timothy imperturbably.

The party was something to be remembered by everyone who went: all the Rogiers, including Mary Ann's part-time husband, Professor Dearson, and a host of Timothy's friends. It had snowed for two days, blanketing the mountains under a flocculent whiteness and almost blocking the North Cheyenne Canyon road. Timothy was equal to the occasion. From out of dusty storage sheds, carriage houses, and livery stables he evoked every old-fashioned sleigh in town, hung them with bells, and lined the seats with mothy buffalo robes and Navajo blankets.

How beautiful it was, thought Ona, watching the snowy cliff-walls open and close behind them, hearing the jingle of the bells and the songs drifting back from the sleigh of young people in front. And the Lodge! She caught her breath with delight as it leapt at her from the darkness, aglow with lights. The huge, rustic, log structure was festooned with spruce boughs and kinnikinnick; a huge fire in the stone fireplace lit up the polished pine floor; candles gleamed from the big table and piano. A bartender from the Ruxton Club stood behind an enormous bowl of hot punch, bottles of liquor and wine. In the kitchen a white-hatted chef was presiding over a steaming venison haunch, a browning turkey, and everything to go with them.

There was no denying the warmth of the liquor, the high humor that molded them into a friendly group. Timothy was his urbane self; Professor Dearson pungent; Boné keyed to a pitch that left little to be desired from one so royally received. Even Rogier was drawn out of his morose brooding.

Dinner over, they moved to the end of the big hall. Cigars were passed around; the ladies were prevailed upon to sip more wine. Boné; of course, was asked to play. Courteously he deferred to Professor Dearson who snorted an indignant refusal.

"Why, you two sticks!" exclaimed Mary Ann. "I'll play!"

She flounced over to the baby grand and launched into her favorite ragtime. Everyone applauded but Professor Dearson who pushed her off the stool so he could give his own famous version of the "Black Hand Rag." Boné played and then after conversing lowly with the Professor gave up his seat. Professor Dearson sat down, laid his fingers lightly on the keys, and looked up at Boné. The boy nodded. With all the force of wrist and fingers the old man crashed down in a loud chord, began a wild rhythm strange to all but Ona.

"The Corn Dance! I remember!" she shouted.

Boné did not reply. Slowly he began to circle round the room, head down and back bent, lifting his knees high, bringing his feet down with a powerful stamp. Once again, after all these years, Ona saw and felt him as she had when he had practiced the steps in Bert Bruce's trading post. Finished, Boné came over and patted her hand. "I thought I'd forgotten, but it all comes back."

The party was growing serious now. They pulled their chairs up to the fire and quietly listened to both Professor Dearson and Boné who gave their best. Ona grew annoyed; somebody in the corner was whispering interminably. She looked around. Rogier was emphatically shaking his head and Timothy was scrawling on a scratch-pad balanced on his knee. She thought it rather strange that a man like Timothy would go to such trouble and expense to give a party like this to a family with whom he had no social connections whatever, poor as they were. Now remembering his allusion to the *Cripple Creek Times* report of the Sylvanite, a quick suspicion jumped into her mind. Certainly they weren't talking about a building contract. Resolutely she dismissed it and tried to concentrate on the playing.

It was after midnight before they left. On the way home the snow stopped falling. The moon came out. The drivers had taken off the straps of bells, and through the eerie blue light the sleighs sped home swiftly and silently as ghosts.

4

For two days Boné stayed in bed upstairs in the barny third floor. Only for supper each night did he come down in brocaded slippers and a black silk dressing gown emblazoned with a golden dragon. He was tired out, he said.

On the third morning Mrs. Rogier sent for Dr. Beverly. He sat talking for a half-hour, then got up and casually announced that Boné was not tired out; he was on the verge of a nervous breakdown. Two weeks rest in bed and no excitement, he prescribed, and after that a good three months' rest from work in quiet, agreeable surroundings. Bone pooh-poohed the verdict, but stayed in bed; it was the easiest way to avoid all engagements. His cheerfulness gave way to a sullen apathy that withstood all interference. He tore dinner invitations to bits, shouted down the stairs that he was out whenever the doorbell rang, and refused curtly to see again the people whom he had greeted so cordially the week before.

In the darkness they all passed in parade before him: the plump-breasted dowagers who had used him to further their social ambitions, the bejewelled hangers-on of the exclusive rich, vapid wives and yawning husbands, music club members repeating technical phrases from their textbooks—the whole tribe who had sung his praises, lauded his meager accomplishments, and by their extravagant flattery insulted his integrity beyond repair.

Suffering under his own accusations, he saw himself charmingly accepting their ovations, gracefully acceding to every request, and passing for what he knew he was not—a composer of national stature. True enough, his work was known over all the country. His tour had been successful. In Cleveland, Pittsburgh, Philadelphia, Boston, Chicago, even New York, his audiences had been receptive, the press notices kind. But it was his songs, those light melodious airs and ragtimes dashed off in San Francisco that had recalled him to their minds. Not the solid composition of his "Indian Suite" that had cost him so much sweat and worry. Never his two piano sonatas to which he had given the best of his talent and skill. Here at home these were hardly known. Humbled by the work of masters to whom he had always bent in obeisance, shamed by the standards of an art to which he meant to give his own best, he felt himself a poseur, a charlatan, for accepting the unwarranted praise. And those who gave it he despised.

Songs, songs, songs! They had grown to be the bane of his life. Melodic fragments that came to him from every possible source and that once built upon still leapt at him derisively from a piano in an obscure Barbary Coast saloon, from a boy's whistle, or from a shop girl humming on her way to work. If he could just quit writing songs and get down to honest composition!

There was a sudden creak. He sat up, realizing it was only the Kadles on their nocturnal rounds. He could hear the regular, intermittent squeak of the deliberate steps coming up the stairs, pausing at every door. Mechanically, with a nervous hand, he began to mark a beat. A crazy, simple tune tried to jump into his head. He flung down, ear to pillow, and swathed his head with covers.

Matie Vrain, who was in town for the first time in two years, came to see him. The very sight of her dark wrinkled face brought back those days when life was sharp and simple as the smell of sage, colorful as the cliffs flaming red under the turquoise sky. Matie was still working on the Reservation, and thinking of moving to the hospital near the new Navajo Indian Mission sponsored by the Women's Home Missionary Society.

"You remember the old mission in Jewett Valley, near the Hogback? Well, it was sold to the Presbyterians, and the Society moved to its new site, up the San Juan about twenty-two miles. It's across the river, near the La Plata suspension bridge west of Farmington. Miss Tripp, who started the school for Navajo children, is the one. And you remember Mrs. Aldridge, the field matron? Oh yes! There's a big trading post at Shiprock, and another one started."

Matie sighed. "That's the reason I'm going to move. Lew's getting queer, Boné. Seems like she's more Indian than white. Says the country's getting too civilized for her, and keeps talking of going off alone, way downriver."

"And Bruce?"

"Oh, Bert's all right except for his leg. It keeps going numb on him. He has to lie on a bed behind the counter most of the time. He kind of liked you, you know. Always figured you'd be coming back."

Boné lay staring at the lumpy, weather-beaten face before him. "Before you go back, Matie, I want to see you," he said at last, with a flicker of hope in his eyes.

As the winter wore on Rogier spent an hour with him every day, usually late in the afternoon when no one else was around. He would stamp up the stairs, sink into a chair, and after the barest greeting launch into his talk. Things looked fine up at Cripple Creek. The mines were being drained in great shape by new drainage tunnels. Freight and treatment charges had been reduced considerably; $5 ore could be shipped at a profit.

With this as a background, he began to elucidate the excellent prospects of the Sylvanite. One afternoon he brought up the results of the latest assays and pulled out of his pocket two new samples and a magnifying glass. On another he explained in detail the planned development workings. On still another he cheerfully imparted the news that the Zebbelins had finished their cabin and built two bridges across the creek.

Boné was quite aware of the intent of this continued harangue and tried to forestall it. "Sounds like it's going to be a great mine. I'll be so glad for you and Aunt Martha. After all these years! But it's not my line, mining. Frankly, I'm at a crucial turning point in my own career – if you can call it that. I –"

"You're right, my boy! Wait'll the snows melt. Then we'll go down. On the best working you ever laid eyes on, son!"

An equal measure of compassionate pity and extravagant admiration infused Boné as he listened to him talk. An old white-headed man, eyes bright with an almost unendurable gleam. But still the man who had loved and raised him as a father, who had understood and condoned his own dream, and whose monthly checks for years had enabled him to preserve a sense of independence against Lockhart's munificent hospitality. How indomitable he was, as if possessed of inexhaustible energy! Still Boné refused to ride up to Cripple Creek with him, although more and more often he was helplessly drawn out to the shop where Rogier could talk without fear of interruption.

It was on one of these days, early in March, that Rogier finally and outrightly came to the point. "I'd sure be willing to take you in with me, boy. It's just a family affair, Cable and me, and Abe and Jake. No outsiders if we can raise the money to go down."

"Wish I could," answered Boné slowly. "If I were only sure of some money coming in, so I wouldn't have to stop work to go on tour and write these everlasting ragtimes!"

"If the Sylvanite runs into a blanket vein you won't ever have to worry, any more than Cable and Ona. You'll be independent for life!"

Boné stared out the window, unable to face him.

"As a matter of fact, son, I'm in something of a pinch," Rogier went on. "I'd counted on a little money to cover the invoices for some machinery I ordered. It's at the freight depot now. How long they'll hold it I don't know. But – Well, it's a problem that has me worried."

Boné flung around. "I've got about five thousand dollars to carry me through a siege of serious work. I have the feeling that if I don't make it now, I never will. There's no telling when I'll have another chance." He hesitated. "You can have it. I'm going back to the Navajo Reservation where I won't be disturbed and expenses will be low. So if you want, put me down for a share in the Sylvanite."

Rogier nodded his head, but the sudden gleam in his eyes betrayed him. "I'll take it! It's not much you understand, considering the cost of mining these days. But it will get that machinery off the depot platform. What about that, eh?" He slapped Boné on the shoulder. "Son, you've got yourself a share in a good mine! It's going to pull us both out of a hole! Don't you worry!"

Boné laughed. "You know, Uncle Joe, we're both after the same thing. If we hit it, we hit it. If we don't, it won't be our fault!"

Two weeks later Boné left home as he had left years before, sick and worn out. He was off to the Reservation with Matie Vrain,

Early that April, Rogier began packing hoist and boiler up the canyon from Bull Hill junction east of Victor. Jake had written that they had better start moving before the spring freshets and while the snow was still hard enough to support a sled.

It was the news Rogier had been waiting for. He hired four laborers in town to help – to avoid talk in Cripple Creek – and took the train next day. With them went Cable. The real estate deal, as Ona had foreseen, had petered out; for the present he was out of a job and could spare the time.

The men worked swiftly in the cold clear morning. Abe and Jake had built two sleds and engaged two spans of mules. On the stoutest of the sleds the heavy steel drum was loaded and buckled to the iron supporting bolts; on the other was lashed the cable reel. "Where's those jackasses I told you to get?" demanded Rogier. The burros were driven up. "Pack those boxes on 'em. No need of wasting time. Here, don't you know how to throw a hitch?" He set his foot against the shaggy ribs, heaved on the ropes. "Cable, you and Jake take a couple of men and go ahead with the burros to break trail. Mind you, now: a level route where the sled can't topple. Watch the bridges and keep out of the swamps. It's liable to be wet along the base of that aspen grove."

They started out, crossed Grassy Gulch shimmering white with snow, pulled around the base of the Calf. For two hours they labored up the pass behind Cow Mountain, finally reaching the mouth of the canyon. In the cold dry air the breaths of men and beasts puffed out like smoke against the somber blue-clad mountains. The aspens were grey along the creek bottom, the cliffs tall and frosted white. In the eerie silence the men plodded on with an occasional curse, a snap of rawhide echoing like the report of a forty-five and arousing the chatter of a flock of magpies in the grove.

A deer leapt out of a thicket, stood quivering, then turned and bounded up the slope.

Late that afternoon Cable, wiping the sweat from his face, stood looking up the slope at the Sylvanite. There was the last bridge of rough hewn pines over the stream, the big new cabin, and the shaft and tool house ready to receive the machinery. Even the corral was shiny new with unpeeled green aspens.

"You sure have done your work," he said quietly to Jake.

"You know the Colonel!" Jake replied shortly. "He's goin' after it, no mistake. And we'd better be gettin' back to help him."

It was early evening before drum and reel were unloaded from the sleds, the miscellaneous boxes stacked in place. "Let's close up now, boys, and get back after the other load. We'd better be fetchin' that boiler up while we got easy going," Rogier called.

The men did not move except to congregate at the door of the cabin. "What the hell!" expostulated one. "We been at this all day long on nothin' but a dinner of bacon and beans. What's the all-fired rush?"

Rogier pointed at the sky. "Look for yourselves: clear as a bell. The sun will be comin' out in the mornin' and melting the trail. You know how much that boiler weighs. We'll be sloggin' down in slush, gettin' stuck at every crossing."

"It's gettin' dark. We want to eat," the men began to mutter.

"What's the difference whether you work two days or a day and night?" Rogier demanded. "We've got to get this job done. Double time for the night, boys! What do you say?"

"We say we don't want to. We'll do it tomorrow."

"I'm tired out as the men," Cable remonstrated. "We can't work in the dark anyway. A good night's sleep is the thing for all of us."

"Dom lazy jackasses – every one of you!" Rogier grumbled, turning away.

Abe already had built a fire in the cabin and was busy mixing biscuit dough.

The hearty meal put the men back in good humor. They lit their pipes and lounged before the fire, picking spots for their blankets. Betweentimes they warily cracked jokes at Rogier for being in such a goldarned hurry – he having walked up the hill with a torch to inspect the machinery and see that none of the boxes had been lost. A half-hour later he returned, threw open the door and stood looking out at the patch of star-stung sky flung like a banner over the opposite canyon wall.

"You boys better be rollin' up in your blankets. It's goin' to be a good day and we've got to hit the trail early."

True to his word, he roused them out at the first faint streak of dawn above the cliffs. It was still dark in the cabin; and the men got up grumbling at the cold, at the icy water, at Rogier. Aspens, pines, cliff, and stream emerged slowly but distinctly in the break of day; the stars still shone, but without luster. Abe, man-wise, took his time at the stove; he kept heaping the platter with pancakes until every man was stuffed. Rogier, idling at the fireplace with a cigar, could restrain his impatience no longer.

"Abe, I've never seen you so slow. What's ailing you, man?"

Abe took off from the stove a fresh bucket of coffee and set it on the table without answering.

One of the men let out a goodnatured laugh. "What's the rush, Mr. Rogier? Them gold nuggets will be here when we get back!"

Rogier angrily flung out the door. The sun was just showing over the pine-tips.

A half hour later they were on their way, mules and burros fresh and frisky as an early squirrel in a nearby spruce-top, the men laughingly taking turns riding the empty, ungainly sleds.

By mid-morning they presented a different appearance. They were wet to the knees, splattered with slush and mud until they were hardly recognizable. One stopped to wipe his face with his hat; another straighteded up stiffly, his hand to his back.

"Dom it! I told you men that sun was comin' out to raise hell. Cable! Get these burros off the trail. They've tracked up too much already. What're you tryin' to do—get us stuck in slush?" Inflexible, merciless, and unwearied, Rogier drove them on.

It had been a fight from the first. The cylindrical, slippery boiler kept springing the ropes as if they were made of rubber. Cleat after cleat it broke on the sides. Heavy, cumbersome, too long for the sled, its back end bumped the ground at every rise. They were continually cutting a new trail through snow. But now the warm April sun was melting the crust and the frozen stream.

By noon they had made it up the difficult grade and down the other side. Somber, wordless, and worn out, the men flung themselves down in the wet. Cable pleaded their unspoken need for food and rest. Rogier, grim-lipped and indomitable, shook his head. He stood facing the small meadow threaded by the stream over which they must pass. The snow field, lit by the sun, gave back a dazzling brightness. Only for yards on each side of the stream was there a patch of dirty gray. The men rose to their feet, knowing what it meant: the snow was melting and in the soft wet marsh grass underneath the heavy sled was likely to bog down. An hour's wait would never do.

The quarter-mile stretch took them over two hours to cross, with every jack-man of them heaving beside the mules at every step. Rogier was triumphant; like a victorious general he was all for pushing forward immediately before luck turned against him. Despite him the men scattered for wood, built a fire, boiled coffee, and ate.

The trail leading off the meadow into the mouth of the narrow forested canyon, made a sharp turn to the right along a thick grove of aspens. Just above it the stream had been blocked by beavers and the sudden thaw had sent it pouring over the dam and spreading a thin flood almost to the edge of the grove. Not until they were in it, did any of them realize how deep it was.

"Look out! Whoa-up! Whoa, boy!" shouted Jake, digging in his heels and throwing himself backward with the reins wrapped round his fists.

"Dom it to hell!" growled Rogier, running up. "Now, we've done it! Just like I told you. Stoppin' to eat, eat, eat. That water wasn't up an hour ago."

The left runner of the sled had sunk almost out of sight; the heavy boiler, listing precariously, looked likely to go over.

The men worked fast and furiously. New ropes were slung from the boiler and half-hitched to the nearest aspens to hold it in place. All four mules were again strung out to pull at the sled – the ropes to be tightened at every step. Aspen trunks were cut and trimmed of branches, laid corduroy fashion in front of the sled runner. All the men bent backs to the downoff-side. Finally the mules were whipped up. The sled did not budge.

Again and once again they made futile efforts. Rogier shut his mouth in a straight, grim line and began walking slowly over the ground, scrutinizing every foot. The mouth of the canyon rising upward into the blue shadows of pine and spruce was so tantalizingly close.

"If we could just get up there on that gravel slide where the snow ain't melted yet we'd be plumb outa trouble fer all the rest of the way." The remark came wearily from one of the men leaning against a panting mule.

Rogier walked up to him. "And just how do you propose to do that?" he demanded.

The fellow flushed and moved off with an apprehensive look over his shoulder.

Two of the burros were hitched with the mules. They were able to stir the sled an inch, but the minute they let up it settled back again.

"If we could get them other two on we might do somethin'," Jake said quietly.

"Well, why don't we?" cut in Rogier.

"Ain't no traces, no straps, no nothin'. All we got's up in the tool house."

"I'll go after them," spoke up Cable, motioning for another man to follow him.

It was a long stiff hike, and loaded down with their heavy burden they took over two hours to make the trip. For still another hour the men sat around clumsily fashioning traces and harness from ropes and straps.

The eight animals and eight men, working together now, made another effort. The sled jerked out of its clutch, but the back end of the boiler snapping two of the ropes slid off into the mud.

Of cool, calm Rogier, master builder and contractor for $100,000 jobs, there was now no semblance left. The back end of a boiler resting in mud – no more than that! – made him out a madman. He stood there on the edge of that white virginal valley faced by the dark slope of immemorial pines, and heedless of the knot of men and beasts around him, raised his face to that of the great icy Peak rising above him. For a moment he was silent. Then he took off his hat, ruffling his white hair, and threw it on the ground. He beat his fist into the palm of his left hand. Suddenly he began to swear. It was an epithetic denouncement of valley, canyon, Peak, the snow, men, and the weather—and it frightened a mule which shied from the impassioned intensity of his voice with a sudden squeal. The men backed away, silent and embarrassed, as if taking upon themselves the unwarranted guilt for the unfortunate mishap. Cable alone seemed to remain untouched. Dark and taciturn, he sat down on a log and calmly lit his pipe.

When Rogier finally quieted and backed away, Jake picked up the fallen hat and began in a shame-faced manner to beat off the snow and muck with a cold, bare hand.

"I reckon they ain't nothin' to do but wait till evenin' when it freezes up again," muttered one of the crew.

"And the sled and boiler too? Hell, we'll never get it out then," replied another.

Abe walked over to Cable. They talked, finally went over to Rogier. "We figure there's only one thing to do," Cable told him decisively. "Send the men back to the Sylvanite. Cut off cable from the reel and use it instead of rope. It's the only thing that'll hold her."

Rogier stared at them as if they had proposed to violate his own personal integrity. "Use that cable?" he shouted. "You must be mad! That's hoisting cable, you fools. I figured it to fifty feet. Just what we need to get down to where we're goin'."

"Order more if you need it—which you won't. That shaft's not goin' clear through to China."

"And be delayed weeks—never!" Rogier flung around, shouted to the men. "The man who lays hand on that steel cable is responsible to me for destruction of personal property. Do you hear, men? You stay here, understand? We're goin' to get this out tonight. Now, by Jove!"

He began to give orders. Two pines were felled, stripped of branches. The logs, slantwise, were driven into the ground to keep the boiler from rolling off. Mules, burros, and men laboriously snaked the front end of the sled around to face the aspen grove. By dark the back end of the boiler had been raised on the sled again.

"Jesus, where we goin' now?" swore a voice from the deep dusk. "We can't go through no grove of aspens."

"That," answered Rogier quietly, "is exactly where we're goin'."

And now began the heartbreaking task of chopping a pathway through a hundred yards or more of thickly growing trees to get back on the trail. Foot by foot sled and boiler were snaked ahead, and finally slid upon the hard packed snow and gravel base of the canyon trail.

Torches were lit, the flames rousing from the dark canyon the cry of a wolf; in the flickering red light the men resumed their march. The night was cold, a bitter biting cold that froze the wet boots and leggings of the men and formed a thin white fringe on the shaggy hair of mules and burros. It was long after midnight when they at last pulled into the clearing where sat the cabin and big corral of the Sylvanite.

Abe worked up a hasty meal, put on a pail of coffee. The men, worn out, ate and flopped on the floor in their blankets, feet to fire. A half hour later Rogier came in; it was he who had remained outside to unhitch and feed the animals, to break the ice at the creek and carry back and forth buckets of water, to carefully hang up their harness and throw the bars on the corral gate. He sat down at the deserted table, poured out the dregs of the coffee and dug a single scrap of bacon from the cold grease in the pan.

"Dom fine work, men! Double time for both days. Every one of you. Hey?"

No one answered. Already asleep, they were stretched out like stiff corpses on the floor before him.

Rogier got up slowly, ran his hand through his tousled white hair before putting on his hat; he figured there had better be some wood split to build the morning fire before he turned in.

5

When Cable returned to town, it was with news that all the machinery had been set in place despite a new fall of snow and that work sinking the shaft had commenced. Rogier, he said, would remain at the Sylvanite for yet awhile, but would soon be down again to see about his building work.

Ona, sitting with her mother when Cable returned, said nothing. Throughout supper and all the way home she maintained the same heavy, negative silence. She put the children to bed, waited quietly until Cable had finished his few chores. "Jonathan," she said then, "you can't do this to me."

"What?"

"You know what, Jonathan. Going up to help Daddy for a few days and staying more than two weeks. But it isn't the work or time that really matters. You know what it is. I could tell it the minute you walked in the door. 'Our mine!'—'When we get the shaft down!' After we had ironed it all out once, for good, that you weren't going in on the Sylvanite."

"I agreed to nothing of the kind. If I did, that time has passed. Last fall. What do you want me to do?"

"Do?" She looked at him with an ironic smile that did not hide her anger. "So you have to be told that your precious prairie land turned out to be a miserable deal Bennett tried to palm off on you! That he didn't even own it—just held a short option. That you wouldn't get into first class real estate, and now you're out of work at all. Do you have to be reminded that we, myself and children, must be considered too? Or are you planning to move us home?"

This last brought a slow flush to his swarthy cheeks. "You wouldn't be so hoity-toity if the Sylvanite came in a boomer! It would be a different story then. You'd be Rogier enough to share in the profits. Why the independence now — for the first time in your life?"

She rose, crossed the room to sit down beside him where she could lay her hand on his. "Let's don't quarrel, Jonathan. You know how afraid of the Sylvanite I am. And Daddy too. All my life I've been plagued with mines, mines, mines! They're all alike, good ones and poor ones. They ruin a man every time. I want you to keep out of such risky ventures. Daddy's too old to change. It's in him for good. But you—you're still young, Jonathan."

He withdrew his hand from under hers, deliberately filled and lighted his pipe. "Now that you've begun it, let's see the thing through. First of all, I married you and expect to take care of you and the children. I'm not a Rogier, nor am I a waif picked up and added to the family, expecting to be provided for out of the Sylvanite. I stand on my own feet."

"What are you doing wasting your time on the Sylvanite for, then, when you could be about your own business?"

"Because," he said simply, "I've put in part of my bank account on the Sylvanite."

Ona had risen, let down her hair. The news caught her, hands under the tresses. She sank back down with shocked amazement, flung back her hair, tried to speak. The long brown hair, soft and fluffy from washing, crept over her face as she leaned back and turned her head. "You couldn't! Oh, you couldn't be so foolish. Not if you loved me—or thought of the children."

"But I did," he said quietly. "All of you."

It was midnight when they finally went to bed, worn out and sleepless from a quarrel whose end neither could foresee. It dragged through summer and fall into winter—a futile wrangle whose objective both seemed to have forgotten.

Cable kept returning to Cripple Creek, a week, two weeks or more at a time. Between trips he studied and tried to sell insurance; Ona was still bent on his being a businessman, and fought his moving permanently up to the mine. The arrangement kept them all on edge: Rogier who was after him continually, Ona who resumed her quarrelsome pleas the day he returned, and Cable who each day drew more closely into himself.

Work on the Sylvanite progressed steadily. The shaft was down a hundred feet, commonly assumed the proper depth for a level, but Rogier was insisting on another forty feet before cutting a station. Cross-cutting would then be commenced to tap the vein traversing the property. Overhand stoping, working up on a raise instead of down on a winze, he had figured would be a good thirty percent cheaper; they could take advantage of gravity instead of having to install a small lift. He already had bought an old iron bucket of 900 pounds capacity to use instead of a cage, a supply of drills and hand tools, and enough dynamite for the winter—box after box buried halfway up the hill in back of the cabin. He was well satisfied with the assays and counted on shipping ore soon.

But it cost so much—the dom hard country rock! He had to spend half his time in town, not daring to let his business drop; it was the only source of income to carry the mine. Hence his frequent calls for Cable to take his place with Abe and Jake.

Rogier's current contract called for a two-story annex to one of the schools; it amounted to comparatively little money, but upon it hinged his bid for a new group of schools for the West Side.

"It doesn't amount to an awful lot, Rawlings," he told his old foreman, going over the plans. "You can do most of it yourself. You know how rushed I am up on the hill—and where to find me."

Rawlings assented to boss the job after taking a few days off, Rogier digging the foundations while he was gone. Returning to the job, Rawlings methodically and carefully checked the work done. The foundations had been dug three feet too deep. He sent a man for Rogier, catching him just as he was leaving for Cripple Creek.

"Doggone it, Joe! Look what you went and done. You know we can't have that."

"Shoot!" growled Rogier, winding up his steel tape. "How the devil did I let that happen? And so all-fired deep."

"Exactly three feet to the inch. We can't fill in with dirt, it'll settle. And if you pour cement, it's goin' to cost too much."

Rogier got out his pencil. "Right you are, Rawlings! You do have a head on your shoulders. We'll fill it in with coarse gravel from the west pits and add water. It'll set hard enough to bottom the concrete."

In a few days Rogier's mistake had been rectified; and leaving Rawlings in charge to begin pouring cement, he left for Cripple Creek.

There were no mistakes made at the Sylvanite. He went over every detail a dozen times, sat up half the night figuring and brooding over his plans. Two months later, on the 140-foot level, Abe struck the vein. It was solidly filled with gangues and tellurides which assayed a sylvanite ore running, at best, almost $30 to the ton.

Cable at home was elated at the news, and got ready to join Rogier at the mine. Ona watched him pack with a frown. "Don't get too excited. Mines are like prostitutes. They all promise more than they give."

"What do you know about prostitutes?" demanded Cable.

"And what do you?" she countered in a level voice.

She kissed him goodbye warmly enough, but when he had gone compressed her lips in a stubborn line. Rogier, for the time, had won. But it was not the end. She knew men and mines too well.

That month by month regular shipments of ore were made changed little the consensus regarding the Sylvanite. A few old-timers straying up the gulch held it to be a freak pocket. Timothy and his group of club members speculated on its actual existence; the mine was not listed and they could obtain no information from Rogier who had stopped coming to the Ruxton. Even the family, oppressed by the specters of previous failures, regarded it with awe tinctured by a spot of fear and wondered where all the money went.

To be sure, Mrs. Rogier was given a generous contribution for her sugar bowl. Jonathan and Ona, with new furniture, moved up the street to a bigger house. Boné was sent a little money as a cheering token, and a case of books. Such were the visible dividends from Rogier's investment. Every other cent he was putting back into the mine, determined to go down another ninety feet to a second level.

"We're out of money again," Ona told Cable one morning.

"I'll get another check from Joe. Forgot it last time I was up there," he answered casually.

"It's awfully embarrassing, this having to ask you for money all the time. And you having to go to Daddy. I don't see why you can't be paid your share at a certain time every month. Then I'd know what to count on."

"Oh, that's all right. You know how it is. We don't have enough ore for a carload yet. When we do get a check from the mill we'll have our money, and you can pay off the bills."

Ona bit her lip. "No, it isn't all right, Jonathan! It's wrong all the way around. You know how Daddy is. So bound to put everything back in the Sylvanite, he forgets we have to live. It just gives me the feeling we're living off him. And we're not! We've put our bank account and all our savings into it, and you give him most of your time. I do wish you'd stop and go on with your insurance. Something substantial to fall back on when the Sylvanite peters out. Let Daddy hire a man."

"What makes you talk like that?" he asked irritably, walking into the kitchen and pouring himself a cup of coffee.

She followed him, and disregarding March who was playing with a wooden pistol on the table, continued her tirade. "From knowing a hundred mines! They're all alike as soiled women. Entrancing for awhile and then poof!—they've eaten up all your money and the best years of your life, and vanished. Look at Hartsel. Famous Hartsel! When I was little, he was worth a hundred thousand dollars from his Bluebell. And now, look!" She jerked up from the back of a chair where it was hanging a bit of blue ribbon. "Where did I get this band for Leona's hair? At Pelta's Dry Goods Store. From the little clerk at the ribbon counter. Hartsel!" She lowered her voice. "Jonathan, I'm afraid of the Sylvanite. It's playing us a trick. It won't last."

His brown inexpressive face might have warned her. He was usually so kind, so gentle—gentle as an Indian's cupped hands replacing a baby trout in a stream. She had seen him, in a hurry to catch a train, stopping to unknot the laces of March's shoes; and watched his patient brown hands untangling Leona's hair. A slow rhythmical man careful of insignificant details and content to let the big things take care of themselves – yet likely for no reason at all to erupt like volcano.

What he said now was inconsequential; it was as if his voice carried a spectrum of tone audible only to the boy hacking at his wooden pistol with a butcher knife.

March jumped up from the table, pointing his pistol at his father. "Don't you be mean to my mother! I'll shoot you!"

With unbelievable swiftness, and without a word, Cable turned on him. Grasping the boy by the collar and the seat of his pants, he flung him through the screen door and over the back porch railing. It was a good six foot drop, but fortunately the earth of the garden was soft from recent spading. The boy lit flat on his belly, legs and arms outspread. By the time Ona reached him he had regained his breath, unhurt, white-faced, but too scared to cry. It was the first time his father ever had lain hands on him. Cable, without waiting to see whether the boy had been hurt, had flung off to town.

That afternoon Cable was strolling up Tejon Street and happened to glimpse March walking downstreet toward him. The boy saw him at the same time. He halted with the look of a scared rabbit about to hide behind a lamp post or dodge into the crowd of passers-by. Before he could move, Cable crooked his finger. The boy obediently followed him into the drugstore.

"About time for a dish of ice cream, eh?" said Cable. "How about a nut sundae?"

March grinned sheepishly as they sat down at the long counter flanked by big red and blue glass jars, and in back of which hung the large Red Raven sign he liked so well. Cable watched him eat. Then taking out his pipe, he said casually, "Too bad about that business this morning, March. But the first thing a man's got to learn is not to mix in other people's affairs. Nobody's. Just what concerns you. I guess you'll remember that, won't you, son?"

March licked off his spoon, glancing up at his father. A quick, shy smile passed over Cable's face. March grinned. "Yes, sir!"

"I see Buffalo Bill's Wild West Show is coming early this summer. The posters are already up. A lot of Utes'll be here too. Reckon we ought to take it all in. I'll make it a point to come down from Cripple Creek. What do you say?"

"Ohh! Will they attack the stagecoach and scalp the soldiers and burn the women at the stake and all?" March sat up, talking garrulously.

"The whole bloody business, I reckon," Cable assented complacently.

They walked out of the door hand in hand –

Buffalo Bill's Wild West Show! To the boy of those years it was always to stand out with a preternatural clearness and tragic intensity undimmed by time, like something not seen but recalled by a memory hidden deep within him. Not the mock heroic figure with long yellow hair leading the morning parade on his white horse and shooting his clay balls with less markmanship than birdshot. Not those who followed him, sitting limply in their saddles and swaying unconsciously as reeds in the wind: the hunters in broad hats and buckskins, the silent mountain men, the prospectors in red flannel shirts, the masked badmen and those who brought them to dust, the chiefs regal in paint and warbonnets, the braves naked but for a clout and a single eagle feather, the squaws with papooses lashed to cradle boards on their backs. Never just these, framed by the colored posters with the melodramatic Buntline touch, the shouting crowds filling the grandstands with the drunken loafers below, the dust, the flies, the war paint dripping from a warrior's chin upon a copy of the *Denver Post* spread across his knees, a lounging chief noisily sucking ice cream shortly after his demise, a squaw begging pennies.

Not the sorry form he saw, but the splendid substance of a life, an unbelievable century drawing to a close, through whose still-open gate rushed at him sight, sound, and smell of something he could almost touch. A story without plot and without end, music without melody, a kaleidoscopic panorama still too new to be confined in a frame. The vast sunlit plaines, the slow red rivers, the heaving blue walls of the great male Rockies – what horizons could hem in these backgrounds of America's only true legends? Tomorrow their tales would stand beside those of Arthur of Pendragon and the Knights of the Round Table. The hazy picturebook figures of Launcelot and Sir Galahad faded at the crack of a forty-five. Toward him galloped the warrior horsemen of the Great Plains, lances up, feathers streaming in the ceaseless wind, in phalanxes that would have put Ghenghis Kahn to rout. What names these heroes bore, so earthy and commonplace they sent a tingle up his spine! Sitting Bull and Roman Nose, Red Cloud, Rain-in-the-Face, Kicking Bear. Crazy Horse shouting his battle-cry, "It's a good day to die!" Old and unarmed White Antelope calmly singing his death song on the dawn when he was massacred with a whole village of women and children not far east. Siegfried and the dragon, Jason and his Golden Fleece, the journeys of Ulysses had nothing to compare with these epics of grassroots America. Still their cadence was not yet measured, their tones not yet suave and polished. The veil of time had not yet blurred their sharp outlines. They unfolded here, close and touchable, they moved here before him truthfully, formless, and without fault. They were a part of him who needed not to be told they were the priceless and unmeasured substance of his birthright, so completely did he respond as he sat spellbound upon his plank seat while the sun rode from south to west and dipped behind the mountains that had seen it all an incalculable number of times.

And now the long procession of covered wagons came crawling slowly over the plains. The creaking wooden wheels, the ceaseless jolting that churned butter, the canvas wagon sheets drawn tight over the bows. The patient weary women sitting limply under their starched sunbonnets, the wail of a child, the men plodding behind with a cow whose teats had been chewed off by wolves.

But now, so suddenly, that single, eerie, high-pitched cry! Almighty God! Who could ever forget that long, loping crescent of Cheyennes! The thunder of their hooves, their sea of feathers breaking over the crest of hills. A single shot. The chiefs swerving to the right and left, riding in a circle about the wagon train, the warriors bent low over their spotted ponies and shooting arrows under their necks. Gracefully the feathered shafts tore through the canvas wagon sheets. Men with rifles knelt patiently behind the wagon wheels, shot steadily and deliberately, and spat on their hot breeches. A woman handed one a supply of fresh bullets. An Indian fell headlong; the riderless pony trotted off and started eating grass. And now a band of brave cowboys dashed up, in the nick of time. The Indians withdrew. And then over the horizon galloped a troop of Dragoons! Bluecoats! The wagon train had survived the attack, but it must go on to water. It slowly unwound and passed out of sight over the plain –

The show was over. Buffalo Bill rode out on his white horse and took off his hat. He raised his right hand aloft, palm outward. Then with a quick turn, he galloped off. The hard plank seats emptied. Boy, man, and crowd trickled between Indians washing the war-paint from their cheeks. Dead white men had come to life, brushing dust from their clothes. The beautiful cowgirls were selling their photographs. The corrosive shadow of the mountains obscured all these imperfections. Only the vision of beauty persisted because seen with an inner eye.

Mama and Leona were probably waiting at home with a hot supper. But upon March the spell still held. "Daddy, did you ever kill Indians?"

Cable brought up short. His swarthy brown face set; his big Indian nose jutted out like Pike's Peak; his soft black eyes seemed to grow hard and shiny as flint. He strode to the buckboard and said curtly, "Get in."

They drove silently out of town to the encampment along the creek. In the darkness the pale gray tepees loomed up against the willows. They got out, and March followed his father up the long lane. In the red glow of small cooking fires dark taciturn faces leapt at him. The shadows of blanketed figures writhed on the stretched skins and canvas. A tepee flap yawned open into the mysterious blackness within. A dog barked. Somewhere there sounded the soft beat of a drum.

Cable did not pause. With March at his heels, he picked his way between moccasined feet that did not move to let them pass. At the end of the lane a big fire was burning down into a bed of coals. Around a carcass spitted over it sat a circle of men loosely wrapped in blankets that revealed their naked breasts. Cable stopped but said nothing. Then one of the men looked up and grunted; he had on a red shirt with some colored porcupine quills worked on it. Cable nodded, pushed his way into the circle of eating men, and squatted down cross-legged as they.

How funny he looked among them, it seemed to March standing behind him. His suit was neatly pressed, his high collar was white and stiff in the flamelight, his shined boots tucked under his haunches. And yet March sensed in him something he had never felt before. A strange solidarity with the blanketed figures around him, as if he felt completely at home. One of them said something to him in a guttural tongue. Cable for reply made a queer sign with his hand. The rest of them grunted or laughed.

Cable reached down with his delicate brown hands and tore off a chunk of bread to put on a tin plate at his feet. Then he got out the toad-sticker with its long razor-sharp blade which he always carried. Leaning over the carcass spitted on the coals, he deftly laid back a flap of thick fat and cut off a slab of lean meat underneath.

March stirred uneasily at his shoulder, expecting his father to pass the filled plate to him. But Cable seemed oblivious of his presence. Holding up the slab of meat to his mouth with one hand, he cut off a bite with the knife in his other hand, and continued eating. When he was through, he wiped his fingers on his straight black hair. Then picking up a tin cup he raised it to his shoulder. "Water!" he said curtly.

A wave of hot resentment flooded March as he took the cup. His father had known he was there all the time, but he hadn't given him anything to eat, and now he was ordering him to go get water. Just like a maid or servant girl or something. For the first time he noticed the squaws and children hanging around the outside of the circle. They hadn't been given anything to eat either. And now suddenly he was oppressed by a feeling of male domination exuded by this circle of lazy, lordly, and impolite men over all those who stood patiently waiting outside. It magnified his own helpless childhood, increasing his resentment, and at the same time its force compelled him to step back into the darkness.

Water! Where was he to get it? Down at the creek. Through the lane of lodges and dark hairless faces with strings of braided hair tied with strips of red flannel, the greasy store-pants and stretched-out moccasins. Into the frightening darkness, the thickets of willows. His heart pounding, he filled the cup and hurried back to hand it to his father. Cable took it without thanks and without turning around.

For another hour now the men sat there smoking and talking about the show. Then as the circle broke up and the women came in, Cable filled a plate with meat and bread for March. "Good meat, son. Eat that juicy strip of fat. Indian candy!"

And now at last, in pale moonlight, they drove silently home to a world March had almost forgotten.

6

The long day they had spent together at Buffalo Bill's Wild West Show somehow had established an intimate relationship between March and his father that had been lacking before. Ona realized this one evening when, cuddling him on her lap, she waited for Cable to come for supper. She had been talking of his growing up into a big boy, maybe going to college, and becoming a famous man like his uncle Boné.

"Daddy's more fun!" March interrupted. "He takes me everywhere and let's me do what I want. He doesn't keep sayin' 'don't do this' and 'don't do that.' That's why I like him. And guess what. When school's out he's going to take me with him up to Cripple Creek. To stay with him and Grandad and learn all about the mine in the ground. What do you think of that?"

Her body stiffened, then slowly relaxed. She put him down and led him into the kitchen, her face strangely grave. "I'll give your supper now, March, so you can go to bed. And get that idea out of your head. Your father knows you're too small yet to go up to the mine. You're going to stay down here and have a nice summer helping Mother. Now ssh! No talking back, mind!"

Disappointed, the boy soon crept off to bed. Ona tucked him in, kissed him, and went back to her seat at the window to stare silently into the darkness. At the sound of Cable's steps, she rose and slowly opened the door; her face was pale and set.

"What's the trouble?" he asked. "Either of the kids sick?"

"No. I want to talk with you. But come have your supper first."

Cable ate silently but deliberately, then put down his napkin and slowly filled his pipe. "A good supper, Ona. Now do you want to go into the other room?"

Ona ignored the remark, pushing aside his plate and leaning forward. "March tells me you're planning on taking him up to the Sylvanite when school is over."

"We're great chums now. It'll be good for him."

"Jonathan, you know I'd never stand for that. Never! If it were the last thing in my life."

He leaned back without replying, his face dark and expressionless.

"No!" she went on, her voice thickening. "I remember how Tom and Sister Molly's lives were ruined. I've done what I could with Mother to keep Daddy out of Cripple Creek, until now I know nobody can help him. I've tried to encourage you to make a success in business—real estate, insurance, anything to keep you out of mining. All of you are alike. Cursed by a damned mine—whatever name it's called."

Cable, elbows on table, drawn tight into himself, let her continue.

"And now you want to take March up there and get the thing started in his blood too. To make it seem so natural to him that when he grows up he won't know he's accursed like the rest of you. Jonathan, you're a fool if you think I'll let my boy go like that!" She drew a deep breath; her voice grew quieter, more resolute. "He's my boy, a Rogier to the marrow of his bones, and he's going to have his chance. He's going to get an education, do something, be somebody. He's never going to see a mine! My foot's down now to stay, Jonathan. I'm not fooling. My boy stays with me if I have to take in washing. You can do what you please, but you leave him alone. Understand?"

It was the climax of that quarrel which long had been beating them apart as with ceaseless waves upon the shore. And it resolved into an open fight for the possession of a boy who still saw them undivided. Only for a time did they maintain in his presence a commendable behavior. Cable was quiet, taciturn. Ona was quiet, reserved. Then gradually they broke out into sudden eruptions at any cause. Twice Ona spanked March for innocently asking when his father was going to take him up to the mine. To atone for the unjust chastising, she began to coddle him like an infant child. Her maternal poses, arms around the boy at every opportunity, aroused in Cable a sullen resentment.

"What do you think he is, a little tin Jesus? Let the boy alone. He can live his own life and form his own ideas without so much harping on the subject by a doting mother."

The last week of school dragged by. Rogier, surprisingly, came up to the house. "Where you been?" he demanded of Cable without prelude. "Don't you know with this good weather we've got to make hay while the sun shines! Thought you were coming up for the summer to help us on the Sylvanite!"

"I might," said Cable quietly. "Been thinkin' of bringing up March for company. Then again I might not. I like to see the rest of my family too, you know."

"Move them all up to the district. I'll get you a house in Victor."

The suggestion roused Ona to justifiable fury.

"Dom it!" growled Rogier. "Minin's minin'. It's no picnic. But there's no call for you to get so riled up." And mystified by the unbearable tension in the room, he strode out without an answer.

The quarrel, now that a decision was at hand, came to a head. Ona, on her knees with her arms around March, was a she-animal defying anyone to take away her cub. The posture was so silly and melodramatic that Cable flung out the door. When he came back from town that evening, Ona was waiting for him with March on her lap.

"Jonathan," she said in a quiet, resolute voice, "this can't go on. We both know that. So I've settled it for good. I telegraphed Boné that I was sending March down to the Reservation to spend the summer. He'll live at Bruce's trading post – Bert is lame and never gets out. Boné is there most of the time. And Lew will get up there often, so it won't be like he won't have a woman to look after him."

She bent down, brushing the boy's hair from his forehead. "You'll like it, Sonny. Remember the story of the rug beside your bed? And there'll be lots of Indians like your father tells you about, only kind and friendly. Won't that be nice?"

"Ohh yes," the boy muttered, too excited to talk.

"Now get to bed and go right to sleep. When you wake up I'll have your suitcase all packed to take to the train right after breakfast."

When he had gone, she turned a pale stern face to Cable. "I'm sorry if you don't approve, Jonathan, or if I've hurt your feelings. But it's the only thing left for me to do. And if you insist on going up to the Sylvanite, I'll miss you both and pray for the time we can all be together for good."

"So you'd send the boy to strangers, a hundred miles from a railroad, just to keep him from being with me?" Cable asked quietly.

"No! To keep him away from the Sylvanite!"

Cable, without answer, walked out of the room.

The next morning they rose early. Ona had packed March's suitcase the night before. Now while he ate breakfast, she sewed a $10 bill with his name and address in the waist of his pantaloons. Meanwhile she kept calling Cable for breakfast. After a time he came out with a suitcase and a dufflebag which he set down beside March's in the hall.

Cable poured himself a cup of coffee and, ignoring the bacon and eggs, stood munching a piece of toast. "The trip is too much for a boy alone. I'm going to take him down there myself."

Ona stood biting her lip, her hands clenched together at her breast. Neither seemed aware of March's excited chatter about having his father for company. There was an awkward silence, broken when a neighbor girl came in to mind Leona.

They walked in silence to the depot, stood waiting for the train. There seemed nothing either could put in words. When the train pulled in, Cable boosted up boy and bags and waited beside Ona until the conductor called, "All aboard!" They kissed.

"Take good care of yourself," he said calmly.

"And you, Jonathan," she answered, too proud to confess her fears and longings.

He swung aboard and without a backward glance strode through the vestibule into the coach.

Ona stood watching the train until it vanished around the bend. Then, the tears beginning at last to fall, she plunged sobbing up the tracks to home.

A week passed and then another before a postcard came from March in Cable's handwriting:

"Tell Mama this is a big country a long way off. I got wet when the wagon swum the river. There are lots of Indians. They ride horses and mostly wagons. They wear bracelets like girls and ain't the scalping kind. They ain't no post office or even town so maybe you won't get this. But we're here anyway with love."

There was no postscript from Cable, but she expected him to return any day. When he did not come, she began to worry. Rogier did little to ease her anxiety. He demanded to know why Cable hadn't returned to work in the Sylvanite as he had promised.

"I expect him soon," she said. "Probably he's taking a short vacation first."

Rogier returned to the Sylvanite in a devil of a temper. Abe and Jake had lost the vein and were piling up non-shipping ore on the dump. "No more drifts!" he ordered. "Just fooling around, you are. We'll go down some more. Another level, two if necessary, by Jove! I tell you boys, you've got to keep going down. What became of those men I sent you?"

"Just one, Colonel," said Jake mildly. "When we stopped shippin' ore we let the other go. You can't pay a man outa nothin'. We figured that."

"Bah! Leave that to me. I'll get the money and see you get help for that shaft work. Cable. He's long overdue."

There was no doubt about it; he was feeling a squeeze. Cable had not returned to help Abe and Jake, and it was necessary to call back the mucker they had let out. To pay his wages Rogier gave Ona only half the monthly allowance she had been receiving as a return on Cable's investment in the mine. This seemed quite reasonable, for with Cable and March away, the family had been reduced by half.

To sink the shaft would be expensive. He had turned in a bid for the group of six west-side schools in Little London to pay for it, but the contract had not yet been awarded and the money would not be forthcoming for several months. Rogier could not wait. He wrote Boné . The Sylvanite, he asserted, looked better than ever despite the fact that the present stope had been exhausted. They were in hopes of sinking the shaft still deeper when money from a forthcoming building contract became available. Meanwhile they were losing time. There was no doubt Boné would receive a substantial return from his investment so greatly appreciated. He hoped the lad was writing good music and his health was improved. He must remember to let nothing, nothing, come between him and the dictates of his inner self.

An answer came in due time—a draft for another two thousand dollars. Enclosed with it was a letter stating how sorry Boné was that it was no more, but not to hesitate a moment in applying it to the further development of the mine. He had finished his long orchestration and was leaving for another winter's concert tour back east.

Rogier, disappointed by the amount, did not let Mrs. Rogier read the letter. He simply told her of Boné's success. "They won't let the boy alone, Marthy! He's got to go on another piano playing expedition to keep them satisfied." Nor did he mention the money he had received; he was too busy estimating how many feet down it would sink the Sylvanite shaft.

A week later he received an unexpected windfall. He had stopped in the Ruxton for a cigar, the first time in months. It was a dull cloudy afternoon and a group of men sat talking over a small corner table in the barroom. There was nothing for it but to stop and pay his respects.

"By George, boys! The old prospector has returned. How's that hidden mine coming, Rogier?"

His mine was hardly more than a rumor to them; their sallies were extravagant and preposterous. They accused him of boring under Bull Hill and tapping the Portland and Independence. They demanded he empty his pockets of gold nuggets, suggested that at least he let them in on his secret. They meant to be kind and friendly, but their witless jokes were barbs which stung Rogier to the quick.

"Fools, the whole pack of you!" He lit his cigar and stalked into the lounge.

The group set up a delighted cheer. For the first time they had got under his skin; he seemed really human.

Rogier in the lounge bent down over a paper covered with figures. So absorbed was he in his ever-present problem—how far down he could get with Boné's money, how far down the profit from his school contract would carry him, how far down he must get sometime, somehow—that he did not at first notice the elegant figure of Timothy seated beside him, his creased trouser leg thrown over the arm of his chair.

"Well!" he looked up startled.

Timothy negligently lit a cigarette. "Those esteemed friends of ours don't believe you have a mine."

"So they sent you to find out, hey?"

"No indeed, Mr. Rogier. I came myself. As you might remember, I'm interested."

Dom! He had forgotten completely the $2500 Timothy and Pearson each had invested in the mine during Boné's visit! His forgetfulness or his remembrance of it now irked him beyond measure. "Timothy, when I permitted you to participate to a small extent in my mining venture, I gave you to understand that it was strictly a family affair. It is not listed on the Exchange. I have no fancy printed share certificates and no fool stockholders calling for reports and worrying about their money. I allow no one on the premises. My mine is my mine! I own it, run it, and am not under obligation to reassure you that you'll make a fortune out of your modest investment. On the contrary, you may lose it!"

Timothy unwrapped his leg from the arm of his chair. He sat up straight and slapped Rogier on the shoulder. "Old man, you do me a rank injustice! You underestimate me! Don't think for one minute I came here to ask for a confidential report on its development, to plague you with a single question about it. No sir! From the day I first heard about it, I had a hunch you had something tremendous in mind. You're too good a businessman not to have something sound. And what is good enough for Boné and Pearson and your son-in-law is good enough for me!"

Rogier unbent. "It's a good mine, Timothy. No mistake about that. But whether it'll pay off is another matter."

Timothy unbuttoned his coat and turned back the satin-lined flap. From his waistcoat pocket he drew a blank check from an

English-leather wallet calling for a pen from the desk, he filled it in for another $2500, and slid it toward Rogier.

"Understood, Mr. Rogier. I shall never interfere or ask questions. I ask merely to let me take a sporting chance. You know I'm rich enough. I've never worked a day in my life and never will. Why, man, I've wagered that much on a horse! Win, lose, or draw, this five thousand means nothing to me. I want the fun. And to pay for it, I can keep my mouth shut – about some things!"

Rogier grinned. He folded the check and stuffed it in his trousers pocket. "You're a lazy dom fool, Timothy. Don't know what kind of an agreement to give you."

Timothy stood up and airily buttoned his coat. "Such things never interest me. But mind – however it turns out, I would like a gold nugget to hang on my watch chain."

"You shall have it if it takes all the gold in the workings!" Rogiér scrawled on the side of the paper not already filled with figures a briefly worded receipt, giving Timothy a share in the Sylvanite. Timothy thrust it into his flowered waistcoat, and breezily walked out to the barroom. His cronies were still joking about Rogier's mythical mine; and as Rogier left, he could hear Timothy's voice raised louder than the rest.

7

The queer retentiveness of the human mind that blanks out the significantly important only to grasp the trivial! Sunlight on water, shadows of clouds upon the plain, the smell of father's pipe – of such things, evanescent and enduring, may be woven a boy's memory.

Sitting small and still upon his plank seat, he watched beyond the ears of the team the illimitable desert keep spreading out, cut by deep arroyos and shallow washes. A vast emptiness without a frame, a monotone never monotonous. He remembered the swirling brown river at the ford, lit red by the setting sun; the streaming horses and the muddy water clutching at his knees; the two braids of greasy black hair before him and the pattern of the blanket they hung upon. He remembered the smell of sage. The gray ghostly wash of the Gallegos under the rising moon. Then the long, low adobe trading post squatting in the draw. A fire glowed outside. About it lounged blanketed figures with dark and somber faces, tinctured with a strange racial smell. He was carried inside, stiff and sleepy, past a hawk-faced man sitting silently in lamplight. In ten minutes he was asleep in his shoes. This is all he remembered of a tiresome three-day journey, fragments of a dream of time; for he had made an interplanetary transition from a known world to the unknown—to "a big country a long ways off," isolated in time, whose rhythm and meaning like the beat of a drum erased from his mind all that had gone before.

In the morning when March awoke, the post leapt out at him in the cruel clarity of sunlight. A great adobe fortress with walls almost four feet thick and windows latticed with iron bars. Shaped like a cross, its trading room or bull pen was almost forty feet long. The walls were flanked with shelves of staples and canned goods; *ahzay* —patent medicines, iodine, cough syrup, castor oil. Sloan's Liniment, colored shirts, and Levis. On the floor were stacked bags of flour, salt, sugar, pinto beans, bushel baskets of onions, and huge sacks of raw wool beside a pair of scales. Around a huge wood stove were boxes of sand to spit in. On wooden posts hung saddles, bridles, bits, cinches, and harness. From the *vigas* overhead hung slabs of mutton ribs, strings of jerky, a *ristra* of dried chiles. A glass candy case boasted licorice sticks, jelly beans, gum drops, and Christmas candy. At one counter were displayed bolts of rich, solid-color velveteen and lengths of flowered gingham; and in another case pawn jewelry; glowing silver, mellow turquoise, rings, bracelets, eardrops, huge squash blossom necklaces, and heavy concho belts.

The focal point of this vast marketplace was the long wooden counter which extended down one side of the room. Behind it, on a raised couch covered with a Navajo blanket, lay Bert Bruce, the trader, the master of a wilderness domain. Partially paralyzed, his hair turning white, he looked out like a reclining emperor upon the room crowded from sunrise to sunset with the slim-hipped Navajo men with their dark arrogant faces, the scrawny and the fat women in their flounced skirts and numerous petticoats and richly colored velveteen blouses slithering around in fawn-pink moccasins twinkling with silver buttons, and the children rubbing dirty noses against the candy case.

Off from this trading room lay the windowless rug room behind a massive locked door. Here, stacked from floor to ceiling, were the blankets for which The People exchanged the necessities for their primitive existence. Rare old *bayetas*, brilliant Germantown weaves, fine, striped Chief blankets. Soft glowing red, deep indigo blue, simple white, natural brown and gray; in stripes or in intricate patterns; with simple bold designs whose origin could be identified at first glance; tight enough to hold water, to outwear a century. A minimum $50,000 worth maintained at all times; Bruce had never been known to buy or sell a blanket of spurious weave or dye.

In the other wings of the post were his kitchen, always cluttered with dirty dishes, and his own bedroom; and the rooms he had added to accomodate his two helpers, a stray missionary or government agent, the Vrain Girls, Boné, Cable, and March.

This was Hon-Not-Klee, Shallow Water, the trading center for a 3,000 square-mile patch of desert, the hub of all the life that revolved around it.

Far west across the sandy Gallegos stood Shiprock. To the south and east stretched the sage-studded desert broken by Canyon Blanco and El Huerfano, the sacred peak. To the north the muddy San Juan marked the boundary of the world March had left. Here squatted the little towns of Farmington and Bloomfield, the hospital and Navajo Methodist Mission. Even these seemed far away and as unreal as the railroad junction seventy miles farther north across the Colorado line.

If the desert around March seemed like a sea, life at the post was conducted with shipboard routine. At sunrise the great doors were unlocked, the windows opened behind their bars. March could see the squeaking, springless wagons of the Navajos rising on the swells and drifting in to the courtyard. All day the trading went on. There was no hurry. The tall, slim-waisted men would stand around smoking, spitting, talking. The women in their voluminous petticoats and brilliant velveteen blouses would pick lice from their hair. The children would nose the glass candy case. Then a man would lug in a Pendleton of wool – some forty pounds sewed in a Pendleton blanket with yucca strips – and inquire how much the trader was paying. Bruce would open a can of tomatoes, the great delicacy, or put on a pot of Arbuckle coffee. Then came the great nine-foot-long regulation wool sacks holding sorne 300 pounds of wool to be weighed on the scales.

Bruce would remember how much the man owed him that his pawn silver did not cover. The amount of the debt he would jot down, subtracting it from the trade slip which he handed to one of his clerks. Then the women would step up with the man to trade out the remaining sum for flour and sugar, a new coffee pot, yard goods, and a Pendleton blanket. To conclude the trade, a little candy in a striped-paper sack would be given to each child.

There was no transaction too small to escape Bruce's attention. His Navajo speech was equal to theirs. He knew their superstitions, traits, and customs; he had worked with their medicine men in preparing for their ceremonial Sings. He met their haughty arrogance with bland self-assurance, their cunning with shrewdness, their stubborness with tact. Hard, practical, and wise, he proved himself every day the recumbent master of Shallow Water.

At sunset the great doors would be closed, the windows drawn behind their bars. All inside would gather at the table for the evening meal, and March would be sent off to bed.

Famous Uncle Boné was not much fun, really. There was no doubt he was Bruce's pet. For when Bruce had given up his post in town he had built here a little one-room adobe just like the one Boné had stayed in there a long time ago. Moreover, he had moved into it the piano Boné and Lockhardt had used. It was a good thing Bruce had put him away from the post, thought Boné, for the Navajos, hearing the tinkle of his piano far down the draw, would shake their heads as if the *Belicana* were crazy.

March wandered down there often. In the morning Boné was grouchy, and during his spells of work untouchable. He would be at the piano, touching a key at a time and then turning around to make a funny dot with a twisted tail on a sheet of paper ruled with lines. On the table sat a square box with a tin arm sticking out. It swung back and forth, tick-tock, like a clock.

"Is this how you make music, Boné ?"

He spun around. "What the devil you doing here, boy? Haven't I told you to keep out of here this time of day?"

And when March backed to the door, Boné was likely to jump up. "Well, as long as you're here, go make the bed. Not that anybody cares, but see you tuck the covers under the foot better this time. And don't bother stirring up dust with that broom again today."

Something was bothering Boné. Worn out, worried, and irritable from his nervous breakdown, he acted like a man no one dared approach – like Lockhardt, whose place he had subtly usurped. Goodnaturedly, Cable would take him out a hot lunch. In the afternoon Boné would take a nap. Then, near sundown, he would dress up and come to the post wide-awake and cheerful.

One night he asked Cable abruptly, "Jonathan, is that Sylvanite Mine all right?"

Cable turned around, giving him a sharp look. "Boné, how do I know? I put all I had in it, and it was doing all right when I left."

Boné jumped up, strode around the room. "Every week I've been getting letters from Daddy. He must think I'm made of money! I've sent him all I have. I'd counted on a couple of years – a long rest and time for good work. But now I can't finish this long orchestration. I'm facing another long concert tour, with just two new songs between me and starvation. Lord man, what'll I do? Be honest. What do you think my chances are?"

Cable spread his hands. "Boné, you know Rogier better than I do. Why ask me?"

A couple of weeks later Boné left the Reservation.

March missed him, but a few days later he got a horse. A small pinto, just his size, that an old Navajo was holding in the courtyard of the post. "That's the one I'm going to ride, Daddy!" he exclaimed at once.

Cable walked up to the horse, lifted a foot, swatted him on the flank, watched his ears go back. "We'll get you a horse, sonny. No hurry."

"This one! I'm going to ride him now!" March insisted.

The old Navajo, whose graying thin hair was tied in a chignon in back, said something in a low gutteral voice. Cable shrugged and lifted the boy into the crude saddle, shortened the buckskin stirrups to his short legs, and stepped back. The nice little pinto laid his ears back again. He crow-hopped a few steps, broke out into a short run. Then he plowed up short, arched his back, and March flew off into the sand, scraping the skin off his nose and cheekbones.

When he got up, ready to cry, the Navajo was holding the pinto by the bridle. Cable was looking at him with a stare which gave him that feeling the boy had experienced the night after Buffalo Bill's show. "You said you were goin' to ride him. Then do it," Cable said coldly.

It was the Navajo this time who boosted March back on the pinto, loosening the reins. With a swat on the rump, the pinto broke away. March gripped the saddle with both hands, shut his eyes. Unchecked, the pinto ran through the sage, plowed through a dry wash, whirled round a clump of chamisa. March clung on desperately, bouncing around like a cork in a heavy sea, and staring at the tossing horizon. After a time the pinto trotted back and let himself be caught by the old Navajo.

The boy could not stand up when Cable took him off the saddle; his legs were numb and there was a terrible pain in his crotch. Cable laid him down on the sand and wiped the blood off his face. "Well son, you did what you said you were going to do," he said kindly. "Just take it easy awhile; you'll be all right." Then he walked off with the old man to dicker for the horse.

During the next couple of days he gentled the pinto. He sure did! March watched him ride him from hell to breakfast, slap him with a saddleblanket, and jingle the bridle in front of him until he wouldn't spook no matter what you did. Then, of course, they had to go on a long ride together with their blankets and saddlebags.

Maybe it was the last of the three nightcamps of the *Entah* ceremony, ending with the Squaw Dance, they were sleeping in their blankets, feet to fire, when across the boy's mind, or rather across that mysterious narrow plain which separates the sleeping and the conscious minds, there was traced the path of a new and wonderful sound. An abrupt, shrill piercing yell soaring to the midnight sky, then breaking like a rocket into a parabola of eerie song. How it splayed out across the naked stars, those clear male voices with their strange and wild intensity! Indians singing! No other sound could ever hold for him the indescribable power and freshness and haunting strangeness of that song gushing forth into the soundless desert night.

Now wide awake, he heard the faint splashing of horses' hoofs at the ford. The singing stopped. Cable was already on his feet, stirring the coals awake. Little fire-tongues licked at his lean brown hands propping up the blackened coffee pot with stones. The flickers became flames, their glow filling the clearing in the brush.

"I'm awake!" March called out.

"Lie still," his father answered without looking up.

Abruptly a yelp thrust at the boy like a lance from the darkness. He could feel his scalp tingle, as if his hair had jerked up stiff as the quills of porcupine. The brush crackled. Raising his head, he saw them behind his father: three somber figures sitting on their horses.

Cable, squatting on his haunches, back toward them, did not turn around. Deliberately he set out on the ground three tin cups and a small stew pan. They reflected an accurate gauge of the mixed-up clatter of four horses up the gravelled slope, subtly betraying his seeming unconcern. The three horsemen knew it. They dismounted and strode into the flamelight without greeting. They were Navajos in dirty Levis, their ragged black hair bound by headbands of red and green cloth.

The silence was oppressive. No one moved or spoke. About each was the wild sanctity of aloneness, a sense of guarded self-effacement. Above all, the boy felt their terrifying awareness: the gathered-in strength, the easy casual grace fortified by a thousand quivering nerve ends. So it was with Cable. He stared indifferently into the fire without a look at his visitors. And yet March could feel his own awareness, sounding to the full all that moved and did not move at the edge of the circle of which he was the vibrating center. Terrible really, this silent, guarded sense-appraisal between the three men and the one.

Then the fourth Navajo strutted in and yelped once beside the fire, cruelly and derisively. He was plainly full of whiskey. Cable filled the three cups and stew-pan with coffee.

"I want some white man's thin meat!" the drunken one demanded.

"Bacon can be bought at the post," Cable said quietly. Gently but decisively he waved his hand toward the cups

All began to drink, smacking their lips over the black, twice-boiled Arbuckle. The sugar tin went around and was emptied.

"He is from the Gallegos," said one.

"The tall dark man at Shallow Water."

"This is the one," Cable assented listlessly.

"It is said a pony was stolen from the white man's ranch up by Red Rocks."

This was common gossip; a native policeman had come to the post a week ago, trying to trace the thief, the drunken son of Mrs. Black Kettle. "Who knows?" asked Cable softly.

There was no answer. He took out his black stub pipe. And now March sensed a subtle change. It was his father now, not the strange dark man who could so instantly and effortlessly slip away from his son. The others sat rolling cigarettes.

"I want tobacco!" arrogantly demanded the drunken one.

Cable carelessly tossed out his pouch. The drunken Indian filled his brown Wheatstraw, then slyly hid the pouch under his blanket. Cable appeared not to notice. "The *Entah*. Is it over?"

"Three camps. Three nights, as is proper. It is finished."

Suddenly, without moving his feet, Cable rose. He thrust out his long arm toward the drunken Navajo who jerked back. Then he opened his hand, palm up, sternly but silently demanding. The pouch fell at his feet. As he stooped to pick it up, a snicker sounded. The men stood up.

"I shall walk with you to your horses," said Cable easily. "Our two might stray off with yours. That would cause us trouble."

The sky toward the east was beginning to pale. March could hear the receding hoofbeats of four horses. Cable came back with their two mounts, picketing them nearby, then flung himself down on his blanket without speaking. March snuggled in his own blanket, knowing that their horses would not be run off like the rancher's pony by the drunken son of Mrs. Black Kettle.

There weren't many of these trips; Cable was too busy. Quiet, somber, and unsmiling, he stood all day beside the recumbent master of Shallow Water. In his faded denim shirt and Levis, his dark face burned darker and his straight black hair grown longer, he seemed to have been there always. He got down cans from the shelves, bundled up sheep and goat hides, prepared blankets for shipment, sorted silver, kept accounts, rode to the bank in Farmington. Like the other store clerks, no task was too menial for him. But as he spoke Navajo more fluently every day, Bruce relied on him more and more. Cable had a way with The People. He knew their idiocyncrasies and their tricks. For all their barbaric splendor, they were to him just like himself: alive with human passions, cursed with fraility and folly, blessed with the gifts of the inscrutable Most High—men alone and lonely under the same unchanging stars as he, confronting the encroachments of an alien civilization.

Hosteen Day-u-gi, a giant and rich man whose wives owned a great flock, brought in a load of wool packed in the regulation sacks holding 300 pounds or more, and opened negotiations with Bruce. The trader, with a slight gesture, surprisingly referred him to Cable beside him. The two men began to dicker, comparing prices offered at other posts, and the length of the haul. After a time they agreed on a price, and a bag was thrown on the scales. Cable figured the amount on a scrap of wrapping paper. Hosteen Day-u-gi, smarter than he appeared, indignantly pointed at the marker on the scales and accused Cable of short-changing him thirty pounds. It was true, but Cable stood firm on his offer.

The argument brought a crowd of Navajos around them, all protesting with shocked looks at Bruce. Bruce, resting on one elbow, refused to arbitrate. Hosteen Day-u-gi threatened to reload his wagon and go to another post. Still Bruce said nothing. Finally he shrugged and called to Cable. "Open her up then!"

The floor was cleared, the bag emptied, and the wool shaken out – revealing a big heap of sand. A titter of restrained amusement ran through the bull pen. Hosteen Day-u-gi, six feet tall under his high-crowned Stetson, was not at all embarrassed. He leaned back his head and roared with laughter. Bruce, lying behind the counter, enjoyed the joke as much. He clapped for a clerk to open a case of canned tomatoes and to put on a big pot of Arbuckle. Cable grinned his great relief.

It seemed so obvious that Cable belonged here, March did not notice that his father never mentioned going home. When he received a letter from mother, he read it out loud but avoided all talk about it afterward. One day March was talking about the rug Bruce had given her years ago. He had picked out another for her, his very own present. Although he didn't know it, it wasn't a hand-woven Navajo blanket but a Pendleton woven of pure wool in gorgeous colors in Pendleton, Oregon for the Indian trade – superlative weaves beloved by all Navajos, those with fringes being called shawls, and those without, robes. Cable said nothing; it was expensive, more than he could afford. But Bruce simply folded it up and threw it at the boy as a gift.

"We'll take it home with us, won't we Daddy? And wrap sage and cedar inside it to make it smell nice?"

"Might as well send it, son," Cable answered tersely. And he wrapped it up next day for the boy to address.

Matie Vrain came to spend a couple of days. The first thing she noticed were a couple of blankets hung up on the wall in Bruce's room. "Humm. How in the world you get these?"

"Come in yesterday. Cable got 'em."

"Humm," Not in twenty years had she known Bruce to allow anyone in the post to appraise and buy a ceremonial blanket. "He must be pretty good."

Bruce shrugged; Cable was standing at his shoulder.

Matie turned around to Cable. "It's a good thing you're here to help out. Bruce isn't getting any better. He needs a good man to rely on. Why don't you move Ona down and settle in?"

Bruce and Cable glanced at each other for an instant, then Cable turned away.

During supper Matie talked continuously; it had been a week since she had spoken English. "Lew left yesterday with a man and two pack horses. Clear down the San Juan. You know there's nothing there. Guess she's just turned Indian."

"Don't blame her. Times are changin' too fast," said Bruce.

Matie, over sixty years old, withered and brown as a frost-bitten pumpkin, still was strong with the Spirit. "Our Navajo Methodist Mission is all set to open school this year. The one about four miles west of Farmington, right on the San Juan near the La Plata suspension bridge. Buildings fixed up. And a new superintendent coming, Mr. Timmons. Come down and see it sometime."

That evening after supper Bruce drew Cable aside. "Matie mentioned something that's been on my mind. There's plenty of room here for all your family if you want to bring 'em down. Fact is", he finished lamely, "with this leg I could do with a partner."

A sudden warmth lit up Cable's eyes. There was no chance to reply. Somebody was beating on the locked door; he went to see who it was.

A little bit later when he was putting March to bed, the boy asked sleepily, "Daddy, are you going to take me down the mine this summer too?"

Cable laughed. "What do you mean, this summer? Don't you see the chamisa turning yellow? Summer's almost over. Now into bed!"

But, the boy thought as he dropped off to sleep, his Daddy hadn't even mentioned going home.

8

No! Never did he mention returning home; and sitting with his letter in her lap, Ona stared with dull eyes out the window at the cottonwoods beginning to turn yellow along the creek.

One, two, three months, and in not a single letter had Cable said he was coming home. With his first letter she had got over her resentment and assumed that he would soon return. Day after day she had listened for the train whistling around the bend and waited for his step on the porch. He did not come. And then he had written again. The letter was kind in tone and informative of content, but between the lines she could read that he was stubbornly entrenched at Shallow Water.

The surprise and the injustice of his action stunned her. To leave her so, on the pretext of taking March to the post, was an inexcusable and petty revenge she could never forgive. And facing the long summer, alone with her pride and hurt, she wrote him a long letter that betrayed nothing of her feelings. Nor did her manner; she acted as if he might be spying on her every move.

She kept the house spotless, maintained a cheerful composure. Occasionally she took Leona and Mary Ann's Nancy on a picnic to the park. She worked on Rogier's books and went to church with her mother. Yet as the weeks dragged by she found herself gritting her teeth on the way to spend the customary Sunday evening in the big old house on Shook's Run.

Mrs. Rogier, catching up Leona in her arms, would exclaim, "The only Rogier in the bunch! And what do you hear of that brother of yours, child?"

Rogier, worried and restless, was always grumbling. "What's Cable mean, loafing down there! When is he coming back to help me? By Jove, Ona! I told you to write him a week ago."

And then over their teacups Mrs. Rogier would say in a confidential tone that had become almost unbearable, "Ona, I do declare it seems strange how he can stand being among those dirty heathen so long – him so neat and clean all the time. What in the world's he doing?"

"He's tending to business!" snapped Ona. "Jonathan's a grown man and quite capable of deciding his own affairs. It's all right with me if he stays all winter!"

And then each morning toward ten o'clock her heart would begin pounding and she would stand peeping through the curtains at the postman coming down the street.

"A letter from the Territory today, Mrs. Cable," he would say – so infrequently, for all her watching.

"Well!" she would answer with a smile. "I hardly expected one today, the boys are so busy down there!"

Inside the house she would read it through hurriedly, and with a dull stab of pain and resentment resume her work. The afternoons and evenings were hard enough to bear. But the nights! Dear God! Then she knew what he'd done to her. A Rogier whose passions were enclosed within the sound shell of self-restraint. Ona could never have been swept off her feet. Nor had he taken her thus. But quietly firm, gently insistent, he had insinuated himself into her life. There was no prolonged love making, but the passion was there. An engulfing fire that, once they had come together, seemed to consume her utterly. What became of her then when she seemed to resolve into an unholy flare that fused with him! The memory made her flush. And then by day he left her as completely as he had come. This was the Indian in him, without constant endearments and caresses. And she had grown content to feel him slip away, knowing he would always come again.

So she lay there, realizing that in the husband she had the lover too. It was as if for the first time she had awakened to her woman's need. Why didn't he come back? She loved him! She had to have him! Didn't he need her too? She flung over in bed with the hot blood staining her cheeks in the darkness. Yes! No man could come to her as he did, enshrouded in the mindless passion that made them one, without the same deep need.

But his letters! She could have torn them into bits, these only letters she had ever received from him, yet she read them again and again. They were terse and impersonal; they mentioned the weather, the trading, the occupants of the post – everyone but himself. Like his love making and his quarreling, they were subtle and deep-felt. Yet, taciturn and matter-of-fact, he betrayed himself by the very medium with which he thought to cloak his thoughts. The astounding communicativeness of the written word, that no man can ever hide behind.

She saw it so clearly—the squat adobe post, the well and the willow, The People coming in their squeaky wagons—as she remembered the even tenor of her own early days at Shallow Water. Him too she saw quietly working as if in rhythm to something within himself alone. She loved him so! Simple, subtle Jonathan, slippery as the adobe banks of the Gallegos, whom she could never hold against his will.

Looking forward to the opening of school, Ona bought March a new little corduroy suit with brass buttons on coat and pantaloons, drawing him a picture of it in her letter. His childish answer almost broke her heart. He thanked his mother, but wouldn't she send it to him in case Daddy didn't bring him home? Enclosed was an unembroidered statement from Cable that Bruce had offered him a share in the post at Shallow Water if he would stay. It was more than Ona could bear. She went into the bedroom and flung herself down beside the scorned little blue suit and wept.

It was thus Rogier found her when he stalked into the house in a devil of a temper. "When in the name of Almighty God is that man comin' to help me out? He ought to know Abe and Jake can't manage things while I'm away! He –"

Ona waved Cable's note in front of him. "He's been offered a share in the trading post, Daddy! Oh, I'd give anything if he'd come back. Even let him go to Cripple Creek. We miss him so!"

Rogier frowned. "A share in a backwoods grocery store selling canned peas to Indians? When he's got a share in one of the greatest gold mines on Pike's Peak? No, he's not that crazy. Don't you worry. I'll get him back!"

Rogier returned to his shop, composing with all his craft and skill a lengthy letter to Cable. The Sylvanite had been developed to the point where Cable's help was imperative. Four men were needed to run it – Jake and Abe below, a man at the dump above, and somebody to run the hoist and take charge. In Rogier's own absence. Cable would be relied upon to keep things going. The value of the ore was increasing so steadily there could be no delay.

Hardly had he mailed this than he was struck by the obvious fact that these youngsters of his were having a family squabble. So he wrote again that Ona, dear girl, was wasting away with worry over her husband and boy. This would never do! Reassured by this appeal to the emotions of a family man, Rogier mailed his letter that night. Only in the cold light of morning to have another practical thought. That dom Indian trader would be paying him actual money for his work. What did he, Rogier, have to counter that? Belatedly he realized he had cut down Ona's allowance from Cable's investment to the point where she was having a hard time making ends meet. Was this what was worrying Cable? Ah, he knew how to fix that! He scribbled out a check to Ona for five hundred dollars, writing Cable he had advanced this on Cable's salary, adding that the ore from the Sylvanite amply justified the payment. This, he was sure, would win over his son-in-law; and he could borrow it back when Cable returned.

September came and school opened—without March. And now Ona plumbed the depths of a loneliness she had never dreamed existed. The Rogiers, rooted in the passionless stability of the old house on Shook's Run, were no longer a refuge. She stood alone and separate, but incomplete. Dear God! why wouldn't he come home? Because he was a man and thus possessed the inherent right to pursue his own folly, forcing her to admit at last that it is a woman's lot to love blindly or clearly but without pride or shame. It was a bitter lesson and she learned it well, these long weary evenings as she rocked alone in an empty house.

She began to write him honestly and clearly. He answered kindly, but the steel was there behind his words. He had no job at home; the Sylvanite was not a dependable future. But Bruce, laid up and getting old, had offered to take him in as a partner. Besides, here at Shallow Water he felt in touch with things. There would be plenty of room for them all in the post if she ever thought of coming down. "In touch with things" – "a dependable future!" The phrases opened before her a chasm she could not cross. She could see him, like Bruce, spending a lifetime in a remote Indian trading post, becoming with his own Indian blood more untouchable than ever; and herself, with never a soul to talk to except an occasional government agent or wool dealer. For now, a woman and a Rogier, she no longer saw with a romantic eye that symphonic summer spent with the Vrain Girls. She saw only those two old women, burned black by the sun and wrinkled by the wind, who had given their lives to a nomadic tribe of Indians only at last, like Lew, to ride away forever into a wilderness still more empty. No! She wanted a home and schooling for the children. She wanted him back with March, to resume their normal life together.

Hurrying to the corner to drop her letter in the box, she knew her appeal was vain. Heaven itself would have to send him back. As if in answer a single drop of rain fell on her hand as she posted her letter –

The rain traveled from the high Colorado peaks south down the Continental Divide and kept spreading over the vast upland desert: from the Brazos west to Black Mesa, as far south as Hosta Butte and the Zuni ridge. One could watch from Shallow Water the ominous thunderheads changing from white to dirty wool-gray, the mist blanketing the late September chamisa, the interminable showers. The Gallegos swelled, burst its banks, and flooded sparse cornfields and squash patches. There was nothing to do in the post but sit and listen to the driving rain.

Briefly the weather cleared; and Matie, marooned at the post by muddy roads, insisted on driving March to the Mission. "We'd better go now while I have the wagon," she told Cable. "If it rains once more, we'll never make it. After all, what's here for him to do? He'll enjoy being in school, even for a short time."

Her proposal to put March in the Navajo Methodist Mission

brought to a head the impasse that had faced Cable and Bruce all summer. Bruce, old and ailing as he was, was too wise to ask questions, to push Cable. But his generous and flattering offer had perturbed Cable as much as Ona's and Rogier's letters. He had a deep-rooted, atavistic desire for the simplicity and subtlety of life at Shallow Water; something about the solitary post, the vast sweep of unbroken desert around it, The People themselves, recalled the Great Plains of earlier years. With Ona there, and a school for his children not more than twenty-five miles away, he knew he could face life with equanimity and gratitude all the rest of his days. So until he could think things out, he assented to March's enrollment in the Navajo Methodist Mission School.

Early Monday morning Matie and March drove away in a light spring wagon. By noon it was beginning to rain again. Soaked to the skin and worn out from the long drive through slippery adobe, they stayed in Farmington overnight. The little town lay some sixty miles south of Durango, at the base of the Colorado mountains, and on the northern edge of the immense upland desert of the Navajos. The San Juan River was the natural boundary. Draining the high mountains, it swung down in a great curve to its confluence with the Animas River not far from town. Two miles west it received another tributary, the La Plata. From here it swept westward between high clay banks through the sandhills past Shiprock toward its junction with the mighty Colorado.

Farmington's straggle of houses and apple orchards lay a mile back of the river between the junctions of the Animas and La Plata. It had nothing to recommend it to March save a warm fire and supper in the house of a friend of Matie's. He was glad when next morning she again lashed over the wagon the heavy tarpaulin, bundled up March on the plank seat beside her, and drove off. The horses plodded deep in mud; the wagon slid from side to side in the slimy adobe. The boy, huddled in blanket and greasy canvas, sat staring at the great brown river rolling past. From the bottomlands to the clay banks on the other side the muddy flood was choked with debris and cottonwoods torn loose from its banks.

When they reached the suspension bridge Matie pulled up the team. In good weather the bridge hung high above the river. Now it seemed to have sagged until the floor boards were almost level with the water. Even the approach to it was obscured by the muddy wash. Matie compressed her lips. "Bet we get our feet wet!" she said cheerfully. One of the horses balked, setting up a frightened neighing. The woman lashed out with her whip, and gingerly the horses stepped upon the bridge.

For an instant March was terrified by the feeling of being set afloat; the wagon had depressed the bridge the few inches necessary to bring it to the level of the river, and now a thin wash obliterated the planks. He had the sensation of walking, like a Sunday-school picture of Jesus, upon the swirling stream. He closed his eyes; the sweep of water made him dizzy. When next he opened them the team was halfway across. And now they were lost indeed. The opposite bank seemed miles away. From upstream the river, a half-mile wide, poured down upon them with a force that made him huddle close against the woman as if for protection.

"Sure, boy, you're not scared?" Matie demanded, warily watching out for floating debris.

"No, Ma'am," he answered, drawing an inch away. His hands were cold and stiff from clenching the wagon seat, his feet numb. Scared solemn, he fixed his gaze upon the building that now loomed up across the river.

"Thank goodness!" ejaculated Matie, once again on firm but slippery land. "Those horses sure were scared, weren't they?"

At any other time the small hospital she and Mrs. Mary Aldridge had established might have seemed a cheerful refuge. Yet the minute they stepped into the waiting room, March was oppressed by the crowd of Navajos squatting around the walls. Water trickled from their hair and oozed from the corners of their blankets, making puddles on the bare floor on which they sat, patient and enduring. On all their faces was the same look of helpless incertitude.

Matie opened the door to the inner room, then swiftly closed it. His one quick glimpse inside at two bloody, recumbent figures was enough for March. Matie took him into the kitchen.

Mrs. Aldridge was boiling water and laying out shiny instruments on a clean towel. "Oh, you're back, Matie? Just in time." She nodded toward the next room. "Horses bolted at the bluff. Hosteen Tso got his leg caught in the traces when he jumped for the reins. Almost off – we've got to finish it. Don't know where the doctor from town is, this weather, but we can't wait. Oh yes, the wagon went clear over. The others in a bad mess. Look 'em over while I get ready. You brought the anesthetics with the supplies?"

Matie pulled off her coat, rolled up her sleeves. "There's been an accident, March. I'm going to be too busy to take you to the Mission. I'll find somebody else. But here's a cup of coffee and a piece of bread while you're waiting. Tell Mr. Timmons I'll see him later."

March couldn't eat his bread for the sight of the bloody figures he caught every time the door was opened, and a sweetish sickening smell coming from the table at which Mrs. Aldridge was working. But a Navajo man came to drive him in the wagon to the Mission two miles downriver.

The Navajo Methodist Mission compound of three buildings and corrals and sheds for stock and chickens looked imposing in the rain. But once inside the two-story adobe, March found the room in which he had been left cheerless and cold for all the heat of the stove. It was a half-hour before Mr. Timmons came in. The superintendent was tall and lean, with a cadaverous face and a big Adam's apple on which, like a ball bearing, his small head revolved within a high starched collar. He wore a black bow tie, vest and coat, his boots alone deferring to the country and the weather. Entering the room, slicking his wet and fresh-combed hair, he stopped short at sight of the bedraggled boy standing at the stove.

"Well! What is the meaning of this? What are you doing here?"

"The Indian brought me."

"What Indian? Where are your papers? Bless my soul! Speak up, boy!"

"Aunt Matie's Indian. He brought me here to go to school."

Mr. Timmons stealthily approached the boy who backed away; then shot out his cuffs and began warming his hands at the stove. "Matie – Matie Vrain. Oh, yes. She'll have to fill out papers. You're not a Navajo. But this is indeed a house of refuge. No favors and God's loving kindness to all." He turned to a woman who had just come in. "Miss White, another member to join our happy family. Take him to the dormitory, and see that he marches down with the rest for supper. Six o'clock sharp, mind!"

9

How repellently and frigidly repressive it was, this primitive outpost on the Jesus Way. Confined indoors by the rain, March exhausted its meaning on his first day.

The "happy family" of six adults and twenty-seven Navajo children marched into breakfast promptly at seven o'clock, standing at the table for Mr. Timmons' morning prayer. " – and the blessings of our Holy Father, Jesus Christ, Merciful Provider, be upon this our daily bread, Amen." He pulled back his chair, shot his cuffs over his plate, and sat down. Beside him sat Mrs. Timmons. At the other end of the table sat Miss White, a teacher. To her right, neat in collar and tie, was Mr. Pike. He was new to the country and kept talking about "conditions back east" and "conditions out west," particularly the "condition" of the San Juan roaring by outside.

"It ain't no bad condition a'tall!" boomed out the hearty voice of Mr. Monta, perhaps seventy-five years old, who boarded at the Mission. "No, sir! I been in this here country since the year One, and seen rains worse'n this by a long shot. The river ain't never been within a stone's throw of this here ground!"

"But Mr. Monta, it's already up to the foundation of the

laundry." Mrs. Timmons' weak voice carried no conviction and her husband silenced her with an upraised hand.

"It is my opinion," he stated loudly, "that we are in no danger of being discommoded by an overflow. Moreover I would remind you we are safe in His sacred palm, as sparrows one and all. Miss White, there will be no deviation from the day's schedule."

At her signal, March and the Navajo children filed out of the room behind Frankie Damon, the half-breed interpreter. From the start March liked Frankie. Middle-aged, he was human, kind, and attentive to the needs of every child. His eyes were peculiar though: smoky gray and expressionless behind dropping eyelids. Suddenly the boy realized Frankie was blind. Yet so well did he know the whole compound of the Mission, he could walk unhesitantly from room to room, and building to building.

Lessons were conducted in the downstairs portion of this large two-story adobe, whose upstairs served as a dormitory. The twenty-seven Navajo children ranged in age from eight to fifteen years. Many of them had left their *hogans* for the first time, their brown little faces stolid but still expressing their terrified amazement at this new world of the Mission. All were dressed exactly alike: the girls in white pancake hats, starched white slip-ons over their gingham dresses, and high-buttoned shoes; the boys in denim shirts and pantaloons, their hair cut short and thoroughly deloused. To contribute to their loss of individuality, Mr. Timmons, who could not understand Navajo, had peremptorily assigned them English names: Abigail, Alice, Hortense, Geraldine, Percy, John, Joseph, Ira –

Mr. Timmons was present with Miss White to begin the first lesson with a hymn:

> Jesus a-yo a-so, 'nih,
> Bi nal-tsos yeh sil, hal-ne,
> Al-cin-i-gi-a-nis-t' eh
> Co si-dzil dah, Ei bidzil –

Mr. Timmons stopped the singing with an upthrust arm. "Now we have the tune! In English now!"

> Jesus loves me,
> This I know –

Again he stopped the singing with a protesting arm.

"What is this I hear? Somebody is singing native pagan words! English now, everybody! Hear me, Frankie?"

So inch by inch, hour by hour, they plodded on the Jesus Way towards Salvation.

At noon they ate, rested, and went back to study the colored lithographs and stories of Jesus. After supper they were all marched upstairs to sleep. There were two rows of beds for male and female, separated by a thin wooden partition at whose end slept Frankie Damon. How terrible these nights were to the sole white boy! For now, after a day of repression among the Belicanas, the Navajo children were free to talk in their own language, of their own families, customs, and traditions. An alien in a strange new world, March would listen to their sibilant whispers.

Only Frankie Damon tried to bridge the gap. He told the children about Shallow Water and March's two aunts whom their parents knew; and March the place names of the children's homes. Through him March learned the real names of his companions, and began to get acquainted with them. His favorite among the girls was spunky Kigpah, "On the Warpath;" and his closest friend among the boys was Yabatya, "Brave," who had earned his name because as Frankie said he always "dared to do right." Then the light would be turned off, talk ceased, and in the darkness he would lie sleeplessly listening to the lash of rain outside . . .

Matie, after sending March to the Mission and helping Mrs. Aldridge to hack off Hosteen Tso's leg before gangrene set in, stubbornly walked back across the suspension bridge with an empty saddlebag to fill with crucial medical supplies. Now, marooned in town for a week she found it still impossible to return to the Mission. It was still raining.

Messages from Colorado expressed fear that the Rockwood Dam above Durango was weakening, and warned people in the lowlands to move to safety. Knots of townspeople, ranchers, and traders stood on the corners oblivious of the rain, watching the steady rise of the river. The floor boards of the bridge were under water – if they still held; only the suspension cables were visible, cluttered with debris, and likely to snap at any moment.

"I've got to get this stuff to Mary!" Matie kept muttering forlornly as she wandered from group to group.

"Forget it!" a man answered gruffly. "If that one-legged Navajo dies – and they never do! – what's one dead Indian? The hospital's on high ground. Do your worryin' about that Mission. All those kids ain't got a chance down there on the bottoms."

His remark eased Matie's obsessive concern over the crude hospital so short of supplies. "Warn Mr. Timmons! He's got a telephone. Tell him to move everybody to the vacant homestead a half mile back up on the ridge."

The man did not budge. "That damn fool Timmons! He's been called like everybody else. Says his buildings are safe. What do you expect from a greenhorn?"

Matie grabbed up her saddlebag and hurried to the telephone office. After a long line of people, her own turn came. She called the Mission; no one answered. She called the government Indian agent at his home and office; Mr. Shelly could not be found. There was nothing to do but spend a sleepless night, hoping that the rain would stop and the river go down.

In the morning more news came in. The railroad tracks from Durango had been washed out by another cloudburst in the mountains, and a flood was expected that night. At Shiprock the Agency buildings were already flooded, and hundreds of Navajo gathered for a Sing had fled to higher ground. Many of them on their way home had made it to the La Plata only to find they could not cross. They were still huddled under their wagons on the high bluff above the San Juan.

Worn out and desperate, Matie found in a trading post two Indians she had known from boyhood. To one of them she gave the saddlebag stuffed with medicines and a message to her co-worker, Mrs. Aldridge: she was to send word to Timmons that the Mission was to be emptied immediately. To the other she gave a packet of letters and a telegram that had lain waiting a week for Cable, and a hastily scrawled note of her own. She minced no words. A flood was expected down the San Juan that night; March was in the Mission which was expected to be washed away; and that whatever happened, Cable should be on hand.

The two Navajos rode away, slimly erect under their dripping stovepipe Stetsons, both headed upriver where there was another bridge beyond the Animas' junction with the San Juan: the one to ride back on the opposite side of the river to the hospital and the Mission, and the other to ride down the Gallegos to Shallow Water. Matie watched them fade into the mist, praying that the bridge would hold, and computing wearily the twelve or fifteen hours it would be before Cable reached the Mission. If Timmons would only move!

It was noon when she finally got a call through to the Mission, but Timmons refused to talk. Imperiously she demanded Frankie Damon and talked to him for five minutes in Navajo in case Timmons might be listening at Frankie's shoulder.

Late that afternoon a report came from high country: they were to expect the first rise about 2:00 a.m. and the second – the rise from both rivers – between 3:30 and 4:00 a.m.

Not until evening did she locate the Agent, Mr. Shelly. He was in his office, splattered with mud, and still supperless. He listened patiently to her as he waited at the telephone. "We've all been as worried as you about the Mission. It's no use to call again. They've all gone to bed on schedule, and Timmons as usual has given orders the telephone is not to be answered."

"Try!"

"Of course! Don't you see me ringing?"

There was an answer.

"Frankie," Matie whispered. "Thank God!"

Shelly demanded the superintendent and was informed Timmons refused to talk.

"You tell Timmons I demand that he vacate the Mission immediately with all the wards of the government. Do you understand, Frankie?"

Damon promised to deliver the message and went to bring Timmons to the telephone. Neither returned or if they did, could not talk. The line had suddenly gone out.

There was nothing more Matie could do. Sick with fear, she stumbled home to spend another sleepless night listening to the increasing roar of the river –

That noon, when Matie had called the Mission, the happy family had been gathered at table for the midday meal. Miss White had answered and called Mr. Timmons, who refused to answer. Before she could hang up, Frankie Damon quietly took the receiver.

March saw Mr. Timmons jump up from the table and rush toward him. "You know I don't allow any such interference! You —"

Frankie silently handed him the receiver spouting Navajo.

"We speak English here!" shouted Mr. Timmons.

Frankie calmly took back the receiver and listened for a long time. When he finally put it back on the hook, Mr. Timmons, hands on hips, demanded, "And what was that about, if I may ask?"

"The river will flood tonight. We must move out to high ground right away," answered Frankie.

"We will not move! God will protect us! Take your seat at the table!"

Mr. Pike smirked. "I'm an expert swimmer."

The meal ended in silence. Lessons resumed. At three o'clock came the playtime recess. Mr. and Mrs. Timmons went back to the separate adobe house in which they lived. For the children there was no play outside in the rain. They sat on the floor listening to the patter on the roof and the roar of the river. Frankie sat with them, head against the window, listening. In a little while he rose, fumbled for his coat, and called for Yabatya to go outside with him.

"Frankie, please can't I go too?" begged March.

The three of them left the building, March hanging to the blind man's hand, Yabatya holding his other arm. To March it seemed that Frankie had eyes as they began a circuit of the buildings and corral. Then suddenly they stopped; water was swirling over their ankles. Frankie and Yabatya talked in Navajo for awhile, and they went back indoors.

Mr. Timmons didn't come back until suppertime. Then he and Frankie had a terrible row in front of everybody. Mr. Timmons was real mean, though he talked like God's prophet. Frankie, usually so good-natured, talked right back. He insisted they all move out, before it got too dark, to that old homesteader's place, a big adobe of four rooms, all vacant. The livestock too.

"Never!" roared Mr. Timmons, forgetting his oratory. "I'm not going to have all the people in town running my business and I'm not going to be dictated to by a blind interpreter on my payroll who can't see his hand in front of his face, let alone hear God's command. I'm not answering that telephone anymore or listening to another word from you!"

No one ate much. Mrs. Timmons and Miss White were frightened. Mr. Pike kept grinning at the hearty reassuring boom of Mr. Monta's voice. The children sat still, oppressed by the restless undercurrent that swept the room. Foxy, the little terrier the children loved, scampered in.

"Get that dog out of here!" shouted Mr. Timmons. "Lock him up in the laundry!"

Frankie took him out. Evening prayers were said early and the children were marched upstairs. March didn't feel like going to bed. A vast inquietude, a nameless fear, filled the room. The other children too sat stiffly on their beds, peering out the window. Frankie began to talk in Navajo. After a long time, he turned to March. "I've been telling every boy in the room not to undress, but get in bed. Keep on your clothes and don't talk." Then he went into the other room and told the girls the same thing. The lights were put out. March sat on his bed, listening to the stealthy sound of blankets being pulled off the beds around him. The air was charged with excitement, with fear. He could only sit there, trembling, waiting, and wondering where Frankie had gone.

Miss White's steps and the light of her lamp appeared on the landing. From the girls' room he heard her shouting through the partition. "Frankie! What did you tell my girls, I want to know? The very idea! They won't undress or go to bed. When I undress one she puts her clothes back on the minute I go to the next. I demand to know the meaning of this rank insubordination!"

The next minute she stalked into the room with her lamp. Frankie wasn't there, but every boy was sitting on his bed fully dressed and with a blanket wrapped around his shoulders. "Oh, you too!" she screamed. "I shall report him to Mr. Timmons this instant. And you and you." She pattered downstairs and they could see her lamp bobbing across the courtyard.

Then Frankie called and they all trooped down, boys and girls. Yabatya lit a lantern. In its light they saw that Frankie had hitched the horses to the wagon and opened the corral gate, letting loose horses and cows and chickens. By the time the Timmons had dressed and come out, followed by the two men and Miss White, they were ready to pull out: Frankie holding the reins on the plank seat with Yabatya beside him to serve as his eyes; the little children crowded in the box; the bigger children, who were to walk behind, hanging to ropes. And now it was all a nightmare in the pouring rain. The stock milling around, Foxy barking in the laundry, lamps and lanterns flashing, Mr. Timmons yelling. "I forbid you to leave! Hear! Get out of that wagonbox!"

Instead, Mrs. Timmons climbed up on the seat beside Yabatya, weeping bitterly. "I've got to go. I'm afraid. Please go with us!"

"That team and wagon is Mission property!" screamed Mr. Timmons. "Pike, you see that it's brought back here!"

Miss White began to show signs of hysteria. Adding to the rank insubordination of Mrs. Timmons and the rest, she waded through the water in her pearl button shoes, grasped the end of a wagon rope with one hand, and hoisted an umbrella with the other.

Frankie could wait no longer. He laid the whip on the horses and the wagon moved off. March looked back behind the children and Miss White plodding through the rising water to glimpse the three men in the light of a lantern. Timmons was still shouting. "Go, then! Go! I shall put my trust in the Lord!"

And now all was dark save for the lantern lights bobbing up and down in the water lapping against the wheels and the legs of the plodding children. It was too late to reach the abandoned homestead only a half-mile away; the approach was under water. Frankie drove on. March could think of nothing save Foxy barking in the laundry.

Eventually a light appeared ahead, then the hospital loomed up. It was as crowded as when he had left it a long, long time ago. But Matie wasn't there, Mrs. Aldridge couldn't tell him from the other children, and he could no longer see the bloody recumbent figures in the inside room. There was no space left in the reception room for all the people from the Mission. Frankie took some of them into the storage room. March, with Yabatya and Kigpah, squeezed into the kitchen between the Navajos huddled about the stove. He was wet and cold and hungry, scared and miserable. Worn out, he wriggled into a corner and slid down against the broad haunch of a squaw. It was warm and soft as the flank of a horse. In this cramped position he went to sleep.

10

Cable at Shallow Water had just stood up and yawned, stretching his long arms above the pot-bellied stove in the bull pen. "Might as well turn in, Bert!"

On the floor, propped against the walls and stacks of pelts, lay a dozen Navajos sleepily swathed in their blankets despite the stuffy room. They had been there for a week or more, and if it kept on raining confidently expected to stay another spell. Bruce got up on his crutches and hobbled off to his room as if they were not there, leaving Cable to see the post through another night.

Cable turned down the lamp on the counter, took off his shoes, and lay down on Bruce's narrow cot. He slept soundly but lightly, back to the faint glow of the lamp, a hidden revolver within easy reach for emergency.

Minutes or hours later—which, he never knew—he was awakened by the slosh of a horse's hoofs outside, the click of the door latch, and a gust of cold air. They were almost simultaneous, so swiftly had the messenger leaped from his horse and opened the door—and before he had reached the stove, Cable was on his feet and turning up the lamp. The Navajo, sopping wet, stood silently watching Cable put on his shoes. Then, without greeting, he handed his message to Cable.

"When did you leave?" asked Cable. It was his only question. He roused Bruce, got into warm clothes and boots. The letters and telegram from Ona and Rogier he thrust into his pocket without opening.

Bruce came out, read Matie's note, and talked with the messenger. "I'm sorry, man," he said simply turning to Cable. "If you can get across the Gallegos, follow up the bluffs to Two Trees, then turn due west. But mind the alkalai flats. Hear?"

Cable nodded, threw on a torn slicker. The master of Shallow Water turned to the Navajos on the floor. It was not what he said, but his inflexible commanding spirit that roused them to their feet as if he had cracked a whip. There was no need to flatter them with his friendship, to remind them of the coffee and food they had been gorging for days. He simply called for their best pony and lightest saddle, and they jumped at his bidding.

To Cable he gave a light buckskin pouch containing a box of crackers and a cake of unsweetened chocolate. He grabbed from the pawn case a squash-blossom necklace of silver and turquoise, thrusting it into Cable's hands. "Don't know what he'll do with it, but the boy always fancied one of these things. Give it to him for me."

For an instant their eyes met and held. Cable thrust the useless ornament into his pocket, and flung out of the door to his horse.

It was pitch dark and still raining; for a moment, as he swung around the post, he could see nothing of the willow, the wagons, shed, and stable. Guided by the roar of the creek, he picked his way carefully downstream. At the ford he paused. The Gallegos was swirling over its bank. Suddenly, with his slap, the mare plunged into the stream. The shock of cold water as the pony went down was like a blow. Stunned and gasping, he clung to the horn with both hands. Finding footing, the pony made its way to the opposite bank. Cable came alive again. Feeling the ground firm beneath him, he headed north and swung at last into the sage.

The little mare was a good one. She lay down to the ground in an easy rhythmic lope, nose out, fighting for the reins. He let her have them; she could pick her way among chuck holes and clumps of sage better than he. Easing his weight on her by riding on the point, he settled down for the long ride.

The rain began to let up. He could make out the dark floor of the desert extending to the sand hills along the river. So close! And yet hours, miles away! Resolutely he tried to fasten his mind upon the mare, Shallow Water, any trivial remembrance, only to find himself a moment later staring across those miles of sage that separated him from the endangered Mission and his boy.

He remembered the compound well: the three adobe buildings, the corral and sheds, the big cottonwoods flanking the road, the flowered bluffs behind. Yet its pleasant aspect in summer when he had seen it kept fading into the new and terrifying vision before him. He knew the dry, sandy Gallegos too well after a rain not to be able to imagine the San Juan in flood. The Mission was on bottomlands, on the west bank of the river where it made its turn – at the one spot where the buildings would receive the full force of the flood. Again and again he saw the children, the teachers, March! caught like rats in a trap. Why didn't they move? There was no answer to his ceaseless conjectures. He kept riding. And with him rode a dragging sense of guilt that slowed his pony's pace and kept whispering with those voices he had long ignored – Ona's letters asking for her boy, Rogier's blunt requests to return, and Matie's suggestion that March would enjoy school after so many months. Most clearly it spoke to him with phrases of the boy himself: "Aren't you going to show me the mine this summer, Daddy?" – "Are we going home?" Nothing could shut out the thin boyish voice. Cable could only tighten his lips in a straighter line and dig spurs in the laboring mare.

The junipers of Two Trees appeared against the horizon; warped and twisted, they looked in the mist like weeds at the bottom of the sea. He knew then the rain had stopped and the night was on its wane. He swung to the left and was caught in the soggy alkalai patch. It was necessary for him to retrack and detour with fury in his heart for the delay.

It was almost dawn; the inky blackness had paled to a thin purple against which the far sand hills flanking the river stood out almost imperceptibly. He became aware of other lone horsemen and lumbering wagons, all heading with him toward the growing rise of hills. One by one he passed the wagons, seeing without noting the soggy figures huddled in their blankets, the drawn but immobile faces that never looked around as he galloped by.

Reaching the crest of the hills, Cable reined up the panting mare. It was lined for a quarter of a mile with horses and wagons as if the desert night had spewed up all its human life. Some of the people were squatting on the ground, others sat their ponies like cardboard figures against the horizon, still others mounted and on foot were crawling and slipping down the slope. There was no talk, no noise, no confusion. All, like him, seemed withdrawn inside their impenetrable shells.

It was dawn, a dirty woolen skein blanketing both earth and sky. From far down below, still too dark to see, came a sullen ominous roar. Cable knew what it was. He sat fighting back the insane desire to ride madly down the slope before he could get his directions. Only a minute, a minute more, and it would be light!

At no other time in his life did he show more clearly the inner texture of his obscure breeding. That inexhaustible Indian patience! Covered with muck to the crown of his hat, muddy hands crossed over the saddle horn, he sat immobile as a figure modeled from mud.

It was light. The opposite bank emerged, dotted with people. Then the valley and the river. Two miles upstream a thin column of smoke was rising from the shadowy-gray outline of a building on the high river bank. Then suddenly and without warning the sight burst before him.

Below and a little to the left of him, the river swung past the site of the Mission. The buildings were gone. Only the floor of the laundry, to which was bolted the machinery, remained on its foundations. On this stood a man waving his hands frantically, and a dog going through the contortions of barking. Behind it the river was tearing out the big cottonwoods. As he watched, one of them slowly went over. For an instant it seemed suspended in air, roots upward with a ton of dirt, then it vanished to come up stripped of branches. Farther behind in a quiet eddy a pig and a dozen chickens swept round and round with a scatter of debris. Still the great brown river swirled down with inconceivable force, rising in a high wall, then breaking away, leaving a hole gouged out bigger than a house.

Cable did not flinch. Slowly he gathered in the reins. And with a dull glance upstream at what he knew now was Mrs. Aldridge's and

Matie's hospital, he urged his tired mare down the sandy slope –

That night at the hospital no one had been able to sleep for the roar of the river. March couldn't even hear Mrs. Timmon's blubbering in the next room. He had been awakened from his short nap of an hour or more by a muffled crack and snap when the first rise of the river took out the suspension bridge. The warm fat haunch underneath him stirred. He sat up. All the Navajos were sitting up, wide awake too. He could sense running through them, like animals, a curious awareness and nervous expectancy. What they were waiting for, he didn't know; but he kept waiting too.

Finally it came: a roar like that of a train over the crossing near Shook's Run back home followed by a loud crash. Mrs. Timmons screamed and dashed outside. Mrs. Aldridge, Miss White, March, and all the Navajo refugees followed her as she ran toward the edge of the rise.

The rain had stopped; the sky was clearing. Across the river the bank was black with people from town. On the high bluffs above the La Plata was another group. The first rise had taken out the suspension bridge. Now the second rise was pulling out the east anchorage; girders, spans, and cable work were swept loose and whirled away like string. But it was not at this the watchers were staring. They were watching the flood take out the last of the Mission buildings farther off. One adobe wall after another crumpled like wet paper and vanished in the waves of muddy water. To March it was incomprehensible; he could not relate the sight to the Mission of last night. But Mrs. Timmons lay on the ground hysterically screaming.

Then suddenly Mission, bridge, and river were replaced by another drama more compelling because human. One of the Navajos who had slid his horse down the slope of the sand hills and was riding slowly upstream, stopped and gave a shrill cry. Then lashing his mount forward he rode into the crowd from the hospital. He had spotted the Mission children.

As if it had been a signal for an attack, the horizon like a bow string shot forward horsemen, wagons, running men, and waddling squaws. March watched them plunging down from the crest, rushing toward him – whooping, yelling, waving arms and blankets, lashing horses. It was like a charge in the Wild West Show. Like a spring roundup when branded cows are loosed to hunt their calves. From around him the twenty-seven children of those fathers, mothers, brothers, and sisters who had believed them washed away with the Mission acted themselves like dead who had returned to life. Soggy new shoes flew over the sand, quilts and store blankets dropped on the ground, and from bedraggled gingham dresses and buttoned little coats, from beneath round hats and floppy bows, brown stoical little faces burst into bloom as they rushed to meet the charge.

March stood watching a fat mother kneeling on the ground before her girl, pinching her legs, stroking her arms, her hair, her face. Then he turned around to see something that he would never forget to the slightest detail – the sight of Cable who had slowly ridden up to see, without warning, his own son standing safe before him. He was sitting loosely on his mare, his hands clutching the saddle horn. From his high cheek bones down, his dark face might have been hewn of rock. His jaw was clenched until the knotted muscles stood out, his lips a thin straight line. The rest of the face the boy could not see for his father's eyes. Always black and big, they were now like caves into which he fell headlong. Suddenly he saw that tears were gushing down his dirty cheeks, leaving streaks through the mud. Cable sitting there on his mare, unmoving, unspeaking, but weeping in the early morning light!

"Daddy! Is that you?"

Cable, loose-jointed as a sack of meal, seemed to fall out of his saddle and on his knees. His long arms swept the boy to him, head on his shoulder. His whiskers scratched, his tears splashed down the back of the boy's neck. He didn't say a word.

All morning they watched the man and dog marooned on the laundry floor. Mr. Pike kept waving his hands for help, but poor little Foxy didn't know what to do. He'd take a step one way and peer down into the raging torrent, then turn around to look down on the other side. Some cowboys on shore were waiting with lariats to lasso the machinery when the river went down, but the floor rose and topped them both into the river. Mr. Pike disappeared instantly, his body to be recovered twelve miles downstream three days later. Foxy was washed toward shore and lassoed by the cowboys.

About noon a crowd of Navajos came, bringing a bedraggled and unconscious old man. It was Mr. Monta who had jumped from the roof and had been washed to a mud bank. For a long time Mrs. Aldridge worked over him. He was still alive but he had lost his mind.

That afternoon they all rushed out of the hospital again. The river was going down, revealing a black clump stationary in its flow. It was Mr. Timmons clinging to the top of a tree, somebody said, looking through field glasses. Not until next morning could the men lasso and yank him ashore, more dead than alive.

Matie was in the first boat to cross the river after the flood had receded. She brought food and coffee for all—and a big hug for Frankie Damon who had saved the lives of the Mission children. "I don't have a single pinch of tobacco for you, Frankie! But you'll get more than that when I tell Mr. Shelly and everybody else at the Agency what you've done! We'll find a better place for you, with good pay too!"

Cable, holding March on his lap, looked up. "I know a place you'll like, Frankie—mine, at Shallow Water," he said quietly. "Once there, you'll never want to leave. Can I take you down?"

Matie stared at him a long time. "I - I thought you were staying, Jonathan, and Ona might be coming down, and March would stay with me while he went to school in town. I wish you would, Jonathan—on account of Bruce. Shallow Water needs you, and Frankie too."

Cable looked out into the desert. The sky was clear; the outline of a distant mesa was etched against the horizon; stars were coming out bright as silver buttons. He hugged March more tightly. "I reckon not," he said with a slow smile. "Son and I — Mother needs us both, and we need her, don't we, March? We're going home, Matie."

And yet on that first morning home, when he rose and looked out the window, it was with a feeling he had turned his back upon something that would haunt him always.

Henceforth that high Peak gleaming pale silver with early snow was to encompass his life and hopes: its bare frost-shattered granite slopes cutting him off night and day from the world below; the clank of machinery and the creak of the cable the only sounds penetrating the cloying darkness within; and the cold slimy walls of the stopes, resistant and enduring, mocking the futile expenditure of his strength. There would be Jake and Abe, simple-minded orphans without roots in fertile earth, hard-rock men in every sinew. And Rogier, warped and unpredictable—a man, he knew now, who would stop at nothing until he had plumbed the utmost depths of his folly.

Behind him lay Shallow Water, a flowering of something atavistic and dormant within him. For there did exist, always, that one earth whose unique place-rhythm found an echo and an answer in every man, as if the soul of each race and tribe had been fecundated with the mystery of its own earthly womb. And he who had been long away or returned for the first time to the earth of his flesh felt then the deep and wordless but triumphant cry of his inner self, "Home! At last I am come to home!"

He felt like Cable the fierce proud morning break open the eyes of his soul that had never seen before. He saw the lofty amphitheatre of sage-gray desert tilting upward to the pine-studded foothills and hemmed by the immense wall of the Rockies in their curve: blue as smoke, blue as chalcedony, blue as turquoise. In the splendid terror, in the wild silence, in the cruel and magnificent clarity of the day, everything stood out pure, serene, virginal. So new! And yet so immeasurably old that it was as if he had known it all long, long before. In the house made of evening twilight, in the house made of dark cloud—in summer sun and winter snow, he remembered it all, all like a wordless voice, like the voice of an inner consciousness.

For what had he forsaken this manifested outer form of his secret inner self, this land and its people whose blood-beat was tuned to his? Not for the cold sweaty darkness of the Sylvanite or for the petulant, driving Rogier. He had left it and willingly, with all that it contained of him, for that single moment when he had stood again on the threshold of his home. When Ona had opened the door and into his wife's arms he had gently pushed his son, alive and safe from harm. Never, never! could he have faced her or himself, had he stood there alone.

And so late that October he picked up his duffle bag and strode off toward that high snowy Peak—strode off like Sister Molly's Tom, Rogier, a thousand others, all loved by someone like her who sat behind uneasy and troubled by disquieting dreams but powerless to do aught save smile and hope and wait.

PART III

SYLVANITE

1

Now, late in the afternoon of a sunny spring day, Rogier sat on a rickety chair in front of the Sylvanite hoist. The wooden shanty, cluttered with tools and muck-smeared overalls hanging on the walls, and rank with the smell of an open carbide can, was cold as an ice box. The door was open and across the greasy planks of the threshold the western sun lay thin and yellow. Rogier stamped his feet, slapped his gloved hands, and continued staring fixedly at the big hoisting drum before him.

At the sound of a bell he jerked erect and let out the big lever to his right. The huge drum began to revolve. He watched the black steel cable swiftly unwinding, layer after layer of coils slipping off smoothly from right to left. The old cheap hoist was without an indicator; he watched instead for a bright mark chiselled on the greasy steel rope indicating the layers unwound. When it flashed into sight he drew the lever toward him for half-speed and stood up to look over the high reel.

The window glass of the shanty was cracked open. Through it the long line of cable inclined upward to the top of the gallows frame outside, revolved in the pulleys, and stretched tautly down into the open shaft. In a moment the rusty half-ton iron bucket rose into sight above the shaft collar. Rogier jerked and locked the reel lever, dutifully pushing a wooden peg in his punchboard to indicate the bucket was up.

Now, after maneuvering the bucket to the wooden ore chute, he pulled on the catch and listened to the dull rumble of more than a thousand pounds of ore sliding down to the sorting dump. Outside he could see Cable, bundled against the wind, standing on the runway behind his empty little tram car.

"Hey!" Rogier shouted through the window. "You keepin' track of all these buckets?"

Cable nodded curtly.

"How's it sorting?" he yelled again. "I want some good samples!"

Cable nodded again; and scraping out the chute, went on with his work.

Rogier swung the bucket free again, and ringing his bells, lowered it to Abe and Jake working below. Then marking his punchboard, he relapsed into another cold half-hour's wait. Up the trail he could glimpse the stout log cabin and the neat corral of green aspen poles for the shaggy burros used to pack in supplies. Compared to these works of axemen's skill the surface plant in which Rogier sat was not much to look at, but it was sound. Sound as a bottom dollar! The timbers of the gallows frame were of well-seasoned pine; the shaft was cribbed for the first fifty feet; the dump was held on the slope below with heavy log baffles.

Little it mattered to Rogier that the plank shaft house and tool shanty looked like backhouses in Poverty Gulch, that everything was covered with muck and dust. He had not installed a single line of electric lights; the men were compelled to use carbide lamps. Nor had he put in a compartment shaft or cage. The men had to be lowered in the empty ore bucket, coats over their heads to keep out the drip of water. The huge iron boiler that had been so laboriously hauled up the trail still sat unused on its frame. Rogier had been in too much of a hurry to install a hoist engine. He had brought up a light gasoline engine to run the hoist; it would require less time than for the men to cut wood.

No, nothing mattered to him if the plant was good enough to

pass inspection. His one concern was to go down, down below grass roots. And so he had. Abe had found the new lead perhaps a hundred yards from the old outcropping which had petered out. The vein dipped downward at a steep angle. Abe had proposed another inclined shaft along the plane of the vein, but Rogier held out for a vertical shaft. Dom the expense! It would give him the greatest vertical depth for the least footage. And measuring the dip of the vein he had stepped off the site of the shaft house and gallows frame.

Sinking the shaft vertically, they had established station levels at 150 and at 250 feet, making crosscuts eastward to intersect the vein. For a time they had taken out shipping ore—a fair grade of sylvanite. When this gave out Rogier had sunk the shaft still deeper and repeated the process: establishing levels every hundred feet and cross-cutting into the inclined vein again. Anything to get down, down! Thirty to forty dollars a foot through solid granite meant nothing to him if only he could feel himself sinking, sinking down into the depths of that resistant and enigmatic Peak which forever plagued him.

The windfalls of money from Cable, Boné, and Timothy had given him the means; he was down now to below 450 feet, and figuring how to go down another hundred feet. But to get money for it, to keep Abe and Jake from grumbling, and to appease Cable and the family, he had to strike more shipping ore. And for that he was dependent not only on the Sylvanite, but on the whole Cripple Creek District.

Abruptly he picked up the binoculars from the floor beside him. Adjusting the screws again, he stared once more out the open door and down the gulch toward the far rise of Battle Mountain.

Cripple Creek, the "$200,000 Cow Pasture," in its first decade had produced with its 475 mines more than $100,000,000 worth of gold from an area of scarcely six square miles. In those ten years Rogier had watched the annual production jump from $200,000 to the stupendous amount of $18,149,645—and that barely scratched from under the grass roots.

Then had come the turn of the century and the turn of the tide for Cripple Creek. What now in the last ten years had happened to the district?

The labor strike had called the turn. During the disorders, with mines closed and mills shut down, the production had been cut almost in half. Gradually the mines had opened up again, new ore discoveries were made, and mills were running overtime. But still production kept dropping: to $14,000,000; $12,000,000; and last year to $10,562,653. And worse: to get $10,000,000 worth of gold now it was necessary to treat 756,900 short tons of ore as compared to only 451,082 four years ago, so greatly was the value of the ore decreasing.

If to the decreasing population of the greatest gold camp on earth this was indubitable warning that the gold was petering out, it only confirmed the secret and unalterable conviction of the white-haired, erratic, and cranky old man who now sat in the rickety hoist house of a temperamental mine staring through his binoculars at the imposing surface plants on Battle Mountain.

His former carpenter Winfield Scott Stratton, the late and world-renowned Midas of the Rockies, had believed that all the gold veins in the district converged under Gold and Globe Hill. To monopolize this center he had spent $7,000,000 of the $10,000,000 he had received from the sale of his Independence in buying up more than one hundred claims and control of eight mining companies, practically one-fifth of the whole district.

How wrong and foolish he had been! Now, scarcely ten years since his death and the collapse of his stupendous scheme, his theory had been proved false. Why, his multi-million dollar properties on Gold Hill were producing less than eight percent of the district's output! The greatest producers were still the Independence, being gutted of another $10,000,000 by its British owners, and the fabulous Portland. These and the other mines on Battle Mountain were producing almost forty-three percent of Cripple Creek's gold. And Battle Mountain rose directly across the grassy valley down which Rogier looked from his lofty perch; a signal mountain located on the shaft of that arrow whose point struck deep into the high gulch on the slope of Pike's Peak where he now sat!

Years ago he had divined the goal of his impassioned quest. There had not been one vast upheaval through the granite walls of the ancient volcano. There had been several different blow-offs; and of the many pools of eruption, that on Battle Mountain and Bull Hill was only one. The last and greatest pool of all still lay hidden beneath the solid granite where the eruption had not been able to break through. And where was all that superimposed granite thicker, deeper, more resistant than on Pike's Peak itself? Pike's Peak, the culminating point, the highest stub remaining of the great extinct volcano which had towered so high in the skies!

If it seemed inconceivable that no one had thought of it, it had revealed to him with cosmic perspective the vast subterranean world whose life went on unceasing and unhurried beneath his feet. A life that in turn gave life to plant and bird, beast and man. An earth that like the sea flowed in rhythm with the moon and stars, obeying the same unknown universal laws that kept the sun in place, maintaining an isotatic equilibrium under which mountains crumbled and washed away, old sea floors subsided under the weight of their conglomerate ooze, and new mountain peaks rose with sea shells on their summits. It was a revelation. He could almost feel beneath him that great arterial fountain bursting from the mysterious hot center of his earth. And he—he only!—was boring down, down through it to the living heart of the Peak itself.

Occasionally an old-timer would stray up the gulch to the Sylvanite. "God A'mighty, man! Don't you know this here workin's too far north? Granite, plumb hard-rock granite. You won't find no gold here!"

Rogier, imperturbably chewing on his cigar, refused to answer a single question. With a face indomitable and serene as one of granite, he pulled the lever which again released the ore bucket from the chute. It caught on the shaft cribbing; he stood up and yanked at the chain until it was free and dropping swiftly down the shaft. "Get down! You!" he muttered masterfully, throwing the lever to high speed.

Punctually now at four-thirty, as every afternoon, sounded the three-bell signal which meant passengers coming up the shaft. Rogier, with a slight frown, slid the hoist lever to slow speed and watched for the ore bucket to rise above the shaft collar. The rusty iron bucket was of half-ton capacity suspended on steel cable capable of lifting forty tons in compliance with the safety factor required by law. It was nevertheless too small in size for two men. Jake squatted in the bucket, arms in and head down. Abe stood on the rim, one hand holding the supporting cable, the other gently pushing against the cribbing of the shaft to prevent the bucket from revolving and crushing him against the timbers. Hoisting them was a slow process. One saw first the bent head of Abe with his metal hat dripping slime, then slowly his spread legs and between them the muddy face of Jake blinking eyes at the sunlight. Cable, up from the dump, was on hand to steady the bucket while they climbed out.

"Kind of early, ain't you, boys? It's still the middle of the afternoon," said Rogier.

"We've always quit at four-thirty and we ain't goin' to stop now. It's regular," answered Jake, putting out his lamp. Neither of them reminded Rogier that since early morning they had been working down below in cold and damp and darkness, drilling, mucking, tramming – doing the work of four men; he wouldn't have been satisified with a twenty-four hour shift. Both crawled out of their jumpers, kicked off their boots, and stood rubbing their hands.

There sounded underground a sudden dull rumble, followed by another. The last thing before coming up each night, Jake set the blasts; the dust would be settled before work next morning. The four men continued talking. Standing before a long plank shelf, they inspected the ore Cable had brought in – a chunk from every bucketful that had come up the shaft. They selected samples to thrust in Cable's small canvas sack. Carrying this, Cable walked to the corral and straddled a burro. It was his last job each night to ride down the gulch to a box nailed on a fence post. Scattered throughout the district were hundreds like it. They were the boxes in which were left the day's samples from the mines for the assayer to pick up on his rounds.

Arriving at the Sylvanite box, Cable drew out the limp sack used the day before. In its place he stuffed the laden sack brought with him and jogged back up the gulch. The sun, just sinking below the mountains, flooded the high open meadow and lit up the tips of the highest peaks. Below in the canyons it was already dark. Only the snow patches among the pines gleamed palely as shards of moonlight. Wondering what the previous day's run had assayed, Cable stopped the burro and drew out of the sack a slip of paper. The flare of a match lit up the figures on it.

"Doggone!" he said to the burro. "The Old Man will be glad to hear that. It might give him an appetite bigger'n a canary's."

Thrusting paper and sack into his pocket, he dug his heels into the little one's ribs. The burro continued mincing along. Cable leaned to one side, tore off a willow switch. "Now you get along! Jack!"

Under the switching the burro pattered quickly and daintily up the trail, Cable's long legs dangling almost to the ground. A fire was going in the cabin and the men were just sitting down to supper. Cable tossed the assayer's report in front of them. "It isn't high, but we can start shipping," he said, washing in the corner. "Abe, I told you you were sending me up some better looking stuff."

Abe looked at the figures. "Humph – .74 ounce ore! We had a full ounce showing on the level above. And how long did it last?"

Jake swiped his mouth from elbow to wrist and picked up the slip. Even to his slow mind the figures represented something more than intelligible news. "We git maybe $15 a ton. It cost us $8 to mine and treatment charges run close to $5. I reckon that leaves us about two bucks a ton and we got to haul it down the gulch to the siding. Slow pluggin', I say."

Rogier, at the head of the table, had been angrily and impatiently listening to Jake's long monologue, watching him scratching his head and biting his nails to aid his laborious calculations. He could restrain himself no longer.

"Give me that paper!" he shouted, leaning forward to sweep it with an eager glance. "Three-quarter ounce ore! The average of every ton shipped to the mills from the whole district. What in Sam Hill's wrong with you fellows? A man would think you were sittin' at a wake."

Abe gave him a curious glance from his mild blue eyes. Then opening a half-dozen biscuits on his plate, he began covering them with a stream of black molasses. In the lamplight his bald head glistened like a billiard ball. His shirt front was open; under his beard his massive chest was white and hairless as a baby's. The muscles of his arms moved like ropes as he wiped the rim of the can with his forefinger, set it down, and went on eating in a passive silence that gently rebuked Rogier's noisy exhortations.

"Yes!" Rogier was yelling at Jake. "I told you it costs about $8 a ton to mine. But that's the total cost of mining development, sorting, and every other dom thing. Now that we've got our shaft and plant it costs us only $3 stoping to get it out. That's why half-ounce ore has always been good to mine."

"Maybe Jake's hit the nail on the head," interrupted Cable. "All that money for development has been paid out and ought to be included, raising the cost to $13 a ton milled, easy. This is a business we've got to make pay."

Rogier's face flushed under his white hair. He brought down his fist on the table so forcefully that the plates and saucers rattled. "Business! Who told you this was a business? This is a mine, and more too. It's a shaft to Hell if I can get her there! There's going to be no fool business cluttering up the Sylvanite. Get that through your head."

The silent, shocked surprise that greeted this heresy made him pause a moment. "It beats me how you boys could figure such a thing," he continued in a lower voice. "All that development is paid for. Way behind us. We can't let the past drag at our coattails. We've got to look ahead. See? A good sound plant, and hundreds of tons of three-quarter ounce sylvanite costing only $3 to stope and $5 for treatment, leaving us a tidy little profit of $7 a ton. Money all the way around, eh boys?"

Cable pushed back his plate and lit his pipe. With a dark expressionless face he listened to Rogier with incredulous amazement. By no effort of his will could he make himself believe this was the man who, when he had come to Colorado, was leasing two of the biggest mines in the district for $10,000 a year apiece. Mines with miles of underground workings and double-compartment cages taking crews below in three shifts. Mines he had given up for this erratic and remote working that at best produced ore that might bring a dollar or two profit on the ton.

"Yes, sir!" Rogier was saying, jabbing at Jake with his fork.

"You don't say, Colonel!" Jake was muttering, his eyes wide with childish amazement. "I'll swan! Wouldn't it beat the band?"

"I'll stake my bottom dollar on it, Jake. A thousand feet or more down. Then one day you'll lift your pick and break into a stope that'll make Aladdin's Cave look like a junk shop, that'll blind you with a radiance brighter than a May sunrise. Ore, Jake, the world has never seen. In crystal formation. Glimmering like glass prisms. Stuck to the walls like frozen drops of water. Hanging from the ceiling in icicles of solid gold. Glistening on the floor like sands of crushed jewels. So precious you'll get down on your knees and scrape it up into little canvas bags. Not by the ton. By the ounce! By precious little pinches between your fingers. God Almighty, man! Can't you see it?"

Suddenly aware of the deep silence becalming the room, he turned around. Cable, dish towel in hand, was standing motionless at his shoulder. Behind him Abe had stopped trying to unscrew the cap from a bottle of horse liniment. No trace of a smile lurked at the corners of their mouths; no echo of disbelief was reflected from their eyes. Rogier stood up and faced all three men.

"Have you ever known me to deliberately falsify?" he asked in a calm voice resonant with that fey quality which imbued his profound conviction. "What I have just said is not idle fancy. How I know it I don't know, save that I already see it and feel it within the touch of a pick. Here in Cripple Creek will yet be found the greatest ore deposit that the world has ever known. A treasure greater than Croesus ever took from the sands of the Pactolus or Solomon from the mines of Ophir." He stared deliberately at each of the three men. "And it will be here in the Sylvanite. Under our very feet."

With an abrupt snort he broke out, "Jake! For two nights running you've forgotten to lock that tool house. Good God, man! We just got through layin' in a supply of hand tools."

"Yes sir, but nobody ever comes up here and the coyotes can't eat picks, Colonel. I – "

He went out the door followed by Rogier.

Cable finished his dishes. Smoothing out the wrinkles, he neatly draped the wet cloth over a chair. Abe was standing in front of the fire in his long underwear and massaging his leg with liniment.

"What's the matter, Abe?" Cable asked quietly. "Aren't things up here going all right for you?"

Abe nodded his bald head. "The Colonel ain't so steady as he used to be, is he?" He squinted at his knotty muscled leg, then with horny hands resumed his patient rubbing.

Cable did not reply.

2

With Cable up at the Sylvanite most of the time, Mrs. Rogier besought Ona to move down with her. Ona demurred; she wanted her own home. But she did move closer to the old house on Shook's Run in an old-fashioned clapboard shaded by cottonwoods. It was set on the street parallel to the high railroad embankment through which was cut an underpass leading down Bijou Street to Shook's Run.

The location had its disadvantages. Passing trains marked off the hours. One heard first the shrill blast of the whistle at the grade crossing two blocks north. Then with a rush and roar the train swept by, shaking the house until the very dishes rattled, raining cinders on the roof and stripping the cottonwood branches of the last clinging leaves. A minute later came the piercing scream of brakes as it slowed down at the station. If it were a northbound train, the agony of its passing was more acute and prolonged. Heavy freights required a helper on the grade; and the two engines, belching smoke and buckling the cars back and forth as they tried to get under way with a full head of steam, seemed trying to jerk the train in two. On rainy days they let out a steady stream of sand on the slippery rails, the spinning wheels grinding it to a shower of sparks that could be seen a block away. Most of the neighbors were railroad people. Under their influence March and Leona were soon calling out, "10-5! Number 6 right on the dot!" when the train went by.

Yet all this sound and movement was muted for March by that snowy Peak rising at the end of Bijou. "Is that where Daddy's working, way up there in the sky?" he would ask his mother.

"On the left side, just a little way down the south slope from the top, son."

"Ain't I ever goin' to get to see his mine?"

Ona ruffled his tousled hair. "When school is out, if he'll take you, maybe you can go."

And sure enough he went; and until his dust had given up its share of native granite it would still be there unchanged, not so much a landscape as a state of mind that opened in full bloom at his first look: the high bare hills seamed with gulches, hirsute with gallows frames, smokestakes, and shaft houses, corroded by glory holes and splotched with ore dumps; the shabby little towns cluttering the gulches with squalid shanties and whose stubby streets were blocked by canyon walls or mountainous tailing dumps; the refuse-laden gullies below and the dizzily winding roads and railroad spurs above; the pale sparse aspen groves and dark patches of pines, the clouds filling the canyons; and rising above all, the snowy summit of the Peak itself. He heard the snorts of the 2-8-0 iron ponies clawing their way up from Phantom Canyon on the Florence and Cripple Creek narrow-gauge and the puffing of a bigger 4-6-0 Ten-Wheeler on a spur; the dull, resonant roars of underground blasts; the tinkle of a honky-tonk piano. He smelled the yeasty buckwheat cake batter working in the buckets on the back stoops, the smell of raw whiskey spilled on a bar. Stark of outline, shamelessly blatant, and always crude, the district still carried inexplicably something of the romantic and unreal; and like the memory of a loved face it was always to reflect the unchanged vision of a boy of those years who saw neither its beauty nor its sordidness, but only its ever tragic freshness.

When he finally arrived at the Sylvanite, Jake and Abe had just come up the shaft. Besmired and unshaven, in boots and overalls, they stood blinking in the bright sunlight at the brass-buttoned little cowboy Cable held by the hand. "My boy, the one I been telling you about!" he said proudly. "Reckon you can put him to work?"

They nodded stiffly, without speaking. Rogier came out of the shaft house. He walked around the boy, looking at the thin leather chaps, the shiny tin buttons, the colored kerchief around his throat. "Great God! What's this?"

"My new cowboy suit," said March. "Mother bought it for me so I could ride the burros."

Rogier scowled. "Don't expect to wear that fol-de-rol around here. You'll get those chamois skin pants wet and freeze your little bottom off. And those boots – where's your rubbers, boy?" He snatched the hat off March's head, slapped it on again. "The first time you go down the shaft the wind'll take care of that. Humph! Mad as March, like I always said."

That evening after supper Rogier retired to his own corner of the cabin. His bunk was along the east wall, and at its head in the corner was a small table covered with papers. Here he spent his evenings puffing on a cigar and figuring. Cable washed the dishes and March wiped them. Jake sat at the big center table reading his newspaper with moving lips and forefinger. Abe, shirt and shoes off as usual, squatted on a chair close to the fire. Across his lap lay an old pair of dungarees gone through the knees. These he was reworking with a solemnity as forbidding as Rogier's absorption. From time to time he threaded his needle, squinting through the eye like a marksman taking aim at a difficult target.

Cable and March sat down and played checkers. No one spoke. The flames crackled, a coyote howled. Every once in awhile Cable let out a tiny, irritating cough. And sitting there in the silence the boy was reminded of the trading post at Shallow Water. There too had been solitude and silence, the kind but blunt companionship of only men. But everything there had seemed so vibrantly alive and resilient, so subtle and rhythmic. Here he sensed an ungiving hardness, a tautness in the very air. What this difference was, as between adobe and granite, he didn't know. "It's kind of like Shallow Water, isn't it Daddy, but different."

"I reckon so," Cable replied carelessly, with a tiny cough.

Later, when March crawled into his bunk, he whispered to his father, "I don't think Jake and Abe like me. Abe hasn't said a word or even looked at me."

But in the morning when he rose, there on a chair beside his bunk lay a little pair of dungarees. Abe, sitting up half the night, had cut down his old pair to fit him.

In these he went down the Sylvanite.

Those big resplendent surface plants, the great steaming boilers and electric dynamos, the hoist operator sitting enthroned before his double drums with their indicator dials and winking signal lights, the two-compartment shafts and cages filled with men, the electrically lighted level stations and miles of tidy drifting— "Why, Granddad, your mine's not as big and nice as the Mary McKinney, is it? Daddy took me down it with all the tourists when the train stopped, and it had electric lights and everything."

Rogier slammed back the hoist lever, stood up to see over the greasy cable reel, and rang his bells with a frown. "No, by Jove! We're not runnin' a tourist excursion. When you go down this hole keep your head down or you'll get some sense knocked in it."

March watched his father scoop up a handful of carbide for his lamp and add water, saw the narrow pencil of flame spurt out and hold steady when he applied a match. "Come on, son." The ore bucket was lowered to the shaft collar. Cable lifted the boy in and stood on the rim holding to the cable.

Slowly the bucket began to descend, sliding down the slimy cribbing to straighten out into a vertical drop. Crouched in an inch of water at the bottom of the rusty iron bucket, March stared upward at the fading light. He could barely see his father. The jagged rock walls dripped water, seemed to bump against the bucket, and oozed a cloying coldness that penetrated his thin jacket. He shut his eyes, still feeling earth and darkness rushing upward. "Level Number One!" called Cable's reassuring voice. The boy opened his eyes to see a blank hole shoot upward. At the fifth hole the bucket stopped.

Jake came pushing a little iron car down the narrow tracks. March stood back against the wall, watching the two men load the ore into the bucket. Then he followed them through a long dark hall into a slope almost as big as the bedroom at home, where Abe was mucking.

"What keeps the roof from falling down?" he asked apprehensively.

"Hard rock," said Jake. "It don't need no timbering."

"Where's the gold?" he asked again, looking vainly for chunks of glittering metal hanging from the walls.

Cable and Abe were on their knees, tracing downward a thin

grayish blue streak in the wall. Cable took his pick and broke off a piece that crumbled between his palms. "Heavily oxidized, isn't it?"

"Never know what we'll run into," said Abe, "As crazy a workin' as he ever said it was."

Cable frowned, then turned to March with a smile. "There's the gold vein, Sonny. Jake and Abe follow it wherever it goes. See those holes they've drilled there? That's where they'll put the dynamite tonight. Tomorrow they'll shovel all the blasted rock into the bucket to send it up to me. I'll sort out the ore that holds the gold to send to the mill. The rest I'll throw on the dump. See now what makes dumps?"

"But don't it get all mixed up, Daddy?"

"Oh, sure. That's why your granddad needs me to sort it, even though Abe and Jake do all the work! Now come on. Let's don't interfere."

Even as they turned away there began the deafening sound of the drills. Dust filled the stope. March began to cough. Just as they reached the level station there was the sound of bells. Jake and Abe came running.

"What's the trouble?" they demanded. "It's not noon yet!"

Cable and March went up first and waited for Abe and Jake, then all four walked into the hoist house. "What's up, Colonel? Ain't nothin' wrong?"

Rogier locked the hoist, picked up his binoculars, and walked out to the dump. Here he squatted with the others gathered around him, staring fixedly through the glasses at the bald summit of Pike's Peak. Even with the naked eye one could see the tiny jet of smoke from the cog-train crawling up the slope.

Rogier passed his glasses around. "It's June 17th and near high noon, isn't it? Well, if the Maharajah can realize the significance of the Peak, I reckon we can knock off work a little early and meditate with him. We need it, so close to our work we forget our real purpose."

All three men knew what he meant, remembering the article in the paper. The Gaekwar of Baroda, illustrious Maharajah of India, was stopping in Little London with his retinue on his trip around the world. Today he had chartered the cog-train to the summit of Pike's Peak, one of the famous sacred mountains of the world. He had requested the officials to prohibit anyone else on top for the duration of his visit. For at high noon he was going to kneel for a half-hour on a golden rug and – so close to Heaven – commend himself and followers to the mercy of Allah.

Yes! That mighty potentate of the East was not too humble to render obeisance to the divine will on this great manifestation of its living power. They themselves could not do less, Rogier had declaimed; they who also vibrated in unison with the pulse of that mighty heart into which they were driving so relentlessly.

Nor now at the appointed hour had he forgotten. Jake and Abe walked off to eat and rest an extra half-hour, followed by Cable and March, leaving Rogier alone to meditate in undisturbed silence with the Maharajah above him.

This then was all there was to the Sylvanite – cabin, corral, tool shanty, hoist house, and a vertical shaft; and March fitted unobtrusively into the hard and simple life constrained by the routine the mine enforced. By night Rogier sat figuring how to go down still deeper. By day he sat at the hoist, an inexorable taskmaster. Abe and Jake worked down below, blasting, mucking, drifting. Cable above sorted at the dump, and occasionally spelled off Abe or Jake. Upon March fell the disagreeable, homely chores: washing dishes, sweeping the cabin floor, sunning blankets, tending the burros, and running errands. Infequently he sat at the hoist, providing a helpless and unargumentative target for Rogier's vehement mutterings.

The men now selected their assay samples earlier in the day so March could ride down the gulch with the sack. How lovely were those June afternoons when jolting slowly along on his flop-eared Pike's Peak Canary, the boy gave himself to the wild and serene beauty of the long narrow canyon. The aspens had leaved, new grass was sprouting among the old. Everywhere were flowers: wild sweet peas and yellow wall flowers, anemones and fragile columbines among the pines, tall penstamons along the rutted trail, and in the flats blankets of wild orchids. Color everywhere, rich and full. Only the thistleberries white as snow remained to tell of winter. The little creek poured merrily over the beaver dam; a red-tailed hawk launched itself with a scream from the cliffs; a porcupine waddled up the slope. Everything awoke and moved with delicious abandon to transient summer, and March could feel it rush through him without restraint.

On Saturdays there came a break. Abe and Jake after work dressed up and went to town. "What do you do there?" March asked them. Neither answered and strode off stiffly in squeaking boots.

"Don't ever ask them that again," Cable said sharply. "This is the one day they can live private lives. It's nobody's business."

Sometimes they staggered home shouting at dawn. Mostly they didn't return until Sunday afternoon, morose and sullen, to lie snoring on their bunks. On alternate weekends Rogier, and then Cable and March, went down to Little London. The train rides back and forth were exciting. There were two standard-gauge lines into the district besides the narrow-gauge from Florence. The Midland Terminal crept up Ute Pass from Manitou to Divide, the summit of the continental watershed, passing the little resorts of Cascade and Green Mountain Falls with their ornate hotels. Entering the district from the north, the train detoured around Battle Mountain to Victor, and cut over Raven and Gold Hill to the brick depot in Cripple Creek at the head of Bennett Avenue. Sitting on his green plush seat, nose pressed against the window, March could hear the big Mogul puffing up the grade, the thunder of the exhaust against the blackened cliffs. He could see the smoke shooting high at every stroke of the pistons when the engine swung round the horseshoe curves, crept across the high, spidery trestles. Then entering a tunnel, the coach was suddenly enveloped in darkness and smoke and a rain of cinders.

For one of the Midland's locomotives he developed a strong attachment that began one Sunday when he was down in Little London. Cable had taken the family to Manitou for a day's outing, and they were walking up to the Iron Springs Pavilion to fill their water bottles and to buy some of its famous salt water taffy in all colors. Shortly after they had passed under the high wooden trestle by which the train spanned the narrow canyon, they were halted by the sound of a tremendous crash. Running back, they confronted a terrible sight. A number of boxcars and flats in a freight had plunged off the high trestle and were dragging down more after them. One car after another was derailed, toppled over, and plunged down to crash into kindling on the great boulders below.

"Oh my God! Why don't they jump!" exclaimed Ona.

March knew who she meant—the engineer and the fireman in the locomotive. He identified it at once: Number 60, one of the 2-8-0 mountain-climbing Moguls he had ridden behind often. "Look!" he shouted. "Old Sixty's hangin' on!"

The Mogul was indeed. Her eight drivers were clawing at the rails like a mountain cat, pistons shooting fire and smoke pouring from her straight stack. The engineer had his throttle wide open, and the fireman was sweating in a frenzy on the apron. All the cars but one had been dragged down now; and as he watched, it toppled over.

"Don't look!" shouted Ona, grabbing Leona and turning her back.

Old Sixty was still hanging on. And as he watched, the coupling parted with a loud snap. The car plunged down, leaving the locomotive alone on the rails high above.

Always thereafter March boarded the Midland with fervent praise. "It's Old Sixty, Daddy. She'll get us there!"

The Short Line was different but just as exciting. It followed the old stage road from Little London, climbing up the steep canyons behind Cheyenne Mountain. No resorts, just scenery along the way. A trip that bankrupted the English language, President Teddy Roosevelt had asserted when he visited the district. And the scenery was easy to see, for the train carried an open observation platform on the back coach where March always insisted on sitting. Here he could hear the clickety-clack of the wheels on the rail joints below him, the squealing of the flanges on the sharp curves. Far ahead he could see the sleek-boilered Consolidation engine rounding the bend, hear the mournful wail of the whistle from the quill. High above him loomed cliffwall and mountainside. And down below on a siding in an open meadow the Wild Flower Special, a train of roofless coaches, waited for its picknicking tourists to gather armfuls of wild flowers. They were always jerked up by roots, March knew, and so wilted in the sun by the time the Special got back to Little London that the picknickers dumped them in the trash cans; but there were always plenty with more. And now again, out of this serene and yet brooding mountain wilderness, he climbed into that high granite domain swarming with human ants.

He was becoming bolder now, riding throughout the district on its interurban system during the long summer afternoons. It had two tracks between Victor and Cripple Creek: the Low Line and the High Line which on Bull Hill near Midway reached an altitude of 10,487 feet, the highest trolley point in the country, Cable told him. It was a fine ride for a nickle. He learned the hills, towns, camps, and mines; the great producers like the Independence, Portland, Ajax, Pharmacist, and Gold Coin, and those with funny names like the Pocohontas, Butcher Boy, Red Umbrella, The Ore or No Go, the Lulu, Lizzie May, and the Nameless. Like other urchins he partitioned empty cigar boxes to hold samples labelled "Native Ores of Cripple Creek". These he hawked to tourists on the railroad platform at Cripple Creek.

One afternoon there he ran into a gang of boys from Poverty Gulch, the slum of the Tenderloin. The leader, a sturdy miner's son, stalked up to him. "Where you come from?"

"The Sylvanite!" March boasted. "We own it!"

"That ain't no mine!" shouted one of the boys. "Everybody knows old man Rogier is crazy!"

"And it's over by Victor!"

This was enough for the big bully. For if the main producing area was around Victor, the "City of Mines," Cripple Creek was the oldest camp and largest town, giving its name to the district. And so between them had grown up a rivalry that extended from the most influential mineowner to the sorriest mucker. "Ain't nobody from Victor goin' to steal our customers! Let's run him out!" Knocking the cigar box of samples from March's hand, the leader attacked with flying fists. In an instant the platform erupted into a melee of fighting urchins that was broken up only by the station agent and two brawny bystanders. The boys took to their heels.

March found himself slinking down Myers Avenue. Looking back to make sure he wasn't followed, he sat down on the curb to wipe the blood and mud off his face and clothes. Behind him stood a long row of big houses with funny names: "The Homestead," "Ol, Faithful," "The Library," and "Sunnyrest." Huddling there, muddy, bruised, and miserable, he watched the ladies coming back from their afternoon drives or walking down the street. They weren't dressed in drab clothes like the miners' wives, but in bright taffeta from which daintily protruded little slippers. A plumed hat ruffled in the wind, a parasol glowed with color in the sun.

Suddenly he felt a hand clapped on his shoulder. "What's the matter, Sonny? Lost your last friend or a nickel down the gutter?"

March spun around, looking up at a slim young girl, kind of pretty but pale, and wearing a flowered dress.

"Here, you come with me," she said, taking his hand and leading him into the house behind them. The parlor was more like one in a hotel, with a red carpet, three sofas, and a potted rubber plant. In it several more ladies were sitting. One of them stood up, an older woman with sharp features who looked bossy. Immediately March took off his hat.

"What's he here for?" she demanded of the girl.

"I'm going to clean off the boy's jacket and pants a little so he can go home without gettin' the tar beat out of him."

She took him down the hall to a small bedroom and was right nice about it too. She didn't look when he took off his pants until he was in bed, and she gave him a magazine to look at while she was gone.

"There!" she said, coming back. "I scrubbed off the mud slick as a whistle. They're still a little damp but they'll dry out in no time when you get into them. 'Course your shoes are still muddy, but so are every boy's."

The older woman came in and the three of them talked a long time. "My name's Charlotte," the tall girl said. "Now what's yours?" March told her; and impulsively told her also about his father and grandfather, Abe and Jake, and the Sylvanite. He liked the way Charlotte laughed; it made him forget her pale face. And she had the funniest little wrinkles at the corner of one eye – just two of them. "And what's your name?" he asked the older woman abruptly.

"Madame – Madame Jones," the woman answered with a frown. "But you better be running along. Here's a quarter. Keep out of the mud."

March stood up. "I sure am much obliged, Madame Jones. And maybe I'll bring you some flowers, Charlotte. Daddy would sure like you too!"

The girl laughed, but Madame Jone's face got thundery. "Now boy. I don't want you bringing your menfolks here a'tall. I won't have it! And if you don't want a licking, you won't say anything about coming here."

Charlotte smiled. "Let's keep this to ourselves, just for fun. And sometime if you don't forget you can bring me two flowers, a big one for my room and a little one to wear!"

March did not forget his promise. The following week he came back with an armload of wild flowers. The Madame met him at the door with no recognition on her face. "What do you want, boy?"

"Why, it's me, Madame Jones. You remember me. I brought Charlotte the flowers."

She stared at him queerly. "Charlotte's busy." Then seeing his face quiver with disappointment, she pulled him inside the parlor. "Oh, I remember now! What was I thinking of?"

In back of the parlor was a short bar. A few men, half-drunk, were wrangling with some of the ladies. To escape the noise, said Madame Jones, March could wait down the hall in another small sitting room. Shortly afterward Charlotte came in, her pale and fragile face lighting up at the sight of March waiting stiffly in his chair with an armful of wild flowers.

Every week thereafter March stopped at Madame Jones' to see Charlotte. Sometimes she was busy and he had to wait almost an hour. There were times when they talked for only a minute before she sent him away with a quarter to spend. On other days they spent nearly the whole afternoon together. Once they were interrupted by a hoarse voice shouting down the hall, "Goddamn it! I know who I want! Where's Charlotte?" Then the boy could hear Madame Jones' hard voice calmly telling him to close his trap before she rammed his tongue down his gullet with a poker. "It's my uncle," said Charlotte, her brown eyes clouding. "He's such a noisy one!"

There were other girls living at Madame Jones': Lulu, Belle, Flora – many whose names he could never recall on seeing them in the parlor. But invariably he took off his hat, grinned shyly, and was answered with kind and hungry greetings, good-natured jokes, or by a polite civility in which he detected a hurt resentment because his loyalty never wavered from Charlotte. Madame Jones, he knew, did not approve of him; but she was always polite and whisked him in and out as if he might soil the red carpet with a speck of dust.

What held them together, March never knew. At each visit he

found in Charlotte something new. She was changeable as a chameleon: somber, tired, and listless, abnormally cheerful, or burning with a quiet vitality whose depth or origin he could never fathom. Only her pale girlish face and the astounding contrast of her dark hair and big brown eyes never changed. If her lips were violently red some days, they were hardly pink on others, and one day they were almost cold blue. She was very young, but to March at times she seemed old and weary-wise as his grandmother. He liked her best when she was a child with him, remembering familiar fairy tales. But at all times, whatever her mood, they met as friends should always meet – two lonely souls stripped of age and sex, caring little of the paths behind them and grasping the precious moment of contact from which sometime, and forever, they would be withdrawn by the mysterious and irrevocable power which swings each man and each star into an orbit which is his alone.

3

Early in June the old house on Shook's Run began to fill again. Matters between Mary Ann and her husband Cecil Durgess finally had come to a head. A divorce had not yet mantled them with disgrace, but Mary Ann had traipsed off to start a delicatessen store of her own somewhere, leaving Nancy in Mrs. Rogier's care. She was a fair-haired, light complexioned girl about the age of dark-skinned Leona who came down every day to play with her.

Two weeks later Sally Lee arrived to spend the summer. In her entourage were a beribboned baby who went by the name of Sugar Lump, a fat and pouty Negro nurse named Josephine, and a tall slim girl who was introduced as Miss Evelina, one of Sally Lee's rich neighbors. Getting out of the carriage, Miss Evelina stood with folded hands staring at the Negro boy hitching post while Sally Lee embraced her mother.

"Oh, he does need a new coat of paint! And the old house too!" exclaimed Sally Lee, noticing the look. "You know, Mother, Miss Evelina and I just wracked our poor brains wondering where to spend the summer. No one, simply no one, stays in Memphis. Then I thought, 'Miss Evelina must see Pike's Peak and Sugar Lump will adore cool Colorado.' She has a little heat rash already, our drawing room was so stuffy. Josephine, you must bathe and powder her immediately."

Mrs. Rogier watched her carelessly pass a crumpled bill to the driver. "Oh, keep the change. I do detest these silver Colorado dollars; they're so heavy to carry in my purse."

Still talking, they walked inside and sat down in the front room. "You received my telegram?" asked Sally Lee.

"All three of them," answered Mrs. Rogier. "The last two really weren't necessary. It made no difference whether the train was late. For your first visit home we'd have stayed up all night to welcome you."

"It's so much easier to send telegrams than writing letters. Why, you don't even have to write them. Just tell the porter what to say."

Miss Evelina spoke up. "Sally Lee has promised to show me the Garden of the Gods, Seven Falls, and all the sights. Says I shall like cool Colorado better than Canada and the other places where one usually summers, you know. Too, she has been telling me of Colonel Rogier and his gold mine and charming idiocyncrasies."

"Just Mr. Rogier would be better than Colonel, I think, my dear," remonstrated Mrs. Rogier. "He was never an officer, not even a soldier, and he detests all the military. And our mine isn't really a treasure chest. But we will do our best to make you comfortable." She turned to Sally Lee. "How about Sister Molly's big room for you and the baby? Josephine can sleep in the alcove where she'll be handy at night. Nancy will move her things upstairs so Miss Evelina can have the middle room next to yours."

"Of course, Mother. And see that the big redwood closet is cleaned out for our furs."

"Furs?"

"Now, Mother! You know we can't be driving up the canyons without wraps, after just coming from the South."

Mrs. Rogier did not blink an eye. She was staring at visions of Sally Lee in a skimpy gingham dress galloping by on one of Rogier's horses or climbing barefooted up the cliffs after wild raspberries.

"Josephine, you come along with the baby. I'll show you where you can bathe her." Her tone and manner showed Josephine instantly a woman who knew how to handle Negroes.

"Yas'm," she said obediently, and followed Mrs. Rogier upstairs.

A moment later Mrs. Rogier stuck her head in the middle room. Nancy was pouting on the bed. "I won't give up my room to *her*!"

"You will be very quick about it, honey. The Third Floor. And don't leave a single finger-mark on the bedrail either."

Something of her calm, decisive manner remained after she had gone downstairs and was left alone with Sally Lee. "You haven't changed a bit, Mother, but the house has," Sally Lee said defensively. "Why don't you make Daddy paint it and the Blackamoor, and re-gravel the driveway?"

"Oh, I wouldn't pester him about such little things."

Sally Lee felt suddenly abashed, as if her mother's smiling look had stripped her to her silver shoe-buckles, sheer hose, and lace-trimmed lingerie—handmade and imported from France, Aurand the darling! "But I can't understand. After all your wishing and waiting for a big house in the North End and a pair of matched bays. And teaching us always to demand the best. Nothing but the best!"

"I'm sure you will always have it, Sally Lee. And what a nice start with a husband like Aurand and your baby. I can't tell you how glad I am."

Sally Lee gave her mother a hug and backed away. She expected now, at last, a sniffle and then a deluge. There was no sign of either. Mrs. Rogier stood before her, small and slim and straight—all steel. Her eyes were clear and untroubled; and in a firm voice she said casually, "And now dear, you'd better run up for your bath. Miss Evelina probably finished ages ago."

Now alone and rocking in her chair, Mrs. Rogier looked back upon a past that would have seemed unbelievable had she not seen it preserved and reflected in Sally Lee. It was all there: her craving for a mansion in the North End and a position of social prominence, the ostentatious display to flaunt before her neighbors, her false pride and foolish vanity, the old Rogier attitude of divine superiority before man, God, and the Devil, and the placid assurance that no plum hung too high on the tree of this world's approbation for her to pick at will. Sally Lee, of all persons! Penned up in that gaunt house on Shook's Run, deprived of friends because they were too "common," and nurtured with the outmoded traditions of a vanished aristocracy, Sally Lee in every act now betrayed the pathetic snobbishness that once had been her mother's.

Mrs. Rogier, being a mother, did not condone Sally Lee's manner and aspirations; she simply ignored them as one from whom all these same foolish trivialities had been burned away. And rocking in the warm June sun, frail and indomitable, she never realized that now, stripped of pretense and faced with certain failure, she was at last a real lady.

Every day she showed it. Alert, courteous, resourceful, she began the battle, knowing the inevitable end. For Sally Lee had learned her lesson well—the insidious corruption of wealth that blinds the most sincere. Two or three times a week she hired a carriage for the day. With Miss Evelina beside her in the back seat and Josephine up front with Sugar Lump, she drove to Seven Falls, Garden of the Gods, Cave of the Winds, and up both Cheyenne Canyons. She came home laden with souvenirs: Indian moccasins and bows and arrows manufactured in Chicago, carved gypsum bookends, polished agate paper weights, spoons, little boxes of Cripple Creek ore specimens, and views of the region by the stack. That she had no use for this tourist fodder made no difference; it seemed the thing to do. She attended shows and concerts as a matter of course, usually leaving in the middle of the program. She bought clothes that hung in the closet yet unworn months after her departure. And when she needed still more money it was only necessary, after an apologetic "Dear me! How frightfully expensive this town has become!" to send a telegram to dear Aurand.

This careless extravagance she carried on at home in a delightful manner that impressed Miss Evelina with the indubitable fact that she was indeed the daughter of the owner of a gold mine in fabulous Cripple Creek. Every day she took a notion for some rare or unseasonable delicacy that was ordered by telephone and sent down in a hurry before she changed her mind. That all this bulged Mrs. Rogier's accounts to astounding proportions seldom entered her head. When it did, Rogier's gruff delight at the new dishes dispelled any qualms.

He came down from Cripple Creek every other weekend. Because Josephine was fat and black, he assumed she could cook.

After sixty years he was determined to taste corn pone that embodied all the memories of his childhood.

"I'se a nuss-maid," objected Josephine. "Ah ain't no cookin' Negra."

"Oh, go ahead and try," urged Sally Lee. "We'll all help."

They made a day of it – Sally Lee, Miss Evelina, and Josephine. Mrs. Rogier was forbidden to enter the kitchen and ordered to rest. This rest was punctuated from early morning till supper time by falling pots and clanging pans, by Miss Evelina daintily emptying the closet in search of the egg beater hanging over the dripboard, by Josephine prying into every nook and cranny with the insatiable curiosity of the black, and by Sally Lee wasting a week's groceries in cooking a miserable meal.

For of all gathered around the table, including Ona and Jonathan, no one save Rogier but acknowledged the truth of the old maxim that too many cooks spoiled the pie. Despite two quarts of champagne the ham was dry and tasteless; the candied yams were too sweet and soggy; the asparagus tips were scorched; and the whipped cream on the glazed strawberry tarts had been allowed to turn.

But Rogier, engrossed in the memory of a boy of ten eating corn pone taken off an open fire, chewed happily on his crumbling square and kept up a long harangue on Negro cooking that left no word for anyone else. Through it all Mrs. Rogier sat at the end of the table with a pleasant smile and politely sipped her half glass of wine.

Not until next morning did she have a word to say. She took only one look at the kitchen. The stove was covered with dried batter; the sink piled high with unwashed dishes; every pot and pan was dirty and the room completely disordered. At nine o'clock the carriage drove up outside. Sally Lee and Miss Evelina, with Josephine carrying Sugar Lump, came down for their drive.

"Goodby, Mother. Don't know when we'll be back. Be sure and save my letters!" Sally Lee called cheerfully.

"Just a minute!" said Mrs. Rogier quietly. Nancy behind her, almost in tears, was slumped down at the dinner table waiting for the inevitable summons to clean up the mess. "Josephine! You don't think you're going out driving and leave that kitchen the same way you left it last night, do you? If you're going to play at being a cook you're going to finish the job. Now you get upstairs and into some old clothes. I want every pot and pan scoured till it shines, the silver polished, and the floor scrubbed!"

The woman's fat pink lips pouted; she glanced at Sally Lee for help.

"You heard me!" said Mrs. Rogier. "I'm not going to tell you a second time. Now git!" She turned around. "Nancy! Put on your hat and wrap. You're going out riding with the folks to mind the baby. And see that you do mind her." Without a look at Sally Lee, she walked back to her rocking chair and picked up the morning newspaper.

Sally Lee and Miss Evelina, a little shamefacedly, slid out the door with Sugar Lump to wait in the carriage for Nancy.

Thus Mrs. Rogier began to wage that heroic and womanly battle of which she only was aware. Never once did she utter a word against Sally Lee's and Miss Evelina's extravagance, giving them her best as if it were not quite sufficient for their needs. And when in return they brought her a bag of candy or a foolish bauble she accepted it gratefully. Yet all the time she was checking her bills for the slightest error, wracking her head for ways to utilize every scrap of food so no one would realize she had used it. And alone with Rogier, she was sharp and grasping as a miser.

"Just half enough, Daddy," she would tell him, counting the generous allowance he gave her. "It's a downright cryin' shame you have to feed so many extra mouths with all your other expenses. I've made up my mind to tell Sally Lee she must do her share."

"What? And make a boardin' house of the girls' own home? The first time she's been back?"

"Well, I shall let them give up some of their running around. There's no reason for setting such a table every day. We shall all get sick with so much rich food."

"By Jove! You'll be wanting next to feed them sowbelly and beans. Never do get anything to eat in this house 'less they order it!"

"Well, Daddy, I can't pay the bills on this."

And staring at her with incredulous eyes, Rogier would storm about the vast sums he was pouring into her lap, threaten to hire a cook who knew her business, berate her for her extravagance – and end by giving her another hundred dollars; a hundred precious dollars that he might have used in the Sylvanite.

4

It was a hot sultry afternoon that now, just past three o'clock, was cooling off for the daily shower. Summer was ending and Sally Lee and Miss Evelina were leaving next morning. Watching the sweating Josephine strapping the last of the overloaded trunks, Sally Lee looked up at her mother. "There! I'm tired enough to drop. All I can think of is a breath of fresh air."

"It's going to rain," said Mrs. Rogier. "You'd better lie down instead."

"No! I'll tell you what. We'll order the carriage for five o'clock. That'll give us an hour to drive around. We'll stop by the Ruxton to pick up Daddy, then take dinner out. Mother, you do the calling while I take my bath. Be sure and tell the club to tell Daddy to wait for us."

"I don't believe I would," protested Mrs. Rogier. "Daddy hates to have anyone come after him, anyplace, and this is a men's club."

Sally Lee laughed. "We won't compromise him!"

Promptly at six o'clock the carriage swung round the corner and stopped outside the club. Rain was coming down in a steady drizzle. The three women waited patiently: fifteen minutes, a half-hour, and still Rogier did not come out. "I won't go in after him, Daddy or not!" Sally Lee declared with sudden vehemence. In dreary silence they continued to wait.

Of a sudden Miss Evelina drew up erect, and with a tense embarrassed face stared at the club entrance. Sally Lee looked out. As she did so there began a loud and prolonged guffaw from a dozen men standing in the doorway –

Rogier, some time before, had entered the club and asked for Timothy. He was told that Mr. Timothy had not come in yet, and that Mr. Rogier's own family would call for him there. Snorting with impatience, he flung into a far corner of the lounge and ordered a drink.

Dom it! He wanted to see Timothy now, only for a minute, and get home before his family traipsed in. Fishing out of his pocket the token he had promised Timothy, he laid it beside his glass of whiskey. They were both the same color, and both stimulants to his imagination.

The solid was a large burnished gold nugget looped by a fine gold wire whose clasp could be attached to Timothy's watch chain. Naturally it wasn't a nugget of free gold, nor was it exclusively of gold mined from the Sylvanite. How could it be! A mill didn't work that way, reducing the ore from each mine separately. Nevertheless the nugget was of gold minted from the run in which had been included a shipment of ore from the Sylvanite. There was no use explaining all this to Timothy. But he would be pleased. The thing cost enough, what with shaping, burnishing, and mounting; and it did look fetching, glowing soft and dark yellow beside the coppery gold whiskey. For that matter, wasn't it congealed liquid itself, bled from the veins of the breathing earth? Lost in his reverie before it, Rogier was startled by a hand clapped on his shoulder.

He looked up. It was Timothy who had come up with a group of his cronies. Rogier rose to his feet. There was no use thrusting the nugget back into his pocket; they all had caught sight of it. "Here. Put this on your watch chain," he said gruffly, handing it to Timothy. "And my compliments go with it."

Timothy let out a yell of delight and snapped it on his chain to dangle against his showy waistcoat. "A tear-drop of pure unalloyed beauty, man! A radiant smile from eternal darkness! It deserves a drink and toast from all of us!"

None of his companions knew of his investment in the venture, but for Rogier the cat was out of the bag. The men set up a chorus of unmerciful joshing.

"A gold nugget! Just like that, boys!"

"Where's mine? You heard me say I wanted one too!"

"Why, he has got a gold mine, men!"

To all their quips and sallies Rogier was immune, affable and good-natured. Then, as usual, somebody threw at him a serious question. Rogier answered thoughtfully, but was indignantly refuted; the man's wink to his cronies he did not catch. And now Rogier was led into a long harangue on the subject ever in his mind—the auriferous structure of the Cripple Creek volcano, its history, geology, and philosophical significance. With sly grins his listeners settled down in their chairs. The room was gray; the rain drizzled persistently down the window panes. Across the thick carpet the boy trod lightly back and forth from the bar with more drinks. The hour passed, the chimes in the lobby tinkled the half-hour. Still Rogier talked, stimulated by the whiskey and brooking no opposition.

Abruptly, his glass halfway to his lips, he happened to look out the window. Setting down the glass, he rose to his feet. "Well!" he muttered, a little thickly. "My girls have come to fetch me!"

Without more ado he hurriedly strode out of the room. Flinging on a coat and hat from the rack in the hall, he swung open the door. Behind him trooped all his listeners. At the door they stopped and set up a guffaw that could have been heard to the corner and which aroused the three women in the carriage in front.

Sally Lee, looking out, stared transfixed at the ludicrous figure of her father stumbling down the front steps in a strange hat and coat. The hat was an old derby that, as he hit the bottom step stifflegged, jolted down over his ears and eyes. He stopped to push it back. His hand caught in the torn lining of a black-and-white raincoat, several sizes too large and flopping around him like a blanket, the tail dragging on the wet sidewalk.

" 'Where did you get that hat?' " sang out one of the men in the words of the popular ditty.

"Throw her, cowboy!" yelled another. "She's gettin' you

down!"

Then a howl of glee went up as somebody recognized the clothes. "He's tryin' to steal the porter's hat and coat!"

Sally Lee reared back in her carriage with a mortified face that suddenly went white. Was this her father—this ludicrous and pathetic old Ichabod struggling in a greasy old coat like a netted hawk! Her own father acting like a fool in front of the Ruxton, and with her in plain view of all those men! Never – never! – would she be able to hold her head up in town. And to face Miss Evelina – Then she did gasp.

Mrs. Rogier was out of the carriage and swiftly walking to Rogier. She gave one level glance up the steps at Timothy bent over and howling with laughter like the rest. Then she said quietly to Rogier, "Here, Daddy, let me help you." In a minute she had disentangled him and handed the coat and hat to an attendant who had come out with Rogier's own.

He dug in his pocket for a dollar and handed it to the boy with a grin. Then putting on his own coat and hat, he waved good-naturedly to the crowd and walked out to the carriage with Mrs. Rogier.

"You'd better drive straight home, Jim," Mrs. Rogier told the driver in an even, unexcited tone.

"By Jove!" exclaimed Rogier with an amused grin. "That was the domdest fittin' coat you ever got me out of, Marthy. I figured I was caught in my shroud."

Mrs. Rogier patted his hand, and the carriage drove on in a silence unbroken by the water splashing against the wheels. Miss Evelina leaned back languidly, looking straight ahead. Sally Lee did likewise but with every muscle tense. She was biting her lip; and she too considered it quite expedient to forget the farewell supper uptown promised them all.

Now, just past midnight, she lay sleepless in her bed. Something in the familiar squeak of the Kadles' steps that she would not hear again remorselessly cracked her heart at every step. For a moment they stopped outside in the hall. Sally Lee dug her face into the pillow. She could feel upon her, even through the closed door, the condemnation of those two faithful family ghosts. They alone saw through her, knew her for the child of that old house she would be always.

She had the wild desire to fling out of bed and confess her shame to them who had known all her childhood worries, hopes, and trespasses. The clear thought of how she would look standing in the empty hall held her back. Sugar Lump would be awakened. Josephine would be angry and sulky. And Miss Evelina in the middle room – Sally Lee, clenching her hands, lay listening to the Kadles' footsteps retreating down the stairs.

Too late! For tomorrow morning she was going home. And not until now, with that devastating picture of the afternoon before her, had she realized how much she loved her father. Roll and toss as she might, she could not shut out the vision. But strangely it was not his ludicrous appearance she saw now. It was the calm, unembarrassed manner with which he had met a perfectly normal and amusing incident. Even then, jeered at and a little confused by liquor, he had maintained, without effort and without being conscious of it, an easy dignity too sound to be affronted. And her mother – she too had acted impulsively, thoroughly right.

Nor could Sally Lee escape the memory of her own actions and the frigid manner successfully maintained all evening in front of Miss Evelina. Her last evening home!

"Oh, God." she breathed into her pillow, "Why didn't I laugh and shriek at Daddy, and jump out and fling my arms around him in a big hug, and josh him for cutting up so? Why didn't I take them all to the Antlers for a jolly farewell supper?"

She knew too well; and she could have rushed to Miss Evelina's room to rend that stuck-up nitwit tooth and nail. And all the time she knew that in the morning she would be casual and polite, and that for months after they reached home the subject would never be mentioned.

Oh, she was a coward and a fool, fool, fool! She was the same little girl in gingham who in the "poor days" had eaten little but biscuits and molasses, the freckled young woman who alone had been permitted to work out Rogier's horses on the track. What had happened to her to make her act as if her mother had all kinds of money? Not once all summer long had she taken the family out for supper, or offered her mother a dollar for expenses. But tomorrow morning she would thrust a roll of bills into her hands – and get it back with a gentle smile whose ironic meaning only Mrs. Rogier could manage! Sally Lee knew she couldn't even send a check from home. That would be worse; Rogier wasn't a man to be paid off like an inn-keeper.

Oh, she knew now how much she loved them both. When she got home she'd write often, send them expensive presents, and see that they would always have plenty of money. And the small, still voice of the Kadles' silent condemnation whispered the lie back to her heart. Back home she would drift again into the easy, forgetful life made possible by Aurand's success. She would relapse into that habit of mind which believes everyone must have as much as she because, "Dear me, how can one possibly get along on less!"

No, not then or tomorrow morning was the time to make amends. Now! This instant she would tiptoe into her mother's room and light the lamp. She would smooth back the hair from her forehead, kiss the loved lips that had scolded her so many times, and sit there with her, hand in hand, for one long talk at last.

Then, so quietly, she would sneak down the hall to her father's room. The instant she laid a hand on the door knob he would awake and grumble, "Who the devil is this, this time of night?"

"Your own ornery and contrary Sally Lee, of course! Came in to tell you I still love you and to ask when in the Sam Hill you're going to buy some new fast pacers and a trotter or two."

And he would sit up with a twinkle in his eyes. "Dom me, girl! You know the track's all gone. But, by Jove! We sent Aralee around, didn't we? And if Silver Night—Sally Lee, you go on back to bed and don't be givin' me none of those smacky kisses you give that man of yours!"

Sally Lee lay motionless on her bed. She wanted to get up and she couldn't. Dear God, she couldn't and she didn't know why. And torn between her two bitter selves, wracked by an anguish greater than she ever had known, she finally burst into blessed tears.

A half-hour later she lay quiet and limp as a wrung-out towel. For now at last she knew as a mother herself that nothing in this world could sever the bonds that held her to this gaunt old house on Shook's Run and those within it. In pride and shame, in all the misery of success and the comfort of false hopes, she was still a Rogier.

5

They were all familiar to March now as he whizzed past them on the Low and the High Line, those great mines that had made Cripple Creek the most famous gold camp in the world. Not only the fabulous Independence, Portland, and Gold Coin, but the Dr. Jack Pot, Mary McKinney, Elkton and Ajax, Strong, El Paso, Granite and Golden Cycle, dozens of others whose tales of discovery and production almost rivaled his grandfather's ranting prophecies of still greater wealth to be found. Why, in the Cardinal on Globe Hill had been discovered wire gold assaying 800 fine or $500,000 to the ton! And only thirty-seven pounds of highgrade from the Pike's Peak Lode had brought $11,840!

But now in the last weeks of summer March learned a new side of Cripple Creek. It began that Saturday afternoon in Victor when his father took him into a saloon with a long, polished mahogany bar, a spotless mirror behind it and a glittering array of glasses. Even the brass rail and the hour-glass spittoons were shiny as gold. Then at the end of the bar he saw an array of food that made his eyes pop: crisp green onions, radishes, and olives on ice, a whole baked ham stuck full of cloves and a steaming roast beef oozing pink juice, butter cut into little squares, rye bread and hard crispy rolls, all kinds of pickles, and slices of white or yellow cheese, and – "Sandwich, Sonny? Free lunch, you know!"

Cable had two drinks while waiting for March to finish his heaped plate. When he paid for them with a $20 bill, the bartender gave him back all his change except a $10 bill which he passed to March with the terse remark, "Here's a souvenir for you!"

On the margin of the bill, scribbled in ink, the boy read: "The last of £10,000."

Cable explained what a "pound sterling" meant on their way home, telling him about the young man who had come from England to make his fortune in Cripple Creek. Here he had spent all his patrimony except this ten-dollar bill without making a strike. With it he had bought a bottle of whiskey in the saloon, walked to Arequa Gulch and blown his brains out.

"The last of £10,000" – it was a refrain that now continually sounded in the ears of a boy who for the first time perceived that not every venture, every man, is unavoidably marked for success. He learned of the solid foundation of lost hopes and abysmal failures upon which Cripple Creek, as every other success, had been built.

There was the First Chance on Mineral Hill into which Louis Perrault had sunk three different shafts and spent £10,000 without obtaining enough ore to make a single shipment.

He heard of the death of a poverty-stricken, ninety-year old man in a cheap lodging house on Larimer Street, Denver. He was Hall A. Premo, who had just refused a settlement of more than a quarter-million dollars for his share of the C.K. & N. on Beacon Hill. Premo in the early days of the Cripple Creek rush had been rich, respected, and generous. One day he had grubstaked a down-at-the-heels prospector named Horace A. Granfield for one-half interest in any strike he made. Granfield made a rich strike on Beacon Hill, and Premo footed the bills for development. The C.K. & N. was a boomer. But Granfield, dressed up like a Thanksgiving turkey and swinging a cane, passed Premo on the street without a nod. Shortly afterward he sold the mine and went to New York to become a financier on the profits. Premo smiled wryly; it was the same old story of rank ingratitude. Yet he was still rich and consoled himself with the thought he had helped the fellow out. Then his own mines petered out, his investments crashed, and the labor strike finished him. He found himself as destitute and forlorn as Granfield had been. Granfield! He wrote Granfield in New York, reminding him of his agreement to share in the mine, begged at least a grubstake from the man he had once grubstaked. Granfield refused. Premo finally obtained a law firm which instituted suit against Granfield. Year after year dragged by. Premo was ninety years old and living in poverty when the lawyers came to him with the news he had at last been awarded $265,000 by judgment in favor of his suit. "It's not big enough – appeal the case!" he quavered. There was no time. He died penniless in his lodging house.

Often March stared wonderingly at a heap of rubbish on Crystal Hill – all that remained of the magnificent gesture of J. Maurice Finn, an unscrupulous lawyer who had served Stratton, and who had wrung a fortune from the Mountain Beauty and the Caledonia on Gold Hill. Again and again March tried to envision Finn's Folly as it had been when President Teddy Roosevelt had addressed the miners from its front steps. A three-story mansion it had been, with twenty-six rooms, and surmounted by four towers each flaunting an American flag. The grand staircase in the reception hall was elaborately carved. On the wall behind it was painted a mural of the Mount of the Holy Cross, and from one of its gulches spurted a real stream of water into a circular pool filled with mountain trout. But Finn's mines had petered out, his law practice failed. He became an alcoholic, and of all his preposterous dreams and hopes there remained only this pile of rubble.

How many stories like this there were of failure and betrayal, how many deserted mines and glory holes gaping on the hillsides like graves empty now of even foolish hopes. Yet how perversely strange it seemed to March that men pointed out these great failures with the same curious pride they directed attention to the notable successes.

The most heartbreaking failure of all, and of which Cripple Creek was inordinately proud, was the Coates Prospect Hole, owned by the St. Patrick Syndicate of Scotland. It boasted a shaft 700 feet down, and 3,500 feet of lateral work. The plant had been almost totally destroyed by fire three times. One million dollars had been expended for development. And not one ounce of pay ore had been taken out. "Not a damned speck of color, mind you!" – a statement told visitors with consumate pride.

This negative aspect of the district lent a new and disturbing significance to the Sylvanite. March began to be aware of chance phrases he heard about it and his grandfather. They were confirmed by more and more visitors coming up the gulch to see the crazy venture located so far outside the producing area. Most of them were hardy old pioneers with time heavy on their hands who had left their saloons and rooming house chairs. They were followed by a few curious townspeople expecting to see in Rogier an Acherontic, white-bearded maniac. They found him morose and untalkative, but undeniably in full possession of a blunt wit that flayed their hides whenever they managed to goad him into an argument. When towards the last of the summer a few tourists began to ride up the gulch upon hearing exaggerated tales, Rogier could stand it no longer. At the first sight of a stranger approaching he would shout out of the cracked window of the hoist house for Cable to throw rocks at them from the dump.

Cable instead erected a "Keep Out – Private Property" sign at the turning. This, for the time at least, stopped the flow of visitors. The mere appearance of brawny Abe and Jake at their Saturday night orgies was enough to halt the talk in town. Work on the Sylvanite went on as usual. If March was infected by a doubt that the Sylvanite might not be all that Rogier promised, he did not show it.

Perhaps he was dreading his last visit to Charlotte. It came as it had to come. Madame Jones let him in, nodding toward the back sitting room. When Charlotte came in, he was still standing beside the taboret, his face flushed, a distressed look in his eyes.

"Charlotte!" he blurted out at once. "I'm goin'. I can't be comin' back no more."

"But March. School doesn't start for another week. You can come two more times."

"No. Daddy's taking me down tomorrow."

The girl stood still, smiled, bit her pale blue lips. One of her thin hands gently caressed her throat in a pathetic gesture of resignation. The boy's brown eyes clouded, filled with tears; and at sight of these, the girl's face took on an expression of unendurable hunger. Still she did not move.

"Good-bye, Charlotte. I like you – I – " Suddenly, one foot in the doorway, he blurted out with a sob, "Charlotte. You never have – aren't you going to kiss me good-bye?"

The girl, in one stride and with a face suddenly transfigured, was on him like a panther. Frail, light, and all nerves, she lifted him off his feet with unbelievable strength and kissed him with rapacious ferocity.

When finally she loosed him, the boy backed hastily away and stood looking at her with an astonishment sharpened by an edge of fear. He lifted a hand to his burning lips; one of them was slightly cut and bleeding. "I never knew you were so strong, Charlotte. You hurt my lip."

Charlotte backed to a chair and sat down stiffly. Her two hands raised to clasp her head; the long loose sleeves of her dress fell down to reveal, in the thin white sunlight filtering through the curtains, her frail white wrists through which could be seen the tracery of blue veins. Her face, from the color of wet cement, changed to a white marble. Then, giving way to the pressure of a flood of some long damned up desire, it broke into a horrible grimace of pain and guilt that disfigured forever the boy's memory of her girlish smile. "God forgive me!" she whispered. "Not you, March. Not you!"

The boy could endure it no longer. "I don't care," he shouted hoarsely with a frightened sob. "I like you better than ever!" Flinging open the door, he fled down the hall to the street outside without stopping to tell Madame Jones good-bye.

Charlotte never saw him again.

But the boy saw her once more. It came about through one of those inexplicable juxtapositions of time and place that men are wont to call coincidences, but which in long perspective sometimes reveal a deep intent. The occurence was rationally simple. Cable up at the mine had been sick, and Ona was worried. "Oh, if I only could be sure he saw a doctor or took medicines or something. He just won't buy them, I know!"

The difficulty was solved simply enough when March offered to ride up to the mine Saturday morning, promising to return Sunday afternoon. So he had taken the train with a bulky package of cough medicine, liniment, a hot water bag, and a miscellany of cold remedies.

It was late October. The bare hillsides had lost the yellow scarlet, and russet cloaks flung over them by aspen, scrub oak, and ivy. The Peak was white, the mountains marine blue – a cold, clear background against which the unpainted timbers of the frames and the shanties of the camps stood out as desolate refugees from approaching winter. March got off the train at Cripple Creek, intending to take the Low Line to Victor. Abe or Jake was to meet him there with a burro so that he would not have to walk up the gulch to the Sylvanite. The cold wind whipping down Poverty Gulch rustled the paper package under his arm. His cheeks were red as apples. He was smiling as he turned down Myers Avenue; there was just time to say hello to Charlotte.

He was too wrapped up in his anticipations to surprise her to notice the black crepe hung on the door, and the solemn row of girls sitting in the parlor. Madame Jones appeared. She was wearing a stiff black taffeta dress, long silver earrings, and a cold officious manner that set off her sharp, frigid face.

"Boy, what are you doing here now?" she demanded.

"Can I see Charlotte – just a minute, Madame Jones?" he asked, frightened a little.

"She's not here. Still over at Fairley and Lampman's. Maybe they'll let you see her," she said harshly.

The boy backed out, feeling a chill premonition congealing all thought. Slowly, as if on wooden legs, he edged around the corner, down the street. There it was, inescapable: Fairley Bros. and Lampman's Undertaking Parlors.

Somehow he managed to walk inside. The parlor for the moment was empty. A big fern hung down from a stand at the window. Several chairs stood on the plush green carpet. Then on a table he noticed a large glass case. It was filled with relics of notable people who had been laid out at the mortuary: a lock of red hair from famous Pearl De Vere of the Old Homestead, the combs of Two-Go Ruby who had swallowed strychnine, the pistol of a gambler who had shot himself through the mouth. "The last of £10,000!" flashed through March's mind.

Abruptly there exploded behind him the voice of a man who

had walked out of the morgue. "A pretty collection of doodads, hey!"

March spun around, all his insides suddenly melted. "Charlotte! Is she here? I mean – "

The man let out a guffaw. "If it don't beat all hell! Kids in knee pants, old codgers with canes, muckers, and gents. What that skinny slip of a girl had to draw'em all is beyond me!" When the boy did not answer, he added gruffly, "Sure. Till the funeral this afternoon at three. Want a look?"

March followed him to the morgue in back. He had never seen a corpse; but under the compulsion of a horror whose meaning he had not yet fully accepted, he looked into the coffin. It was Charlotte and yet it wasn't Charlotte. Her head, framed by her dark brown hair, rested on a small silk pillow; her bony fragile hands were crossed over her breast; she appeared at first to be sleeping a sleep profound and restful. It was her face that appalled him: white with a whiteness no rouge and powder could color; immobile with a frigidity that forebade anything to open eyes or lips, to crinkle those two tiny wrinkles at the corner of one eyelid. Something was gone – a mysterious something he had never thought about till now, when he first noticed its absence; the one mysterious something no man has ever fully defined.

With one wail, "Charlotte, she's dead!" he flung out the door.

Cable was waiting for him with two burros at Victor, and during their long jog up the gulch March sobbed out at last the story of his meetings with Charlotte all summer. It was a confession, for it was impacted somehow by a sense of guilt he could not quite define. "Myers Avenue? Madame Jones' place, eh?" murmured Cable gently. "I don't recollect the name. The third house from the corner, you say? Well, anyway, I reckon we better go to the funeral, son."

Dinner was on the table in the cabin when they arrived. It was a miserable meal. Abe and Jake had shaved and were dressed up in their Sunday suits of black and bulldog-toed shoes, ready to leave for Cripple Creek. Rogier was grouchy because they were taking off so early. And March couldn't eat.

Abe and Jake kept squirming on their bench. Finally Jake broke out, "Don't say nothin' more about her! It's disrespectful to keep harpin' on the dead! If we're goin', let's go!"

Cable gave them a quick penetrating look. "Is that what you're headin' for?"

"We done sent the Madame our contribution," Abe said defiantly.

They straggled down the gulch: March and Cable, still a little weak from spending several days in bed, on burros; Abe and Jake, grim-faced, striding beside them without speaking. The funeral services had begun when they arrived at Fairley and Lampman's. The small parlor was full, forcing them to stand in back for the sermon, prayer, and hymns. Not until they stepped outside did they realize the loyalty death engendered. The coffin was being loaded in an open hearse. Along the walk and behind it in the street a crowd had gathered: all the girls in Madame Jones' establishment, inmates from the other houses on Myers Avenue, people of the Tenderloin, miners and muckers and children from the shanties of Poverty Gulch.

Abe, who had bought a nosegay of flowers, thrust it into Jake's hands. He, just as abashed, edged up to the hearse where Madame Jones was standing. She gave him one withering look, and another to Jake and March and Cable.

"Well, I'll be Goddamned," she muttered, but with no other sign of recognition. "Put 'em on the hearse, you fool! They ain't for me, are they?"

Slowly the hearse moved away, followed by a dozen rigs and buggies, and people on foot. As the procession headed up Bennett, men lounging along the street, too ashamed to attend the funeral, accelerated their pace until they caught up with the crowd. Others loafing in the saloons drank up and hurriedly left the bars. March trudged along silently with Cable, Abe, and Jake. The sun was gone; a raw wind whipped coat tails and scarfs. The grade was steep. He could hear the squeak of wagon wheels in the dreary silence. Utterly miserable, he kept blowing his cold nose every few steps. Up the hill he looked back. Gray clouds were beginning to droop over the tops of Mineral and Tenderfoot Hill, and Gold and Globe Hill were hazy in the mist. Cripple Creek below him looked like a jumbled mass of toy brick buildings and wooden shanties that had been let down from the sky in a handkerchief. It was all so desolate, so dreary and cold; the boy shivered in the wind, remembering the flowered hillsides of summer. The Mt. Pisgah cemetery they now entered was more desolate still.

It lay on the slope, sparsely covered with withered brown grass. The graves were dug in the frost shattered granite, many of them blasted out of the solid rock. Each was surrounded by a picket fence to keep out wolves and coyotes. The wooden headboards which still resisted wind, rain, and snow were gaudily covered with scrolls and sentimental epitaphs.

> Here lies Richard Dunn
> Who was killed by a gun
> His real name was Pryme,
> But that wouldn't rhyme.

Nearby stood a great granite boulder with no other marking save the simple statement. "Here lies the only man who called Bill Smith a liar."

The cemetery was divided into two sections: the lower half for good, respectable folk; the upper half, on the high saddle of the hill, for the unknown and poverty stricken, the denizens of the Tenderloin. Here the procession stopped and grouped about an empty grave. The coffin was lowered. The preacher, the long tail of his frock coat flapping about his legs, finished speaking and praying. Now a group of girls began singing a hymn. One of them turned to mumble in another's ear. The Madame in front whirled around. "You there! Shut up!"

Across from them miners, gamblers, workmen and parasites, pimps and prostitutes, storekeepers and druggists appreciating the Madame's trade – they all stood there in the profound silence of the hills, attesting by their own silence the solidarity of mankind, bound together for the moment by her whose fraility was at once their weakness and their strength, the invincible bond of final brotherhood.

March, for the life of him, could not reconcile his memory of Charlotte with the body in the grave being sealed in the granite slope of Mt. Pisgah. Frail Charlotte, who with her short and awry life, her folly, grace, and alloted wisdom, was yet among the applauded and successful, the dissolute and the damned, the failures and forgotten, who had lent their lives in the desolate region for uncounted others to build upon.

The ragged hymn stopped. The grave was filled in and a few bunches of flowers placed on top. And now March saw a bare-headed scarecrow stagger up toward the preacher. From the pocket of his long coat protruded the neck of a bottle, and in his arms he bore a wooden headboard lettered in black. The sharpened end of the stick on which it was nailed he stuck into the head of the mound. March recognized him from the purple sash worn around the outside of his coat, and the brass horn stuck inside it – Joe Dobbs, the Poet Laureate of Cripple Creek.

Turning around, Mr. Dobbs pulled the bugle out of his sash, blew "Taps" upon it. Then pointing to the epitaph on the headboard, he recited:

> Here lies the body of sweet Charlotte,
> Born a virgin, died a harlot
> For fifteen years she kept her virginity;
> A damn good record for this vicinity.

The preacher intoned a sonorous "Amen!" Madame Jones with a curt, "Let's get going, girls!", herded her flock into their hired rig. And behind it, in the bitter dusk, March trudged back to town with Cable, Abe, and Jake.

6

Rogier was worried. There was no doubt the world was beginning to turn against him. He was equally convinced the world was wrong. Julian Street, a journalist of great repute, had come to cover the Pike's Peak region for *Collier's Weekly*. Rogier read his write-up after he was feted and dined by the elite of Broadmoor and the North End. To his bread-and-butter compliments, his superficial appraisal of Little London, Rogier paid no heed. But when Street referred to the Garden of the Gods as "a pale pink joke," he began to smile. Rogier continued reading:

"Houses elaborate as the Grand Trianon – lend themselves best to formal, park-like country which is flat; while Elizabethan and adopted Tudor houses seem to cry out for English lawns and great lush growing trees to soften the hard lines of roof and gable. Such houses may be set in rolling country with good effect, but in the face of the vast mountain range which dominates this neighborhood the most elaborate architecture is so completely dwarfed as to seem almost ridiculous. Architecture cannot compete with the Rocky Mountains; the best thing it can do is to submit to them: to blend itself into the picture as unostentatiously as possible."

Rogier leaned back, slapped his leg, and roared – his only laugh in months. "By Jove! The same thing I told that Mr. Andrews years ago! Thank God for one honest newspaper scribbler!" He immediately rushed out for an armload of more copies. The clippings he pasted to his own lettered stationery and mailed out to all his potential clients.

A few days later Julian Street rode up to Cripple Creek and got off at the Short Line depot. Walking up Third Street, he turned east on Myers Avenue, and was invited into a crib by a Madame Leo. He talked with her possibly an hour, then rushed back to catch his train on its return trip to Little London. Rogier, with all the district, anxiously awaited his reportage on world-famous Cripple Creek.

His article appeared that November. Of the town itself, which he hadn't seen, Street had little to say save that it was "one of the most depressing places in the world. Its buildings run from shabbiness to downright ruin; its streets are ill-paved, and its outlying districts are a horror of smokestacks, ore dumps, shaft houses, reduction plants, gallows frames, and squalid shanties situated in the mud." The Madame's remarks he reported at length, including her request to send her up some "nice boys" from Little London for business was poor. Street also casually mentioned that Cripple Creek was above "cat-line" as well as timber-line, as domestic cats couldn't live at such high altitude.

At this view of itself as seen by the unprejudiced eye of the world below, Cripple Creek set up a furious howl. Housewives and whores had cats by the hundreds sent up from Little London to prove Street's assertion false. Indignation meetings were held in churches and parlors. Protests were wired to *Collier's Weekly*, demanding refutation of the article. When nothing availed, the City Council formally passed a resolution changing the name of Myers Avenue to Julian Street.

Rogier, deeply hurt, sulked through the excitement. The world was contemptuous of Cripple Creek. The district was on the wane; everybody knew it. Production was still falling, the population decreasing. Electric cars over both the Low and High Line were more infrequent. Two men were overcome by gas in the Star of Bethlehem.

Up at the Sylvanite things were worse. Rogier was quite aware that insidious gossip was calling the mine the Pike's Peak Bubble. Even Abe and Jake kept talking of giving it up and finding a better one for him to lease. And Cable had a bad chest, coughing for hours after drilling down below with the Zebbelins, and writhing in agony each night with pleurisy. Moreover, there was no money to pay him to meet the expenses of Ona and the children. Reluctantly Rogier sent him back down to Little London for the winter.

"Just for the winter, mind!" he insisted. "We'll hit shipping ore again by spring, and need your help!"

With Cable gone, Rogier himself carried the weekly samples to the assayer's office. Grim, aloof, and dignified, he would mount a shaggy little burro and ride down the gulch, his legs dangling, his white head swathed and bent in contemplation. The errand took all day; for he no longer trusted the assayer's report, and insisted on watching the handling of his precious samples.

The assays were cheap, being simple fire assays for gold in low-grade ore instead of expensive and complete chemical analyses. Too, the assayer was an old, mild, tobacco-chewer whom Rogier could bully without rousing a frown of resentment on his placid homely face. His office was a dilapidated brick building from which one end had been torn out to make a great furnace. He usually ran through twenty to thirty assays at a firing. Rogier stuck with him to the end, shivering with cold in the outer room where the ore was crushed; sweating in front of the great furnace as he waited for the small bone-ash cups to be removed with long tongs. But never in his own cup a globule of gold and silver bigger than a pin head.

"No!" he would exclaim. "Sure you didn't get my sample mixed up with one of these others, Simms?"

The old assayer did not reply. He only sat there spitting tobacco and gazing mildly out of his rheumy blue eyes at one of a thousand men who had read their success or failure from the work of his hands. Then, with a benign glance he continued his work, weighing the infinitesmal speck and computing its contents.

"Less than a quarter ounce! Good God, man!" Rogier would snort. Then throwing down a dollar, he would stride out into the bitter dusk, straddle his mousy burro, and jog slowly back to the Sylvanite.

Supper was waiting. Rogier announced the assay, and sat down to eat in silence. In a few moments he pushed back his plate. It was time for the usual before-bedtime argument. "Dom that old fool Simms!" he began. "Reckon he's trying to pull the wool over our eyes?"

"Told you that sample wasn't no good," said Abe gently.

"You watched him run it," added Jake.

"I tell you we've got gold here!" boomed Rogier. "What I want to know now is why we're not gettin' any place?"

"It ain't you, Colonel. You're a smart man, like I always said. And it ain't us either; we do our work. What I think" – Jake looked around with a solemn expression of deep wisdom – "is that it's the Sylvanite. She's just played out. Now I was a-talkin' the other day," he continued swiftly, "and found out we could lease the Paint Brush real cheap. Just givin' up the Sylvanite for a spell."

At this Rogier's fist came down on the table with a bang. The Zebbelins had anticipated it, merely raising their refilled coffee cups. "No, by Jove! Never! You boys are stickin' to the Sylvanite till Hell freezes over! There'll be no more such talk!"

Jake, always scared half out of his trousers by the demoniacal fury in Rogier's eyes, scraped back his chair an inch. Abe dropped his glance, stroked his whiskers, and took a long swig from his coffee cup.

Rogier changed his tactics by reiterating his prophecy that here someday would be found treasures greater than Croesus ever took from the sands of the Pactolus or Solomon from the mines of Ophir. Right here!

"Ain't never heard of them fellers or mines either, and I asked about them," grumbled the sulky Jake.

"Exceeding the amount of gold Cecil Rhodes took from the mountains of South Africa, then," went on Rogier. "Deposits that will make the fortunes of Tom Walsh, Tabor, and Stratton look like a poor man's bread tax. You've heard of them, hey? Not gold *ore*, Jake, you dom fool, that has to be shipped to the mill in carloads. You remember what I told you about breaking into a stope floored with grains of gold sand you can scrape up in sacks, whose walls and ceilings are hung with gold crystals? Glistening, glittering like an Aladdin's Cave! It's here under our feet somewhere. No, boys, I won't let you leave me now. You've been too faithful and suffered too many disappointments for that. You've got to stay and get your share!"

At night he could not sleep, so vivid were these images he had evoked. Tossing in his bunk, he would grit his teeth, compose himself, and command his tense body to relax. And through the planks of the bunk, through floor and earth and granite, from the deep heart below, would come the measured rhythmic beat of the cosmic pulse of the Peak. With it throbbing in his aching head, he would get up, wrapped in his blankets, and stare out the window.

It was winter now, clear and bitter cold, the mountains white and blue—a deep marine blue from which foamed like crested choppy waves the snowy peaks. Hemmed in on three sides, the little cabin looked down upon the pale and pitiless world of frozen white. Now at night and in moonlight the long narrow gulch took on the pale violet aspect of a frozen arm of the sea or the greenish cold glitter of an alkaline river bed. From his window Rogier could see the formless shadows of deer trafficking like ghosts to the corral for scraps of hay. An owl hooted dismally from the top of the gallows frame; the faint howl of gaunt cruising timber wolves carried over the ridge; a dead pine cracked with the cold; a cougar screamed like a frightened child;—and all these sounds seemed woven from the same warp and weft as the eerie silence.

What made him so sure of what lay deep below? Instinct was not enough. Nor was reason, the strata above it. But superseding both existed that mysterious realm of intuition to which Rogier gave full allegiance. For if the one was the perception of the bodily senses, and the other that of the calculating mind, this was the apperception of the spirit transcending both. A consciousness timeless and spaceless, so limitless that it informed every drop in the sea, every grain of the earth, every breath of air, every cell in the tiny organism of man. Formless and unproven, denied and refuted as it might be, he knew it for the one ground fact underlying all lesser facts reflected from it. Yes, by Jove! It told him, over and over, what he had always known without knowing that he knew. It told him all he wanted to know. And every trip down into the Sylvanite confirmed it.

Getting into his boots and overalls, he would crawl into the rusty iron bucket with his sputtering carbide lamp. As he began to slide slowly down the shaft his troubles and worries flitted upward like the faint splotches of daylight on the cribbing. Now, dropping swiftly down, he gathered to himself the consoling mystery of the deep velvety blackness rushing up to engulf him. He took no heed of the rude jolts as the bucket knocked against the sides of the shaft, the dull somber ring of iron against stone, a flurry of sparks, the quick spin of the bucket. Crouched inside, Rogier watched over the rim the roughhewn rock glimmering in the faint light of the lamp held on his knee. He could see a micaceous glitter in the granite like that of artificial snow sprinkled on a child's Christmas tree. In the glint of pearls in the cracks he imagined that he could hear and see the slow musical drip of water from above in a silence thick, cloying and profound.

At the first level Rogier would get out and walk the length of the drift, exulting like a man returning to his native haunts. Quick, sharp, and hollow, the sound of his steps echoed along the abandoned passages, his lamp crawling through the eternal dusk like a phosphorescent bug. Always he could have flung his arms aloft with joy, feeling above him the solid mass of rock. He was below the horizon of mankind's eyes; the wrinkled crust of the earth men trod so lightly, heedless of what lay beneath; below the tides of river and sea, ever contracting and expanding under the influence of moon and sun; the dreary surface of an earth stained by men's blood and tears, fought over and furrowed—below grass roots at last! And staring upward, he fancied he saw the ends of those mortal roots of a life he had escaped at last. On top of him stood the mighty Peak—a reassuring weight that gave him comfort.

But still on the sheer sides of winze and stope he saw evidence of surface life: brown streaked rock oxidized by the carbolic acid contained in seepage water from melting snows. And he would walk back to the level station and impatiently ring the bell. Then he would go down to the second level, to the third and fourth in turn, prowling alone through abandoned drifts, stopes, and cross-cuts. And the deeper he descended, the more secure he felt. Often he hooked his lamp to the wall and stood staring into the unfathomable gloom of a cavernous stope. The darkness and silence were thick, impenetrable; they merged into what seemed a new element. Then suddenly it congealed about him as if frozen into the resistant immobility of solid rock. Now he stood motionless. The old queer sensation came upon him that he too was of that stony flesh which pressed against his own, that it too lived and breathed and echoed to the pulse of a hidden heart. He could feel its rhythmic beat, feel it close around him and adhere with the familiar and comforting illusion of adding to him another strata of being.

And now for an instant he lost his sense of balance, direction, and gravity. It was as if he were metamorphosed into a creature who, like a fly, could walk and stand head down. He faced only the earth's depths which so intrigued him: the hundred miles or less of the upper crust from which had been thrust the Peak and its shoulder mountains; the underlying 2,000-mile-thick mantle; and the vast hollow core at whose center, 4,000 miles down, lay the fiery heart which radiated solar energy throughout the arterial structure of the earth's stony flesh with a temperature of perhaps 6,000° Fahrenheit under a pressure of some 3,000,000 tons per square foot. The conjectured measurements meant nothing at all to him. His own divinations, like X-rays, cut through distance, pressure, and temperature without rational impedance. Rogier, dizzy with the vision that suddenly possessed him, sank down on his haunches, bent over, and held his head in his hands. It was as if he were on the verge of a vast abyss, at the perimeter of the aura of an undiscovered sun in the center of his planet, fixed and immutable within a universe duplicating the one outside.

The vision,, with all the force of indisputable truth, vehemently refuted the unsubstantiated theories that the interior of his planet was solid, molten, or gaseous. What need had his earth of another sun millions of miles away in outer space? Here it had its own. Was not every soul, mineral, plant, animal, and man answerable alone to one immutable law, and sufficient unto itself? Was there not a living world constructed within a drop of water, a grain of sand, a microscopic cell invisible to the naked eye? Let men stand alone then, self-reliant and serene in their own completeness, admitting the universality within their own earth as within themselves, and ceasing their scientific prattle of other alien worlds far off in space.

Here beneath their feet was the one disregarded mystery of all time: a vast subterranean universe upon whose surface they trod without a thought for what lay below. Where, oh where, were the intrepid explorers of modern scientific thought? Diving like frogs into the shallow seas, ballooning aloft into the air; thoughtless fools to whom the subterranean core of their own earth was so mysteriously unknown that they ignored it to conquer others! Thousands of years behind the intuitive ancients, they did not yet know that at the center of their own earth lay the golden sun of life, surrounded by its galaxies and constellations.

And crouching there in the abysmal darkness until his spell wore off, Rogier felt rise within him the power of his unalterable conviction. He would get down yet, through porphyry, through granite, to that golden heart.

Abe, working in one end of the drift, caught the tiny flicker of Rogier's lamp and glimpsed his shadowy figure staring off into the invisible depths. He walked up quietly. Rogier straightened up, and they glanced into each other's eyes.

"Quittin' time, Colonel. Let's go up."

And ringing the bell for Jake at the hoist, they rose again to surface. Suppertime came when they could not escape the inevitable.

"What we goin' to do now, Colonel?" asked Jake. "We finished cross-cuttin' like you said, and there's no more sign of a lead than of a jack rabbit in heavy brush."

"Go down another level. You'll find it," answered Rogier promptly.

"Shaft sinking costs money and you ain't got it," Abe said tersely.

Rogier jumped to his feet. "I know you haven't been paid for a month! Why don't you say so!" he screamed.

Said Abe quietly, "We ain't said nothin' about that, Colonel. We said shaft sinking costs a might of money. That's all."

Rogier sat down. "I'll get the money. I don't know how. But I do know there's an almighty power in which I trust completely. Whatever you call it, whatever it is, it won't let the Sylvanite down."

Four days later the letter came. Rogier's bid for the construction of two big additions to the high school in Little London had been accepted — a job running to almost $90,000.

Rogier was jubilant as he left to board the train. "Keep goin' down. The money will keep comin' up. Hey? I'll see you come spring!"

7

When Cable came down from the Sylvanite, Ona was shocked at his appearance. He was gaunt, hollow cheeked, and coughed continually. Shaved and cleaned up, he looked worse. His high Indian cheek bones seemed ready to protrude from a skin that had lost its dark swarthiness and was now an unhealthy yellow. His big dark eyes were somber and without luster. At night as he lay wrapped in her arms, she could feel his ribs, hear his labored breathing, feel the damp cold exuding from his pores in a perspiration that left his pajamas wet next morning. Only after a stiff drink of whiskey upon arising was he warm at all.

"Jonathan, you're sick. Really sick. Please see a doctor."

"Just a cold and that pleurisy," he answered. "Nothing to worry about."

And yet she did worry tremendously. He was not like himself – alert and rhythmically alive, though silent, to everything about him. He was dull, tired, apathetic. Not even their long guarded talks of what to buy the children for Christmas aroused him.

"We haven't got much money, as you know," he said with a quiet smile, "but buy them just what they want. Let the rest of the folks slide; they don't matter."

How he loved his children! Always his patient smile rested upon them like a benediction; his long brown hands, once smooth and tender as a woman's but now hard, calloused, chapped, and split open, were forever finding excuses to touch them – tying hair-ribbons, lacing shoes, brushing tousled hair back from their smooth foreheads.

For days he was content to sit at home by the fire, warming, resting. Oh no! This was not her Jonathan! What business had he being confined in a cold dark mine high up in the snowy mountains? He belonged to the wide wind-swept plains he loved so well.

That Saturday, a warm and sunny one, Indian Poe, the vegetable huckster, came by as usual with his rickety wagon. He was an old Cheyenne, dark, wrinkled, with long greasy black hair. Because he and Cable long had been friends, Ona always patronized him – although, too, his vegetables were always fresh and cheap. Cable walked out to the street with Ona to see him, giving him the tribal sign. Indian Poe for answer merely laid his dark hand on Cable's arm. For a minute they talked in Cheyenne while Ona looked at lettuce and radishes. Then Poe asked in English, "Long time. Where you been?"

Cable replied that he had been up in the mountains hunting for gold. "Gold. Big nuggets, see?" Grinning, he marked the size of a marble in the air with his thumb and forefinger.

The old Indian gave him a penetrating stare and grunted. Then he reached into his wagon and brought out a clump of unwashed beets. From it he picked a lump of dirt the size of a marble and handed it to Cable. "Gold no good for Indian. This more better."

Cable laughed. Slowly his face changed as he crumpled the dirt between his fingers. "No, no good for Indian."

When Ona had filled her apron with vegetables, Cable climbed up on the plank seat to ride with Indian Poe on his rounds. Ona watched them drive off. The old Indian in his ragged coat was humped over the reins, head down. Cable beside him, in his tidy coat and shined boots, duplicated the posture. Like blood-brothers bowed under the same insupportable weight, they sat mutely staring at the plodding feet of the broomtail team.

Every Saturday it was the same. Cable made the rounds with

Indian Poe: up and down the streets, ringing a little brass bell, stopping to let housewives inspect the trays of vegetables in the decrepit wagon. Ona, upon seeing them, bit her lip. The ride was getting Cable out into the sun, of course. But God had made her a Rogier, and she could not restrain an involuntary shudder at the thought people might think Jonathan was a vegetable huckster with that ragged old Indian.

He finally got a job, but it did not deter him from making his Saturday rounds with Indian Poe. His position was that of a salesman for a life insurance company. The opening was fortuitous. The incumbent had died suddenly, leaving a section of town to be covered, weekly collections to be made, and new policies to be written. A man who could be trusted was needed at once; and that man was the son-in-law of the builder Rogier, whose work crew the company wanted to insure.

The opportunities seemed boundless. Cable was representing a fine company, associating with businessmen, and making new friends throughout a fast growing town. Ona and Cable were both delighted. So every morning he would stride off to work in his neatly pressed suit and freshly shined handmade boots. But every night it seemed he came home later. There had been a sales meeting he had to attend after work, or a prospect to talk to in the evening, or something else.

One morning the head of the office, Mr. Perkins, dropped in to invite Ona to the sales meeting that evening. It was the policy of the company, he said, to enlist the support of the wives of the representatives in the great effort being made to insure the welfare of the community. "We're all one big family, you know. We want you with us."

Ona was glad to go with Cable, and took along March. The small office uptown was crowded with the "one big family" of twelve salesmen, their wives, and a few children. Mr. Perkins, big-boned and florid, with a gold-mounted elk's tooth swinging from his watch chain, was in his element. He stood before them, making a speech like that of a football coach urging his team into battle. He expounded the prime importance of life insurance in the health, wealth, and happiness of the entire country, and the recalcitrant Pike's Peak Region. He revealed the necessity of bringing this divine message to every man and woman in the community. It could only be accomplished, he reminded them, by the constant, unremitting, and devoted work of those chosen twelve representatives who, like the chosen twelve disciples of another cause whose name he did not need to mention, were dedicated to this task.

"Every minute of the day," he thundered, "they must carry this sense of obligation to duty. Every person they meet must be regarded as a possible candidate for a policy. And when they go to bed at night, they must review in detail their accomplishments and how to better them next day. And to aid them, they need the whole-hearted, unstinted support of their wives and children—this one big family.

"The reward will be great," he continued. "We are making a sixty-day drive, and the family of the winning salesman—the one who writes the largest dollar amount of life insurance—will be given a free, all-expense-paid trip to Denver with accommodations in the world-famous Brown Palace Hotel!" He paused a moment. "Now, for the results to date!"

Mr. Perkins wheeled out from behind him a large blackboard and turned it around to face his audience. On it was chalked the names of the twelve chosen salesman with the dollar amounts of the insurance they had written up to date. Cable's name was at the bottom of the list.

Ona glanced at Cable. He sat there stiffly upright, his face impassive above his high white collar.

Mr. Perkins expostulated the virtues of Mr. Devoe at the head of the list. He reviewed the eminent qualifications of Number Two and Number Three. He kindly pointed out the methods and means by which Numbers Four to Eleven could improve their lagging records. "And now, Number Twelve, our Mr. Jonathan Cable. He is new to us. His feet are not yet solidly rooted in the ground of insurance, of life insurance. He needs our support, the support of his family who are with him tonight. And let me postulate the hope, let me prophecy, that with their whole-hearted endeavor, their unstinted devotion to the cause, they well may rise step by step, and perhaps win three whole days, magnificent days, at the Brown Palace in Denver!"

Cable, Ona, and March trudged slowly back home. Cable went

down to stoke up the furnace while Ona put March to bed. "Was Mr. Perkins makin' fun of Daddy in front of all those people?" asked March. "Why didn't he get up and hit him?"

"On no," answered Ona. "That's business, son."

Next week Cable bought a bicycle. Having no buggy or automobile, he had found that it was too tedious walking to make his rounds. The bicycle was a short, squat one, with the paint peeling off its rusty iron, and it had no brakes. Cable had leather toe-clips installed on the pedals; in these he thrust his handmade boots – the foot fetish of every Indian. The seat was small, the handlebars high. Often March saw him peddling past school, a long, lank Ichabod from whose coat pocket protruded his long stiff-covered account book.

"He looks like an Indian who oughta be ridin' a horse!" shouted his schoolmates. "Why don't you tell your Dad he needs a haircut!"

March had nothing to say. He remembered the father he had known at Shallow Water, the dark and taciturn horseman who had faced down Black Kettle's son. He remembered the strong and gentle man who had sorted ore on the Sylvanite dump at Cripple Creek, and cooked suppers for Abe and Jake and Rogier in the cabin at Cripple Creek. And he couldn't reconcile them with the man he saw now. Cable on his bicycle and on the plank seat with Indian Poe had become another strange character in town. But when Cable arrived home at night, jumped off his bicycle, and clasped him, heart to heart, in a quick and close embrace, then he knew this was his father, his only father, the guiding hand at Shallow Water, at the Sylvanite, the strange and wonderful man who was his father whatever he seemed now.

That winter Mary Ann returned home to the old house on Shook's Run for the first time since she had left town. There was no doubt she expected to stay, for her trunk and bags arrived with her. Nancy took one look at them and let out a scream of joy. "Mother! You're back! Oh, I've been so lonesome!"

Mary Ann gave her a hasty kiss. "Lonesome? With your grandmother and grandfather here, Ona and Jonathan coming down, and March and Leona to go to school with? Why don't you run up to their house now and tell them all to come down to supper tonight? Tell them I'm back and I've got somebody I want them to meet."

When Nancy had gone, she settled down in the parlor with Mrs. Rogier for a short preliminary talk before the rest of the family arrived. The need for it was soon obvious. Mary Ann during her absence had been divorced at last from her husband Cecil Durgess. Mrs. Rogier shuddered. She had been spared the disgrace of a public court hearing, with hundreds of persons flocking in to witness the severing of bonds of holy matrimony between a member of the Rogier family and a husband to whom she had sworn to be faithful till death did them part. There had not even been an announcement in the *Gazette*; it had been simply a matter of signing some papers sent to Mary Ann by mail, or something. Still it was a blow.

"Now, Mother," said Mary Ann pertly. "It's nothing to be sorry about. Cecil was a no-account bum, and you know it. I was glad to get rid of him. And besides, divorces are dime-a-dozen these days."

She then led up to another subject just as delicate. She had brought back with her a fine gentleman, a firm friend, to stay with her until they found another and better business opportunity. "Jim's a dear. You'll love him. I met him in Salida while I was in business there – but I'll tell you all about that this evening. Anyway there's a possibility, a distinct possibility, that Jim and I may establish a closer relationship than one of business associates, if you know what I mean. That's why I think he should stay here with me, so we can all get acquainted."

"Here? Living in this house? Mary Ann!"

"A roomer, Mother. Just like Jonathan before he and Ona got married. Certainly you have no objection to that!" she said sharply.

"But wouldn't it be more circumspect if he found accommodations elsewhere?" murmured Mrs. Rogier.

"Rats! Neither one of us has much money left after settling up our business. We'll take the two middle rooms on the second floor. Nancy can move up to the third floor."

"But – "

"Good, It's all settled then. I'll have our trunk moved up there before Jim comes."

Supper that evening was something of a strain. Not that Jim wasn't a big, simple, likeable fellow. But Nancy was jealous of the attention her newly restored mother gave him, and resented giving up her room to him. And Mary Ann dominated the table with talk of her new business career. Having been married to Cecil Durgess, she had obtained from the famous Durgess catering firm many fine recipes, formulas, and trade secrets, and she had become an excellent candy maker and chocolate dipper. Resolving on a career for herself, she had opened a "Cande Shoppe" of her own in Salida. Here she had met Jim, temporarily out of work, and began teaching him the trade. Unfortunately, Salida, in the Rockies south of Leadville, was a rough and backward town that did not appreciate high quality candy and delicatessens.

"Chocolate creams with pure fruit centers, real butter instead of glucose, they could not appreciate at all," she indignantly proclaimed. "Of course I had to price them at seventy-five cents a pound. But they preferred peanut brittle at a quarter, sloppy fudge made out of cocoa instead of Swiss milk chocolate, which they could buy at any counter. And I simply refused to lower my high standards. No! Salida was not the place for me. So we simply closed up our Cande Shoppe and came here to stay until we can select the proper town."

She was a pert little woman with a face that seemed to have become sharpened of late; and Rogier, listening to her decisive voice, felt doubts that she was the shrewd businesswoman she fancied herself to be. For like most of the Rogier girls, brought up in the passionless stability and holy confines of the old house on Shook's Run, she had never betrayed any sense of business whatever. She had never been able to add up a row of figures, in fact. And this big fellow, Jim, likeable as he was, probably was no great help. Certainly Rogier would never have put him on his own payroll.

Still he viewed Mary Ann's return with something like a philosophical objectiveness. To him, high above human frailty and men's follies, she was like ore that the world had not assayed as pay dirt and had been returned home like a useless tailing. Yet he knew that a tailing thrown out on a dump might contain valuable minerals that would pay for extraction when the market price of the metal was high. So that what today was regarded as a tailing may not be such at another time.

Mary Ann and Jim settled down in the big house. Impractical and feisty as she was, Mary Ann was generous. She had brought

Nancy, Leona, and March handsome presents, and Jim could always be depended upon for a stick of licorice or a chocolate bar. That they soon quit paying Mrs. Rogier money for their board and room was not too much of a hardship. Mrs. Rogier simply kept drawing more from Rogier's advances on the High School Annex he was building. And from these large demands for household expenses, she always extracted a little to add to her sugar bowl. The time would come, she knew, when it would be their only bulwark against disaster.

8

Rogier's finally amended contract of $87,000 for the High School Annex called for one large classroom building adjoining the present structure and another to house the manual arts shops. Because the grounds were located within view of North Park, the plans had been drawn with an eye not only toward utility but also a pleasant appearance to offset the old tower-like school. Rogier understood it was one of his most important jobs. He was getting old—just turned seventy—and competition from younger builders had been very keen. Only his reputation as the town's oldest and most reliable contractor had won him the job.

Pressed to obtain money for the Sylvanite, he jumped into the job with abandon, letting sub-contracts as quickly as possible. Never in his life had he gone into partnership without losing money, and Ona warned him against doing so.

"Lighting and heating and plumbing are all very well, Daddy. But this concrete work is different. It's pure construction work you've always done yourself. And this man Deere you want to sub-contract – what do you know about him?"

"Nothing except he's in the business and you're not!" replied

Rogier irritably. "Besides, I'm in a hurry and can't do everything myself!"

So he signed. The work got under way with Rogier's large construction force managed by his old foreman Rawlings, a plumbing crew, and Deere's concrete men. Deere was a fat, jovial man with small, shoebutton eyes. Neither Rogier nor Rawlings liked him and kept out of his way as much as possible. The excavations were completed; concrete was poured; stone masons and brick layers were brought in; the walls went up quickly.

As the work advanced, Deere became more and more over-bearing, stalking about the job, criticizing and applauding, over-harsh with some men and unduly familiar with others – acting in general like the lord and master of them all. This familiarity was unbearable to Rogier. He grew to abhor the sight of Deere, stalking away with contemptuous indifference whenever he saw the man approaching.

Rawlings, usually so mild and uncomplaining, remonstrated to Rogier about something Deere had done. "Why, the other night an hour before quittin' time two two-ton trucks pulled up there at the side. And there was that gosh-blamed Deere having the day laborers collect scrap lumber for him to take home! It ain't his wood. They wasn't his men neither; they were on our time."

Rogier blinked at the petty trick. Always it had been understood that on all his jobs the waste lumber was to be given to his men to haul home for kindling.

"Now, Rawlings," he said, holding his temper down, "you tell the men personally that after quittin' time they can gather up all the scrap lumber. Every jack-man can make his own pile to carry home or save until he gets a truck load. Then he can pay his own fifty cents to haul it away. That'll keep the place cleaned up. But no squabbling, mind!"

Rawlings noticed more incidents. Whenever Deere's concrete mixers needed moving on the job or in the town, it was always Rogier's teams or trucks which were called to do the work. And it was Rogier's carpenters whom Deere used to construct his forms. He was running a skeleton crew augmented by a vast amount of work done by Rogier's men which was not provided for in his sub-contract. Rawlings also noticed Deere hanging around the desk of the timekeeper Moody whenever Rogier was out of the office.

Rawlings said nothing of his suspicions to Rogier. His employer always had been a man for facts. Too, he had a stiff-necked pride so rooted in his own integral honesty that he could never believe in baseness from any man he once had accepted. Even in his few squabbles with Deere he had been courteous enough to lead the man out of ear-shot from all employees. And invariably he addressed him as "Mr. Deere," a formality that Deere never reciprocated.

But what was wrong with Rogier, to be so blind to the obvious? Rogier, he observed, was more nervous and erratic than ever before. And forgetful! In his office, half the time, he was staring at a sketch of a mining shaft instead of his own blueprints. And what was worse, he was gone days at a stretch – up to his blessed mine in the mountains.

Patient, faithful Rawlings! He could – and did – cuss Rogier daily with mild ejaculations of extreme annoyance. But for the man he had served for years beyond recall, whose family accepted him as an integrated part of Rogier's professional life, Rawlings had a deep affection and loyalty which never wavered. Unknown to anyone and long after hours, he began to feed his suspicions with fruitful observations.

One night just past eight o'clock when Rogier was in his shop, engrossed in a schematic of the Sylvanite, a knock sounded on the door. Thinking it was Mrs. Rogier or Ona come to disturb him, he did not even raise his head. Again the knock sounded, louder, more insistent. Rogier impatiently let down his legs from the high stool, and flung open the door to see Rawlings.

"Come in, man, come in!" he said gruffly.

"No sir. You come with me. I've got something to show you!"

There was that in Rawlings' sharp and obstinate voice which Rogier obeyed without question. The two men walked swiftly and in silence to the unfinished job. Rawlings produced a flashlight and led his employer into the tunnel connecting the two buildings. Here on a bench, his lantern and a half-empty pint of whiskey beside him, dozed the night watchman. With a kick Rogier sent the bottle splattering against the brick wall. At the sound of the shattering glass the watchman sat up, blinking his eyes. Before he could utter a word Rogier swung around, grabbed up a water pail, and drenched the man from head to toe.

"Where'd you get that bottle?" demanded Rogier.

"Mr. Deere give it to me," he whined, sputtering. "He said a little drop don't do a man no harm."

"Get off this property and get your time in the morning! If I see you hangin' around and whinin' to Deere, I'll have you arrested. Git!"

Then turning to Rawlings as the man vanished down the tunnel, Rogier demanded irritably, "Doggone it, man! Why can't you tend to things like this instead of bothering me?"

For answer Rawlings led Rogier out of the tunnel and pointed to the lighted window of Rogier's small wooden construction office across the lot. "Two or three nights a week they're in there, both of them."

The two men cautiously approached the shanty and peeked through the window. Moody the timekeeper was pointing to an entry in his big ledger. Deere, seated on top of Rogier's desk, threw back his head and let out a roar of laughter. Then, awkwardly bending forward, he patted Moody's arm.

Rogier, followed by Rawlings, yanked open the door and stepped inside. His sudden appearance snapped off Deere's laughter like an electric switch; the man's jaw dropped and hung as if caught by the fold of fat under his chin, his eyes opening wide with fright. Moody pushed back his chair, nervously closing the ledger and hugging it to his vest, his face red as a radish.

"You conniving yellow-livered poultroon!" thundered Rogier in the deathly silence. "And you, Moody – what are you doing here in my office this time of night? You and your tricks! Why, you ignorant little pen-pusher – I was in this business when you were in diapers. You can't fool me. If you can't keep up those books in the daytime there's a dozen others who can. You're keeping them for me, understand? Not Deere here. And the next time I catch you conflabbin' with him I'm going to kick you off this property so hard your pants are going to burn your back-side. Get out of here now!"

Nor could he wait for the frightened timekeeper to rise and crawl around his desk. He reached out a hand, grasped the man's high celluloid collar, and flung him out the door. For a moment he stood staring at Deere sprawled across the top of his desk.

"And you. By God! If I ever saw an unprincipled fat skunk, you're it. Struttin' around here like Mr. Jesus H. Christ himself. The Big Boss of the Whole Works. Tellin' Moody how to keep my books. Using my men. I told you once, like a gentleman, you were nothin' but a concrete pourer hired to do your work and keep out of my way. Are you deaf? Well, I'm tellin' you again you're workin' for me just like any hod carrier. Who told you to come in my office and lounge on my desk like a whore on a sofa? Get off!" He lunged forward, banging his hand down on the desk.

At the resounding slap beside him, Deere scrambled off and backed against the wall. His face was white; the muscles of his heavy jowls trembled; his small eyes blazed with fright and anger.

And still Rogier kept shouting with magnificent vituperation. He had jerked off his hat. His thin white hair was touseled, his face red, his body trembling with rage. He called Deere every name he could think of, insulted him beyond the endurance of any other man —and began again as if his insults and epithets were inexhaustible. Deere edged forward, intending to brush past and leave the shanty. Rogier stepped in front of him. "No, you don't, Deere! You're going to stay right here till I'm good and finished. And by God, man, if I have to thrash you within an inch of your life, it won't be here. I'll do it in front of every jack-man on the job!"

Deere slunk back.

Rawlings interposed. "Now that's settled! Mr. Rogier —" He was utterly shocked; and staring with unbelieving eyes at Rogier, he nervously began to pull his ears with hands that itched to shut out the astounding outburst. He could see so clearly the Rogier of years ago: walking in quietly and divining the truth of the situation at a glance; could hear him tersely ordering both men out with a cold merciless voice that forestalled talk; envisioned him swiftly going through the books, putting his finger on any discrepancies, and replacing both men at once — all without a trace of visible perturbation. Why, scarce half-dozen years ago he would never have forgotten himself thus. He simply would have called in an expert accountant and acted on the facts. But now! Rawlings kept pulling his ears with trepidation.

He suddenly noticed the ugly leer creeping into Deere's face. With a start he realized that Rogier had overstepped himself. A minute ago he could have walked out leaving Deere and Moody scared to death that he knew perfectly all their machinations. Now it was too late. Rawlings knew that Rogier did not realize the truths he had spoken. His anger was simply derived from his own injured pride and personal animosity against a man whom he could not help but instinctively hating—an outburst occasioned by perhaps no more than the sight of Deere sprawled across his own desk. And by the sneer on Deere's face, Rawlings knew that he too suspected as much. Rogier had only made an implacable enemy of the man who with Moody would resume his scheming more adroitly, now that he had been forewarned. And nothing that Rawlings could ever say would convince Rogier of his folly.

He turned suddenly as Rogier stopped talking and stood glaring at Deere. The concrete man returned his glare with a frightened but contemptuous sneer, grabbed up his hat and strode toward the door.

Rogier stepped back to let him pass. After a minute he slouched down at his desk and carefully smoothed out the rumpled blueprints. "There, by Jove!" he said finally. "That ought to teach him to behave himself!"

Rawlings, with a long sad face, sat pulling the lobes of his ears. He surmised correctly that this was to be Rogier's last big job.

9

Boné had written another immensely popular tune. He sent home a music sheet on whose cover was imprinted a picture of nebulous ghosts, and on whose margin was scribbled in pencil, "With apologies to 435 and the Kadles. Love. Boné." Mary Ann and Ona spread it out on the piano that evening; and sitting down on the bench, sang and played it to the family:

They squeak, they creep
And yowl and prowl,
Whoo – whoo – whoo?
Our old family ghosts!

Ending it with a crash of chords, Mary Ann spun around laughing. "Can you imagine a crazy thing like that! One of the best selling pieces in the country. Boné's done it again. Just like 'Ching, Ching, Chinaman'!"

"Nonesense!" ejaculated Rogier. "From a grown man, too. What about that symphony or something he was supposed to be doing?"

"His letter says it's going to be published in Vienna. But he's on another tour back East. When it's over he's going back to San

Francisco," answered Ona quietly.

"I do think he could have restrained himself from being so publicly facetious about our own home," added Mrs. Rogier.

Nancy scowled. "There's nothing funny about it. There's something I been meaning to tell you." She hesitated. "You know that bed I've sleeping in on the Third Floor. Facing the door of the little south room at the head of the steps. There's where it happens just after midnight."

"What?" asked Ona.

"A light. A pale round sort of light. It shines on the wall at the head of the steps for a long time. Then, just as slow, it slides along the wall and stops on the door of the little room on the landing." At the look on Rogier's face she raised her voice. "Granddad, I'm not fooling! I'm not a fraidy-cat either! It happens when the moon's shining and when it's dark. I pulled down the window blind so there wasn't any shine from the arc-light outside, I hollered once and I threw my shoe once. I tell you, it wasn't anybody and that light isn't natural. It's spooky."

Rogier's reaction was immediate and decisive. "Dom those Kadles! They've been keeping up this tomfoolery long enough. Their everlastin' squeakin' is bad enough without any more nonsense. I won't have it!"

He moved Nancy downstairs and hammered into place a big plank across the Third Floor stairs.

"Daddy, see what you've done!" said Ona testily. "Driven nails into the polished redwood bannister. And how is Mother to get her sheets and blankets off the bed, I'd like to know!"

"What's wrong with her crawling underneath that plank, she's little enough. But I say, let them rot." Gathering up his hammer and saw, Rogier clumped noisily down the stairs.

Nancy's resentment at sleeping on a cot was soon dissipated; she got her old room back. One night Jim left the house without saying goodbye. A week later Mary Ann, murmuring vaguely of another business opportunity offered her, left to open a Sweete Shoppe in Silverton.

Early that summer Rogier's High School Annex was finished and both buildings formally accepted. When the books were balanced, all men and accounts paid, there remained for Rogier a few trifling hundred dollars. Due to his own lack of acumen, the rascality of Moody and Deere now vacationing in California, and the fact that he had been diverting his profit to the Sylvanite, he was financially little better off than when he had started.

But he had put down the shaft another eighty feet – at the drilling rate of $36 per foot through solid granite – where it had broken into a great vug or underground chamber. Rogier immediately established a new level station and ordered exploratory tunnels cut. He was jubilant as all get-out.

"Look! A forty-five foot vug. Right in solid granite. Didn't I tell you we'd be running into something?"

Jake and Abe nodded gloomily. "Sure, Colonel," said Jake. "A vug like that cave of Aladdin's or somebody. Floor and ceiling of solid gold. Crystals big as walnuts. All that. But we haven't found a single trace."

"The whole thing's clear enough now for me," added Abe. "There's been a big blow-out here. The little veins we worked were close to the surface. The farther down we come the worse they got. And now with this big poop hole it's plain there's no use goin' deeper. It's an empty air-bubble. A Pike's Peak Bubble. I'm for quittin'."

For Abe it was a long speech and a significant judgment.

Rogier was aghast. "Hold on, Abe! You can't mean what you say! Didn't I tell you we'd hit a chamber full of gold crystals in solid granite? Now you've hit a chamber. A forty-five foot vug, man. It's only a sign of another to come. Then you'll see what I told you!"

Having heard this prophecy so often before, Abe turned away. Rogier grabbed him by the arm. Abandoning his grandiloquent descriptions, he got down to brass tacks. "You're too good a minin' man to quit now, Abe. A short exploration tunnel first. Just to be sure. You wouldn't throw me down before a last look, Abe? God Almighty, man! You're my right arm!"

It was an outright, desperate appeal the faithful Zebbelins could not withstand. They firmly protested against sinking the shaft deeper, but agreed to work the new level for all possible leads. The drilling crew was released, and again Abe and Jake took up the labor of cutting laterally through hard rock. Scarcely ten feet to the northwest they blasted into another hollow chamber or poop hole.

Splayed on one wall was a thin tracery of sylvanite ore.

Rogier went wild with excitement. "It's just as I told you, boys! We're reaching the cardiacal center of the old Peak herself! The golden heart of the Rockies!" He could not be kept out of the big chambers. How vast and cavernous they were, greater than any stopes he had seen, even in the Elkton. How silent, how black! They evoked in him a sense of wonder that instantly dispelled any thought of mining. Their mystery was more profound, shrouded in that Cimmerian darkness whose velvety texture was like sable. Lost in this eternal labyrinth of time, he crawled deeper inward, oblivious of surface time. Only Abe could get him out.

"Look, Colonel. With you down here below, Jake's got to man the hoist above. That don't leave nobody to work but me, and it's more'n a one-man job."

Rogier blinked at the truth in the sunshine.

"Somethin' else," went on Abe. "The assays have come in. It's shippin' ore again. Just barely. But I say there won't be enough for a shipment. That stuff is just splayed out thin on one wall. It don't look like it goes through."

"How do you know?" shouted Rogier. "Let's go through and see!"

"Who's goin' through, with Jake up above on the hoist? And who's goin' to do the sortin'?"

"Cable of course," Rogier answered without hesitation. "Didn't I tell you last winter I'd have him up here again? Don't you worry. I'll get him up here." He rushed down to Little London.

Cable had reached the end of his tether as a life insurance salesman. Under Mr. Perkins' merciless driving he had climbed up four places on the blackboard of endeavor: riding around town on his bicycle all day, visiting prospective clients every evening, buttonholing acquaintances on streetcorners, fretting at night. The effort had worn him out. Even Ona knew that he was not cut out for a businessman. And when, bored and listless, he dropped back to the bottom of the list, they both knew he and Mr. Perkins had come to the parting of their ways.

"Jonathan, you know what I want?" Ona asked him one night, flinging her arms around him. "To build our house out on your prairie lot, and move away from everybody where we can be happy!" They had not driven out there all spring, and she was worried at his unaccountable loss of interest in it.

Cable smiled gently. "To build a house would cost a lot of money. And I won't be getting it selling insurance any more than I got it selling neckties."

"But surely there'll be some other way."

"What?"

Ona could not answer. A week later Cable quit his job before he was fired, and began hunting another job while the bills began to pile up. It was during this propitiously discouraging time that Rogier arrived with the electrifying news that he had struck pay ore in the Sylvanite and needed Cable immediately

Cable was not impressed. Still he muttered, "Shipping ore, eh? Well, that's something."

"Something?" growled Rogier. "Steady wages to meet all household expenses. Your share when we hit it big. It's opening up now—hollow chambers that'll give way to the treasure vug I've been telling you about. Why,—"

"No!" said Ona, cutting him short. "That's the same old story I've heard all my life. Jonathan's never going up there again if we have to starve!"

And now it began again, the same old battle between her and her father. This time she knew it for the last, remembering Cable's condition when he had returned from the mine last fall. Too well she knew the danger of miners contracting phthisis from drill dust; that pneumonia was almost invariably fatal in the high altitude; and the additional dangers from falling rock, bad air and gas, a hundred other risks. She did not blame Rogier now; she knew him too well. It was only that accursed worthless mine which for years had been the bane of all their lives – draining their purses, their hopes and lives, enslaving them like a monstrous machine, warping Rogier, and now at last trying to draw Cable within its relentless greedy maw. It was no use; she'd said it all before.

She knew it that night when in her thin silk shift she flung herself upon his lap and against him. By the pressure of her breast, the demanding clasp of her warm arms, she appealed without shame to the slow fire within him to burn away her fear, to enwrap her within its passionate shroud against all else. She could feel the answer in his embrace as he ran his hand under her arm, along her bare side and up to close upon her breast. But so slowly! It was warmth, but not fire, without the swift fusing passion. Of a sudden she went cold with fear.

"Jonathan! Why don't we cut loose and go to Shallow Water? Write Bert Bruce!" she gasped, astounded at the thought which had suddenly leaped out unbidden.

He raised his head, staring out the window as if at the fleeting vision of sage and sand, the sandy Gallegos in moonlight. "Too late," he said, "I reckon I'm in the Sylvanite to the end."

Next evening he told Rogier at supper he would return with him to Cripple Creek. Ona kept pestering her father with questions: Was the cabin really warm and comfortable?—Did they have enough to eat and plenty of blankets? – Jonathan did use the hot water bag and rub his chest at night, didn't he?

The questions remained unanswered then and for months afterward. Ona could only sit at her window and wait and hope, and then get up and write another letter to Cable.

Up at the Sylvanite, he read them through slowly and dropped them into the fire. This listless release of her words of encouragement and love was not the index of his character. He was like a man whose mainspring was broken, who no longer cared to retain his hold upon a life so devoid of meaning. When a sock wore through at the heel, it too was dropped into the fireplace instead of being retained for darning. One by one he discarded his belongings, gave up his hold on the mine. With Abe and Jake he did his work without shirking but without interest. And when he was through, he refused to discuss the mine's prospects.

Most of the summer he felt well. He sat in the sunshine upon the dump, sorting ore, the breeze hardly disturbing a thread of his coarse black hair. On infrequent weekends he went down to Little London, his healthy appearance reassuring Ona, and his listless air disturbing her. March came up, doing the chores and rushing off to spend the day rambling around the district. What was happening to him Cable did not know. But it seemed he was cut off from a vital relationship with his wife, his son, from Rogier, Abe and Jake, from the mine, life itself.

Then, unannounced, came fall. March returned to Little London to go to school. Cold rains set in, then frost. Cable, spelled off from work on dump and hoist, went down into the mine where he found it even colder. In the evening he sat bowed and cross-legged on the cabin floor in front of the fire. Jake and Abe never minded him, so early they went to bed. And he seemed to exude a dark repellent aloofness that forebade communion. He had begun to cough again.

There was beginning to resolve within him the struggle which meant the end. How often had he witnessed on the Reservation that hopeless confusion of the Indian trying to adapt himself to the advancing civilization of the white. Yet it was a trivial problem compared to his own. No Vrain Girls, no government agents could help him. For in Cable was not a racial unity of character that had only to adapt to an outward change of conditions. Deep within himself, the mixed-blood, was the turmoil.

It had always been so, as if his very bloodstream raced all ways in hopeless contradiction. Educated, loving Ona and his children, he had found himself time and again in a position to succeed to a dull and comfortable existence. And then from somewhere within him rose without warning a wave of black negation washing him adrift on the other side of that vast gulf in which lay the centuries between the red and the white.

His months at Shallow Water had marked the turn. The vast sunlit desert of sage and sand, the dark-faced People – to these his long submerged atavistic instincts had leaped exultantly, obliterating all his life since childhood. Only Ona and Rogier, the one who held him by emotion and the other who tugged at the strings of his outward existence, had brought him back to a meaningless routine that little by little crushed out of him all spontaneous life. Living rhythmically, devoid of ambition and competitiveness, and with an attitude that implied an acceptance of his oneness with the animate universe, Cable never reasoned by analysis. He simply felt.

And now caught without escape he did not, like the white, fight violently against the unbeautiful. Like an Indian, he refuted it as if it did not exist. But there was nothing left. Nothing but the heaviness of frustration settling in his heart, the stifling sense of self-unfulfillment. So he sat there, high in the cold granite canyon, stolid, taciturn, without hope. Sat as thousands before him had sat wrapped in their blankets: in dwindling Reservations, in Indian schools, in jails; fed, clothed, administered to, but with the mainspring of life broken within them—a race of men never assimilated, not understood. What they lacked no one seemed to know. It was as if their whole inward existence had been geared to a rhythm that once broken could never be attuned.

So Cable, staring into the flames. He had made his fight. The turmoil had died within him. Money from the mine, a position down in town, his lot out on the prairie, even Ona and his children, meant nothing to him now. Nor did a renewal of life at Shallow Water. It was too late. He wanted nothing. He remembered an old Plains Indian shut up in jail years before who had sat for a month without speaking, and when finally released had crawled off to sit on the edge of town and die. He remembered a little Navajo boy placed in a Reservation school who had stolidly refused food, preferring to starve unless sent back to his *hogan*.

They did not grieve nor brood. He knew now what it was they felt: that black stifling sense of negation clouding his mind, gathering in the pit of his stomach, paralyzing his deep nerve centers. That impenetrable Indian stolidity against which nothing could avail. Nor did he fight against it now. He was content to give himself to it wholly. Only, growing cold, he reached to the bunk behind him for a blanket. With a gesture seemingly habitual, he wrapped this around his shoulders, and sat staring at the dying embers with a face dark and immobile as if of carven wood.

10

A week before Christmas, Rogier in Little London received a telegram from Abe and Jake. Mrs. Rogier rushed with it up Bijou to Ona's house. "Now don't get excited none! You know how a cold scares people to death that high up!"

Ona grabbed the telegram. Atrociously worded, misspelled, and unimproved by the busy railroad agent and telegraph operator at Victor, it said simply that Cable was "more terrible sicker" and to "blanket him conclusively" when he arrived on the afternoon train.

All the family went to the station to meet him, but Cable did not get off the train. Not until Rogier had asked the conductor and turned to stride up the platform toward the engine, did Ona comprehend the Zebbelins' message. Ignoring the children who clamored, "Where's Daddy?—I thought he was comin' on the train," she ran swiftly behind Rogier to the baggage car.

She stopped abruptly, stuffing her handkerchief in her mouth to stifle a scream. The big door of the car had been slid back, a hand truck of trunks and express unloaded and wheeled away. Inside on a collapsible canvas cot partially covered with a greasy tarpaulin, lay

Cable.

With Rogier she sprang toward the car. Rogier put a foot on the wheel hub of a second truck pulled up to the open door and tried to clamber inside. Two men, heavily armed, pushed him down and ordered him to stand back, pointing to a stack of bricks half-covered with a canvas and stacked in the car opening. Ona knew what it was: a shipment of gold bullion being sent down from the mill to the Denver mint. "Make 'em take Jonathan out first!" she screamed at Rogier.

"It won't take a minute, lady," one of the guards said gruffly. "Can't you see the stuff's all piled up and ready? It's got to catch the Denver express."

Gold, always the gold that had to come first! She stood back, breathing a wordless but anguished prayer, her gaze on the still form of Cable. Times on end she had seen men thus rushed down from Cripple Creek on the first train; pneumonia at that high altitude was swift and fatal. At last the cot was lowered to a truck and hauled down the brick platform. Ona walked beside it, holding her coat over Cable's drawn face to shield it from the stinging blasts of snow. He was awake and tried to smile. "We figured I'd better not wait," he muttered thickly. "Abe's a good horse. He carried me most of the way down the gulch."

And now began another anguishing delay inside the waiting room; they had forgotten to order an ambulance. Leona muttered plaintively, a little frightened. March, ever so sensitive, was ashamed of his father's appearance. He kept shrinking from the rude, curious travelers gawking at the group around the cot. It was bad enough to be stretched out helpless before so many people. But his father was so dirty! His long, black, uncombed hair hung over the edge of the cot. He was unshaven, his ears brown with dust, and from beneath the tarp his half-boots stuck out caked with muck.

By the time they reached home Ona had got hold of herself. They laid Cable on the sofa in the parlor, Ona jerking down from the winuow the Christmas wreaths which collected soot and dust.

"I wish you'd taken him home and put him in Sister Molly's big front room upstairs," said Mrs. Rogier.

"This is his home and mine," Ona answered curtly.

The doctor Rogier had called arrived. "He ought to be in a

hospital," he told Ona after his examination, "but I wouldn't move him now. Not even upstairs to the bedroom. Parlor or not, this is the place for him. I want you to sleep in the dining room, close and handy, and keep the fire going. Have the children stay upstairs out of the way."

That evening, unannounced, a red-headed French nurse named Suzanne knocked at the door. She had a nice smile, was quiet and unassuming, and after one glance took charge of the house. Thus began a desperate two-day period marked off regularly by the passing trains which shook the house and rained cinders against the rattling windows, the only noise in the quiet house.

For hours at a time Mrs. Rogier sat stiffly in the dining room. Cable from the first had captured her fancy. Between them—a woman flushed with the pride of a Southern aristocracy however false it might be, and a shy swarthy stranger of Indian blood—had grown a strange attachment, if only to attest the solidarity of aristocratic humility and peasant pride, their equal strength and courageous honesty. Neither was ever only common. Rogier, helpless, restless, and erratic, stormed back and forth a dozen times a day. The children, peeking inside the parlor, ate quietly in the kitchen and crept upstairs. Suzanne was capable and indefatigable, earning forever their blessings. In her precious few moments of rest she read European war dispatches in the newspapers, admitting she was waiting for her call. And Ona every moment gave the sick man her undivided care, if only to sit uncomfortably dozing beside him but still grasping his hand.

But he, the beloved object of their unceasing attention, seemed oblivious to all but the thin streak of light, like the eastern horizon at dawn, which showed below the drawn window blind. At this, hour after hour, he stared with black unfathomable eyes. He had been shaved and washed, and yet with a swift and almost imperceptible change his foreign aspect increased; his cheek bones stood out high and gaunt, his big Roman nose became increasingly prominent, his eyes grew blacker, and as his color ebbed his swarthiness seemed ingrained to the very bone. He lay there as if impenetrably cloaked at last, not alone by the dark shadow, but by a racial fortitude summoned from a long past. He never asked for his children and took no cognizance of whether it was Ona or the nurse who administered to him.

"Is your husband a drinking man?" the doctor asked Ona the afternoon of the second day.

She drew herself up proudly. "Certainly not!"

The doctor left without comment.

Now, that evening, four days before Christmas, Cable's labored breathing developed into the faint sound of a rattle. March upstairs, wide-eyed and sleepless, had forgotten to say his prayers; an omission he tried to make up for thereafter until grown by murmuring, "Oh Jesus, help nobody dies tonight"—a terror-stricken appeal from a guilt he could not forget. He got up and crept down the stairs. The door to the parlor was closed. He knelt and peeked through the keyhole. His mother was lying on the sick-bed with her arms around his father. She had taken off her shoes, and the boy could see in her cotton stockings her toes crooking stiffly with anguish. The nurse was sitting across the room.

The boy retreated to sit mid-way up the stairs in the cold darkness of the shabby hall, shivering in his thin nightgown. His mind was too numbed by a nameless fear to think. But against the fear he ground his teeth and clutched the wooden bannister. A strange compassion gripped and squeezed his bowels. He felt almost sick enough to vomit.

In a little while the nurse found him there. She helped him into his warm coat and boots. "Go down to your grandfather's house and stay there," she told him. "Tell him—just tell him we sent you."

March crept downstairs, past the parlor, and out the front hall door. It was snowing heavily. There was a Christmas party in the house next door. Through the window he could see the lighted candles on the tree. He crossed the road to the railroad underpass. A single light faintly illumined the sandstone blocks on either side. Through the underpass he emerged at the end of Bijou Street. There was not another arc-light between him and the bridge across Shook's Run, a half-mile west. To his left, in the vacant prairie between the railroad and the curving creek, stood a deserted wooden shanty. Two weeks past, a Negro inside had killed his wife with an axe. The following day the boy had peeked inside to see the besplattered blood and the black hair sticking to the slashed walls. So now he walked in the middle of the road.

The snow was almost up to his knees. The flakes drove down his unbuttoned collar, melted and wet his nightgown. Somewhere a dog whimpered. It sounded more lonely than a wolf at timberline. And to his side under the falling snow, as if they were the shacks and shanties of Poverty Row, a sparse row of buildings held still more people asleep and insensible to the misery, pain, sorrow, and mystery forever bestriding the lonely roads across the wide and bitter earth.

Alone in the dark snow-stung night! Alone in the glare of the midday sun, in crowds and work and worry, in the illusions of success and proverty. He would always be alone, but never more than now.

He crossed the bridge over Shook's Run, cautiously approached the gaunt old house. All three stories were dark. For awhile he stood on the steps. He was here—from back there. Why? It was all preternaturally impressed upon him, to carry always. And now the fear and pain and strange compassion made him more sick than ever. He began to shake violently. And yet he began to dread seeing anyone, as if his only wish was to hide his misery in perpetual solitude.

Finally he rang the bell, kept ringing.

A lamp appeared inside, and beside it the face of Rogier. March watched him part the curtains, set down the lamp. Unlocking the door, he stood there in his nightshirt holding open the screen.

The boy did not move or speak. He clenched his teeth in a vain effort to stop the echo of a rattle that shook his whole body. With big brown eyes he stared at the wisps of white hair sticking up above the rough-hewn face, the steady, suddenly comprehending eyes.

Then an arm reached out and gathered him against that old body already half consumed by the strange fire within. Pity and compassionate silence, they weld us together without the need for words. The door banged behind him.

Thus did he too come to his grandfather's house.

Near midnight the death rattle stopped in Cable's throat. The nurse rose, looked at him and the woman in whose arms he lay, and went out to the dining room to stare at the headlines of the newspaper spread out on the table. Then she went upstairs to sit quietly beside Leona, restlessly tossing in bed.

With the cessation of the rattle, the dying man turned slightly and fell on his back across Ona's arm. The silence was profound and oppressive; it seemed to lie in a stagnant pool filling the room. The fire had gone out, and a cloying cold seeped through the window cracks. Ona raised slightly in order to stare at the beloved but unfamiliar countenance of him who was slipping now, without effort and forever, from her love's grasp. It was less serene than implacable, a face devoid of expression save for the unfathomable black eyes which stared fixedly, without interest or indifference, into that realm which opens to all more indifferently still. Yet, unaccountably, she could still feel something within him still mortal as wet adobe. Slippery, unconstrained, it seemed to overflow that ungiving barrier over which he stared with rapt indifference – overflowed and then slipped back again.

Suddenly, and without warning, a flicker of intelligence lighted his eyes. It was as if the gates of his inmost being had swung open and shut. He smiled, the barest withdrawal of lips from his white even teeth. In reflex his hand closed upon hers. And then, passing from sight forever, all that was mortal of Cable slipped the fetters which had bound his wild freedom and elusive strength – passed effortlessly as a feathered shadow over the sunlit plains which had ever called his vagrant spirit.

A few days after the funeral Ona and the children moved down to live in the gaunt old house on Shook's Run. Mrs. Rogier had prepared Sister Molly's big redwood bedroom for them. "It's the best room in the house, like you know, and big enough for a half-dozen. March can have the alcove and the front balcony all for his own, and you and Leona can make yourself at home in the rest."

Ona, grim-lipped, shook her head. "The Third Floor will be plenty good enough."

Mrs. Rogier gave her a penetrating look. "You can't possibly feel that way, child. Of all persons, you should know best that this house is like your Mother's heart – you really have never been gone from either."

It was this incontrovertible truth that hurt the most. A woman who had returned at last to that inescapable old home, at once a womb and an oubliette, she knew now that her marriage and life with Cable had been but a brief absence during which it had been given her to experience for once and always the outside world, to taste the joys and fears, the freedom and responsibilities of one who stands alone. It was as if she had completed—so soon!—the circle of her life, only to realize now the precious independence for which Cable had stood against the Rogiers. Henceforth she was to be not an individual but a part, indistinguishable from those others who had failed to escape from their ancestral womb.

Resolutely she ripped off the plank boarding up the stairs and marched up to the barny Third Floor. In the crepuscular winter light it looked altogether forbidding. Dust covered the plank floor, the rafters, the bedsteads. Spider webs and cocoons clung to the corners. And from the ceiling, like sewed-up bodies, hung the sacks of bedclothes and pillows. After two days of washing, scrubbing, tacking down carpets, laying rugs, and hanging curtains, it still looked depressing but presentable.

March, big enough for a room of his own, was given the little south room at the head of the steps. On the floor he spread Ona's Two Gray Hills rug, and on the bed the one he had sent her from Shallow Water. On the walls he hung Cable's Plains Indian treasures: a soft buckskin shirt with a panel of crimson-dyed porcupine quills, a gorgeous war bonnet of eagle feathers tipped with red yarn that hung to his knees when he put it on, and a dozen pairs of Cheyenne and Arapaho beaded moccasins. Jewelry given him by Bert Bruce and the Vrain Girls littered dresser and bookcase: Navajo bracelets, necklaces, rings, and belt buckles of silver and chunk turquoise. The barbaric color and strangeness of the room whenever Ona walked into it, gave her a start. It seemed to her that with all these relics he was trying, unwittingly, to evoke the nebulous past of a dead father and a dying race. She was glad to see, much as she hated it, a big case of ore specimens from Cripple Creek.

The barny north room, extending two-thirds the length of the house, Ona reserved for herself, Leona, and Nancy who moved up with them for company. It was long and low, dark and cheerless even in daylight and summer. Nevertheless Ona was content in it. It forced her downstairs to work. Never could she stand the thought of sitting and brooding in Sister Molly's room. For now like one reincarnated, she found herself apeing the despair of Sister Molly whose Tom had blithely set up the Pass to Leadville to make his fortune, leaving his two boys and Sister Molly to grieve herself to death.

As the days wore on, Ona was increasingly troubled by the spector of that memory; it seemed to her that the pattern of life in this gaunt old house never changed. Tom, who had left Sister Molly and his two boys; Jonathan, who had left her with Leona and March; Cecil Burgess and Mary Ann who had abandoned Nancy here in this graveyard of lost hopes. And behind them all, the same enigmatic mountains, the same wild lust for gold or silver, the same curse that had killed Tom, old man Reynolds, and Cable.

A stray suspicion leaped into her mind. Shortly after Cable's death, remembering the doctor's question whether Cable had been a drinking man, she had asked him what he meant.

"He was sinking so rapidly I thought a drink of whiskey might rally him, but didn't know whether he could stand it," the doctor had replied. "No offense meant, of course."

"Of course."

And now she lay writhing under that question which would forever remain unanswered: did Cable's morning glass of whiskey make him a drinking man?

But what if she had encouraged him to refinance his haberdashery store, to settle on his prairie lot east of town, to remain with Bert Bruce at Shallow Water? Vain regrets, unanswered questions which, alone at night, she knew futile. She, with March, Leona, Nancy, and Mrs. Rogier were imprisoned hostages to Rogier's monomaniacal search for gold in the Sylvanite, come what might.

BOOK THREE

The Dust Within The Rock

PART I

CONCENTRATE

1

Shipments of ore from the Sylvanite were returning so little that Rogier accompanied a carload down to the mill to make sure he wasn't being cheated.

The mill was the former old bromide and hot chlorine plant at Colorado City, three miles west of Little London. Several years before, it had been changed to handle the new cyanide process and was destroyed by fire. It had then been bought and rebuilt by the Golden Cycle Mill Company which owned the Golden Cycle mine, then commonly believed to be the third richest gold mine in the United States, and a consolidation of one hundred other mines in Cripple Creek. The mill was an immense structure whose long and high dump rose against the blue mountains like a barren gray mesa.

Rogier, wandering through the roasting rooms, noisy and hot as the inside of a furnace, finally ran into the superintendent who accosted him at once. "Hello, Mr. Rogier! You got my letter?"

"No," Rogier answered sourly. "I came down to see if you're going to give me a decent control assay on my carload of sylvanite. You've been running me short."

The superintendent shook hands. "Another little carload of that stuff? Every time I get one I swear it's nothing but granite, and the assay almost bears me out."

"Never knew a mill man yet who wasn't ready to steal you blind and swear the best ore didn't run half an ounce! What're you trying to do with all those Company mines, run us little fellows out?"

The superintendent frowned. "We're a custom mill. Don't forget that. We give everybody a fair deal." Then he grinned. "What I want to know is why you've gone in for mining gravel. You haven't given up your work?"

"Why not? Last time I talked to you, you were going to call me about an estimate on enlarging the mill. That was a long time ago. How do you expect me to pay my boys' wages?"

"That's what my letter was about. Here, let's get out where we can talk."

Rogier followed him outside and listened to his quick, precise explanation. The Golden Cycle Mill was ready to enlarge its plant. The plans provided for an extension of its huge ore bins, offices, and more space for facilities to increase its capacity to handle 1,100 tons daily – based on the firm expectation of treating 400,000 tons a year. When completed, the Golden Cycle would be the largest and most modern wet chemical plant for the treatment of gold ore in the world.

"That was what I had in mind when I wrote you, Mr. Rogier. The job will be put up for bids. But the Old Man knows the work you did for us some years ago has stood up sound as a bottom dollar, and if you can give us a fair figure it'll probably be given preferential consideration on the basis of your previous work. That is," he added, "if you don't hit a jackpot in that gopher hole of yours."

"Much obliged to you," muttered Rogier. "I'll get the specifications and put in my bid right away!"

"Sure thing – but don't ship us any more granite. This job will pay better!"

Rogier's bid, as expected, was accepted. The job pulled him out of a nasty hole and allowed him to hire a man to help Abe and Jake up at the Sylvanite. Rawlings, his old foreman, agreed to boss his crew only on one condition. "I handle the men. You do everything else. But I handle the men. We ain't goin' to have any more fusses like you had with Deere and Moody."

Rogier solemnly agreed, and the work went along smoothly. The construction was no fancy piece of architecture to grace the scenic landscape of Little London, to be sure, but one in which Rogier took unusual interest. Wasn't it the mill to which Abe and Jake were occasionally sending a carload of ore from the Sylvanite? And striding along the railroad spur lined with carloads of ore from Cripple Creek, he would eye each one of them with a tingle running up his spine. Any one of them might be from the Sylvanite!

During the long days he spent at the mill, he came to know every room and every process in the plant as he followed the run of ore. Never did a long train of ore cars fail to evoke in him instant enthusiasm. He would scramble up the steep embankment to watch the cars being shunted up the high trestle above the bins. In the glint of sunlight he could distinguish instantly the grayish sulphide ores from the brown-streaked oxides and tellurides. By their feel and color and a peculiar sense developed from long familiarity, he could tell where they came from: the west or east side of the district, Battle Mountain, Bull or Globe Hill. The oxides he knew were from a depth not exceeding a thousand feet; over the others he wasted time envisioning the deep dark stopes from which they had been mined. With the tremendous roar in his ears as the cars were emptied into the receiving bins, he strode past the great crushers, watched the ore being sorted to mesh sizes and transported into the sampling works.

The cavernous roasting room entranced him most. Till his shoe soles grew hot and his collar wilted, he would stand before the great roasters. Brawny men stripped to the waist walked past him, reflecting the red glow from their grimy, sweaty bodies; the clang of furnace doors, the roar of the flames echoed in his ears. Rogier never looked up. He stood watching the ore on the hearths. It was fine and powdery, glowing red; in little ripples, like that of sand, it passed underneath the spindles and was slid to the cooling hearth to become the color of dirty brick dust.

Often he sauntered along the narrow gangway over the tops of the huge flotation tanks. Looking down, he could see the dirty spume of the concentrates sluggishly rising to surface like the gold-flaked soap suds in the washtub of the woman who had discovered the principle while washing out her husband's mining clothes. He watched the dirty red flow streaming into the ball mill, being ground in a cyanide solution. He followed it to agitators, to the slime presses where it was washed free of gold-bearing solutions. He then watched the gold being precipitated, treated in the refinery, and finally reduced to bricks of gold ready for shipment to the mint in Denver. Bricks worth $5,000 each. Day by day the repeated process, by which men refined from the great masses of mountain rock the tiny living sparks of gold, became more familiar to him.

Invariably the day's end found him standing on the long, high tailing dump outside the mill. From the flume beside him poured out a steady sluggish stream of waste pulp ore being discharged as tailings. He watched it, a reddish slime like the slow red rivers which had given Colorado its name, a vast ejecta which would harden into another layer of the powdery mesa stretching eastward toward town. A gust of wind would whip off sprays, like fine sand from a desert dune, and elite Little Londoners would make haste to close their windows to the dust, noses up to this irritating reminder of the riches which had built their mansions on Millionaire Row.

Behind him a whistle blew. Workmen – his own among them – streamed from the mill and down the trail. He could hear the jingle of their empty lunch buckets across the creek and into the rows of shacks at Colorado City.

Technically competent, a good construction and mining man, Rogier was more engrossed in an aspect of the mill seen with his own peculiar inner eye. Standing on a narrow shelf between the high wall of mountains and the plains, he could envision beyond Little London the skyscrapers and minarets, the lofty proud cities of America. All built from the gold in the mountains behind him – from that tiny area of only six square miles on the south slope of Pike's Peak which was producing as much gold as both the Mother Lode of California and the Klondike combined!

Here to this high continental plateau, to these mysterious mountains and snowy peaks, had flocked the treasure seekers of the world. This was their treasure chest, the backbone of the continent, the ultimate source of the rivers and the natural resources for centuries to come. And standing there in the twilight, Rogier could see them coming from the cities of cobwebbed steel with their swarming streets and busy marts, from the ships crawling like ants across the seas. Foreigners speaking in strange tongues, shrewd city men calculating how to make an easy dollar, awkward country youths and shy girls in gingham, bashful lads in black string ties sounding their r's with a harsh Western twang, women who enfused strength and freshness and simplicity into the stagnant pools of life for all their blushes and nervously spilled teacups.

They were all ore. In the vast mill of the yet crude West, they all went through the run. Rogier could see his own – poor Tom, Sister Molly, and Cable; Mary Ann, Sally Lee, Ona, and Boné still in their own roasters; March, Leona, and Nancy whose tests were yet to come. Some of them would assay as concentrates. The rest, for all his hopes, would be tailings cast aside.

The devil roast them all! What could he do to help them? A power greater than he had spoken.

"I have graven it within the hills, and my vengeance upon the dust within the rock."

"He who has no roots beneath him has no god."

But he! – he knew to what led his own roots down through the breathing mountains, divined the heart that beat deep inside the fleshly rock. The secret of all men's alliance with the earth would soon be his. No mill of men but would show that he, at last, through the Sylvanite, had reached the final oubliette.

If an inconsequential splatter of shipping ore had been for Rogier a significant discovery, a slip of paper found in the safe constituted a more significant one for Mrs. Rogier. The huge iron safe stood in a dark corner of the dining room for want of a better place to keep it. In years gone by, Rogier had locked in it his valuable papers and a considerable amount of currency. Of late it was unused; the door swung open whenever Mrs. Rogier's dustcloth caught on the combination knob; and occasionally odd papers fell out. So it was that she discovered a note that betrayed Timothy's investment in the Sylvanite to the tune of $5,000. Mr. Timothy! That rich, spoiled, pampered wastrel! It was all clear to her now; buttering up Boné with that party at the Deer Horn Lodge, introducing Rogier into the Ruxton Club, and then dropping the family altogether. He had got what he wanted, a share in that fabulous gold mine certain to make him another fortune!

If this was reprehensible, Rogier's acceptance of the money

was worse. Knowing him, Mrs. Rogier was certain he had taken it under false pretenses as surely as if he had stolen it out of Timothy's pockets. There was no talking to Rogier now. It was up to her own honor to be ready to clear the debt when that awful day of judgment should surely come. Five thousand dollars! It would take months of saving, scrimping, slicing expenses to the bone in ways that no one could suspect.

She began at once. No longer did her sugar bowl contain savings for a rainy day, but contributions to her honor fund.

Rogier began to be suspicious; his profits from the mill job were vanishing too fast. "What do you do with all the money I keep giving you?" he demanded, glaring across the breakfast table at Mrs. Rogier, slimly erect and indomitable in her demands.

"Jonathan's doctor bills and nurse bill, medicine and funeral expenses were all large, Daddy. And you must remember I'm not here alone any more. There are six of us now, and the three children must have milk and eggs and fruit."

"They don't eat a peck apiece. I never see them going for anything but cornbread and molasses. Didn't Ona pay those bills? And didn't she give you some money when she moved down here?"

"Money doesn't last forever," she answered calmly. "A thousand dollars, Daddy."

"A thousand! God Almighty! I've got three men up at the mine to pay and feed, and they're running into trouble. Five hundred. That's all you get, and make it last as long as you can."

Before long the argument came up again, this time before Ona. She was embarrassed. "I don't like feeling that the children and I are sponging off you. I thought that keeping Daddy's books and accounts for so long without wages would pay our way. Maybe I could get a job somewhere else. All I have left is Jonathan's lot east of town."

"It's in Nob Hill now, being built up fast. You'd get a good price for that piece of land," suggested Mrs. Rogier.

"It isn't the money, Mother. But Jonathan's land! Oh, I can't! He loved it so. Remember how he used to drive out there every Sunday just to look at it and feel the dirt in his fingers? Why, that was to be our home. He'd turn over in his grave!"

"Nonsense," said Rogier. "You'd be paying taxes on it as long as you live – with what? Or lose it. You know you'll never have a house out there. This is your home now."

The shamelessly spoken truth broke Ona's will. She sold the five-acre lot for the handsome price of $2,500. That evening she laid the check on Rogier's plate and went to bed supperless and weeping.

In the barny Third Floor she could not sleep. Oh God, she missed him so! The slim straight shaft of his body, his dark head on the pillow, the stubborn independence of that strange man whose only spot of beloved earth had been sacrificed, like himself, for a worthless mine.

Leona and Nancy in their own beds stopped giggling and whispering. The light in March's room across the landing finally went out. Ona lay listening for the creaky steps of the Kadles making their nocturnal rounds. Suddenly, about midnight, she awoke from a doze, stiff with fear. She was staring down the long dark room and across the landing at a spot of light which hung on the closet door at the head of the stairs. It was about as big around as that from an electric flashlight, so bright that she could see the polished grain of the wood it illumined. Suddenly it moved – scarcely six inches to the left, then stopped. Ona, too terrified to move, lay staring at it as if mesmerized. The light kept slowly moving across the wall of the landing and coming to rest again. It was accompanied by no sound, no stealthy fumbling of hands in the dark, no restrained breathing, no sound of steps. Then at last it wavered across March's closed door and stopped on the door-knob. With the flickering reflection of the polished knob, Ona screamed. The light vanished instantly and without a sound.

Nancy woke up, sleepily muttered, "The light? Just like I told you," and dropped off to sleep again. Ona lay sleepless, unmoving, till dawn.

Now began for her a fear-ridden existence she cautioned Nancy to reveal to no one. Mrs. Rogier would have insisted she move downstairs. Rogier would have stormed and stamped around again, doing everything but tearing down the house. And March – she trembled lest he learn of the light that hung on his door like a phantom. Her concern each night was that his door was securely closed.

The light reappeared again and again. It might appear twice within a month or it might be weeks, but it was sure to reappear sometime. She began to try to trace its source. There were no lights kept burning in the house at night. The only light outside was the arc-lamp suspended over the bridge at Shook's Run, too far away to cast a reflection through the one north window of her room. There were no other windows on the third floor it might shine through except the small west window at the head of the stairs. Nor was it moonlight. Like as not it would appear on the darkest night. The eerie light was round and small, undiffused and never varying in size. There was only one other possible source – the new revolving searchlight on Pike's Peak whose thin ray swept the trails and canyons to guide lost hikers. Ona knew this was a foolish assumption. People didn't hike up the mountains this late in the year, nor was the Summit House kept open except during the summer tourist season. Nevertheless she drew the blinds on the stairway window and the windows in Sister Molly's front room downstairs, even closed the door to shut off every possible source of light. And still she would awake to see the cold malevolent eye fixed on the wall before her.

She bought a flashlight, throwing it upon the wall when the phantom light appeared – and saw nothing. The doors she locked securely; no one could possibly get into the house. She began to suspect Rogier, or even her mother, of walking in their sleep. But when she jumped out of bed and rushed to the landing, the light vanished instantly and there was no one on the stairs or in the hall below.

Many a time when the incomprehensible phenomenon appeared, she was on the point of screaming out to the Kadles for help, trusting to those two old faithful family ghosts to make their nocturnal rounds and set the seal of their benediction upon the house. But in the morning sunlight, looking at the reflection of her worn and sleepless face in the mirror, she would think of this folly with amazement: appealing to ghosts for help against the supernatural!

"Am I – are we all crazy?" she muttered to herself.

She only knew that this gaunt old house on Shook's Run was haunted by specters of the unforgettable past and the dreaded future, by the ghostly flow of all time; haunted by worries and doubts and futile hopes; haunted, oh haunted, even by the aimless ancient winds forever prowling about the creaking timbers which stood where once tall slim lodge poles raised firm and straight.

2

And now it was October again, the time of change; and haunted by the ghostly flow of time March lay in the attic of his grandfather's house grieving for his father and listening to the aimless ancient winds. It was October and autumn, the season that the Americans call fall, said James Fenimore Cooper, because it was the time when the leaves fall. Of all the months of the year, it was America's month, the corn-ripe moon, when corn came in by wagonloads: Indian maize, the crop of America's soil, blue ears and black, blood red, bronze, yellow, white, and speckled. The first frost had come, "the thunder sleeps." So now to Shallow Water, from out of a desert wilderness of sage and sand, of mesa, butte, and canyon, came hundreds of Navajos in their squeaking wagons to gather for their great Sings. And the nine bitter frosty nights drew down upon the river's elbow, the muddy San Juan, upon the plain of flowering campfires.

But where was his father now, on this cold October's night when he lay alone and lonely in his bed in a ramshackle old house on Shook's Run? Not to Shallow Water had his spirit fled. Not to the mountain Utes, the desert Mojaves, the fierce banty-legged

Apaches. Nor to the mud-brown pueblo dwellers, the reverent Zunis, the Acomas and Hopis isolate on their remote high mesas, the swarming pueblos along the Rio Grande. But farther, over the last range, had fled his long-legged, lonely spirit. Back to the tall slim ghosts of arrogant warrior horsemen who slashed their wrists and were strung up by the sinews to dance, showing how they could endure pain.

Where were their lodges now? Where now the smoke-gray ghostly tepees once strung out along the thousand-mile water courses of the Arkansas and the Platte, the Arickaree and the Red, that clustered in Bijou Basin, at Smoky Hill, standing out like gray anthills against the great blue Rockies? Where did the aimless ancient winds cry to his father's ghost as they prowled across the great plains, stirring the dust in huge wallows where phantom buffalo rolled, and whipping the smoke rising from a thousand campfires of invisible tribes? Was it among the Kiowas and Comanches, the Pawness, the Shawnees, the Crows and innumerable Sioux of the Seven Council Fires? Or was it rather among the Blue-Cloud Arapahoes and the fighting Cheyennes in whose tongue he spoke to Indian Poe?

Where had fled his ghost over the long trail where the pony tracks go only one way, the ghost of that strange dark man, his father, who seldom spoke and now would never speak again? Oh sweet medicine, by the four sacred arrows I ask: "Who was my father, the strange dark man I never really knew?"

It was October, the time of change, when the great male Rockies turned blue and white, and the pines grew smoky in the haze, and the aspens turned yellow and pink. It was the crack of Jake's rifle bringing down a deer, the smell of bacon sizzling in the pan, the tall tales of ore wagons creaking up the Pass to Creede, Tin Cup, Fair Play, Leadville, and Buckskin Joe high in the Colorado Rockies. It was the time when Cripple Creek, two miles high, drew in its horns for winter and the first snow whitened the shaft houses on Battle Mountain. At night the long train of empties puffed slowly up to the Bull Hill junction under the steam of four engines and from high above, you could see the furnace-red glow from their tenders. Then when the great mines, the Independence and the Portland, the Golden Cycle, Jack Pot, Mary McKinney, the Wild Horse and the

American Eagles looked like great liners dry-docked on the mountain slopes; and miners' wives lined the insides of their shanties with the pink-sheeted front pages of the *Denver Post* to keep out the wind; and the little fellows boarded up their tunnels and drifted to town to make a stake for next year's beans.

Shallow Water and Cripple Creek, adobe and granite. And lying there sleepless in bed on a cold October's night, listening to the aimless ancient winds whipping the leaves from the trees and whining under the eaves, he stared through the darkness at the case of ore specimens from the Sylvanite, at the single eagle feather tipped with red yarn that hung from the rafter. They were symbols of things which were themselves symbols, imbued with a terrible fixity and at the same time reflecting a terrible change. Who knew what they meant? To himself he seemed unreal, worn out with the vain effort to discern what in him was the transient, what was the enduring. He knew only that he too was an eternal stranger, and that always he would be alone as now. And all that he had known and felt and loved and lost had been swept away by a current too timeless and immense to give him the sense of its onward course. For he had lost his father and something else – his childhood; he was twelve years old.

The mysterious flow of time that does not move, yet ever moves. Who am I, he wondered. The leaf that falls into the flow or the leaf that sprouts anew? Am I the mountain rock shattered by frost and disintegrated by time, or the timeless dust within the rock, carried to the sea to rise again a lofty peak with sea shells on its summit?

There is no beginning, no end. I am all that ever has been and will be, in me is rooted all that I have ever met. I am my mother's worn shirtwaist, the shining crystals of sylvanite and calaverite in their dusty cases, the deep black stopes of my grandfather's worthless mines and the fiendish laughter that pursues him, the wind that warps the pines at timberline and the cry of the wolf it carries. I am my grandmother's false pride and envy, the crumpled magnolia leaves and the moth-holed Confederate flag in her old trunk. And I am my father's dark hawk face and the smoke of a thousand camp fires in his blood.

I am the dark adobe world of my father which lies behind, and the white granite world of my grandfather which lies ahead. In me the great flow of time is a leaping fountain which will water both. For I am the feather, the flower, the drum, and the mirror of the old gods who have never died.

And yet as he lay listening now to the wheels of a milk wagon rumbling across the bridge, he wondered, What or who is in me that knows these things I do not know? Who and what am I?

Columbia School did not teach him.

There were seven public grade schools in Little London: two each in the north, west, and south, and one in the sparsely settled east section. The geographic boundaries of these sections were as definitely fixed as patented mining claims. Each of them reflected the exact, rubber-stamped social status of its residents. For Little London by now, ignoring the hoarded gold it had wrung from Cripple Creek, had completely forsworn its environmental heritage. Built on the ideal of a European spa, it self-consciously proclaimed itself a cultural oasis in the crude American West, a culture possessed by its various sections according to their positions on the rising stairsteps of distinction:

$$$$$$
$$$
$
¢
0

No liquor could be sold within town. Newspapers were prohibited from carrying funny papers in their Sunday issues. the *Odeon* and the *Princess* movie palaces were closed on Sunday. And all manufacturing within town limits was forbidden. The ore reduction mills which it ignored were restricted to the sandy mesa west of town. Here on the west side and in the suburb of Colorado City lived the brawny Golden Cycle mill workers who trooped on Saturday night to riot in the block-long array of saloons nearby called Ramona. So of course their children and the two west side schools they attended were on the lowest step.

Lowell School on the southern edge of town reflected the haphazard, listless nonentity of the ramshackle buildings and fringe-area residents. Liller School, farther in, stood just a block from the railroad yards and drew its rowdy children from the houses at the bottom of Bijou Hill and the nigger shanties of Poverty Row along Shook's Run.

The North End was the elite heart of Little London. To its wide and gracious avenues, particularly Wood Avenue, had flocked the lucky who had struck it rich at Cripple Creek. Their rococo mansions filled block after block. The side streets accommodated the mere comfortably wealthy, the leading business men, and the barnstorming social climbers. So naturally its two grammar schools, Steele and Garfield, were the best in town.

Columbia was across the tracks in the sparsely settled prairies east of town. A tidy, two-storied, red brick building, it stood beside an unfinished white brick church holding Sunday services in the basement. Around it lay a vacant expanse of prairie playground stretching eastward to the pine bluffs. But the district was clean and tidy; more and more tradesmen, professional men, and newcomers were coming in. There was even a big house or two, rows of cottonwoods, and fresh cropped lawns. It was here that March and Leona had gone to school before moving down to the bottom of Bijou Hill in the old house on Shook's Run.

"And I don't see why March can't keep coming here just one more year," pleaded Ona, seated with March in the principal's office. "He's in the eighth grade and will graduate next June. Naturally he wants to finish up with his old classmates and teachers."

"You have moved into the Liller district. That is evident," said Miss Trumble coldly.

Miss Trumble, the principal, was almost six feet tall. Her backbone was an iron ramrod, her jaws a steel trap, her eyes a pair of rifle sights that drew a bead on any youngster who showed a streak of wildness. She was a capable woman who formerly had taught school in a mining camp. Now the muzzle of her ambition was pointed at Garfield School. *Excelsior* was her favorite poem, and "Old Excelsior" her nickname among students.

"It's not Leona I'm thinking of," replied Ona. "She's young and can adapt to Liller. But March would be distressed; you know how high strung he is. And such a short walk, too. Just up Bijou to the railroad embankment, then north, and four blocks east. For only one year!"

"It's too irregular. I will not recommend it." Old Excelsior rose.

Ona set her own square jaw as she stood up. "I don't want to have to pass my simple request any higher, Miss Trumble."

"I and my pupils obey the rules. That is the spirit of Columbia. Mrs. Cable!"

Ona returned to Mrs. Rogier storming with indignation. "It's not the education. Goodness knows the boy does nothing but read, read, read. But I won't have the stigma pinned on him of being a Liller boy. With all those niggers and numbskulls!"

Mrs. Rogier laid down her spectacles on her Bible. "A Rogier is a Rogier in any company. Blood tells, always. Now if his demeanor and deportment are worthy – "

Ona whirled around to face the boy. "I'm goin' to get you back in Columbia and you're goin' to have demeanor all right! And deportment too! You're goin' to brush up on figures if I have to burn up every book in the house. I won't have you runnin' wild as a jack rabbit any more!"

Mrs. Rogier nodded. "Your father built Columbia, every other school in town. Mr. Ford is still on the School Board – one of Daddy's best friends – and if you were to ask him, casually like – "

"And there's a precedent already set!" interrupted Ona. "That pretty little girl who lives up on Bijou Hill. Leslie Shane, whose father owns the Saddle Rock Grill. She's going to Columbia even though she's out of the district too."

"What's good for the goose is good for the gander," agreed Mrs. Rogier. "But easy-like. No hard pushin'!"

It was done. March was allowed to finish eighth grade at Columbia while Leona and Nancy were transferred to Liller. The triumph was all Ona's; she didn't have to taste each day the bitter fruits of her success. For one thing it alienated March from his neighbors, the twelve Caseys and two Kennedys on either side, who went to Liller. Occasionally he played with them in the street: marbles, cricket with tin cans and baseball bats, and kick-the-can. But there was no bond between him and them, no mutual dislike or like of the same teachers and lessons, no confidences to be exchanged as they walked back and forth to school. He was there for the moment in their midst. But in the morning, a stranger, he walked away.

Many of these neighbor boys never knew his last name; to them he was March Rogier or simply the Rogier kid. His tribal affinity with the Rogiers set him apart too. For the Rogiers were different. One knew this without question early on the morning of every Fourth of July when Mrs. Rogier took out from her trunk the large Confederate Flag and hung it over the front railing of the second-story balcony. By mid-morning clumps of neighbors began gathering to point at it and protest with scowling faces. The telephone rang. The caller was a man on the *Gazette* who had received protests from people in town, and wanted to know why a good old American flag couldn't be displayed in its stead on this patriotic Fourth of July.

"And I don't see why not, Mother!" protested Ona herself. "You know hanging that old rag out there is just like waving a red flag in front of a bull. It always creates a stink and a rumpus. Damn it, Mother! Don't you know yet the Civil War's over and forgotten?"

"It is far from me to forget that many brave and true men died nobly for that old rag as you call it, Ona," Mrs. Rogier answered quietly. "The Stars and Bars is just as much an emblem of our family faith as the Stars and Stripes to other people. As long as this is a free country I see no reason to take it down."

So there it stayed all day, the rest of the family hiding as if in shame behind it. Peeking out the window, March could see neighbors putting up their noses at it or spitting on the sidewalk as they walked past, hear the firecrackers hurled at it. But when the Casey and the Kennedy kids began to throw mud balls, plastering windows and the front of the house he felt rise within him a curious stubborn pride.

"General Grant beat Lee, didn't he?" they shouted. "And we can take the Rogiers like Grant took Richmond! Come out, you little Reb, if you ain't scaired of us boys in blue!"

And then he would rush out to get his nose bloodied, knuckles skinned, and clothes muddied; and the glorious Fourth of July, as usual, would turn into another shameful, noisy, family row.

Even at Columbia he felt deracinated and alone. He was dark and thin, beginning to grow tall and skinny, with his father's small hands and feet. The Cable in him made him grave and shy, the Rogier in him too sensitive and stubborn. After long months at

Shallow Water and up at the Sylvanite with none but the companionship of taciturn men, he did not know how to get along with children of his own age. His schoolmates often seemed childish, but none were as gullible to pranks and jokes as he. He was easily wounded. A word, a look, would thrust into the quick of his being, and he was slow to forgive. Still he was never bullied by the bigger boys from outlying ranches, for in him was a cold cruelty and he could be sly as an animal when pressed in combat, kicking into the groin or jabbing a thumb into an Adam's apple.

Arithmetic was his despair, fractions his nemesis. Miss Thomas, the teacher, was a plump little woman who stood at the blackboard in front of the class, the horizontal line of her corset showing across her round posterior.

"Above the line we place four. Below the line, what? March! What do we have below the line?"

A thumb poked his shoulder. A steamy breath whispered in his ear, "Plush Bottom!"

No; he had no mind for figures.

Nor for geography. The United States of America were forty-eight. They were tidy parallelograms, properly fenced: pink, green, red, blue, brown. But really, the Rocky Mountains marched right through. You couldn't tell Kansas from the wasteland prairies of eastern Colorado on a clear day from the slope of Pike's Peak.

History, you might say, was in the same boat. The country was England's, Spain's, France's. Then came the Louisiana Purchase and it was the United States of America. But what about it when it was comprised of the great united nations of the Iroquois; Pontiac's confederacy of the Ottawas,Ojibwas, Hurons, and Delawares; Tecumseh's alliance of Shawnees, Wyandots, and Kickapoos; the mighty nations of the Cherokees, Creeks, Chickasaws, Choctaws, and Seminoles; the Seven Council Fires of the Sioux; the Cheyennes, Arapahoes, Kiowas, and Comanches; Apacheria, land of the Apaches; the combined clans of the Navajos; and the multi-storied mud cities of the Pueblos? History, like geography, had nothing to say. But the snow drifted over the bunch grass just the same, and the great mountains shouldered aside races, customs, governments, creeds. And the aimless ancient winds whispered of a mighty continent with its own spirit of place that was and would always be beyond political division.

At his desk during the writing lesson he sat like one automaton of many. Feet down flat, back straight, left arm curved above the paper, so!

"Ready now? The vertical strokes first. Very lightly. Don't move your fingers. The whole arm, remember. Ready? Dip pens! Stroke!"

Hail Columbia, the Gem of the Ocean! You can't tell one's handwriting from another's. The same slant, the same shading, the same size. Stroke! The light ovals this time! Procreation next by the Palmer Method.

March was awarded the thirty-ninth Palmer Certificate of the class with a gold seal and tags of purple and white ribbons, the school colors.

Drawing in the public schools was a negligible diversion. Miss Marion made the rounds every two weeks, coming to Columbia on alternate Thursdays. A big breasted woman with a deep and fertile voice, she wore leather gloves and a floppy coat, like a man's. March adored her. Like a plain faced daughter of Ceres, she brought the grasses, fruits, and flowers of the fields, and all the secret beauty of an earth he had never noticed before.

In the spring, Indian paint brushes, bluebells, an armful of pussy-willows. In the fall, milkweed pods, one to a child, to be drawn in charcoal. Often when the snow lay deep she trooped in with pine branches, a sheaf of barley, or merely alfalfa purchased from a feed store. Or they painted apples. But always these trivial things took on an astounding vitality; they still clung to the stem of all life.

"Let's open these windows! Let the day in!"

The boy's soul leaped up to meet it. He saw outside, waving in the wind, the brown prairie grasses, the sere weeds, the withered stalks he had blindly ignored. On his desk lay a brittle, green-gray milkweed pod on its leafless stick, and beside it his charcoal scrawl.

Miss Marion, prowling silently down the aisle, stopped beside him. "Not bad. But look!" She dug him playfully in the ribs. "You're making a submarine out of it. All iron, closed up tight against the water. Look here."

She turned it, gently pried open the narrow tapered lips, drew out the white silky spume with its enmeshed black seeds. The breeze from the window sent the tufts floating across the room, landing on desks, papers, backs. "See? It's got hinges. It opens to the wind so the parachutes can drop out. Remember, everything in nature is alive."

She sauntered on; and the boy, smeared with charcoal, began again.

But for Miss Watrous' grammar class March trod willingly the treadmill of his school existence. Miss Ruth Watrous was tall and bony, wore glasses, and maintained an habitual air of disassociation from the mechanical grind around her. Old Excelsior didn't like her. Neither did Miss Plush Bottom. But against her easy mannered immunity both were powerless. She kept perfect order. Instead of sending a pupil out to stand in the hall for whispering, or making him eat crackers in front of the class for chewing gum, she would turn around listless at the sound of any fuss.

"You might think this grammar is dull, but you need it and I'm the one to give it to you. However, if you don't want it, just quietly walk out. But remember, you don't come back. Now who is the first to leave before the rest of us diagram this sentence?"

No one ever left. She rewarded them by reading out loud for the last twenty minutes of the day. Greek and Roman mythology at first. Gradually for March the world of Old Excelsior faded away. Pike's Peak rose higher, more majestic, into Mount Olympus. The great Labyrinth yawned blacker than the deepest stope of the Sylvanite. He was in a new world watching the sowing of the dragon's teeth, the phoenix rising anew, the salamander in the flame; hearing the sea maidens cry, the crash of shields before Troy, and in the woodlands the pipes of Pan. Now, from the waters of Babylon came the sacred hawk-headed, ram-headed, and winged beasts; and from the great Nile the god Osiris and the goddess Isis, and the sacred bull with a beetle under his tongue and the hair of his tail double. And now the many-headed gods of the east, Vishnu and Siva, and all the rest, ivory and peacocks, and streets that quaked to the tread of elephants. Then the new and mighty world of the north and the frost giants, and the lusty Vikings swilling mead from great horns. It was Thor hurling his hammer, Odin seated on his throne, two ravens perched on his shoulder, two wolves crouching at his feet, and the Valkyries thundering over the rainbow bridge to Valhalla with fallen warriors. Then, late one afternoon, he was transported from the shadows of the Druids' sacred oak and mistletoe to a land he knew well, his own great continent of the hereafter, so unutterably old and unknown that men called it the New World. High above it towered still-smoking Popocatepetl, and Ixtaccihuatl, the sleeping woman covered by a snowy mantle. Below them the war god Huitzilopochtli hungered for blood-dripping human hearts torn out from the breasts of victims on top of pyramids greater and higher than those in Egypt. Yet he, Quetzalcoatl, the Feathered Serpent, the Lord of Dawn, the god of gods, had not forgotten his children. Someday he would return. And darkly, in his blood, March could hear beating the tall drum *huehuetl* and the flat drum *teponaztle*, echoing in the deep-toned belly drums and the little water drums. And he could hear again the deep-voiced singing out beyond Shallow Water. This was the altar, the high flat mesa across the desert, and burning cedar the incense. For we of America, its children, are the feather, the flower, the drum, and the mirror of the old gods who never die.

The bell rang. In a daze March walked out into the late, gray October afternoon, under the honks of wild geese passing overhead. What a wonderful woman was bony Miss Watrous! She was a priestess seated on a moonlit rock lapped by a glimmering sea. The boy knelt before her on the lonely shore. And she dipped her fingers into that sea of ethereal plasma and sprinkled his bowed head. Thus was he baptised in the living mystery. Mythology, the only true history of the soul of man!

And then suddenly he saw riding past the schoolhouse the ghost of his father. Mounted stiffly, knees up, on his old paint-peeling bicycle. Dressed in his black business suit, his handmade boots stuck into the leather toe-clips provided instead of safety brakes. And still wearing on his hip, hidden beneath his coat, that long-bladed, razor-sharp toad-sticker with a bone handle! That strange dark man who was his father, who had faced down the son of Black Kettle, peddling past like an Ichabod with his life insurance premium book protruding out of his pocket!

This then – Old Excelsior, Miss Plush Bottom, Miss Marion, and Miss Watrous, with their straggly classes – was for March Columbia School.

There was also Leslie Shane.

3

Leslie Shane! Oh magical and musical name!

He had seen her first during one afternoon recess. She had been up in Old Excelsior's office with her mother, arranging to enter school; they had just moved into town. Now they came down the sandstone steps outside. Old Excelsior pointed out the girls' playground on the left and went back upstairs. Her mother walked away. And she was left alone to look about and see her new companions.

One like her sees more than this. In a group of children one sees the whole of society: the cheat, the coward and the bully, the quick wit, the dullard, the sensitive, and the vulgar. Each has his own capacity for understanding and spiritual growth that never enlarges; it only fills. The world of childhood is not so childish as the adult world that pompously proclaims it so. It sees this immediately with an intuition not yet dulled by experience nor clouded by reason. They *are*, simply, unaccountably, they are. Tall, strawhaired Grace already superficial and cheaply elegant; Eunice, beautiful and butter-mouthed; German Marie whole-souled and stolid; Two Bit Liz eyeing the big boys from the ranches; Torchy swaggering in another new suit; the hunchback Thompson kid, smarter'n a whip. And another skinny lad leaning against a tree, fumbling with a jackknife. The casual proper pose of a boy too superior to notice a mere new girl who has entered school. But she catches the sudden tautness of his body, the furtive glance. Clear across the gravel and the strip of lawn the glance holds. A swift red stains his brown cheeks. He squirms like a grub impaled on a pin. And still the glance holds. It is a moment of strange truth that time will never alter nor explain. She knows that his soul streams out toward her like a flood, and that he mysteriously seeks to dam it, powerless as he is. A queer, contradictory boy! She simply, shyly smiles.

It releases him like an arrow. He leaps forward, grabs Torchy's cap and throws it into the drinking fountain, and dashes off as if pursued by a thousand shrieking demons.

She had seen him! She had seen him!

A mighty song filled him, a great strength leaped into him. By a single glance, like the touch of Moses' rod, the hard rock fastness of his being had been split asunder. Beauty and wonder, joy and life gushed from him. For the first time he felt whole and sound, the premonition of manhood. Out on the prairie he stopped, panting. Inside him wrestled a boy and a man. Then the two merged into one that was neither; sheepishly it crept back to where, unobserved, he could stare helplessly at her who held him in such magnificent bondage.

She was leaning against the balustrade, watching the girls playing around the drinking fountain. The wind had blown back her spruce-green sweater, played with the hem of her corn-yellow dress. She was small but well formed, with the suggestion of early maturity. Her hair was a mass of apricot-colored curls, her face pale and covered with freckles. She had large brown eyes, a wide mouth, and a stub, sympathetic nose – a face that never in childhood was childish, but only unawakened. Later he was to see and remember always her thin, delicate hands with their tiny network of blue veins. The hands that already, before her face and body, had become a woman's.

Leslie was in his class and sat in the next row. Mr. Shane, after managing Fred Harvey railroad lunch rooms for years, had just bought the Saddle Rock Grill. The family lived close to March, two blocks west, on top of Bijou Hill. Mrs. Shane impressed March as cold and shrewd; it was she who had managed to enter Leslie in Columbia, establishing the "precedent" Ona had used to insure March's own return to school. The family owned an automobile in which, on rainy days, Mrs. Shane drove Leslie to school. On good days she walked, and March longed to walk with her. Instead, tortured with his own cowardice, he straggled homeward a block behind her.

Before he could screw up courage to catch up with her, his turn came to stay after school and dust erasers. A few afternoons later he came out to see her ahead of him. Alone. Sauntering along, a step at a time. Panic overcame him. The blind urge which drove him to her, and that equal force which restrained him before they merged – this was the eternal craving and the stubborn integrity of every human soul driven by loneliness to seek that which must be found only inside itself. Suddenly she looked around. Just as suddenly he was beside her, roughly grabbing her books to clench under his own arm.

"You're awfully slow walking," she said quietly. "I've been waiting for you."

"I'm done beatin' erasers," he muttered.

"I'm glad. I was wondering if you were going to walk home with me."

She looked up at him. Her eyes were clear and unquestioning, dark and fathomless. Into them he plunged helplessly, as if into a mindless oneness that absorbed him wholly. He came up naked and clean of shame, stripped of pretense and fear.

"I am. I'd rather walk home with you than anything." Then in a rush of feeling he added. "I like you, Leslie. Oh, I sure like you!"

Lightly she laid a hand on his arm. "Yes. I know. You don't have to tell me. I know!"

And sedately, in silence, they walked on.

Bad weather set in. Her mother drove her back and forth to school. Then, late in October, Old Excelsior called a meeting of the eighth grade. "Marie is giving a Halloween party for the members of her class and its teachers on Friday night. You are all graduating next June and should know how to conduct yourselves like grown-ups. So every boy in the class must escort a girl. Boys, be gentlemanly! Agree among yourselves whom you will ask. And tomorrow after school report to me the name of the young lady who will accompany you, and for whom you will be responsible."

Boys and girls went out giggling in two groups. A few bolder boys made a rush across the lawn, then swaggered triumphantly across the street to congregate in front of the drug-and-candy store. March slunk across behind them.

"I got Eunice!" boasted one. "And didn't waste no time either!"

"That's nothin'! Didn't you see me givin' Grace the wink right when Old Excelsior was talkin'? Ferris did. He seen me!"

"Who's goin' to take Two-Bit Liz behind her old man's barn afterward?" snickered another. "Not me this time! Her old lady purt near caught me last time!"

March waited apprehensively for what would come.

Cecil James spoke first. "I asked the new girl – Leslie Shane. I guess she's pretty enough to ride in my dad's new car if he'll drive us."

"So'd I," said a lanky redhead named Bob Schwartz. "She nodded yes and didn't say nothing about you."

March's face had gone sallow. "She's goin' with me," he said quietly.

A titter went around. "Fight it out, all three of you!"

Cecil drawled, "She must think she's popular, sayin' yes to everybody. Who does she think she is?"

"Well, I asked her," said Bob, "and I'm goin' to take her."

"I said I'm takin' her," March insisted in a low monotonous voice.

A curious, cold expectancy held him as he looked at Schwartz' long rangy body lounging carelessly against the fence. He remembered the long sharp blade his father always carried on his hip, and he felt the comforting shape of his own jackknife in his hip pocket, knowing triumphantly that he really meant what he said as he had meant nothing else before.

Schwartz lit a cigarette. "Oh, the hell with anybody so far gone on a girl! But I've got a good mind to turn her name in too, just to see what she says!" He spat and walked away.

There was no triumph in March as he slunk homeward, obscessed by the fear of asking Leslie and hearing that she already had promised to go to the party with Cecil or Bob.

She had been sitting on the gutter down the street for nearly half an hour. "Hello, March!" she said cheerfully, rising like apparition before him.

They walked in silence to the railroad tracks before she asked quietly, "Are you going to Marie's party?"

"I guess so," he answered fearsomely. And then, "Why don't we go together, seeing that we live so close?"

"All right."

He was bathed now in a wonderful aura of delicious warmth and self-assurance. As always, once they were alone, he lost his fear of her. He took her books, his gaze caressing hungrily her slim white hands with their fine blue veins, her freckled face, the apricot curls protruding from her green wool tam.

"As long as you live a ways on the other side of me, why don't you just drop by on the way to the party?" he suggested casually. "I'll take you home, of course, but there's no need climbin' the hill twice."

"Sure. Why, sure I will, March. I'm glad you're going with me. We haven't talked together for a long time."

That Friday evening as he dressed in his blue serge suit, pinning to the lapel an enamel Confederate flag given him by Mrs. Rogier, March was conscious-stricken. He ought to go after Leslie, but he dreaded knocking on the door and meeting Mrs. Shane's cold, inquisitive face. So, dressed up, he lingered downstairs, waiting for supper. It was always late; the Rogiers could never pull themselves together.

"Is Leslie Shane going to be at the party?" asked his mother.

"Everybody in class," he mumbled.

"Do you like her?" asked Leona. "She's a pretty girl."

"Maybe you can bring her home," suggested Nancy.

The family finally settled down at table. What an array it was, thought March. Mrs. Rogier, Ona, Nancy, Leona, himself, and Rogier for a change. He could hardly eat. There was a sudden loud knocking on the front door. March lunged to open the front door.

By the dim light behind him he saw the figure of a burly man, grinning humorously from a considerate, benign face. It was Mr. Shane.

"Well, young man!" he roared in a heavy jocular voice. "I've brought your girl here for you to take to the party. But see that you bring her home. Understand?"

He reached around behind him, pushed Leslie over the threshold, and walked away.

March, petrified, brought her into the dining room, managed to introduce her.

Mrs. Rogier rose up in wrathful indignation. "You mean to say, March, you are escorting this young lady and didn't have the courtesy to call for her? I am ashamed, deeply ashamed. Young lady, you have my full permission to resent this insult by returning directly home!"

"March! How could you?" gasped Ona.

Leslie was not at all embarrassed. Perfectly composed, she said easily, "March and I understand each other. Here, have a piece of the candy I'm taking to Marie." She passed around a satin box of chocolates. March's eyes met those of his mother with the same unspoken guilt: why hadn't he thought to bring a gift?

Rogier indecorously was the only one to take a piece. He took two. After which he rose and put his arm around her. "Young lady! You've confronted with courage and equanimity a bastion of outmoded conservatism! You have given me some mighty tasty candy everybody else was too polite to touch. I welcome you into this house!"

It was awful, Rogier touched with port after starving in Cripple Creek. March backed Leslie hastily of of the room.

"Take care of that boy!" Rogier boomed out behind them. "You can see he's got a chicken-heart!"

"Don't you worry, Mr. Rogier!" Leslie called back as they closed the door. "We'll get along all right!"

Her mature assurance oppressed March as they walked in darkness to Marie's house. Yet all these insults and injuries to his pride, his own angry shame, were dissipated by the fragrant perfume of her proximity, the feel of her arm through his. "It's too bad we're so young and have to wait so long till we're grown up," she said.

He stopped and turned her face around, his thumb caressing her cheek. Then he kissed her on the mouth. He had never kissed a girl before and it was a funny feeling. The touch of those warm, dry, velvety lips which clung to his, and through which stemmed the indefinable essence of all that was Leslie Shane! Charlotte, sweet Charlotte, born a virgin, died a harlot, had kissed him once before. She was his first love, but the rapaciousness, the hungry loneliness of her kiss had frightened him. It had bruised his lips! This was different. It was something he couldn't understand or ever forget. He only knew, even then, that whatever became of them both, they were sealed together by a bond which could never be broken.

They reached Marie's house. The lights were blazing. All the members of the eighth grade class were there and their teachers. Blindfolded, they pinned the tail on the donkey, played blind-man's bluff, dropped the handkerchief. In the cellar they paraded through dark tunnels illuminated by ghostly skeletons and Death's heads. They bobbed for apples in wash tubs, ate sandwiches and pumpkin pie with ice cream. Through all this childish fun, the flow of ghostly time, the boy was acutely aware of Leslie's face gently smiling at him across the room. And now they gathered to sit on chairs arranged in a semi-circle around the fireplace.

"Just this one game before we leave," announced Miss Plush Bottom, holding up one of the forfeits given her by the students for the game. "What shall the owner do to redeem it? Just this one last game!"

The forfeit was March's jackknife. He sat deathly still. "Bow to the wisest, kneel to the prettiest, and kiss the one he loves best!" somebody shouted.

"And it's March's! March's!" shrieked Grace.

He was pale and shaking. It was the first forfeit in the game, and the voice sounded in his ears the irrevocable sentence he must pass before Old Excelsior, Miss Plush Bottom, Cecil James, Bob Schwartz – publicly, before everybody.

In silence and loneliness he got unsteadily to his feet. He tried to smile and the pitiful attempt contorted his dark face. To pass it off as a joke! To kneel in front of Marie or Two Bit Liz! This was his only frantic desire. And yet as if in a dream he saw her to whom he was so irrevocably committed. She was sitting head down, hands clasped, modestly withdrawn.

He stumbled across the room to stand in front of her, bowed stiffly, got down on his knees. She raised her face. He could not look into her eyes, and quickly and gently kissed her on the forehead.

Then he rose and with hands clenched at his sides stalked back to his chair.

Old Excelsior rose at once. "That's enough of that! Don't you think, Miss Thomas, that kissing games are out of place among children of this age? Like March. They are simply too intense! And besides, it's late. We should all go home."

They walked silently out of the house into the darkness, arm in arm. Through the gloom of the great cottonwoods along the creek.

"It wasn't just a game? You really meant it?" asked Leslie.

"Sure, or I wouldn't have done it."

"Thank you, March."

"That's all right," he said. "That's the way it is, that's all."

A light appeared: the single bare globe in the railroad underpass at the head of Bijou Street. Self-consciously they walked through to the street. A strange feeling followed March. This was the way he had come to his grandfather's house that other night long ago. In its feeling of aloneness and loneliness, he could hear faintly behind him a rattle that kept increasing in volume and meaning. Leslie, he noticed, was glancing apprehensively sideways at the wooden shack now haunted by the murderer and the murdered and the bloody axe that had served as the final bond between them. In silence he walked her down the middle of the dusty road, over the bridge at Shook's Run, and past his grandfather's house to the arc-light at the corner. From its aura into more darkness they climbed Bijou Hill to Leslie's house.

The porch light was on. "I think I'd better go in. They're waiting up for me," she said.

He hesitated. "Wait here in the porch light, will you, till I get to the bottom of the hill? Then I'll wave and you can run inside."

"Yes, that's better!" she agreed at once. "But run fast, March!"

They gasped hands, stared into each other's eyes. Then March ran quickly down the hill to turn, wave back, and run on home in darkness.

4

Late that November Abe and Jake, in their cabin at the Sylvanite, were preparing to go to town. It was unusually early, before noon. They put on their black suits and black string ties, rubbed their boots off, brushed their hats. They moved somberly and quietly, as if preparing themselves for a funereal ordeal rather than a weekly spree. Finally dressed and ready, they closed their duffle bags and stood looking at each other's long sad face.

"It just don't seem right to be leavin' here before we tell him, man to man. The Colonel's been mighty good to us fer a long time," said Jake.

Abe rubbed the moisture off his sweaty hands, pulled at his mustache – irresolute movements that betrayed his own reluctance. "We can't be waitin' here till he comes to tell him the hole's worked out and we're finally leavin'. You know the Colonel! He'd talk us out of it, and we'd be stuck again. That's why I say we'll meet him when he steps off the noon train. It'll be easier tellin' him there – And I reckon a drink beforehand won't hurt none."

"Well – "

They gave a last look at the cabin they had tidied up, latched the door behind them, and duffle bags over shoulder strode down the trail –

Rogier, unable to catch the noon train, did not arrive till midafternoon. Jake and Abe, with their duffle bags beside them, were waiting on the platform when he swung off the train. Rogier did not notice the bags for the knots of people, all excitedly talking. A strange air of expectancy seemed to imbue the very air.

"Well, boys!" he greeted them warmly. "Never expected to see you here! Come on! Let's have a drink at the Mint before we go back!"

Jake nodded and walked off with Rogier. Abe dallied behind to leave the duffle bags in the depot, then joined them in a comparatively quiet corner in the Mint. Rogier could not help but notice his companions' unusual animation. Cold sober, their faces were flushed; their eyes sparkled with a mysterious expectancy like those of two boys waiting for Santa Claus. Nor did Rogier fail to observe the tremor of excitement running through the men at the long bar. Occasionally above the murmur of conversation rose the name "Cresson."

"Dom me!" he said at last. "What's goin' on up here? You both look like the cat that swallowed the canary. Hit another streak of shipping ore?"

Abe leaned forward. "Colonel, it's not the Sylvanite. It's the Cresson."

"That old workin'?" snorted Rogier. "Well, tell me about it!"

Jake looked solemnly around him before he spoke in a low voice. "It's a mighty big thing, Colonel, and still secret even if it's leakin' out. But we know Luke, and he says he'll give us a peek – just a peek, mind! – if we come up right away. So we been waitin' for you."

A curious tremor of foreboding shook Rogier. "Let's go then!"

Abe and Jake strode out of the saloon. Rogier followed them. The Cresson was sunk in the gulch between Bull and Raven hills. They rode the Low Line to the Elkton and walked up the gulch to the portal of the Cresson.

What had got into these two old fools, Rogier kept wondering, to make them so excited about anything here? The Cresson had been a marginal working ever since its discovery in 1894; the government report on the district in 1906 didn't even list it. But somehow the mine had been foisted on a couple of real estate men in Chicago who periodically sold a few shares of stock and leased its working levels to different operators who could never make its low grade ore pay. The shaft was down to 600 feet and the mine was $80,000 in the red.

Then three or four years ago, as Rogier recalled, Dick Roelofs had taken over its management. He was a young man, a graduate of an engineering college somewhere in Pennsylvania, but unable to find steady work he clerked in the Green Bee Grocery on Second Street. Rogier had pricked up his ears when Roelofs, with a small crew under Luke Shepherd, began to lift the Cresson out of debt. He sank the shaft to 1,000 feet, blasted out great stopes, and by economic management began to make the low grade ore pay dividends. Ore which averaged only $15.67 a ton! Why that was no better than the Sylvanite! The Cresson however seemed to have plenty of it, but still the mine was barely making out and Rogier had forgotten it till now.

The surface plant looked tidy enough he admitted when he reached it: a great smooth-rolling drum, clear indicators, a commodious new cage. The place was crowded with men. From them stepped Luke Shepherd.

"We come like you said we could, Luke," said Abe.

"We'll have to hurry," replied Luke. "Roelof's bringin' the officials to go down, and the whole workin' will be closed tighter'n a drum. Maybe we oughtn't, but if we get out before they come – just a peek, understand?"

They stepped into the cage, dropped swiftly, smoothly to the twelfth level. A man with a sawed-off shotgun met them when they stepped out.

"It's all right, Sam," said Luke. "Hold the cage. We're only goin' to take a quick look."

He struck off into a drift, turned into a lateral, another drift, another crosscut. Behind him plodded Rogier, Abe, and Jake. "He's tryin' to mix us up," whispered Abe, never a man to be lost underground. "You countin' your steps?"

"Why? You ain't figurin' you'll ever get in here again?" asked Jake.

Rogier began to tremble with a curious expectancy.

The four men brought up short against a huge bank-vault, steel door. Luke sounded a signal, and it was opened by three guards with drawn revolvers.

"It's me," said Luke, "I'm givin' these boys a quick look. The cage's waiting."

The guards stepped aside to reveal a large hole in the back wall about the size of a doorway and just above the level of lateral. "Go on up!" directed Luke.

Rogier, pushed ahead, climbed up the platform, followed by Abe and Jake. Then Luke behind them lighted and raised over their heads his magnesium flare.

Rogier uttered one gasp – a gasp that seemed to empty his lungs and bowels – and then was silent. What he saw was a geode, a vug, a "poop hole" as Abe called it – an immense hollow chamber in solid rock nearly forty feet high, twenty feet long, and fifteen feet wide. A cave of sparkling splendor that almost blinded him, a cave from whose walls and ceiling hung crystals of sylvanite-and calaverite crystals, and flakes of pure gold big as thumbnails glowing in the light. A cave floored with gold particles thick as sand and glittering like a mass of jewels. Everywhere he looked was gold tellurium of astounding purity, sparkling gold crystals, glittering gold sands; even a protruding small boulder of quartz gleamed golden. Here it was as he had envisioned it so clearly: an Aladdin's Cave transported from an Arabian Night to the twentieth century, a treasure greater than Croesus ever took from the sands of the Pactolus, or Solomon from the mines of Ophir.

Somebody with a hand on his collar jerked him back. In a daze he was walked back to the cage, ascended, found himself back in the Mint. "We got to pick up our bags," said Jake. Abe stopped at a corral for burros. "It's too far to walk," said Abe. "The Colonel looks played out."

Voices shouted in his ears. Vague phantasmagoria flitted across his mind. Arriving at the cabin late that afternoon, he insisted on going down into the Sylvanite. "Man the hoist, Jake," ordered Abe. "I'll take him down."

They went down to the bottom level. In the darkness, lit only by the flare of their carbide lamps they traversed the drift to the crosscut, turned into a giant stope, the vug Abe had opened up. Rogier knelt on the floor, sifted blasted granite through his fingers. He got up, ran his hands over the sheer rock walls, stared up at the ceiling. "Abe! Lock off this vug. Keep out all trespassers. Nobody comes down here but you and Jake and me! Understand?"

"Colonel! There's nothin' here!" remonstrated Abe. "Not even $15 ore! That's why me and Jake were goin' to leave the old hole. That was Cresson vug we saw! Remember! Not here in the Sylvanite!"

"The Cresson! Not here!" Rogier clawed at the bare rock walls. "The Cresson! No, not here!"

Abe picked him up bodily, carried him to the station, furiously rang his bells. Once up, he carried Rogier to the cabin, laid him on his bunk.

"He's havin' a spell," he told Jake.

"What'll we do?" asked Jake.

"Cool head, warm feet," said Abe. "That's all I know."

Jake bathed his face with cold water. Abe put a hot-water bag at his feet.

"Leavin' me and the Sylvanite?" Rogier kept crying with a piteous voice. "Is that what you said, with your bags all packed? Just when what I said—"

"We were, but we ain't now, Colonel!" shouted Jake. "Everything you told us was true as all get out. We saw it! Gold crystals hangin' from the walls and the ceilin'! Gold dust thicker'n a carpet on the floor! All them riches of Midas shinin' in our faces! Just like you told us, Colonel, over'n over! We ain't leavin' you now!"

They found some whiskey, mixed it with hot water, and poured it down his throat. He stopped mumbling. His lips grew still. The old body stiffened, then relaxed in sleep.

Abe and Jake, their backs to his bunk, sat before the fireplace.

"It was just like he said," Jake kept muttering. "Everything! Just like the Colonel said!"

"The twelfth level, and we're on the fifth," said Abe. "How're we ever goin' to get down?"

Day after day Rogier sat there on his bunk or at the table, reading the newspapers brought him. Some 1,400 sacks of crystals and flakes had been scraped from the walls and ceiling of the

Cresson vug and sold for $378,000. A thousand more sacks had been gathered from the gold-littered floor, bringing $90,637. Eight four-horse wagons with armed guards had transported a shipment of surrounding ore from the collar of the shaft to five broad-gauge cars sealed and marked for the Globe Smelter at Denver, which brought more than $686,000. And then, when at last Rogier was induced to go to town, it was only to see exhibited in the window of the bank a cancelled check showing an amount of $468,637.29 for a shipment of 150 tons.

Rogier, like all Cripple Creek, the whole world, was stunned by these richest shipments of ore ever made. They raised the yearly mean ore value of the Cresson to $33 a ton, yielded an extra dividend to its stockholders of more than a million dollars, and raised the annual production of Cripple Creek to $13,683,424, the highest in a decade.

All taken from a vug in the Cresson, that worthless mine, not the Sylvanite! He could not believe it, and every day he went down the shaft to examine the bare rock walls. Coming back up, he sat for hours envisioning the rewards had the discovery been made in his own mine. The different tune of the townspeople who had ridiculed the Sylvanite, the way his idiocyncrasies would have been miraculously converted into marks of genius, the ready acclaim of the Ruxton Club and all Little London. He thought magnanimously of the money he would have wired to Boné, of the check he would have stiffly handed to Timothy, of the fortune with which he would have rewarded ever-faithful Ona. And Martha! Dom! He would have built for her at last a mansion in the North End that would shame the palace of an Oriental potentate, though to be sure she had not mentioned this old desire for a dozen years or more. And Abe and Jake, who had stuck with him through thick and thin! God Almighty!

—and all these mundane rewards, long past due, were yet but the trivial by-products of his one desire. A million dollars profit would have been but a bank account on which to draw means of continuing his search into the black chasm of the world below. At $40 a foot, say—he began to compute the depth to which he might drive.

And then into these resplendent daydreams obtruded the harsh insistent truth: it was in the Cresson, not the Sylvanite, the miracle of wealth had happened. And with a shriek of despair he would fling over in his bunk to pound the log wall with his fists.

Jake would roll him back with a brawny hand on his shoulder. "Colonel! Don't take it so hard. We never believed you, Abe and me, until we saw it with our own eyes. And there it was, just like you told us. The gold and the glory, shinin' plain as day. We seen it. With our very eyes. We ain't givin' up the Sylvanite. Why, we might hit it right here!"

Rogier sat up to listen to Abe. "Colonel, let's don't go off half-cocked. They never hit that rich stuff till they went down to below 1,000 feet. And they couldn't get down that far without the Roosevelt drainage tunnel that opened up the district to lower levels. It's that simple. Now I figure that with depth we're all goin' to open up more ore bodies."

How strange it was to hear these two old obstinate faithfuls preaching the sermon he had expounded for years! He began to come to himself, to eat a little, to sleep.

"We ain't leavin' yet," Jake assured him. "Take it easy, Colonel. Things will work out."

And shortly before Christmas, Rogier returned to Little London shaken but not shattered.

5

Mary Ann and a gentleman friend also had come down for Christmas from the small mining town of Silverton. They were a day late; the little narrow-gauge train had been blocked by a snowslide for eighteen hours. She and her friend Sam had eaten five of the fifteen pounds of candy she was bringing home, but that afternoon a new mahogany-red box phonograph was delivered from uptown with ten records.

"It's the very latest: a Victrola! I want my family and dear little girl to enjoy their Christmas present the year around!"

Mrs. Rogier did not have the indelicacy to inquire what had happened to Jim, and obligingly installed her and Sam in the two adjoining middle rooms on the second floor. Sam was a brawny, middle-aged man who for years had been a railroad man, and still wore the traditional polka-dotted blue shirts starched stiff as iron. He had been a great help to Mary Ann in Silverton and she intimated that he might continue to be a great help to her in business in years to come.

At supper she left the family no doubt of her acumen as a shrewd businesswoman, and that it was unforseen conditions which had made her Chocolate Shoppe a failure.

"No, with conditions the way they were, Silverton is no go. ABSOLUTELY no go! And such taste you NEVER saw! Sticky nougat, colored gum drops, plantation sticks – all glucose, mind you, the Greek across the street used. Did they see the difference in my pure sugar creams, my bitter-sweets?"

"Maybe the difference was the price," suggested Ona. "Silverton's a dwindling mining town isolated half the year. You didn't expect poor miners' wives to buy your chocolates at eighty cents a pound when they could get ordinary sweets at forty? Or a really nice bag of mixed candy for a quarter?"

"That's beside the point. You just don't understand business, Ona. But I'm considering a new location. Alamosa. A thriving town in San Luis Valley. Sam tells me it's just the place to appreciate quality. Perhaps in the spring – "

How difficult it was for her to find the niche where she belonged as a maker of fine candies in a shop catering only to the elite. This was where she had started, in Durgess' Delicatessen which served the North End trade. She had heard the ring of the cash register, known the self-importance of being proprietor of her own "Shoppe," and after her divorce she had wedded business. And yet within her was a streak of wildness that impelled her to one remote mining town after another in the Rockies instead of to the populous marts of the state.

She was a small, nervous, opinionated woman. She spoke sharply but with a husky voice the jargon of commerce without understanding the one hard-rock basis of its function: distribution only at a profit. Like all Rogiers, she had no conception of the value of money. She might be down on her uppers, head over heels in debt, but the dollar in her pocket came out with free-handed generosity at a moment's whim. Her judgment was usually in error, her heart never.

Nancy she loved volubly, extravagantly – and was always ready to abandon her at the next beckon of Business. Nancy, during her mother's infrequent visits, accepted her protestations with a pleasure tinged by a sense of wonder. She was small, rather chubby, with dark brown hair and a dead white skin. The antithesis of Leona, she was somber and quiet as a mouse, preferring her own little corner to the world outside. No! – never like Leona was she joyous, active, swift as an arrow. And never like March, cruelly alive with an intolerable awareness, a stranger to all men. She was always quiet, tender, gentle, a passive pool.

To Sam she was pleasant but remote, as was the whole family. Nobody could fathom Mary Ann's attraction to him. Always the first at table, he ate heartily, spoke little. After meals he wandered down to the station to watch the trains come in. Between times Ona and Mary Ann washed and starched and ironed his blue shirts.

One evening Mary Ann, for want of something more important to say, imparted a scrap of information to Mrs. Rogier and Ona that they had awaited nearly thirty years. In Silverton an old prospector with white hair and a long beard used to ride down into town on a shaggy burro for supplies. He always stopped in Mary Ann's Chocolate Shoppe for a quarter's worth of taffy "chews" to carry back. Every month, regular as clockwork, said Mary Ann. Early that winter he had failed to come. The cold was terrible; the drifts in the mountains were six, eight feet high; even the elk were starving in the high valleys.

A group of men broke trail to his solitary cabin up the gulch. The old man was in his shanty, frozen to death. He had burned up the flooring and all the rude furniture, and was lying in bed wrapped up in his blankets with a half-chewed-up slab of raw salt pork. The drifts were too deep to bring his body down to Silverton. The men had simply placed it in his tunnel and blown up the entrance.

His next-to-worthless claim was registered as the "Molly H." His own name was unknown. He had been called only "Old Tom."

"Tom Hines! Sister Molly's Tom! Our Tom!" Ona's voice rang out with all the cloying pain and bitterness of thirty years suddenly washed away. "Oh, why didn't he ever come home?"

"Maybe so," said Mary Ann. "Of course I never knew him."

There was nothing else for her to say; it was the end of a tale that needed no epitaph.

Yet to Ona, clenching her lands in her lap, it was more than this. Tom, Cable, and Rogier—each in his way had given themselves as hostages to this deep and spacious earth high above the hopes of men, close under the inscrutable eyes of a Heaven that attested the heroism of their labor, their greed and ambitions, their faithfulness or their unfitness to the futile task of its subjection. Tom was ours, she thought, and yet he was America's too. He dies, the Strattons die, and the Tabors and the Walshes, but the immense and wild and lonely earth endures forever. The earth with its haunting ghostliness, its secret terror, and the savage exultant cry that rises by night from these lofty Rockies when moonlight floods its canyons, and the cougar screams from the aspen thicket, and the tall pale peaks hunch up their shoulders to brush the frost from the stars. They die; great new cities arise from their campfires; the gleaming rails span gorge and creek and gulley; the steel bites deeper into granite. And when in a forgotten gulch, on a lonely hillside, one comes upon their bleached bones, their upturned skulls seem fixed in a derisive grin. For the earth endures forever and is greater than its masters. Yet why do men, mere men, forever and always, without stint, hurl their strength against the rock, plod on towards a star that gleams and fades and dies?

"I think, Mary Ann," said Mrs. Rogier quietly. "that we shouldn't mention this to Daddy right now. He seems a little upset. Maybe because of that excitement about the Cresson discovery. At a later time, perhaps, a marker would be appropriate. But not now! Do you understand?"

Rogier, confronted daily by a strange man in his house who wore the starched blue garb of heaven dotted with stars but who never contributed an earthly dollar for his board, stayed in his shop out back. Seated on his high stool, his frail shoulders hunched over the drafting board, he seemed bent under the burden of an invisible and insupportable guilt.

The Cresson vug, shining, sparkling, and glowing with a wealth and splendor greater than the Aztec treasure room of Montezuma or that of Atahualpa the Inca, Son of the Sun, had been too much for him. He had been betrayed by something within himself he had never suspected. Never! – no, never in all his conscious life had he craved with the greed of most men wealth for its own sake, the power and luxury it bought. Yet at one glimpse of that incandescent chamber a dormant and hidden desire, a karmic predisposition inherited from a previous existence, had leaped forth. He had ignored the golden sun within him, reflected for his edification in the chamber before him, thinking only of the mortal debts its earthly treasure could cancel. Betrayed! Betrayed in his pride by the secret propensity, that hidden increment in his cumulative character of ages past! Bowing his head, he contritely accepted the verdict of his own accusation. No wonder that luminescent vug had been placed in the Cresson rather than in the Sylvanite! To teach him, old as he was, the lesson every man must learn in his time. But he would learn it now. He would root out every vestige of inherited desire, all the shreds of false pride, envy and jealousy that embroidered it. Yes, by God! he swore not profanely, banging his fist on the board. Now he saw that chamber for what it really was: a dim reflection of that deep golden heart of the earth which mirrored the golden sun within him, a promise of his eventual self-fulfillment. Nothing would ever betray him again. He was consecrated for the last time to his search.

That search, he reflected in calmer hours, still led down. It was no longer he who constantly proposed and preached the sermon of depth. He didn't have to. Abe recognized it too. If the Cresson vug had been opened on the twelfth level, why wouldn't high-grade stuff be encountered at equal depth throughout the whole district? And the Roosevelt drainage tunnel was unwatering the region down to a thousand feet or more. So Abe and Jake were still staying on the job, at least for a time. To keep them there, Rogier had to pay their keep.

But how?

Suddenly, in a lucid moment, he happened to think of the life insurance policy Cable had taken out while trying to sell insurance. Straightway he rushed into the house to ascertain if it had ever been cashed. Ona was uptown fortunately, and it was with Mrs. Rogier he had his first battle. It ended an hour later with Rogier flinging back out to the shop in a fine rage. Mrs. Rogier sat rocking away before the front window. Not for a minute did she fool herself the matter was ended. And at the first sight of Ona coming down the street, she jumped up, threw a coat around her shoulders, and hurried out to meet her.

Arm in arm the two women walked up Bijou to Wahsatch, turned on Platte, and came down El Paso. Talking like parrots, they discussed every phase of the matter except the most important – Rogier's frantic obsession with Cripple Creek.

"Of course he's just Daddy and always will be," admitted Ona. "I'd give him anything I owned. But Jonathan did plan so much on leaving something to the children. He loved them so much! That's why I'm saving this policy to put March through college. Mother, he's got to have a chance! He can be just as big a success as Boné with an education. And this is all I have left in the world, Mother – all I ever will have. But Daddy –"

"Don't be a fool!" Mrs. Rogier told her sharply. "Didn't I tell him all that and more too? I tell you Daddy's – well, you know how he is. And he's gettin' far worse. The minute we get back to the house he's going to hit you up for that money. Don't you do it, Ona!"

"Mother! My own father! What'll I do?"—the one agonizing plea she asked over and over.

They turned through the underpass to Bijou again; it was getting late. "How much will that policy pay?" asked Mrs. Rogier.

"Five thousand dollars."

Mrs. Rogier walked a few steps in silence, then turned to Ona. "There's no use deluding ourselves. Something about women makes them all fools. They know it but can't help themselves. Daddy's going to get that money. I'm as sure of it as I am of Judgment Day. Now let me tell you what to do! Tell him it was for $3,500 and give it to him if you can't help it. Give me a thousand. I'll see it goes for a better purpose. And you hang on to the rest. Don't let a soul know you have it. Keep it for the time you just have to have it."

So it was when Rogier cornered Ona alone, begging the loan and promising rich returns, she gave him $3,500. That night was the first of many which they all passed in peaceful sleep. Ona with her conscience at rest because she had not withheld help from her father, and Rogier momentarily at ease because he could resume shaft drilling. Mrs. Rogier slept the most soundly of all. She had added another thousand dollars to her honor fund.

Early that spring Mary Ann and Sam left to open a new Chocolate Shoppe in Alamosa. Rogier hardly noticed their absence. He had gone up to the Sylvanite to encourage Abe and Jake. They had been convinced by the resplendent Cresson vug that an equal treasure might be found at depth here, or anywhere in the district. But Rogier had run out of the bulk of money Ona had given him before he had sunk the shaft to another level. So he persuaded them to open another exploratory drift on the level above with hand drills.

It was dull, hard work. But things were slow, and the remainder of Cable's insurance provided them wages. So they kept hammering away.

Rogier down in Little London could hear, like an echo, the faint tap of their hammers. For awhile it would cease. Then a rasp of gravel underneath his shoe or the sound of Mr. Pyle next door hammering nails into his fence started it again like a painful tooth or a phrase of remembered music. A faint tapping that began on top of his head, increasing into a staccato hammering on his skull that shook his whole bone structure. A devilish tattoo ceaselessly urging him to hurry down the shaft another level.

Where and how could he raise more money for shaft drilling he kept wondering. As he lay in bed at night, the loud hammering increased in volume and tempo. He could hear the hiss of escaping air under pressure, the reverberant thunder of steel drills biting down into granite, swelling into a full-bodied orchestration of musical and meaningful sound. Then suddenly, with a great crescendo, the finale was translated into its visual counterpart: the glorious spectacle of a golden sun whose facets of sylvanite and calaverite crystals reflected all colors of the spectrum. And this combined both light and sound, a music he could hear and see, in whose ineffable beauty he began to dissolve in peace and fulfillment.

And then, too swiftly, it faded. And again, like Boné's right hand fingering on a piano the few notes of the motif of the whole orchestration, there began the faint tapping of Abe and Jake's hammers.

6

Late one afternoon the Rogier's next door neighbor, Mr. Pyle, came to call. It was such an unusual occasion that Rogier and Mrs. Rogier, Ona and March, received him in the now somewhat shabby front room. The Rogiers and the childless Pyles were barely on speaking terms. Mrs. Pyle remained shut up in her house all day long, and Mr. Pyle was always out on business. Rogier characterized him as a bald-headed, sanctimonious, Presbyterian plate-passer and a sneak thief of a real-estater.

Ona, regarding Rogier's presence with trepidation, made haste to be cordial. "Why, Mr. Pyle! It's so nice of you to call. I do wish Mrs. Pyle had come too. May I make you some tea?"

"Nothing like that!" Pyle asserted. He seated himself in a rocker, carefully thumbed the crease in his trousers, and brushed his bald head. "This is not exactly a social call. I came to see why you do not join the church. This young man, particularly, should be in our Sunday School."

"I've told you before, Mr. Pyle," answered Mrs. Rogier testily. "We can't join the Presbyterian. We've always been Southern Methodists."

"But you are no longer members."

This was Mrs. Rogier's sore spot. "My husband built that church. He donated the work and lumber for it. It was I who in the early days scrubbed the floors, scoured the windows, washed all the curtains. For a quarter of a century or more our family served God in that church!" She paused to sniffle. "But then, Sir, when we suffered reverses, when our mining venture declined, we could no longer afford our large contributions. The new minister had the temerity to ask that we give up our pew to someone else. Mr. Pyle! I asked for my letter from the church! Now Sir, we serve God right here in this house, and expect God to serve us. It's His turn now!"

Pyle adjusted his cravat, frowned. "But what about the boy here? A young untried soul searching for the fold?"

"Please, Mrs. Pyle," answered Ona. "When March is older will be soon enough. When he can choose for himself. Understand?"

Rogier, figiting in his chair, could contain himself no longer. "Dom this snifflin' women's religion of yours! What are you going to dig below the grass roots of all this tomfoolery? What we need now is a man's religion, a religion with granite guts, the faith of mountains. No more Saviors will come walkin' across the Galilees. No more angels will come flittin' through the air like flocks of doves. The almighty God-power of Creation is locked in us all, in the earth itself. We've got to dig in, blast him out. The GRANITE GOD, by Jove, you keep locked up in the mountains, in the hard-rock canyons of your own flinty souls!"

March was embarrassed. Mrs. Rogier squirmed. "Daddy!" protested Ona.

"Very well, then. You refuse." Mr. Pyle got up, bowed, and stalked out.

"That skinflint!" snorted Rogier. "If I thought he'd take that boy in with his petticoat religion I'd switch his bony behind to kingdom come!"

"Enough of that, Daddy! You know he didn't come here to rile you up!" Ona whirled on March. "Nobody's making you go to church and Sunday School—although it might be good for you, the way you're running wild!"

March fled out to the shop behind his grandfather. The old man was sitting on his high stool at the drafting board. There was growing up between them a curious intimacy that dispensed with casual preliminaries. "I reckon you saw what I meant when Pyle came, didn't you boy? Sittin' in Sunday School listenin' to his stuff and nonsense. Or lettin' your mother send you to school to learn how to sit uptown in a stuffy office and do your thinkin' with a pencil, pilin' up money in the bank and whorin' after Broadmoor society trulls, and drivin' to church in a fancy automobile. It's a disease that's mighty catchin'—money-eczema, the uncontrollable itch, the national disease. You'd be better off sneakin' away from home and makin' a man of yourself."

"Yes, sir."

"But you have to learn your lessons, hey? Fairy tales, every one! Do they teach you what time is, space and the earth, and the cement that binds them into one? Bah! Look at me? Do you know who I am?"

March stared up at him wonderingly. Rogier's hat was off, a wisp of white hair stuck up above one ear like a horn. He began pounding on the drafting board with his fist.

"I'm the great eunuch, the wind between the worlds, the frost of glacial epochs yet to come. I'm the maker of seas, the destroyer of mountains, the biggest joke of Eternity and the invisible hand of Infinity. Time—they call me Time—a great worm crawling through Chaos eating up worlds and leaving in the dung behind me the seeds of worlds to come. I'm Time, boy, whose other name is Space, the unmeasured and measureless, the great uncreated without beginning and end, the nothing from which is created the all. If I can be shrunken to here"—he jabbed a pencil-point on the paper—"I can also expand to everywhere, just as I can be both now and always. Call me whatever you want. Divide me with clocks and calendars, fence me off with foot-rulers and surveying lines, and I vanish into the nameless One I am."

March crouched on an apple box before the old man's oratorical outburst. "Yes, sir."

"Get up from that box. Let's have it out here in the middle of the floor."

March obeyed.

Rogier slid off his perch and knelt under the long work bench, sliding blocks of wood out between his legs. These he gathered and stacked on the upturned box. "Come on," he demanded gruffly. "Scrape around. Let's have a stack."

Ransacking the barny shop, they stacked up a column of blocks reaching almost to the lofty ceiling. Rogier clambered down the ladder and stood looking at the faintly swaying pillar. His sleeves were covered with sawdust, shavings stuck to his coat and white hair. "There, by Jove! That column of blocks represents space-time, geologic time—the age and surface depth of this one little earth we think we know all about. Do you get me?"

"Yes, sir."

"Then tear off a piece of that onion-skin tracing paper on the drafting board." When the boy brought it, he ordered, "Now skite up that ladder and lay it on the top block. Better spit on it so it'll stick – It don't make the pillar much higher, hey?" he called as March leaned over carefully from the top of the ladder. "Well, come on down and see that it makes a lot less difference from down here."

For a minute they stood together, staring.

"Now, son," Rogier went on, "the thinness of that piece of paper you can hardly see up there represents ALL the time of the existence of ALL mankind, of all your recorded history and unwritten legends, your dom fairy tales. In the thinness of that paper is buried Nineveh, Carthage, Thebes, and Tyre. All the antiquities of Babylon and Egypt, the lost cities of Africa, and the templed cities in the jungles of America, Uxmal and Chichén Itzá, and proud Cuzco high in the Inca Andes. And more than that! The great civilizations on lands that sank under the sea ages before naked savages were roaming through the forests that grew in the streets of Paris."

He climbed up to sit on the work bench.

"Look now at that top block—that piece of red cedar about an inch thick," he demanded. "In that little time of up to sixty million years ago was formed the oldest rock here in Colorado, and the mountains and the seas began looking pretty much like they do now. Vertebrates started to stand on their hind legs. The hairy ape changed into a hairy cave man spearin' hairy elephants, mastodons with mighty tusks, and monsters seventy feet long with even longer names. A dom little time ago when what we call modern life began!

"To six inches down from the top there were great crawling reptiles a hundred feet long and weighing thirty tons, snaky-necked reptiles swimmin' in the seas, and snake-like birds flappin' through the air with leather wings. And the earth was just cooling off, coal red, making the Painted Desert in Arizona and the Great Red Valley in the Black Hills.

"And to a couple of feet down – maybe as far as that chunk of quarter-sawed oak – are fossils and the prints of insects, fish, and oyster-like things that lived in the hot mud and seas that took the place of the mountains. Everything was hot and stinky, the oceans were meanderin' through America, and plants were beginning to form and creep across the land bridges from Brazil to Africa, and from Asia to Alaska – jungle plants.

"Yes sir!" Rogier slapped his leg. "All this in just the top three feet or so in that column of blocks. Seven hundred million years or thereabouts. Below that – you see that piece of maple sticking out? A single rock stickin' up in Russia, the oldest rock in the world, two billion years old. And below that, in all the rest of the column down to the floor, no plants, no animals, nothing. Eight billion, ten billion years, who knows, nothing but the mysterious, eternal earth, the dust of the rock that endures forever. There, boy, that's time as we think we know it!"

A vacuous look crept into his eyes as he sat picking sawdust from his sleeve. Then they brightened as he lowered his voice. "I reckon you're catchin' on now to what a man might find out if he could sink a shaft to the bottom of that column, to the beginning of time, eh? Why, he's likely to discover that he's had all his work for nothing! All that time, the whole dom column, is condensed in that piece of paper on top; in a pencil point marked on it; right in himself, by Jove!" He tapped his head. "And the reason is, like I told you before, he's the Beginning and the End which meet like the ends of a great circle. Like this."

Jumping down from the work bench to go to the pillar of blocks, he raised his right hand toward the top, his left hand to the bottom, as if to bend them together.

At his touch the pillar swayed.

"Look out, Granddad! The blocks are comin' down!" yelled March.

Rogier tripped and went sprawling, as with a roar the stacked-up wooden blocks came tumbling down. He threw both hands above his head, diving from his knees to safety behind a floor post. But a piece of falling wood had gashed his forehead; he came out from the vast wooden talus with a thin trickle of blood running down his temple.

'I told you to lay them blocks on straight! That's what your education's doin'!"

March contritely held out his handkerchief. "I'm sorry, Granddad. I didn't mean to. But I got the idea. Honest."

Rogier whipped around upon him. "Who says you got the idea? That's the idea on the floor! Diastrophism. Crustal unrest, continual uplifts and subsidences. Why, these mountains have sunk under the sea a dozen times. Didn't you find sea shells on the slope of the Peak?" He kicked the heap of blocks on the floor. "They build up again, and not with your help either, to maintain the isotatic equilibrium of the whole earth. And none of these blocks are ever destroyed. Cut 'em up for kindling, make sawdust out of them. The wood's still there. Burn it. You can't get rid of the ashes. Why? Palingenesis. Eternal palingenesis. No death. Just change. What you need, son, is to get out of school and suck some wisdom from the teat of a granite outcrop!"

He stalked out grumbling to the hydrant to wash the blood off his face.

A few days later when March came home from school he saw a strange young man sitting in the front room with his mother.

"Come in here, March," called Ona. "I want you to meet Mr. Austin. Mr. Howard Austin. He's the assistant in the Fred Harvey news stand at the big new Santa Fe depot, and boards with Mrs. Jenkins up the street. We've been thinking you'd be just right for the newsboy they need. Now run upstairs and get into your blue serge suit so you can go down with him to see the manager."

"Mr. Warren is very particular about neatness," said the young man, himself neatly dressed in blue serge. He was blond, blue-eyed, about twenty-five years old. "The Fred Harvey uniform is blue serge. We furnish the cap and the brass buttons. I have mine in my pocket."

The buttons were in his hand when March came back. "See? Hollow, round brass buttons with the name 'Fred Harvey.' They slip over your regular buttons like this." He fitted the buttons on

March's coat. "Now, do you think you'll like it? Your commission will be a penny for each paper you sell, paid at the end of the week. You work the platform alone and the trains that don't have our own butchers. But there are other small duties in the news stand between trains. You open it up at six-thirty in the morning – I come down to meet Number 5 at seven. Then you empty the trash, dust magazine racks, wash the cases, jerk paper heads, and so on."

"But school?" asked Ona.

"Mr. Warren sees no problem. March will miss only the train at noon and at two o'clock. Most of them come between four and seven. Then he's through. Now what do you think, March? Maybe you can wait on customers and become a Fred Harvey clerk like I am." He was simple, straightforward, earnest.

"What about it, son?" asked Ona. "Do you want to earn money so you can go to high school? To help your mother? To learn business from the ground up?"

March nodded dumbly. If only there weren't those awful brass buttons.

"Mr. Warren is sure to take him," said young Mr. Austin. "He's really very neat and quiet."

Together, silently, they went out the door.

Ona leaned back with a sigh of immeasurable relief. March would learn punctuality and strictness, which Columbia hadn't taught him. He and his grandfather would be separated. And thank God! – there would be no more talk about mining, no more trips to Cripple Creek. He was on the safe and sane road to business!

Yet as she watched him walk past the window, she caught the quick flash of his metallic dark eyes – the same kind of a look that Cable once had given her when she had engineered him into a foolish real estate venture. And now, as then, she felt the premonition that she was losing something wild and perverse, but hauntingly precious – something she could never quite regain.

7

Still it kept up—that devilish tattoo on the top of his head, echoing the sound of the Zebbelins' hammers. He hated it and perversely feared it would stop for the simple reason he had no more money to keep it going. So he went up to the Sylvanite.

There was little to do. Abe and Jake kept up a show of work, but it was evident their brief enthusiasm had worn off. Rogier descended the shaft to add depth to depth. He would squat down, holding his head, waiting for the drills to crash through the last wall of granite to the mysterious world below. When the crash did not come, Rogier knew it was the incessant hammering on his own skull. Then Abe would touch him on the shoulder, and lead him back aloft. Rogier began to worry over his mind; there were periods now, he realized, when it could no longer think consecutively. It kept whirling him about and ever downward into a chasm of despair blacker than any stope.

A letter from Mrs. Rogier climaxed his worries. One night, without warning or apparent cause, one of the big spruces in the front yard had toppled with a crash into the other, which also had to be cut down. There was no wind and the tree looked sound, she wrote, and March had watered it faithfully. Just age and internal rot, she supposed. The trees had been Rogier's favorites; among their tangled roots, when they had been brought down from the mountains thirty years before, he had discovered his first traces of tellurium. Their sudden toppling now seemed ominously significant. He seemed to see himself in the clear perspective of time and as if at a great distance: an old white-headed man cursed with a mine into which he had emptied all his substance, without money for his dependents, too old to work, and with a mind that was beginning to wander frightfully.

All that day he lay in his bunk, refusing to get up to eat. In the evening after supper Abe and Jake sat playing dominoes. In low tones they talked about the decline of gold and silver now that the Kaiser was on a rampage with all the Frenchies and Britishers in the Old Country. Iron, copper, and molybdenum. Manganese ores for the steel plants. That was the thing now. Ain't Leadville shipped almost 100,000 tons of manganese ores to the steel mills?

The evening dragged on. Rogier lay gripping the edges of his bunk. God Almighty! Something was coming to a verge. With a queer sense of impending disaster, he jumped up and heartily wrung both Abe's and Jake's hands as soon as they had finished their games. He said nothing, although with the turmoil in his head it seemed he was emptying his heart in a rush of words.

"Colonel! You ain't feelin' sicker!? Shall I go get a doctor?"

Abe raised his hand in protest and quietly laid back the blankets on Rogier's bunk. Rogier lay down again in his clothes; he merely wanted to rest, he said. Jake and Abe, with apprehensive glances at him, undressed and went to bed.

After awhile Rogier turned over. The lamp was out, but by the light of the fire he could see they were asleep. An hour or more he waited for the flames to die down. Then he laid back his blanket carefully and sat up. For an instant he debated whether to scribble a note. Deciding that the flicker of a candle or the scratch of a pencil might waken Abe, a light sleeper, he got up and flung his coat over his shoulders. Quietly now he tiptoed across the plank floor, opened the door carefully, and stepped outside.

There was a half-moon. In its light he could see the dark ragged fringe of pines along the gulch and the gauntly outlined timbers of the Sylvanite gallows frame. He hurried to the shaft. The iron bucket was lashed securely above him to the frame, its rusty side faintly scraping in the wind against the wood.

Gathering his coat about him, Rogier kneeled on the shaft collar. Before and above him, looking down with passionless serenity, stared the enigmatic face of the high Peak. Ever and always since his first glimpse of it from far down on the Fontaine-qui-Bouille, its white seamed face had drawn him step by step, without compassion, merciless and compelling, to this insignificant aperture into its unsounded depths. All his vain conjectures, the deceptive glitter of success, and his countless failures he saw now as milestones of a monstrous folly which could have no end but this. He bent his head, leaned over to stare into the velvety blackness of the open shaft.

He was now quite calm, his mind clear. Death for Rogier held no terror. No man of more than superficial perception but has contemplated at some time the voluntary and willing destruction of his faulty, mortal cast. And this deep soft darkness, oozing from the subterranean world that had ever evoked in him the comforting assurance of the mysterious immortal, now seemed to him a cloak of final authority which would at last insure his admittance to the deep unknown. A single movement and to the secret of that mighty Peak he would consign himself forever.

Still he hesitated. For if his mind was lucid enough to confront without trepidation the course before him, it could also clearly perceive the turbulent wake of his carefully considered action. He thought of his family. Mrs. Rogier's quiet disregard of his erratic storms, Ona's obstinate faithfulness even after Cable's death, the children's hushed playing in the yard lest they disturb him in the shop—they all took on for him now a somber beauty enhanced by their family undemonstrativeness. In a blinding flash of reality he saw himself among them through the years, repaying kindness with curtness, and draining them of hopes to fling down this shaft below him. And now this: to reward their enduring faithfulness with an abrupt wordless departure that would inflict upon them the wounds of a lasting cruelty. No! He could not! Secure in his integrity, calmly facing his own fate, he yet was bound to those innocent and unsuspecting loved ones in the shabby old house on Shook's Run—to their trivial follies and childish hopes, to smiles, laughter, sorrow, and discontent, to the eternal sadness that binds us each to the other and all in our loneliness to that of which we are a part.

These quick, searing thoughts roused in him a fire of furious resentment. The devil take them all! They had their own lives to lead, as he had had his. To be free forever from the shame, the poverty, the ignominious narrow life to which he had committed himself! To escape that continual hammering on his head!

It had begun again, driving through his skull with resonant strokes whose vigor he had never experienced before. All his sentiments of the previous moment fled before the blows; he became what he had been, was, and would be always – a man consecrated since birth to a search far below his personal surface. For an instant, confused as he was, the hammering on his skull became synonymous with the blows of the Zebbelins' jack hammers below. One last crack, and he would burst at once through the resistant granite and the walls of his skull to the secret and resplendent heart of the obdurate Peak rising above him, his last ally, his final adversary.

He rose from his knees, threw off his coat, and confronted its dual aspect across the gaping shaft. That great white sentinel of a continent had entranced him, beckoned him, comforted him in his lifelong search. But also it had repulsed him, rejected him, fought him at every turn, because he had not fully, wholeheartedly, sacrificed himself to it without stint. Always from his impassioned search he had held back that fatal modicum of personal egotism remaining from his long inherited past. But not now! If this were all he had left, he would hurl it into the depths of his own granite self and crack open at last its golden heart. This time he would succeed! Crack! Crack! The hammer blows were crashing through his skull now, confirming his resolve. Bathed in sweat from the unendurable pain, he raised both arms, poised on the collar to leap down the shaft. At that moment the blow came, shattering his skull and driving into his brain. There was a terrific explosion of sound and light, of a golden radiance into which both he and the Peak dissolved with a final shriek torn from his bowels.

Inside the cabin, Abe stirred in his bunk. A cold wind was blowing across his bare arm hanging outside the blankets, and fanning into flames the dying fire. He sat up quickly and looked around, his first thought of Rogier. The bunk was empty, the door open.

Abe jumped out, grabbed a burning stick from the fire, and ran outside. There was no need to search for Rogier; Abe knew well enough where to find him. Almost immediately he saw him, a dark huddle on the shaft collar. Lifting the torch above his bald head, he ran forward on bare feet with stark fear. The old man was slumped across the collar, arms outspread, his white head hanging down the gaping shaft. With one hand, Abe pulled him back and turned him over. His tortured face, the frothy white sputum covering his lips, the glassy look of his open and unseeing eyes, were too much for any man to see. Abe flung his burning brand down the shaft. Then he knelt beside Rogier, gently wiping the froth from his mouth and smearing his face with a handful of snow. After a time the old man's body twitched, his eyes flickered with life.

"Colonel! Colonel!"

In the light of the half-moon the stiff lips quivered.

"I know, Colonel! I know!"

Abe's long arms gathered him to his breast in an embrace more tender and less awkward than it had been given him to hold any woman. On his strong and simple face was the profound sadness of a child confronted with something he could not understand but only feel. Faithful, simple Abe, one of the great unsung who in the gloom of the mine, the glare of the furnace, or the isolation of the range does his work unrewarded with but his daily bread—and yet carries forever the unspoken tribute of less humble men.

Mrs. Rogier and Ona were waiting when the Zebbelins and a Victor doctor brought him home to Shook's Run. Rogier was carried up to his own bedroom where he lay like a wasted, wax image in a glass case, insensible to the pain and horror of the last ordeal it was possible for him to withstand.

Just what had happened to him none of the family could understand from Abe's and Jake's confused account. He hadn't fallen down the shaft or been crushed by a rock; nor had he suffered a stroke of paralysis, for he was able to move all his limbs. The family doctor came, replacing the one Jake had roused in Victor. He murmured indecisively something about a seizure, epilepsy, a mental breakdown.

Mrs. Rogier asked abruptly, "You mean – ?"

He nodded. "But it may not be permanent. We shall see."

Mrs. Rogier fled to her room to pray. "If only God will spare him that," she murmured repetitiously, remembering his once firm step, his square calm face and steady eyes. Gradually this memory of him aged into the nervous old white-headed man she had known for years. His increasing irritableness, his prolonged abstractions, and lapses of memory took on sudden significance. "Daddy, oh Daddy! If we'd only known!" For though he was more untouchable than ever, his grasp upon her had strengthened. And now, fearful that her prayers might have been misinterpreted, she murmured into her wet pillow the simple request, "Don't let him die, God. No matter what."

Two mornings later Jake and Abe, who had slept in the shop, came in and dawdled over their breakfast until none remained but Ona and Mrs. Rogier.

"I reckon the Colonel will get over it after a long time maybe," said Jake awkwardly. "They ain't much use of our stayin'."

"You know how grateful we are to you both," said Mrs. Rogier.

Both men nodded vehemently. "About the mine," stuttered Jake. "We ain't figurin' on stayin'. She's all played out, like him." He jerked his thumb at the upstairs bedroom.

"We got to find work somewhere's else. The district's playin' out too," Abe said straightforwardly. "We'll just close it up, hey?"

"Of course!" said Ona. "The Sylvanite will never be worked again. If there's anything you can sell, do it before you leave. And God bless you both always, for the way you stuck to Daddy!"

Abe began counting off his calloused fingers. "The plant ain't much, but there's the cable reel and the hoist engine maybe somebody will want. That old boiler we'll have to let rust away. But there's some boxes of powder, the lamps, drills, and all the hand-tools. And of course the cabin fixin's. A few hundred dollars, all told. We'll send it to you all right."

Ona's eyes flashed. "All these years of working in a no-good, worthless hole when you might have been in a big producer! And I'll bet you haven't been paid regular wages for weeks, have you Jake?"

Jake flushed and hung his head, acutely conscious of that

inward glow provoked when a man's unheeded virtue has finally found him out. "Aw – Miss Ona!"

"No, sir!" went on Ona. "You boys go back up there and sell every bit of steel and timber you can get rid of. Keep the drills to take with you. The money will be little enough. You'll need railroad fare. And let us hear from you, mind. You're Daddy's best and only friends."

Abe rubbed his bald head as he turned to Mrs. Rogier. "It just don't seem fair. We're both strong and powerful well. But him up there – sick in the head, and doctor bills and all – "

"No!" protested Mrs. Rogier decisively but with effort, thinking of her honor fund. "Ona is right. We wish it were a lot more."

The silence was unbearable. Ona broke it by hurling herself in turn against the breasts of the brawny giants before her. "Abe!" – "Jake!" Abashed, each patted her clumsily on the back; then they fled out to the shop, and thence up the back alley to catch the train. It was over, all over at last – the monstrous folly of that stricken man upstairs who was insensible alike to all hope and despair.

Day and night he lay there, not dead nor yet alive, neither immune to light but not yet absorbed by darkness. He was like a man caught between the surface world he had rejected and that subterranean domain which, except for one quick glimpse, had not opened to receive him. And lying in his pellucid dusk, in an unbroken tranquility that was not repose, he moved, breathed, was fed – and seemed conscious of nothing.

The doctor was cheerful but cautious. "He's going to pull through. Rest, care, absolutely no worry. But it'll take time and patience, Mrs. Rogier."

And as Rogier finally began to respond to voices and the touch of familiar hands, Mrs. Rogier braced herself for a glimpse into the inescapable future. It loomed so terrifying before her frail little figure, she snapped the catch on the door and sat down on the bed to confront it with all her courage and resources. Jake had sent a postcard saying he and Abe had been able to sell some five hundred dollars worth of salvage, gutting the mine and cabin of everything to Rogier's boots and wool shirts. They had sent back only his old-fashioned miners' candlestick, the one pathetic reminder of the

Sylvanite which now, like countless others, was gradually being absorbed like a wound into the healing granite flesh of the Peak. Mrs. Rogier sighed as she tore the postcard to bits. That money would have come in mighty handy.

Now on the bed beside her she opened her sugar-bowl, a white Chinese porcelain jar, on which was wreathed a dragon, that Boné had sent her from San Francisco years ago. It was stuffed with bills and envelopes so neatly folded and pressed she had to pry them out. No amount had been too small to add: dollar bills left over as change from her grocery payments, a gold piece received as a Christmas present, portions of the allowances Rogier had given her for household expenses. As the money had accumulated she had changed it into $100 bills, each little stack of ten snapped together with a rubber band and sealed in an envelope. There were five of these, her honor fund. Five thousand dollars—her savings of years, Cable's inheritance, March's education, food taken right out of the children's mouths; a fortune that attested a frugality and duplicity that no one would ever know but her. She had saved the amount at last.

But spread out on the bed in smaller amounts there remained but $180.75 for household expenses, taxes, doctor bills and medicines for Rogier – to last, for all she knew, forever. She did not expect help from Sally Lee, Mary Ann, or Boné . They all had been written of his illness, letters that did not explicitly explain the nature of his illness and the fact that money could be used. They ought to know it! And if they couldn't guess it, Mrs. Rogier would have bit off her tongue before saying more.

Five thousand dollars! And to that man Timothy! Never—no, never!—would she forget him laughing at Daddy that day in front of the Ruxton. For if once she had been impressed by his social prominence, friendship, and waistcoats, she was now more impressed by the five fat envelopes in her lap. If Rogier had lost every cent he owned and his senses besides, Timothy could afford to lose what was to a rich man a measly, speculative investment.

Mrs. Rogier got up and walked to the window where she stood braced against temptation. Always she had imagined evil and dishonor cloaked in the gorgeous raiment of unreality. By their seductive whispers of temptation she would know and be able to flaunt them easily. Now she realized that they, like virtue and honor, were born of the same need, walked side by side, and could be distinguished only by the discerning gaze of one's own integrity. It wasn't fair! A simple thing like doing nothing, just not giving back Timothy the money he didn't expect. Listening to the Devil's promptings, she stuffed the envelopes back in the jar, envisioned it hidden on the top shelf of the closet where she could withdraw money for every need. No bolt of lightning from Heaven seared her hands for their wicked intent, no angel perched on the jar to protect it. Yet a deep quiet voice, peculiarly her own, whispered authoritatively that Daddy might die, they might all starve and the house be sold over their heads, but never would Timothy or any other man be able to say a Rogier had played him false.

If it was to be done, it had to be done now! Resolutely she flung on her coat and bonnet, and walked swiftly uptown with her handbag clutched to her breast. There was just time before the bank closed to change her currency into a draft made out in Timothy's name and enclosed in a manilla envelope. This was more businesslike; currency would never do. Now a new fear beset her. She could not send Timothy the draft by messenger or by mail; a note would have to be enclosed, which she could not write. She owed him the courtesy of delivering it herself.

Stepping into a tourist hack at the curb, she drove to the Ruxton. Prohibited as a lady from entering a gentleman's club, she sent the driver inside with the request that Mr. Timothy step outside a moment. Luckily he was inside. On seeing him approach, faultlessly groomed, Mrs. Rogier remembered how Rogier had looked that rainy afternoon in a porter's hat and coat.

"Mrs. Rogier! How happy I am to see you on any excuse. I do hope that Mr. Rogier, Boné, and the rest of your family are as well and happy as you yourself appear!"

"Forgive my intrusion, Mr. Timothy," she replied, thrusting the envelope into his hands. "I stopped by only to return for Mr. Rogier the money you wished him to invest in his mine."

Timothy took it with a puzzled expression on his face. "That was some time ago. I had almost forgotten it. A sporting venture he agreed to let me in on. Strange he didn't say something if he never intended to use it."

"Not at all," she replied pertly. "You are well aware how

absentminded my husband is. The Sylvanite was never more than a highly speculative venture restricted to his own family members."

Timothy frowned, fiddling with the gold nugget on the watch chain strung across his waistcoat.

"We regret having not accounted for this so long," Mrs. Rogier continued. "It was only on suddenly discovering it that I came up without waiting for Mr. Rogier to fulfill his own obligation."

The phrase illumined for Timothy the careworn look on her face, her rusty bonnet, the cheap tourist hack in which she was sitting instead of a taxicab.

"Mrs. Rogier, no man with the dormant but not dead instincts of a gentleman could possibly refuse to deny the generous prompting of a true lady. A lady of the old South, particularly. Please convey to your husband my sincere thanks and devout congratulations. How is he, by the way?"

"He's had a little upset, Mr. Timothy, but doing quite well. No visitors, of course. But if you will pardon my intrusion – "

Timothy stepped back on the curb, watching the hack drive away.

8

Creeping quietly past his stricken grandfather's room and out of the house each morning at six o'clock, March walked quickly to the Santa Fe railroad depot and into a life as uniquely, indigenously American as that he had known at Shallow Water and Cripple Creek.

Little London was a health resort; manufacturing, with its soot and noise, was prohibited. It was a tourist resort, its mineral springs, bath houses, scenic drives, country estates and summer pavilions modelled upon the pattern of a European spa. It was a college town, a New England seat of learning nestled in the shadow of Pike's Peak. A city of churches—and of five polo fields. A center of classical culture in the crude and vulgar West.

But a railroad town—merciful Heaven! A railroad town of grimy shops and roundhouses with hordes of men carrying lunch buckets and thick Waltham watches and wearing starched blue shirts, and disgorging smoke and grime into the rarefied, mile-high, sparkling champagne air? Never! shrieked the pamphlets and posters and the ladies on the hotel verandas.

And yet Little London had been a railroad town since its

inception. Don't talk of romantic gold rushes. The Pike's Peak Bust had been over a decade and more before Little London sprouted on the plain, and it was a railroad survey that planted its seeds. Johnny-come-lately Cripple Creek, whose gold and sweat created the great mansions flanking its wide avenues, was still discreetly hidden in the mountains and now politely ignored by the best society.

Yes! Little London was a railroad town, as all towns of western America are railroad towns. Where the rails stopped to wait for supplies, a survey farther ahead, the tents went up. Then bunk houses, board shanties, a water tank. It became a junction, and then a town. "Rail-ends!" This was the "Land-ho!" shout of our prairie voyagers. It was as if we sailed across a measureless and unmarked sea, and wherever we made landfall a port of call sprang up. In other lands the market place, town square, or plaza marked the heart of the town anciently grown up around it, and its pulse echoed the beat of the country. But here the railroad depot was the community center, the focal point of life.

Who has not on a dreary Sunday gone down to see the train come in? What do we expect, whom do wait for with a curious and hopeless expectancy on our faces? It is all there in a whistle, a long drawn-out shriek, that sounds round the bend. It tugs at the heart, stirs deep within us that nameless ache and haunting rapture that lies at the bottom of every soul. There is a momentous hush out of all proportion to the event, as if it is imbued with a mystery too profound and too common to be remarked. The train is coming in!

She'll be comin' round the mountain
She'll be comin' round the mountain
She'll be comin' round the mountain
When she comes!

She comes, and here in this vast and lonely hinterland it is always round a mountain's shoulder. And hissing, steaming, a horribly beautiful monster with one glaring eye and a long serpentine body snorts reluctantly to a stop. For what, to where has this monstrous iron sauropod hurtled across prairies and wind-swept plains, spanned gulch and gulley, gorge and ravine, puffed up the grades and rolled drunkenly through smoke-blackened cuts and tunnels, crawled soberly along the mountainside, and swept down twisting and turning from the snowy roof of the world?

Why, to this grimy depot with its crowd of loitering towns-people, its carriages, buckboards, and mud-splattered Tin Lizzies, a row of blanketed squaws squatting with their pots, a horseman engraved against the sky. And behind the dreary grass square, a row of shabby all-night lunch counters, a third-rate hotel, a sinisterly shuttered lodging house, pawnshops, and the street that led uptown.

This is America—all the towns, magnified or miniature, that lie upon its spacious and lonely breast. And to all, for this immortal moment, the arrival of a train assuages their nameless and haunting ache, appeases their hunger for the strange and far-off, lifts the weight of their loneliness under the immense and empty skies.

And when it leaves, pouring sand on the upgrade, and finally cleaving the dusk full stride over the trestle, shrieking once, wildly, at the last crossing, it is as if it has carried out of our lives something that has been there forever—bone of our bone, flesh of our flesh, and the wild and turbulent spirit of our unrest that if it wanders far enough, long enough, must again return home.

So it seemed to March when with papers under his arm he stood on the platform to meet Santa Fe Number 5, northbound, sweeping round the bend of Cheyenne Mountain, that he was standing at the hub of Little London and at the core of whirling time.

Number 5 was a breakfast train. A white-jacketed bus boy was standing beside the door of the Fred Harvey Lunch Room beating a brass gong. To its summons the long train emptied already groomed and toileted ladies from the Pullmans who had reserved seats by telegram a half-hour before; a lazy slattern in a nightcap and purple silk robe who rushed past, haggard women with children, their faces still crinkled by the gritty red plush cushions of the day coaches; well paunched businessmen hungry for ham and eggs; thin, sallow men from the smoker for coffee and a doughnut.

"Get the morning news! *Denver Post* and the *Rocky Mountain News!* Read all about it while you eat! *Pueblo Chieftain!* The *Springs' Gazette!* Git your mornin' PAPer!"

The platform teemed with people. Among them March shouted, his black uniform cap too large even with paper stuffed under the sweatband, his brass buttons glowing conspicuously as red-hot coals. Then suddenly the platform was deserted. Now he shouted himself hoarse outside the coaches to rouse those within, and then posted himself outside the slowly emptying lunch room. People read more on a full stomach. Particularly news and trash.

"All aboar-art!" Highball. And as the train pulled out, he was left alone again on the deserted platform, alone at the core of time, the dead center of the maelstrom whirling about him. That was the everlasting mystery. Trains, crowds, newspapers vanished, only to be replaced by others new and fresh for their brief moment. Nothing varied, nothing changed, yet everything constantly changing. The mystery of movement, this for March was the fascination of railroading.

Quickly he gained friends: the ticket clerks, telegraph operators, and baggagemen, the lunchroom manager and the Fred Harvey girls who smiled at his bashfulness. He began to be brusquely acknowledged by the yardmen, switchmen, and yard clerks, and finally by those lords of the rails themselves, the engineers, firemen, and conductors. They seemed men whose lives of the spirit might never have existed or of which they were never aware. Like the monsters they served, they ran on rails, definite, fixed, punctual to the second. Rain, snow, family, friends – nothing mattered. Their one eternal gesture of prayer to the god that ruled them seven days a week, night and day, was a hand reaching to a watch.

Ghostly flow of time, how far now the sandy Gallegos and those who told time by the first frost and the spring thaw? Number 2 in the block, four minutes late!

After the breakfast train's departure at seven-thirty, March emptied the trash, dusted magazine racks, polished apples with a cloth moistened with olive oil, and cut newspaper heads. Then after coffee and doughnuts, he walked a mile up the tracks and turned east to Columbia School. After school he came back to stay until seven o'clock, helping to ready the newstand in the new station.

There were two railroad depots in Little London: that of the Denver and Rio Grande in the western part of town, below the Antler's Hotel; and that of the Santa Fe to the east, not far from Shook's Run. Both were small grimy stone buildings fronting their exposed yards. But now with the growth of Little London and the booming railroad traffic, a huge new Santa Fe station was being built behind the old one. There was no doubt that it was to be an impressive monument to the prime importance of railroading, and a credit to Little London. Built of red brick and white stone, its huge vaulted waiting room was floored with red tile and furnished with great stained-oak benches, Mission style. In addition, there was a waiting room outside with concrete seats. There was not only a new Fred Harvey lunch room with a horseshoe counter, but a well-appointed dining room. Upstairs were the sleeping rooms of the waitresses; and above the barny baggage room, the telegraph office and private offices.

March, helping Mr. Warren and Mr. Austin to ready the news stand, was impressed. It jutted onto the station platform outside and into the big waiting room inside. There was a little office for Mr. Warren and a checking room for baggage. Also it boasted magazine racks that could be locked at night, eliminating March's chore of emptying and refilling them daily.

"You see now, March, why we wanted to break in a newsboy," said Mr. Warren. "A young man, neat and efficient, who'll be ready when we move into the new station."

The day came when the transfer was made. The grimy old depot was pulled down and the Main Line tracks were re-routed over the site. Between them and the new station a high, iron picket fence was erected, and the subway finished. The first tunnel emerged between Main Line 1 and 2, the second between 3 and 4. Down at the end of the platform were two spurs for the Colorado Midland and the Cripple Creek Short Line. To add to the new station's modern and formal aspect, a Station Master attired in a uniform of golden-tan serge with brass buttons was hired to call the trains.

How proud March was, how he loved it all! Most of the men were now his friends. But there was one exception, an angular, hard-muscled man named Wadkins who worked down in the yards and kept walking up to the station for coffee. His face was long and furrowed, and held a look of furtive cunning and cruelty. Coming up to March, he demanded a paper. March obediently drew one out for him. Wadkins read it through deliberately, his greasy blunt fingers turning each page.

"Please sir, will you pay me now? I can't wait any longer."

The man grinned, "Pay you? You little greenhorn! I work here!"

The newspaper by now was a mass of splotched sheets. He

finally wadded it up, flung it at March, and strode off. March threw it in the trash can and turned in one of his own nickels for it.

A few days later Wadkins again demanded a look at a paper.

"Not till you pay me first," insisted the boy. "I ain't payin' for the ones you spoil!"

Wadkins' thin lips twisted into an angry leer. "You little son-of-a-bitchin' brat! I'm goin' to take the starch out of you right now!"

Some people came up; he turned away and walked quickly into the lunch room.

Ten minutes later the passenger swept in. March, standing entranced as ever by its majestic sweep, was struck violently on his left elbow. His armful of papers splattered on the brick platform, some of them being sucked under the passing wheels. He dropped to his knees, arms outspread to hold the remainder, and flung around. Wadkins was standing behind him, a look of pustulate evil upon his grimy face.

"You big bully! By God, if you ever touch me again, I'll kill you!" the boy shrieked against the roar of the train.

Thereafter he kept a sharp lookout for Wadkins. At sight of him he grew cold and hard, felt his face change to stone. But sometimes the man, passing behind him in a crowd, managed to jerk his papers into the mud or snow, or rip a front page with his thumb. March said nothing to Mr. Warren or Howard Austin of his persecution and the many papers he was obliged to pay for. He shrank into himself, with an intense awareness and silent inscrutability. Wadkins was conscious of it, and became more wary and malicious. It was a strange feud between boy and man, but its strangeness March never questioned. It was as if the hate between them was a chemical fusion that would endure forever.

Through it he saw with preternatural clearness the inherent meanness of the man, the warped and sadistic character whose mirror was Wadkin's deeply-furrowed, thin-lipped face. By it too the boy first glimpsed the depths within himself. He had experienced quick flashes of childish temper, the sudden violent storms that left him weak, frightened, and ashamed hours later. But now it was as if from the bottom of his soul there welled up unceasingly a flood of terrible and savage passion. It filled his thoughts, ran like hot lead through his veins. He absorbed it wholly as he stood grasping his papers, day after day, with a face as blank and set as Cable's.

It was a hate that left him cold and nerveless; a tremendous and formidable fact, a part of his life as ancient and timeless as the earth he trod. In his terrifying aloneness and with a strange awareness, he knew simply that between him and this man stood something that some day must be resolved.

One winter afternoon Number 11 whistled at the bend. Standing at the subway entrace, March could see the black snout nosing through the driving snow. Then suddenly he recognized Wadkins, fifty feet away, plodding up the platform in front of the train. March dodged back hidden from train and man. He was calm, pitiless, resolute. Wadkins would pass him on the narrow platform just as the train would hurtle by. A hand pushed abruptly against him would throw him across the tracks in front of it.

The earth was trembling now. There was a great clanging, the hiss of stream, all the insensate force of a million pounds of iron driving forward on two narrow rails.

In the snow, head down and hands in pockets, Wadkins shuffled by the unseen boy. The next instant the train also rushed past.

March remained crouching in the snow. He was too weak to stand; his face was white and drawn; he gagged until he was unable to cry his papers. An hour later he fled home up the back alley, and knelt in the cold barrenness of Rogier's shop.

"Jesus in Heaven – Blessed Jesus," he prayed inarticulately. "I pretty near killed him. I was goin' to – Oh God, you saved me from bein' a murderer in the nick of time – I don't know what happened, God. But I'm awful glad and don't let it happen again – Save my black wicked soul. Don't let me be bad!"

He could feel the cold, hear the pigeons on the roof. His black hate settled, sediment once more. He emerged as if from a horrible dream. But he knew now, deep in his heart, that within him prowled a strange god whose power he had never dreamed existed.

Now, strangely, he saw Wadkins for what he was; was filled with disgust and pity at the thought of him; and resolved to keep away from him at all costs.

But then a queer thing happened: Wadkins let him alone after weeks of persecution. Why? Had Wadkins seen him, guessed his intention? Had the Lord worked another miracle with Wadkins as He had with March himself? He only knew that the man still ambled up the tracks for coffee, his face evil, cruel, and cunning, but he never jostled nor molested him, never spoke a word.

A month or so later March was standing at his post in front of the subway entrance. A light rain was falling; the brick platform was wet and shiny.

The Cripple Creek Short Line came in slowly: a baggage car, a smoker, and a chair car whose back observation platform, due to the shower, was empty save for one man who clung to the outside railing. March noticed that it was Wadkins, who had jumped on in the yards below for a ride up to the station. As the train rolled past, Wadkins jumped off. His heels slid out from under him on the slippery bricks; he lit flat on his back, then flopped sideways under the rear trucks of the observation car.

March was not twenty feet away. He could hear the sudden jolt and crunch as the wheels passed over the man's legs, the awful greasy swish and a sudden sweetish and nauseating smell, the hollow bumping of his head upon the bricks. Within a second or two the train had passed, leaving the legless trunk of Wadkins flopping in blood and rain on the ties. Then suddenly rose the piercing shrieks of terror and naked fear from a man numbed by the shock of pain, but not yet mercifully blinded by unconsciousness.

The boy did not stir or utter a sound. As if turned to stone in a posture of deathly horror, he stood there until men came rushing with a blanket and the ambulance had come and driven away. Then throwing away his papers, he fled home. All that night as Ona sat beside him pressing wet towels to his head, he could see, as if indelibly engraven in his memory, that searing accusation of his own secret guilt.

"Thoughts are power," Rogier had told him once. "Thoughts are deeds before they take form. Be careful what you think, boy, if you don't want it to happen."

There was no praying now. Nor could he betray his anguishing guilt to his mother. He could only lie there in darkness, frightened by a mystery whose meaning he could not quite fathom. And years later when he tried to piece together this experience as a whole, he still felt something of its hidden meaning – something whose moral, if it could be called a moral, might be no more than an evanescent light cast on a pattern formed in the darkness through which we blindly grope.

9

Rogier was pulling out of his spell, but taking an agonizingly long time. His firmly built, broad shouldered body had wasted away until his clothes hung on him as if on a scarecrow. He had lost some of his hair and the remaining white wisps, after his many days in bed, stuck up above his ears to lend him the aspect of a frightened child. His voice was still gruff and resonant but no longer irritable. He used it only to supplement the mild inquiry of his dull gray eyes, voicing a simple question that might have shamed a child. When he smiled he revealed the emptiness within him. If a smile is always an index of a man's character, his was a grimace that contorted a purposeful face into a foolish mask. Ona and Mrs. Rogier shrank from it, waiting for those instants when his eyes brightened with comprehension like shutters blown open by a draft within. He would be all right! They knew he would! And each look of comprehension and sensible remark they would treasure like mothers elated over a baby's tricks.

It was a joy to them that he was still fastidious in habit and dress; for an hour he would sit carefully smoothing the shawl across his lap. Ona taught him to file his nails, an occupation in which he delighted. Always reassured by the dark, he remained awake to wait for the sound of the Kadles' footsteps. Mrs. Rogier would be aroused by his excited cry and rise to light the lamp. He would be sitting up in bed, bright-eyed as a child who had seen Santa Claus. "The Kadles! They still come to see us!"

"Yes, Daddy! Now get to sleep. They'll come back to see us again tomorrow night."

They never failed to creak up the steps and pause at his door on their nocturnal rounds – those two faithful, family ghosts who had found in the master of the shabby old house on Shook's Run a kindred soul at last.

After a time he was allowed to come down stairs for awhile in the afternoons and evenings. Like a man held in the invisible bondage of a world profound and enigmatic as the one he had envisioned below grass roots, he was always summoned back into it when his visit on this one reached its unpredictable duration. Rogier never minded the abrupt summons which none but he could hear, nor did the ceaseless commuting seem to harm him. A gesture, a flicker of his eyes, a word, and what there was of him that the family could recognize would flit away instantly and silently as a bird from a branch to return again as unbidden and unannounced.

He was getting better! During the long winter evenings he sat before the fireplace in the parlor with Ona and Mrs. Rogier, listening to the three children wrangling noisily over their school books on the dining room table. Mrs. Rogier read her Bible. Her sugar bowl had been emptied, but she managed to sell some of Rogier's contracting machinery: gasoline motors, concrete mixers, winches, and cable reels. Then she had taken a mortgage on the house. It always had been in her name, a hostage given her by Rogier against the time when he would build her a mansion in the impeccable North End. Mrs. Rogier did not worry. When this money gave out, He would provide. Were not they all, like Rogier, in His hands?

Ona sat listening to the children's voices, alert to discern in the wrangle the first let-up of work.

"Mother!" called out March. "We're learning about gold and silver and bronze, what the Greeks made swords from. Shall I say Cripple Creek's got bronze mines too?"

Ona answered sharply. "No, son! It never had a bronze mine,

and it doesn't have much silver and gold any more. The district's all played out. Don't bother about it. Just stick to your ancient history."

At the mention of Cripple Creek, Rogier's head snapped back. His eyes brightened with a look timeless and profound as the face of that immutable Peak which had stood before him and would stand for those to follow, an eternal jest of nature at men whose folly and salvation is the blind perpetuation of a quest that has no truth but this – a flashing vision, darkness, and eternal rest.

Late that spring he suddenly snapped out of it. In the warm sunshine he meandered among the currant bushes, the garden, and the now empty barnyard in back. "What became of those concrete mixers? How do you expect Rawlings to get along without them?" he would demand. "Where's March? Where did you say Abe and Jake went?" Like a man returned from a long absence, he was avid for news, interested in every triviality. The impetus of this miraculous recovery was soon spent. He began to retreat to his shop where he sat for hours at a time, wondering what had happened to him.

The doctor couldn't tell him; he knew the effect but not the cause. You've got to go down into the earth and learn the subtle, mysterious affinity between it and man, the image of his earth.

The crusty shell, what is that? The flesh that warps, erodes, rhythmically reacts to the pull of moon and sun, whose cells like radioactive elements dissipate heat and life. Below, a skeletal bone structure of darker, heavier rock; and within this, a visceral cavity whose central sun radiates psychical energy to all the organs in its constellation.

Doctor! Slip a thermometer down the throat of a volcano. Poke a proctoscope up the hind-end of a mountain, switch on the little electric globe, and take a squint through the tube. What do you see there deep in the bowels of the earth? Slit the epidermis, cut down through flesh and bone. Let's have a look at the liver and lungs and guts of this whirling dervish of a monster. A pretty anatomical puzzle, another smooth machine that runs like a watch. But how? Why? That's the end of all probing. An autopsy on the dead body. You've got to deal with the living soul at the center, its mysterious sun and unknown heart.

We die and rise out of the dead flesh like the phoenix; the

mountains crumble and wash away and rise again in eternal palingenesis; and we all are forever kept in isotatic balance.

But suddenly, from deep within, there is a great displacement. From some focal center the shock travels upward and outward in great undulating, seismic waves. The body trembles with the oscillation; there is a sudden yielding to the strain along a fault, at one or many epicenters; the doctor rushes in: a stroke, a fit, an epileptic seizure. A human earthquake. The diagnosis of the effect is correct. But what about the cause?

A necessary internal readjustment to maintain isotatic equilibrium. But why? A nervous strain, a mental stress, a correction of a displacement at adolescence, or the last organic settling at old age?

Diastrophism, the great earth movements by which continents, ocean basins, and mountains have been continually reformed. That's all his spell had been, decided Rogier. A human diastrophic change. Dom! The earth itself was epileptoidal, its pulse too kept mounting to another crisis. What was he to worry about his own eruption, he felt worn out. Head in hands, his mind suddenly blank, he sat gazing vacantly out the window.

Ona opened the door and stepped inside. "Daddy! I want to talk to you!"

Rogier switched around. "You talkin' to me or a boy you caught stealin' cookies?"

"To you, man to man. Like we have always. What've you been doing out here?"

He blinked his eyes.

"You've been out here brooding. Now Daddy, we're coming to an understanding right now. You've been a sick man and we're all doing our level best to keep you well. But you've got to cooperate. No more brooding on the past, on Cripple Creek, all that stuff."

"Ona, I won't be dictated to!"

"We're past the point of being childish," she went on quietly. "We're down to rock bottom. Neither of us are frightened by your spell, but we can't ignore it. Sitting around brooding's likely to bring on another one. You've got to do something to keep busy."

"Forbidding me to think, by Jove! A half-wit, eh?"

"No more mining. No more contracting. All that's over, Daddy. But you've got to do something, and I've decided what. Raising chickens. This big empty barnyard's just the place for a nice flock. They'll keep us in eggs, and a chicken in the pot once in awhile will taste mighty good. God knows, we need every bite, what with March buying groceries with his paper money."

"Chickens! Almighty God, that you should bring me to this!"

"I've already ordered some hens, a rooster, and baby chicks. You'd better build a coop before they come. We're facing a tough pull, Daddy, all of us."

Rogier began work with hammer, nails, and saw. Never a man with the pride of Mrs. Rogier, he still felt the ignominy of his task. Here he had raised his buggy and carriage horses, his racing trotters and pacers; Pet and Lady-Lou, Dorothy, Tolar, the ornery Little Man, Silver Night, the great Aralee, and the supreme lady of them all, the loved Akeepee. For what? That these magnificent, satin-coated aristocrats, now shadows of the past, be replaced by a straggle of squawking hens! Thoroughly humbled, he drove his nails with methodical precision.

It soon became apparent that Rogier's management of his small flock of sleek white Leghorns, plump and plaid Plymouth Rocks, and Rhode Island Reds was not an unqualified success. True, they kept him busy outside in the sunshine and provided the family with fresh eggs; and he was constantly filling his coat pockets with corn and bread crumbs to feed them. But occasionally they roused him to maniacal fury. He would let them out for an hour to pick among the currant bushes. Then patiently he would endeavor to herd them back into the chicken yard, one at a time, in some strange order of precedence he was trying to teach the whole flock.

The silly hens! He gave up his vain cajoling and bribing, and began throwing dry clods. Always with a quick, underhand snap of the wrist that sent the dirt thudding into wing or tail feathers.

"Not you! Fool!"

Head out and squawking, a slim Leghorn streaked through the open gate, out of turn. Rogier lunged in after her: across the big yard, past the old carriage and ash pit, cornering her finally in the tool house now used for a chicken roost. "There! Dom you!" he screamed, hurling the offender back over the high fence. "Wait for your turn. First the Reds, then you Whites, and the Plymouth Rocks. Now walk in like a lady!"

Order, decorum; a stately marching line of prim hens, beaks up, breasts out, daintily lifting their langorous yellow claws – this was the deep need for order his disorderly mind demanded.

So out he rushed again, tearing his coat on the currant bushes, tripping on the walk, and spilling corn from his pockets. About him and between his legs dashed, flapped, and squawked the fool hens. No matter! Still shouting, bombarding them with clods of dirt, he leaped about, a white-headed old Ichabod brandishing his stick.

"Mr. Rogier! Stop! This very minute!"

The porch steps next door had suddenly sprouted the cadaverous Mr. Pyle. "What did I tell you I'd do the very next time you carried on such a disgraceful scene? Call the Humane Society – that I will! Look at the crippled fowl! I won't have it in this neighborhood!"

By now the righteous Mrs. Pyle was out, as well as the grinning Caseys next door west. The old man let out a mighty howl of rage. "Tend to your own business, Pyle! You sanctimonious Presbyterian plate-passer. You real estate horse thief. You gold-toothed bastard of greed and envy, you tailing from a manure dump, before I take off those striped pants of yours and switch your bony behind to Kingdom Come! Dom me, Pyle, I'll – "

What he did do was to grab the wire netting of the fence between them, lunging back and forth, his white head flung back, uttering piercing shrieks which roused all the neighbors.

"Rah for the Colonel! Tear her down, Crazy Man!" yelled the Casey kids. On the other side Mrs. Kennedy stood on her back step piously fingering her beads.

Rogier by now was oblivious to these customary spectators of his fusses. A peculiar and faint tap-tap-tap was sounding on his head. Increasing in tempo and volume, it was suddenly translated into its visual counterpart: a number of yellowish petals rushing toward a common center to form a golden flower. Before they could assume shape, everything went black. He dropped to his knees, then spread out on the ground.

Aroused by the commotion, Ona and Mrs. Rogier and March at her heels, rushed out of the house to kneel beside him. In a few minutes he quit jerking, his eyes began to clear. "Daddy! Why, Daddy! And your nice hot bath waitin' for you too! Land sakes!"

And he was led into the house.

"March, get those chickens in and close the gate. Mind you, no talkin' back to the neighbors now!"

Then together, wife and daughter got Rogier upstairs for an hour's hot soaking and a nap.

By dark his *petit mal,* his "little absence," was over. Out in the gloomy tool house echoing a muffled cackle from rows of feathered throats, he stood gently stroking a slim white hen. "My little lady! You're not hurt, my child. But we've got to learn. Yes, by Jove, we've all got to learn."

Yes! Colonel Joseph Rogier of the Ca'olinas, Suh, a prominent mine owner of Cripple Creek, and the outstanding contractor and builder of Little London since its founding, was slowly returning to the surface of the earth from depths known only by himself.

10

It was now late May and March's last year at Columbia was drawing to a close. Engrossed in his work at the railroad station, he had seen little of Leslie Shane. But now with the rumor of a class party, he resolved to ask her boldly like a man, and to call for her at her own house. For graduation he had bought new shoes and would have money to carry in his pocket.

Everyone seemed to know about the party. It was to be held in the basement of the unfinished church next door to school. Members of the graduating class, their mothers and teachers were to come. There was to be a Grand March, Virginia Reel, and folk dancing.

Then he discovered that invitations already had been mailed, but one had not come for him. He grew sick with shame that he had been omitted, and a stubborn pride prevented him from inquiring whether it was a school, church, or private party, whether Old Excelsior had perversely forgotten to include him, or whether his own invitation had been lost in the mail or misdirected. He knew only the most horrible suffering of childhood – that of an outcast.

Assidiously he avoided any chance meeting with Leslie; and on the Friday afternoon of the party, immediately after school, he fled down the street. Before he had reached the railroad embankment Will Hapsworth caught up with him. "You goin' to the big party tonight?"

"I'm workin'."

"Well I guess we're the only ones not goin'," said Will, more honest. "I didn't get an invite. They think I ain't good enough to sit watchin' Cecil James show off with the girls. And Leslie Shane's goin' to do a dance all by herself. A real classy party. I'll bet there's lots to eat."

"I wasn't invited either," confessed March.

Miserable and silent they walked home to the Hapsworths' frame house along the dump on Shook's Run. Will's father was a mucker in the coal mines north of town. He had just returned from work, his face black and streaked with sweat, his clothes grimy with coal dust. He was not a dull-witted nor narrow-minded man, but he was a bitter one. "'The *Denver Post* has a heart and a soul', eh?" he was exclaiming. "Why, it's nothin' but a mouthpiece for Capitalism. This ain't America for Americans no more. It's America for the Industrial Lords. Look what happened in Cripple Creek. Remember what they did to us coal miners in southern Colorado. The Battle of Ludlow! Women and children shot down like dogs. Colorado, the richest state in the Union. With your blessed Governor, boughten Senators, and your red-sheet, bull-shittin' *Denver Post* of Tammen and Bonfils – the stinkpot of political intrigue! I tell you, the only hope of common working men, the real Americans, is Eugene V. Debs!"

Will's mother, a plain, scrawny woman, did not reply to his tirade. They were pitifully poor; and to make ends meet, they watched the dump like hawks to salvage uncracked glass, old picture frames, broken furniture, and household articles which they cleverly mended.

"They're common, March! They live on the town dump!" This was Mrs. Rogier's unalterable judgment, though no one was kinder to Will when he came. Yet underneath the Hapsworths' hopeless struggle bubbled a homely warmth, an appetite for life, and a rebellious spirit which March found exciting. It was this that cemented his friendship with Will although they had little time together.

"Let's go," now whispered Will. "Meet me here after your last train. I got something in mind."

That evening at dusk March saw what it was: a big can of thick black grease Will had found on the dump. "The only way they can get out of that church basement is the stairs in front," explained Will. "When the party gets goin' we'll smear every step. They'll have to clean off every one before they can leave. The sons of bitches! That'll teach'em to snoot us! What do you say?"

It was dark and the party was in full swing when they reached the church. The shades on the side windows were drawn, but they could hear shouts, laughter, the tinkle of a piano. Quickly and furtively the boys smeared the steps and the handrail with thick black grease. "Let's hide and watch, or maybe peek through the window," suggested Will.

"They can all go to hell!" answered March, thinking of Leslie Shane dancing with Cecil James inside. "If I'm not invited I won't stand outside and peek in like a dog!"

"You're right! We might be caught. And we better ditch this grease bucket and the sticks we used. Let's go!"

Back at the dump they hid bucket and sticks, then scrubbed their hands in Shook's Run. "I'd sure like to see Old Excelsior scrapin' off that grease with her lace hanky!" March grinned.

"Swear you won't tell!" muttered Will in a voice already husky with anxiety.

"Wash your hands with soap and don't leave any marks on the towel, Will. And look over your shoes and clothes again." They parted and ran for home.

Now for the two boys began an agonizing two weeks. On Monday morning the school talked of nothing but how the steps had been smeared during the party. A group of boys had been the first to rush out, running for seats in Cecil James' new automobile. In the dark they had slipped and fallen on the greasy stairs. Shirts, pants, and shoes had been ruined. Miss Watrous had brought out a chair and tried to clamber through the railing, spoiling her white gloves and splotching her organdy dress. It had been necessary to telephone the janitors to bring a ladder from outside. Up this and out a window the rest of the party had climbed, snagging more clothes. The place had not been emptied until nearly midnight.

March slunk back and forth from school thoroughly ashamed. He dared not watch the men scrubbing the stone steps of the church next door. He thought of Miss Watrous' spoiled dress, and of Leslie Shane abjectly crawling through the window in her pretty dancing dress. Will still gloated over the news of each spoiled garment. But he was deathly afraid of being caught, and with reason. For Old Excelsior called a meeting of the upper classes.

"You all know about the disgraceful occurrence of last Friday night," she announced curtly. "We have our suspicions who are the culprits. I merely want to announce they will be given another day to confess of their own free will. Otherwise every boy in school will be interviewed separately in my office by the Superintendent of Public Schools and the guilty one will be expelled. If he is present here now, it will be best for him to come to my office immediately to avoid more serious consequences."

Two days dragged by. The church had refused to pay the bill for cleaning the steps, sending it to the school with a curt note that the party had not been a church function. The Superintendent of Schools in turn had referred the matter to the Chief of Police. The following week – the last week of school – the Chief arrived. He questioned without results Schwartz, an overgrown ranch boy; the grocer's clerk who had been in previous scrapes; and a few notoriously "bad" boys. Then another assembly was called, presided over by the Chief, the Superintendent, Old Excelsior, and Miss Watrous. The Chief's announcement was brief. No regular classes would be held, but every student must be present in school to await questioning when called. The inquisition would start next morning. No one would be omitted.

The following morning March, on the way to school, waited vainly for Will on the railroad embankment. Finally he ran down to the Hapsworths' house. Will was sick, said his mother. March went in to find Will dressed, but white with fright.

"You've got to come!" hissed March when they were alone. "They'll know in a minute why you're stayin' out. Face 'em down, like I'm goin' to. What the hell!"

A moment later he told Mrs. Hapsworth calmly, "Will's comin' to school with me. He feels better, and the fresh air will do him good."

They walked slowly along the railroad embankment to certain doom. "I'll tell. I know I'll tell if they get me up there alone," moaned Will.

"They won't. You're in the seventh grade, not the eighth, and you're a new boy. It's me they're after. And I don't give a damn! I'll quit school and work on the railroad." March's face was set, his eyes contracted to wary, dark glass in his impassive face, yet underneath his taut awareness his nerves were stretched to an almost unbearable tension.

All morning they sat in assembly, waiting to be called up in front of the battery of inquisitors. Old Excelsior was figiting, the Chief was growing impatient. Then Miss Watrous stood up.

"This is taking a great deal of time. Graduation day is Friday, as you know, and there's lots to be done. May I offer a few suggestions? Most of those present were at the party, and can be excused from questioning. Nor do I see any need for interviewing the girls and several boys. Leslie, I know, is due at her dancing lesson uptown. Cecil's mother is waiting for him in her car outside. March, as you know, must be down at the Sante Fe station. And Will, as a seventh-grader and new boy at Columbia, certainly was not implicated. I suggest that all of them be excused at present. If you will allow me, I'll answer for all of them personally until they can be interviewed later if necessary."

She spoke quietly, but with a sharp voice. Her casual glance, however, held on March. He, with his stubborn will and nervous strength, might have withstood the probing of the Chief and Superintendent but not that calm, yet searching beam from Miss Watrous' eyes. It flooded his soul, lit up its black guilty sediment, revealed every nook and cranny wherein lay hidden the dream stuff of the hundred myths she had woven for him. She knew! She had forgiven him for her ruined gloves and dress, and was trying to save him from public exposure. If she had spoken the word, he would have risen and made a clean breast of his part in the atrocious crime.

The Chief and Superintendent nodded agreement; and at the imperious wave of her hand, March and Will rose and fled. On Friday school was let out. Each eighth-grade pupil was given at assembly a certificate tied with purple and white ribbons, Columbia's colors, and dismissed. As March accepted his from Miss Watrous, he detected in her eyes a look of ironic amusement. Thus elated at his narrow escape and yet weighed by a sense of guilt, March left Columbia School.

He was growing fast, tall and thin, small-boned like his father, and that summer he bought his first long pants, his "extensions." He had hoped to buy the suit in "The Boys" stylish haberdashery. But the family was so poor Ona prevailed upon him to order it from a large mail-order house.

"A splendid suit, March, really. Look at the picture in the catalogue. Only $7.69. You'd have to pay two or three times more uptown."

"But out of a catalogue! Like ranchers way out of the city!"

"Oh shoot! Who'll know the difference? And you've got to have it to start in high school!"

Late in August the two-piece suit came, a fuzzy brown worsted. To be sure of getting the trousers long enough, March had insisted on stretching the tape an extra two inches. They now dragged on the ground over his shoes, but he turned them up until Ona could cut them off. Very proud, he wore them after dark until school started in order to get used to his strangely mature, long-legged appearance in the mirror.

And now came September: rich Indian Summer, like the lingering mellow glow of blazing summer. The crowds of tourists departed, the trains grew shorter, fewer. Summer cottages and resort cabins were boarded up; great homes were closed while their owners now in turn fled elsewhere with the same unrest that had brought their guests. And now after the first frost up at Cripple Creek the aspen thickets blazed among the pines, and the deer trooped daintily, stiff-legged, down from timberline; and down at Shallow Water the wagons of The People creaked through miles of yellow chamisa. All this the ghostly flow of time had carried behind him. He was entering high school now, grown up, in long pants. But as he lay at night in his grandfather's house listening to the ancient aimless winds prowling along the eaves, he heard the haunting voices of his father and his father's fathers whispering that there is no changing constant change; that all must pass only to come again; for always and forever we are the feather, the flower, the drum, and the mirror of the old gods who never die.

PART II

TAILINGS

1

Often during his first semester Ona asked March how he liked high school. He answered her with a shrug.

High school. What was it, really?

Down from the mines of Cripple Creek came trains of ore to the unloading chutes of the reduction mill. Inside, with faultless precision, the ore was crushed, ground, sent to the roasters and flotation tanks. What gold there was, came out in standard-sized bricks. The waste pulp, the tailings, was sent to the dump. The economic process was simple. It was too expensive to handle low grade and high grade ores separately. They were mixed together and the same treatment was given to the whole run of the mill at once.

The one high school of Little London was no different. So down the chutes went March with all the rest of the ore: a ragged-shirted boy from the West Side; a frightened, handsome Negro girl from Liller; Cecil James sporting a vest and a gold watch chain; Leslie Shane, beautiful and demure; poised children from the North End discussing between classes where they had spent the summer.

"No. You've got to take algebra – Yes, English is required – Here's your card now all filled out. Go get it signed – Next!"

Round and round they went, as if on a moving belt. One room sucked them in and an hour later spewed them out. The teachers regarded them all with the calm scrutiny of gang foremen who had handled ore too long to be surprised at any trivial variations in the run. March wrote on the required notebook paper punched with two holes, learned to use a cheap fountain pen continually leaking. And all this monotonous routine went on with precision to the harsh clanging of the hourly bell.

To escape it he managed to schedule his study periods at mid-morning and mid-afternoon when he could meet the trains at the Sante Fe station instead of being confined in school. A secondhand bicycle which be bought with his savings enabled him to make these quick transitions.

This was March's first impression of high school. It was changed with Will Hapsworth's entrance during the second semester. Then he saw that the high school, like Little London itself, was divided strictly and impassibly as by railroad tracks. Each section of town, each class of society, was as segregated and inviolable within its walls as if the students wore the brand of their social status. Democracy was not a rubber stamp of society which could be imprinted on all men, for no impress could make all men equal. There was nothing in common between boys from the elite North End who drove their own cars and those who came from the West Side with their lunch buckets; between the girls of Liller who wore the gingham of their hard-working mothers and those who spent their summers in Europe. At the bottom of the scale were the poor and orphaned children of the Myron Stratton Home, the charitable institution which had been founded by Stratton, the Croesus of Cripple Creek, for destitute miners' families. The snobbishness involved was creating in them such a hopeless sense of inferiority that the officials of the Home were arranging to remove them from the public high school.

All this was reflected by the two boys' literary societies: the Senate which controlled the weekly school paper, *The Lever;* and the Delphian which controlled the dramatic club. Their functions were primarily social; their parties, dances, and steak fries in the mountains were in reality the school's only social events except one or two farcical school dances which few students attended. The two societies dominated the high school; they were sponsored by the most influential teachers, and their members were invariably drawn only from the North End. Neither March nor Will was admitted.

"God damn their thick hides!" swore Will. "Let's blast the hell out of 'em till they let us in!"

What they would do if they were admitted, they didn't consider. Neither boy owned an automobile, nor could he even drive one. Neither could dance; had no money for outings, even to buy the pearl-encrusted pin denoting membership; and would have been aghast had their fraternal brothers and their girls entered his home. They thought only of the chasm between their poverty-stricken life and their resplendent aspirations.

To bridge it they composed a letter headed "Little Brothers, Big Brothers, and Fathers," a masterpiece of naive candor. Its theme was simple. The Little Brothers of wealthy North End families dominated Little London's grade schools and high school; their Big Brothers dominated The Colorado College in town; and their fathers ran the town with the same selfish arrogance. This whole "un-American" regime should be abolished, beginning with the transformation of the Little Brothers by opening the two literary societies to membership on a purely scholastic basis. They would then, as Big Brothers in college, and later as City Fathers, be more democratic and generous of spirit. The letter was signed "The Well Wishers," and mailed to *The Lever*.

For a week the two boys anxiously awaited the result.

The Lever came out. On the back page was printed a travesty of their letter. Its meaning was mangled and distorted; sentences were cut and replaced by shameful grumblings. It was headed, "Anonymous Socialists Indict School," and signed "The Grumblers." Underneath was a curt paragraph signed by the Principal. It stated sanctimoniously how pained he was that some of his students were so jealous of the popularity of others, warned against the evils of socialism, and lamented the cowardice that had prevented the writers from signing their names.

March and Will were aghast.

"The son of a bitch!" declaimed Will. "Too afraid of the truth to print our letter. The damned coward!"

"No!" answered March. "You forget the Senate Society runs

The Lever. They're the ones who rewrote our letter before they showed it to the Principal."

Unable to endure the accusation of cowardice, they fell headlong into the trap laid for them. They wrote another letter daring the editor to print their first letter just as it was written, and signing their names. Within a week it was obvious that almost everyone in school knew who "The Grumblers" were. Then something happened which brought this trivial occurrence to a disastrous climax.

Late one afternoon Ona, March, and the two girls were sitting on the front porch when Will came walking home from school. Hands in pockets, coat collar up, he was slouching past on the other side of the street as if ashamed of being seen.

"Why, what's the matter with Will?" asked Ona. "You boys haven't quarreled, have you, March?"

"No. He was all right this morning," answered March, giving a shrill whistle.

The two girls yelled, waved their hands. Will turned and slowly, head down, slunk up to the porch. His face was pale and strained; he looked shamed and frightened.

"Oh, Will! Your coat!" Leona's sharp eyes had spotted it first. On the right side of the jacket, directly in front and between shoulder and lapel, the cloth had been burned away to a huge hole. They could see the scorched and ragged lining.

"Will, I'm so sorry!" Nancy's sensitive left eye twitched with pity. "It's the new coat your father bought you to wear to school."

The boy's face constricted. He tried to sneer, to laugh it away; and these pitiful attempts at an unwarranted nonchalance only intensified the pain and fear in his wild, troubled eyes.

"How'd you do it?" demanded March.

"The sons-a-bitches. They done it a-purpose. But my Dad – " Gradually he became coherent. That afternoon in the chemistry class the teacher had asked for an assistant to help demonstrate an experiment in the laboratory. Will volunteered. As he stood bent over the counter with the other students gathered around him, the teacher was called outside. He left them for a few minutes with instructions to handle the acids with care.

"Maybe it was the nitric or maybe the sulphuric acid. But anyway it was them North Enders. Cecil James on the staff of *The*

Lever who rewrote our letter and told everybody who wrote it. He was the one, the rotten, dressed up bastard! He reached around from behind me and poured the nitric in the sulphuric, just what we weren't supposed to do. They mixed like hell-fire and brimstone. The whole mess spouted up like a geyser and burned my coat."

"Now Will!" remonstrated Ona. "He didn't deliberately try to harm you. He's just like other boys and girls."

"What did the teacher say when he came back?" asked Nancy.

"He said he'd told me to be careful, and after this to buy a rubber apron."

"Land alive, boy!" said Ona. "Your face might have been disfigured for life. It's only a coat."

Will's face hardened; a sullen resentment emanated from him. "The whole class was laughing at me fit to kill."

Frightened and ashamed, he crept home to the tawdry frame house on the dump along Shook's Run. The Rogiers had little to say. The coat was irreparably ruined and could never be worn again.

That evening after supper Ona called March aside. "Son, wouldn't you like to run over to Will's a few minutes? I've got the feeling it's going to be a bad evening for him, Mr. Hapsworth and all. You know – Just a cheerful word."

"Why sure, Mother," March reluctantly agreed, knowing Hapsworth better than she.

When March arrived at the Hapsworths' kitchen door, Hapsworth was sitting backwards on a chair, his grimy hands resting on the back and swinging his leather belt. In the corner where he had been flung across the wood box, Will straightened up. March could sec he had been whipped badly; a lash of the belt had caught him on one cheek; a welt was rising. Mrs. Hapsworth sat at the kitchen table. Her worn, tear-spotted face wore a look of peculiar hardness.

"I'm sorry," said March, abashed and hesitating at the door. "I guess I won't come in."

"Come in, I said!" thundered Hapsworth without removing his glance from Will. "We got nothing to be ashamed of!"

As March sank upon a chair, Hapsworth stood up in his dirty blue socks and brought his heavy belt down, whistling, across the back of his chair. "I told you those filthy capitalist brats would try to keep you from gettin' an education! And you were fool enough to step up and volunteer. Not them others with two, three, or likely four suits to home. No! When a drift's plugged up and the air's bad, do the rich mine owners in their white collars go down? No! It's a call for volunteers among the workers. And when Hansen gets stretched out, turns yellow, and we haul him up pukin' green slime to stay home for weeks, it's nothin' out of their hides. They try to beat him out of his compensation. And you! The professor ain't buyin' you a new coat, or those rich brats either."

His coarse dirty dungarees had slipped down to his bony hips; his shirt tail crawled out; his black face was beginning to drop beads of sweat thick as shoe polish. "You mind what I'm sayin'. You was sent to school to learn to get what these capitalists have got, and then it'll be us crackin' the whip!"

March stole a look at Will. What he saw filled him with a strange fright and disgust. The boy's fear and resentment over his beating had faded from his face; his eyes were steady upon his father's; he seemed intent upon this vindictive indictment and promise of revenge as if it were already salving his wounds.

Hapsworth, however, was not through. He lifted his foot to the chair and gave his knee a loud whack with the belt. "Now!" he said ominiously. "I'm goin' to see you remember this lesson. Your ma and I saved months for that new coat. And you're goin' to keep on wearin' it, understand?"

Will's eyes widened with new fear and shame. He looked appealingly at his mother wiping away a tear with her apron.

"I can't mend it for him. The hole's too big," she stammered.

"Wear it the way it is, then. Every day!" Hapsworth thundered at the boy. "Let 'em see that hole – the rich brats, the professors, you too. It'll remind you of somethin' you better not forget." He stepped forward, lifted the belt, and stared at the boy shrinking back against the wall. "And if I ever catch you forgettin' it, I'll strap the hide off your bones!"

With this he turned, grabbed up his shoes, and flung into the bedroom.

Will stood up, gazing at his mother with a look March could not bear. March stammered his excuses and fled home.

Next morning he stood at the front window with Mrs. Rogier, Ona, and the two girls, waiting for Will. "Of course he won't come!"

he boasted. "Do you think I would?"

"Never mind," answered Ona. "I'll run over later and talk to Mrs. Hapsworth."

Suddenly Will appeared. He did not stop for March as usual, but walked past stiffly, head up. He was wearing the coat; on it was a huge and glaring patch. The Rogiers dodged back in embarrassed silence. Old clothes, cheap clothes, worn clothes, all cleaned and neatly pressed and mended – but patches never!

March watched him pass by the window, his own face flushed with shame. Then a mighty admiration filled him. Will had a courage greater than he could ever have assumed; and that horrible patch seemed to him now a heraldic symbol of something that the Rogiers with their monstrous false pride could never equal. He ran out quickly and caught up with his chum.

But in the days that followed March saw the difference in Will. For awhile Will kept aloof, a little truculently, until his classmates' glances no longer helplessly strayed to the enormous patch. Then little by little he began to ingratiate himself among the Senate and Delphian boys. March could see him in the halls and on the grounds between classes. His smile seemed open, his pats on their backs spontaneous, his admiration of their society pins profound. And yet with a curious disgust, March divined in his manner a bitter homage, and a sly and eager hunger. Will, seeing him walk by, winked furtively.

"It's like my dad said," he told March later. "You got to get in with them to lick them. I'm goin' to be in a society if it kills me."

How little we know one another! March, confused and disgusted, knew only that he himself was as out of step at high school as he had been at Columbia. But to make up for it, he pedalled furiously back and forth to the Sante Fe station, his one great love.

2

That winter was a crucial one for the Rogiers. The United States had entered the war to make the world safe for democracy, and the wartime rise of prices increased their difficulties. The $30 to $40 a month that March earned selling newspapers helped greatly on the grocery bill, but there were other household expenses too. March came home one night to find the piano moved out of the parlor. The next week another one of the concrete mixers in the back yard was gone. Soon men in a truck came after the great steel safe in the obscure corner of the dining room. Mrs. Rogier was on her knees before it, scraping Rogier's name off the door.

"Daddy's safe that's been in the family all these years. I won't have it carrying his name!" she hissed melodramatically.

"Oh shoot, Mother!" comforted Ona. "The combination lock's broken, and we've only kept the Haviland in it for years!"

Then one day the little cast-iron Nigger-Boy out in front was sold to a wealthy North End family which had long fancied it for their garden. No one said a word while it was being removed. They didn't have to. The Blackamore's outstretched hand had held the reins of Akeepee, Little Man, Aralee, Silver Heels, Tolar, and Silver

Night. From it Sally Lee, Mary Ann, even March when little had clambered upon Rogier's horses. But that night when Mrs. Rogier called the children to table, she was stern, grim-lipped, and deadly serious.

"Now children, before you sit down, I think it's right for you to realize we're having a hard time," she began. "We've eaten up Daddy's concrete mixers, the piano, the safe, and now the Nigger Boy. Where more will come from I don't know, but the Lord will provide. There'll be enough each meal. But only help yourself to what you can eat. Don't leave anything on your plate to be thrown out."

Abashed by her vulgar frankness, the children sat down to a silent meal. Suddenly March blurted out, "Everyone around here goes up to the railroad track with gunny sacks to pick up coal. I don't see why we shouldn't if we're so poor. I know the fireman on Number 6. He'll throw off some coal just where I tell him to. Nobody will see him in the dark, or me when I bring it home."

Mrs. Rogier flung back stiffly in her chair. "Must I point out the difference between poor people and poor white trash? I thought we all instinctively understood!"

"Let the boy bring home all he wants!" growled Rogier. "At the price it is, a good big chunk of anthracite ought to be worn on a watch chain!"

Mrs. Rogier flung down her fork and left the table.

"Never mind, son," cautioned Ona. "We haven't come to that yet. You're helping Mother splendidly with the money you give her. We can pay for what we need; just let's be economical."

Yet in March who sat there, secretly worried as they all were, his grandmother's unhappy spirit roused a savage and uncontrollable shame for the deathless pride and valor of which she was still an untarnished symbol.

The family's usual fare during the winter, with the restrictions on sugar and flour, was corn bread and potatoes covered with "compound gravy." This synthetic spread they all disliked. They ate it for the first taste which vaguely reminded them of the meat they could not afford, and because it hid the absence of butter. Leona could not endure it. Cheerful and light-hearted, she forebore mentioning her disgust at table. But to Nancy and March she had plenty to say.

"Compound gravy! Compound gravy! Isn't it ever going to end? I'll bet it's made of axle grease, it's so yellow and greasy. How do you stand it?"

"Oh, it's not so bad if you squeeze the lumps out flat," murmured Nancy.

"What do you want – T-bone steak and asparagus, with a chocolate cake thrown in?" demanded March.

"Yes!" laughed Leona. "Two helpings please. Mine and yours, since you'd stick up your nose at it!"

That night at supper she was passed the bowl of compound gravy. "No thanks!" she said airily.

March stared down at his plate. In it was a slab of corn bread and two boiled potatoes, all butterless. Abruptly he took the bowl and thrust it at Leona. "Take some!" When she did not move, he grabbed and squeezed her wrist. "Take some, I say!"

Leona took the bowl and rose to her feet. Then without warning she began to fling handsful at him, spattering him from the top of his head to his waist.

"Take some, I say!" she shouted hysterically. "And this and this!" Her light body shaking, her dark face a sickly yellow, she continued to scream. "Tell me what I should eat! Who do you think you are? Compound gravy! Compound gravy! Fill your belly full – Your face – Your ears!"

March, blinded, kicked back his chair, dug out his eyes. What he saw was not a girl's hysteria, but the savage fury and violence of his father when he was finally aroused. She too was a Cable, as well as a Rogier. He stood transfixed, slowly wiping off his face, hair, and clothes.

Leona hurled the bowl at him wildly; it hurtled past his head and crashed against the wall. Then she rushed, wild-eyed and panting, to fling herself kicking on the shabby sofa in the parlor. Ona and Nancy followed to kneel and stroke her hair. "Honey! Quiet down now. It's all over."

Mrs. Rogier, still seated at the table with Rogier, raised a tense white face, and asked calmly, "You'd like some more corn bread, Daddy? A hot piece from the oven?"

The bottom of family misfortune was reached just before

Christmas. The weather was terribly cold and dry; and to conserve coal, they kept only the downstairs rooms heated. In the evening all gathered about the kerosene lamp on the dining room table; it always seemed to be smoking, no matter how often the wick was trimmed. Rogier, years before, had torn out the electrical wiring in a fit of temper because the light bills were so high. He had then installed a carbide gas lighting system at enormous expense. The folly was soon apparent. Great cans of chunk carbide had to be emptied into the plant in the basement. Water was then added to generate the gas. A month later, when the gas was exhausted, the slimy, milky residue had to be carried, bucket by bucket, outside and emptied. Because of the work and expense, the plant was abandoned and kerosene lamps used.

The feeble light of the one on the table was enough to illuminate the family's hopes for Christmas. Mary Ann, bewailing poor business in her Chocolate Shoppe, sent only a box of her bittersweets. Boné sent a lovely card. And Sally Lee from whom they expected a big box of munificent presents, sent a $20 bill to go around. Of this, $15 went for coal.

"I know you're all a little disappointed," said Ona, "but this Christmas we must all be sensible. With the remaining $5 March and I have bought a family present, one we can all use. Guess what it is! A new fangled lamp to use instead of this kerosene one. A Coleman lamp. You pump it up with air, and it's got mantles, and gives the brightest light. Now what do you think of that?"

"What about our Christmas dinner?" asked Nancy.

"Daddy's going to kill that big red rooster he's always chasing with a stick. It'll take two hens if he don't, and we need the eggs."

But Rogier balked at killing his arch enemy, the big red rooster, beginning an argument that lasted till the afternoon before Christmas. It was settled by a ring of the doorbell. Ona and Mrs. Rogier rushed to the door. No one was there, but at their feet lay a grocery basket containing a dressed turkey, celery, and cranberries. The card on top read: "Merry Christmas to my friends and best customers from their groceryman, Mr. Bryce."

"And we've owed him over $50 for two months!" muttered Ona, her eyes misting with tears. "I'm going right over and thank him!"

After a devoutly enjoyed Christmas dinner the Rogiers returned to their meager fare. It was enlivened by one delight — lettuce. Crisp, green lettuce with its crinkly leaves and its reassuring taste of summer and the fertile earth; the great green bunches which lighted up their cheerless winter evenings when the snow whirled against the window panes. The one place where they could buy fresh, cool leaves was Aunt Fanny's jerry-built greenhouse a half-mile up Shook's Run. Almost every evening March and Leona walked up there for the dime purchase.

Shook's Run below the Bijou bridge was a horror of trash and tin cans culminating in the dump along which lived the Hapsworths. Above the bridge, the creek still retained vestiges of its original charm. Cottonwoods lined the steep banks, weeping willows hung over the stream, patches of watercress showed under the ice. Leona loved these evening walks when the yellow lamps in the shanties and small wooden houses on each side seemed lit by the red glare of the sun setting behind the snowy peaks. She tripped along cheerily as the little creek, spurting out her frosty breaths like puffs of tobacco smoke.

She was a head shorter than March. Her hair was lighter than his, and her eyes gray-blue like Ona's, but she had Cable's dark skin which drank up the summer sun and never blistered under the brightest rays. She was sensitive about it, no doubt due to Mrs. Rogier's constant repetition of the family joke. "The stork didn't bring you like all the rest, Leona. A nigger man left you on the doorstep. Or maybe it was old Indian Poe."

March always had seen her as light-hearted and easy-going. Now since her blow-off over compound gravy, he detected in her casual manner the lackadaisical unconcern and deadly fury of his father. But beneath this was also Cable's intense awareness, gentleness, and frightening intuition — qualities which he lacked, possessing instead a black sediment at the bottom of his soul and the fumes of unceasing storm.

As they approached the home-built greenhouse Leona nudged March. "Look at her hair good this time."

March nodded. Aunt Fanny was a Negress. It was said of her that she had become bald because her hair had grown inward instead of upward. She had then bought a wig to cover it. This, Leona insisted, did not stop the ingrowing hair from penetrating her skull and brain. "That's why she's kind of funny at times – like Granddad," explained Leona.

March discounted the explanation. Big and jovial, Aunt Fanny let them select their own lettuce and wrapped it carefully in a newspaper. Also her hair looked perfectly natural to him. "Bosh!" he said as they walked home. "You can't believe everything you hear, Leona." Yet he secretly respected Leona's judgment. She was a strange one, his sister.

As spring ate into winter it became obvious that Rogier was bored with his chickens. They made him too irritable, screwing him up to a pitch of nervous tension that brought on another seizure. Light and infrequent as these were, they still were to be avoided at all costs. Hence Ona suggested that he keep the chickens fenced in the barnyard, and plant a few rows of vegetables in the garden.

Rogier agreed. The work was difficult but he kept on, stooped shoulders and thin back bent over the spade. He overturned the black earth, smoothed it with a rake, laid out rows of lettuce, radishes, green onions. Peace and quiet worked their change. He became calmer, more agreeable. An excellent sign! He was recovering, taking an interest in things, keeping busy!

Then over the high fence sailed his arch enemy, the big red rooster, to scrape up the emerging green shoots in his garden with long sharp claws.

"You cocky little cavalry-spurred Hohenzollern! I'll teach you to strut around and rake up my plants like a Prussian army general!" And grabbing up hoe or rake, Rogier would chase the flapping rooster about the garden till he was cornered. For a minute the old man would stand panting, stroking the rooster's proud arched neck, feeling his sharp spurs. "Next time I'm going to wring your neck, boy, for being so contrary. But now I'll let you off, little William. Get in there and stay there!" And he would toss the rooster over the fence.

One afternoon as he was chasing the squawking bird through the currant bushes, he was overtaken by another spell. His foot caught on a protruding root; he fell full length, arms outspread. After a time he slowly rose out of cloying darkness. As sight and senses cleared, there emerged before him, like something risen from the depths of dreamless sleep to the horizon of wakeful consciousness, a shape without clear outline yet embodying the substance of a hope and meaning that seemed as strangely familiar as it was vague. The Peak! He recognized it now, the face of that high, snowy, massive Peak. And suddenly it all came back to him: its undying challenge and its promise, his years of fruitless search. How could he have forgotten it? For there it still stood as it had stood on that day he had first glimpsed it long ago in timeless time.

He sat looking at it and at the squawking rooster with contrite shame. What had he come to, a seventy-six-year-old man, chasing a dom rooster out of a two-by-four vegetable garden! Spading up eight inches of dirt! He who had spent a lifetime drilling through hard granite into the depths of the immortal earth itself! But let no man say he was yet too old and his faculties worn too thin to take up his search where he had left off. For now suddenly and full formed there leapt into his mind a new plan by which –

"Daddy! Another spell. Just when you were getting along so well. Oh, that damned rooster!"

It was Ona, kneeling on the ground beside him.

"Oh, let him alone!" answered Rogier gruffly, feeling sound as a nut, resolute, and lighthearted. "He won't bother me again. I got something else in mind."

What it was, he explained after he'd had his hot bath and sat down to supper. "The garden's all planted," he began casually. "March can hoe out the weeds after work. Ona, you and the girls can look after those fool hens. I'm tired of them."

"But Daddy – "

Rogier raised his wrinkled hand for silence. "I've got something more important to do. You folks are so all-fired taken with fresh lettuce in the wintertime, I'm goin' to build a little greenhouse where we can raise our own lettuce the year around."

"Fine, Daddy! A good idea!" encouraged Ona. "You can use all those glass window frames stored up in the loft of the shop. And March can help you put it up."

"I'll tend to it," Rogier replied confidently. "The boy's busy enough."

Yes! He was back now, after so many fruitless "little absences" as the doctor called them, to the grass-roots reality of his only meaningful existence.

3

That June March quit his job at the Fred Harvey news stand. He was too big, too old to peddle newspapers; there wasn't any money in it, he thought scornfully. He became a Red Cap.

There had never beeen one at the old depot. But now with the new station's many gates and subways, passengers needed help and Old Lester was granted the concession. Les was an "old" man of thirty-two, a frail, rachitic consumptive who looked fifty-two. He had broken arches and flat feet, most of his thin sandy hair was gone, and his skin was scaly from cheap and insufficient food; his lungs were in such bad shape that after each busy train he had to stretch out on a bench and fight for breath; and he weighed exactly one hundred pounds. He received no salary. His only remuneration was the tips passengers gave him for carrying their bags to and from trains. To earn this privilege he helped at the gate to read tickets and Pullman reservations, and called trains when the Station Master was absent. The importance of these functions had gone to his head. Out of his pitiful savings he bought a French-blue uniform with brass buttons in which he strutted around like a small gamecock. Yet he possessed a courage, a love of life, and the faculty of appraising people at first glance.

It was he who gave March the privilege of working with him. There was need of another boy. The northbound Denver and Rio Grande trains were now being routed through the new Santa Fe station. And now, in the heyday of railroad tourist travel, trains of two or three sections poured in crowds to see the scenic wonders of the Pike's Peak Region. The Santa Fe and the D&RG – the Dirty, Ragged and Greasy – bringing rich people who had wintered in California and were on their way back East; the Colorado and Southern with Pullmans full of sweaty Southerners escaping the baking heat of the Texas plains and Louisiana swamps; the Colorado Midland rattling down the Rockies from Utah; the Midland Terminal and the Short Line from Cripple Creek with its daily Wild Flower Special.

March, tall and thin but wiry, learned the art of carrying six pieces of luggage – two bags in each hand and a suitcase under each arm, the lid against his body so it would not pop open from the pressure. Les taught him to read tickets, the tracks on which each train came in, and the spurs to which the Pullmans were shunted. Now he began to learn the subtle and intuitive art on which every Pullman porter, taxicab driver, hotel flunkey, street urchin, and cardsharp based his livelihood – the knack of reading faces.

To be sure, there was something in clothes that augered the size of a tip, in the cheapness or dearness of a traveller's luggage, whether he came by taxi or street car, whether he occupied a Pullman or a chair car. But who had time to size up all this? The bus drove up to unload fifteen passengers and thirty-five bags. Simultaneously two taxis squealed to a stop behind it.

"Here, boy!" – "Take mine, son, I'm in a hurry!"

The train pulled in. Spot the bags on the platform. Help the Porter to unload the vestibule. There was just time for carrying a quick load out to the taxis, and a dash back to the train to collect tips from outgoing passengers – There wasn't much time to load six parties on, and take two off, staggering heavily loaded in a crowd. You've got to work fast, and you can't pick any duds.

By a quick look at a face – this was the only way you could gauge the size of a tip. Faces that in the busy press of a great railway station dropped their masks and unsuspectingly revealed the open generosity, the spendthrift habit, the strict budgeting, or the miserly selfishness of their souls. If you would know a man, rather than his financial status, observe how much he slips into an open hand in the dark when he is leaving town.

How marvelous they were, these thousands of faces ever swarming the station platform like bees and taking flight again! They became for him symbols of some inner texture of their lives he learned to evaluate instantly but never quite explain: the faces of travelling salesmen whom he hated and avoided; the spoiled and demanding faces of women from the South with their Negro maids; the frank and generous faces of prostitutes whom he always tried to serve; the cunning faces of Little London's political bigwigs; those of gawking Eastern tourists; and above all, the faces of those few men and women, whatever their clothes and baggage, that proclaimed them as true gentlefolk and citizens of the wide earth they trod.

He made his biggest tips from handling a truckload of bags from a large escorted tourist party travelling under the auspices of the Raymond and Whitcomb, Cook's Tours, or other national agencies. Many of these parties were comprised of foreigners, Japanese, Chinese, French, or English. Yet it never seemed strange to him that so many of his own countrymen were so ignorant of the Wild West that they let themselves be herded like sheep to see its scenic wonders.

There were other sources of money: occasional tips given him on the sly by tourist drivers and keepers of third-rate hotels for directing tourists their way. This was against the rules. The transportation company of Diggs and Handel, with whom Rogier had fussed over a mine some years ago, had secured the station franchise. All itinerant baggagemen and tourist drivers of both automobiles and horse-driven hacks were banished to the street where they stood shouting at the curb. Only Diggs and Handel's bus and taxis were allowed to stand at the edge of the station platform. March did his best to chisel the edge off their monopoly. He would hold back his most influential-looking parties till the Diggs and Handel bus had driven away, then call a tourist driver and a baggageman from the street.

The tourist drivers repaid him by taking him with their parties, by carriage or automobile, to the scenic wonders of the Pike's Peak Region: through the Garden of the Gods, up North and South Cheyenne Canyons, to Seven Falls and Helen Hunt Jackson's grave on top; to the Ancient Cliff-Dwellers, the Cave of the Winds, General Palmer's English castle of Glen Eyrie.

There was no doubt about it; America, having saved the world for democracy, was suddenly curious about itself. "See America First" was the thing, at least until Europe was swept up for visitors. And so Little London swarmed and trainloads of the newly rich, war profiteers great and small, hordes of tourists from everywhere. She had mastered at last her environment, stamped out all traces of the little pioneering town at the foot of Pike's Peak. *Little London! The spa of the West with Old World charm.*

Driving around with young Hanlon who had just replaced his carriage with a new automobile, March saw gaudily painted, cast-iron Indian Chiefs on every corner advertising soda water. In Manitou the old street car pavilion was replaced by a huge cement tepee. Hot dog stands boasted imitation log-cabin fronts. A high board fence was erected around Balanced Rock to make sure no one saw it without paying twenty-five cents. Picture show palaces were no longer named the "Majestic," "Princess," or "Odeon," but the "Ute" and the "Chief."

At the end of a trip March complained to Hanlon, "Weren't you ashamed givin' that spiel? The Cliff Dwellers is a fake. It's just copied after the ruins in Mesa Verde. The shards are broken Hopi bowls buried in the sand, brand new. Helen Hunt isn't buried above Seven Falls. It's only an empty grave and the rocks on top are put there for souvenir hunters." Bitterly he went on. "And that Petrified Indian at the Garden of the Gods! You can see he's even got paint and bracelets on. And all that fake Indian jewelry you made people buy. Why, those Ute moccasins were manufactured in Chicago!"

"Hold on!" interrupted Hanlon. "What the hell's the difference what I tell 'em? You can see their mouths gapin' open for flies at anything. That's what they pay their money for. Jesus' underwear! If this town told the truth, nothin' but the truth, most of us would go hungry." He shook his head knowingly. "We only get these suckers three months a year. We've got to make enough out of 'em to last the other nine. That's why everything costs so much. Everything! Every hotel, salt water taffy stand, and souvenir shop's got our number. We get a commission on every dollar they spend. See? Now for God's sake keep your trap shut the next time I haul you around."

A week later Hanlon picked up a party of distinguished visitors, wealthy Chicago meat packers and their wives. Unfortunately he had caught cold on a sunrise trip up the Peak and was too hoarse to deliver his spiel, and asked March to point out the sights as they drove about.

"Really overwhelming. The vastness, I mean," one of the ladies in back remarked, glancing at the folder in her hand. "Now Fraunce does have a chahm. A quiet chahm. Don't you think so, Stella? But here, it's the distances, the sparkling champagne air, the coloration you know, that really gets one, don't you think?"

"Yep!" answered one of the men. "But it's the good ol' U. S. A. for hogs and cattle ever' time. Pork chops and T-bones. But likely scenery hereabouts. Now what do you suppose made them rocks stand up like that?"

March answered bashfully with a remembered bit of Rogier's geology.

"Hummmm. The boy sounds like he knew what he was talking about," growled the other man behind him.

"Yes sir," hoarsely responded Hanlon. "Born and bred of old pioneers. Knows ever' inch of the country. I sometimes bring him along to give the low-down to my smartest customers."

By the time they had reached the Garden of the Gods, March had lost his bashfulness. After dutifully pointing out the post-card-famous Kissing Camels, the Seal and the Bear, he pointed toward a pile of formless rocks. "That's the Shark's Head, lady. See it sticking up against the sky?"

For a moment there was silence.

"Sure, Stella! Look there!" Her husband stretched out his arm.

"Oh yes!" the woman shrieked. "I see it now. Plain as the nose on your face!"

Rapidly now March pointed out more nondescript cliffs and pillars, calling them by any name that jumped into his head: the Two Doves, Lady in White, Manitou's Headdress. He concocted lies that would have choked him with anger had he heard them from another. Here a bear had eaten a child; off this cliff a lovelorn Indian maiden had jumped to her death; there the pioneers had made a last stand against bloodthirsty Utes. "The Massacre of '72 – or was it '73?" he asked with a solemn face.

"It was '73, I believe," spoke up one of the men authoritatively. "I read about it in history. But then," he added modestly, "I'm better at figures than dates."

They bought boxes of ore specimens, glass wampum beads made in Germany, moccasins manufactured in Chicago, souvenir spoons, bows and arrows, salt water taffy, dozens of postcard folders. And when at last they clambered out at their hotel, each shook hands with this all-knowing boy-wonder whose family was among the oldest Pioneer Winners of the Far West.

"And by Gosh, if you ever come to Chicago, son, you look us up. You sure showed us a wonderful time. We were lucky you came along."

Hanlon finally found his voice as the car drove off. "Christ!" he muttered hoarsely. "You told them ignorant meat butchers more lies than there's in all Little Lunnon. How much did they slip you?"

"A five dollar bill," March answered smugly.

Such munificent windfalls came seldom. But March took other rides between trains with Old Dutch, delivering trunks. Old Dutch was a big-boned man, strong as a buffalo but with a squeaky hip, who stood beside his rattletrap truck at the curb soliciting baggage in a bellowing voice. Number 11 from Kansas City, Chicago, and all points east, arriving in two sections at 3:05 p.m., brought him the greatest number of trunks. He delivered them before Number 2 arrived at 5:35, taking March with him.

Panting up a narrow flight of stairs on one end of a big Hartman wardrobe was hard work for the boy, but he was amply rewarded. The Rogiers, penned with their poverty and pride in the shabby old house on Shook's Run, received no visitors and never went calling. Except for the homes of a few schoolmates to which he was occasionally invited to a party, March had never been out. Now, day after day, he saw the nooks and crannies into which flowed the vast streams of people that poured off the trains.

The little summer cottages and cabins with their "cute" names – "Dew Drop In" and "Rancho Costa Plenty" – forty steps up the steep hillside streets of Manitou. The tawdry tourist homes and rooming houses with their florid wallpaper, cigar butts on the dresser, and silk stockings hung over a chair to dry. The Sanitoriums—Star Ranch in the Pines, Cragmor, and the beautiful Woodmen Sanitorium—where the tuberculosis invalids, the "lungers," sat on open porches with their sputum cups, gazing at the mountains which would, of course, restore their health. The hotels he loved to peep inside. Each in some strange manner had a character and an atmosphere all its own: the historic and beloved Antlers fronting Pike's Peak Avenue as if set at the very base of the great Peak itself; the beautiful gray stone Cliff House at the entrance to Williams Canyon; the Mansions with its rose-walled ballroom; the Ruxton, named for the young English explorer who gave his name to the mountain stream it straddled; the sedate Alamo and the family style Alta Vista; even the little Joyce, so cheerful and sprightly.

The great homes of Little London's aristocracy held him spellbound. All his life March had heard his grandmother bewailing the unproductiveness of Rogier's mines that had prevented her from building a proper Rogier domicile in the divine North End. The barny mansions, the rococo palaces, and the enormous brownstone houses on Millionaire Row were impressive enough. But like Cripple Creek gold, they were out of date; their owners had made their piles and settled down to a staid career of preserving them against change. The really showy places were the spacious and luxurious estates in the new Broadmoor section. Each reflected the tastes and whims of its builder: Gothic, Tudor, and Elizabethan houses, Italian villas, Spanish and Mexican ranch houses, Swiss chateaus, even imitation Indian pueblos. Into each one March walked entranced by a spaciousness, cleanliness, and luxury he had never dreamed existed; awed by maids in spotless white uniforms, slipping on smooth polished floors, eating a cookie given him by a cook. And coming out, he stared just as entranced at gardeners tending the great expanses of lawn and garden.

The crowning jewel of this newly developed suburb was the magnificent new Broadmoor Hotel. Built on the site of Count Portales' historic Broadmoor Casino, which March's mother remembered with such an accountable and nostalgic fondness, it upheld with new splendor Little London's tradition of European elegance and luxury. Its multi-storied tiers of white stone gleamed palely from afar against the dark slopes of Cheyenne Mountain. To each side lay the polo fields and nearby a new golf course. The gravelled approach to it lay through a magnificent formal garden and directly behind the hotel a tiny lake boasted on its shore an Italian chapel.

Its setting was so beautiful that the famous artist, Maxfield Parrish, was brought to paint it—the reproductions to advertise a brand of coffee, and the original to hang in the hotel as Little London's most revered work of art. Its artistic integrity no one dared to deny while humbly making obeisance before it; and none ventured to remark that the Master of Blue with an artist's license had moved the lake from behind the hotel to place it in front, so that his masterpiece would conform with all his other paintings.

The Broadmoor was a royal hostelry. Its color was a rich plum-purple, its crest emblazoned in gold. Its own private bus and taxicabs, which met all trains, were so painted and emblazoned. So were all its servants' uniforms, with gold buttons. How wonderful it was, with its beautiful setting, its majestic facade, its luxurious interior with its open terraces, dining rooms, commodious rooms, and a swimming pool whose water was purified by ultra-violet rays!

Madame Jones' parlor with its rubber plant in Cripple Creek, the Palace Hotel, Finn's Folly, were nothing compared to this! All of Cripple Creek's gold had built nothing like it. Times were changing. The perpetual, ever-flowing, constantly changing stream of time. That was what March read in the changing aspect of Little London, in the faces swarming before him on the station platform only to vanish a moment later.

But there came a moment when time stood still, and he stood looking at its unmoving core, remembering his father, the feather, the flower, the drum, and the mirror of the old gods who never die.

4

He saw them one afternoon when Number 11 pulled out, leaving them stranded far down the platform with their bags and bundles. A large group of dark, fat, and dirty Indians, the men wearing ten-gallon Stetsons, ragged trousers and moccasins, the shapeless women wrapped in bright silks. Sullen and bewildered, all squatted under blankets in the blazing summer sun, eating peanuts and bananas.

March watched them with shame and sadness, remembering the proud and arrogant Navajos at Shallow Water. The Indians stared back without moving. And now there began a curious duel, a tug of war, between him and them. "They can't just squat there all day," he thought. "If they want help or to ask directions or something, let 'em yell or wave."

The Indians did neither. They just squatted there, calling him across the tracks with the silent stare of their black, unblinking eyes. Finally March walked over to the undeniable leader of the group, a man big as a hill, dark as new-plowed earth. Inquiringly, March raised both hands to his temples, brushed backward and upward with a light, swift motion in the tribal sign that Cable had taught him signified Osages – "Shave Heads."

Big Hill scowled, "Ho – Hah! – Boy knowin' somethin'. Humph!"

"Where you goin'?" March demanded.

The men around Big Hill found their voices. "Eat. Sleep. Smellin' good air. Drinkin' good water. We goin' somewhere!" Out of their pockets they pulled rolls of bills big enough to choke a cow. Off his, Big Hill peeled a thousand dollars which he handed to March. "Good place! We goin' now!"

March grinned. "Yes sir! Let's go!"

Loading them with all their bags and bundles, rolls of blankets, a stalk of bananas and a case of soda pop, into two yellow tourist Cadillacs and an old red Hudson, he drove them to the Antlers Hotel. The supercilious clerk looked them over, then down at the thousand dollars March laid on the desk, and called the manager.

"Oil-rich Osages from Oklahoma, eh?" he asked. "We're full, but I can let them have the Presidential suite and the bridal suite."

When they were safely installed, March returned to work. But only to be met by a worried Big Hill a few hours later. Their spring had gone dry, he complained. Taking a taxi to the hotel, March discovered the cause of their trouble. They had been drinking out of the toilet bowl, their "spring," which was now empty. He explained its purpose, showed them how to turn on the faucets for water, and returned to the station.

The following day the chief came back. His people were tired of being cooped up in the hotel. "Good air. Good water. Grass. Trees. You find 'em, eh?" He pressed a dollar bill into the boy's hand.

"No!" said March. "No good!"

Big Hill promptly handed out his whole roll. From it March peeled off another thousand dollars. And now in Hanlon's tourist car with a real estate agent, they toured Little London for suitable accomodations. The place they found was a beautiful estate in Broadmoor with a huge lawn threaded by a stream. Here the Osages settled for the summer, learning how to turn on the electric lights and cook on gas, but sleeping under the trees on their blankets.

Occasionally Hanlon drove them to see the sights, their favorite ride being the sunrise trip to the summit of Pike's Peak. And every week or so Big Hill came after March to spend the evening. Over a fire in the garden they cooked huge slabs of steak, then to the beat of a drum they did a stomp dance, finally spreading out to sleep under the stars.

In Little London they became a sensation. Hotels, cafes, and stores refused them nothing. Money to the Osages assumed its only real significance. It was merely green paper. Oil had been struck on their homeland and they had been forced to trade their birthrights for headrights, becoming fabulously rich. But what, wondered March, did they buy with the former slow rhythmic tenor of their days, the awareness of their oneness with their earth? Good air, good water, grass, trees – and with these, a blinded vision, atrophied senses, glutted appetites, an ever-fresh inward life stagnating within them, a putrid decay! Like Indian Poe, like his own father's people, they were lost and alone, restlessly prowling a new America for something they had lost and would not find again.

They oppressed him with a sense of guilt. They annoyed him, irritated him, and laughed at him. And all that summer and the next, when they returned, he kept wondering what drew him back, again and again, to this growing horde of shiftless, ignorant Osages. Big Hill and his band seemed oblivious of their tragedy. Big Hill knew exactly what he was. His rough-hewn face with its jutting big Roman nose paled to anonymity the swarms of transient faces flitting past. His massive body rooted to the earth by his small moccasined feet, he stood like a pillar around which flowed all time and change. Nothing could ever dwindle or change him; he would endure forever. And so to March, caught in the swirling tide of constant change, he loomed up like a monument of something fixed and immutable but which he could not grasp.

March had seen little of Leslie Shane in High School. The family had moved from the top of Bijou Hill to a house in the North End. She was quite popular, becoming a promising dancer who appeared frequently at women's clubs. Now this semester he found her in two of his classes. Sight of her in his geometry class upset him. She had developed quickly. Her small body was strong and firm; her apricot-colored curls glowed like a halo about her pale freckled face; her delicate blue-veined hands were swift in movement. March found it impossible to stand before her in front of the class to prove a theorem on the blackboard with a pointer. Time and again he refused to get up when called.

One day the teacher, a dried-up spinster, held him after class. "March, you have a good, sound mind. Your paper work is excellent. But I won't be dictated to any longer. Unless you get over your bashfulness, or whatever it is, and go to the blackboard like the others when called upon, I shall be forced to fail you at the end of the semester."

"I can't," he replied calmly, with unfounded, unreasonable stubbornness.

Nor did he, even though the teacher failed him as she threatened.

To offset his miserable appearance in the geometry class, he showed off in front of Leslie in their physiography class. The teacher, Mr. Lyle Ross, was a small, wispy-haired, nervously energetic man who reminded March of Rogier with his talk of ancient marine floods and the re-emergence of the earth as the sea retreated, of changing tides and air currents. This was old stuff to March. Already he knew the limestone, sandstone, and granite formations of the region; and brought specimens of ore from Rogier's shop to display.

Wispy, absent-minded Mr. Ross did not restrict himself to books, maps of oceanic currents, U.S. quadrangles, and geology reports. He taught from nature. And so one afternoon the class met at the Busy Corner, rode a streetcar to Adam's Crossing, and walked to a long north-south hogback terminating in an asymmetrical fold where they could see the exposed stratified layers of rock.

"Fossils!" Mr. Ross announced from underneath the umbrella that shielded him from the sun. "Sharks' teeth imbedded in limestone. Let's see how many you can find and dig out with your hammers."

The class spread out to hunt likely spots along the limestone ridge. March and Leslie drifted together as if caught by the same invisible and powerful tide. The sun burned like the heat of an oven; a hawk wheeled overhead; far away sounded the pecking of their companions' little candy hammers. The girl sat quietly before him. She had on a big straw hat, sand-colored with a pinkish weave, to protect her white freckled face from sunburn. The boy worked steadily: cutting away the gray weathered top rock with Rogier's small miner's hammer to expose a small dark speck imbedded in the limestone.

"You've got to be careful," he said, conscious of the steady communion between them. "Sharks' teeth are small and brittle and liable to break." How beautiful she was with her small stub nose, tiny freckles, and soft warm eyes! He remembered the night he had bashfully caressed her cheek with his thumb before he kissed her. Magically now, the mark emerged upon her cheek: broad at the top over her cheekbone and dwindling away down her soft cheek, like a shark's tooth imbedded in white limestone.

"There it is! You chip it out now!" he directed. "Careful!"

With a slight blow of her hammer she exposed it: a beautifully curved shark's tooth, the point imbedded in limestone.

They laughed together with delight. "It's yours. You dug it out," said March.

"No, it's yours. You discovered it," she insisted.

Facing her, looking into her eyes, he suddenly grasped her fine, blue-veined hand. "You're runnin' around with that Cecil James and his crowd."

"He lives near us, he's got a car, and he takes me to dances and parties, March."

He knew now, as every child knows, the tragedy of youth: of mature emotions and longings balked by years of development and attainment that could not be hastened, a barrier that could not be broken through.

"I don't belong to a society. I don't have a car. And besides, I'm too busy at the station for that stuff," he said straightforwardly, without bitterness. "That's the way it is, I guess. But it makes no difference."

Leslie knew it too. Gazing steadily into his eyes, she said just as calmly. "Yes, that's the way it is. But it makes no difference to me, either."

Far up the ridge Mr. Ross was calling. "Fossil hunters! Shark tooth diggers! Boys and girls, one and all! Gather here!"

March and Leslie got up and walked sedately toward him.

A few weeks later she vanished. Shane had sold out his cafe and moved his family away from town – to where, March never learned. He never saw her again.

He also lost Will Hapsworth's friendship. Will had got a job in the "The Boys" haberdashery, sweeping out the store in the morning and selling neckties after school. Immediately he blossomed out in a new two-button, pinch-back suit, striped silk shirts, and brocade ties. Continuing to ingratiate himself with the Delphian Society, he was admitted as a member. His rise to glory was rapid. He brought trade to "The Boys" which promptly made him a clerk; and he in turn became the store's fashion model with his lavish spending. He developed a passion for jewelry, and successively bought a synthetic ruby ring, a tie-clasp mounted with seed pearls, and a silver belt buckle on which was engraven his monogram. Assuming the nonchalant and sophisticated ease of manner of a young-man-about-town, he seemed years removed from March. The two now seldom met. But that winter Will stopped March in the hall.

"You're going to the big school dance at the Antler's Saturday, aren't you? Some of the Delph Boys are taking me in their car. But you show up with your girl, and I'll slide you in our party afterward. Eh?" He winked. "You got to get in with the right people to get along, you know."

March had no girl. He decided to take Leona who had just entered high school. They both were excited, having never been to a dance in the great hotel. Ona, working feverishly, made up a dark brown wool dress for the girl—a simple school dress square cut at the neck and with an embroidered girdle of green yarn.

"It's not quite the thing," she sighed, "but we can't have a fancy party dress now. And besides, you're just a little girl yet."

When March gave Leona four dollars to buy a brown velvet hat with a green feather, her joy knew no bounds. Like Cable, she lived only in the moment, utterly un-selfconscious.

"Now remember," he told her condescendingly, "I'm going on a private party with Will afterward. So don't squawk when we bring you right home from the dance."

Saturday evening after supper they polished their shoes, dressed up, and walked uptown. A wet snow was falling; through it the lights of the hotel, blocking the end of the avenue, glowed softly, warmly. A long line of cars was drawn up at the entrance, disgorging guests. March suffered a pang of shame that he and Leona were walking. Inside the lobby he was more embarrassed. Groups of schoolmates congregated in corners, chatted on lounges, but to his anxious and appealing looks they seemed blind.

He shook loose Leona's arm and took off her coat. "Keep your hat on, it's more grown up," he muttered savagely. "And don't gawk like a ninny!"

After an intolerable wait, they followed the groups downstairs to the ballroom. It was already crowded and in the forefront stood Will with his party. Nervously March walked up to him.

"Why hello, March! What brought you here on such a stormy night? Or rather, what little damsel brought you?"

March reached for Leona's arm and hauled her forward.

"Will!" she exclaimed spontaneously. "How nice you look in that new suit. And how lovely this place is! Do they call it the Rose Room because of the pink walls? And are those the curtains Lon Chaney decorated? It's just like I heard about!"

To Leona's childish exuberance, her sparkling eyes, and rapt face, the group gave a stony indifference. Will fumbled his watch chain, wiped his face with a flourish of his silk handkerchief, and finally mumbled introductions. A boy or two offered a curt "Hello." But Will's partner—the reigning belle of school—set the tone of response. A dreary silence.

Leona did not notice it for looking at the young lady's dress. "What a pretty party dress! All silver! And silver slippers to match, too!"

The young lady arched her eyebrows and backed away. "Really!" she said. Then languidly taking Will's arm, she led him away, followed by the group.

The encounter awoke March to the fact that almost every girl there wore flimsy white, pink, or blue party dresses beside which Leona's plain woolen dress, hat, and brown face seemed suddenly to have sprouted with all the homely familiarity and fresh vigor of the earth itself.

"Take off that hat!" he muttered savagely to Leona. "Can't you see nobody's wearin' hats! And while I'm checking it, wipe off your shoes. They're wet."

"I like my hat. You bought it for me. And I'm going to wear it!" She was a Cable talking to a Rogier, and he could do nothing about it.

The music began. " 'The Beautiful Blue Danube', Brother! This is the way it ought to sound on our phonograph. Oh, I wish Nancy could hear the orchestra too – You can dance this! It's a waltz. But be careful when you turn, you know."

She was small, light, an excellent dancer, and seemed surcharged now with an incandescent joyousness and aliveness. March trudged around the floor with her, his body stiff, his face set in a dark impassive mask. For Will never came up to ask her for a dance.

"The bastard! You taught him how to dance, too!"

Nor did anyone else ask her to dance, or come up to chat with them during intermissions. If this were required or customary, Leona didn't notice it. Questions, ejaculations – "Look at that beautiful girl! Her hair's like gold!" – sly pinches of his arm, her low light laugh – life and enjoyment flowed from her in a bubbling stream. And when at midnight they walked upstairs for their coats, she gripped his arm. "It's been the first dance and best time I ever had, Brother! I hate to leave!"

And he – sullen, shamed, flooded by anger – he too was as much Cable as Rogier. They walked out of the lobby. The snow had left a blanket on the street; the moon was out; the stars gleamed sharp as glass. "I'm glad you wore that hat. Just a match for that brown dress of Mother's. It made those cheesecloth dresses look cheap and flimsy," he said. "Now what do you say, let's stop at one-armed Alex's and get us a hamburger with chile and beans?"

March never had anything to do with Will after that.

Big Hill and the Osages, the loss of Leslie Shane and Will, his obvious failure at high school, all contributed to his delinquency. Abruptly he quit school without saying anything to Ona or to the school authorities, and spent all day at the railroad station. Not until two months later did the Station Master tell him that Mr. Ford wanted to see him.

March walked up the stairs and into the office warily. Mr. Ford was the local agent of the Sante Fe Railroad, managing all its activities and property in Little London. He was a short, rather stout, and benign man who was sitting leisurely at his seldom occupied desk. Across from him sat a truant officer from the school board.

There were no preliminaries. "March," said Mr. Ford, "the

truant officer here tells me you have quit school and are spending all your time here as a Red Cap."

"I'm done with school. I'm going to be a Railroad Man," answered March.

"A laudable goal," answered Mr. Ford. "The Santa Fe needs men with your calibre and ambition. But only after you have satisfied the legal requirements of the school board. March, I'm afraid you've got to go back and finish school."

"Mr. Ford, you can't fire me!" March said boldly. "I'm not on the Sante Fe payroll. All I make is tips."

Mr. Ford looked disconsolate. He uncrossed his legs, smoothed the creases in his trousers. "How right you are. True, so true." Then looking up, he said softly, "There is only one thing I can do. As the Agent of the Santa Fe Railroad, I must forbid you on the property of the Santa Fe for the purpose of gainful occupation."

"Mr. Ford! You couldn't! You can't!"

"I've known you a long time, March. I would like to see you continue in your work till you are old enough to take an official job. But only part-time until you finish the schooling required of you. Do you understand?"

Ona, when March reached home, was in a torrential rage. "So all this time you've been playing hooky! The truant officer told me. Sliding out of the house every morning, staying away all day, while I thought you were in school. Lying, cheating, losing a whole semester!"

"I didn't say I wasn't going to school! I didn't say anything!"

"Don't give me that!" she shouted. "I know your secretiveness. That goddamned Indian business of keeping a straight face and saying nothing. And those dirty, filthy-rich Osages haven't done anything to help it. You'd quit school, give up your chance at an education, being a successful businessman. Now, March, when I'm about to die and leave you as the whole support of Leona and Nancy—God Almighty, son, you're all we got left to carry on! I ought to horsewhip you. And I'm only asking you to show mercy to those who'll depend on you after I'm gone!"

It was a disgraceful scene March left disgusted. But an hour later he went up to the Third Floor to confront her again. "All that talk of dyin'. What'd you mean?" he demanded.

For answer she tore open the bodice of her gingham dress. There on the upper part of her breast, just under the shoulder blade, was a hard red swelling. "That's a breast cancer, March," she said calmly now. "I don't have much time left."

"What's the doctor say?"

She gave him a derisive look. "I didn't ask. We can't afford a hospital, one operation after another as it keeps spreading. No! I've tried ointments, applications, massages. Nothing helps."

And now suddenly compassion gripped him for this incomprehensible woman who happened to be his mother. He could see her washing, mending, cleaning, cooking all day for three children and two failing old people, and saying nothing. And he could see her lying in bed night after night, grim-lipped and silent, feeling that horrible growing lump, and trying to hold back her mounting fear. While he, all these months, was playing hooky from school – and her approaching end.

"Mother!" He dropped to his knees before her and burst into tears. "I didn't know. You can't die! What would we do without you?"

She calmly stroked his head. "Now not a word to anyone, March. Maybe there's a way to do something."

Several days later they walked uptown and boarded a westbound streetcar. Ona in her neat but shabby clothes wore on her square-jawed face a look of determined composure. March beside her squirmed uneasily, staring out at the tawdry buildings and whorehouses of the West Side. Ona patted his hand. "You know, I always liked this ride. 'Member when we all used to ride out this way to Manitou for Sunday picnics in the mountains?"

At Colorado City they got off and trudged to a dilapidated brick building. The doctor's office was up a flight of dusty, creaky stairs. It was crowded with workmen in overalls, shabby housewives, and dirty children. The doctor, they had learned, tended to most of the mill workers, was honest and cheap – and March had the five dollar fee for his examination of Ona. After an hour's wait Ona's turn came. She stood up, thrust a tattered magazine into his hands. "Read the jokes in this. They're real funny. And son, remember that whatever happens is the Lord's will."

A half-hour passed. Then another. Finally she came out, white-faced and shaken. Hand in hand they walked to the corner, boarded a streetcar. Ona, sitting next to the window, began to shake. From this tremor erupted a heart-rending sob. She bent over, stuffing a handkerchief into her mouth, and began an uncontrollable weeping. "I'm going to live! I'm not going to die! It's not malignant, he's sure. He'll treat me or cut it out for twenty dollars."

A fire sprang up within the boy, melting his insides, eating at his brain. Still he sat beside her with a dark, impassive face. The woman flung around, her eyes streaming tears, and gripped his shoulders with hands of steel. "Do you hear me? I'm not going to die! I'm going to live to take care of Granny and watch Granddad build his greenhouse – live to raise Leona and Nancy! Live son, and see you grow into a successful businessman your father would be proud of! Dear sweet God! He's goin' to let me live!"

It was late afternoon. At every stop more mill workers got on. The aisle was crowded with standing passengers. All listening to the hysterical shrieks and sobs of a shabbily dressed woman. "For Pete's sake, mama!" hissed March. "Stop it!"

Ona reared erect, smeared her face with a wet hanky. "For Pete's sake yourself, March! If you don't cut out all your tomfoolery, and help Daddy build his greenhouse, I'm goin' to horsewhip the hide off your bones!"

5

Building a greenhouse by himself was hard work for a man in his late seventies, even though he had been an apprentice, a journeyman, and then a master carpenter in his younger days. There were stout corner posts to anchor, timber wall frames to be squared, glass window frames to be fitted, a door installed. Rogier persisted, with little help from March.

One would have thought that with an enormous shop so completely fitted out any master carpenter would have enjoyed it, the boy would develop into a craftsman. But March had no bent for carpentry. He couldn't drive a nail straight. He was too scatterbrained. So after an hour's work, Rogier dismissed him. "That's fine. You can take off now, son. But if I were you, I'd sneak out the alley. Your mother's a sharp timekeeper, you know."

As the boy gratefully laid down his hammer or saw, Rogier would add, "How about some tenpenny nails? I'm plumb out."

"Sure! I'll buy 'em, Granddad!" And the boy would clamber over the alley fence.

After a time the old man would lay aside his own tools and turn to the Peak watching his indomitable efforts with compassionate understanding. They were great friends again. Rogier had forgiven it for blocking his impassioned search after years of toil. His failure had been his own fault. His human pride, engendered by propensities born in him for generations, had played him false. He had been led astray by the tantalizing promise of mere gold—thrown off balance by the entrancing splendor of the Cresson Vug. And he had paid his debt. Now at last he was consecrated as he had been at first, to the pure and immortal sacredness of his mortal calling.

Winter stopped his work. He couldn't stay in the barny shop while mapping out his campaign; it cost too much to heat. Nor could he spend the evenings in the house. How could he compose his soul in tranquility to the squeak of Mrs. Rogier's rocker or plumb the depths of spirit in a nest of chattering magpies? So after supper he would stamp down into the basement, slamming the kitchen door behind him.

It was a great, warm, clean room. In the far corner sat the unused carbide lighting plant. Next to it was the small wine cellar of more opulent days, empty now save for a few jars of jams and jellies. At the other end was the coal bin filled from the driveway and shut off from the rest of the basement by a plank door. In the center bulked the massive furnace. Through its small door-panes the roaring flames cast a rosy warm glow upon the clean cement floor and walls of rough square-hewn rock.

Something about the room reminded him of a stope deep below grass roots. He would light his candle. It hung to the wall in his old-fashioned miner's candlestick—the simple and ingenious tool which could be thrust into a crevice like an ice pick, hung from an edge like a hook, or set on a level plane. In its glow he sat musing in a chair drawn up before the furnace.

"The Sylvanite was a dud, like the Magpie and all the others before it," he would mutter to himself. "I should have had better sense. 'Whoever needs the earth shall have the earth.' And this time I'm drivin' straight in as soon as I get that lettuce house built."

One cold winter evening when he stamped downstairs, he saw a man sitting in his chair in front of the furnace. The man rose instantly. "Am I taking your chair, sir?"

"Humm. Didn't know you were here. Who let you in?"

"No one, sir. I came down through the coal bin from outside to toast my toes. In fact, I'm toasting my supper too." He nudged with his toe a potato baking under the furnace.

"Humm," Rogier muttered again. "I allow a little bread and jam might go with it." He trudged upstairs and back again, settling on another chair beside his visitor.

The guest slept all night in the basement and was invited upstairs for breakfast. "What are you having?" he asked Leona.

"Shredded Wheat with sliced bananas!" she replied promptly.

"My favorite breakfast!" he replied, sitting down beside her.

There grew up between them a warm intimacy during his two-day visit. The man, slightly built, middle-aged, with uncut sandy hair, was a professional railroad tramp. Year after year he crossed and re-crossed the continent, riding the rods or the blinds, sleeping in off-track jungles with his fellows, splitting wood here and there for a meal. It was a great profession of which he was proud. Every top-notch tramp had his own mark or sign which he inscribed on railroad trestles and the walls of freight stations. The greatest of these tramps was the man whose mark was "A-1." The Rogier guest once had raced him across the continent from New York to San Francisco, losing by only a few hours. Leona related these facts with pride.

"Stop it!" Mrs. Rogier commanded her. "Why, a tramp's liable to cut our throats while we're asleep. What's his precious sign? And pray tell, what's his name?"

Leona shrugged. "You have to be a professional tramp to know his mark. And his name—why, it's 'Shredded Wheat!' He said so!"

Every few months Shredded Wheat would appear, sleeping in the basement or in the shop, then disappearing suddenly as he had come. Leona loved him, making sure he had Shredded Wheat with bananas, wild strawberries, or raspberries every summer morning for breakfast. Everyone else in the family liked him and saved old clothes for him. Rogier especially would permit no criticism of him or his professional career. "Every man's huntin' for somethin' or got some kind of a quirk, I don't care who he is. If every one of us thought just the same, this world would be a mighty dull place to live in!"

Mary Ann returned home. The whole family sighed when she walked in the house that evening, unannounced, with still another gentleman friend. Yet there was a glint in her eyes revealing that this time she meant business. Pulling him into the aura of lamplight, she announced curtly, "This is John, my husband. We were married last week. I know you will all love him. We're going to move in with you and be one happy family together."

John nodded shyly and sat down to table. Unlike big, robust Jim or Sam, he was a rather frail-looking, middle-aged man with graying hair and a gentle sensitive face. Within a few minutes his overwhelming shyness became evident; he didn't talk and could hardly eat.

It was just as evident that Mary Ann could handle all situations. Always brisk and aggressive, she now had a sharp edge honed by adversity. After opening one Chocolate Shoppe after another throughout the mining towns of the Colorado Rockies, all failures perhaps abetted by her shiftless gentlemen friends, she suddenly had come into focus.

"Mining is a bust. The ore's all played out. Mines are closing, camps are shutting down, towns are dwindling. How foolish I was to chase that will-of-the-wisp when home right here is the center of the biggest money-making industry in history!" Pausing to let this conclusion sink in, she continued briskly. "I mean the Pike's Peak Region is drawing more people than the Pike's Peak Rush, Cripple Creek, and all the rest of them put together. Tourists from all over the world. With pocketsfull of money! And so I'm—John and me—are opening a Chocolate Shoppe right here."

"Where?" asked Ona.

"Manitou. Up Ruxton Creek. The center of the mineral springs. I'll wait trade and keep the books. John's going to learn to make candy and manage the candy kitchen. We sign the lease tomorrow."

Within a week the place was open for business. For a chocolate dipping stone Mary Ann carried off the marble slab that graced the ornate hall tree. More changes came. John's overpowering shyness prevented him from eating at the table with a tribe of strange people around him. He began coming home late from work. When he could be induced to sit down with the family, he fled up to his room with a headache immediately afterward. Mary Ann acted promptly. She fitted up the second story back room as a kitchen, reserving the middle room as their bedroom.

The Rogiers downstairs grumbled and stormed at the smell of

cooking above. "A housekeeping apartment in our home!" snorted Ona. "We might as well take in roomers, too!"

Mrs. Rogier sniffled in her hanky.

As the months wore on, their resentment died down. John was a hard worker who soon became adept as a maker of fine candies of every description. He brought home to the children almost every night a big box of the batch of pinoche, fudge, nougat, or peanut brittle he had made that day. It vanished instantly. "If you kids weren't half-starved you wouldn't eat so much!" complained Mary Ann. "I swear, you're all sugar drunks!" Shy as John was, he was gentle, patient, and forgiving; and he eventually won over the family. The children began to call him "Uncle John."

And the Chocolate Shoppe was making money.

There was no doubt about it when Mary Ann ordered the house rewired for electricity. Then a team of men showed up with her to measure the living room and dining room, the size of the front windows, and to shake the sofa loose from its broken leg. "The place is so run down and worn out, it's disgraceful! Downright shabby!" she complained. "Those old-fashioned lace curtains are a joke. The rug's been threadbare for years. And look at that tottering sofa. The whole place looks like a shanty of poor white trash. I'm going to freshen it up!"

March, in his last year at high school, had become self-conscious and just as ashamed of the run-down house. With Mary Ann's announcement, a glow of pride suffused him. He could envision a thick Oriental rug on the floor, tasteful draperies at the windows, a modern couch and a few excellent "occasional" chairs, all softly glowing under electric lamps.

Instead, there was laid on the floor stiff, rubberized, imitation rugs made of linoleum with a blatant design of roses. On these was set an array of furniture stiff as iron, shiny as shoe-polish. At the windows were hung curtains screaming with violent purple iris. There were no lamps; a white porcelain lighting fixture was hung from the ceiling.

That evening when Mary Ann came home to proudly survey her "freshening up," all March's outraged sense of good taste, his rejection of vulgarity, erupted. "What do you mean sending down this trash? Our home was shabby and old-fashioned maybe, but in good taste. Now it looks like the parlor of a whorehouse on Myers

Avenue! An imitation rug of linoleum. It would look bad enough in the dark, without those ghastly white lights shinin' on it!"

"Hold on!" interrupted Mary Ann. "Not linoleum. Congoleum. The latest thing. The edges'll soon flatten down! And what, may I ask, do you know of whorehouses on Myers Avenue?"

"The furniture! Grand Rapids veneer. Not even honest wood. Purple flags screaming from the curtains at the roses on the floor. And that picture. It makes me sick at my stomach to walk in here!"

"And who are you, smarty, to put up your nose at your own home?" shouted Mary Ann. "I took down that old landscape over the fireplace because we're all tired of staring at it after fifty years. This print of the Master of Blue with a beautiful Greek temple and a bunch of grapes is his most popular masterpiece. It hangs in the window of every furniture store in town!"

It was a stormy disgraceful row from which March stalked out in fury. "The lad's at an impressionable stage," observed Rogier mildly, not too enthusiastic about Mary Ann's changes himself. Uncle John fled upstairs with a headache. Mrs. Rogier sniffled.

"And this is the thanks I get for trying to improve our happy home!" Mary Ann flounced upstairs.

Ona glanced sharply at Mrs. Rogier. "Mother! Quit sniffling! And make it plain to Mary Ann she's not to do any interior decorating of the Third Floor!" Then she too trudged tiredly up to bed with the two girls in that cavernous attic where she lay feeling the scar on her breast, listening for the steps of the faithful Kadles, and waiting perchance for another appearance of that mysterious, frightening light. Listening too, sleeplessly, for the sound of March's footsteps—that strange son of his strange father whom she loved most and understood least of all the persons given her to meet in her narrow but mysterious life.

Rawlings came to call. "Mr. Rogier—Joe!" He rushed up to his former employer of uncounted years, shook him by the shoulders, gave him a hearty hug. "When I saw you last I thought the game was up. You was in bed, your eyes blank as a hoot owl's, you didn't know me for nothin'. And now I see you sound as a nut, still kickin', hey! Joe!"

"Thought I'd gone crazy or was dyin', or both, hey? You old son-of-a-gun. Finally got up enough backbone to open an office as a building contractor on your own. Well, match this!"

Rogier led him out to see his greenhouse. It was set a safe distance from the house. The building was about the size of an average room, running east to west so that it would get the full swing of the sun by day. On winter nights buckets of hot ashes and coals would keep the plants from freezing. Rawlings looked it over carefully. "Just the thing for a retired businessman, Joe! I'm right proud of you. But that roof's a little out of plumb if I can see straight." He squinted along a timber. "What you need's a couple of two-by-tens or two-by-twelves laid straight and set solid. But what's this?"

He walked to the west end closed off from the rest of the glass room by a wooden partition in which was set a solid door locked by a huge padlock. Over it hung a sign, "Private."

"A tool house or a storage room? Mighty funny in a greenhouse. Why don't you use the big shop in back instead of cluttering up this nice glass buildin'? What's it for, anyway?"

"The sign says 'Private,' " muttered Rogier.

Rawlings shrugged. "Well anyway Joe, I'm goin' to send down a couple of men and a load of timber to help you out."

"Rawlings! I'll build that myself just the way I want it, without your help!" His voice was sharp and decisive.

Rawlings' embarrassment was eased when Ona called him into the house for tea. His hands still horny and his clothes ill-fitting, he grinned at her. "I ain't no Britisher yet, to be drinkin' tea in the middle of the afternoon. Just a plain old American cup of coffee'll suit me fine."

When they had settled down Ona said casually, "Mr. Rawlings, we're all proud of you for getting into business for yourself after all these years. Without your help Daddy could never have finished those last jobs of his. Now I hope you're contracting for some fine big buildings of your own."

"As a matter of fact I ain't, Miss Ona. I'm tearin' down. More money in it." He turned to Rogier. "Yep, Joe. Been up to your old stampin' ground, Cripple Creek." Rogier sat up straight as Rawlings continued. "The whole district's on the toboggan. Hardly 5,000 people up there now. The High Line and Low Line cars ain't runnin' no more. Nobody to ride 'em. The mines are closin' down. And most of the towns – Elkton, Anaconda, Arequa, Mound City – are plumb deserted. And that's where I'm making my money."

"How's that you say?" asked Rogier, a dangerous glint in his eyes.

"Why, it's simple man. Why should contractin' firms in Little London here buy timber from mill yards when there's all kinds of it in Cripple Creek for the takin'—big seasoned timbers from gallows frames, lumber galore from abandoned houses, window frames and doors too. That's what I'm doin'. Runnin' a wreckin' crew instead of a construction crew. And cartin' it all down by truck."

Rogier's face seemed to have turned to stone, a faint pallor showing through his stubble of beard.

"It might surprise you to learn I tore out that stout cribbing you built. The logs was still sound," continued Rawlings. "I even got some good brick from that little hotel in Goldfield."

Rogier leapt to his feet, his face distorted with anger. "Stop it, damn you, Rawlings! I went up there when it was still a barren cowpasture. With my naked hands I helped to build it up, log on log, stone on stone. The very cornerstones of some of those buildings you've torn down carried my name. That earth, that granite, is the soil of my flesh. And now, blast your soul, you come here—in my house—and think to tell me this!"

"Joe!"

"Daddy, please!"

Rogier could not be stopped. "You've betrayed me. Everything I stand for. A man's a builder or a destroyer. And you—I know you now. You've gone rotten. Get out of my home! Keep out of my sight!" he howled, lunging toward his old foreman.

It was all Ona could do to hold him. Rawlings, who had witnessed too many of Rogier's ungovernable rages before his breakdown, fearfully backed away; and with a look of sadness and forgiveness on his mild face, hastily pressed Ona's hand and slipped out the door.

Rogier sank down on a chair, still shaking. Ona stood before him. "Daddy, do you know who that was? Your construction foreman for thirty years or more. Your most loyal and faithful friend."

"Rawlings is the name," Rogier said imperturbably. "A man who's turned traitor. It was high time I found him out."

6

The June when March finally graduated from high school, Boné came home for another visit. The reason for his coming was the "Pike's Peak Carnival." Not for years had the traditional Shan Kive been held, when Buckskin Charlie and his Utes were brought home from their reservation to pitch their lodges on the mesa west of town; when in feathers and buckskins they paraded the street with prospectors, miners, hunters, old pioneers; when a downtown block was roped off for their last night's dance. But with the tremendous influx of tourists it behooved Little London to put on a show of sorts. A few Utes had been brought in. Dressed in dirty blue denims, they disconsolately roamed the streets between iron casts of noble Indian chiefs advertising soda water. Fat-bellied bankers and thin store clerks boasted two-color boots and ten-gallon hats; loyal Rotarians grew beards; society women descended from limousines to shop in sunbonnets and silk plaid dresses; polo ponies sported Western stock saddles.

The grand climax of the carnival was to be a "Pageant of the Past" in the Garden of the Gods. Boné, "our own famous Colorado composer," had been engaged to write the music for it. Boné had not written the family, but the details were fully reported in the *Gazette*. All the Rogiers titillated with excitement and anticipation except March.

He was now almost six feet tall, slim and wiry like his father. He had given up his work as a Red Cap, considering it too menial to accept gratuities, and had been given a job by Mr. Ford as a baggage clerk with a regular salary. The conviction of Will Hapsworth for stealing clothes from "The Boys," and his internment in the reformatory school, had made March suspicious. And his continuing friendship with Big Hill and his Osages inclined him to view the approaching carnival as merely an exploitation to ensnare tourists.

Continuing newspaper reportage of his famous uncle did not allay his doubts. If Boné's first recognition had come with his "Indian Suite" written under Lockhart at Shallow Water, his first success was the lyrical "Song of the Willows." He had then achieved national fame as a song writer with his popular ragtime "Ching, Ching, Chinaman," and "Our Old Family Ghosts." These nonsensical tunes followed by others had recouped the nest egg wheedled from him by Rogier for his mine. During a trip to Europe he had written an opera, a few sonatas, and a string quartette which had been competent enough to give him some small reputation. But they were not popular. And so he had returned to write "Songs from Plain and Prairie," "Tepee Tales," and "Melodies in Red," for which he was best known throughout Europe and America. Perhaps he realized that he had great talent but not greatness; that America's music was not Indian melodies, Negro spirituals, or folk songs; but that these pure and full-throated voices must be absorbed, built up, and combined in one symphonic peal of passionate avowal from the great integrated soul of all America. He had set his heart on such symphonic structure. Yet driven from coast to coast by the economic necessity for concert tours, weakened by ill-health, and consumed by an ambition perhaps too great for his strength, he had relapsed into security. In Oklahoma he had picked up a talented Indian soprano, Princess Bluebird, with whom he was touring the country. For two weeks now they had been appearing in Denver, from where they had been brought to Little London.

Princess Bluebird was an Osage, a half-breed, Big Hill told March at sight of her photograph. But there were no Indian "princesses" among the Osages or any Plains tribes. The beaded headband supporting an eagle feather, which she wore, had been an indication of sacredness or high rank restricted to warriors. Not until recently had it been adopted by women for so-called "Indian Princess" contests sponsored by whites.

Two days before the Pageant they arrived at the house. Hardly had they got out of the taxi before the whole family was on the porch to greet them.

" Boné, my dear boy!"

"Aunt Martha! The finest mother a boy ever had!" Hugging her with one arm, he reached out the other to Rogier. "And Ona!"

"This is Leona and Nancy, Boné. Not little any longer. Do you recognize March, this big man? You've been his inspiration all these years!"

"And my Princess – My family, Bluebird."

Kissed and hugged, they were finally led into the house. March thought he had never seen a woman more beautiful than Princess Bluebird, dressed in full buckskin and beaded moccasins, wearing the band on her dark hair. Boné had changed little, but seemed smaller. He had the round head of a musician, his black hair turning gray above his ears; and the thin, big knuckled hands of a pianist which he began at once to drum on the arm of his chair. March knew he had contracted phthisis – although Boné called it asthma, and was so high strung and nervous it was impossible to hold him on one subject for a full minute. He gave the impression of great talent and assurance, but not the wholesome soundness of a great artist, the strange completeness of a world within himself.

There was so much to talk about, and so little time for it! "We've got to go," Boné said, rising. "The Brown Palace sent me to the Broadmoor. I'm always at the mercy of hotels, you know. Have to make a few changes in the score before the rehearsal tomorrow. You're all coming, of course?"

"We wouldn't miss it for the world." said Ona.

March expected Boné to take or to provide tickets for the family. Instead, he winked as he left. "Come up in back afterwards. It'll help swell the crowd. Tricks in every trade, you know!"

The Rogiers stood on the porch, watching his taxi drive away. The cost of the long drive and keeping it waiting, thought March, would have bought all of their tickets.

Ona was disappointed too, she told March when she drew him aside after supper. "But that doesn't mean we're not all going – except Mary Ann and Uncle John who have to keep their shop open. We'd never forgive ourselves if we didn't."

"At two dollars apiece? Hell with it! Boné's too rattle-brained to think of anybody but himself."

"For shame, March! He's a great artist. Your own uncle, absentminded or not." Her voice grew stern. "You're going to take us out of your Saturday pay check. If need be we can take it out of the grocery money later. But we're going! Understand?"

"Twelve dollars! And how're you going to get there and back? It's too far for Granny and Grandad to walk from the streetcar line. Am I hiring a taxi too?"

"That will arrange itself," she said calmly, putting her arm around him. "He was like yourself once, son. Poor and perplexed, not knowing what the future would hold. Be inspired by what he has achieved – our own Boné. I know you will, son!"

They went, all six of them: Rogier and Mrs. Rogier, Ona and the three children. Their next door neighbor, Kennedy, took them in his car on his way to work in Colorado City; they would have to find their own way home.

They walked into the roped enclosure, spread a blanket on the ground. The summer night was warm and fragrant; the high sandstone cliffs stood out like a painted background behind the raised stage covered with sod and dried grass; off to the side peanut and popcorn stands littered the grounds under flickering gasoline flares.

Nancy's somber face with her drawn left eye twitched into a smile. "It's pretty as a circus. Thank you for bringing us, March!"

"Dom!" said Rogier. "I haven't seen a show for years!"

Their obvious delight in this unusual outing did not melt the hard core of curious resentment within March. He sat sullenly chewing a blade of grass.

The lights went out. There was suddenly a high pitched yell. An Indian brave bounded across the stage in a spotlight, paused with a hand to forehead in the immemorial gesture of all calendar Indians, and leaped behind a piñon. There came a burst of music.

The Pageant of the Past had begun.

It lasted almost two hours and consisted primarily of three processions across the stage: a group of feathered and painted Indians; a covered wagon containing red-shirted miners and their wives; and finally, with a screech of a fire siren, a train, painted on a screen, propelled across the stage.

Each of the processions stopped on the stage for its act. The Indians deplored the vanishing game; made a treaty with an Explorer; and finally sang a dirge to the Great Spirit lamenting the Passing of the Red Man.

In Act Two some of them came back and tomahawked a woman who fell across a wagon tongue, showing a beautiful silk-stockinged leg. But the miners struck pay dirt – a nugget big as a fist. "Pike's Peak or Bust!" they shouted. "By God, boys, we got the Ransom of an Empire!"

The third act portrayed "The Founding of the West – The Dawn of the Future." From the painted train poured the Empire Builders. They hammered on anvils, revolved spinning wheels, hoisted cardboard masonry into high walls; and eventually Little London was wheeled into view, painted on a beaverboard screen with Pike's Peak in the background. The West Was Won!

"But to us in the future," a frock-coated orator recited to soft music, "this legacy of beauty and courage must forever be our bulwark. Let us not forget the unlettered but noble Pioneer Fathers who opened the gates of this free and unsullied America. Let us lift our eyes unto the hills, and be ever renewed by the pure and serene mountains, the cloudless skies of Colorado" –

Finale. "The Red Rock Garden March." Writer, composer, singer, actors on the platform. Then the pudgy, tuxedoed Little Londoner who had promised to make up any deficit in the budget.

It was a ghastly travesty: colorful but empty, all form and no substance, expensively produced but cheap and sentimental. March sat through it appalled, listening to the tremendous applause with bewilderment. Those miners in squeaky new cowboy boots! That gold nugget! March knew nothing of music, but it seemed to him that Boné's was but little better than its vehicle. Only Princess Bluebird's clear soprano lifted a few songs out of their uninspired melodies. The short prelude he liked, and in the "Red Rock Garden March" he felt the youthful vigor he remembered in Boné. For the rest, it was a dull accompaniment. He got up at the end feeling done out of twelve dollars.

"Brother! Wasn't those colored lights pretty at the end? Red, white, and blue! And did you see the Indian waving the American flag?"

"We've got to go down and congratulate Boné," persisted Nancy. "He told us to. He did!"

They walked up to the edge of the crowd around Boné. He was dressed up, his cheeks were rouged, he was laughing and shaking hands.

"A marvellous touch, sir! I recognized your hands at the piano!"

"Authenticity in every note – so – so commanding! Our foremost native composer. He lived his early life among the savages, I hear."

"The scope, the vastness – the sweep of history, I mean. I tell you drama here is just emerging." –

There was no getting to him. March herded his little flock out of the enclosure to the road. It was impossible for the two elderly Rogiers to walk two miles in the dark to the streetcar line. Nor was there a taxi in sight. Standing at the edge of the road, beclouded with swirling dust, March yapped angrily, "I told you, Mother –"

At that instant there sounded a high-pitched yell as a Cadillac limousine stopped beside them. Out of it leaned Big Hill. "Boy walkin'. No good! Ridin' better!"

"I've got my family!" March shouted back.

Big Hill imperiously waved his hand toward the car in back. It was Hanlon's tourist car with still more Osages, and in back of it was still another. Big Hill was in no hurry. Keeping the long line of cars waiting, he moved Osages from car to car to make room for his new passengers. Leona and Nancy were put in one, Ona in another, and March with his grandparents in Big Hill's limousine. It was a little crowded, of course; Mrs. Rogier had to sit on the lap of a blanketed gentleman three times her size.

"Mr. Hill," she exclaimed. "Your Indian Princess was beautiful! She sang like a bird!"

"Bluebird. Good song."

"And it was my boy who wrote the music, Mr. Hill."

"Good boy."

Big Hill was in high humor. His broad face and great body exuded pleasure, contentment, and approval. "Good show! Seven shots shootin' from a six-gun. I count 'em. Ai. Ai. Some gun!" There was nothing ironic in his acute observation. He was as pleasurably excited by the performance as were the Rogiers.

If it seemed his driver was taking the Rogiers the long way home, they were more surprised when the limousine rolled into the driveway of Big Hill's house. "But Mr. Hill," began Mrs. Rogier. Imperiously he waved them across the lawn to a barbecue pit where a huge chunk of beef was roasting. Two Osage women took it off, throwing on the fire armloads of fresh wood. A man came out of the house with a suspiciously-shaped bottle and a box of tin cups which he set on wooden table.

"Mr. Hill! Meat at midnight! Why!" Mrs. Rogier was more shocked at the size of that mammoth roast.

"Good meat. Eat 'em anytime. We dancin' first," answered their host.

The stomp dance around the fire began, one Osage at a time flinging off his blanket or shawl and moving into the circle. The big men lifting their knees high, bending low, then jerking erect, eyes to the sky. The women hardly raising their feet, dancing demurely but in perfect rhythm.

Another car rolled up. Out of it jumped Princess Bluebird, still in costume, to join in. "Boy sick?" asked Big Hill. March got up and moved into the circle. Then Leona. The Princess grabbed Nancy by the hand. "Come on, honey! Use your hips, not your feet!"

At last Big Hill sank down on the grass beside Rogier. "Good time! We eatin' now!"

"Dom!" said Rogier. "I'm hungry!"

They all ate, sitting on the grass in the light of the leaping flames. Paper plates filled with thick slices of roast beef and chunks of bread. Tin cups of strong black coffee. Apples and bananas. Mrs. Rogier began to figit. "Why, it must be almost two o'clock in the morning!"

"Catchin' train?" Big Hill inquired. "Got all night, all mornin'." But finally he sent them home with his driver.

When had all the family been out together? Long after Big Hill's hired car had taken them home, they laughed and prattled about the Pageant and Big Hill's party; Ona could hardly get them off to bed. March, who worked the morning shift from three o'clock till noon, stayed up. He dressed in his work clothes, laid out his bowl of cold breakfast cereal. Then he made a cup of coffee and carried it out on the porch.

He was not aware of a taxi slowly cruising down the street, lights out, until it had stopped in front. Then he noticed a man sitting on the running board. He rose as March walked toward him. It was Boné. His breath smelled faintly of whisky. "What're you doing here this time of night?" demanded March.

"Big reception at the Broadmoor. Bluebird skipped out early to hunt up some Osages nearby. These Indians! Wanted to take you all to the reception, but you didn't come up on stage. You saw the show?"

"Of course. An went up to see you, but you were too busy."

"My God, boy!" The man shook him by the shoulders. "Never too busy for all of you. Damnation! I've spanked your little bottom, March. This is my home. I couldn't leave it – for years perhaps – without one more look at it. Why, I remember Sister Molly's old elm, when Shook's Run had a wooden bridge –"

"Ssh!" cautioned March. "You'll wake up Mother and the girls."

They sat down on the grass in front of the dark waiting taxi.

"You liked the Pageant?" inquired Boné.

March hesitated a moment. "No! It was cheap and trashy, something a real artist wouldn't have stooped to. No! It was a tinhorn show!"

Boné hiccoughed. "Boy! You're bitter and intolerant, and it takes the sting out of the little truth in your words. Do you think every composer is a Beethoven, every pianist a Liszt? Oh, you're so young, so idealistic!"

He moistened his hands on the damp grass and wiped his face. "Don't you realize, you young fool, we musicians have to live? How do you suppose I make my money – on my best work? Hah! By being a monkey at the piano in Chicago, New York, Denver, Oshkosh! By dressing in Indian feathers in Vienna and Stockholm. By writing scores like this tonight. It took me only two days! March, forget it. Before long you'll be up against the same problem. Then you'll remember your uncle more charitably. You'll think of the old days at Shallow Water. And we'll have a good laugh together, eh!"

He leaned forward, flung his arms around the boy, stooped to kiss him on the cheek. At that instant it happened – a sudden fright and revulsion whose cause March could not explain. But whatever it was, Boné's rouged cheeks, delicate hands, and effeminate sensitiveness immediately translated March's feelings into action. Roughly he pushed Boné away. "Don't you ever lay your hands on me again!"

Boné recoiled as if struck. A tear rolled down his cheek. "March!"

The boy rose. "Three o'clock. Time for me to go to work." He strode quickly down the street.

At noon when he returned home, the family was bubbling with excitement. Boné last night had sneaked into the house, slept on the sofa, and taken breakfast with them. He had bought all kinds of good things at the grocery store and given each of them a souvenir program. "The kind that cost a dollar!" said Nancy. "And he wrote something on them for us too, about our being the inspiration for the 'Red Rock Garden March'!"

The big surprise came when Ona took March upstairs and showed him a check for $100 that Boné had left before he drove back to Denver. "For you, son. To start to college on. It'll pay for the first semester's tuition, and if you make good, he'll send more!"

And now the talk began, lengthening into days and weeks; a wrangle in which every member of the family participated. March had no intention of going to college; he hated school. He wanted to be a Railroad Man, and already he had a job. But everyone insisted: Rogier in his baggy trousers, Mary Ann and Uncle John, Ona, even the two girls. What were they, wondered March: a tribunal, a group of seers laying out his life, assuming the prerogative of God and Chance, or merely one of a million families striving in ignorance, poverty, and pride to advance a son one step farther than any of them had taken?

"No Rogier has ever been to college," added Mrs. Rogier. "All you have to do is go one day to set a new record for the family."

Reluctantly March walked up to the registrar to find out if he could meet the entrance requirements. Despite his poor high school grades, he was allowed to register and given a catalogue of the courses offered. To Ona it was the menu of a delectable feast over whose *entrees* she smacked her lips. "Medieval European history – Greek drama – Calculus – Political science! Me, oh my!" But if all the plums of the world's knowledge lay at her boy's feet, she was childish and shrewd enough to see that he picked up the right ones. Doctor, Merchant, Lawyer, Chief: what careèr was he to follow?

The college offered three basic curricula: classics with a major in Latin and Greek, business administration and banking, and science. It was obvious to Ona that March was not cut out for a Professor of Greek. "Business, banking, finance. That's the thing for nowadays! You have to be a business man, March, in any line."

Rogier objected. "Why stuff that down the boy's gullet? Business is money-grubbin', pinchin' pennies, figurin' how to skin your neighbor before he skins you. Call it Economics, Business Law, or anything else, that's all it is. By Jove, he ought to take engineerin' and learn somethin' about his own earth and Natural Laws!"

The disgraceful scene that followed brought out at last Ona's resentment of a lifetime and the family's secret grudge against Rogier for his failure to strike it rich. She jumped to her feet, hands clenched, shouting. "Stop it! I know what you mean by engineering – mining! My boy won't be saddled with your crazy ideas. I won't have him ruined like Tom, Jonathan, you and all the rest! I tell you, I won't!" She flung around to face March. "You're going to take Business or I'm going to tear up this check!"

March trudged back to the campus, miserable and confused. Here he signed up for the four subjects required of every freshman. The family's mighty discussions had come to nought. And in September, on Boné's $100, he entered college.

7

Rogier's greenhouse was finished, a tolerable job of which the family was proud. On each side of the center aisle were banks and shelves and boxes of growing green: not only crinkly leaves of "pickin" lettuce, but onions and chives and herbs, and potted flowers of every kind. None of the family questioned the windowless plank room adjoining it on the west end, undoubtedly a tool house. The stout door, locked with a big padlock and marked "Private," was enough to proclaim it one of Rogier's foibles.

That the old man was working himself to the bone was evident. All day long he was outdoors or in the greenhouse: digging fresh earth, weeding, nursing, and in the winter carrying out coals and hot ashes to keep his plants from freezing at night. He was thin and shrunken, a mere skeleton inside his baggy trousers and sagging coat. But the family rejoiced. He had found something peaceful to do. His spells were less frequent. He ate heartily, slept soundly at night, and he had developed a peculiar humor.

It was the custom of Mrs. Pyle next door to whistle from the back door whenever she wanted Pyle. He then tripped to the house in a ludicrously dainty fashion from the yard. Leona and Nancy for fun often whistled for Roger to come to dinner. He would grin slyly, spread his arms, rise on his toes, and come prancing down the back walk in imitation of Pyle – and often under his very eyes.

Yet Ona began to grow suspicious. He insisted on emptying the ashes from the furnace and fireplace without March's help, lugging bucketsful out to the alley. Even in the winter he spent hours locked within the closed tool house at the end of the greenhouse. And during the evenings he sat down in the basement in front of the furnace, his miners' candle flickering on a scratch pad upon his knee.

"Daddy's up to something!" Ona exploded one evening to Mrs. Rogier. "What in God's name is it?"

"All that Cripple Creek business is out of his mind. Rawlings put the kibosh on that," Mrs. Rogier answered smugly. "Let him alone."

Downstairs in the basement, Rogier continued to figure the obstacles and advantages of the tremendous plan that had leaped into his mind, full grown. Up in Cripple Creek, at the Sylvanite, he had begun work at an elevation of almost 11,000 feet. He had sunk his shaft to five levels through solid granite in his prolonged effort to bore into the very heart of the Peak. He was wise enough to realize that a man's failure is due to causes hidden within himself rather than to outward circumstances. Yet despite these intangible factors in the mysterious equation of a man's fate, he knew that mere lack of money had stopped him from driving deeper. There was no need to recall the details of his abysmal failure.

No, by Jove! Not when his new plan illuminated success with all the bright glory of a promise fulfilled at last. Here in Little London he was at an elevation of only 6,000 feet – a mile below the collar of the Sylvanite. What a head start! He had only to dig a lateral tunnel into the base of the Peak to achieve his objective.

He was quite sensible. There were great difficulties. The base of the Peak was six miles away, a long distance for one man his age to dig. He would have to bore underneath Little London and Colorado City; there were water mains, sewage pipes, and underground conduits to avoid. And above all, he must preserve utmost secrecy.

Yet the advantages were reasonably greater. The tunnel would not have to be too deep – a mere fifty feet; and what was that to a hard-rock man! Moreover, the ground rose swiftly, and by maintaining the same level he would gradually be sinking. The farther he got, the firmer the earth – gravel, shale, sandstone; he would not need cribbing. In any case, the digging on an average would be neglible compared to driving through solid granite.

Scratching away with his pencil in the flickering light of the candle above him, Rogier compared the vertical and horizontal approaches to the glowing golden heart of the Peak. Driving a mile straight down from the portal of the Sylvanite through hard granite at a cost of $40 a foot or more, would have cost him dom near a quarter-million dollars – a fortune he never could have made from the profits on his contracting business. But a lateral tunnel, while six times longer, would have to be dug only through soft earth at little expense. A man could do it with a pick and shovel, given time. And when it was finished – Rogier could have let out a shout of triumph! He would be 5,000 feet below the Sylvanite. Three thousand feet below the bottom of the district's mines and the thousands of men working above. Rogier laughed and slapped his leg. What would Cripple Creek stockbrokers and mining engineers think, the townspeople of Little London, when they found he'd burrowed beneath them! And Pyle, the sanctimonious hypocrite! He'd never guess what had gone on under his very nose.

For then, after years of toil and frustration, after a lifetime of devout concentration, Rogier would feel like Atlas the weight of the mighty snow-covered Peak above him; hear the breathing pulse and rhythmic throb of the great heart of the continent. And suddenly, with one last stroke of his pick, he would break through to the brightness and the glory, the incandescent mystery of that secret and immortal Self which had forever hovered in his mind like something risen from the depths of dreamless sleep to the horizon of wakeful consciousness.

Elated and disturbed, Rogier climbed upstairs and walked out into the snowy back garden. It was nearly midnight. The moon was in its first quarter. In its glow the Peak stood clear in the cloudless sky. Rogier stared at it a long time. Something between them still remained unresolved, friends and enemies though they had been; but this time, old as they both had grown, their synonymity would be established.

March was too relieved to get out of helping Rogier empty ashes to notice how often the old man trudged with his loads to the ash pit in the alley. One afternoon when he was in the shop, the dump man called to him. "What's goin' on here, son? I'm gittin' mighty tired of emptying this pit of yours so often. Half of it's dirt. Not ashes."

"Can't you see we've got a greenhouse?" March answered just as testily. "Dirt's got to be changed!"

Promptly he forgot the incident; he had his own troubles.

Already disgruntled, he found his first year at college a continual horror of disillusionment. Little London's college since its founding had been "A New England Seat of Learning Nestled in the Shadow of Pike's Peak." Popularly known as an outpost of Boston, its large and beautiful campus lay in the heart of the North End and was called "New Massachusetts." Most of its professors, benefactors, and donators of buildings were staunch New England Congregationalists whose eyes like General Palmer's looked back to Mother England.

The present Administration Building formerly had been the ornate home of a Cripple Creek tycoon. Yet all the other buildings, from the first historic Cutler Hall, whether built of gray stone or peachblow sandstone, reflected in some measure New England architecture. Their crowning glory, and the first addition in twenty years, was the new memorial chapel being built at a cost of $350,000. Not a single stone from the granite mountains shut off from sight by its stained glass windows rooted it to its own earth. Romanesque style, its stone had been shipped from Indiana. Its pretentious cornerstones, however, had been brought all the way from Merrie England. There were four of them. One from Winchester to symbolize "the relation between Church and State which has been the peculiar characteristic of England's history." One each from Oxford and Cambridge. And one from Gatton Surrey which "speaks to us of the parish churches of England, where the people who really count received their training. For it is characteristic of the Gospel that it makes little account of influential people." The speeches made when they were laid embroidered the theme to relate the history of the donor's ancestors who came from the localities.

An expensive mausoleum of England's past, and with no roots

in its own living earth, it and the school epitomized to March Little London itself. A college located at the mouth of the Pass that had led to two of the world's greatest mining booms, it no longer taught mining and metallurgy. The historic assay furnace in the basement of Cutler Hall which had been made and used by Stratton, founder of Cripple Creek, had been knocked to pieces and sold for junk. In a region where the great open pages of geological structure were visible from the campus, the school had no major course in geology. The few courses in engineering leading to a degree in general science were pathetically inadequate and attended by a mere handful of students. The school of business and banking was no more than a concession to the times. The college in short emphasized the classical arts, and its faculty ran to type.

Mostly from New England, they were old, unimaginative, passionately conservative. They were like cloistered monks who had reduced life to a symbol, named it truth, and now proclaimed its formula. They were agreeable and dull. They were dead.

There was every excuse for the hopeless stagnation and stupefying conservatism which March found infecting the school. Unlike a state university, the college depended upon subscriptions and endowments. This limited its size and growth. There were just over 400 students in school. For them were seven national fraternities, and three girls' societies pledged to national sororities. In all, one house for every forty of the total enrolled students.

Most of the students, March found, were from well-to-do families. They had to be: tuition and living expenses in the fraternity and sorority houses were high, and there were no industries in Little London to provide jobs for working students. With little engineering and science in the curriculum, demanding long hours of laboratory work, the students were usually through classes by noon. And Little London, a tourist playground with its mild weather, mountain trails, golf courses, polo fields, dining rooms, dance floors, and mineral springs, provided them an indolent and delightful sojourn.

Little wonder that the college was commonly known throughout the state as "The Country Club," and was even a bit proud of its nickname.

There was no place March could have gone more unsuited to his needs and temperament. Nineteen years old, he had all the failings and good qualities of his breeding: he was proud and timid, reserved in action and bold in thought, stubborn, sensitive, passionate in feeling, but appearing cold when most aroused. His high school companions like Cecil James had merely moved from their literary societies to the fraternities. March was not pledged to a fraternity. As a "town boy" he found himself as isolated and alone as he had been farther down the street in high school. For him "College" as the Rogiers regarded it did not exist.

To add to his discontent, Boné did not send the additional $100 he had promised for the second semester. Nor did Ona know where to write him. Mr. Ford, the Santa Fe agent, came to his rescue by giving March a job as a "number grabber" on the "Graveyard" – the third shift Yard Clerk, working in the railroad yards from eleven at night until seven in the morning.

Carrying a lantern and a packet of Switch Lists, one for each track in the yards, he was required to keep record of every car on every track every hour of the night. To accomplish this he had to know the yards so well that when he swung off a yard engine – a goat – anywhere on the darkest night, he knew immediately where he was. What a maze of tracks there were: Main Lines 1, 2, 3, 4, 5, 6; Pass 1, 2, 3, 4; Main Line Pocket, Pass Pocket; the Spurs, Stubs, Warehouses, and Terminals. Below the station the yards flowed south and west around town – a great river of steel whose tributaries crept along warehouses, into coal and lumber yards, between grain elevators. Old frame houses, a night watchman's shack, a grimy all-night lunch counter, nigger shanties, and decrepit whorehouses flanked the right-of-way. Then the river of tracks thinned out, creeping on west to Colorado City and the big Golden Cycle mill on the mesa. It was nearly four miles long, a world known best by the people of the night. In it March was still alone and lonely.

Then at seven o'clock in the morning he had barely time to rush home on his bicycle, clean up and eat breakfast, and pedal furiously up to the Country Club for an eight o'clock class. How dull, dead, and impractical it seemed!

Ona couldn't sleep at night for worrying about him down there in the yards, prowling around with a lantern, jumping on and off freight trains in the dark. She would go to bed early in the cavernous Third Floor with Leona and Nancy in their beds across the room. In a little while she could hear Rogier come up from the basement to join Mrs. Rogier in the big master bedroom on the second floor. Business was good in the Chocolate Shoppe in Manitou; Mary Ann and Uncle John worked late. Ona could hear the streetcar squeak to a stop on Kiowa, their steps coming down Bijou. She listened to them enter the house and climb the stairs to the middle room below. Soon the murmur of their voices ceased. Now there was silence, and Ona lay gripping the sides of her bed.

She had not been able to keep her fears to herself, and had told the family about that strange, ghostly, and malevolent light. It kept appearing intermittently despite Rogier's grumbling efforts to ascertain the cause. She had then angrily confronted March. "You're in college now! What with takin' physics, electricity, chemistry, and all, *you* ought to be smart enough to do something about it!"

So for days and nights March investigated lights and shadows, measured angles of reflection, traced all possible causes to no avail. Then, angry himself, he had on three different nights off, slept in Ona's room with a loaded twenty-two rifle beside him. On the third night it appeared again, a narrow beam of light shining on the closet door at the head of the landing. Ona silently reached over to grip March's shoulder. He awoke instantly, picking up his rifle. Together they watched the light swing slowly, hesitantly, across the wall. When it reached the knob on the door of March's room, he rose up in bed, shouted "Stop!" and fired. The light disappeared instantly.

All of them – Ona, March, and the awakened girls – rushed to the landing. The bullet had torn a hole through the door. Nothing else was to be seen; nor was there any reasonable explanation to offer the rest of the family when they came running upstairs.

So Ona lay gripping the sides of her bed, dreading its appearance. Instead, long after it was due, she heard the reassuring steps of the Kadles making their nocturnal round of inspection. The dual mystery of all existence, the perpetual unseen battle between good and evil, the comforting Kadles and the malevolent light.

After a cat nap she was awakened by the milk man rumbling by and the scrawny red rooster crowing out in back. It was nearly dawn. Time for her son—that strange son of his strange father—to blow out his lantern. She rose on one elbow and in the graying light looked at the faces of the sleeping girls. Leona's was dark on the pillow, a happy face. In her make-up was none of March's brooding sullenness and tragic intensity. Alert, intuitive, all light, she was tripping through high school on her toes, the most popular girl in her class. Despite made-over dresses and shoes which she shined herself, she was taken to parties and picnics by both high school and college boys.

Nancy was cut from another cloth. An old soul in a young body, she was quiet, compassionate, humble. Perhaps it was her left eyelid that made her so unpopular. Heavy and without reflex, it drooped over her eye. Sometimes when she was happy and laughing in a crowd it would be all right. Then suddenly it would droop down again as if in a solemn wink that refuted her gaiety. She became content to stay home, sitting in the rocker up in the front second-story bedroom.

"What's the matter, dear?" Ona had asked her once. "I thought you were going out on the picnic party with the rest."

"They didn't ask me," Nancy said with a somber smile. "I guess they don't want me with my droopy eye. They want girls like Leona, she's so pretty and lively."

"Don'd you worry, dear." Ona gave her a hug. "Business and running around isn't for homebodies like you and me. We'll keep the home fires burning and be the happiest of all, won't we? When are you going to have your Sunday school class of little boys down again?"

Now in the gray dawn Nancy's pale face was somber on its pillow. Ona sighed. In that chair downstairs her grandmother had rocked away the last years of her unbelievable life, chewing at the wart on her diamond-covered finger. Sister Molly had died while waiting there with hopeless abandon for Tom who had never returned; and Mrs. Rogier, forever sitting out Rogier's absences at Cripple Creek. Here too she herself had waited, unloved and ignored, until Jonathan had caught her up for a brief and passionate interlude; and now, in empty dawn, she was still waiting for March. Suddenly and intuitively she knew that it would fall to Nancy to sit at a window bearing in turn their burden of hope and courage, of folly and futility.

"What is this strange pattern stamped upon our lives?" she wondered, blindly seeking the thread that bound them all together in the mysterious life swirling around the passionless stability of this shabby old house on Shook's Run. "Why, you'd think it was all laid out for us from the start, and we had no choice!"

Rogier, Tom, Cable, March – the men were all alike, vibrating to far horizons, ever restless and uprooted. But in each of three generations, in each of these men's lives, had appeared a woman loved, left, and forgotten, to bear for them trivial burdens with strength and uncomplaining patience.

Who will ever understand a woman, she thought. We are sweethearts and wives, we are daughters and mothers of men. Yet our fathers forget us and the passion that begot us; the touch of our husbands' hands grows cold and falls away. The fruit of our wombs is severed so soon from the bough. By our sons we are forgotten.

And still and forever we endure. We are the red lips smiling through parted lilac blossoms in spring, the passion of summer storms when the lightning crackles around the granite peaks, the ripe fruit of the harvest. Toothless and wrinkled we huddle against the winter storm, beside the dying embers, sewing moccasins for the long trail. And still and forever we endure – greater than the promise, the passion, the harvest of our flesh.

We are women but there is something in us greater than any woman. How then can we be understood? Men seek gold and silver, the riches of the earth, and yet it is the common flesh of that earth they tread underfoot which is the most precious of all. How then shall women be understood, when their riches are the most precious and secret of all?

We are the Earth Mother, our flesh is her flesh, we are the womb of all life. So still and forever we endure.

My father, my brother, my husband, my son – all these have plumbed and are plumbing the depths of the earth. Yet in their daughter, their sister, their wife, their mother lies the mystery they sought and will seek forever. Like the earth, I am the secret of life and I shall never be known.

And so she sat, heavy with the mystery, gazing out the window at the earth-heaped mountains rising into the dawn as endurable and unknowable as she. All things pass. But in her secret oneness Nancy would endure as had she.

8

It was inevitable after his first year in college that March drifted into engineering. The small group of science and engineering students contained a few older men who had returned to school to brush up on theory with the hope of advancing in their technical work.

Professor Thomason, because of ill health, on loan to the college from his permanent post in New England, was the head of the department. He was a tall, sandy haired man about fifty. His aversion was Art; his religion Theoretical Physics; his creed the Electron Theory. In his way he was brilliant; a hard worker and a tyrant. But without any knowledge of men, industry, or practical engineering, he was a hot-blooded theorist.

It was his aim to reduce his students gradually to a select group, for each of whom upon graduation he would secure a teaching fellowship in an Eastern university where he could obtain his doctorate. To achieve it, he supervised the selection of all their courses; saw to it they took no more English, history, economics, and language than was barely necessary; laid out all their outside reading; and gave them keys to the basement laboratory where they had to work nights, Saturdays, and sometimes on Sundays to keep up. The effect of all this was to divorce his small department from the mainstream of college life. His students were further alienated by being quartered in old Cutler Hall across the campus.

March found himself perched on a high stool at a drafting table in the historic old building his grandfather had erected. The place reminded him so much of the shop at home that he had the uncanny feeling Rogier was perched on the stool beside him, sharpening his own pencil by pushing the knifeblade outward with his thumb.

Professor Thomason insisted that his students sit with their slide rules in hands during his lectures. He would abruptly, stop talking, scribble an equation on the blackboard, and demand they finish the computation "within one-tenth of one percent – the accuracy of your slide-rules! Who's the first to give me an answer?"

He had another irritating idiocyncrasy. He would whip around at any time, point his bony finger at a boy, and ask out of context, "What causes the Aurora Borealis? The rainbow?"– "Jameson, what is thunder?–lightning?"

Oh, it is the red forked tongue of the great serpent when the white-bellied clouds gather over the parched desert of the Navajos, over the shrivelled little corn patches below the cliffs of Oraibi. In the dusty plaza the dancing Snake priests shake louder their rattles; the resonant stamp of their moccasined feet on the *pochta,* the sounding board, sounds like the faint rumble of thunder. And with writhing rattlesnakes firmly but gently clenched in their mouths, they lift their horribly painted faces upward to the darkening sky. Oh yes, it is the red forked tongue of the great serpent whose image is wrapped around the mouths of the huge water jars, the fertility serpent, the feathered serpent who summons the tall walking rain majestically striding sky and desert, bringing life to shrivelled corn and shrivelled people.

"Lightning, sir," said Jameson, "is an electrical discharge caused by an electrical potential set up as a result of rising air currents blowing off the edges of the larger water drops in the cloud, and carrying away the smaller drops of spray which remain. Thunder, following the flash, is caused by the vibrations set up by the sudden heating and expansion of air along the path of lightning."

March's gaze strayed outside to the sun gleaming through a

haze of autumnal gold rich with the ripeness of Indian Summer. He was suddenly recalled by a young lady saying, "Indian Summer is only a figment of a poet's fancy. It does not exist as a meteorological entity. The haze is simply composed of collected and suspended smoke and particles of vegetation, and is caused by a stagnated high pressure area."

"Correct!" The professor rapped the desk. "Cable! What is this? This desk, the chair you're sitting on?"

March sat up. "All matter, sir, is nothing but an elemental charge of electricity, you might say. The molecules of all substances are broken down into atoms, and these atoms are composed of electrons with their satellite protons – positive and negative charges of electricity whose numbers and arrangements determine the outward form of matter which we call by different names. We will eventually break down this ultimate unit, and release its locked-up energy for the industrial uses of man."

"It will do. It will do," said Professor Thomason. "What I'm trying to get all of you to do is to regard even simple phenomena in terms of your calling. Clear your minds of old beliefs. Think freely. All nature, everything that exists, is nothing in itself. It has no life, no meaning. We have reduced all to its simple expression in scientific laws. Now, by learning to apply them, we will at last be masters of the universe, of life itself."

This was his interpretation of the mysterious, all-pervading life force flowing through interstellar space, a stone, a blade of grass, ourselves; the mysterious flow of undifferentiated and unlimited power informing the great breathing mountains, the rutting deer, the passions and thoughts of man. It was clear, mathematically precise, but it denied the mystery of creation, the secret unknown gods who whisper in all men.

Some of the students were amazed and amused, like children robbed of Santa Claus. "Murder – social subtraction, eh?" they joked.

But March sat through these lectures as if Professor Thomason had him by the throat. He was inarticulate, unable to voice his misery. It was not as if he did not understand. His mind worked well enough, but something within him passionately refuted the view of life that science held out before him. Rogier, for all his queer ideas, had at least an appreciation of life's mysterious profundity, its torment and beauty. Thomason, never.

Perhaps his opinion of the professor was not entirely unjust. For there was one aspect of life Thomason's rigid theory did not include – sex. And this was the strange god within him now crying with a voice at once terrifying and compelling. During high school he had attended a compulsory lecture and movie on the evils of unsanctified and promiscuous sex. The preliminary lecture was innocuous enough. But the movie was disastrous. It showed in a few brief scenes a man meeting a woman of ill repute and their casual courtship ending with an embrace in her bedroom. Then followed in tedious medical detail his trips to the doctor, the spread of a horrible venereal disease as he was taken to the hospital. Shots of other patients in the ward, faces distorted, bodies covered with sores. Finally a close-up of the hero, the victim of his passions: legs spread and held up by ropes, screaming with agony. March could stand no more. Dripping sweat, unable to breathe, he reeled up the aisle. A nurse caught him before he fainted, squeezed an ammonia capsule under his nose, and finally let him stagger outside, frightened, revolted, and ashamed.

The movie accomplished more than its purpose. It brought out the Puritanical streak in March that proclaimed sex and sin as synonymous. And it buried deep within him the first faint urgings of his developing maturity.

But now for some cause he could not understand, he became aware of women's smiles and women's shapes. Madame Jones' parlor on Myers Avenue in Cripple Creek, the women in their cheap lodging houses near the Santa Fe station, the whorehouses west of town, became meaningful. The lewd jokes of taxicab drivers took on new significance. Whenever he thought of them his mind grew cold, and at the same time his body seemed to leap into flame. Lying in bed at night he thought ceaselessly of thousands of naked women in their beds, in narrow Pullman berths; of beautiful nymphs with long hair and pink-tipped breasts floating in the sea of desire, calling, calling.

Evidently many of his campus friends were not as tortured with secret longings. There were too many girls and young summer widows vacationing in Little London while their husbands slaved in the heat at home.

"I never seen such a place!" Hanlon cried enthusiastically to him one day. "The hotels, cabins, and streets are full of hot-breathin' hussies pinin' for somebody to take 'em out. Seems like you young bucks at college have got a hell of a harem to work over!"

Indeed several students with cars openly boasted of the women who had paid their expenses all summer for their sturdy favors.

The Country Club at Stud for Visiting Tourists.

March wondered if he were going mad; he had no doubt his mind was diseased. His feeling was intensified one morning in chapel when Valeria Constance's hand fell on his knee.

Seats in the chapel were assigned to students alphabetically. For more than two years he had been sitting beside Valeria during the compulsory chapel period each morning. This was the only time they ever met, and they never talked. March had taken a dislike to her from the start. Valeria's father was a well-to-do editor of one of the Denver newspapers. Even as a freshman she put on airs. She had a room of her own in one of the halls, dressed well, and became immensely popular. In her second year she sported a bright red roadster. Then the girls began to edge away from her. She became known as a sweetheart of Sigma Chi, then of every other fraternity in turn. In her junior year she dropped everyone, refused all dates, got rid of her car. Whether her father had lost his money or she had taken up philosophy, no one knew. Valeria kept them all guessing and went her way alone.

She was good looking, tall, and thin; but aside from a chance word to her, March ignored her. Yet more and more often of late he felt a hot and quickening throb of desire when near her. Outside, the spell passed.

He cursed himself for a fool. "She's getting skinnier every day," he thought. "I don't know what's worse – the smell of her perfume or the smell of the cigarettes she's always smoking."

To crave her while near, and to hate her while absent – this was the paradox that baffled him. Until that morning when she casually dropped her hand on his knee. March jerked erect with embarrassment. It was an important day: a noted speaker had come to address them and the faculty were dressed in their black robes. March had put on his old brown suit. The knees of the trousers were threadbare, and Ona had reinforced them on the inside with slabs of mending tissue. They looked excellent when pressed, but were stiff as a board.

Valeria appeared not to notice the knife-edge crease on which her hand dropped. "Meet me outside when this farce is over," she whispered.

She was waiting for him when the talk was over. "I see you had to dress up today like all the other sheep. I thought better of you than that."

They took a side path to Palmer Hall. Valeria continued, "We've been sitting together now for over two years. You've never asked me for a date, hardly been civil. Are you bashful, a grind, or got an inferiority complex? Let's call off the feud. Ask me for a date and see what I'll say."

"What fraternity house are you trying to spite now? Why pick on me?"

"Because you're so damned blunt and rude. At least you're not like these simpering idiots. What do you say—tomorrow night at seven-thirty? I'll get my leave till eleven-thirty."

"Dinner?" asked March.

"Don't be a fool!" Without another word she ran up the steps of Palmer Hall, leaving him feeling exactly that.

Next evening March dressed up as best he could and sought out Hanlon. He was positive Valeria would want to go to a hotel to dance. "I'm in a hole," he explained. "You can't take a girl to a dance on the street car – not this one. The drug store clowns on the corner would laugh us out of school."

"Oh hell, jump in my car!" replied Hanlon. "I'll take you there at least."

Valeria was waiting in the hall when March got out of the car. "What's that for?" she asked.

March explained.

"You're trying to run to form, but you're out of character," she said sharply. "Tell him to go on. I want to walk and talk."

They walked down to the creek and up the long park to Third Lake. The moon was coming up, reflected on the water like a floating silver dollar. A beaver slapped his flat tail, a fish splashed noisily. Sitting beside her, March could see the outline of her long thin legs, the shape of her small firm breasts as she leaned forward to light a cigarette. March shuddered. He put his arm around her, leaned back and clasped her breast.

"Never mind," she said listlessly. "I don't have to be loved. Every time I go out with a boy, he seems to think it's only an excuse to neck. I like to get out. That's all."

The simple assertion, with the friendly pressure of her body, instantly quenched the flame within him. For a moment he was angry, frustrated, then he relaxed and listened to her talk.

She seemed to have had everything: an excellent home, friends, three summers in Europe, every wish fulfilled. Nothing mattered. She hungered for something she had never known. She was like those strange insects of night that live but a few hours, beating their wings in a mad flight of ecstasy, and expiring at dawn. But if this explained her actions during her first two years in college, what had happened now to change her so completely?

Valeria didn't know. "You've seen me in the college plays?" – she always took the vampire part. "Well, that's the way I feel. As if I were born to be a prostitute or something. Never good.' I feel that if I were married, settled down for an easy existence in the house my father bought for me, it would kill me. But I can't be 'bad.' Not with my family. So I'm at the end of my rope. Already!"

"Oh, you just want to sow a few wild oats. All women are like that," he said knowingly. "You'll snap out of that when you're married."

"I'm engaged," she answered abruptly. "A fellow in Yale. Nice but dull. He's coming to help my father. I can't hurt either of them. But it will mean the death of me. I have a premonition."

March laughed, but nervously. There was something horribly real and bitterly sincere in her listless tone that belied her melodramatic assertion.

"I've got one year more!" she cried. "And everything is stale. I've slept with a dozen boys. Nothing matters. I feel alone always. And all I care for now is to lie and look at the mountains. Something's happened to me. I don't know what."

And so that night March went home from his first date in college having spent ten cents for two cups of coffee, feeling somehow thwarted and taken in.

He was now working at the Santa Fe station only in the summer, leaving him free during the school year to get up into the mountains on weekends. Valeria took long hikes with him often. He grew to know her quick and brilliant mind; she was an honor student. If he resented the quick hot wave of desire the first sight of her aroused in him, he also appreciated the casual sympathy between them that took its place. But they seemed never really to meet as he had met Leslie Shane. There was something that did not fuse between them. She was like a vampire greedy to suck from him the warm blood of intuitive understanding which she sensed in his dark brooding face. He too was as selfish. Resenting the animal desire in him which she throttled by her quick mind, he drew back deep within himself against her.

How unsatisfying it was for them both, this constant attraction and repulsion. We all desire the passion of the flesh, the understanding of the mind, and the intuition of the spirit, all in one. So we refuse the priceless gifts that come to us singly.

Late that fall March, who had been up the mountains, caught a ride down on a freight. Snow was beginning to fall, yet the air was warm and vibrant. It was nearly dusk when the train rolled across the high trestle above the upper end of North Cheyenne Canyon. March could see a group of cabins, the falls below, and Bruin Inn. From here he could walk down the canyon and catch a streetcar to town. Waving back to the conductor, he swung free with his duffle bag, and slid down the gravel slope.

As he walked down the narrow trail, he suddenly met Valeria sauntering along in walking shoes and fur coat. "Hello, Figure meetin' you!"

She answered surlily, in one of her moods. "You look dirty as a miner, an Indian," she said eyeing his boots, corduroys, and leather jacket. "What's in the bag?"

"A slab of bacon and some cans, coffee, bread. Want to eat 'em up?" he asked jokingly.

"Why not?" she assented listlessly. "Down at the Inn a crowd of fools would ruin supper by playing that squeaky phonograph." She stared at him steadily. "Go down to Lavely's and get us a cabin for the night. Just tell them you've got a friend. I don't want to go back to that stuffy dorm."

He walked down to the cabins. The caretaker nodded. "Two of yeh? You can have that little one-room cabin across the creek. No need of my goin' up there with you. There's wood. Just pay now and leave the key here in the mornin'."

It was done. In abashed silence March lit the lamp, built fires in the fireplace and small cook-stove while Valeria huddled on the bed, smoking. They ate hungrily. Then March heated water, washed the dishes, repacked his duffle bag. Valeria watched his rhythmical, capable hands with amusement. "How neat and methodical you are!"

"In the moutains it's a good habit to be ready for whatever comes," he said simply.

The room had warmed up now. In the ruddy glow of the fire the oilcloth covered table seemed less shiny; the smooth log walls took on a mellow tone. Valeria took off all her clothes except her brassiere and silk panties. Then putting back on her mink coat, she sat down on the bed.

"I suppose you feel righteously wicked. A man always does. Even Professor Enderly, for all his philosophy."

At the boy's start of surprise, she went on obdurately. "Oh yes. I first thought him the freest, most intelligent man on the campus. I took every course he gave. I joined the group meeting in his apartment – Agh! It was just talk. All in his head. He made love like a silly schoolboy – That's philosophy for you. Words!"

She pulled him down to sit beside her. "You're not like that, March. You're strange, somehow. Different. You don't think, really. You've got a sense-intuition that'll be stronger, truer than your mind will ever be. But I'm afraid you'll take it on yourself to think your way instead of feeling it."

She lit another of her interminable cigarettes. "Be yourself, always. Remember me, who can't. Oh, remember me, March, when I'm lost and gone!"

March shuddered. A terrible conviction that she would really die–soon, so soon!–swept over him. He put his arms around her but without desire, as if he were embracing the fleshless voice of a truth he had never known till now. He perceived now what had kept them apart. His flow of life, except for a spurt of passion when always he first met her, had sunk down to coagulate deep within him. And yet he was afraid.

Valeria rose and threw off her coat. "Unsnap my bra, will you?"

Fumblingly he unfastened the snap, watched her step out of her panties and walk up to the fire. He had thought her thin and bony. Now he saw how full and rounded were her thighs and hips, how firm and pointed were her small breasts. And yet he was shocked by the whiteness of her smooth skin; it was like that of a candle, a candle that was swiftly burning out. He hastily flung off his clothes, walked up behind her, and put his arms around her.

She leaned back her head and smiled reprovingly. "Now March. You're in a hurry because you're shy. Or do you think I'll run away? Let's get good and warm before we get into bed."

Even till then he had misjudged her, with her cold and analytical mind. Then suddenly he found himself immersed in a mindless passion that endowed her long frail body with a physical strength and inward power beyond his comprehension. Out of it he emerged weak and spent to lie quietly beside her. Valeria snuggled up close to him. "How cosy you feel. Now don't talk. You might say something."

Would he ever forget her he wondered when he awoke next morning: this haunting face so childlike now in sleep, her narrow mouth curved slightly in a smile, her yellow hair sprawled over the pillow? Would he ever forget her who for the first time had eased the misery of his pent-up passion, and forever laid the Puritanical ghost of sin and sex which had haunted him?

It was still early. He rose quietly so as not to disturb her, and bounded to the window. The sky was cloudless; the thin fall of snow was soggy already. The storm, and that within him, was spent. He felt cleansed and whole, buoyantly alive. Stretching on his toes, he flung wide his arms, arched his chest, and gulped great breaths of air.

"Shut that window and light a fire!" Valeria's petulant voice demanded behind him.

He ran back, knelt and kissed her eyes, stroked the hair back from her eyes. "Oh, Valeria! I never felt like this before!"

"Light that stove too. I want some coffee," she demanded sharply. then, when he'd put the pot on, she said in a soft voice, "Now come back here and lie with me. We've got all morning, haven't we?"

How different it was now, holding her slim full body against him, feeling the warm moth-like texture of her lips! He had no more inhibitions. They were strangers no more. They had met at last.

9

Glancing out of the Third Floor window one morning, Ona happened to see Rogier across the street. He was squatting on the high bank of Shook's Run, one hand shading his eyes, and staring intently toward the house. A moment later he moved west, kneeling on the ground and squinting along his outstretched arm. She immediately stalked downstairs and across the street to confront him.

"What are you up to now, Daddy?" she demanded. "I know it's something!"

The old man looked her steadily in the eyes. "There's some people in that big three-story house there tryin' to spy on me! I aim to find out who!" Indignantly he strutted across the street and into his greenhouse.

Yes, Rogier had encountered an unforseen difficulty in digging his tunnel into the base of Pike's Peak. Closing the plank door behind him, he had only to walk a few steps down into the passage to see it: a pool of water, a shallow well filling up with underground water. Dom! He should have known better, digging so close to Shook's Run! Hence he had gone across the street to the bank of the creek to ascertain, without benefit of surveying instruments, if there were a slight rise in altitude behind the house where he could avoid the seepage. There was not. He would have to make out where he was.

Indomitably he installed a small hand pump, running the hose out into the currant bushes where it would not be noticed, and pumping most of the night. Next day seepage water filled up the hole again.

Well, he'd have to bridge it and extend his tunnel through the slightly higher properties of the Pyles and the Caseys next door. So over the well he constructed a footbridge of planks. Beyond this he dug an inclined plane cleated with slats from apple boxes to keep him from slipping on the wet earth, and resumed driving his lateral tunnel.

The hard wórk with pick and shovel he didn't mind. Getting rid of the excavated dirt was the difficulty. Some of it he could mix with ashes and dump in the ash pit. The rest of it he would have to trundle up the alley in a wheelbarrow and dump in a vacant lot. If sometimes his thin back gave out, or the muscles of his skinny shanks knotted with cramps, he had only to sit and stare at the Peak. Its compassionate face condoned his efforts. It encouraged him "Time!" it said. "All anything takes is time!" And Rogier knew his tunnel was getting along. Already it was through Pyle's lot and beginning to burrow under the Casey's backyard. Digging now would be easy.

March was not as satisfied with his own progress. Professor Thomason's picked group had dwindled to a sparse dozen under his tyranny. Stuffed with theory and mathematics, they clamored for something concrete.

"We're not a technical trade school like a state university or the Colorado School of Mines," Thomason reminded them. "Basic principles, the principles underlying every field of science and engineering. That is what we're after."

But under their prodding, and without technical facilities, he arranged for them to obtain field work. He sent them separately to make detailed reports on the old steam power plant east of town, the hydroelectric plant at Manitou, and the new power plant at the Broadmoor Hotel. For high voltage, X-ray, and ultra-violet work, he sent others to hospitals and tuberculosis sanitariums. Another was sent with a railroad division lineman to learn how to locate grounds and crosses. To March, whom he understood had a mining background, he suggested some field studies in Cripple Creek.

"I hate mining!" answered March.

"No mining or geology. Just a look at the new electrical plants supplanting the old steam hoists. A report on the proposed new drainage tunnel," Thomason said imperturbably. "No industrial applications. Just the underlying principles, mind. Take your time. You'll be excused from class work. And we can pay you laboratory assistant fees to defray your expenses."

So early that spring March packed his bag and announced to Ona he was going up to Cripple Creek.

"Up to the district? Mining!" she shouted. "Like Tom, Daddy, your own father! And now you, son! Is this what you've been doing to me all this time in college while I thought you were learning to be a successful businessman? Betraying me! Behind my back!"

Her childish ignorance and distorted image of his purpose made him furious, but her real anguish clawed at his heart. She looked so old and tired today—a wash day; her hair was turning gray, the crows' feet growing deeper around her eyes.

"Mother! Don't be so dumb!" he pleaded. "I'm not taking up mining. I'm just going up there to see the electrical plants as part of my outside laboratory work in physics. Lord, you'd think I was leavin' with a pick on my back!"

"Well, don't tell Daddy where you're going," she cried despairingly. "It might bring it all back. Or even bring on another spell." She began straightening the room, a woman's only answer to success, failure, and hope alike.

It was just daybreak when March swung off the freight caboose and walked down into the district. There was no fault in the vein of his memory as he stared through a light stinging snow into that vast granite cup which held so precious a part of his childhood.

Above him a seamed, mute, and impassive face stared back at him through the gray and ghastly morning light. In a wrinkle up its cheek lay what had been the Sylvanite, still manned by the ghosts of Abe and Jake, his father, and the undying spirit of his grandfather whose outworn body still puttered like a mechanical robot in a makeshift greenhouse far below. Around him rose the old familiar hills: Bull Hill, Squaw Mountain, Tenderfoot and Globe Hills,

Mount Pisgah, Big Bull, and the Nipple. And cutting below them the deep arroyos: Arequa Gulch, Poverty Gulch, and Grassy Gulch. A dreary landscape scarred and pitted with gallows frames, smoke-stacks, shaft houses, glory holes, ore dumps, and squalid miners' shanties; the features unchanged, but their expression lifeless. A world gone dead.

Down the slope huddled a clump of apparently abandoned cabins. From one a slatternly woman came out, stared at him sullenly from a pinched blue face, then gathered up a dishpan of snow to melt for the morning coffee. March turned up his coat collar, lit the new pipe he was affecting, and trudged on.

From Victor, once proud "City of Mines," a scarce dozen chimneys were sending up their streams of smoke. Stores and houses were deserted or torn down, their gaping excavations filled with snow. Scores of shaggy half-wild burros roamed the empty streets even though the town council had appointed a man to keep them off the sidewalks—sidewalks with weeds growing in the cracks. He peered into a deserted saloon. The mahogany bar was gray with dust, an empty whisky bottle was standing on the shelf behind it. But as the end of Fourth Street, a block from the central downtown corner, he ran into a few miners coming down from the working on the hill. The lamps were still burning on the front of their caps. Their dirty faces were pinched with cold.

He followed them to a narrow brick building whose lower front had housed the Opera House, and climbed upstairs to what he remembered as the Gold Coin Hotel. Here he entered a small drab parlor containing a stove surrounded by rows of stiff chairs. Soon Mrs. Okerstrom came in. She was a fine, fat old Swedish woman with a brogue thick as pea soup, one of the old-timers of the district. She was the landlady of the place – the Gold Coin Boarding House.

"Vat it iss you want?" she demanded.

March explained timidly, mentioning his grandfather. Her stern weathered face, flushed like a drunk's from cooking over the kitchen stove, broke into blossom. She grabbed him by the shoulders. "Ya! Vy don't you say who it iss you are? Old man's Rogier's boy! Vell, vell. I don't know how to belieff you have grown!"

A clock struck six. From their rooms around the dreary parlor miners in stiff muck-smeared clothes and boots clumped in, carrying the chairs into the long dining room. March had breakfast with them: oatmeal with canned milk, hot biscuits, eggs, bacon, fried mush, stewed prunes. They ate silently and ravenously, raising their stony white faces from their plates only to call Mrs. Okerstrom from the kitchen with another heaping platter.

While she washed dishes, March watched the men off to work. From the window he could see them trudging up the trail from the end of the street to the working on top of the hill. It was beginning to snow again. The seven o'clock whistles were blowing. The sun was not yet up.

In back of the boarding house lay the long disused corridors of the Gold Coin Hotel. Cold and dark, they were strung with cobwebs. On each side lay the honeycombed cells, heaped with old dusty furniture. From one of these rooms Mrs. Okerstrom pulled two chairs and a small table. In the kitchen she gave him a bucket of soapy water to wash them off with.

"No empty rooms have I," she explained. "So few boarders. Ah, so bad these mines!" But up the slope of Squaw Mountain there was a log cabin March could use.

They set off through the snow with the three pieces. The cabin was not far away. The road led past the great brick shaft house of the famous Gold Coin. The walls had caved; the machinery lay broken and rusted under the debris. Nearby stood a group of weathered shanties. Only one family lived in the best and was gradually knocking down the others for firewood.

Farther up the slope stood the cabin he was to use. It was of good sound logs, and contained a bed, cook stove, and a gunny sack of blankets hanging from the rafters. When Mrs. Okerstrom left him, he cleaned up, made the bed and fire. He bought an axe, borrowed a lamp and a few dishes. His near neighbor loaned him a bucket, showed him where to get water, and cautioned him against the open, unprotected shaft that gaped downward a hundred feet just outside his door. He was settled. And during the weeks he returned to it for days at a time, the little cabin became the first home of his own.

To save money, he cooked most of his simple meals. But sometimes he gorged at Mrs. Okerstrom's table. He loved to listen to the hard clipped talk of the miners, especially the old-timers. In manner, speech, and appearance they seemed to have taken on the hard-rock durability of the earth in which they spent their lives. One evening a writing woman from Denver came for supper. She wanted a story: not the usual thing, she insisted, but "a true tale of glamorous Cripple Creek."

A sudden hush fell on the long table. The men coughed, scraped their boots, looked down at their plates. March himself felt embarrassed. Then abruptly a former old faro dealer and bartender named Bill Rankin spoke up.

"Hell yes, lady! Damned if I can't deal you one right off the top of the deck: how Cunningham Mountain got its name of the Nipple!"

Mrs. Okerstrom hastily retreated to the kitchen. March squirmed as he stole a look at the speaker. Rankin's rheumy blue eyes were dead serious. He rubbed his white whiskers reflectively, then lit his stub pipe with a flourish.

"You can place the Nipple right likely, Ma'am," he began. "It sticks up just south of town here. A tolerable bit outside the porphry spread, but in them days ever' hill and gulch was worth a look.

"Well up there in its granite side Cunningham sunk his shaft. He put her down and didn't hit a speck of color. Now Cunningham was a mite on the stubborn side. He couldn't believe that hole of his wouldn't pan out sometime. So he stuck there in his shanty. But ever' Sat'day he come into town, got roarin' drunk and paraded up Myers Avenue to see the girls, a-shoutin' and a-cussin' the purtiest you ever heard. Oh, but he was a likely man with his curly yellow hair and his way with a wench!

"Now I'll be damned if Mrs. Hancock didn't take a fancy to him. She was a widow woman, rich, right good-lookin', and lively as a plump young mare what with her husband bein' dead a good year. But she was stuck up and proud as all get-out, one of the High Society.

"Now nature, lady, is a fickle hussy. And when Mrs. Hancock got that ace-deuce look in her eyes, and the nipples on them plump breasts of hers got to stickin' out her fancy shirtwaist, and she panted like a lizard on a hot rock – well, Cunningham was a mighty likely man as I been sayin'.

"Before long ever-body knew what was goin' on. Hell's fire! The whole town missed his paradin' up Myers Avenue ever'

Sat'day, shoutin' and cussin', slappin' the girls across the bottom and snappin' their red garters till he found one to suit him. Instead, he rode in quiet like, and hitched his horse in front of Mrs. Hancock's big house.

"You can bet she was still persnickety. She marched to the Ladies Club carryin' her nose higher'n ever. 'Really', she would say, 'I do believe Mr. Cunningham's claim on Cunningham Mountain has excellent prospects. I'm doing everything possible to encourage him to develop it.' That's what she was lettin' on: that they was talkin' business, them two.

"Well, Ma'am, one of them fine Sat'days when Cunningham come in for some of that tall encouragin', he bit off one of her nipples – plumb off, slick as a whistle!"

March saw the Denver lady's face redden; involuntarily she drew her coat across her bosom. Mrs. Okerstrom, listening in the doorway, ducked back into her kitchen. March grinned slyly. Yes indeed, Madam, Glamorous Cripple Creek abounds in legend. The staunch spirit of its Pioneer Fathers and Winners of the West should awaken us to their valor and unimpeachable idealism. But withal, we must remember that they were human.

Rankin refilled his pipe and continued. "Now I ain't sayin' Cunningham carried that pink nipple of hers back to his mountain. But I am sayin' that Mrs. Hancock didn't have it no more. She went around swishin' her skirts, trippin' in to the Ladies Club with her nose up just the same – but with one of her nipples gone. It didn't phase her a good God-damn. But all the ladies in the club got to sniggerin' when they saw one side of her shirtwaist flat as a pancake, and wonderin' what had become of the nipple that used to stick out. But nobody said a word. She was that uppish.

"Now there was a kleptomaniac woman in town who went callin' on all the ladies regular, but couldn't help herself from sneakin' out of their parlors some little doo-dad or somethin'. She didn't mean to steal none, and she was ashamed to bring them back. So they kept pilin' up – and gettin' scarcer and scarcer in all the other ladies' parlors.

"Finally they got together to give her a lesson. They made her bring all the what-nots and doo-dads to the Ladies Club, so they could pick out what was theirs. About four o'clock in come Mrs.

Hancock. Nose up, hoity-toity like, she ambled around lookin' at the sea-shells, hair brushes, paper roses, and flower vases and all, to see if anything was hers.

"By this time the kleptomaniac woman was mad and tired of bein' rawhided. She rose up on her hindquarters, looked Mrs. Hancock up and down, then spoke up sharp and loud for ever'body to hear:

" 'Mrs. Hancock! Don't you go snoopin' around here any more for that nipple of yours. I certainly didn't steal it. You just better go look for it on Mr. Cunningham's Mountain!"

"Now blast my soul to hell, Ma'am! If that ain't why Cunningham Mountain's called the Nipple, I hope the livin' God strikes me dead on the spot!"

Glamouous Cripple Creek! With its 475 mines producing from an area of six square miles more gold than the Mother Lode of California and the Klondike combined; three railroads hauling ore down and empties back, with thousands of passengers; the High Line and the Low Line whizzing through its dozen towns and innumerable camps; the great houses on Myers Avenue, "The Homestead," "Old Faithful," and "Sunnyrest" and the swarming cribs behind. Madame Jones and Charlotte, oh sweet Charlotte! Abe and Jake, the tall dark man coughing on the dump who was his father, and the indomitable master of the Sylvanite, his grandfather. God Almighty! And the columbines among the pines, the red hawk sailing above, and the mousy burros trotting down the trail with twinkling feet. Always and forever it would still exist, throbbing with vitality, rich with wonder and magic, the mystery of the last of £10,000 sterling. But not here, where from a cabin on Squaw Mountain he stared out upon a frost-shattered world dreary and lifeless, oppressive with its high remoteness and capitulation to decay.

Making friends with Bill Rankin, who took him around, March presented his letter of introduction from Professor Thomason to the superintendents of the largest mines and continued his studies.

Statistics bore out his observations. There were now only forty-eight mines working: production had dropped to a bare $4,000,000 a year; and there remained less than 5,000 people in the entire District. Of course there were new modern plants and methods of operation. Immense syndicates and powerful corporations controlled the mines, mills, railroads. The few miners worked on a royalty or split-check basis, merely operating a single level, one stope or drift. They supplied the work and tools; the company supplied the pneumatic air and operated the hoist. If there were no pay ore, the company was out little but the men were out their work and time, and without bacon and beans. If there were a strike of sorts, the discoverers got only their stipulated royalty.

Of course there was a little hope; the most barren desert and desolate heart is not without it. There was talk of another drainage tunnel to be built. Five miles long, it would drain the district down to 3,000 feet on the premise that ore would be found to continue at depth. But what good would that do, wondered March; the big corporations would reap the profit.

"No industrial applications, mind!" Professor Thomason had told March. "Just the underlying principles!" And the underlying principle, March found, was that the days of independent mining, when a man relied on his own initiative, strength, and love of life, were over. A corporational profit of six percent was squeezing out here, as it was in the beet fields, the cotton and wheat fields, the juices of the living earth. He found himself staring at a huge industrial machine. And he knew that if he became a successful engineer he would be no more than one of its inconsequential cogs.

Why he kept coming back long after his report was finished, March didn't know. Maybe it was just to get away from the deadening constriction of the Country Club; from the more oppressive miasma of defeat and decay that permeated the shabby old house on Shook's Run and all his crazy tribe; from the constant clatter and rumble of goats and freights in the railroad yards. Or to simply sit here high above them all, feeling the snowcap melting on his head and running in rivulets down his cheeks, the avalanches ripping great hunks out of his winter-fat sides, the columbines and anemones springing up between his rooted toes — Perhaps, after all, it was the wedges of wild geese flying past overhead, tearing a wordless cry of longing from his heart. The strange and haunting cry of the tormenting unrest that was the legacy of his father and of his own mixed blood, of America itself.

10

Walking down Bijou Hill one afternoon on his return from Cripple Creek, March was disturbed to see an unusual commotion in the street ahead of him. Mrs. Jackson was dashing down the walk, dish towel in hand; the grocer Mr. Bryce in his white apron ran frantically across the road; swarms of children came flocking across Shook's Run. Good Lord! They all were making for his own home! With a premonition of disaster he broke into a run.

At the entrance to the driveway he halted and dropped his duffle bag. A throng of people swarmed before him shouting, crawling up on the fence, pushing forward. Mrs. Pyle next door was leaning out of her upper window, hands over her face, but peeking between her fingers.

"Granddad!" The cry seemed torn from his bowels as he suddenly went sick with fear and compassion. He dashed forward, brutally cleaving his way through the packed neighbors.

A devastating sight flashed before him. The west end of Rogier's greenhouse had collapsed; broken panes of glass were strewn over the back walk. In the middle of the driveway loomed a gaping hole. Farther west the earth had caved in under Pyle's fence, leaving a post sticking up with a flag of chicken wire. Even as he looked, Pyle's freshly planted garden caved in. Then he noticed the flimsy wooden garage in back of the Casey house. It was ominously tilted to one side as if upset by an earthquake.

"Stand back!" someone shouted. "The whole ground's undermined!"

Now March saw Leona and Nancy standing with arms around each other, stiff and frightened. Mrs. Rogier was waiting in broken glass and lettuce leaves, her hands clasped over her breast. March pushed on. Six feet down in a hole crouched Ona and Mr. Kennedy, tugging at a protruding foot.

"Here he is!" shouted Kennedy. "Help us get him out!"

Two men dropped down, clawing back the earth and prying off with a crow-bar a timber fallen across Rogier. March helped to drag him out as a car rolled in the driveway. A man hopped out, carrying a respirator. Rogier lay on the ground in front of the collapsed end of his greenhouse, his head in Ona's lap. He was unconscious. A thin trickle of blood oozed through his white hair. He was covered with dirt: his ears, mouth, and nose were full; his hands clenched it; damp earth stuck to his clothes, his shoes. It was as if he had been buried alive and yanked out like a fishworm. As the doctor worked on him with the respirator, March noticed the clipping tacked on the lintel of his greenhouse door: "Whoever needs the earth, shall have the earth."

Around him swarmed the crowd, looking down at him who had fallen the lowest a man can fall this side of the grave, his talents quenched, his dream besmirched.

"Look at them holes! Ain't it a scream? Boy, he was headin' straight for China!"

" 'Spose he was a German spy, goin' to blow up the town?"

"Look at my garden!" shrieked Pyle. "My radishes and spring peas! MY garden!"

"Aw, that old codger was batty as a hoot owl! But what in the name of God was he up to?"

No one knew except Rogier, and he was still unconscious though breathing when he was driven to the hospital.

It really had been very simple. Elated though he was by the progress of his tunnel, Rogier had been alert to the difficulties. The ever-continuing problem, of course, was getting rid of excavated dirt. With the coming of spring, he could no longer mix it with furnace ashes to dump in the ash pit. The vacant lot up the alley, to which he trundled it, was covered. There remained only two more locations for disposal: the banks of Shook's Run across the street, and the dump almost two blocks away. While he was debating these alternatives, another problem posed itself to his practical mind.

The base of Pike's Peak was some distance away. A declination of a degree or two to the north would bring his tunnel under Ute Pass; or a few degrees to the south, under the Cheyenne Canyons. No! He would have to hit it square, full on! To achieve this accuracy of aim, he mounted on a board an old mariner's compass bought at a pawnshop on Huerfano Street. Taking a reading on this as he sighted the Peak from outside, he carried it inside the greenhouse to mount at the entrance of his tunnel.

Then he became aware of another difficulty. How was he, deep in darkness below grass roots, to know whether he was driving at a level instead of inclining or declining his tunnel? He strung a plumb line from the entrance of his tunnel to its farthest end; and as he progressed he took readings with a carpenter's level.

A man had to think of these things, he reminded himself.

What he did not worry about—being a mining man who for thirty years had blasted and drilled tunnels, drifts, and crosscuts through hard granite without the need for cribbing—was the soft black loam, soggy with spring moisture, through which he was digging. Occasionally a clump fell in from wall or ceiling. No matter! Adequate cribbing, with stout pine A-frames and two-inch lagging boards, was beyond his means. It was enough to plant a two-by-four here and there, with a protective sheath of slats from discarded apple boxes.

Yet aside from these practical considerations of an alert, professional mining man, Rogier was screwed up to a high nervous tension. His mind felt like an alarm clock about to go off. Something was driving him to greater and greater haste. Hurry! He was getting old. Hurry! His pulse beat faster, his hands trembled. When he got up that morning he stumbled on the bathroom step. At breakfast he gobbled down his bowl of mush and ran out to his greenhouse. He could hardly force himself to putter at his shelves and boxes in plain view of family and neighbors before opening the padlocked door.

Loosening a chunk of the black loam, he carried it into the light for a better look. How richly black, finely textured, and fragrant it was! Crumbling the clod on a plank, he picked out a couple of fish-worms to look at their translucent amber bodies against the light. Then a snail, another fellow-creature who lived unnoticed in these depths. There came to view a small arrowhead beautifully flaked. Yes, the people who chipped it knew their Mother! But exactly what was it?

He sat down to look at the earth through a magnifying glass. There was no need to send it to an assayer. It was a composite unity of miniscule particles bound together by almost invisible threads of vegetable matter. Living roots and trunks and branches duplicating in miniature the great giants of the forests. He looked closer: at the infinitesmal specks of multicolored stone, the granicular texture of fine clay mortared with salts and minerals in solution, the almost invisible interstices which breathed in air. How beautifully composed and integrated it was—this organic cornerstone of all continents, of a small planet that whirled through interstellar space. No wonder it gave life to his lettuce and radishes, to whole civilizations of mankind.

But what was the ultimate secret of its fertility, the source of the life it engendered? That, not fools' gold, was what he sought. The subterranean sun. So he returned to the mouth of his shaft, lifted the hatch, and lit his miner's candle. For a moment he stood there before his mariner's compass and carpenter's level, like a pilot about to embark on a subterranean voyage no man had ever charted. Ahead of him in the flickering light stretched the long and narrow passage like a vulva into the hidden recesses of living flesh. Hurry! He walked in, and resumed digging. His pick was dull. He seemed short-winded; his legs trembled. He was getting old. There was no time to be lost.

Suddenly the earth caved in. He retreated, but only to confront another avalanche. A serious miscalculation, no doubt. He dug his way through. Then a rush of falling dirt blew out his candle. A clump of dirt dropping on his head knocked out his wind, made him weak and dizzy. Staggering forward, he dropped into the pool of water. Cussing, he clawed his way up. His efforts dislodged another stream of heavy black dirt. As he reached the entrance of the tunnel, the daylight seemed suddenly cut off. Simultaneously the alarm clock in his head went off. In explosive darkness he lurched forward, grabbed at a support and locked his hands around it. He did not feel the flimsy two-by-four give way as he fell backward. A few faintly colored, fish-shaped petals had already begun to whirl around a yellow-bright spot before his eyes as if trying to arrange themselves in a pattern he had never seen but which he seemed to know would be that of a great golden flower. He did not see it take shape. There was a tremendous crash as the timbers came down, followed by the shattering of glass. Then he was flooded with darkness and silence.

PART III

DUST

1

Rogier, back home from the hospital, lay silent and unmoving in his darkened room. Coincident with his seizure, he had suffered a serious blow on his head, a deep cut over his left eye whose scar gave him a sly and sinister look, and a rupture which necessitated his wearing a tin and leather truss – injuries enough to have killed a dray horse. It was miraculous that he pulled through. But he had come to the end of his tether. The greatest gift to which he might look forward now was a peaceful death. So thought the family.

"It might have been a mercy," began March, "but good Lord! Won't anything stop him? Fits, ruptures, cracked head, cut eye, old age! He's worse than a gopher." Yet humbled to the dust as his grandfather was, March saw in the flicker of his eyes the glimmer of an inner fire that could never be wholly estinguished; the imperishable, eternally groping spirit of man that made him invincible to success and ease, failure and shame.

His last pitiful folly was at once the pride and disgrace of the neighborhood. Pyle stormed, threatened suit, and finally paid to have his hole filled in and the fence rebuilt. The Caseys propped up their leaning garage, joyfully shouting insults as they worked. March boarded up the remnant of the greenhouse, filled in the collapsed tunnel under the driveway. Yet long after the scars of the crazy old man's backyard digging had been obliterated, neighbors brought visitors to view the scene. The Shook's Run Gold Mine had become as locally famous as its Cripple Creek prototype, the Sylvanite.

The Rogiers retreated into the decrepit old house as if sealing themselves up in a tomb. Over them all had come a change. They were exhausted and numbed by years of work and worry. Rogier had outworn them all. Lying upstairs like a lump of decomposed granite held together by tin and leather, he was still a man of stone.

"Hasn't that pampered pip-squeak in Memphis answered your letter yet?" Mary Ann demanded of Mrs. Rogier when the hospital and doctor bills arrived. "You wrote her a stiff one, didn't you?"

Mrs. Rogier had written Sally Lee indeed; a hasty note saying that Rogier was quite ill, a delicate reminder that a check would be accepted. A month later an answer came, a postcard from Paris. Sally Lee was in Europe, showing dear little Sugar Lump at her impressionable age the scenic wonders across the sea. Sally Lee was saddened to hear of Daddy's illness, hoped he was now recovering, and wished he were with her on tour.

"What about Boné?" asked Mary Ann sharply.

Mrs. Rogier spread out her hands emptily. Boné had not sent his current address.

Mary Ann, disgruntled, settled down with Uncle John to pay off the mounting debts.

March too had come to the end of his rope. The miasma of defeat and decay that penetrated every pore of the house roused him to fury. It was like a cancer; he was afraid lest it fasten on him and eat into his own flesh. Little London he abhorred. At the Country Club he saw Valeria seldom. They were like stars, each in its separate orbit, which had touched in a moment of truth and passed. Neither would forget the other, but there was nothing that permanently bound them together. He began cutting chapel, lying outside on the grass watching the clouds and listening to the pipe organ wheezing inside. The departing professors passed him with angry looks. He did not notice them, but lay drawn tight within himself, impenetrable. Through the daily class lectures he sat quietly but uninterested. His afternoon laboratory work he did lackadaisically and left early for home to read. Summer was coming, but he did not ask Mr. Ford to save him a job in the Santa Fe yards. In a mindless calm he wondered vaguely what had come upon him. Spring fever, he thought, unable to overcome his lassitude. Something was coming to a crisis.

Early one Friday morning in May he walked to school to take an important examination. Only the six major students of Dr. Thomason were taking it. The end of the school year was some weeks away; yet the students passing this test were promised immunity from the final examinations and approved applications to larger technical schools for teaching fellowships.

"Bring your slide rules and all the notes you want," Thomason had told them the day before. "It won't be necessary to write anything on your cuffs. Only don't talk among yourselves."

The professor was in his office when March arrived, and did not come out. He merely handed March a notebook as he walked into the basement laboratory. March sat down on a chair below a window. The other five students were scattered around him. The short, solid pillars of brick topped with immense slabs of slate had been cleared of apparatus. On them lay textbooks and lecture notes, engineering handbooks, and logarithm tables.

Where were the examination questions?

There were none. One of the men turned around to March. "Professor Thomason said we were simply to solve the circuit on the blackboard." It was the only word spoken.

The blackboard on two sides of the room was covered with a drawing of one vast compound electrical circuit. At first glance it seemed to begin with a generating plant, run to a main switchboard through several circuit-breakers, and thence to an amazing network that seemed to contain every problem March had encountered during his three years' work. A devil of a mess!

March leaned back in his chair. There was no hurry; they had four hours. He was not sure, but he believed that he could work it out. Still, he did not begin.

Staring at the generator diagram, he remembered the old steam plant east of town he had visited, the whirling drums cutting the lines of force in the magnetized rims to generate the power drawn off from the plant to supply the town. Was this the source of power? No, because the drums had to be set whirling by steam from the old boiler. What made it go? Coal. What was the nature of coal, the inherent power of fuel itself, deriving from the enormous pressures of earth and time? The beds of coal were simply great forests that had been washed out upon the plains and covered with sediment from crumbled, vanished mountains. And the life of these forests—It all went back to a beginning no one knew. This was merely an industrial application of the one sacred power of life that flowed through everything that lived and breathed, the stone, the blade of grass, beast and bird and man. The Great Spirit, stripped of its divinity and mechanically employed only for monetary gain in a materialistic civilization.

Lazing in his chair, March could see the bleak future spreading out before him. A big technical school. Years of work in more basement laboratories. Degrees. Then with a doctorate his priestly initiation into the cult of Science. Why, in time he might concoct a tidy little theory himself and be acclaimed a genius. March was vaguely aware that just as there were but few true artists, there were also pitifully few real scientists. Like Thomason the rest of them were merely industrial engineers. Their consciousness did not deepen with the perception of nature and her laws; they were mastered by their own machines. They believed they were geniuses, forgetting that genius is the power of evoking life, not throttling it. It was the love of truth, the love of life, that led to pure science. But these men were interested only in the application of science to commercial ends. They were industrialists.

March felt this strongly enough, if not clearly, to realize fully for the first time he could never give up life for industry. He was on the wrong trail, and spring was pounding in his blood an aching restlessness that no longer could be denied. He could see out the window, on a level with his head, a single clump of grass sticking up against the cloudless blue and shouting all the mystery of his youth.

Spring, the wanton hussy! Who has not smelled the perfume of her passing, heard the rustle of her skirts when the apple blossoms flutter to the ground and the rain flicks against the window pane, seen her steps in the long black furrows behind the plow? But who knows her? In all of vast America she is never twice the same.

It is Corpus Cristi in the little Mexican settlements, when the people stream out from Mass and kneel chanting in the rock street before doorways hung with evergreens. Good Friday and Easter, the time when the *Penitentes* come out from a *morada* and straggle up a remote arroyo, lashing their naked backs with whips of cactus, to hang a limp member on a cross. It is San Juan Day when all the waters of the world are blessed, and old grandmothers creep out in the dawn to bathe their flabby, wrinkled bodies in the muddy creek; when exactly at four o'clock it rains.

It is Holy Cross Day at Taos when the Indian races are run, the men and boys giving back with bursts of speed their energy to the sun who will return it again to mankind; when at San Felipe the green corn dance is held on the bank of the swollen Rio Grande, a hundred old men singing to the beat of a belly drum while 300 dancers stomp the dusty plaza from sunup till sundown. Over Cochiti and Zuni, cliff-high Acoma, the white-bellied clouds gather, and the thunder cracks open the gates of sky.

Here in the high hinterland of America the snowcaps shrink on the peaks, the water pours down canyons to three seas, the anemones push sturdily erect through snow. But now come the late and heavy snows. The freshly budded lilacs bend and break. Paper ice forms over lake and pond. Wild ducks drop from the mists into the marshes. A lone robin chirps disconsolately underneath a bush. The running sap congeals on the spruce bark into hard globules of chewing gum.

Fickle spring! A blizzard one day and a dry gritty wind the next. A vast and slow birth with horrible travail. All aboard behind the snowplow for the first ride to the summit of Pike's Peak! The high passes begin to open: La Veta, Hoosier, Rabbit Ear, Monarch, Tennessee, Whiskey, Slumgullion, and Mosquito. The little mining towns watch for the first train in, muttering incoherently of fresh vegetables. Now the road crews hit the ball. Avalanches make all trains late. The D&RG is stuck again.

The shaggy bear leaves his den, the deer climb higher and rub the moss-growth from their prongs. Who sees the wild geese, hears the woodpecker, for the bitterness, the sweetness, the wracking birth pangs of spring?

It is a state of mind, a wordless cry, a resurrection, misery and hope sharped and flatted by the wailing winds. Above all, it is a tormenting unrest, a wild passion to hit the lonely trail over the last horizon into the forever unknown and unknowable, wearing a single upright feather – not defiantly as men flaunt the faded cockades of their decadent heritage, but proudly, like the everlasting insignia of the wild earth's nobility.

An hour had passed. March rose, wrote his name in the empty notebook and laid it on the table. Without stopping at Dr. Thomason's office, he walked out and crossed the campus to the Administration Building. At the cashier's window he collected twenty-two dollars due him for work as a laboratory assistant. He was supposed to turn it in at the next window as payment on his tuition. Instead, he jammed the money in his pocket and walked slowly home.

The two girls were in school. Ona was over at the grocery store. Rogier was lying on the sofa, and Mrs. Rogier was dusting. March went upstairs and packed his leather-rimmed canvas duffle bag. Before long his mother came hurriedly up the stairs.

"What's the matter, son? Home this time of day! Are you sick?" She suddenly saw the duffle bag. Her glance swept the bare top of his dresser and the empty hooks inside the closet, flew back wildly to his face.

"Don't get upset, Mother," he said quietly, standing before her. "I've quit school, and I'm leaving home. Sit down, Mother."

He pushed her down gently on the bed, sat beside her and put his arm over her shoulders.

"You're mad, son. Mad!" she gasped. And yet there was something in his quiet tone, assurance and unusual gentleness that sent a chill up her spine.

He explained patiently as best he could. "And so you see, Mother, it's no place for me. I'd got all I could out of it a year ago, but never knew it till now – Don't look so! Wouldn't I be leaving soon anyway to go to work? We're poorer now than ever with Grandad the way he is. You'll be needing the money I can send you."

"But where are you going? God in Heaven, boy!"

"The Wyoming oil fields, Mother. There's a big boom on. Work for everyone."

"What kind? What can a boy do? It's a wild goose chase, son.

Be sensible. Don't leave yet."

She knew it was futile talk. The moment had come that she had dreaded and waited for, day by day, ever since he had gone to Cripple Creek. Tom, Rogier, Cable, and now her son, her only son! How could she repeat now the pain and anguish, her protestations of love and affirmations of faith, go through that scene of parting in which she had participated nights on end? It was like a play she had rehearsed for years, and now at the rise of the curtain she found herself tongue-tied and frozen. Only the pain stabbing her heart was real.

Indomitably she stood up and wiped away a tear as if ashamed of that single priceless pearl formed within her years before by the tiny grit of her first fear. "Well, son!" She grasped him sturdily by the shoulders, her big heavy body hard as stone, her square jaws clenched. "So you're really goin'. Well!"

If she'd only wept or stormed or something! Anything but this slow fusing of despair and strength, a tear and a smile – this Rogier undemonstrativeness! It was more than the boy could bear. He flung his arms around her, stroked back her graying hair, kissed her beautifully white, girlish smooth face.

"I'll be comin' back soon. Hell! Sure I will!"

"I'll be fixin' up a few things for you," she answered simply and walked head up into her room.

March told Leona and Nancy good-bye when they came home for lunch, answering their joshing with quiet grins. Mrs. Rogier was perplexed but loyal. "It beats all how things happen. But I count on my boys every time. Just remember you're a Rogier, March!"

For Mary Ann and Uncle John he left a note. But when he went to bid his grandfather farewell, something hard and bitter within him dissolved in a sudden glow of pride and compassion. Rogier, lying on the sofa, stood up: bent over, both hands clutching his truss.

"Don't stand up for me Grandad!" March cried, cut to the quick.

Rogier, wincing with pain, adjusted his contraption and straightened up to grasp the boy by the arms. His white head barely reached March's shoulder.

"I just want to tell you I'm leavin'," March stammered.

The old man had snapped out of his usual haze; his eyes were clear, his voice resolute. "I heard you at the table. And boy, I think it's good. Every tub's got to stand on its own bottom." He paused, as if trying to dig out from the shaft of a collapsed memory at least a specimen of pay dirt. "Minin' you say? No, not minin'. But you're diggin' in, hey!" He dug futilely in his empty pants pockets. "Dom, boy! I hate to see you leavin' without a cent. If things had panned out different –"

"Grandad!" The boy caught him to breast, this shrunken bag of bones, and over his head cried to all the years behind and those ahead, "Grandad, everything I know about mining, construction, geology, and all that, I got from you. I won't forget it, ever. Or you, Grandad! Ever!"

He grabbed up his duffle bag, kissed Ona for the last time, and ran out the door. Walking swiftly to the station, he felt the sadness lifting from him. He was alone and free at last! The world lay immense and naked before him.

He had turned his back forever upon college without gratitude, shame, or regret for his wasted opportunities and the unlocked doors he'd never entered. But when he stood for the last time in the Santa Fe railroad station, he knew this would always be his Alma Mater. These were the classrooms where he had learned the lessons of life: the great waiting room in which he had shouted his newspapers, the Fred Harvey newsstand in which he had polished apples, the huge baggage room where he had wrestled loads of trunks, the grimy little freight office down in the yards. It was a coeducational institution, of course. Look at the Misses Fred Harvey majoring in – should we say home economics? – or coffee and pie? Dining Room juniors and seniors in starched all-white. Not a frowsy head among them at six a.m.

He could remember his campus in starlight: the Upper Yards and Middle Pass Pocket and the Lower Yards. He knew it instinctively as on the dark night he was caught between Lower Four and Main Two, with twenty seconds to reach, unlock, and throw the switch for a cattle train. And the hot steam spouting like geysers, the red-bellied furnaces of the 4400's and the shriek of the great steel cats racing around the bend. The slippery roofs of jolting freights on a rainy night and the cold grab irons – these were his athletic field and gymnasium. "By God, you made it! I thought when she hit the turn you was a goner!"

His Technical Advisor, the Yard Master, knew both practice and theory; in a pinch he could replace a broken driving rod, swearing with the best. His Dean of Men, the Station Master, spouted no sanctimonious quotations from the Bible, but he knew the vagaries of men and women. And his President, the Station Agent, Mr. Ford, had fired him twice but still slapped him on the back.

Change, change, change. The constant, ever-flowing movement of life that changes all things. This was what he had learned here, the stage and the institution created by the phenomenon of the great American unrest. Just as he had learned at Shallow Water and Cripple Creek its dual counterpoint: the verities that lay embodied within the hub of time, the core of life itself. And there came over him again the mystery of his own being: Am I the leaf that falls into the flow or the leaf that sprouts anew; the rock disintegrated by time or the timeless dust within the rock?

A whistle sounded. The train swept round the bend, clanged in with hissing jets. "Come on, Mister Cable, before you miss it."

"Aw, say, Les!" he protested, grabbing futilely at his duffle bag. "I'll tote this damn thing, Quit your kiddin'!"

But it was Old Les who stuffed it aboard the smoker and came back to join the men gathered around March, joshing, shaking his hand.

"He'll never get away! From force of habit he'll be jumpin' off at the water tower!"

"Don't spend all your money on the girls!"

Behind all the rude jocularity March could sense a deep good will, the farewell of men to one who could never outgrow them, succeed to a niche higher than it was their lot to attain, but always remain, as he once was, a comrade of their stature, no better and sometimes less than they.

But now the stop was up; the platform was almost empty. The Station Master left the gate.

"Well, son," he said simply and directly, sticking out his hand. "I'm wishin' you good luck. We've had our squabbles and they're forgotten. When you get to sittin' in a fine big office with secretaries and such, or somethin' else, don't forgit us and how you used to bust through these gates bulgin' with suitcases. And when you come back, big and important, remember us boys will be glad to see you."

With this baccalaureate sermon echoing in his ears and heart, March swung on board. He found his seat. And pressing his nose and clouded eyes against the window pane, he saw dimly from the high trestle over Bijou that Shook's Run and the ramshackle old house were passing irretrievably by.

In the middle of the street stood an old white-headed man with his arm upraised, and beside him a woman waving her handkerchief.

Behind them, their eternal background and his, stood Pike's Peak.

2

Rogier, still wearing his truss to hold his rupture in place but vehemently refusing to carry a cane, limped around house and yard like a man bound by invisible hobbles. His white hair, thin as corn silk, hung down in sparse strands to his stiff white collar – still fastened by his diamond button and worn without a necktie. His powerful body had shrunk to a bag of sticks draped in coat and pants that hung on him in folds; he looked like a scarecrow. He had lost most of his teeth and lived on mush, French toast, and sweet potatoes. His spells were infrequent and mild, often lasting but a few minutes. He did not read, being content to sit out in the sunshine or on the high stool in his shop. He gave no trouble at all.

This was the pathetic and sometimes ludicrous caricature to which had been reduced the proud yet humble and always indomitable "Colonel" Joseph Rogier as viewed by his family, the neighbors, and the children who occasionally jeered at him and his backyard mine across the fence.

Rogier did not mind if he ever noticed them. For after a lifetime of work and worry, success and abysmal failures, and the loss of his few old friends, he had come at last to the threshold of his greatest discovery.

Like something risen from the depths of dreamless sleep to the horizon of wakeful consciousness, without clear outline yet embodying the substance of a hope and meaning as strangely familiar as it was vague – thus had he first glimpsed it years before, believing it was that high snowy Peak which had drawn and held him like a lodestone he could not escape. Into its granite depths he had drilled and blasted toward its glowing heart, the luminescent sun, the golden flower of life. But now, sitting in the afternoon sun, he stared at the Peak without seeming to see it objectively manifested before him. It was where it had always been – inside him.

He could see it when he sat in the shop on rainy days, down in the basement on winter evenings, in bed at night. Daylight and darkness meant little to him now. For if at intervals he was consciously bright as a silver dollar just struck from the Denver mint, most of the time he lived in that curious realm between dreamless sleep and wakeful consciousness; as if becalmed in that immeasurable interval between two breaths when the mind is stilled and the mysterious faculty of intuition bridges the gap between the tyrannical reasoning of the finite mind and the all-embracing comprehension of an infinite and universal consciousness. In that pellucid dusk everything was all one to him now; success and failure, sloth and ambition, poverty and riches, acclaim and derision, all merged into one indivisible whole. The great snowy Peak itself was no longer a friend to be coerced, an enemy to be combatted. It was like himself, a material shell, a transient symbol. What its purpose and meaning was, or his own, he could not yet read clearly. He no longer anticipated its taking shape as faintly colored, fish-shaped petals slowly revolving around a yellow-bright center as if trying to arrange themselves into the pattern of a great golden flower. Being timeless it was also formless; and he was content to accept it as it was.

No, Rogier gave no trouble at all. Ona did not worry about him. But in bed at night she worried about March. Leona she loved and understood. But always at sight of March's dark, sensitive, and stubborn face, her soul had streamed out to him as if she had been pierced with a knife. And yet she had never been able to touch him. There was between them a curious and imperceptible barrier. In him the ghost of Cable prowled. Not the careless, gentle husband, the casual companion of her days. But the lover, the soft sensuous flow that had enshrouded her in a mindless passion, the subtle awareness her analytical mind could never fathom. He was the wildness of the night to which she succumbed so completely, but from which next morning she shrank as if in terror. In him was intuition, not reason; cruelty, not coldness. He was the eternal stranger who had appeared from nowhere, made her his, and departed swiftly, silently, still unknown.

He is my son, my only son, she thought, and yet to me he is a stranger. It is a strange thing and a bitter thing, but true. Boné of my bone, flesh of my flesh, he is closer to me than was my husband. And yet I cannot touch him. For in the immense and lasting loneliness of their separate selves, it is given to a man and woman to meet, to touch, and break away. And a woman ever after would reach out her hand to her son and draw her husband back again, who is forever gone. And this cannot be. So he is a stranger.

Why this strange and bitter thing? she wondered, listening for the comforting steps of the Kadles in the darkness. He is his father's coarse straight hair, his black bottomless eyes, and his slim straight body and strange living awareness. But he is also the fruit of my womb. To him I was the tree of life; my sap runs in his veins, he is a limb torn from me, whole. I know my son! I know him as no woman, no man will, ever. But because I see myself in him, and no one can believe it is herself she sees, I see him always a stranger.

"Damn him! He treats me like a squaw!" she cried to herself in bitter loneliness, knowing that it was the shame and hurt, the pride and glory of every mother to be treated like a squaw by her son.

"But where is he, and what in God's name can he be doing all this time?" she cried to the Kadles making their nocturnal rounds.

Infrequent, short, scrawled notes from him began to arrive. He was in the Salt Creek oil fields of Wyoming, working as a roustabout or day laborer in a gang laying six miles of eight-inch pipe. Like Cripple Creek, Salt Creek was a place-name for an immense oil structure that included many fields: Big Muddy, Poison Spider, Lost Soldier, Crook's Gap, Teapot, and Salt Creek. He himself lived in a construction camp not far from Lavoye, a squatter camp that reminded him of early Cripple Creek with its squatters' shanties, drab wooden stores, company commissaries, and dance halls. The work was hard, but the food was good and the pay fair: fifty cents an hour, with a dollar and a half subtracted for meals and the use of a bunk. Enclosed was a money order.

Mary Ann sniffed at the small amount. "At least he's showing a sense of responsibility!" Next day she mailed him a box of candy.

That fall postcards came from Malott and Okanogan, Washington in the Columbia River valley, where March was picking apples. One weekend he had gone up to Canada. The immense valley did not appeal to him. It had been formed by glacial action; he was a Leo, a sun-child, preferring a country of volcanic origin.

Ona sighed. "A sun-child! Of all things! Where could he have got that zodiacal notion except from Daddy?!" She settled down for a long wait, knowing that he was heading south.

His Christmas card came from Oregon, where he was working at a timber mill. Ona did not know just where; the postmark was blurred.

And now came no word from him at all.

March, still working slowly through the vast immensities and lonely little towns heaving gently on the back of the sleeping earth-monster of America, felt his mind go numb, his soul expand into space. There rushed through him again the rich flow of life he had known as a child – a tempestuous rush of sensory impressions undefined and unconstrained. And ever he could hear the aimless ancient winds cry hauntingly to him with the voices of his father's people:

Brother, where do you go now in the new moccasins of manhood, with a brave heart, and a lean and hungry look?

Brothers, his heart answered, I do not know. I have known the short-grass plains of my father's people, the Cheyennes, the Kiowas, the Blue Cloud Arapahoes. I have seen the great male Rockies where Buckskin Charley and his Utes pitched their smoke-gray lodges, the cold campfires of the mighty Sioux, the buffalo grounds of the Crows, the sacred Wallowa of the people with pierced noses, the Nez Perce. Old and familiar are the *hogans* of the Navajos, the mud-brown terraced towns of the Pueblos, and cliff-high Acoma with those of the mesa-top Hopis. New to my moccasins are the deserts of the Shoshones and Piutes, the baking river valley of the Cocopahs and those giant, naked war-clubbers, the Mojaves. Now I am come to *Apacheria,* the barren parched rock mountains of the Apaches. Where my trail leads I do not know. I have forgotten what I seek.

And around his solitary campfires the ancient aimless winds cried back derisively: Break your own trail, brother! We work for no man nor people!

That spring March reached the Mexican border. It was a separate country unmarked on any map. On one side the United States with its rabid commercialism and industrialization, its plumbing and stock markets. On the other, Old Mexico with its pride and poverty, its obduracy to change. The border was neither, but a world between; the last frontier. It was a chasm a thousand miles long, whose deepest sink-holes were the towns – Tia Juana, Tecate, Mexicali, Algodones, Nogales, Naco, Agua Prieta, Juarez – into which poured all the vices and perversions, the brutality and cruelty, the tailings of both races.

Bars and cabarets, *cantinas* and *casinos.* Chinese lottery counters, *refresqueria* stands on the corners, *taco* venders carrying their tables on their heads. Phonographs blasting from every doorway, stacks of sugar cane, strips of drying meat, and tubs of guts in open meat stalls beclouded with flies. A Packard limousine and a burro loaded with firewood; brown bare feet and high French heels treading the dust of Mexico's infinite dryness. Ragged *pelados,* somber old señoras wrapped to the eyes in black *rebozos.* Forty dollar panama hats and silver braided, high peaked *sombreros.* French champagne, Spanish sherry, and Portuguese port; and in the mud floor drinking dens raw *mezcal* and cheap *tequila.* Pigs rooting in the *plaza;* a guitar whining "La Paloma." The stench of beer, the acrid smell of urine in the dry dust – A thousand screaming contradictions resolved into the harmonic whole.

And the faces he saw! The arrogant faces of strutting fat Mexican generals and their scrawny mistresses, the red faces of bluff Anglo cattle ranchers and rustlers, the white anemic faces of American politicians and those of obsequiously polite Mexicans who aped with equal greed and cunning their American neighbors' "Beeg Business" methods. And in the sputter of *ocote* torches the evil faces of petty criminals of both countries, the cruel masks of the half-breeds, the disintegrated faces of the *peones* deprived of their land, the yellow faces of Chinese long run out of Arizona and now being driven from Sonora, the cheap powdered faces of prostitutes from rows of open cribs, the pock-marked diseased faces of beggars, the hopeless faces of decadent Indians sprawled in a stupor in the gutters or asleep on the steps of the cathedral.

And all these faces, so dark and haunting by night and so timelessly imprinted in his memory by the hard glitter of the sun, resolved into one face in which he glimpsed the mystery and howling terror of its single soul. It was the savage fusion of two blood streams, the white and the red. It was the clamorous cry of the mixed-blood – the *mestizos, ladinos, creoles, coyotes.* Here he was staring into the racial soul of mixed-blood America. And as if in a mirror, he saw the violence, the mystery, the dark beauty of his own soul. He too was a mixed-blood. He loved it and hated it, and he felt at home.

Wandering from town to town in crowded auto stages, sleeping in lodging houses and four-bit throws, and eating where he could, March wound up at Nogales. Here he became friends with John Bratling, head bartender of the "Cave" on the south side of the Line. The Cave was a new *cantina* built into the rocky side of the hill. It formerly had been the Mexican jail, and the small rocky cells from which the iron latticed doors had been removed now served as private dining rooms. The cabaret was large and beautiful, boasting the finest food and wines available. The barroom in front was long and narrow, with a sawdust floor. Despite its tacky appearance, it was a famous rendezvous.

Bratling was a suave, polished Englishman ruined by the war, who had put to work his knowledge of wines and liquors, and was obliged to live in this dry desert climate for his health. He knew every man worth knowing on both sides of the Line – Mexican generals, immigration and railroad officials, engineers, bankers, politicians, gamblers, and owners of the big ranches south. He also knew their first names and their favorite drinks, a memory worth a fortune to the Cave. He had only one failing. For months he neither smoked nor drank, he kept reasonable hours, and he saved money for his one wish – a walking trip through Italy. Then one day, without warning, he would go on a "high lonesome:" locking himself in his room and drinking himself into a delirium until he was carried to the hospital.

He lived in a ramshackle hotel, the Santa Caterina, where most of the dealers and entertainers had rooms. Off duty at midnight they gathered in his room to talk until morning. March visited with them often. It was a strange Bohemia that flowered then for once and always, and which was to remain with March as a never-to-be-forgotten fantasy of his youth.

One night Bratling asked him abruptly, "March, what kind of work are you doing down here?"

"I'm a malaria control engineer."

Jose, an ecarte dealer, laughed. "A mosquito chaser!"

March nodded glumly. He knew his payroll title merely glossed the job of draining irrigation ditches and swampy fields of stagnant water.

Bratling said simply, "We ought to be able to do better than that for you, March. Eh. Jose?"

Jose eloquently spread out his beautiful, narrow hands. He was a *mestizo*. His face was the color of *café con leche*, with high cheek bones and full lobed ears from which dangled long turquoise ear-drops. He wore gray gaberdine shirts with mother-of-pearl buttons, and black string ties. He was on duty from five until midnight, and was paid twenty-five dollars a day. While dealing he never recognized a friend, never spoke. When March came to his table to place his $2 bet, Jose allowed him to play until he had won enough to buy a good dinner. If March persisted in playing, Jose broke him flat.

Now for a month Jose in his room had been trying to teach him to deal. Jose was a born dealer. He could shuffle a deck with either hand; deal six hands of poker rapidly face down, and then call out each card in each hand; he could deal from top and bottom too adroitly for March to observe; could palm a card; and lay down any hand March could order, as if it came out naturally from the deck. That the cards were marked seemed impossible until Jose showed him how they came so in sealed packages from the manufacturers. Yet there was more to it than craftsmanship; something that made Jose one of the best dealers along the border and that prevented March from ever becoming the worst.

Jose had put it bluntly at last. "It just ain't in you, kid. You got guts although you're too stubborn. You got a flat face, and you could get your hands in shape with glycerine. But you just ain't got the feel of cards in your bones. So lay off. You ain't cut out that way."

Three days later Bratling sent word to March to come to the Cave that evening. When March arrived, he saw a party of Americans celebrating in the cabaret. Heading the group was a portly man named James Finnerty – Vice-President in Charge of Operations of Western Mines, Incorporated. At least once a year, said Bratling, Finnery came down for a spree, leaving it to him to provide food, liquor, entertainment, and plenty of girls. "We're good friends," added Bratling, "so speak up when you meet him."

A few minutes later when Finnerty came out to the bar, Bratling introduced March. "This is the young man I was telling you about, Mr. Finnerty. It seems to me that Western Mines ought to have a place somewhere for an ambitious young fellow."

"Shurtinly!" mumbled the Vice-President, putting down his fourth Martini. "Lots of mines, good mines, all over the worl' – I want some more lil' onions, John, on lil' sticks – What'd I say, sir?"

"You were telling me what an extended corporation Western Mines is sir," answered March, "and how you needed trained men all over the world."

Finnerty blinked. "Technical school trainin'? Minin'?"

"Colorado. Cripple Creek."

"Hmm." Finnerty's small eyes steadied. He was worth his salt, for despite the flush suffusing his face and his thick tongue, he was wary and cautious. "I don't hire men. No shure! Got an Employment Supervisor. College professors send him their kids. You go to him. Maybe he can use a young engineer in one of our copper pits on the Sonora boundary. Hey? Tell him Finnerty sent you."

"Perhaps a note from you would help, Mr. Finnerty," said Bratling, laying a pencil and paper in front of him. "And here's another Martini. Not quite so dry, sir; you mustn't spoil your dinner."

When Finnerty had ambled back to his crowd, Bratling winked at March. "Hold on to that note, boy! It's a ticket right into the payroll of Western Mines. How much railroad fare are you going to need?"

3

Familiar only with the deep hard-rock mines of Cripple Creek, March thought the Copper Boy the damndest looking hole he'd ever seen. It wasn't a mine, really. Western Mines had simply sliced off the top of a hill with a butter knife and was dipping out spoonsful of reddish sugar rich in copper. But the spoons were huge steam-driven buckets that travelled on railway tracks around and around the great open pit in concentric circles which descended deeper year by year.

This immense pit, surrounded by company offices, shops, tool-houses, and railroad sheds, lay on the backbone of a narrow parched-brown range which rose out of the desert like an immense gila-monster turned into stone.

To the south, on the barren dove-gray plain from which rose the smoke-blue Sierra Madre, lay the Mexican town of Dos Ritos – a single dusty street lined with *cantinas, casinos,* cribs, and squalid adobes.

To the north, lining a narrow steep-walled gulch, sprawled the American town of Piedras Blancas. About desert mining camps there was always the feeling of hopeless, hard dreariness, as if the land had gone dead. So it was with Piedras Blancas. Even the big Copper Boy Hotel, built by Western Mines to accommodate its occasional guests, held a look of careless abandon despite its old-fashioned, ornate architecture. The one lively spot in town was Mother Brenet's boarding house, where March roomed and boarded. The dining room sat fifty men at a meal. The long oilcloth table at night supported huge bowls of vegetable soup, platters of roast beef, loaves of French sour bread, vegetables, stewed fruit, two kinds of pie, and gingerbread cake. The charge per meal was forty cents.

At work March found that a junior engineer was a jack-of-all-trades who did everything but fill his superior's pipe. He trudged along with the timekeeper and crew bosses, was ordered out of the shops and roundhouses, was found in the way of the assayers, tried to check car loadings and compute tonnage. His little successes were attributed to "fool's luck" and his inexperience was the excuse for loading him with a thousand distasteful jobs.

"Here, Cable, work out these figures for me, will you? It'll give you good experience."

"It might pay you, March, to come back on your own time and spend a few evenings on this. I feel you ought to know what these reports include."

Jackson, the superintendent of the camp, was a typical company official. He wore shiny boots, whipcord trousers, and a large Stetson. He and his wife lived at the hotel and spent their evenings playing bridge.

The chief engineer was an old bowlegged Scotchman named MacGregor. He was a bachelor, and despite his large salary lived in a small company cottage which he kept neat as a pin. Mac wore an old wrinkled suit, flannel shirt, and a black bow tie sewed on a rubber band.

Between them existed an unexpressed antipathy. The cause for it March understood one evening when he had dinner with the Morrels in their cottage. They were plain, homey people. Morrel was the chief clerk, an excellent man but without the technical training and personality that might have made him outstanding in the company.

"Yep, that's what it takes to get along in this company —

politics and personality," he explained. "Take the boss, Jackson. He runs the whole camp—payroll, production, all that. But he doesn't know a whoop about mining. He doesn't have to. Just look at our reports, the same standard forms for every one of Western Mines' holdings. And the mines are no different. Look at the Copper Boy. The old-timers took all the chances. And when the thing proved good, the ore all blocked out, Western Mines bought it for a song. All they had to do then was haul out ore according to its market price. It might be a factory, a chain grocerystore – anything. It just happens that it's ore the company deals in.

"All the selling, buying, transportation, milling, hiring is done for all mines in the General Office. The superintendents are like store managers: men who know the company policies and routines, and see they're followed to a T. And the fellow that gets the job is the politician.

"But on every job technical problems come up. Too expensive for the General Engineering Office to send out a man each time. So they have an old-time mining man directly handling the removal of ore – Mac here, for instance. He knows his stuff and gets a good salary, but he reports to Jackson and will never get any higher.

"Do you catch on? Imagine Mac dressed up, playing bridge, entertaining company directors and visiting stockholders at the hotel! So the Office has Jackson. He's got personality. Look at those boots and hat! The Romantic Engineer in the Wilds of Arizona. Do the New Yorkers eat that up? You ought to hear the ladies!"

"Now, now!" remonstrated Mrs. Morrel.

Morrel laughed and refilled his pipe. "Keep all this under your hat, March. You're a bright young chap and I'd like to see you get along. I've seen too many young engineers just out from school, thinking that technical training is all they need. It isn't. So here's my advice. Forget all this stuff about the brave engineer conquering nature. Mining is a business now, like any other. It's the stock market that rules the game. Learn all you can from Mac; he thinks a lot of you. But for Pete's sake, boy, play up to the Boss. Jackson's the man who'll make or break you. Drop over to the hotel where the officials stay and make yourself agreeable. And when Finnerty brings down a big party for another 'inspection' trip across the Line, you bust a gut to be included!"

March walked home slowly in the moonlight. Below him, like a sea beating against a rock, lay the unbroken chaparral desert. What would that ruined old man, his grandfather, have thought of Morrel's exposition on mining? And how strange it was, March thought, that he was now caught in what he had tried to escape.

Months later he was reminded of it when Finnerty arrived with a large group of company officials and stockholders on a tour of inspection. Piedras Blancas drew a deep breath and stood at attention. The hotel was scrubbed and polished, the Copper Boy put in apple-pie order. Jackson stalked around with a fixed and oily grin on his face.

For two days the party went over plant and pit. On the third day, during which the men held conferences and read reports, the women were driven on a sight-seeing tour over the Border to Dos Ritos. March was one of the drivers of the company cars. He had shined his own boots, put on a necktie, and did his best to be agreeable.

"Now, Mr. Cable, be sure and stop when we get to the border. I want to say I stood with one foot in America and the other in Mexico – No? Isn't there a line drawn on the ground or something? Well, I declare! All the country looks the same. It ought to be different!"

"So you can speak Spanish, Big Boy! You gay young dog! Now I know where you spend your time. How about showing me a Place – you know, the kind our husbands hit for when we're not along? I'll bet these little Mexican cuties can really shake it up!"

March managed to get them back to the hotel in time for the banquet to which all of the engineers, clerks, and their wives were invited, the laborers having been given the afternoon off. Finnerty and Jackson were talking on the front steps when he drove up.

"Oh, James!" screamed Mrs. Finnerty who had been in the party. "We've had the loveliest time. We had Lombardi cocktails at the Foreign Club. Pink. In tall glasses. Young Mr. Cable here ordered them for us. Do you know him?"

Finnerty blinked.

"You probably don't remember me, Mr. Finnerty," said March, "but you gave me a note in Nogales during your last business trip."

"Yes, yes," recollected Finnerty. "I see you got your job.

How's he doing, Jackson?"

"Developing nicely, sir!" spoke up Jackson, turning to March with a sudden air of cordiality. "I didn't know you had met our Vice-President, March."

The boy detected a sting in his remark. "Mr. Jackson has given me the run of the place, Mr. Finnerty. I appreciate his changing me about."

Both smiled; Jackson in a peevish temper had lately handed him over to Mac.

Politics! March grinned as he drove off.

After the banquet Finnerty and Jackson drew him aside. "Ah - March - ah," began Jackson. "I've told Mr. Finnerty you might be the one to do us a great favor. Your wide acquaintance across the Line – escapades one might say – Tut, tut! my boy. Only natural. And they have never interfered with your work."

"Hell!" said Finnerty. "Speak out! We're all grown up, eh, Cable?"

"In short," went on Jackson, "Mr. Finnerty wants to give his guests a stag party before they return to New York. A touch of the border, of Mexico."

"You know John in Nogales, Cable. That's the kind of a party I want. The real stuff!" demanded Finnerty. "A hell of a good meal with lots to drink, entertaining, and plenty of girls. Get me?"

March nodded.

Jackson resumed. "Mrs. Jackson and I, with my staff members and their wives, are entertaining the ladies at bridge while their husbands are away. Mr. Finnerty gives you a clean bill as far as expense goes. If you can arrange it, take tomorrow off and the next day also."

"I'll do what I can," March replied soberly.

"Fine!" said Jackson. "We trust you implicitly. I'll have a voucher cashed for you tomorrow morning, and meet all bills beyond that."

The party began at nine o'clock in *El Zorro Azul* on the single dusty street of Dos Ritos. When Finnerty and his men arrived the bar was empty save for a group of Mexican army officers March had invited. The night was warm, the stars hung low over the chaparral, and down the street they could hear the hoof beats of an occasional horse. The men drank as most Americans drink across the border: hastily, gulping one after another. Then, faces flushed, they gathered in the back room.

The table was already set on the polished dance floor, lighted candles glowing on the white cloth. On a plank dais behind, four musicians dressed in gaudy *charro* costumes were thumbing their guitars. On one side of the room stood a long buffet stacked with liquor bottles, trays, and glasses. Around it stood a group of Mexican girls dressed in cheap evening gowns, their black hair freshly oiled, and their dark faces splotched with white powder. The Mexican officers nodded to them casually without showing undue familiarity, but Finnerty stopped at the door in amazement.

"Jesus Christ! What's this – a formal dinner? I told you I wanted a stag party."

March nodded at Lola, who had supplied the girls for him. She grabbed Finnerty by the arm. "Come weeth me. A leetle drink, *verdad*? I show you!"

She sprinkled some salt on her left hand in the hollow between thumb and forefinger, and with one quick motion adeptly smeared it over her gums. Then she tossed down a jigger of white liquor, and noisily sucked a slice of lemon. *"Puro Mexicano, no?"*

"Tequila! That's how you drink it, boys! Watch me!" shouted Finnerty.

Now they all stood poking salt in their mouths and sucking lemons like children. The strong cactus brandy, on top of the many cocktails they had taken out front, was beginning to shake them loose from their shamefaced air of restraint. Even the corpulent, uniformed *generales* began to unbend. The girls, observed March, were behaving nicely. Their full breasts shook as they laughed, and they took no offense when a hand negligently slapped them across the bottoms.

Ceferino announced dinner. But there were chairs only for the men.

"Dinner without the ladies? It isn't fair!" sputtered one of the men, who had his arm around one of the girls. "What're you going to do, honey?"

For answer she undid a button, drew down her dress. A laugh went up. She stood before them in dancing trunks, shoes, and stockings. "Damn me! They're entertainers. Here, Cutie, let me help you out of yours!"

The dinner, served to music and dancing, was superb; fresh shrimp from Guaymas, *guaycamole* salad, venison cutlets surrounded by quail; and scattered along the table by way of novelty, fried beans, *enchiladas*, and *tortillas*. Wines of course, Spanish and Portuguese, duty free.

All restraint ebbed. The *generales* were gorging on the free feast, cursing fluently in Spanish the waiter who did not keep their plates and glasses filled. The New Yorkers clapped and yelled for the girls, pulling them on laps to feed tidbits while feeling a knee or breast.

Finnerty, seated at the head of the table with March on his right, kept slapping the boy on the back. "By God, boy! As good a party as John ever got up, and at half the expense. Western Mines won't forget you. No shure!" On his lap sat a girl in a worn black velvet dress, to whom he was giving champagne. She had slapped on his head an orchestra player's huge sombrero. Whenever he tried to kiss her, she yanked the brim down over his eyes and punched him jokingly in the ribs.

Now the fun began. More men jumped up from table and ran to join a group surrounding a girl in the far corner. "Hot damn! *Carramba!* Give us the works!" Someone tossed a dollar at her feet. She took off her shoes. With a clatter of more silver on the floor, she took off stockings and brassiere. The men went wild.

A fat general sitting next to March said quietly, *"Estan hecho los zorrillos, no?"*

March was not too drunk on wine and Finnerty's praise to appreciate the play on words. *El Zorro Azul* meant in English "The Blue Fox," and its drunken and drowsy guests could rightly be regarded as acting like *zorros* or foxes. The general instead had changed the word to *zorillos,* skunks. March could not resent the insult to his own countrymen, nor could he ignore it. He mumbled quietly, *"Me hace uno el zorro"* – "I am pretending to be a fox and not to hear, *mi General*."

The tenor of the room began to change. It was now after midnight and drawn by the noise all the *pelados* and beggars of Dos Ritos were crowding into the bar hoping for a scrap of something to eat, a drink, or a piece of silver. Most of the Mexican officers had slipped out with their girls. Finnerty and his American guests were demanding from the remaining girls an all-nude chorus. The girls did not object to stripping, but were greedy for money and demanding $10 apiece.

In the midst of the hubbub March raised his eyes to see framed in the open window a face he would never forget. It was dark, somber, hard as flint, with a few black whiskers on the chin. The man's steady reptilian eyes were black as obsidian, timeless and fixed as the sierras themselves. His tattered straw hat was pushed back, a ragged splinter of coarse black hair lying on his forehead. Below his brown muscular throat his wrinkled dark hand was holding the corner of a *serape* up to his shoulder.

March knew the intent awareness that held the man there, unmoving. The smell of food and spilled wine, the sound of shouts, and the sight of naked flesh did not disturb him. His flinty eyes refuted them all with a blank indifference that held neither envy nor contempt, but was only a fixed negation.

Sight of him sobered March instantly. Once again he felt himself set between two worlds incomprehensible to each other.

But now there was another commotion. One of Finnerty's guests, a director of the company, was missing. March hurried out in back to a long courtyard lined on each side with cribs—narrow cell-like rooms above which were crudely lettered the girls' names, and in front of which were hammocks strung from a few tamarisks. In back stood an open sheet-iron *mingitorio* rankly smelling of urine.

Here, as he suspected, he found the bespectacled director shouting for help. He was backed against a wall, surrounded by a pack of *putas* clad only in dirty shifts. One of them, with a sweep of her hand, had jerked open his fly, tearing off the buttons. Another had yanked out his shirttail. The others were now massed to tear off his clothes and ransack his pockets.

March strode forward, jerked the man free by his collar, and flung the girls all the silver in his pocket. Then they fled out front.

The night was nearly spent. Down the dusty street pattered a burro laden with firewood. A coyote yapped from the hills. Dos Ritos seemed desolate and dwarfed as a scatter of ant hills on the plain. And against all this, enduring and unchanged under the glitter of the desert stars, only the few lights of the Blue Fox glared pitifully. In their glow a man was puking on the portal. The party was over.

4

Something was happening behind carved mahogany desks in a great spider city that shook Piedras Blancas in its far flung web. Stocks were falling on the New York Exchange, prices were tumbling, the bottom was dropping out of copper.

Jackson called March into his office. "March, there's no need to tell you what's going on. We've all been following it in the papers. Western Mines is letting men out all over the country. We're not going to close the Copper Boy. But we've got to shut down to a skeleton force until this Depression is over."

"I understand," said March.

"Not yet!" contradicted Jackson. "You're one of the youngest engineers on the payroll, and we're letting out others with more experience. But Mr. Finnerty—and myself!—think you're very promising material. So he offers you an alternative. Western Mines has an undeveloped silver property in the Mexican back country. One of our men is down there blocking out ore in case we can use Mexican silver. It's an out-of-the-way place. But if you want you can go down there and help him until we make a decision as to what should be done about it. My advice is to take it. It's an opportunity."

March agreed heartily and went home to get ready.

Next day Morrel took him to the auto stage that was to carry him to the train junction. "You're lucky, boy! The axe is chopping off everybody here. You know what your new job, is, don't you? A sentimental sop because you threw that drunken brawl for Finnerty. That's what you get for following my advice. Good luck! And when you get laid up with maleria, dysentery, and God knows what else, don't say I didn't warn you!"

Two mornings later March boarded the slow mix-train that crawled twice a week down the west coast of Mexico. He wore short boots, corduroy trousers, leather jacket, and a gray Stetson. All else he owned was packed in his duffle bag, chained and padlocked to the arm of his seat against the ever-present *rateros*.

The grimy plush seats were jammed with people, bags, and bundles. Dust blew in the windows; the toilet was a horror; and the aisles stank of green orange peelings, pink banana skins, and pomegranate rinds. The rank smell of spilled tequila mingled with the acrid smoke of hand-rolled cigarettes.

In the second-class coach rode the peons and the Indians, sitting immovable on the hard plank seats and in the aisle, wrapped in their *serapes* and *rebozos,* and holding babies, great clumps of pomegranates, and crates of chickens.

Behind was a Pullman carrying four passengers. Up front were three boxcars and a flat car on which sat a guard of scrawny little soldiers in pinkish cotton uniforms with half the buttons gone; there had been another Yaqui uprising.

All day the train crawled southward over the cactus-covered plain. The blue mountains following on the left. To the right the fetid jungle and the slimy rivers running down to the sea. Mountain, plain, and jungle on a sloping shelf: all of Mexico at once. And Indian country. The last "Far West."

The train stopped beside a water tank and boxcar station. An Indian boy got on carrying a small spotted fawn all eyes and legs. *"Cinco pesos,"* he whined, staggering down the aisle. Outside March saw a man sitting on the ground beside his horse. He wore leather chaps and held a rifle across his knees. After a time the boy appeared; he had sold his fawn. The man hoisted him to the horse's rump. Then he swung into the saddle and they vanished into the chaparral.

At dark the train stopped for another hour. The town was not to be seen. But in the flare of ocote torches March saw the platform crowded with people noisily greeting each other, the men clasping each other in an *embrazo,* cheek to cheek. Friendliness with a revolver on the hip.

"*Café con leche! Granadas mejores!*"

March got out.

Women in black *rebozos* squatted beside charcoal brasiers warming pieces of meat smothered in red sauce. Others shuffled up to him, barefooted, offering *tortillas,* huge red pomegranates strung on twisted vines, *tamales,* and earthen mugs of muddy coffee which might have been dipped from the river. Mangy dogs ran yelping from pot to pot; an old woman on the edge of the crowd squatted down like a hen to urinate.

A group of *Indios,* Mayas, stood haughtily aloof, blankets drawn up to their hard glittering eyes. One had blankets to sell: pure white, with borders of black or blue. "*Serapes! Serapes de Mayo!* he called softly. But always the hard glitter of eyes and an intense awareness.

A people like a black obsidian knife sheathed in soft adobe, thought March. Who will draw it from the land?

But now from the darkness he could see the four passengers in the Pullman. An American businessman and his wife, and a fat Mexican general and his scrawny mistress splattering her pock-marked face with more white powder.

Here, as everywhere, was all Mexico with its proud poverty and rapacious aristocracy, its unplumbed past and unfulfilled future. Mexico, the motherland of western America as England was that of the east. The meeting place of time and timelessness. March felt a wriggle up his spine. He was coming home at last.

In the dark and ghostly flow the train moved on.

The catch on the vestibule door was broken; all night it kept banging back and forth. The paper drinking cups were used up and scattered in the aisle. A woman stood at the empty container wailing, "*No hay tazas . . . no hay!*" until somebody loaned her an earthen mug. The little pink-clad soldiers had come in for the night, stacking their rifles; the train was now out of Yaqui territory. There were no seats. They squatted in the aisles, gnawing open little green oranges and spitting out the pulp.

And still the train crawled on in the dark still night with a subdued apprehension; no longer a train, but the spirit of the boy's own unrest drawn effortlessly into the imperturbable stillness, the infinite mystery and wildness of the earth.

At daybreak March awoke. Outside in the dawn-dusk he saw a plodding burro loaded with a jag of wood. Behind followed a man in *huaraches* and *serape,* his full white cotton pants flopping about his sturdy Indian legs. He did not look up. Then, flooded by sunlight, the earth emerged with all its nascent wonder, its timeless visage and indestructible freshness.

That afternoon at a boxcar junction March transferred to a weekly train which chugged up into the sierras. It comprised a donkey-engine, a boxcar, and a coach with eight seats, the rest of the car being used for freight. The rails followed a brown river up a rocky gorge. The heat was oppressive; the dense green growth gave off a sickly smell.

A *pueblocito* appeared, Las Minas, said to be the site of some mines which had been worked soon after the Conquest and then abandoned. Here a few passengers got on with baskets of watermelons hardly bigger than two fists. They did not talk as the train moved on, but sat clutching their fruit and staring out at the steadily rising hills.

It was nearly eight o'clock and still light when the train reached the end of the line. There was no one to meet it save the driver of a rattletrap *arrana.* March clambered into it with his four companions. The driver lashed his team with that inherent hate for horses March sensed in all Mexicans, and the coach bumped away.

They reached the town plaza before dark. March got out and looked about him. A crippled peon was lighting the few lamps with a torch. Dusty oleander and bougainvilleas, *seda* and *alamo* trees lined the square. From a forbidding black-walled cathedral a mellow bell rang softly in the warm, dark silence. A few men stood on the corner, indifferent, sterile, and sullen as the rough stones paving the plaza. A beautiful town, dead and indifferent, but still resisting the pressure of the encircling mountains. El Tazon de las Montanas. A Mexican Acropolis in the Sierra Madres.

Picking up his duffle bag, March walked to an enormous inn on one side of the plaza and was given a room. It had a lofty ceiling, stone floor, and walls two feet thick. Lost in it was a bed, chair, and a washstand. He was glad to come out for a miserable meal of greasy chicken, beans, and tortillas in a tiny dining room. He did not join the man at the other table. A distant politeness: it expressed the wary aloofness of Mexico. They nodded, warily observing each other. March saw a well-built man of about forty-five, sloppily dressed in boots, baggy trousers, and khaki shirt. He was strangely youthful looking despite a scar over his left eye, thin brown hair barely covering his flat-topped head, and stony blue eyes that held the fatalistic indifference of one who had been too long in the lonely places. Not until March leaned back and lit a cigarette did the man speak.

"*Ja!* American cigarettes I have not smoked for eighteen months!"

March handed over the package. "Here, keep these. My name's March Cable."

His companion rose quickly, clicked his heels together, and bowed. "Von Ratlube, at your service," he said curtly but pleasantly.

He was March's new boss: Baron Klaus von Ratlube.

March rose, stuck out his hand, and gave him his letter from Western Mines. "How lucky I am. Or you were awfully good to come here and meet me."

"That hat. Klaus knows when you come in, here is a young American mining engineer who will have some cigarettes." Von Ratlube read the letter, crumpled it, and threw it under the table. "Klaus will call you March, and you will call him Klaus. We shall get along, the only two white men here."

Klaus was in no hurry to get back to his mine, *La Mina Nueva,* forty kilometers back in the sierra. Hearing that he might soon have an assistant, he had come into town a week ago to drink beer while waiting. Now with a companion he still waited, drinking beer. An undeveloped mine and a man awaiting instructions to open it up, forgotten in a timeless country where there was no alarm clock, no calendar.

The immense old hotel, run by a shiftless couple, they had to themselves. It had a strange hard deadness, these great, empty, and formal rooms, and the messy kitchen where the woman squatted smoking among her blackened pots. In back lay a garden overgrown with vivid blue morning glories and bougainvillea blossoms dripping magenta and purple, and with brilliant birds flashing through papery banana trees. In it was a bath: a hut containing a stone basin where one stood up to the knees and splashed cold water in the darkness. There was no *excusado;* one went in the fallen-down shed in the corral.

March and Klaus rose early while it was still cool. They fried their own breakfast eggs, the meals were so distasteful. Then they strolled down to the market, an open courtyard with a roof. Men and woman squatted before their earthen pots, wicker baskets, peanuts, fruits, vegetables. Little melons, bristly *tunas,* limes, green oranges, always stacked so neatly in small pyramids. There was no attempt to sell, to brush away the flies swarming on the hanging meat in the bright hot silence.

From noon till midafternoon they slept. March really wanted to be alone. For afterward Klaus came out to drink beer and talk some more.

At dusk bats began flying out of the cathedral tower. Black chips from black stone walls. Women came to the water fountain to fill their jars and then stalked back, eyes down, through the dark. The crippled lamp-lighter went the rounds with his torch. Big doors slammed shut and were locked with keys nearly a foot long. Iron grillwork barred all windows. And all around the mountains drew closer with oppressive silence. So Moorish really. And Spanish. But holding a down-pressing Indian negation of both.

There were five musicians in town who played for weddings, fiestas, and funerals. They paid their tax by playing twice a week in the plaza. Coronet, flute, trombone, guitars – anything. It all sounded the same. Tax music. No one minded. The people strolled around and around the park. The women on the inside going one way, the men the other. Laughs, greetings, bold stares from the men at the young girls, suspicious looks from the women. All in a subdued key: muted voices, furtive looks. Really two silent, slow, opposite-flowing streams that never mingled, seldom touched. But always with an intense awareness of the other. Then suddenly – slap

– bang! – the musicians put away their instruments, and everyone vanished as if warned of a coming storm.

Late one night March was awakened by a couple singing outside.

Zamboa navajoa cumuripa corral,
Santini pitahaya balmoa algodal!

The man's deep voice was a dark curtain against which the woman's rose leaping and quivering like a brilliant flame; one living flame in the dead, oppressive night. One of the haunting, timeless *aires de la tierra*.

March jumped up and ran to the window. Through the iron grillwork he glimpsed the faint glow of a charcoal brasier, and around it some of the *serranos*, the small quick Indians of the hills, who had come down into town that day. But by the time he had jumped into his pants, unbarred and unlocked the great wooden door, and run outside they were gone.

March was growing sick of Klaus' constant talk. From morning till night, he talked about himself, third person. It was the disease of a man's loneliness. But the death it brought was silence. So March endured it.

The von Ratlube family ranked high in the German aristocracy. Klaus' education at the University of Göttingen was of the best: geology, English and French, with a neat saber-cut scar as a decorative reminder of his days in the Studenter Corps. During the war he joined Richthofen's flying squadron and became one of the leading German aces. His three brothers were killed. He himself cracked up badly.

"Klaus' head was broken like an egg-shell," he said. "Feel his head. It has a flat metal cap on top of the skull. Skin and hair were grafted over it."

At the end of the war he went to Rumania, thence to some remote Russian mines. In Amsterdam he next obtained a contract to work in a group of mines in Belgian East Africa. After three years he caught maleria, and was transferred to Alaska. The sudden change almost killed him. Stricken with pneumonia, he was shipped to a hospital in California. A year later he obtained work with Western Mines in their holdings in Arizona, whence he had been sent down here in Mexico eighteen months ago. Every month his salary check came. Every month he sent in his report. He had blocked out 75,000 tons of silver ore in La Mina Nueva. But still no orders, no money came to develop it into a working property.

"Pagh! The whole country is lousy with silver. Here, Klaus has 75,000 tons blocked out. Who wants it? Nobody. Your country once said it was worth $1.29 an ounce. Now it is worth only the price of a bottle of beer. So Klaus stays here. He is forgotten. Nobody remembers him. It is best so." Leaning over, he slapped March on the knee. "Klaus tells you these things because you are like his little brother."

They were sitting after the *siesta* hour at a table in front of the *Cantina El Club* fronting the plaza. In the hot bright stillness of the afternoon a horse clattered slowly into sight. The rider, the town's policeman, was sitting lazily in the saddle. Attached to the horn was a long taut rope which stretched behind him. Then March saw what was attached to the other end. A *peon*. The rope was looped about his neck. His hat was gone, he was choked with heat and dust. His hands were tied behind his back, his bare feet bloody from stumbling through cactus and over stones. Nobody on the plaza paid him any attention. And in the stifling heat, his head stretched forward like a running rooster's, the prisoner was yanked along.

March felt a little sick at seeing the naked fear in his eyes and his swollen protruding tongue.

"Pancho! Another bottle!" ordered Klaus.

5

Klaus had the German sentimentality; also the German belly for beer, however lean he looked. He drank the excellent bottled beer being promoted by the government to replace the fiery native cactus liquors. It was expensive so far up here. But March too preferred it to the brutal, greenish-white *mezcal* that came so cheaply.

"Klaus can drink more beer than you! Want to see?" Klaus said abruptly one afternoon on the plaza.

It was the day March had received a letter from Ona, enclosing a page of the little college weekly with a paragraph marked in pencil. Valeria Constance, married the week after her graduation, had died while giving birth to a still-born son.

March shrugged assent and drained his bottle.

By evening they were both pleasantly drunk. A light supper of cold greasy chicken had no effect. They returned to their table to sip a bottle of *mezcal*. *"Ja! Der gute, trockene brand!"* said Klaus. But at ten o'clock Pancho closed the *cantina*.

With a fresh bottle under Klaus' arm, they sat in the plaza. Three white shadows gathered around them. The bottle made the rounds. Then Klaus took out another from his hip pocket. One of the *pelados* began to sing.

"Musica! Musica para todos. Eh, amigos?" demanded Klaus.

"*Como no?*" They grinned. In Mexico it was the answer to everything, even death and revolutions. "Why not?" So two of them went to round up the village musicians while the singer roused Pancho for more bottles.

Now they all paraded around the plaza singing to guitars. "*Borrachita, me voy*"... It was all very beautiful, most touching. But no one answered the serenade from the iron-barred windows. And the dark heavy night smothered voices and whining strings.

They straggled down to the market place. Off in the darkness gleamed the tiny fires of a mule train down from the hills. Soon the *serranos* came over, sturdy little Indians in tattered *serapes*. They stood heavy with negation and silence, their black eyes fixed on the *pelados* lounging on a bench.

March retched violently. The clear, greenish liquor had brought out a sweat that ran down his cheeks. Now he felt better. Klaus led him apart from the others. He was very drunk and babbling in his German-tinged English.

"Nobody remembers Klaus. Nobody remembers March. He is like Klaus' little brother. *Blutsbruderschaft!* We shall be blood brothers, no?"

He had already drawn out his clasp knife, opened the blade. Before March could guess his intention, Klaus grabbed the boy's left arm and slashed the inside of his wrist. Quickly now Klaus cut his own left wrist. With his other hand he held their cut wrists together.

"Blutsbruderschaft schwören!" Staggering, he flung his arm over March's shoulder. *"Brüder – auf immer und immer!"*

And so they stood there in the dark circle of trees, wrists still held together, the warm blood beginning to trickle down the finger tips. March was aware of Klaus' proud dignity that drunkenness did not mar, the sincere comradeship he gave with his blood. And yet the rite seemed somehow false and sentimental. Blood communion but not of the blood, he thought hazily. A German schoolboy trick. He remembered the only evening he had spent at a college fraternity house in Little London: the songs, the beer mugs, the theatrically fraternal spirit that was dissipated instantly once the members were off the campus. And he felt a little ashamed and very foolish as he stood wiping off his bloody wrist with a dirty handkerchief. It was just a surface cut; not into a vein, luckily.

One of the *serranos* came up in his thin-soled *huaraches,* his dark brilliant eyes showing an intense awareness. March gave him a cigarette, watching his mobile face as he bent to the cupped flame of a match. And he sensed that between him and this unknown dark little Indian from the hills was more than between him and a lonely uprooted German aristocrat. For we here in Indian America are the feather, the flower, the drum, and the mirror of the old gods who have never died.

"Come, *Brüderlein!*" said Klaus, laying his hand on March's shoulder to accentuate that word of endearment so rarely used. "*Jetzt muss getrunken werden!*"

In the silvery moonlight they drifted back to the white ghosts across the plaza. But the bottles were empty and the musicians had gone. Only two *pelados* and the *Indios* remained. All straggled down the cobblestone street to an adobe hut near the bend of the river. There the *pelados* vanished. Klaus pounded on the door. An old woman looking like a witch opened it and held up a lighted candle.

"*Menudo, mi madre!* We want *menudo!*"

Her seamed brown face searched each of them in turn. March gave her some *pesos*. She bit each of them, then let them in. Across the threshold, sleeping on a *petate*, lay a young boy. Klaus awakened him with a kick, ordering him to rouse Pancho for more *mezcal*.

"*No hay dinero!*" the boy whined sullenly. "*No hay!*"

"Klaus will pay. To Pancho tomorrow, Klaus will pay!"

The hut was one dirt-floored room. But because the old woman was known as the maker of the best *menudo* in the mountains, there was a long table and two benches. On these crowded the two white men and the Indians. The old woman roused the fire in a stove in the corner, put on her pots. The boy came back with more *mezcal,* rolled up in his *serape* on the floor, and instantly fell asleep. The dreamless dog-sleep of Indians that comes so instantly and easily any time, any place.

An hour passed, perhaps two. The hut was steamy from boiling tripe and smoky from cigarettes: cheap packaged "Faros" and *punche* rolled in corn leaves. The raw liquor was bringing out sweat to the men's bodies, and with it the peculiar racial smell. One of them threw back his *serape,* and in the light of the guttering candle March saw his smooth brown chest. Not muscular, but heavy and soft like a woman's. Like adobe. But powerful.

They were singing, talking in their own *idioma.* Klaus began to whistle in two keys a theme from Wagner. When they did not still, he lost his temper. *"Verfluchte Mexikaner!"* he shouted. *"Himmel, Donnerwetter noch einmal! Verfluchte Mexikaner! Maul halten wahrend ich musiziere!"*

His angry demand could not be mistaken. The *serranos* hushed, drew into themselves. Klaus slumped down again at the head of the table. In a conciliating tone he muttered, *"Le gustan Klaus, no? Porque Alemán, sí?"*

"Sí. We like Germans, *Señor.* Mexico likes Germans." It had a flat emptiness. They went on drinking.

"Hermanocito, my little brother! *Alemán tambien, amigos!"* Klaus affirmed, slapping March on the shoulder.

They knew he lied; and March could see their flinty black eyes sweeping him with veiled glances. A dead silence had gathered around them and now endured, unbroken. It was heavy and yet electric, like the air before a storm.

The old woman brought over her pot of *menudo,* a greasy thick soup of tripe with scraps of onions and hominy, ladling it out in earthenware bowls with a dirty iron spoon. Then she brought *cabeza,* the boiled head of a cow. The stuff was horrible. It made March feel sick, but more *mezcal* settled his stomach. He leaned back, fighting against nausea.

Klaus he saw go suddenly pale, his face greenish white and slimy with sweat. He had to go out. March went with him, and the Indians followed. A faint breeze rustled through the papery banana leaves. Down the clearing the river sucked at the stones. Klaus let water, turned toward town. But the Indians stood in front of him, immovable, silent.

"Himmel! Was ist das!" Then contemptuously, with a stiff bow, *"Meine Herren, ich bin ihr Gefangener!"* He stumbled back inside the hut with March at his heels.

Once more Klaus staggered to his feet and lurched out into the clearing with March. No farther. The Indians stopped them again, tried to lead them down to the river. "*Verfluchte Mexikaner!* They want to kill us. Klaus doesn't care!"

March yanked him back inside the hut where, head on his arms, Klaus sat huddled at the table. The old woman had gone to bed, her bare feet sticking out from a blanket. The boy lay snoring on the floor. The only sound was the soft *idioma* of the *serranos* talking among themselves, and it was part of the oppressive silence. Two rows of powerful brown bodies, walls of soft warm flesh hemming in the two white men in the corner.

"You are his little brother, German too?" someone asked March.

"No!" he answered with a quick stubborn pride. "*Yanqui!*"

A little tension rippled around the table although the faces did not change. A foreigner, an Americano, an *Imperialísimo Yanqui.* March felt for the first time the sullen brooding hate of the Indian for his white master. It had always been there, not in the conscious individual mind, but deep in the blood; the subterranean hate of a race whose flowering had been frustrated by another. The brutal liquor had brought it out. He filled his glass again, shoved the bottle across the table.

Beside him, on his left, sat a young *serrano.* Over his bare torso he wore a tattered *serape.* As was the custom, it had a narrow slit in the center called *la boca,* "the mouth," through which protruded his head with its fell of black uncut hair. "*Amigo? Simpático?*" he kept asking in a taunting, malicious tone.

"*Como no? Amigo. Simpático,*" March answered patiently, recognizing the persistent attempts to intimidate him, and feeling grow within him a hard streak of granite.

Once more the Indian asked his interminable question, this time taking March's right hand and inserting it under his *serape,* on his sweaty belly, to feel the bone haft of a knife protruding from his trousers.

March suddenly jerked out the knife, flung his arm backward and upward, and drove the blade with all his strength into the lintel of the window behind him. "Yes! As long as my friend's knife remains there above us!"

The blade quivered in the rotting wood like a reed trembling in the wind. Underneath the table March planted his feet firmly. He pushed back his glass on the table. Drunkenly alert, he gathered himself to turn and lunge for the man's throat at his first move for the knife, sinking his thumbs into the hollows below the ears. "If it's going to come, let it come now," he thought savagely. The Indian did not move, nor did March. A faint flicker, like a ripple, passed over the black eyes across the table. No one spoke.

"There is the power of the blood," March thought hazily with drunken determination, "but there is the power of the will, too. I am my father and I am also my grandfather."

One of the men took another swig. So did March. The edge of the tension dulled. Still the Indians waited with inexhaustible patience. Yet March knew that in his weakness lay his strength: to maintain an unceasing awareness, to give like soft adobe, but to feel within him a core of granite. So he gathered himself in his drunkenness to endure, to out-drink his companions.

They all kept getting drunker, more sullen. March, possessed by a savage exultation, felt as if he were walking a tightrope high above them; a taut line suspended across a deep chasm a thousand miles long.

One by one the *serranos* relaxed, falling back against the wall or lying down on the floor already spotted with vomit. But the candle was almost burnt; he could not trust darkness. He rose. His legs were numb, his mind a roaring furnace. He managed to rouse Klaus and they staggered outside. No one followed them.

Klaus weakly raised March's hand to the flat top of his head. The boy could feel a pulse beating under the platinum cap. "My head," said Klaus.

"Hell with your head! Mind your feet!" muttered March.

The German was too heavy to carry up the narrow cobbled streets. Then the old lamplighter appeared, and together they dragged him to the plaza. The sky was greenish-grey above the *sierras;* it was almost dawn.

The huge door of the hotel was bolted shut. Sandoval let them in, muttering, *"Borrachos!"*

March lurched past him alone, stumbling to his room. Everything suddenly gave way within him. He hit the side of the bed, clutched for the blanket, and fell on the floor dragging it over him.

In the morning his cracked lips were covered with a black scale like soot. His heart was pounding terribly. He could hardly walk across the room. Klaus was even weaker. Neither man could eat.

For two days they sat with drawn faces, suffering mutely in the heat. Perhaps, after all, it was time to return to the mine.

6

La Mina Nueva was a long ride by muleback up in the sierras.

The working was really very old, one of the mines opened by the early Spaniards, perhaps by the Indians before them, said Klaus. He had found in one of the old tunnels a joint of wooden ladder bound with a rawhide which crumpled when he picked it up, and on the walls a few half-obliterated Aztec markings. One needn't believe an engineer when he talked of his own mine, especially in Mexico where all mines are said to have been Moctezuma's. Anyhow it was very old. A dim trail now overgrown led from it across the sierra, a *Camino Real* over which the silver had been carried by mule *conductas* to the coast and thence by ship to Spain. This original working was called *La Mina Antigua*.

It had been reached by an inclined tunnel along the footwall of the vein, big enough to accomodate the little burros laden with sacks of ore. But Klaus, when he had come, had moved east of the opening to a new site on the hillside. Here he had cleared the chaparral and sunk a shaft from which he ran a few discovery tunnels. The hoist was a dangerous make-shift: a small wooden platform without sides, lowered by a wheezing gasoline engine taken out of an American automobile. Gasoline for it was brought up in huge square tins, two to a burro. At the bottom of the hill was a clump of miserable huts with thatched roofs occupied by the *peons* working for him. This was *La Mina Nueva.*

It was early Cripple Creek in the days of the Sylvanite, thought March when he saw it; not the corporation era of huge modern plants operated by Western Mines.

The work was hard but simple; Klaus was a top-notch man with a nose for ore. The two men puttered below, taking samples which Klaus assayed above. Then they ran narrow tunnels and drifts. The blocks of ore between they measured and computed tonnage. Once a month Klaus or March, taking turns, would ride down the trail to the village and take the train to the nearest town. Here letters and a report to Western Mines were mailed. Their checks were always waiting at the bank. Two leather sacks were filled with silver pesos to pay the laborers; supplies were bought; and with a new shipment of gasoline tins, he would ride home with a dozen loaded burros.

Klaus and March did not go together. For then March found he could not pry Klaus loose from the village. He would stay a week or two drinking beer. And when they returned, it was to find most of the workers gone. So the work went on, unhurried, to no end at all.

They climbed one day farther back into the high sierras. Two men walked ahead of their mules, clearing the overgrown trail with their huge steel *machetes*. Wicked-looking knives, thought March; a blow would halve a man like a cucumber. In a clearing lay an adobe ruin: the mill or mint, said Klaus, where the silver from *La Mina Antigua* had been prepared for the long mule *conductas* crossing the mountains. Nearby, fronting a weed-grown plaza, stood a large, magnificent church. Really a cathedral, its stone walls blackened with age and weather.

As they stared at it, a woman came out from a hovel behind it. "*Pobres! Indios!* We have nothing, *Señores!*" The dread, the haunting fear of strangers.

For a *peso* she unlocked the massive carved doors and let them in. The immense nave, lit only by a tiny window high in the thick walls, was empty. There were no seats, no benches of course; in all churches the people kneeled on the hard bare floors. The altar long had been stripped of *reredos* and *santos*. But in front stood a withered stalk of corn, at whose foot lay some withered flowers and the dark stain of turkey blood left by Indians who still came here upon occasion. March was glad to get out into the bright sunlight and rise again on the twisting trail.

On a high ridgetop they left the two men to hobble the mules and sleep in the grass. Klaus now showed March why they had come, tracing across the truncated summit reappearing outcrops in the decomposed granite. They found the fault, followed it down to a steep rocky gorge. Midway across the western wall March could see an exposed jadeite-green vein nearly twenty feet wide.

"Pure copper, Klaus! You've found a deposit that'll beat the Copper Boy!"

"Not pure, but copper. And Klaus thinks it will run to silver at depth." He pointed to the talus slope at the bottom of the gorge. "Down there is lime. A site for a mill where a railroad could reach it from across the plains." He began to whistle, then broke off. "But at first the run would have to be taken out by burros. Why not? Klaus and March could see to it all."

The hot sun was flooding the gorge with a pool of heat. By the time the two men reached the mules they were wet with sweat, their eyes glazed, their throats like rasps. Klaus' flat, platinum-covered head was throbbing like a pulse.

Back at *La Mina Nueva* that night Klaus' enthusiasm had evaporated. "Bah! Klaus has a silver mine here bursting with ore to be taken out. He has found another deposit. The whole mountains are full of silver. What is that? Nobody wants it. And Klaus is kept here, forgotten."

March looked up bleakly from the newspapers Ona had sent him. Back in the States history was repeating itself. Another panic, like that of '93 which had written the doom of the booming silver camps of the Colorado Rockies, was spreading over the country. Prices were tumbling. Industrial plants were closing, men were being thrown out of jobs, a wave of unrest was sweeping the rich heaven of gringoland. And here, sitting on top of 90,000 tons of silver ore while other men stood patiently waiting in ever-lengthening bread lines in all the large cities, March felt the awry balance between the rich abundant earth and men who could not learn how to use it.

Klaus at last had run out of talk. In the adobe where the two men lived together, he would sit after supper reading newspapers over and over, and whistling through his teeth. March could stand it no longer.

"For Christ's sake, stop that eternal whistling!" he shouted, jumping to his feet.

Klaus rose, clicked his heels together, and bowed coldly. "Klaus von Ratlube is disturbing the young American with his odious presence?"

They got along badly. Klaus had forgotten the midnight ritual of blood communion which had made them brothers. He sat glowering across the table at March sewing up a tear in his shirt. Neither spoke. And in their silence grew the strange hate which comes to two men alone in the wilderness. "Cabin fever," thought March.

So one night he said abruptly, "Klaus, I'm not going to bunk here with you any more. It's bad for both of us. Serafina is moving my stuff into the little adobe tomorrow morning."

"*Ja!* Get out then!"

Serafina did their cooking and washing. She was old, fat, and shapeless. But she had been with Klaus two years now and had begun to learn a little cleanliness and to give the pots a good scrubbing. The quarrel between the two men delighted her. Oh, it was good, very good! Soon they would fight. Maybe they would cut each other with knives or shoot off guns. This would be better. There had not been so much excitement for months.

Nothing happened. At night March went home to his little adobe below the bigger one Klaus occupied. In one corner stood a small stove and a packing-case china closet for his few dishes. And he had made a table and chair. A bare little place, but it soon took on warmth. His one distasteful chore was cooking his own suppers, for Klaus had kept Serafina.

Up above, Klaus watched the old woman pattering around in her floppy *huaraches,* looking out the window and murmuring, "*Probrecito!* He is all alone. He misses Serafina, no?"

Klaus got a little ashamed "*Chinga tu madre!* Stop moaning, old pig of a woman. Hurry up with my supper and then go down and get *Señor* Cable's. Every night. *Sabe?*"

So sullenly, every twilight, Serafina scraped together Klaus' supper and then plodded down the trail to fix March's. "It is twice as much work. It is ten times the work," she grumbled.

"*Ándale!* Get on with you!" cried March sharply. "You know you get twice as much money and have two places to steal from."

The old woman grinned. She was devoted to both men.

After supper March carried his chair outside. Klaus above him was already sitting out on his wider *portal.* March could see in the dusk the tiny red glow of his cigarette. To his right the plank hoist house of the mine faded into darkness.

One night, through the velvety blackness, came the sound of Klaus whistling in two keys a bar from Verdi. "How'd you like that one?" his shout came down.

March in turn whistled back a few bars from "Carry Me Back to Old Virginny."

Their relationship smoothed out. Occasionally March took supper with Klaus, or the German came down to spend the evening with him. There was about these "social calls" an air of warmth and hospitality, a faint formality too, which broke the old monotony. Yet March held on fiercely to his quiet aloneness against Klaus' repeated attempts to break it. So they got along better.

The dozen workmen and their families lived down along the stream. In the darkness their cooking fires gleamed red. Sometimes a group of *serranos* spent the night with them, or a burro train on its way to market in the village. A guitar began to whine and voices broke into song. Perhaps there would sound a drum beaten with the heel of a hand to accompany the singers. The deep rich voices, soft and powerful in their maleness, came welling up as if from the earth itself. And from above, Klaus' whistle.

March sat alone in darkness between them, belonging to both and yet of neither. He sat, as had his grandfather, in the lamplight of a single lonely mine in the mountains; and outside he saw, as his father had seen, the red campfires of his fathers' fathers. And it seemed to him that in some curious fashion he had completed a mysterious cycle. Something was beginning to take shape within him. What it was, he did not know, but he felt that he was coming to a verge.

His feeling was manifested by outward events on his next trip for money, mail, and supplies.

Finishing his chores in El Tazon, he made ready to return to the mine. Dawn was scarcely an hour away as he crossed the empty plaza. Behind him the sierras heaved into the violet sky and the black tower of the cathedral began to loom out of the darkness. Demetrio and the *arrieros* were waiting in the corral. They had packed the burros with supplies and gasoline tins, two to an animal, had saddled the mules. Already they had eaten, and now sat smoking around the dying embers of a small fire.

"Esta bien, Jefé," said Demetrio, rising.

March nodded. He tightened the girth of his saddle; went over the pack fastenings—one of the ropes, last trip, had worked loose and spilled a sack of flour; then counted the gasoline tins. Two were missing.

"You brought all the gasoline, Demetrio?" he asked casually.

"Sin dudo, Jéfe. Cómo no?"

"Get the other two! Quickly!"

Demetrio's dark face assumed a dumb, expressionless look. He counted the gasoline tins; he counted his fingers. *"Madre!* Can it really be that two are missing? What eyes the *Señor* has even in darkness!"

"Only to see that Demetrio and his men no longer wish presents of the empty cans. Their woman prefer to carry their water in little jars."

Demetrio peered into the darkness. "Sons of the devil! Cursed *rateros!* Where are you who have stolen the *Jefé's gasolina?* My knife will find the guilty one!"

"Demetrio! Find those tins!"

The men rose quietly and began puttering around. It was Demetrio who awkwardly discovered them hidden under some straw in the corral. "Look! My sharp eyes have found the hiding place of the thieves!" And bullingly, he saw to it that they were lashed on a burro.

In single file they rode slowly out of the corral, past the empty market, and across the river. Dawn was already breaking. March was forever grateful for the delay in starting.

As he splashed across the ford, reined up and waited for the heavily laden burros to pass, he heard a whinny off to the side. He turned quickly into the chaparral. A horse was grazing quietly, a man sprawled limply in the saddle. "Klaus! Here!" He dismounted, grabbed the mare's bridle. Klaus did not stir. Face down, he was lying with his hands twisted in the loose reins wrapped about her neck. When March lowered him to the ground, he let out a low moan. His face and head were dark with clotted blood.

March turned the pack train back to town, carrying Klaus on his mule as gently as possible. Demetrio beside him talked constantly. "The mare brought him safely down the trail. But always she is afraid of water. Remember, *Jéfe?* In the brush she would have stayed. We would have missed her in the dark. Aye! It was the will of God those *rateros* hid our *gasolina*. No?"

"It is as you say – the will of God that we were delayed to find him and not pass by in darkness," assented March. "And the will of God will surely lead me to the guilty if you fail again to guard all animals and packs in the corral."

"I solemnly swear, *Jéfe*. By Our Lady!"

"It is well. There will be many temptations. Chiefly *mezcal*," answered March drily.

He carried Klaus into the hotel, washed off the blood, and sent for the local herb doctor who left poultices and emetics which March tossed out into the garden as soon as the man left.

A gash in Klaus' head had torn loose a piece of the skin and hair grafted over his platinum plate. This could be washed with iodine and plastered back with adhesive – with a prayer his skull had not been cracked. His left arm was broken and beginning to swell. The worst injury seemed to be in his side. Whenever he moved he moaned with pain. From exposure, he also had caught a touch of his old fever. His face by noon was flushed, and he had begun to sweat and chill alternately.

March sat by him, wiping off his face, giving him sips of boiled water with lime juice and quinine to hold his fever down. There was only one thing to do: take him to the train and get him to a competent doctor. "It won't do to wait, Klaus. There's only one train a week, remember? Klaus!"

Klaus did not reply. He was still delirious.

That afternoon March sent Demetrio with the pack train back to the mine, and in the evening loaded Klaus into the ramshackle coach which jolted over the rough road to the train. The tedious journey that night was a nightmare. Klaus was stretched out on a double seat, the other passengers inquiring every few minutes. "He is dead yet, *Señor?* No? But surely soon. See? His breath comes ever shorter."

Klaus was a brave man one minute and a child the next. He lay gritting his teeth to still his moans against pain. Then he would relapse into a petulant whine. "Little brother! You are still angry at Klaus. You won't give Klaus any more water."

They got to town, doctor, and a small hospital. Klaus' lacerated scalp was resewn, his broken arm set, his fever brought down. But something was terribly wrong with his side; he was to be sent to Guadalajara.

The two men joked. "So the mine fell in on you! How do I know you didn't arrange it on purpose?" asked March. "The pretty girls in Guadalajara!"

"*Ja!* And you, little brother, will be sleeping with Serafina! It is what you need to improve your Spanish—a sleeping dictionary!"

He really looked like a ghost. Insisting that he would be back in a couple of weeks, he ordered March to keep the mine open without notifying Western Mines of his accident. "Send another report of 5,000 more tons of ore blocked out. It goes into the waste basket with the others. Klaus is forgotten. But he wants his pay. Eh?"

Next day March set off alone for *La Mina Nueva.*

7

The place was in a devil of a mess. Demetrio finally had stolen his two tins of gasoline – to buy *mezcal* in town, March surmised. Several of the workers had left, as he had known they would. They had to have their silver *pesos* at the end of each day's work, even though they couldn't spend them for a week. At the mine itself the steel drum hung suspended across the top of the shaft; the cable was torn loose; the gasoline engine looked like it had a cracked block. The cribbing of the shaft was loose. Dirt and stones kept falling. And the new tunnel had caved in.

From Serafina he gradually learned what had happened the afternoon of the accident.

Klaus had needed a few more big timbers in a tunnel leading off from the bottom of the shaft. These were usually lowered by the hoist, with either Klaus or March operating the gasoline engine. Now with March gone, Klaus foolishly decided to have someone else lower the timbers instead of dragging them down the old inclined tunnel – an hour's work apiece.

Juan de Dios was selected to sit at the engine above. Klaus showed him how to run it. It was very simple: a hand here, a hand there, and when the little mark appeared on the unwinding cable, this.

"Qué bonito! It is nothing, *Señor.* So carefully I watch. Every *momentito!"*

So he did at first after Klaus went down. Then something happened to Juan de Dios. His body straightened, his strong simple face grew stern, his soul expanded. He had learned the white men's secret of the *máquina. Pues!* Juan de Dios, poor Indian, was now *Señor Ingeniero.* In the wink of an eye, the flash of a butterfly's wing, he had crossed the chasm of centuries.

So he straightened his *sombrero,* stuck an unlit cigarette behind his ear, and called for spectators. They came running: women, children, an old man or two in ragged *serapes.* The two helpers attached the cable hooks to the timber chains, carefully swung the log slantwise to the shaft where it could straighten and drop down slowly. Now they stood back respectfully.

Juan de Dios rang his bell. *Qué bonito!* The motor churned, the exhaust popped, the fumes ran out. As if serenely unconscious of the adulation in their dark eyes, *Señor Ingeniero* Juan de Dios put his hand here, his hand there, and when the little mark appeared on the slowly unwinding cable, did this. So simple! Like a miracle almost.

Down below Klaus unhooked the timber, snaked it with a burro into the tunnel, rang his bell for another.

As the spectators grew braver, venturing a look down the shaft, Juan de Dios grew more important. He whizzed up the engine, retarded the spark to make the exhaust pop, and wound up the cable at high speed.

Another timber was lowered until the tip barely stuck up above the shaft collar. Now it descended out of sight. Now it popped up again, half a length out, to drop again. A woman made a sly, obscene remark. Everyone laughed. An old man clapped his hands. "What a mighty man is Juan de Dios! His wife has never seen such plunging!

Señor Ingeniero affected not to notice them. Power flowed from him. The great log did just as he willed. Dignified and important, he sat up straight, *huarache*-clad feet stuck out before him, bare toes protruding from the leather thongs. His hat, however, needed straightening. He removed his hand and straightened it, of course.

There was a sudden bang and clatter. The cable jerked loose from the drum, whipping round and round like an unwinding snake. *Santísima!* A hand here, a hand there. So simple a moment before. But now in his confusion Juan de Dios had forgotten which was which.

"*Madre mía!*" he wailed, releasing all controls. Jumping to his feet, he stared wildly down the shaft. The huge log was dropping, banging against the sides of the shaft, tearing loose stones and dirt. The drum creaked and rolled. Then the pulleys were torn loose; the cable yanked the drum over; the rocking gasoline engine pulled at the plank platform.

"*Jesu Cristo!*" With a frightened cry he fled with the spectators. And not too soon. The drum, yanked loose, caught across the shaft collar. The cable snapped loose like a thread from a spool. The great log plunged downward.

Juan de Dios, hiding behind a bush, heard a mighty crash and yell. A puff of dust rose out of the shaft. Then silence.

Slowly the people came forth. "It was the devil in the *máquina* which broke loose," explained Juan de Dios authoritatively, his composure restored. "Did you not hear the whistles, the shrieks, the moans?"

But with the Aleman there had been two men and a burro. Lighting candles and torches they trooped down the old inclined tunnel. The two workers they found safe. The burro was crushed. And the *Ingeniero,* the Aleman, was caught like a *tigre* in a pit. They dug him out, administered hot soup and advice. Klaus refused both, insisting he be put on his horse. They hoisted him to the saddle, tied one boot to the stirrups. Alone, he rode off into the darkness. No one accompanied him. There was too much to talk about. Juan de Dios had vanished into the hills: to escape the devil of the *máquina,* he said, and to compose his soul in tranquality –

Resolutely March cleaned up the mine as best he could and wrote Klaus in Guadalajara, asking whether he should order new hoisting machinery. Klaus replied in a shaky hand. Western Mines would have to authorize the expenditure. The company would not do so if it knew he were away and laid up. It might suspend all activity and stop his pay. He advised March to close the mine, keeping an eye on it from town until Klaus returned.

March shut down *La Mina Nueva,* dismissed the few remaining workers, and returned to El Tazón. To avoid the wretched cooking in the hotel, he rented a house. It was really very lovely: faded pink adobe walls, big rooms with a few pieces of furniture, and an overgrown garden through which ran a faint trail to the toilet. The dusty road in front was filled with people going to town. Down the slope in back the curving river glimmered silver between thick growths of mangos.

The house, like most Mexican houses, had a family attached to it as caretakers. They lived in a *barrio,* neighborhood or compound of many families, along the river. Maria Rita Campos was the matriarchal head of the large family. With unbelievable assurance she would come walking down the road and into the house: head up, swinging her hips with a slight *meneo,* in the walk of a queen which blindness had never altered.

Saturnino, one of her sons, was a stocky man who patched the walls, brought wood, and did chores. Then humbly holding his hat to his breast, he would stand around in his quiet heaviness, his eyes alert as an animal's. It was he who occasionally accompanied March back to the mine.

Late one afternoon March walked down to the river. All the women had been washing their clothes and spreading them out on the bank to dry. Now they were bathing in the river with the men who had come to join them. All were naked. Their blue-black hair shone in the setting sun; full breasts, mighty buttocks and strong Indian legs gleamed redly; white teeth flashed. Two children were scrubbing their mother's back, laughing and splashing each other. A man called to him, waving. It was Saturnino. March slipped off his clothes and waded into the river.

It was then he saw her as she rose from a ducking, facing him. A girl and a woman too: her face a child's, her beautifully formed body a woman's. And seeing her ripe breasts so small and pointed, her young vigorous shoulders and iodine-colored arms, March felt a shock as if he had stepped on an electric cable.

The girl swept back the hair from her face. On her toes, she kept bounding up and down in the waist-high water, smiling at him. Who she was, he did not know. And a little abashed, he swam away toward Saturnino.

Early next morning he went to the market for the day's shopping. The place was crowded; in Mexico all life, like the flowers, opened with the sun. Some men from the hills had brought down goat cheeses, big as millstones, two to a burro. March wanted some, but that offered him smelled of burro. While he stood there complaining, the girl he had seen the evening before stepped up. "Burro! Burro! It smells!" With a staccato burst of the *idioma,* she demanded two slices cut from the center and neatly wrapped in a newspaper, which she handed to March. Without more ado, she took over his marketing. Eggs, tomatoes, *aguacates.* Helplessly he followed her from stall to stall, watching her pinch vegetables and fruit, listening to her angry dickering for a squawking fowl. "Bones and feathers! Thief! Where is one with meat?"

When the *bolsa* was full, she took it from him, walking beside him but an appropriate step behind. As they entered his house, a cockroach ran out from the kitchen. He stepped on it, kicked it outside.

"No! Never!" the girl protested. "Where there are *cucaraches* there are no *alacranes!"* He nodded, afraid of the deadly little scorpions.

The girl looked over the house with a peculiar air of proprietorship. Then hands on hip, she asked forthrightly, *"No hay mujer?"*

"No hay mujer. Soltero."

She cleaned the house, cooked supper for him and that night as a matter of course she slept with him.

Her name was Conchita; and as he might have suspected, she was a granddaughter of Maria Rita Campos. The Indian in her gave her at times a sullen, brooding heaviness. This was overlaid with a cheerful brightness, an immense ambition. Most of the year she lived away from home teaching in a small rural school somewhere down along the railroad. Here she had learned to speak English, wear squeaky shoes upon occasion, and splash talcum powder on her dark ruddy cheeks. These railroad-junction airs, as March called them, she seldom affected; she went around in bare feet and *rebozo,* with the submissive meekness and timeless anonymity of the earth itself. But someday she would be *gente de razón* and wear beautiful clothes all day, every day.

That she became his mistress raised the status of them both. March was no longer regarded as a suspicious *gringo* foreigner, and

Conchita was viewed with respect as a woman who had a household of her own to boss. There was no doubt she enjoyed her role. She liked the command of the household money, and to lord it over the big family in back. She did all the shopping in the market. What she saved by merciless haggling, she made up for with what she took home.

"This chicken – you only ate half of it. So I shall take this old tasteless meat to my toothless grandmother. And these *aguacates*. See? Black spots already."

If at times March suspected he was feeding the whole family, he was paying less than before and he liked the life Conchita gave the house. Their relationship lent both of their lives a substance, but it did not alter the form. There was no sentimental love making between them. She was direct and honest, without pretense. When he lay down beside her at night it was as if a secret key shut off his consciousness of self. He remembered at times his childish love for Leslie Shane. It too was mindless but nebulous, a flicker of the pure spirit. Of Valeria Constance he thought also: the queer cold clutch of their two minds, ever wary of the other even in his passionate yearning. How different this! It was without spiritual essence perhaps, yet it was more than physical. It created a world in which sex was master, but in it was much more – timeless and engulfing, beyond analysis.

So they lay together under the open window. Moonlight washed across the stone floor. The leaves of the banana tree scraped against the patio wall with a paperish sound. And over them, heavy with the weight of centuries, pressed down the sierras. In the deep dark flow, in the ghostly flow, he felt himself sink and drift, and sink again.

At sunrise she leaped up to build the morning fire and to half-fill a tin tub with lukewarm water. Every morning March took a bath. Imagine! Conchita preferred the river and lots of company. He ate breakfast alone in the sunlit patio. Inside, she rattled pots and pans. Lord, what a racket! Then off she went to the market to haggle and gossip till noon.

March really wanted the mornings to himself out here in the sun and flowers to work on a report of the mine. For Finnerty, "in view of the alarming state of affairs increasing in this country," was finally evaluating all of Western Mines' holdings in Mexico and elsewhere.

March sent his lengthy report to Klaus, and he with corrections forwarded it to Finnerty. On it Western Mines was to base its final decision whether to open up the mine for production or abandon it until times got better. But Klaus was apprehensive. His crushed side required surgery; there was no telling when he could get back to work. So with the report on the mine he finally sent in an account of his own accident with his doctor's statement, affirming that he had left March in charge of *La Mina Nueva.* March received copies of the report and correspondence, and continued his weeks of waiting.

Conchita at last made ready to leave; she was going to teach this year in a big school in a big town on the main railroad line. For days she talked excitedly of nothing else, but March sensed her reluctance. The family did not approve of her leaving such a fine *casa* and a rich man who had money whether he worked or not. Saturnino especially objected, forseeing his silver for *mezcal* cut off. Only blind old Maria Rita Campos was sympathetic to them both. "*Que lástima.* Perhaps the *Señor* will understand. Girls now-a-days – But we will take care of you. All will be as before."

March was touched. He put his arms around this splendid old woman. "*Mi madre,* I understand. She goes with God. And here all will be as before."

The last night he and Conchita spent together was an ordeal for them both. Conchita wept and stormed, swearing she would never leave. Between deluges of tears she gave way to gusts of passion that exhausted them both of all feeling. Next day, bright-eyed and cheerful, she held court to bid everyone goodbye. March then drove with her in the old *arraña* to catch the train. She was dressed in her squeaky shoes, pink dress, and pancake hat, with more new clothes in two new leather suitcases. She was still waving to him, hat askew, when the train rattled out of sight.

This was the vision of her that plagued him as he lay alone in an empty bed in an empty house night after night. Conchita as he had known her had vanished. Conchita with her ripe, warm, and red-brown body cloaked in a *rebozo,* trudging barefoot in the dust to town. Kneeling on the stone floor, beating out *tortillas.* Clap-clap-clap! An economic fact. Also the heartbeat of Mexico. Yet something within this passionate child of the earth had drawn her away in squeaky shoes, pink dress, and pancake hat; the same mysterious life-force that impelled the leaves of a plant to forever grow upward toward the sun. The same overpowering restlessness that had drawn him here to these remote sierras. A strange unfathomable destiny neither could resist with drawing her upward into the light of consciousness, and him downward into the shadowy realm of the unconscious. But here for a moment they had met and fused, briefly but fully as life allowed. Conchita! She had been his, and would always be his. He loved her. And now she was gone.

Outside, the lightning flashed. Thunder shook the sierras. The lashing rain whipped the banana trees all night. And in the morning, still grieving, he got up to fry his own eggs in an empty, lifeless house. What was happening within him? He did not know. So he kept waiting like a man whose only destiny was to touch bottom before he could rise again.

Eventually a letter came from the Vice-President in Charge of Operations of Western Mines. Finnerty remembered him well. He complimented March for having taken full responsibility for *La Mina Nueva* and submitting such an excellent report. Western Mines, however, could not at this time undertake development of the mine. March was to close it at once. A bonus of three months' salary was enclosed, terminating his services. "Keep in touch with me, however," he requested. "At the first opportunity we want to place you elsewhere." To this he added a pithy statement to the effect that Western Mines always assumed full responsibility for the welfare of its engineers. All of Von Ratlube's medical expenses would be borne by the company, and he would be transferred to a hospital in the States as soon as expedient.

March felt relieved. He closed up his house and for the last time held old blind Maria in a close embrace. *"Mi madre. Mi madre!"* Whom was he ever to call "Mother" besides Ona?

"It will always be your home when you return. Go with God and in the peace, Senor."

Saturnino rode with him to the mine. The shaft still gaped open. March closed the wound in Mother Earth with a blast of dynamite, and turned his back on 100,000 tons of undeveloped silver ore. Saturnino, dumb as he was, understood. They shook hands formally, and Saturnino turned back toward town. March, his duffle bag slung on the back of his mule, began climbing the dim trail up into the sierras.

8

No, nothing now troubled Rogier, who had weathered more storms than ever beset most men. He existed in a dusky limbo between two worlds, the silent darkness of the unconscious and the clamorous light of reason; to both he gave allegiance. He ate and slept well, pruned the currant bushes, interjected pithy comments into the conversation at the dinner table. He took pride in wearing clean shirts, although his trousers were always baggy. He trimmed his nails. And yet beyond these humble confines of his mortal existence in a shabby old house on Shook's Run, he was always aware of that other nebulous, timeless domain of which he was also a part.

If at times he was conscious of teetering on the hairline boundary between these two states of existence, either of which might claim him wholly, Rogier did not care. He felt himself beyond the tyranny of time and circumstance, like the majestic Peak which rose before him. It had suffered cataclysms and submergences only to rise again. So would he.

One afternoon in early spring the two halves of his being began to separate, each world claiming its own. He hobbled upstairs and went into the bathroom. Ona, sitting in Sister Molly's big room at the end of the hall, heard him go in and lock the door. Five minutes passed, then ten. She walked down the hall, knocked on the door. "Daddy! Are you still there?"

He angrily unlocked the door and burst out. The flap of his trousers was open. His face was gray. Without answering, he clumped down the stairs and hobbled through the yard to the chicken house. Here he squared off again and tried to urinate. The effort brought out drops of sweat to his blanched face.

Dom! What was the matter? Fighting against his fear, he buttoned up his pants and strolled out into the sunshine to compose himself. The sky was a stainless blue, the mountains clear and white. Yet all this, the unheeding world about him, seemed suspended in the tranquility of fearful suspense.

Driven by his necessity, he hurried around the shop to stand at the back fence. This time he was wracked by a pain that seemed to rip his groin and bowels with a saw-toothed knife.

"God Almighty!" he groaned. "I can't let water!"

The magnitude of this absurdity burst upon him like a thunderclap. Legs spread, he stood in a strained posture of micturition. His head was thrown back, and with wild beseeching eyes he searched the vast palimpsest of the sky for the faintest trace of help, of hope. There was neither. He howled his anguish; and fly still open, he ran out into the alley to stand at a telephone pole, and thence to the ash pit—to all the familiar spots where he had urinated in years past when too busy on his mining speculations to take time to go into the house. One was no more effective than the last. His every futile effort brought a resurgence of the terrible pain, and with it a mounting horror of what had befallen him. Howling his despair, he ran back into the house, bent over, clutching his groin with both hands.

Ona saw him coming. "Daddy! What's the matter? Your rupture?"

"I can't let my water! God Almighty, girl! I can't!" Doubling up as if caught by cramps, he let out another wild howl.

"Get on the bed and keep quiet. Quick! I'll get the doctor!"

Ona ran across the street to telephone from the grocery store. The doctor—the young one—was in; and fifteen minutes later he drove up in his car. With a catheter he drew Rogier's water and left the old man relieved.

Two hours later Rogier sneaked into the bathroom and came out shouting as before. He was bound up tighter than ever.

A second time the doctor came and relieved him, but now in the bedroom he handed Ona a small package. "A new catheter for you, Mrs. Cable. You'll have to learn how to use it from now on."

"What's that?" Rogier on the bed lifted a face suddenly transfixed.

"Just this," replied the young doctor flatly. "I can't be driving down here a dozen times a day to catheterize you. Mrs. Cable here seems to be the only one who can do it for you—unless you want a full-time nurse or to go to the hospital."

Rogier, unable to reply, turned first to the doctor and then to his daughter a look of unfathomable horror. Ona flinched. Too well she knew his fastidiousness, the monstrous restraint and courtesy of his Southern breeding which prevented him from discussing the facts of life even with his own family. In all his many illnesses he could hardly abide the touch of hands to his person. And now this! To have the secret parts of his body — his water drawn by his own daughter! Ona could read on his face how vile and degrading it seemed to him.

Father and daughter stared at each other without speaking. Then suddenly through his eyes she saw crack and burst asunder the fastnesses of Rogier's granite core. What misfortune and worry, old age and the threat of insanity had never accomplished, shame did in a single moment. His square jaw dropped heavily and hung in defeat. He seemed to crumble, inside, before her eyes.

"Daddy! Don' take it like that!" She flung her arms around him. "We've been through everything together, you and I. And what's this? Nothin'! It'll only take a minute. And besides, what else is there to do?"

"Come, come," spoke up the doctor with professional curtness. "I'll show Mrs. Cable right now how to use this new catheter."

Rogier did not answer. In a hypnosis of acquiescent horror he was led into the bathroom. A few minutes later he stumbled into his bedroom and undressed while Ona showed the doctor out. When she came back upstairs, the old man was in bed with his face turned to the wall. He never left it.

His sufferings increased. Drawing water from him became an increasingly difficult task for Ona and a more painful one for him. He could not masticate, and liquid food had to be forced down him. His feet were cold, even with a hot water bottle in bed. Soon his legs were numb to the knees. All the worn out parts of his body were ceasing to function. He was turning to stone. The earth, of which he had always felt himself a part, was reclaiming it own.

Leona and Nancy kept out of his room, yet the whole house seemed permeated by a miasma of death and decay. Mary Ann, rying to be efficient, stalled the doctor on every possible occasion. 'What is his condition? Is he making progress? What are you going to try now? Perhaps a consultation–"

"My dear madame! There is nothing to try. Your father is a worn-out watch. Old age is something we cannot mend. I'm only doing what I can to make easier his last days. Please!"

Mrs. Rogier accepted defeat the best of all. Something in him precious to her had died years ago; this was but a physical anticlimax. She became aware of this one afternoon while sitting at his bedside. Awakening from a nap, Rogier turned his head toward the open window and brushed back a wisp of white hair. "What's that–Akeepee? Didn't Sally Lee give her her sugar?"

"Land alive!" Mrs. Rogier turned her good ear toward the window. "That's some chickens outside, not a horse nosin' for sugar. Akeepee's been dead for nearly thirty years. You been dreamin', Daddy!"

"I reckon," Rogier assented listlessly.

"Why, I bet my bottom dollar you been dreamin' of all them pacers and trotters of yours," she went on cheerfully. "'Member the day Aralee won from Taffy Lass, and how Little Man tried to climb the telegraph pole? You was mighty proud of them horses, Daddy! Take Silver Night!"

She rambled on, trying to comfort the thin wasted mummy in its sarcophagus of blankets–he who for more than half a century had been the sturdy tree of life to which she had clung as a parasitic mistletoe, frail as she was. "B. N." – "Big Nigger" – that had been her nickname for him long ago, when she married him at sixteen, because he was to her a faithful protector, abundant provider, and unobtrusive master like that big Negro body servant who still lingered in the magnolia-frail memories of her earliest childhood.

Rogier roused, eyes clearing. "Marthy, those mines were no good. None of 'em ever panned out. A wild goose chase, like you always said. I guess you never knew –"

And suddenly she realized there was in him something she had never known. For sixty years she had known him – her own husband: his weaknesses and his strength, his idiocyncrasies, his confounded stubborness and splendid folly. But a secret something in him always had kept them apart. It was not her illness, his busy professional life; not their own children, Boné, or Sister Molly's two boys whom they had reared, the many other mouths he had fed; not even his inborn aloofness, his undemonstrativeness, aristocratic restraint, and independence. It was something more chimerical and hence more powerful, like a star to which his life had been dedicated at birth. It had led him across the wilderness of a continent, to the ridgepole of the Rockies, to a single snowy peak—a star which had gleamed and faded, but to which alone he had been wholly faithful. Not knowing it, she had never really known him. It frightened her.

"Never mind those old mines, Daddy! Who cares?"

Rogier clumsily laid his hand on hers. "You never got away from Shook's Run. To that big house in the North End."

Her slim body rose erect on its straight chair at the bedside. Involuntarily she withdrew her hand from his unaccustomed caress, then quickly clutched it again. This frank avowal coming from him after so many years was more than she could bear.

"Oh shoot, Daddy! I haven't been rememberin' that foolishness for years! Why, this old house has always been a mighty lovin' nest to us and ours!"

Her embarrassed voice dwindled away. Rogier was not to be stopped. "Marthy, I been pigheaded, but not blind. You've missed a lot. Maybe we both have."

His voice, welling up thickly from the granitic stopes of his congealing body, caught and held her. A film was gathering over his eyes again, yet through it blazed a flicker of his indomitable spirit. Mrs. Rogier went stiff. To acknowledge the mystery of their lives, the unbearable truth of their essential separateness through their years together, was something she had no strength to endure.

From the depths of her body she wanted to shriek, "Stop! Let it pass unknown! Let this familiar stranger pass in the loved guise I knew always!" And she silently prayed Heaven to prevent him from unmasking his naked soul at last. With effort she controlled herself, seeking refuge behind the barrier of the plausible.

"We've had a fine, full life together, Daddy," she said, tenderly stroking his head. "You've had ever'thing happen to you and you pulled through. This is a tough time, no escapin' that. But you're goin' to come through with flyin' colors. You're on the stretch, Daddy! Come on, rest and sleep and get strong. I'll be here at the finish."

He did not reply. She gave him a sip of water and leaned back, holding his hand.

Rogier awoke in a heavy darkness, blacker than the space between the midnight stars. All around him pressed walls of rock. They squeezed his body, forced the air out of his lungs. A drop of sweat rolled down his cheek. Still he lay there, unmoving, feeling his flesh congealing and adhering to the granite. Now he knew where he was. In a dark stope in the depths of the Peak. There was the drip of subterranean water, the slow pulse of living stone. He was down — way down. Then up from the blackness rose a faint light.

"Reynolds! Hey Reynolds!" he cried out in a hoarse whisper.

The light swelled like a halo, approached swiftly.

It was Ona setting a lamp on the table.

"You're not worrying about Old Man Reynolds? He's been gone for years," she said softly but resolutely. "Here." She wiped off his face with a warm wet cloth.

"What time is it?" articulated Rogier.

"Maybe midnight. No matter. I'll sit here as always."

He was profoundly grateful. Dom everybody else! Only she comforted him. Cut of a piece, they were more than father and daughter. She understood him.

"Cable had no business bein' in the Sylvanite," he muttered hoarsely. "You're not holdin' it against me, girl?"

"No, Daddy," she answered without subterfuge. "It just happened. He had no place anywhere except with us for the time he was here."

"Good girl, Ona." The old man closed his eyes. Then suddenly, from a wide mouth opened by his unhung jaw, he began breathing great gasps which seemed to tear his chest apart.

Ona stared at him, clenching her fists, then flung herself on the cot across the room. Rogier was dying as he had lived, boring down, ever down. In the last days of his grass roots waking state, he had paid off with pain his mortal debts to the surface world which had borne him. The earth had claimed him. And as he sank into its depths in a dream state, its drifts and stopes of living flesh kept closing on his own, constricting his breathing, pressing out in dreams and memories the last residue of experiences and impressions collected in his mortal lifetime.He was quite aware, in his conscious moments, of the joy and guilt they contained. But these were only momentary judgments and evaluations of the surface world above to which he had never wholly subscribed, irascible and independent as he had been. If for the moment he acknowledged them, it was only to get rid of them. For now, unencumbered, he could sink down more often for longer intervals to a third and deeper level. In this state of dreamless sleep all his bodily aches and pains, his conscious worries, and the memories, dreams, and fantasies squeezed out of his unconscious, were obliterated. He knew nothing. Yet he knew all without knowing from this deepest level of his being—all that he had subtly felt throughout his life, all that he had blasted and drilled for through hard granite into the depths of a mountain peak. A mere lump of fleshy earth like his own, whose heart and meaning were coincident with his own. Rogier at last had reached his deepest, richest stope. And when more and more infrequently he shot up the shaft to surface, blinking at rational daylight, he fuzzily resented these interruptions in his true existence.

Still he did not die. It was taking the earth a long time to claim him, a man made of granite. How horrible, indecent, revolting, this dying man who was denied the grace of an easy death as he had denied an easy life. The family was exhausted; even Mrs. Rogier prayed for him a quick and easy end. But it was Ona who fought the doctor for it.

"I fail to see just what you're hinting at, Mrs. Cable," he said after a long conversation.

"Good God!" she flung back, at the limit of her endurance. "Have you no understanding, no human sympathy? Look at him lying there with his sufferings, his intolerable stench! And yet you stand there like a fool asking what I want, what he wants. Death, I tell you! A quick and compassionate death!" She leaned back against the wall, panting for breath. "A pill under the tongue. Something to put in his drinking water tonight. Anything!"

The young doctor for once had lost his composure. He flushed, gasped, yanked a finger under his collar. "Mrs. Cable! I understand your feelings. But such a thing is unethical in my profession. I cannot countenance it!" He caught up his medicine kit and plunged down the stairs in hasty retreat.

"You cowardly wretch! You poor excuse of nothin'!" Ona shrieked after him. "Don't you ever come here again!"

"I'll stop by in the morning!" he shouted back. "Perhaps I can do something!"

The following night, after an absence in a coma which had lasted some twelve hours, Rogier returned and flicked open his eyes. It was nearly two o'clock. The night lamp was smoking on the table beside Ona across the room She was sound asleep in her chair, completely exhausted.

"Ona!" he called in a tearing gasp no louder than a whisper.

The woman stirred gently, her head wobbling sleepily on its full neck, then limply falling back with a dull thud against the wall. All again was smothered in silence.

It was suddenly broken by the sound as of steps coming up the creaking stairs. Rogier struggled up an inch or two against the head of the bed. His clouded gray eyes lighted with a resurgence of life like that of dying embers before they were wholly consumed. The steps halted on the landing, came down the hall, and stopped in front of his open bedroom door. Rogier could not see his callers in the murky light of the smoking lamp. There was no need to. He reared up with eyes blazing recognition of the presence of those two invisible, faithful, old family retainers. His lips contorted in a silent shriek. He flung up his hand in a synonymous gesture of hail and farewell.

Then it dropped heavily. His head fell back. Something thick and warm rose and clogged his throat—the last organic something not yet congealed into stone within him. He gave one more rending gasp, one last cry to Ona and the Kadles, to all that was human and ghostly in that old house which had been his home.

It was this that roused Ona. She leaped to her feet, fell on her knees at his bedside, clutching his shoulders.

Rogier had already passed—a man who had died as he had lived, alone.

The funeral was held in the house three days later. There was a mass of flowers: enormous wreaths from Sally Lee and Boné, a profusion of bouquets from friends and neighbors, and a small token of white roses fashioned into the shape of a miner's pick. Attached to it was an unsigned card that read: "In memory of a hard-rock man from some of his old workers."

This anonymous offering from a group of men who sometime had worked for Rogier brought tears to Ona's eyes for the first time. It was the one sincere tribute she acknowledged. Stonily she had watched Mrs. Rogier's childish pride at receiving so many flowers: the splendid tributes to the dead from those who had ignored the living; from those whose flower-money would have eased a few moments of his years of suffering; from those who had been too ashamed of him to call upon him during his affliction.

The funeral seemed to her a travesty. The notice of Rogier's death brought a few old-timers more fortunate in Cripple Creek than he. Their big cars made an impressive showing in front of the drab old house. But if their greetings to Mrs. Rogier glowed with sweet memories of their early life in Little London, they discreetly avoided any mention of the years between.

For the most part the house was filled with curious neighbors. The big sliding redwood doors between the front room and dining room had been rolled back; the glass cabinets of ore specimens had been dusted; the Victrola was covered with a moth-eaten Confederate flag. Both rooms and the hall were crowded with those who had hooted at the crazy old man from their stoops, jeered at him across the back fences, thrown stones at him, and slapped each other hilariously as they recounted on street corners his latest frailty. Yet now that he had gone they suddenly felt the absence of a man whose infuriating idiocyncrasies had isolated and made him an individual in their midst—an uncomprehended stranger whose awry and indomitable life yet had echoed something of each one there. So they had flocked here to pay him homage with their final curiosity.

Ona, moving about, could hear snatches of their whispers.

"A fine old man, eh, Mr. Johnson? I won't forget the way he used to chase them chickens with a club, yellin' at the top of his voice."

"Didn't nobody ever find out about that there backyard mine of his? You know, the old man used to be richer'n all get-out. Had race horses and all that. Look at them flowers and the North Enders sittin' up front! What I mean is did the old codger think there was gold in his back yard, or had he buried some there and was tryin' to find where he'd put it? Do you suppose we could get leave to dig out there ourselves?"

There was a sudden stir in the hall.

"Mr. Pyle! And Mrs. Pyle! Well!" Mrs. Rogier exclaimed in a delighted voice. "We been savin' you seats."

"Tut, tut! No trouble to come at all," the Rogiers' cadaverous next-door neighbor declared pompously. And then in a quick whisper to Ona, "You might be sellin'. Or need a new mortgage. Let me know first. I — "

"Sit down!" Ona said curtly, and turned away.

The master of ceremonies arrived: an old friend of Rogier's for forty years or so, the preacher who had married Ona and Cable and who now, after his retirement from the ministry, was eking out an existence as a librarian. Old and somewhat infirm, he took his place up front. Now silence filled the house. Rogier no longer held the principal role in this reenactment of the drama of all humanity; an invisible presence had replaced him. The audience subtly changed into participants. Not now were they curious and gossiping spectators, but people of simple hearts, slow to understand and slower to forgive what they could not understand, but recognizing now as all must recognize the simple dignity of death.

The service, as Rogier would have wished and as Ona had insisted, was very brief: a few words about Rogier's fifty-six years in Little London and Cripple Creek, a prayer, and a hymn sung to the accompaniment of a borrowed piano. Then all filed past to look at the dead man in his simple, sturdy casket. A fairly good job had been done on the corpse. His black broadcloth suit hid his wasted form. He still wore a starched white collar fastened with his diamond collar-button, and without a necktie. His square face, whose cheeks were stuffed with cotton and rouged too redly, looked broad and resolute. Synthetically freed from the ravages of illness and old age, the old man looked better than he had for ten years. And as his indomitable spirit had retreated from his granite body, it seemed to have left it something of its dignity.

Now it was over.

Ona watched the cars roll away with their few occupants. Mr. Pyle, freed at last from the thorn in his flesh, scuttled off quickly. Mr. Bryce had to get back to his grocery store. There were no cars for the crowd in such a run-down neighborhood. Ona and the rest of the family rode in young Dutch's tourist car behind the hearse; behind it followed a couple of others.

The burial place was the family lot in the cemetery southeast of town. It lay on a ridge of the bluffs covered with pine and spruce. The road curved past the great Stratton monument, marble crypts, bronze-door mausoleums, rows of impressive tombstones. The short cavalcade stopped in front of the huge pine which marked the Rogier lot. Ona dug her fist into her mouth. Unable to afford proper care, she saw that the graves of Mrs. White, Sister Molly, and Cable were sunken under their rotting wooden headboards and covered with weeds. On the opposite slope of the ridge one of her childhood playmates had been scalped by Indians while herding sheep. In the gulch between lay an accumulation of refuse and tin cans.

Mrs. Rogier wept into her lace hanky at the sight. "I don't care – I don't care – It's still got one more place."

Between the wide tawny prairies and the high blue mountains surmounted by their sentinel Peak, Ona stonily watched the coffin being lowered into the grave. It had been dug through adobe and loose country rock into hard granite. Here Rogier was finally laid to rest – into that mysterious and eternal earth which at last accepted as its due that dust within the rock with a hospitality it had never accorded the stubborn and futile gropings of his outrageous spirit.

9

Just where he was going and for what, March didn t know. Perhaps, on the surface, to see Klaus in Guadalajara before their lives separated. He could have taken the weekly stub train to the main line and traveled comfortably by railroad. But this would have been only trying to rationalize the irrational. There was still in him an unspent residue of his tormenting unrest. Somewhere, sometime, he had to touch bottom before he could begin his long climb upward. And so alone he crept into the mysterious wrinkled Sierras Madres, the naked profundity of the mother mountains of Mexico.

There kept rising before him a sunlit wilderness of parched brown rock. Jagged sierras studded with chaparral and cactus, and seamed with stupendous gorges and canyons. Suddenly from a high rimrock he looked down into the *Barranca* – that vast chasm with its maze of canyons cut through the backbone of a continent. Far below him he glimpsed the river threading its way through clumps of lemon, orange, and mango trees. And in between, on the steep rocky slopes of the canyons, the Tarahumaras, said to be the least known, wildest, and most primitive of all tribes.

All through the sierras March had glimpsed them. A single man, naked except for a breechclout and with long uncombed hair, appearing for an instant and then vanishing like an animal wary of human contact. Or a couple standing forlornly on a street corner. Little people, with the wonder and the mystery in their dark eyes. This was their homeland, but where were they?

Occasionally he came upon a rock hut beside a tiny *milpa* of corn on a rocky hillside, or a cave in the cliffs. A glimpse inside revealed their life: raising a few stalks of corn, grinding the kernels on a stone *metate;* herding a little band of goats, and weaving the hair into *serapes, cobijas,* and belts on a crude horizontal loom; carrying a bag of tropical fruit to sell in a remote settlement.

But how wary the Tarahumaras were! On the steep hillsides he caught glimpses only of their browsing goats, and heard the shrill plaintive wail of their reed flutes warning of his approach. Thousands of them scattered throughout this vast uncharted maze, but without villages and tribal unity, hiding in these isolate gorges, these uterine folds and cavern wombs of their eternal earth mother.

His encounter with them came unexpectedly. Rounding the end of a cliff wall, he rode into a large encampment on the level floor of a pocket canyon. Sight and sound hit him simultaneously. A *fiesta* of sorts was going on, and many of the Tarahumaras were dressed for the occasion. In the fading afternoon light he could see men in ragged *pantalones* and shirts, with feathers stuck in their straw hats; women dressed in voluminous skirts and red kerchiefs, all packing babies on their backs. Behind them sat others who had come from their isolate huts and caves in the far canyons wearing only breechclouts, *serapes,* and red kerchiefs twisted around their long tangled hair. A few men were shuffling in a dance to the hoarse beat of a small drum, the *kampora,* and the shrill whistle of the *baka,* a reed flute. Across the circle a man was squeaking on a hand-carved violin.

March reined up his old mule at once, and dismounted. A tremor of excitement, perhaps alarm, passed through the crowd. Always the fear of intrusion by strangers. Patiently and politely, March kept waiting. Finally the *Seligame,* carrying the lance which showed him to be their head man or chief, came up to him with two other men. In simple Spanish he invited March to the fiesta, and conducted him to the gathering. As March approached, the dance and music stopped. The people rose to greet him. They slithered up to him softly on bare feet, eyes demurely lowered. Then they raised both hands and gently touched their palms or the tips of their fingers to his own, sometimes murmuring a soft "Kevira." Always this softness of voice, gesture, and manner. Then as they looked up, he could see in the blackness of their eyes the remoteness of the *barranca* itself, the withdrawn look of a people who had never emerged from its dark depths.

Next morning the races began, the men runners kicking a wooden ball over the long course and the women using a small hoop and stick. These races, March learned, were features of all their infrequent gatherings. For the Tarahumaras were famed long-distance runners, accustomed to running down a deer, and able to jog a hundred miles without stopping. Their own name for themselves was *Raramuri,* compounded of the words *rara* for "foot" and *juma,* "to run." There was need for their unbelievable endurance in this rugged wilderness. They were too poor to afford guns, and the sparse game was too wild to approach with bow and arrows. So doggedly they would run down a deer until it was exhausted and then cut its throat with a knife.

What a pitiful *fiesta* it was, compelled by the people's need for communion after months of isolation in their far canyons. Little half-starved men toughened to hardship, women suffering from syphillis and intestinal ailments, rachitic children. Dressed in the pitiful finery of their red kerchiefs, ragged pants and skirts, and feathers. Dancing their *dutuburi* to chanting and rattling. Eating a few scraps of meat and corn, and drinking the little coffee March was able to contribute. A people with the humility of a great pride, the gentleness of a great strength, and a great passion for their freedom. Yet a people who had never broken free of the earth serpent, their mother. March could see in their eyes the perpetual darkness of their deep barrancas.

But if there was little food, there was at last *tesguino,* a strong liquor brewed from the corn they had contributed. Up the canyon the *hechizero,* the shaman or medicine man, had built a fire surrounded by a magic ring of earth. Into it he was dancing, shaking his little bells. Calling forth the powers of the *peyote* taken by the watchers squatting around the ring.

The tinkle of the bells. The reflection of the leaping flames against the cliffs. The puking of men around him. The whole eerie ritual of a people trying to surmount the limits of their earth-bound existence. All this, with the nauseating effect of the few peyote buttons he had chewed on top of the strong *tesguino*, made March deathly ill. He puked into the little hole dug before him. Then he crawled weakly back to the encampment. And here, sunk deep into a shadowy world unlit by the light of reason, he remained.

Now it was over. The sun rising over the rimrock was flooding the canyon with brightness. The encampment was breaking up. He could see the Raramuri straggling off, climbing the steep hillsides, returning to their far canyons. And it seemed that he was watching all humanity streaming out from its common womb of the unconscious, beginning its slow climb into the light and freedom of consciousness. Nothing could stop it, even here among this last great tribe of the Raramuri.

Something had happened to him he could not yet see clearly. But he knew at last he had touched bottom.

The perpetually starved Raramuri of course had killed and eaten his old spavined mule. But one of the young men slung his duffle bag to his shoulders, holding it steady with a tumpline passed across his forehead. He guided March out of the barranca to a small village.

A couple of days later he found a boy to guide him to the next one, each riding a burro. And so he kept climbing.

The villages were few and small. Tiny *ranchitos* of a few adobes or thatched *jacales* in a remote valley or clinging to a hillside beside their corn *milpas*. In one of them he might be marooned for two or three days, even a week. The boy who had brought him had returned to his own village with his two burros.

"Let us go on to the next village," March had urged. "It is only one day further. *Favór!*"

"No, *Iéfe*." The boy's black deer-eyes refused the offered silver. "Already I am one day from *mi tierra*. I must go back."

Mi tierra! Mi tierra! It always waits, this earth mother, for her son. The umbilical cord which binds him to it can be stretched no farther than a day.

And so March waited until he could find someone to guide him to the next *ranchito*. The trail, old as it was, he could never have found himself. March found a man. But first the *Señor* must wait; the earth is crying for its seed. A single day, *Señor!* But the tattered fellow spent a week stubbornly plowing his scrubby little hillside *milpa* with the crotch of a tree. "It is *mi tierra, Señor.*"

And so March waited: sleeping in an adobe, rolled up in his *serape* on a *petate* on the earthen floor with the rest of the family stretched out beside him, a dog and a goat stepping on his legs. Sometimes there would be a sliver of wild pig or scrawny chicken to eat, usually no more than beans, a bit of goat cheese, and a leathery *tortilla*.

He came back to the hut one evening to find the *Señora* in great distress. A terrible thing had happened. March was carrying with him a leather bag of silver *pesos* with which he was paying his expenses. That day while he was gone the naked children had undone the bag, rolling the silver cartwheels across the floor in play. To the old woman the money was an unbelievable treasure, more than she would see during the rest of her life. Yet she was down on her knees patiently hunting lest a *peso* might be lost. "*Señor!*" she wailed. "Tell me there is not one missing! I cannot count!"

He continued on, climbing higher and higher, yet sinking deeper and deeper into the ghostly flow of time, in an aimless journey whose details were always to remain clear but without fixed continuity, like the dream-flow of time itself.

He was in high country now, crossing the crest of the continental divide. Great bulks of heaving mountains dark with spruce and pine. Little patches of paper ice on the streams each morning, and once in awhile a thin sprinkle of snow. March found himself thinking of home, of the glistening silver peaks of the Rockies –

Winter! Who knows winter except the mountain-bred northerner who then comes into his own? Like all seasons it is a world apart, and he who has once known its white and haunting silence feels elsewhere an outcast.

At the first frost the land changes tone, gives out a deeper note. The heaving earth subsides, sleeps under its thickening blanket. The lakes glass over like frosted mirrors; the last mallards and long-legged herons rise from the freezing marshes; the muskrats slide out of the ponds. Long slender aspen trunks turn white. Through the gelid gloom of the forests flap great arctic owls like ghostly white bats. Bears grumble sleepily in their lairs. From timberline deer wind down daintily out of the drifts.

The deep snows come. Softness alternates harshness. The tall peaks rear whiter, clearer, sharper against the amethyst sky; stupendous stalagmites reaching toward heaven from the earth below.

Winter wears the year's most precious jewels. Necklaces of snowbirds are strung between fence posts. Diamong dust glitters upon the fields. Glacé spruce branches droop *lavallieres* of metallic cones. Snowflakes are designs in the abstract, frosted window panes cut glass and rock crystal. The evening sun is a ruby in a platinum setting. Lakes are chunk turquoise mounted in hand-beaten Navajo silver.

But a single, bare, wind-warped juniper hangs to the sheer side of a snowy cliff. This is winter's real beauty, a stark nakedness of line with which nothing can compare.

Now all vibrates to a higher pitch: the hunger howl of cruising wolves muted by the shrieking winds; the music of the wintry stars; the pale sea-green, deep blue, and purple of the spectrum's cold end. Deep winter! It is a metaphysical phrase. For in winter, deep winter, the blood sinks down into its homeland, the hearth is its enduring symbol, and the wanderer yearns for his old seat.

You can smell the buckwheat cake batter souring on the back porches all winter long. It thickens the blood; you can tell in early March when it is time to stop, by the rash coming out on the skin. Then sassafras tea tonight, children, to thin the blood.

Up in Cripple Creek the bare granite boulders crack open like pistol shots. Miners' wives warm up frozen dynamite in their kitchen ovens, and from a carcass hack off chips of meat with a hand-axe. Along the narrow-gauge hay is thrown off to elk, starving, up to their bellies in snow and resting their antlers on the frozen crust. Abe and Jake are splicing a steel cable with frozen mittens. Rogier is damning the delay. And a dark, hawk-faced man is coughing beside the fireplace.

Spectral blue-white winter. In the winter the soul sinks home. It is rest for renewal, a gathering of life for another period of gestation. Oh, the year around I shall restlessly wander space. But in winter I seek depth. In winter my soul sinks home –

So March kept thinking of an old white-headed man and of those with him on Shook's Run, of the ghost of his father and his father's fathers. Yet he could not turn back. There was something, somewhere, he had to find that would tell him who and what he was: the leaf that falls into the flow or the leaf that sprouts anew; the rock shattered by frost and disintegrated by time, or the timeless dust within the rock. So from the top of one high ridge he climbed down into a deeper canyon, into the mindless depths of a timeless land and people.

The Yaquis in the mountain fastnesses of their turbulent river he had left behind. The broader-faced, docile Mayas had disappeared. He no longer glimpsed solitary Tarahumares. Who these Chinipas and Oleros were he did not know. The tribal idiomas kept changing. March was hard put to understand the people in the simple Spanish they both spoke. It did not matter. They were all little hills Indians with soft mobile bodies, arched chests, sturdy legs, and quick poetic hands. The soul image of an old dark race that time had never altered, men in whom the old gods were still strong.

It was difficult to find guides. March discovered that it was easier to obtain a small boy or an old man; they could be better spared from home and persuaded to talk. To induce conversation he made little pencil drawings of plants and herbs, asking their names and uses. The old men knew them all: *herba romero* to place on a cross when the owl cried at night; *guarapio* to put on the stomach for *cholerico;* the spear-leaved *amargosa* which could be crushed and applied to a knife cut; *tepusa* to bind on face and feet; and the small white flower of the *barablanca* for headache. He saw also the small *peyote* cactus which induced strange visions when chewed, and the devil's weed used by *diableros.* Even his boy guides knew the old trails, the sentinel peaks, the hidden shrines. The earth became alive, rich with new meanings.

He came one morning to a rocky hill on whose summit lay a bunch of fresh flowers and a turkey cock with its throat cut. The boy with him answered his questions by simply holding aside the brush to reveal the side of a cut-stone pyramid. *Aye, aye, aye. We are the feather, the flower, the drum, and the mirror of the old gods who will never die.*

A charcoal maker led him down into a village late one afternoon. A spermy white mist hung over the mountains. Water ran down his blackened face, soaked his *serape*. He gave his burro to March. The little beast had no bridle, and for a saddle only two flat sticks tied together with rawhide to keep his rider off the backbone. On this March sat holding his duffle bag, his long legs hanging nearly to the ground. The narrow trail wound downward along the bed of a swollen stream. The water swirled up his knees, rain streamed from his battered hat. The man in front splashed on. He had rolled up his white cotton pants, and at every step emerged his beautiful Indian legs. How smooth and round, never knotted with muscle, but so powerful! There was a strange strength and beauty in these men, thought March, but you've got to see their legs.

It was nearly dusk when from the rimrock of a teacup valley they saw below a great blackened-stone cathedral surrounded by a cluster of squat adobes. The milky white mist was lifting from the sheer wall of cliffs on the opposite side. On top of a crag March glimpsed a crumpled, truncated pyramid of weathered rock, an ancient Aztec *teocalli*.

They jogged down swiftly now to the first stub streets below. The charcoal maker stopped. "My house is off there," he said, nodding to the left.

March slid off the burro. "*Mil gracias*. How much is owing my friend?"

The man regarded him silently. "Fifty cents perhaps? I do not know."

"It is not enough. Will you accept a *peso?*"

The man took it proudly without thanks and turned away.

Darkness had fallen and with it an oppressive deadness. The people of the village, the man had said, still spoke Nahuatl; and like their Aztec forefathers, like the very stones, had sunk back down into the earth at dark. There was no inn for muleteers, no *casa de huespedes* where a chance stranger could find lodging. Not even a light. Wet and hungry, March stumbled around the dark, empty plaza.

A man appeared and led him home to a small adobe. Over a charcoal brasier huddled a woman and three half-naked children. March gratefully sank down in a corner, huddling in his *serape*.

Man and wife talked a long time together in the old tongue.

Then the man turned to March "We would be honored to have you, *Señor,*" he said in Spanish, in a soft proud voice. "But in town there is a bed. You will come, please?"

March followed him across the plaza, in front of the huge empty cathedral. The town was dark and dead as midnight. Not even a torch glimmered. The man pounded on a door. A voice sounded a whimpering, muffled fear. More talk. Then the door opened to show a wrinkled old crone holding up a cup of tallow with a lighted wick.

"This it is, the house which has a bed," explained March's companion. "Peace, *Señor.*"

"Go with God," replied March. "I shall come tomorrow with my thanks."

He followed the old woman through the *zaguan* to an immense, windowless storage room heaped with corn. Two more women came and laboriously moved the corn to one side. Then they brought pails of water, mops, brooms.

"Señoras! Ya esta limpia!"

Against his protests, they swept and washed the floor. Out again they went, leaving him squatting in the doorway, dead tired, soaking wet, hungry, and heavy with sleep. Soon they returned with the bed: a rude wooden frame, chest high, with a bottom of woven hemp cords. Over this they put a *petate* to lie on, and a dry *serape* to cover him.

"Gracias! Mil gracias! Buenas noches, Señoras!"

Their laborious preparations had taken an hour or more. The floor had dried, leaving only puddles on the worn stones. Yet this was not yet enough to do the stranger honor. The old crone returned with a yellowed shawl that had a long silk fringe; a descendant of one of the Chinese shawls lodged here on its way from China to Spain, and now called "Spanish." This she spread smoothly on the bed. At last she left him. "Peace, *Señor.*"

Peace. Always a dead sterile peace. A dark brooding heaviness impregnated with fear—of light and air, of strangers intruding with the clatter of horses' hoofs or the quick dull thud of a knife striking home. Peace. So March could hear them bolting the doors, whispering outside. But always honor and hospitality, despite the fear of betrayal. Warm with gratitude, March slept.

These were the *ranchitos,* the tiny villages, the centuries-old towns he found lost and forgotten in the waves of the heaving earth he breasted. Places having names in a strange tongue, fading into timeless time as one place, one name, the name of the bitter briefness of man's days, his hunger for the ever-beyond, and the haunting loneliness of one who saw on every face the enduring soul of a people rooted to their earth. In each a church, a crumbling mission, a great cathedral whose blackened stone walls would have held twice or ten times the population of the village. The monuments of a race which had impressed upon another a religion and a culture which had not sprung from its own soil. The tombs of *Senor Jesu Cristo,* a limp image of death in every church, gory with clotted red paint, pierced with cactus thorns. And outside, the weed-grown pyramids, the shrines along the mountain trails with fresh flowers and fresh blood, the little stone idols buried in the corn *milpas.* All proclaiming still the dark goddess with all the fertility of the earth itself. Tonantzin, ancient earth mother, in her mantle of sweeping rain. The new Guadalupana clad in the robe of heaven, in a blue mantle dotted with stars like toasted maize grains. Beat the tall drum *huehuetl,* the flat drum *teponaztle,* for the feather, the flower, the drum, and mirror of the old gods who had never died. But neither had they come to full flower, March thought; they too were entombed in walls of living flesh.

10

Eventually he came to a town, a *camion,* a railroad junction, and so reached Guadalajara. His uncut hair hung down his neck, his beard had grown, his clothes were tattered. He went to a barber shop, cleaned up as best he might. Possessed by an insane craving for sugar, he sat in the *plaza mayor* gorging on sticky sweet potatoes baked and smeared with *peloncillo,* on *dulces* bought from street-corner vendors. His duffle bag had fallen into a river while he was crossing on a raft; the old suit inside it was ruined; but in the lining of the trousers under the belt he had hidden a few *Banco de Mexico* paper notes. These he ripped out and went to the Hotel Imperial.

It was an enormous mausoleum of white marble full of overstuffed furniture and decorated with scrolls, doodads, and whatnots. Yet it was modern enough to boast showers and a good dining room in which he feasted on a *biftek* followed by *mole de guajalote.* Then clean and content he slept between sheets.

Next day, while waiting for changes to be made in a cheap new suit, he sat in the *plaza,* almost deafened by church bells: a resonant, deep-toned booming from the Byzantine towers of the 16th century cathedral, chiming, ringing, clanging from a dozen churches. After months of solitude in the wilderness he could not accustom himself to this second largest city in Mexico. Trains, trams, sleek limousines, and beautiful old carriages; men in tidy business suits, well-groomed women, children accompanied by *duenas;* filthy beggars, ragged *pelados,* Indians in their white cotton shirts and *pantalones.* They all swarmed by, faces white, dark, and *café-con-leche* which gradually merged into one face, the face of modern *mestizo* Mexico.

Every continent, March thought, had its own great spirit of place, its own polarity, its own terrestrial magnetism, whatever you chose to call it. The white Europeans who swarmed into this old New World with those two miracles, gunpowder and the horse, were not in tune with the land as were the indigenous Indians; they couldn't root themselves in a new homeland, conforming to its spiritual laws. So up in March's America they killed off the Indians, penning in reservations the pitiful remnants of the great tribes to deteriorate like buffalo in a zoo. But down here, cruel and rapacious as they were, the conquerors were gradually swallowed in the blood they had shed. A fusion took place between the white and the Indian, resulting in a new race, the *mestizo.*

White talcum powder splattered on dark cheeks, high French heels under barefoot Indian feet, the very skulls of the whites gradually tending to conform to the head type of the Indians. One face, one people, growing from the same soil.

A gradual amalgamation of races was an inevitable necessity, March thought. No tribe – not even the Tarahumaras, no race, could forever escape it. In one vast stream all humanity kept welling up from its common cavern womb, the dark unconscious, into the light of consciousness. Nothing could dam its flow; it would eventually wipe out all differences of race, creed, and culture in one great blending of all.

An amalgamation that would not be a scientific mixture of customs, beliefs, and wills, that would not be an economic trade, but which would gather these in its flow. A fusion that would be the death of each, the white and the Indian, as he was today. A death and a great rebirth. And from them, together, the new American – a new continental soul reborn, with new spiritual conceptions and moving to a more profound rhythm than either had ever known.

The shops were closing. The street lights were coming on. The church bells were still ringing. Still March sat there in the gathering dusk.

Mexico! The motherland of his western America, whose remote sierras and faint trails had led him from space to depth, the only answer to the flow of time. Mother Mexico which had settled forever the spirit of his tormenting unrest and given him the answer to himself.

Finally, late next afternoon, he went to see Klaus. The German was living in an old residential hotel with a little private patio where he could be waited upon. His head, broken arm and ribs had long healed; the surgery on his side had been successful; the hospital had discharged him to recuperate.

"*Himmel!* It was nothing!" roared Klaus, giving March the *embrazo*. "Klaus loafs like a gentleman on company expenses! Little brother! Tonight we will drink much beer and see the beautiful girls of Guadalajara together! That suit does not fit. Klaus shall take you to his tailor tomorrow!"

They dined regally at the Fenix, got a little drunk together, and dozed through the antics of an all-blond, nude chorus at the expensive La Azteca cabaret. Then they drove home in a carriage to Klaus' hotel to come awake again on French brandy.

Klaus was eager to get to work again. Finnerty had written him of two possible openings. "Pachuga! Who does not know the mines of Pachuga? So close to Mexico City! But Guanajuato, little brother! The Veta Madre is the richest silver lode in the world. It will not be exhausted in another 500 years. We will be kings together, *cómo no?*"

Stimulated by brandy, he talked on. Suddenly he broke off, slapped his leg. "*Mein Gott!* The *telegrama*. Where is it?" He rummaged through a desk, a stack of papers on the table, and finally passed to March a dirty wrinkled envelope.

March slit it open and glanced at the date, nearly three weeks back. It was from his mother. For an instant he hesitated before reading the terse message. His presentiment of its meaning changed to a certitude that filled him with a tearing pain and anguish such as he had never known – Then suddenly the words gleamed and blurred before him with the evanescent brilliance of the one and only truth of all men's lives—the gleam of a rising star which lights up for each our loneliness, our grandeur, and despair, then fades and dies without leaving a mark of its passage on the eternal skies of night.

Klaus had poured himself another brandy and was still talking. "Guanajuato. *Ja!* That is the place for us, *Bruderlein!* A 500-year-old Spanish colonial citadel high in the hills, like a castle on the Rhine. Great old houses. Good food. And the girls! Ripe little peaches hanging on old family trees. Just waiting for Klaus and March to squeeze out their juice. Eh, little brother? And the silver. Mountains of silver. Klaus will write Finnerty tomorrow."

March stood up, sobered, cold, and resolute. "No Klaus. No more mining. I'm through with Mexico. I'm going home." He lunged out the door.

Klaus went with him to the station next evening. They clasped hands, then Klaus laid his arm over March's shoulder. "We shall not forget, eh *Bruderlein?*" And March, looking into his friend's face, knew suddenly what he had meant to him. The train pulled slowly out of the station, the dusty valley, into the darkness of his own thoughts.

To March that long and tiresome journey home seemed not a matter of spanning space, but of decreasing depth.

Grieving over Rogier's death, irritated at himself for receiving Ona's telegram so late, and ashamed of missing the funeral, he felt like a man slowly lifting from the bottom of a mine. The slow train rocked like an ascending hoist, his ears plugged, he yearned for light. But he was rising, ever rising. The sierras dwindled, muddy rivers slid by, the swampy lowlands fell behind with their matted jungle growth and cloying heat. He felt the rush of cool air. And then one morning he saw what every miner sees with a leaping heart—the source of all beauty, light. It was sunrise over a vast tawny desert hirsute with cactus, the high Sonoran mesa stretching into Arizona. He had emerged at last.

He got off the train at the end of the railroad line and was cleared across the International Line by customs officials. The little border town was hauntingly familiar. *Cantina* lights were beginning to blaze forth, *taco* vendors were lighting their kerosene lamps, Ford *camiones* loaded with big-hipped men and scrawny little *Señoras* rushed past him. The border had not changed, but it seemed different. The brutal pock-marked faces of the half-breeds, the hopeless faces of the decadent Indians, the hard cunning faces of the whites, all seemed to him curiously blended and subdued. That deep dark chasm seemed inexplicably to have flattened out. The border was no longer a depthless pit between two races. It was a bridge. March felt a nameless ecstasy beginning to well from his heart. Neither space nor depth held now for him any fear. He had bridged them both.

He was in his own country. Everybody was talking English. English slang! He stopped at a neon-lit "Cut Rate" drug store. Colored placards swung on strings from the ceiling, decorated the shelves. A raucous voice shrieked from a microphone "Two for a quarter!"—"Ninety-eight cents while they last!"—"One cent sale today only!" He saw thirty-nine brands of tooth-brushes, sixty-two kinds of tooth-paste, rubber gloves, patent medicines, vaginal douches, pure ivory back-scratchers, colored postcards, rayon panties, tobacco, cigarettes, candy, stewing pans, chewing gum, miniature turtles, Siamese fish, electric frying pans, and at the soda fountain signs advertising nut sundaes, banana splits, and Lovers' Delight. All Reduced for Today Only. Mechanistic, materialistic *Estados Unidos* of the *Imperialisimo Yanqui* selling its soul for the good old American Dollar, its standard of culture. But who could buy it? Everybody else was after the dollar too.

How vulgar it was. But it seemed to March the naive vulgarity of children, of a nation, a people who had not yet grown up. This was his country; he loved it all. Imagine! Cellophane-packaged handerchiefs, a dime apiece! He bought three for a quarter, on sale for today only, and hurried out like a thief.

He caught the north-bound train. He had watched the lofty peaks of Ixtaccihuatl and Popocatepetl fade into the turquoise with a sense of irrevocable loss. Now, like a man who must have a snowy peak on the horizon to give his life meaning and direction, he watched for another even more familiar. It began to rise north of the Sangre de Cristos, the slow uplift of a range long and blue as that of a great fish rising out of the pelagic plain. And then he saw it, a great snowy peak too high for any mortal man to climb. Pike's Peak!

March knew now he had come to home.

It was late afternoon when he got off the train and walked through Little London, still carrying his duffle bag. The lilacs were out; the warm sunshine was redolent with spring; tourist cars whizzed past into the canyons. How he had hated his town's smugness and choking conservatism, its gaudy make-believe, and pretentious air. But all this he saw now only as a cosmetic mask. It would crack and wear away as all superimposed cultures must fade and pass away. And he remembered the great pyramids he had seen, the crumbling cathedrals, the haunting look in the eyes of the Tarahumaras. From this Little London with its false ideals he saw rising the Little London of tomorrow—a town rooted to its own *tierra*, with its own traditions, and proudly conscious of its own integral uniqueness.

From the top of Bijou Hill he saw Shook's Run with its new bridge, the haunted old house. *Mi tierra. Mi casa.*

Ona met him in the hall.

"*Mi madre!* Mother! Oh, Mother!"

Blinded, dazed, he heard a rush of feet, felt Leona and Nancy poking him in the ribs, Mary Ann and Uncle John wringing his hand. And then he saw and grabbed the little frail figure of Mrs. Rogier.

"Granny! Why, Granny—"

But deep in his heart was an emptiness that could not be filled. Helplessly he stared into the rickety empty chair in the corner. He had returned to his grandfather's house, but it would never be quite the same.

March had missed Rogier's funeral, but he had arrived in plenty of time for something as distressing—the dissolution of a family that during three generations had endured in this haunted old house on Shook's Run.

The big question had been what to do with the house. Mary Ann had answered it at a family conference shortly before March arrived. "I saw Mr. Pyle yesterday," she announced abruptly. "I told him he could handle the house. There's a mortgage on it which must be met. It might as well be sold."

Ona's face flushed with anger. "Pyle! That shyster! Never! Daddy would turn over in his grave if Pyle ever laid his sticky hand on this house. Who gave you permission to boss this affair, anyway?

It's Mother's own house, in her own name, and she's going to live here as long as she pleases."

"Now, Ona, be practical for once in your life," remonstrated Mary Ann. "Look at it. A ramshackle old barn of three stories and nine big rooms, and the shop in back. No paint for years. No garage. And set in a neighborhood that soon will be really a slum. Besides, it's already been done. I gave Pyle the go-ahead, with Mother's signed power of attorney."

"The devil you say!" ejaculated Ona, jumping to her feet and staring down accusingly at Mrs. Rogier.

"I don't know. I don't understand," wailed Mrs. Rogier. "I just signed the paper like she said."

Mary Ann efficiently took over. When March arrived he observed that a junk dealer already had cleaned out the back yard of the last of the old winches and rusty cable reels which Rogier had held on to so indomitably. His prized hand tools in the shop had been sold in one pile. Ona had rescued for March only his miner's candlestick and a polished bird's-eye maple T-square Rogier had made in Maryland and with which he had drawn all his plans.

"What's become of that big trunk of Indian stuff on the Third Floor?" he asked Ona. In it had been packed Cable's fringed buckskin shirt with its panels of stained porcupine quills, the huge Cheyenne war bonnet of eagle feathers tipped with red yarn buckskin leggings, Arapaho moccasins, a bundle of sacred arrows, and a prized medicine pouch; and with these, the Navajo and Pueblo collection Cable had brought back from Shallow Water. A man's simple and priceless heritage bequeathed to his son.

Ona sighed. "It was gone before I knew it. I don't know where. A museum man or somebody took it. Shall we try to get it back?"

"Let it go!" he said harshly.

Then suddenly one morning a second-hand book dealer arrived with two trucks. A pair of scales was set up in front of the shop. One after another the men came out with armloads of books. They were stuffed in gunny sacks, weighed, and thrown in the trucks: Rogier's library of a lifetime which had lined two walls of his shop. The *Bhagavad Gita, Gilgamesh Epic, Tel-El-Amarna Letters of Babylonia and Egypt,* the *Book of the Breaths of Life,* the *Kabbalah* and *Lament of Lamech*, the *Koran* from Arabia and the *Shah Nameh* from Persia, the Egyptian and the Tibetan *Book of the Dead*, the *Upanishads* and *Suttas*, *Analects of Confucius*, "New Thought" books and books of cheap mysticism, the Masonic plates for which he had paid a hundred dollars apiece, and the pamphlets he could never refuse at a dime; his shelves of mathematics, engineering dynamics, and geology; of philosophy, art, and history; and lastly his countless rolls of maps.

Mrs. Rogier, Ona, and March stood helplessly beside Mary Ann. A book fell out of a sack and split open to reveal a yellowed slip of paper. It was an old signed check made out to Rogier by Stratton at the time he was worth ten million dollars, and the amount was not filled in. March handed it to Ona. "Here. Put this in your family Bible."

"I can't stand it!" moaned Mrs. Rogier. "Next to his mines and horses Daddy loved his books. Almost as much as his children. He spent more time with them."

"Don't be foolish!" Mary Ann answered sensibly. "Books are the most useless commodity in the world. It costs more to cart them around than to buy new ones. And where'd you put 'em?"

March stood watching in silence. There had been the day when he would have regarded this disgraceful scene as a sacrilege. But now, he thought, Mary Ann was right. Forty pounds of religion. Sixty pounds of philosophy. A hundredweight of science, art, and history. Throw on the *Divine Comedy*—that'll tip the scales. Dead weight all of it. Four thousand years of knowledge—and a woman's song on a deserted *plaza* at midnight, the pleading look in the eyes of a primitive Tarahumara refuted it all. It is not dead knowledge we need, but the intuition of the living moment.

So he stood there, raising his eyes to the snowy Peak towering in the blue. In it lay Rogier's life, his triumph, his folly and despair. It was not books that Rogier had plumbed, but the earth itself.

More trucks came to empty the house of nonessential furniture, doodads and whatnots. Pyle stood at the fence rubbing his hands in approbation. He had great plans for the house, he said. Its three stories and many rooms could easily be converted into a lodging house of several flats and separate rooms for individual lodgers; maybe even a boarding house. Also the huge shop in back would make an excellent apartment when adequately partitioned. The family was too shocked to say a word.

That evening at dinner March turned casually toward Mary Ann. "You haven't forgotten a thing. Now tell me, what disposition have you and Pyle made for the Kadles?"

"They can go to hell with their everlasting squeaking—or with you to Patagonia or wherever you traipse off to next!"

It was an unwarranted disapproval of those two invisible but faithful members of the family that shocked everyone at the table, but which revealed to them that even Mary Ann was upset.

11

Where all of them were going became the constant subject of conversation between Ona and March when they sat alone up in the Third Floor. Mary Ann's and Uncle John's Chocolate Shoppe in Manitou had been quite successful, but of course there was always the winter slump. They now intended to move it to Denver. "Little towns have always been my big mistake," she maintained. "For high class confectionery you've got to have a year-round trade that appreciates quality." Mrs. Rogier and Ona, with the money left from the sale of the house, were going to move into a small flat away from this part of town where they wouldn't be troubled by heartaches. In fact, they had looked at one in the North End. "Not too far up, and a bit west," Ona added quickly. "It won't spoil us, and we can see the mountains across the creek. A pretty view. You know it was up in the North End where we first lived. In a house built like a Maltese cross, near the Big Ditch the Indians used to splash across on their ponies."

She was silent a moment. "We haven't told you before, son, but Leona won't be with us. She wants to get married and I guess we ought to let her. A nice young man. You'll meet him soon. And they'll be living here in town where we can see them often."

"And Nancy will be moving to Denver?"

"No, she's not going with Mary Ann and Uncle John. They'll have too much to do, getting a new business started, to give her much company. Besides, Nancy's always been with us. And she's going to stay with Mother and me, still workin' downtown in the ten cent store, pots and pans department. With her droopy eye she doesn't get out often, you know. So like I told her, we'll be three homebodies together, like we always been."

It was this yet unbroken pattern of their lives that was in Ona's mind several days later as she sat at the window waiting for March to return from Cripple Creek. A letter had come to him from the Vice-President in Charge of Operations of Western Mines. Finnerty remembered him well; he had done excellent work for the company in Mexico. Conditions were such that Western Mines had no opening for him at present in the United States, but Finnerty had taken the liberty of recommending him to a large company contracting for a drainage tunnel in Cripple Creek. Would Mr. Cable please follow up and advise? So March had taken the early morning train.

Late that afternoon Ona saw him coming down the street. Her heart beat with pride at seeing his rangy body dressed in new clothes, his lean dark face tanned darker by long exposure to the Mexican sun, the long swinging stride that reminded her of Cable. She jumped up, met him at the door. "Did you see him, son? Have you got a job?"

"Let's go upstairs, Mother," he said quietly.

They climbed the stairs to the Third Floor and sat down to talk undisturbed. March tersely explained the substance of his interview. All Colorado was mining about $20,000,000 worth of gold a year—what Cripple Creek alone was putting out when it led the world in the production of gold. The district's output now had dropped to less than $3,000,000. But the price of gold had just been raised from $21 to $35 an ounce. Old dumps were being reworked, old mines being reopened. Now things looked bright for the district. Its present bottom had been lowered to 8,000 feet altitude by two early drainage tunnels. Now the long proposed third tunnel was going through. It would lower the bottom to 7,000 feet, draining the whole district of thirty square miles. It would cost nearly $1,500,000 but it would open up at least $6,000,000 worth of ore. Who knew how much more lay at even greater depth? Anyway, the firm Finnerty had sent him to had contracted to drive the tunnel and the engineer who had interviewed March had offered him a job.

"You took it?" Ona exclaimed, beaming. "It's a compliment to you, being recommended by the vice-president of a big outfit like Western Mines. You've worked hard for it. I'm proud of you! You're a young man yet. Times are hard now. You likely couldn't find anything else. It won't last long—three or four years at the most. And you can be studyin' for somethin' better."

She patted his hand. "Just think son! I'll have you here with me awhile yet! We'll have an extra room or a bed for you in our new flat. They say in these new-fangled places there's beds in the front rooms. They just pull down from the wall, easy as anything. There you can stay on weekends when you come down from Cripple Creek. Just like Daddy comin' down from the Sylvanite in the old days. Like your own father, son. And we'll be watchin' from the window, Mother and Nancy and me, to see you come down the street puffin' on a black cigar or pipe, like as not."

"Mother!"

With bright eyes, she prattled on. "Why, shoot! Times haven't changed at all. Only you'll be on a regular salary—and a whopping big one too or I miss my reckon, what with your college education and bein' to Mexico and all. No worries about the vein peterin' out. Money in the bank pretty soon, I fancy. A good name as a smart and reliable young man growin' up with the country. Good clothes you look good in—you sure do, son! No dirty old boots or mules to cuss at; you'll be ridin' the cushions. And when I see my son a-stridin' down the street on his way back from Cripple Creek, I'll say to myself, 'That's my boy. He's a Rogier and a Cable too. A regular first rate minin' man, born with the feelin' in his blood!' "

So she went on, sitting in the ghostly emptiness of the barny Third Floor bedroom, clutching at the tattered remnants of an almost forgotten dream of happiness with the invincible and undaunted belief in her son that she had so stoutly and futilely maintained for her father, her husband, and Tom.

March rose, heavy with an intolerable anguish, to stare down at her who all her life had fought tooth-and-nail against their involvement in Cripple Creek. We want so little, at the end, to justify our monstrous faith in others! How could he fail her now?

Disconsolately, guiltily, he stared out the window upon Shook's Run. Then abruptly he turned to face her. "Mother! I turned down that job. I'm through with Cripple Creek and Mexico. I'm done with mining, anywhere!"

A look of blank incomprehension froze on Ona's face.

"No mining in any shape or form," he repeated. "I'm not a hard-rock man, an engineer. I don't want to dig in the ground for gold or silver or anything else. People are more important than places. I'll do my diggin' in them."

"How?" she asked dully.

"I don't know, Mother. I don't know yet how they're put together. Maybe I'll take some premedical courses and then psychology. These new depth psychologists and psychiatrists are going way down below grass roots, opening up new levels of understanding, discovering ore bodies we never knew existed. Just what I'll wind up doing, I don't know, but that's the vein I'm after."

He could see her hackles rise. "Psychiatrists! Doctors to raving mad men! God Almighty! You're out of your own head!" She fixed on him a shrewd accusing look. "Some foreign woman in Mexico hooked you and changed your normal view of life, didn't she? Or did you catch one of those tropical diseases that water the brain?"

"Don't bait me. I just want to find out what people really are, who I am."

She was angry now. "I know who you are, if you don't! You're a young Smart Alec who's forgetting he comes from a fine normal family with a proud background. Rogiers, every one of them!"

"Stop it!" he shouted himself now. "I can't stand that everlasting song of the Old South any more. Let me tell you who we are! We're a decadent family gone to pot! Wastrels, failures, shams, epileptics, homosexuals, half-breeds! What happened? Why? How?"

Ona could not withstand his outburst. She lowered her head, began to twist the handkerchief in her lap. Then she raised her anguished face. "Son! We're no different than any family in the whole wide world. We've had our backsliders. We've made our mistakes. And we've forgiven those who made them. But in us all beats the same warm heart. We all want the same thing, not knowing what it is. We try and fail, and try again. There's somethin' in us that can't be put down. We're people, son, just people the world over!"

She began to sniffle, but her voice was clear and resolute. "Would you be like God, tryin' to know why He put us here, what makes us feel and act the way we do? Let well enough alone, boy. We Rogiers and North Enders, the Hottentots and the heathen Chinese, all of us, are goin' to make out in the end, just give us time. You're young and impatient, boy. Just try to understand without knowin' so much."

The storm was over. March felt contrite and humble as he stared out the window at the Peak rising above Bijou Hill. Yet still there hovered something above it, whatever it was, that committed him to its search. He turned and put his arms around Ona. "Let's don't quarrel, Mother. Things will work out like you say. I'll be stayin' with you all winter while I finish up some courses in school and find out what to do next. No need to worry about money, with all I saved from my salary in Mexico and a whopping big bonus to boot."

"Well, that's something anyway," she said, pressing her tear-stained face against his.

Upset, March left the house for a walk. On a sudden impulse he boarded a streetcar to the south part of town and on foot struck across the prairies to the cemetery. It was sentimental nonsense, this going to gawk at Rogier's grave, he thought; for like Cable he had an aversion to burial places. Mrs. Rogier, however, had been after him ever since he had returned. "Now March, you ought to go out to the cemetery. You wasn't there for the funeral and Daddy missed you. You ought to go, really you ought."

Walking along, he grumbled to himself, "I'll bet two-bits against a buffalo nickel she asks me when I get back if I took flowers." For of course he had been the only one who had not sent a wreath. And yet carting out now a bouquet of hothouse roses would have been incongruous. Rogier would have sat up in his grave and blurted out, "Dom, boy! What's all this? Don't clutter me up with such stuff. Just hand me down a cigar. By Jove, there's nothin' like a good smoke when a man's restin'!"

Still March was a little ashamed, walking along so empty-handed. It was June, the solstitial turn of the year when our Father Sun reaches the northernmost end of his journey. Summer, when full-breasted, full-bottomed Mother Earth comes into her own.

Down in Old Mexico the white glare is blinding, the heat is like an oven's blast. The lush tropical growth along the trails gives off the green sickening odor of chlorophyl. In front of thatched *ramadas,* in the clearings, fires are built, not so much for cooking as to keep away swarms of insects. Delicious pearls of sweat cling to the bottles of *Carta Blanca* beer pushed over the bars of every *cantina.* And from the ground outside arises the distinctive smell of all Mexico, the acrid stench of dust impregnanted with urine. The rivers run soap-green, frothing into white suds around the rocks. In them every evening splash the *Indios* of the *pueblocito,* naked bodies reddened by the sinking sun. The moon rises high over rustling banana leaves and pale white orchids, shines in the open window upon the damp full breasts of a woman of the earth waiting passionately for her due. She shall have it! now in summer when the gently gushing female rain and the hard male rain unite to fructify the sterile earth of human flesh.

But here in High Country end all roads, all trails. From the baking plains and stinking lowlands they lead upward to cottages in the canyons, cabins in the pines. Long-legged colts and velvet-coated calves frisk in mountain meadows. A lone eagle screams from the crag. Magpies and chipmunks follow the smoke of picnic fires. Down from the peaks tumble rivers and rivulets. Trout streams: rainbow, native brook, and the big browns. Kids have got the trick. They load your supper table with butter-fried trout stacked up like cordwood. At the little railroad depots, when a train comes in, they hold up to dining car chefs more basketsfull packed in layers of green leaves. And in every remote Saddle Rock Grill, Sentinel Rock Cafe, and other eating joint a sign hangs at the window: "Fresh Trout—All You Can Eat for Fifty Cents—Spuds Incl."

Summer too is the time for the big rodeos when the broncs come busting out of the chutes, and forty-a-month waddies ride to fame by sticking eight seconds on Five-Minutes-to-Midnight or Old Steamboat, or ride down upon, rope, and tie a plunging steer in seventeen seconds.

Up in Cripple Creek the last big mines open up for tourists, displaying specimens of ore they haven't mined for ages. While in a forgotten gulch a gray-bearded old-timer gives his old working hell while the ground is thawed—for the last time, Mister!

Little London is at the topside of her hour. Crowds throng the hotel verandas, fill the rooming houses and flimsy cottages. Rich people return to open up their Broadmoor mansions. Up the narrow trails from Manitou burros climb with jolting tourists. Everyone wears khaki pants and hiking boots. At the Iron Springs Pavillion they buy saltwater taffy by the ton, dished out in little colored-stripe paper bags. Tourist drivers shout from their hacks and jalopies: "Throw snowballs from the top of Pike's Peak on the Fourth of July!" And the blunt-nosed little engine snorts up the Cog Road pushing its tiny car.

You don't have to look at the calendar. You can tell it's summer by looking at the prices for a bed, a hamburger, and a postcard. Or even at signs posted along the dusty roads a hundred miles away: "Detour here around the Tourist Trap of the Rockies." Who cares? For this is the opulent, full-blossomed season of the year when Little London makes hay while the sun shines—

No, thought March, it wouldn't do to go to his grandfather's grave empty-handed. In the flare of the sinking sun the prairie was a brilliant blanket of white wild onions, bluebells, scarlet Indian paintbrushes, sand daisies, columbines, lupines. He remembered the hundreds of flower stalls in Guadalajara, the remote altars in the sierras covered with fresh flowers. Fresh flowers and fresh blood. His grandfather would have liked that! The old pagan!

March could not resist stooping for an armful. But when he reached the cemetery he had some difficulty finding the family lot. It was unmarked, Cable's sunken grave and Rogier's fresh one devoid of headboards pending the erection of small stone markers which March had ordered. He flashed a look down the gulch. It was filled with tin cans. The pines soughed faintly, a magpie screamed. He knelt and self-consciously but carefully spread the crimson flowers over Rogier's and Cable's graves, side by side. And now as he stood looking down at that patch of earth which held them both, he heard above him the muted whisper of the aimless ancient winds.

Remember what the Indians said of your grandfather's people, that it was the destiny of white men to turn into stone. Remember too your grandfather's square hewn face and figure, his granite will. Look now at the massive granite Peak, son; do you no longer recognize your grandfather's flesh?

Did not your father's fathers and their sons rise out of soft adobe? Out of it and its rich abundance they built the walls of their soft warm-colored bodies. Into it they have returned. Do you no longer recognize your father's flesh? Look down at your feet, son.

And now they both lie before you, intermingled, even as the rising plains merge into the rocky mountains. Here where the chamisa blooms brightest, the sage smells sharpest — who knows which is buried here? Over them both the tall rain walks, the ghost buffalo sweep past, and we, the ancient aimless ones, whisper in the pines. What is adobe and what is granite but the mingled flesh of all flesh, the earth eternal? Look closer, son.

He could feel their cool fingers lifting from him his pride, sorrow, and regret. Their voices comforted him. Yet his inner self cried back, You talk so glibly of the flesh of the earth and the earth of the flesh over whose surface you pass so aimlessly and eternally! But what is the mystery that imbues this flesh with life? Just what am I? That is what I ask!

The aimless ancient winds did not answer; they had passed by already. In their stead answered the resonant voice of the earth, the cruel and immense, the deep and forgiving earth of a continent timelessly spanning the seas 3,000 miles apart.

You are them both, adobe and granite, indivisible and intermingled. You are the flesh of their flesh, and their flesh is of my flesh. We are all one earth. Together, undivided and eternal, we echo the pulse which throbs through stone; the same isotatic equilibrium holds you and the frosty peaks in place; you crumble and wash away, and rise ever again in eternal palingenesis.

You sound like my grandfather! he cried. Flesh and earth! Is there nothing more?

You are the pieces of a broken arrow rejoined. The hand of Quetzalcoatl returned on his raft of snakes to reach forth and lift a people out of their pit. You are the earth of all America out of which shall spring a new and unknown flower — the flower of this mighty, unknown continent risen so soon from the blue depths of time. The flower, the feather, the drum, and the mirror of old gods who have never died. The voice of new gods yet to be heard.

I have heard this before! was his curiously stubborn response. It echoes the voice of my father and my father's people, the wail of the Raramuri you hold in abject bondage!

And once again the mighty earth thundered forth, *Take care, son! Don't be in such a hurry. For in the ghostly flow of time which seems to move and yet never moves, you are the leaf that falls and the leaf that sprouts anew. The rock disintegrated by time, and the timeless dust within the rock. The false pride, crumbled magnolia leaves, and moth-rotted Confederate flag of your grandfather's people. And your father's dark hawk face and the smoke of a thousand strange campfires in his blood. You are all that ever has been and all that ever will be, and from me you are ever reborn.*

For a moment he was silent, feeling a strange resoluteness gathering within him. Maybe I'm all that, flattering as it seems, he admitted. Likely I'm less than that, yet more in a way you neglect to mention. For you sound like my lesser mother, Mother Earth, and I would have you know too I'm not a hard-rock man. I'm done with mining in your bowels for what I seek. And so I must break the umbilical cord with which you also would hold me. Great as you are, there is something greater. What about heaven, Mother Earth, under which you lie so supinely, that fructifies and lashes even you into meek submission?

Oh! You would not only exhaust the meaning of your mother and of your father too, but supersede the duality of all mortal existence! What big boots you think to wear, tadpole that you are! grumbled the earth warningly. *Such impertinence can't question my power. There is in you something that is always mine. Take care! Someday I'll collect my due!*

Your threats don't frighten me, Mother Earth! he cried back with a burst of new self-confidence, staring upward above the western horizon. There is in me something that will escape you. What is the mystery that impregnates your flesh, imbues all earth with life? That is what I'm still asking. The one secret self hidden in the dark stopes deep within our lesser selves. That is what I seek!

The earth gave one last rumble and was still. It did not answer. Perhaps it could not, being itself, like countless other earths in interstellar space, but a part of that vast mystery of all creation informed with life for its own duration.

The sun had set. In the luminous purity of the twilight March could see the pale silvery sheen of the great Peak majestic and immense above the purpling wall of mountains to the west. He stared at it as if at an imperishable monument to a faith he had finally surmounted. And now silence spoke with the voice that outspeaks all. Listening, he saw it before him, like something risen from the depths of dreamless sleep to the horizon of wakeful consciousness, without clear outline yet embodying the substance of a hope and meaning that seemed strangely familiar as it was vague. Toward it he began his long and resolute journey.